Library of America, a nonprofit organization,
champions our nation's cultural heritage
by publishing America's greatest writing in
authoritative new editions and providing resources
for readers to explore this rich, living legacy.

# CONSTANCE FENIMORE WOOLSON

# Constance Fenimore Woolson

## Collected Stories

Anne Boyd Rioux, *editor*

THE LIBRARY OF AMERICA

Published in the United States by Library of America.
Visit our website at www.loa.org.

This paper exceeds the requirements of
ANSI/NISO Z39.48–1992 (Permanence of Paper).

Distributed to the trade in the United States
by Penguin Random House Inc.
and in Canada by Penguin Random House Canada Ltd.

Library of Congress Control Number: 2019940936
ISBN 978–1–59853–650–8

First Printing
The Library of America—327

Manufactured in the United States of America

# Contents

# CASTLE NOWHERE:
# LAKE-COUNTRY SKETCHES

# Contents

# Peter the Parson

I N November, 1850, a little mining settlement stood forlornly on the shore of Lake Superior. A log-dock ran out into the dark water; a roughly built furnace threw a glare against the dark sky; several stamping-mills kept up their monotonous tramping day and night; and evil-minded saloons beset the steps on all sides. Back into the pine forest ran the white-sand road leading to the mine, and on the right were clustered the houses, which were scarcely better than shanties, although adorned with sidling porches and sham-windowed fronts. Winter begins early in these high latitudes. Navigation was still open, for a scow with patched sails was coming slowly up the bay; but the air was cold, and the light snow of the preceding night clung unmelted on the north side of the trees. The pine forest had been burned away to make room for the village; blackened stumps rose everywhere in the weedy streets, and, on the outskirts of the clearing, grew into tall skeletons, bleached white without, but black and charred within,—a desolate framing for a desolate picture. Everything was bare, jagged, and unfinished; each poor house showed hasty makeshifts,—no doors latched, no windows fitted. Pigs were the principal pedestrians. At four o'clock this cold November afternoon, the saloons, with their pine fires and red curtains, were by far the most cheerful spots in the landscape, and their ruddy invitations to perdition were not counterbalanced by a single opposing gleam, until the Rev. Herman Peters prepared his chapel for vespers.

Herman Warriner Peters was a slender little man, whose blue eyes, fair hair, and unbearded face misled the observer into the idea of extreme youth. There was a boyishness in his air, or, rather, lack of air, and a nervous timidity in his manner, which stamped him as a person of no importance,—one of those men who, not of sufficient consequence to be disliked, are simply ignored by a well-bred world, which pardons anything rather than insignificance. And if ignored by a well-bred world, what by an ill-bred? Society at Algonquin was worse than ill-bred, inasmuch as it had never been bred at all. Like all mining settlements, it esteemed physical strength the highest good, and next to that an undaunted demeanor and flowing vocabulary, designated admiringly as "powerful sassy." Accordingly it made unlimited fun of the Rev. Herman Warriner Peters, and derived much enjoyment from calling him "Peter," pretending to think it was his real name, and solemnly persisting in the mistake in spite of all the painstaking corrections of the unsuspecting little man.

The Rev. Herman wrapped himself in his thin old cloak and twisted a comforter around his little throat, as the clock warned him of the hour. He was not leaving much comfort behind him; the room was dreary and bare, without carpet, fire, or easy-chair. A cot-bed, which sagged hopelessly, a wash-bowl set on a dry-goods box, flanked by a piece of bar-soap and a crash towel, a few pegs on the cracked wall, one wooden chair and his own little trunk, completed the furniture. The Rev. Herman boarded with Mrs. Malone, and ate her streaked biscuit and fried meat without complaint. The woman could rise to yeast and a gridiron when the surveyors visited Algonquin, or when the directors of the iron company came up in the summer; but the streaked biscuit and fried steak were "good enough for the little parson, bless him!"

There were some things in the room, however, other than furniture, namely, a shelf full of religious books, a large and appalling picture of the crucifixion, and a cross six feet in height, roughly made of pine saplings, and fixed to the floor in a wooden block. There was also a small colored picture, with the words "Santa Margarita" inscribed beneath. The picture stood on a bracket fashioned of shingles, and below it hung a poor little vase filled with the last colored leaves.

"Ye only want the Howly Vargin now, to be all right, yer riverence," said Mrs. Malone, who was, in name at least, a Roman Catholic.

"All honor and affection are, no doubt, due to the Holy Mary," answered the Rev. Herman, nervously; "but the Anglican Church does not—at present—allow her claim to—to adoration." And he sighed.

"Why don't yer jest come right out now, and be a rale Catholic?" said Mrs. Malone, with a touch of sympathy. "You 're next door to it, and it 's aisy to see yer ain't happy in yer mind. If yer was a rale praste, now, with the coat and all, 'stead of being a

make-believe, the boys ud respect yer more, and would n't notice yer soize so much. Or yer might go back to the cities (for I
don't deny they do loike a big fist up here), and loikely enough
yer could find aisy work there that ud suit yer."

"I like hard work, Mrs. Malone," said the little parson.

"But you 're not fit for it, sir. You 'll niver get on here if yer
stay till judgment day. Why, yer ain't got ten people, all told,
belongin' to yer chapel, and you 're here a year already!"

The Rev. Herman sighed again, but made no answer. He
sighed now as he left his cold room and stepped out into the
cold street. The wind blew as he made his way along between
the stumps, carefully going round the pigs, who had selected
the best places for their siestas. He held down his comforter
with one bare hand; the other clutched the end of a row of
books, which filled his thin arm from the shoulder down. He
limped as he walked. An ankle had been cruelly injured some
months previously; the wound had healed, but he was left
permanently and awkwardly lame. At the time, the dastardly
injury had roused a deep bitterness in the parson's heart, for
grace and activity had been his one poor little bodily gift, his
one small pride. The activity had returned, not the grace. But
he had learned to limp bravely along, and the bitterness had
passed away.

Lights shone comfortably from the Pine-Cone Saloon as he
passed.

"Hallo! Here 's Peter the Parson," sang out a miner, standing
at the door; and forth streamed all the loungers to look at him.

"Say, Peter, come in and have a drop to warm yer," said one.

"Look at his poor little ribs, will yer?" said another, as his
cloak blew out like a sail.

"Let him alone! He 's going to have his preaching all to himself, as usual," said a third. "Them books is all the congregation
*he* can get, poor little chap!"

The parson's sensitive ears heard every word. He quickened
his steps, and, with his usual nervous awkwardness, stumbled
and fell, dropping all the books, amid the jeering applause of
the bystanders. Silently he rose and began collecting his load,
the wind every now and then blowing his cloak over his head as
he stooped, and his difficulties increased by the occasional gift
of a potato full in the breast, and a flood of witty commentaries

from the laughing group at the saloon door. As he picked up
the last volume and turned away, a missile, deftly aimed, took
off his hat, and sent it over a fence into a neighboring field. The
parson hesitated; but as a small boy had already given chase,
not to bring it back, but to send it further away, he abandoned
the hat,—his only one,—and walked on among the stumps
bareheaded, his thin hair blown about by the raw wind, and his
blue eyes reddened with cold and grief.

The Episcopal Church of St. John and St. James was a rough
little building, with recess-chancel, ill-set Gothic windows,
and a half-finished tower. It owed its existence to the zeal of
a director's wife, who herself embroidered its altar-cloth and
bookmarks, and sent thither the artificial flowers and candles
which she dared not suggest at home; the poor Indians, at
least, should not be deprived of them! The director's wife died,
but left by will a pittance of two hundred dollars per annum
towards the rector's salary. In her fancy she saw Algonquin
a thriving town, whose inhabitants believed in the Anglican
succession, and sent their children to Sunday school. In reality,
Algonquin remained a lawless mining settlement, whose inhabitants believed in nothing, and whose children hardly knew
what Sunday meant, unless it was more whiskey than usual.
The two hundred dollars and the chapel, however, remained
fixed facts; and the Eastern directors, therefore, ordered a picturesque church to be delineated on their circulars, and themselves constituted a non-resident vestry. One or two young
missionaries had already tried the field, failed, and gone away;
but the present incumbent, who had equally tried and equally
failed, remained.

On this occasion he unlocked the door and entered the little sanctuary. It was cold and dark, but he made no fire, for
there was neither stove nor hearth. Lighting two candles,—
one for the congregation and one for himself,—he distributed
the books among the benches and the chancel, and dusted
carefully the little altar, with its faded embroideries and flowers. Then he retired into the shed which served as a vestry-
room, and in a few minutes issued forth, clad in his robes of
office, and knelt at the chancel rail. There was no bell to summon the congregation, and no congregation to summon; but

still he began in his clear voice, "Dearly beloved brethren," and continued on unwavering through the Confession, the Absolution, and the Psalms, leaving a silence for the corresponding responses, and devoutly beginning the first lesson. In the midst of "Zephaniah" there was a slight noise at the door and a step sounded over the rough floor. The solitary reader did not raise his eyes; and, the lesson over, he bravely lifted up his mild tenor in the chant, "It is a good thing to give thanks unto the Lord, and to sing praises unto thy name, O Most Highest." A girl's voice took up the air; the mild tenor dropped into its own part, and the two continued the service in a duet, spoken and sung, to its close. Then the minister retired, with his candle, to the shed, and, hanging up his surplice, patiently waited, pacing to and fro in the cold. Patiently waited; and for what? For the going away of the only friend he had in Algonquin.

The congregation lingered; its shawl must be re-fastened; indeed, it must be entirely refolded. Its hat must be retied, and the ribbons carefully smoothed. Still there was no sound from the vestry-room. It collected all the prayer-books, and piled them near the candle, making a separate journey for each little volume. Still no one. At last, with lingering step and backward glance, slowly it departed and carried its disappointed face homeward. Then Peter the Parson issued forth, lifted the careful pile of books with tender hand, and, extinguishing the lights, went out bareheaded into the darkness. The vesper service of St. John and St. James was over.

After a hot, unwholesome supper the minister returned to his room and tried to read; but the candle flickered, the cold seemed to blur the book, and he found himself gazing at the words without taking in their sense. Then he began to read aloud, slowly walking up and down, and carrying the candle to light the page; but through all the learned sentences there still crept to the surface the miserable consciousness of bodily cold. "And mental, too, Heaven help me!" he thought. "But I cannot afford a fire at this season, and, indeed, it ought not to be necessary. This delicacy must be subdued; I will go out and walk." Putting on his cloak and comforter, (O, deceitful name!) he remembered that he had no hat. Would his slender

store of money allow a new one? Unlocking his trunk, he drew
out a thin purse hidden away among his few carefully folded
clothes,—the poor trunk was but half full,—and counted its
contents. The sum was pitifully small, and it must yet last many
weeks. But a hat was necessary, whereas a fire was a mere luxury. "I must harden myself," thought the little parson, sternly,
as he caught himself shuddering with the cold; "this evil tendency to self-indulgence must and shall be crushed."

He went down towards the dock where stood the one store
of Algonquin,—stealing along in the darkness to hide his uncovered condition. Buying a hat, the poorest one there, from
the Jew proprietor, he lingered a moment near the stove to
warm his chilled hands. Mr. Marx, rendered good-natured by
the bold cheat he had perpetrated, affably began a conversation.

"Sorry to see yer still limp bad. But it ain't so hard as it
would be if yer was a larger man. Yer see there ain't much of
yer to limp; that 's one comfort. Hope business is good at yer
chapel, and that Mrs. Malone gives yer enough to eat; yer don't
look like it, though. The winter has sot in early, and times is
hard." And did the parson know that "Brother Saul has come
in from the mine, and is a holding forth in the school-house
this very minit?"

No; the parson did not know it. But he put on his new hat,
whose moth-holes had been skilfully blackened over with ink,
and turned towards the door.

"It 's nothing to me, of course," continued Mr. Marx, with
a liberal wave of his dirty hand; "all your religions are alike to
me, I 'm free to say. But I wonder yer and Saul don't work together, parson. Yer might do a heap of good if yer was to pull
at the same oar, now."

The words echoed in the parson's ears as he walked down
to the beach, the only promenade in Algonquin free from
stumps. Could he do a "heap of good," by working with that
ignorant, coarse, roaring brother, whose blatant pride, dirty
shirt, and irreverent familiarity with all things sacred were
alike distasteful, nay, horrible to his sensitive mind? Pondering, he paced the narrow strip of sand under the low bluff; but
all his efforts did not suffice to quicken or warm his chilled
blood. Nevertheless, he expanded his sunken chest and drew
in long breaths of the cold night air, and beat his little hands

vigorously together, and ran to and fro. "Aha!" he said to himself, "this is glorious exercise." And then he went home, colder than ever; it was his way thus to make a reality of what ought to be.

Passing through one of the so-called streets, he saw a ruddy glow in front of the school-house; it was a pine-knot fire whose flaring summons had not been unheeded. The parson stopped a moment and warmed himself, glancing meanwhile furtively within, where Brother Saul was holding forth in clarion tones to a crowded congregation; his words reached the listener's ear, and verified the old proverb. "There 's brimstone and a fiery furnace for them as doubts the truth, I tell you. Prayin' out of a book—and flowers—and candles—and night-gownds 'stead of decent coats—for it 's night-gownds they look like, though they may call them surpluses" (applause from the miners)—"won't do no good. Sech nonsense will never save souls. You 've jest got to fall down on your knees and pray hard —hard—with groaning and roaring of the spirit—until you 're as weak as a rag. Nothing else will do; nothing,—nothing."

The parson hurried away, shrinking (though unseen) from the rough finger pointed at him. Before he was out of hearing a hymn sounded forth on the night breeze,—one of those nondescript songs that belong to the border, a favorite with the Algonquin miners, because of a swinging chorus wherein they roared out their wish to "die a-shouting," in company with all the kings and prophets of Israel, each one fraternally mentioned by name.

Reaching his room, the parson hung up his cloak and hat, and sat down quietly with folded hands. Clad in dressing-gown and slippers, in an easy-chair, before a bright fire,—a revery, thus, is the natural ending for a young man's day. But here the chair was hard and straight-backed, there was no fire, and the candle burned with a feeble blue flame; the small figure in its limp black clothes, with its little gaitered feet pressed close together on the cold floor as if for warmth, its clasped hands, its pale face and blue eyes fixed on the blank expanse of the plastered wall, was pathetic in its patient discomfort. After a while a tear fell on the clasped hands and startled their coldness with its warmth. The parson brushed the token of weakness hastily away, and rising, threw himself at the foot of the large wooden

cross with his arms clasping its base. In silence for many moments he lay thus prostrate; then, extinguishing the candle, he
sought his poor couch. But later in the night, when all Algonquin slept, a crash of something falling was heard in the dark
room, followed by the sound of a scourge mercilessly used,
and murmured Latin prayers,—the old cries of penitence that
rose during night-vigils from the monasteries of the Middle
Ages. And why not English words? Was there not something
of affectation in the use of these mediæval phrases? Maybe so;
but at least there was nothing affected in the stripes made by
the scourge. The next morning all was as usual in the little
room, save that the picture of Santa Margarita was torn in
twain, and the bracket and vase shattered to fragments on the
floor below.

At dawn the parson rose, and, after a conscientious bath in
the tub of icy water brought in by his own hands the previous
evening, he started out with his load of prayer-books, his face
looking haggard and blue in the cold morning light. Again he
entered the chapel, and having arranged the books and dusted
the altar, he attired himself in his robes and began the service
at half past six precisely. "From the rising of the sun even unto
the going down of the same," he read, and in truth the sun
was just rising. As the evening prayer was "vespers," so this was
"matins," in the parson's mind. He had his "vestments" too,
of various ritualistic styles, and washed them himself, ironing
them out afterwards with fear and difficulty in Mrs. Malone's
disorderly kitchen, poor little man! No hand turned the latch,
no step came across the floor this morning; the parson had the
service all to himself, and, as it was Friday, he went through
the Litany, omitting nothing, and closing with a hymn. Then,
gathering up his books, he went home to breakfast.

"How peaked yer do look, sir!" exclaimed ruddy Mrs.
Malone, as she handed him a cup of muddy coffee. "What, no
steak? Do, now; for I ain't got nothin' else. Well, if yer won't—
But there 's nothin' but the biscuit, then. Why, even Father
O'Brien himself 'lows meat for the sickly, Friday or no Friday."

"I am not sickly, Mrs. Malone," replied the little parson, with
dignity.

A young man with the figure of an athlete sat at the lower
end of the table, tearing the tough steak voraciously with his

strong teeth, chewing audibly, and drinking with a gulping noise. He paused as the parson spoke, and regarded him with wonder not unmixed with contempt.

"You ain't sickly?" he repeated. "Well, if you ain't, then I 'd like to know who is, that 's all."

"Now, you jest eat your breakfast, Steve, and let the parson alone," interposed Mrs. Malone. "Sorry to see that little picture all tore, sir," she continued, turning the conversation in her blundering good-nature. "It was a moighty pretty picture, and looked uncommonly like Rosie Ray."

"It was a copy of an Italian painting, Mrs. Malone," the parson hastened to reply; "Santa Margarita."

"O, I dare say; but it looked iver so much like Rosie, for all that!"

A deep flush had crossed the parson's pale face. The athlete saw it, and muttered to himself angrily, casting surly sidelong glances up the table, and breathing hard; the previous evening he had happened to pass the Chapel of St. John and St. James as its congregation of one was going in the door.

After two hours spent in study, the parson went out to visit the poor and sick of the parish; all were poor, and one was sick, —the child of an Englishwoman, a miner's wife. The mother, with a memory of her English training, dusted a chair for the minister, and dropped a courtesy, as he seated himself by the little bed; but she seemed embarrassed, and talked volubly of anything and everything save the child. The parson listened to the unbroken stream of words while he stroked the boy's soft cheek and held the wasted little hand in his. At length he took a small bottle from his pocket, and looked around for a spoon; it was a pure and delicate cordial which he had often given to the sick child to sustain its waning strength.

"O, if you please, sir,—indeed, I don't feel sure that it does Harry any good. Thank you for offering it so free—but—but, if you 'd just as lieve—I—I 'd rather not, sir, if you please, sir."

The parson looked up in astonishment; the costly cordial had robbed him of many a fire.

"Why don't you tell the minister the truth?" called out a voice from the inner room, the harsh voice of the husband. "Why don't you say right out that Brother Saul was here last night, and prayed over the child, and give it some of his own medicine, and telled you not to touch the parson's stuff? He said it was pizen, he did."

The parson rose, cut to the heart. He had shared his few dimes with this woman, and had hoped much from her on account of her early church-training. On Sunday she had been one of the few who came to the chapel, and when, during the summer, she was smitten with fever, he had read over her the prayers from "The Visitation of the Sick"; he had baptized this child now fading away, and had loved the little fellow tenderly, taking pleasure in fashioning toys for his baby hands, and saving for him the few cakes of Mrs. Malone's table.

"I did n't mean to have Saul,—I did n't indeed, sir," said the mother, putting her apron to her eyes. "But Harry he was so bad last night, and the neighbors sort o' persuaded me into it. Brother Saul does pray so powerful strong, sir, that it seems as though it must do some good some way; and he 's a very comfortable talker too, there 's no denying that. Still, I did n't mean it, sir; and I hope you 'll forgive me."

"There is nothing to forgive," replied the parson, gently; and, leaving his accustomed coin on the table, he went away.

Wandering at random through the pine forest, unable to overcome the dull depression at his heart, he came suddenly upon a large bull-dog; the creature, one of the ugliest of its kind, eyed him quietly, with a slow wrinkling of the sullen upper lip.

The parson visibly trembled.

"'Fraid, are ye?" called out a voice, and the athlete of the breakfast-table showed himself.

"Call off your dog, please, Mr. Long."

"He ain't doin' nothin', parson. But you 're at liberty to kick him, if you like," said the man, laughing as the dog snuffed stealthily around the parson's gaiters. The parson shifted his position; the dog followed. He stepped aside; so did the dog. He turned and walked away with a determined effort at self-control; the dog went closely behind, brushing his ankles with his ugly muzzle. He hurried; so did the dog. At last, overcome with the nervous physical timidity which belonged to his constitution, he broke into a run, and fled as if for life, hearing the dog close behind and gaining with every step. The jeering laugh of the athlete followed him through the pine-tree aisles, but he heeded it not, and when at last he spied a log-house on one side he took refuge within like a hunted hare, breathless and trembling. An old woman smoking a pipe was its only occupant. "What 's the matter?" she said. "O, the dog?" And, taking a stick of wood, she drove the animal from the door, and sent him fleeing back to his master. The parson sat down by the hearth to recover his composure.

"Why, you 're most frightened to death, ain't yer?" said the old woman, as she brushed against him to make up the fire. "You 're all of a tremble. I would n't stray so far from home if I was you, child."

Her vision was imperfect, and she took the small, cowering figure for a boy.

The minister went home.

After dinner, which he did not eat, as the greasy dishes offended his palate, he shut himself up in his room to prepare his sermon for the coming Sunday. It made no difference whether there would be any one to hear it or not, the sermon was always carefully written and carefully delivered, albeit short, according to the ritualistic usage, which esteems the service all, the sermon nothing. His theme on this occasion was "The General Councils of the Church"; and the sermon, an admirable production of its kind, would have been esteemed, no doubt, in English Oxford or in the General Theological Seminary of New York City. He wrote earnestly and ardently, deriving a keen enjoyment from the work; the mechanical part also was exquisitely finished, the clear sentences standing out like the work of a sculptor. Then came vespers; and the congregation this time was composed of two, or, rather, three persons, —the girl, the owner of the dog, and the dog himself. The man entered during service with a noisy step, managing to throw over a bench, coughing, humming, and talking to his dog; half of the congregation was evidently determined upon mischief. But the other half rose with the air of a little queen, crossed the intervening space with an open prayer-book, gave it to the man, and, seating herself near by, fairly awed him into good behavior. Rose Ray was beautiful; and the lion lay at her feet. As for the dog, with a wave of her hand she ordered him out, and the beast humbly withdrew. It was noticeable that the parson's voice gained strength as the dog disappeared.

"I ain't going to stand by and see it, Rosie," said the man, as, the service over, he followed the girl into the street. "That puny little chap!"

"He cares nothing for me," answered the girl, quickly.

"He sha' n't have a chance to care, if I know myself. You 're free to say 'no' to me, Rosie, but you ain't free to say 'yes' to him. A regular coward! That 's what he is. Why, he ran away from my dog this very afternoon,—ran like he was scared to death!"

"You set the dog on him, Steve."

"Well, what if I did? He need n't have run; any other man would have sent the beast flying."

"Now, Steve, do promise me that you won't tease him any more," said the girl, laying her hand upon the man's arm as he walked by her side. His face softened.

"If he had any spirit he 'd be ashamed to have a girl beggin' for him not to be teased. But never mind that; I 'll let him alone fast enough, Rosie, if you will too."

"If I will," repeated the girl, drawing back, as he drew closer to her side; "what can you mean?"

"O, come now! You know very well you 're always after him, —a goin' to his chapel where no one else goes hardly,—a listenin' to his preachin',—and a havin' your picture hung up in his room."

It was a random shaft, sent carelessly, more to finish the sentence with a strong point than from any real belief in the athlete's mind.

"What!"

"Leastways so Mrs. Malone said. I took breakfast there this morning."

The girl was thrown off her guard, her whole face flushed with joy; she could not for the moment hide her agitation. "My picture!" she murmured, and clasped her hands. The light from the Pine-Cone crossed her face, and revealed the whole secret. Steven Long saw it, and fell into a rage. After all, then, she did love the puny parson!

"Let him look out for himself, that 's all," he muttered with a fierce gesture, as he turned towards the saloon door. (He felt a sudden thirst for vengeance, and for whiskey.) "I 'll be even with him, and I won't be long about it neither. You 'll

never have the little parson alive, Rose Ray! He 'll be found
missin' some fine mornin', and nobody will be to blame but
you either." He disappeared, and the girl stood watching the
spot where his dark, angry face had been. After a time she went
slowly homeward, troubled at heart; there was neither law nor
order at Algonquin, and not without good cause did she fear.

The next morning, as the parson was coming from his solitary matin service through thick-falling snow, this girl met
him, slipped a note into his hand, and disappeared like a vision.
The parson went homeward, carrying the folded paper under
his cloak pressed close to his heart. "I am only keeping it dry,"
he murmured to himself. This was the note:—

"RESPECTED SIR,—I must see you, you air in danger. Please
come to the Grotter this afternoon at three and I remain yours
respectful,

Rose RAY."

The Rev. Herman Warriner Peters read these words over and
over; then he went to breakfast, but ate nothing, and, coming
back to his room, he remained the whole morning motionless
in his chair. At first the red flamed in his cheek, but gradually
it faded, and gave place to a pinched pallor; he bowed his head
upon his hands, communed with his own heart, and was still.
As the dinner-bell rang he knelt down on the cold hearth, made
a little funeral pyre of the note torn into fragments, watched
it slowly consume, and then, carefully collecting the ashes, he
laid them at the base of the large cross.

At two o'clock he set out for the Grotto, a cave two miles
from the village along the shore, used by the fishermen as a
camp during the summer. The snow had continued falling, and
now lay deep on the even ground; the pines were loaded with
it, and everything was white save the waters of the bay, heaving
sullenly, dark, and leaden, as though they knew the icy fetters
were nearly ready for them. The parson walked rapidly along in
his awkward, halting gait; overshoes he had none, and his cloak
was but a sorry substitute for the blankets and skins worn by
the miners. But he did not feel cold when he opened the door
of the little cabin which had been built out in front of the cave,
and found himself face to face with the beautiful girl who had

summoned him there. She had lighted a fire of pine knots on the hearth, and set the fishermen's rough furniture in order; she had cushioned a chair-back with her shawl, and heated a flat stone for a foot-warmer.

"Take this seat, sir," she said, leading him thither.

The parson sank into the chair and placed his old soaked gaiters on the warm stone; but he said not one word.

"I thought perhaps you 'd be tired after your long walk, sir," continued the girl, "and so I took the liberty of bringing something with me." As she spoke she drew into view a basket, and took from it delicate bread, chicken, cakes, preserved strawberries, and a little tin coffee-pot which, set on the coals, straightway emitted a delicious fragrance; nothing was forgotten,—cream, sugar, nor even snowy napkins.

The parson spoke not a word.

But the girl talked for both, as with flushed cheeks and starry eyes she prepared the tempting meal, using many pretty arts and graceful motions, using in short every power she possessed to charm the silent guest. The table was spread, the viands arranged, the coffee poured into the cup; but still the parson spoke not, and his blue eyes were almost stern as he glanced at the tempting array. He touched nothing.

"I thought you would have liked it all," said the girl at last, when she saw her little offerings despised. "I brought them all out myself—and I was so glad thinking you 'd like them—and now—" Her voice broke, and the tears flowed from her pretty soft eyes. A great tenderness came over the parson's face.

"Do not weep," he said, quickly. "See, I am eating. See, I am enjoying everything. It is all good, nay, delicious." And in his haste he partook of each dish, and lifted the coffee-cup to his lips. The girl's face grew joyous again, and the parson struggled bravely against his own enjoyment; in truth, what with the warm fire, the easy-chair, the delicate food, the fragrant coffee, and the eager, beautiful face before him, a sense of happiness came over him in long surges, and for the moment his soul drifted with the warm tide.

"You *do* like it, don't you?" said the girl with delight, as he slowly drank the fragrant coffee, his starved lips lingering over the delicious brown drops. Something in her voice jarred on the trained nerves and roused them to action again.

"Yes, I do like it,—only too well," he answered; but the tone of his voice had altered. He pushed back his chair, rose, and began pacing to and fro in the shadow beyond the glow of the fire.

"Thou glutton body!" he murmured. "But thou shalt go empty for this." Then, after a pause, he said in a quiet, even tone, "You had something to tell me, Miss Ray."

The girl's face had altered; but rallying, she told her story earnestly,—of Steven Long, his fierce temper, his utter lawlessness, and his threats.

"And why should Steven Long threaten me?" said the parson. "But you need not answer," he continued in an agitated voice. "Say to Steven Long,—say to him," he repeated in louder tones, "that I shall never marry. I have consecrated my life to my holy calling."

There was a long silence; the words fell with crushing weight on both listener and speaker. We do not realize even our own determinations, sometimes, until we have told them to another. The girl rallied first; for she still hoped.

"Mr. Peters," she said, taking all her courage in her hands and coming towards him, "is it wrong to marry?"

"For me—it is."

"Why?"

"Because I am a priest."

"Are you a Catholic, then?"

"I am a Catholic, although not in the sense you mean. Mine is the true Catholic faith which the Anglican Church has kept pure from the errors of Rome, and mine it is to make my life accord with the high office I hold."

"Is it part of your high office to be cold—and hungry—and wretched?"

"I am not wretched."

"You are; now, and at all times. You are killing yourself."

"No; else I had died long, long ago."

"Well, then, of what use is your poor life as you now live it, either to yourself or any one else? Do you succeed among the miners? How many have you brought into the church?"

"Not one."

"And yourself? Have you succeeded, so far, in making yourself a saint?"

"God knows I have not," replied the parson, covering his face with his hands as the questions probed his sore, sad heart. "I have failed in my work, I have failed in myself, I am of all men most miserable!—most miserable!"

The girl sprang forward and caught his arm, her eyes full of love's pity. "You know you love me," she murmured; "why fight against it? For I—I love you!"

What did the parson do?

He fell upon his knees, but not to her, and uttered a Latin prayer, short but fervid.

"All the kingdoms of the world and the glory of them," he murmured, "would not be to me so much as this!" Then he rose.

"Child," he said, "you know not what you do." And, opening the door, he went away into the snowy forest. But the girl's weeping voice called after him, "Herman, Herman." He turned; she had sunk upon the threshold. He came back and lifted her for a moment in his arms.

"Be comforted, Rosamond," he said, tenderly. "It is but a fancy; you will soon forget me. You do not really love me,— such a one as I," he continued, bringing forward, poor heart! his own greatest sorrow with unpitying hand. "But thank you, dear, for the gentle fancy." He stood a moment, silent; then touched her dark hair with his quivering lips and disappeared.

Sunday morning the sun rose unclouded, the snow lay deep on the ground, the first ice covered the bay; winter had come. At ten o'clock the customary service began in the Chapel of St. John and St. James, and the little congregation shivered, and whispered that it must really try to raise money enough for a stove. The parson did not feel the cold, although he looked almost bloodless in his white surplice. The Englishwoman was there, repentant,—the sick child had not rallied under the new ministration; Mrs. Malone was there, from sheer good-nature; and several of the villagers and two or three miners had strolled in because they had nothing else to do, Brother Saul having returned to the mine. Rose Ray was not there. She was no saint, so she stayed at home and wept like a sinner.

The congregation, which had sat silent through the service, fell entirely asleep during the sermon on the "General Councils." Suddenly, in the midst of a sentence, there came a noise that stopped the parson and woke the sleepers. Two or three miners rushed into the chapel and spoke to the few men present. "Come out," they cried,—"come out to the mine. The thief's caught at last! and who do you think it is? Saul, Brother Saul himself, the hypocrite! They tracked him to his den, and there they found the barrels and sacks and kegs, but the stuff he's made away with, most of it. He took it all, every crumb, and us a starving!"

"We've run in to tell the town," said another. "We've got him fast, and we're going to make a sample of him. Come out and see the fun."

"Yes," echoed a third, who lifted a ruffianly face from his short, squat figure, "and we'll take our own time, too. He's made us suffer, and now he shall suffer a bit, if I know myself."

The women shuddered as, with an ominous growl, all the men went out together.

"I misdoubt they'll hang him," said Mrs. Malone, shaking her head as she looked after them.

"Or worse," said the miner's wife.

Then the two departed, and the parson was left alone. Did he cut off the service? No. Deliberately he finished every word of the sermon, sang a hymn, and spoke the final prayer; then, after putting everything in order, he too left the little sanctuary; but he did not go homeward, he took the road to the mine.

"Don't-ee go, sir, don't!" pleaded the Englishwoman, standing in her doorway as he passed. "You won't do no good, sir."

"Maybe not," answered the parson, gently, "but at least I must try."

He entered the forest; the air was still and cold, the snow crackled under his feet, and the pine-trees stretched away in long white aisles. He looked like a pygmy as he hastened on among the forest giants, his step more languid than usual from sternest vigil and fasting.

"Thou proud, evil body, I have conquered thee!" he had said in the cold dawning. And he had; at least, the body answered not again.

The mine was several miles away, and to lighten the journey the little man sang a hymn, his voice sounding through the forest in singular melody. It was an ancient hymn that he sang, written long ago by some cowled monk, and it told in quaint language of the joys of "Paradise! O Paradise!" He did not feel the cold as he sang of the pearly gates.

In the late afternoon his halting feet approached the mine; as he drew near the clearing he heard a sound of many voices shouting together, followed by a single cry, and a momentary silence more fearful than the clamor. The tormentors were at work. The parson ran forward, and, passing the log-huts which lay between, came out upon the scene. A circle of men stood there around a stake. Fastened by a long rope, crouched the wretched prisoner, his face turned to the color of dough, his coarse features drawn apart like an animal in terror, and his hoarse voice never ceasing its piteous cry, "Have mercy, good gentlemen! Dear gentlemen, have mercy!"

At a little distance a fire of logs was burning, and from the brands scattered around it was evident that the man had served as a target for the fiery missiles; in addition he bore the marks of blows, and his clothes were torn and covered with mud as though he had been dragged roughly over the ground. The lurid light of the fire cast a glow over the faces of the miners; behind rose the Iron Mountain, dark in shadow; and on each side stretched out the ranks of the white-pine trees, like ghosts assembled as silent witnesses against the cruelty of man. The parson rushed forward, broke through the circle, and threw his arms around the prisoner at the stake, protecting him with his slender body.

"If ye kill him, ye must kill me also," he cried, in a ringing voice.

On the border, the greatest crime is robbery. A thief is worse than a murderer; a life does not count so much as life's supplies. It was not for the murderer that the Lynch law was made, but for the thief. For months these Algonquin miners had suffered loss; their goods, their provisions, their clothes, and their precious whiskey had been stolen, day after day, and all search had proved vain; exasperated, several times actually suffering from want, they had heaped up a great store of fury for the thief,—fury increased tenfold when, caught at last, he proved to be no other than Brother Saul, the one man whom they had trusted, the one man whom they had clothed and fed before themselves, the one man from whom they had expected better things. An honest, bloodthirsty wolf in his own skin was an animal they respected; indeed, they were themselves little better. But a wolf in sheep's clothing was utterly abhorrent to their peculiar sense of honor. So they gathered around their prey, and esteemed it rightfully theirs; whiskey had sharpened their enjoyment.

To this savage band, enter the little parson. "What! are ye men?" he cried. "Shame, shame, ye murderers!"

The miners stared at the small figure that defied them, and for the moment their anger gave way before a rough sense of the ludicrous.

"Hear the little man," they cried. "Hurrah, Peter! Go ahead!"

But they soon wearied of his appeal and began to answer back.

"What are clothes or provisions to a life?" said the minister.

"Life ain't worth much without 'em, Parson," replied a miner. "He took all we had, and we 've gone cold and hungry 'long of him, and he knowed it. And all the time we was a giving him of the best, and a believing his praying and his preaching."

"If he is guilty, let him be tried by the legal authorities."

"We 're our own legal 'thorities, Parson."

"The country will call you to account."

"The country won't do nothing of the kind. Much the country cares for us poor miners, frozen up here in the woods! Stand back, Parson. Why should you bother about Saul? You always hated him."

"Never! never!" answered the parson, earnestly.

"You did too, and he knowed it. 'T was because he was dirty, and could n't mince his words as you do."

The parson turned to the crouching figure at his side. "Friend," he said, "if this is true,—and the heart is darkly deceitful and hides from man his own worst sins,—I humbly ask your forgiveness."

"O come! None of your gammon," said another miner, impatiently. "Saul did n't care whether you liked him or not, for he knowed you was only a coward."

"'Fraid of a dog! 'Fraid of a dog!" shouted half a dozen voices; and a frozen twig struck the parson's cheek, and drew blood.

"Why, he 's got blood!" said one. "I never thought he had any."

"Come, Parson," said a friendly miner, advancing from the circle, "we don't want to hurt *you*, but you might as well understand that we 're the masters here."

"And if ye are the masters, then be just. Give the criminal to me; I will myself take him to the nearest judge, the nearest jail, and deliver him up."

"He 'll be more likely to deliver *you* up, I reckon, Parson."

"Well, then, send a committee of your own men with me—"

"We 've got other things to do besides taking long journeys over the ice to 'commodate thieves, Parson. Leave the man to us."

"And to torture? Men, men, ye would not treat a beast so!"

"A beast don't steal our food and whiskey," sang out a miner.

"Stand back! stand back!" shouted several voices. "You 're too little to fight, Parson."

"But not too little to die," answered the minister, throwing up his arms towards the sky.

For an instant his words held the men in check; they looked at each other, then at him.

"Think of yourselves," continued the minister. "Are ye without fault? If ye murder this man, ye are worse than he is."

But here the minister went astray in his appeal, and ran against the views of the border.

"Worse! Worse than a sneaking thief! Worse than a praying hypocrite who robs the very men that feed him! Look here, we won't stand that! Sheer off, or take the consequences." And a burning brand struck the parson's coat, and fell on the head of the crouching figure at his side, setting fire to its hair. Instantly the parson extinguished the light flame, and drew the burly form closer within his arms, so that the two stood as one. "Not one, but both of us," he cried.

A new voice spoke next, the voice of the oldest miner, the most hardened reprobate there. "Let go that rascal, Parson. He 's the fellow that lamed you last spring. He set the trap himself; I seen him a doing it."

Involuntarily, for a moment, Herman Peters drew back; the trap set at the chapel door, the deliberate, cruel intention, the painful injury, and its life-long result, brought the angry color to his pale face. The memory was full of the old bitterness.

But Saul, feeling himself deserted, dragged his miserable body forward, and clasped the parson's knees. With desperate hands he clung, and he was not repulsed. Without a word the parson drew him closer, and again faced the crowd.

"Why, the man 's a downright fool!" said the old miner. "That Saul lamed him for life, and all for nothing, and still he stands by him. The man 's mad!"

"I am not mad," answered the parson, and his voice rung out clear and sweet. "But I am a minister of the great God who has said to men, 'Thou shalt do no murder.' O men! O brothers! look back into your own lives. Have ye no crimes, no sins to be forgiven? Can ye expect mercy when ye give none? Let this poor creature go, and it shall be counted unto you for goodness. Ye, too, must some time die; and when the hour comes, as it often comes, in lives like yours, with sudden horror, ye will have this good deed to remember. For charity—which is mercy —shall cover a multitude of sins."

He ceased, and there was a momentary pause. Then a stern voice answered, "Facts won't alter, Parson. The man is a thief, and must be punished. Your talk may do for women-folks, not for us."

"Women-folks!" repeated the ruffian-faced man who had made the women shudder at the chapel. "He 's a sly fox, this parson! He did n't go out to meet Rosie Ray at the Grotter yesterday, O no!"

"Liar!" shouted a man, who had been standing in the shadow on the outskirts of the crowd, taking, so far, no part in the scene. He forced himself to the front; it was Steven Long, his face dark with passion.

"No liar at all, Steve," answered the first. "I seen 'em there with my own eyes; they had things to eat and everything. Just ask the parson."

"Yes, ask the parson," echoed the others; and with the shifting humor of the border, they stopped to laugh over the idea. "Ask the parson."

Steven Long stepped forward and confronted the little

minister. His strong hands were clinched, his blood was on fire with jealousy. The bull-dog followed his master, and smelled around the parson's gaiters,—the same poor old shoes, his only pair, now wet with melted snow. The parson glanced down apprehensively.

"'Fraid of a dog! 'Fraid of a dog!" shouted the miners, again laughing uproariously. The fun was better than they had anticipated.

"Is it true?" demanded Steven Long, in a hoarse voice. "Did you meet that girl at the Grotter yesterday?"

"I did meet Rosamond Ray at the Grotto yesterday," answered the parson; "but—"

He never finished the sentence. A fragment of iron ore struck him on the temple. He fell, and died, his small body lying across the thief, whom he still protected, even in death.

The murder was not avenged; Steven Long was left to go his own way. But as the thief was also allowed to depart unmolested, the principles of border justice were held to have been amply satisfied.

The miners attended the funeral in a body, and even deputed one of their number to read the Episcopal burial service over the rough pine coffin, since there was no one else to do it. They brought out the chapel prayer-books, found the places, and followed as well as they could; for "he thought a deal of them books. Don't you remember how he was always carrying 'em backward and forward, poor little chap!"

The Chapel of St. John and St. James was closed for the season. In the summer a new missionary arrived; he was not ritualistic, and before the year was out he married Rosamond Ray.

# *Jeannette*

---

$B$EFORE the war for the Union, in the times of the old army, there had been peace throughout the country for thirteen years. Regiments existed in their officers, but the ranks were thin,—the more so the better, since the United States possessed few forts and seemed in chronic embarrassment over her military children, owing to the flying foot-ball of public opinion, now "standing army pro," now "standing army con," with more or less allusion to the much-enduring Cæsar and his legions, the ever-present ghost of the political arena.

In those days the few forts were full and much state was kept up; the officers were all graduates of West Point, and their wives graduates of the first families. They prided themselves upon their antecedents; and if there was any aristocracy in the country, it was in the circles of army life.

Those were pleasant days,—pleasant for the old soldiers who were resting after Mexico,—pleasant for young soldiers destined to die on the plains of Gettysburg or the cloudy heights of Lookout Mountain. There was an *esprit de corps* in the little band, a dignity of bearing, and a ceremonious state, lost in the great struggle which came afterward. That great struggle now lies ten years back; yet, to-day, when the silver-haired veterans meet, they pass it over as a thing of the present, and go back to the times of the "old army."

Up in the northern straits, between blue Lake Huron, with its clear air, and gray Lake Michigan, with its silver fogs, lies the bold island of Mackinac. Clustered along the beach, which runs around its half-moon harbor, are the houses of the old French village, nestling at the foot of the cliff rising behind, crowned with the little white fort, the stars and stripes floating above it against the deep blue sky. Beyond, on all sides, the forest stretches away, cliffs finishing it abruptly, save one slope at the far end of the island, three miles distant, where the British landed in 1812. That is the whole of Mackinac.

The island has a strange sufficiency of its own; it satisfies; all who have lived there feel it. The island has a wild beauty of its own; it fascinates; all who have lived there love it. Among its aromatic cedars, along the aisles of its pine-trees, in the gay company of its maples, there is companionship. On its bald northern cliffs, bathed in sunshine and swept by the pure breeze, there is exhilaration. Many there are, bearing the burden and heat of the day, who look back to the island with the tears that rise but do not fall, the sudden longing despondency that comes occasionally to all, when the tired heart cries out, "O, to escape, to flee away, far, far away, and be at rest!"

In 1856 Fort Mackinac held a major, a captain, three lieutenants, a chaplain, and a surgeon, besides those subordinate officers who wear stripes on their sleeves, and whose rank and duties are mysteries to the uninitiated. The force for this array of commanders was small, less than a company; but what it lacked in quantity it made up in quality, owning to the continual drilling it received.

The days were long at Fort Mackinac; happy thought! drill the men. So when the major had finished, the captain began, and each lieutenant was watching his chance. Much state was kept up also. Whenever the major appeared, "Commanding officer; guard, present arms," was called down the line of men on duty, and the guard hastened to obey, the major acknowledging the salute with stiff precision. By day and by night sentinels paced the walls. True, the walls were crumbling, and the whole force was constantly engaged in propping them up, but none the less did the sentinels pace with dignity. What was it to the captain if, while he sternly inspected the muskets in the block-house, the lieutenant, with a detail of men, was hard at work strengthening its underpinning? None the less did he inspect. The sally-port, mended but imposing; the flag-staff with its fair-weather and storm flags; the frowning iron grating; the sidling white causeway, constantly falling down and as constantly repaired, which led up to the main entrance; the well-preserved old cannon,—all showed a strict military rule. When the men were not drilling they were propping up the fort, and when they were not propping up the fort they were drilling. In the early days, the days of the first American commanders, military roads had been made through the forest,—roads even now smooth and solid, although trees of a second growth meet overhead. But that was when the fort was young and stood firmly on its legs. In 1856 there was no time for road-making, for when military duty was over there was always more or less mending to keep the whole fortification from sliding down hill into the lake.

On Sunday there was service in the little chapel, an upper room overlooking the inside parade-ground. Here the kindly Episcopal chaplain read the chapters about Balaam and Balak, and always made the same impressive pause after "Let me die the death of the righteous, and let my last end be like his." (Dear old man! he has gone. Would that our last end might indeed be like his!) Not that the chaplain confined his reading to the Book of Numbers; but as those chapters are appointed for the August Sundays, and as it was in August that the summer visitors came to Mackinac, the little chapel is in many minds associated with the patient Balak, his seven altars, and his seven rams.

There was state and discipline in the fort even on Sundays; bugle-playing marshalled the congregation in, bugle-playing marshalled them out. If the sermon was not finished, so much the worse for the sermon, but it made no difference to the bugle; at a given moment it sounded, and out marched all the soldiers, drowning the poor chaplain's hurrying voice with their tramp down the stairs. The officers attended service in full uniform, sitting erect and dignified in the front seats. We used to smile at the grand air they had, from the stately gray-haired major down to the youngest lieutenant fresh from the Point. But brave hearts were beating under those fine uniforms; and when the great struggle came, one and all died on the field in the front of the battle. Over the grave of the commanding officer is inscribed "Major-General," over the captain's is "Brigadier," and over each young lieutenant is "Colonel." They gained their promotion in death.

I spent many months at Fort Mackinac with Archie; Archie was my nephew, a young lieutenant. In the short, bright summer came the visitors from below; all the world outside is "below" in island vernacular. In the long winter the little white fort looked out over unbroken ice-fields, and watched for the moving black dot of the dog-train bringing the mails from the mainland. One January day I had been out walking on the snow-crust, breathing the cold, still air, and, returning within the walls to our quarters, I found my little parlor already occupied. Jeannette was there, petite Jeanneton, the fisherman's daughter. Strange beauty sometimes results from a mixed descent, and this girl had French, English, and Indian blood in her veins, the three races mixing and inter-mixing among her ancestors, according to the custom of the Northwestern border. A bold profile delicately finished, heavy blue-black hair, light blue eyes looking out unexpectedly from under black lashes and brows; a fair white skin, neither the rose-white of the blonde nor the cream-white of the Ori-ental brunette; a rounded form with small hands and feet, —showed the mixed beauties of three nationalities. Yes, there could be no doubt but that Jeannette was singularly lovely, albeit ignorant utterly. Her dress was as much of a *mélange* as her ancestry: a short skirt of military blue, Indian leggins and moccasins, a red jacket and little red cap embroidered with beads. The thick braids of her hair hung down her back, and on the lounge lay a large blanket-mantle lined with fox-skins and ornamented with the plumage of birds. She had come to teach me bead-work; I had already taken several lessons to while away the time, but found myself an awkward scholar.

"*Bonjou', madame*," she said, in her patois of broken English and degenerate French. "Pretty here."

My little parlor had a square of carpet, a hearth-fire of great logs, Turkey-red curtains, a lounge and arm-chair covered with chintz, several prints on the cracked walls, and a number of books,—the whole well used and worn, worth perhaps twenty dollars in any town below, but ten times twenty in icy Mack-inac. I began the bead-work, and Jeannette was laughing at my mistakes, when the door opened, and our surgeon came in, pausing to warm his hands before going up to his room in the attic. A taciturn man was our surgeon, Rodney Prescott, not popular in the merry garrison circle, but a favorite of mine; the Puritan, the New-Englander, the Bostonian, were as plainly written upon his face as the French and Indian were written upon Jeannette.

"Sit down, Doctor," I said.

He took a seat and watched us carelessly, now and then smil-ing at Jeannette's chatter as a giant might smile upon a pygmy. I could see that the child was putting on all her little airs to at-tract his attention; now the long lashes swept the cheeks, now they were raised suddenly, disclosing the unexpected blue eyes; the little moccasined feet must be warmed on the fender, the braids must be swept back with an impatient movement of the hand and shoulder, and now and then there was a coquettish arch of the red lips, less than a pout, what she herself would have called "*une p'tite moue*." Our surgeon watched this pantomime unmoved.

"Is n't she beautiful?" I said, when, at the expiration of the hour, Jeannette disappeared, wrapped in her mantle.

"No; not to my eyes."

"Why, what more can you require, Doctor? Look at her rich coloring, her hair—"

"There is no mind in her face, Mrs. Corlyne."

"But she is still a child."

"She will always be a child; she will never mature," answered our surgeon, going up the steep stairs to his room above.

Jeannette came regularly, and one morning, tired of the bead-work, I proposed teaching her to read. She consented, although not without an incentive in the form of shillings; but, however gained, my scholar gave to the long winter a new interest. She learned readily; but as there was no foundation, I was obliged to commence with A, B, C.

"Why not teach her to cook?" suggested the major's fair young wife, whose life was spent in hopeless labors with Indian servants, who, sooner or later, ran away in the night with spoons and the family apparel.

"Why not teach her to sew?" said Madame Captain, wearily raising her eyes from the pile of small garments before her.

"Why not have her up for one of our sociables?" hazarded our most dashing lieutenant, twirling his mustache.

"Frederick!" exclaimed his wife, in a tone of horror: she was aristocratic, but sharp in outlines.

"Why not bring her into the church? Those French half-breeds are little better than heathen," said the chaplain.

Thus the high authorities disapproved of my educational efforts. I related their comments to Archie, and added, "The surgeon is the only one who has said nothing against it."

"Prescott? O, he 's too high and mighty to notice anybody, much less a half-breed girl. I never saw such a stiff, silent fellow;

he looks as though he had swallowed all his straightlaced Puritan ancestors. I wish he 'd exchange."

"Gently, Archie—"

"O, yes, without doubt; certainly, and amen! I know *you* like him, Aunt Sarah," said my handsome boy-soldier, laughing.

The lessons went on. We often saw the surgeon during study hours, as the stairway leading to his room opened out of the little parlor. Sometimes he would stop awhile and listen as Jeannette slowly read, "The good boy likes his red top"; "The good girl can sew a seam"; or watched her awkward attempts to write her name, or add a one and a two. It was slow work, but I persevered, if from no other motive than obstinacy. Had not they all prophesied a failure? When wearied with the dull routine, I gave an oral lesson in poetry. If the rhymes were of the chiming, rhythmic kind, Jeannette learned rapidly, catching the verses as one catches a tune, and repeating them with a spirit and dramatic gesture all her own. Her favorite was Macaulay's "Ivry." Beautiful she looked, as, standing in the centre of the room, she rolled out the sonorous lines, her French accent giving a charming foreign coloring to the well-known verses:—

"Now by the lips of those ye love, fair gentlemen of France,
    Charge for the golden lilies,—upon them with the lance!
    A thousand spurs are striking deep, a thousand spears in
        rest,
    A thousand knights are pressing close behind the snow-
        white crest;
    And in they burst, and on they rushed, while, like a
        guiding star,
    Amidst the thickest carnage blazed the helmet of Navarre."

And yet, after all my explanations, she only half understood it; the "knights" were always "nights" in her mind, and the "thickest carnage" was always the "thickest carriage."

One March day she came at the appointed hour, soon after our noon dinner. The usual clear winter sky was clouded, and a wind blew the snow from the trees where it had lain quietly month after month. "Spring is coming," said the old sergeant that morning, as he hoisted the storm-flag; "it 's getting wild-like."

Jeannette and I went through the lessons, but toward three o'clock a north-wind came sweeping over the Straits and enveloped the island in a whirling snow-storm, partly eddies of white splinters torn from the ice-bound forest, and partly a new fall of round snow pellets careering along on the gale, quite unlike the soft, feathery flakes of early winter. "You cannot go home now, Jeannette," I said, looking out through the little west window; our cottage stood back on the hill, and from this side window we could see the Straits, going down toward far Waugoschance; the steep fort-hill outside the wall; the long meadow, once an Indian burial-place, below; and beyond on the beach the row of cabins inhabited by the French fishermen, one of them the home of my pupil. The girl seldom went round the point into the village; its one street and a half seemed distasteful to her. She climbed the stone-wall on the ridge behind her cabin, took an Indian trail through the grass in summer, or struck across on the snow-crust in winter, ran up the steep side of the fort-hill like a wild chamois, and came into the garrison enclosure with a careless nod to the admiring sentinel, as she passed under the rear entrance. These French half-breeds, like the gypsies, were not without a pride of their own. They held themselves aloof from the Irish of Shanty-town, the floating sailor population of the summer, and the common soldiers of the garrison. They intermarried among themselves, and held their own revels in their beach-cabins during the winter, with music from their old violins, dancing and songs, French ballads with a chorus after every two lines, quaint *chansons* handed down from voyageur ancestors. Small respect had they for the little Roman Catholic church beyond the old Agency garden; its German priest they refused to honor; but, when stately old Father Piret came over to the island from his hermitage in the Chenaux, they ran to meet him, young and old, and paid him reverence with affectionate respect. Father Piret was a Parisian, and a gentleman; nothing less would suit these far-away sheep in the wilderness!

Jeannette Leblanc had all the pride of her class; the Irish saloon-keeper with his shining tall hat, the loud-talking mate of the lake schooner, the trim sentinel pacing the fort walls, were nothing to her, and this somewhat incongruous hauteur gave her the air of a little princess.

On this stormy afternoon the captain's wife was in my parlor preparing to return to her own quarters with some coffee she had borrowed. Hearing my remark she said, "O, the snow won't hurt the child, Mrs. Corlyne; she must be storm-proof, living down there on the beach! Duncan can take her home."

Duncan was the orderly, a factotum in the garrison.

"*Non*," said Jeannette, tossing her head proudly as the door closed behind the lady, "I wish not of Duncan; I go alone."

It happened that Archie, my nephew, had gone over to the cottage of the commanding officer to decorate the parlor for the military sociable; I knew he would not return, and the evening stretched out before me in all its long loneliness. "Stay, Jeannette," I said. "We will have tea together here, and when the wind goes down, old Antoine shall go back with you." Antoine was a French wood-cutter, whose cabin clung half-way down the fort-hill like a swallow's nest.

Jeannette's eyes sparkled; I had never invited her before; in an instant she had turned the day into a high festival. "Braid hair?" she asked, glancing toward the mirror; "*faut que je m' fasse belle*." And the long hair came out of its close braids, enveloping her in its glossy dark waves, while she carefully smoothed out the bits of red ribbon that served as fastenings. At this moment the door opened, and the surgeon, the wind, and a puff of snow came in together. Jeannette looked up, smiling and blushing; the falling hair gave a new softness to her face, and her eyes were as shy as the eyes of a wild fawn.

Only the previous day I had noticed that Rodney Prescott listened with marked attention to the captain's cousin, a Virginia lady, as she advanced a theory that Jeannette had negro blood in her veins. "Those quadroon girls often have a certain kind of plebeian beauty like this pet of yours, Mrs. Corlyne," she said, with a slight sniff of her high-bred, pointed nose. In vain I exclaimed, in vain I argued; the garrison ladies were all against me, and, in their presence, not a man dared come to my aid; and the surgeon even added, "I wish I could be sure of it."

"Sure of the negro blood?" I said, indignantly.

"Yes."

"But Jeannette does not look in the least like a quadroon."

"Some of the quadroon girls are very handsome, Mrs. Corlyne," answered the surgeon, coldly.

"O yes!" said the high-bred Virginia lady. "My brother has a number of them about his place, but we do not teach them to read, I assure you. It spoils them."

As I looked at Jeannette's beautiful face, her delicate eagle profile, her fair skin and light blue eyes, I recalled this conversation with vivid indignation. The surgeon, at least, should be convinced of his mistake. Jeannette had never looked more brilliant; probably the man had never really scanned her features,—he was such a cold, unseeing creature; but to-night he should have a fair opportunity, so I invited him to join our storm-bound tea-party. He hesitated.

"Ah, do, Monsieur Rodenai," said Jeannette, springing forward. "I sing for you, I dance; but, no, you not like that. *Bien*, I tell your fortune then." The young girl loved company. A party of three, no matter who the third, was to her infinitely better than two.

The surgeon stayed.

A merry evening we had before the hearth-fire. The wind howled around the block-house and rattled the flag-staff, and the snow pellets sounded on the window-panes, giving that sense of warm comfort within that comes only with the storm. Our servant had been drafted into service for the military sociable, and I was to prepare the evening meal myself.

"Not tea," said Jeannette, with a wry face; "tea,—*c'est médecine!*" She had arranged her hair in fanciful braids, and now followed me to the kitchen, enjoying the novelty like a child. "*Café?*" she said. "O, please, madame! *I* make it."

The little shed kitchen was cold and dreary, each plank of its thin walls rattling in the gale with a dismal creak; the wind blew the smoke down the chimney, and finally it ended in our bringing everything into the cosey parlor, and using the hearth fire, where Jeannette made coffee and baked little cakes over the coals.

The meal over, Jeannette sang her songs, sitting on the rug before the fire,—*Le Beau Voyageur*, *Les Neiges de La Cloche*, ballads in Canadian patois sung to minor airs brought over from France two hundred years before.

The surgeon sat in the shade of the chimney-piece, his face shaded by his hand, and I could not discover whether he saw anything to admire in my *protégée*, until, standing in the centre of the room, she gave us "Ivry" in glorious style. Beautiful she looked as she rolled out the lines:—

"And if my standard-bearer fall, as fall full well he may,—
    For never saw I promise yet of such a bloody fray,—
    Press where ye see my white plume shine amidst the
        ranks of war,
    And be your oriflamme to-day the helmet of Navarre."

Rodney sat in the full light now, and I secretly triumphed in his rapt attention.

"Something else, Jeannette," I said, in the pride of my heart. Instead of repeating anything I had taught her, she began in French:—

> "'Marie, enfin quitte l'ouvrage,
>     Voici l'étoile du berger.'
>     —'Ma mère, un enfant du village
>     Languit captif chez l'étranger;
>     Pris sur mer, loin de sa patrie,
>     Il s'est rendu,—mais le dernier.'
>         File, file, pauvre Marie,
>         Pour secourir le prisonnier;
>         File, file, pauvre Marie,
>         File, file, pour le prisonnier.
>
> "'Pour lui je filerais moi-même
>     Mon enfant,—mais—j'ai tant vieilli!'
>     —'Envoyez à celui que j'aime
>     Tout le gain par moi recueilli.
>     Rose à sa noce en vain me prie;—
>     Dieu! j'entends le ménétrier!'
>         File, file, pauvre Marie,
>         Pour secourir le prisonnier;
>         File, file, pauvre Marie,
>         File, file, pour le prisonnier.
>
> "'Plus près du feu file, ma chère;
>     La nuit vient refroidir le temps.'
>     —'Adrien, m'a-t-on dit, ma mère,
>     Gémit dans des cachots flottants.

On repousse la main flétrie
Qu'il étend vers un pain grossier.'
    File, file, pauvre Marie,
    Pour secourir le prisonnier;
    File, file, pauvre Marie,
    File, file, pour le prisonnier."*

Jeannette repeated these lines with a pathos so real that I felt a moisture rising in my eyes.

"Where did you learn that, child?" I asked.

"Father Piret, madame."

"What is it?"

"*Je n' sais.*"

"It is Béranger,—'The Prisoner of War,'" said Rodney Prescott. "But you omitted the last verse, mademoiselle; may I ask why?"

"More sad so," answered Jeannette. "Marie she die now."

"You wish her to die?"

"*Mais oui*: she die for love; *c'est beau!*"

And there flashed a glance from the girl's eyes that thrilled through me, I scarcely knew why. I looked toward Rodney, but he was back in the shadow again.

The hours passed. "I must go," said Jeannette, drawing aside the curtain. Clouds were still driving across the sky, but the snow had ceased falling, and at intervals the moon shone out over the cold white scene; the March wind continued on its wild career toward the south.

"I will send for Antoine," I said, rising, as Jeannette took up her fur mantle.

"The old man is sick to-day," said Rodney. "It would not be safe for him to leave the fire to-night. I will accompany mademoiselle."

Pretty Jeannette shrugged her shoulders. "*Mais, monsieur,*" she answered, "I go over the hill."

"No, child; not to-night," I said decidedly. "The wind is violent, and the cliff doubly slippery after this ice-storm. Go round through the village."

"Of course we shall go through the village," said our surgeon,

* "Le Prisonnier de Guerre," Béranger.

in his calm, authoritative way. They started. But in another minute I saw Jeannette fly by the west window, over the wall, and across the snowy road, like a spirit, disappearing down the steep bank, now slippery with glare ice. Another minute, and Rodney Prescott followed in her track.

With bated breath I watched for the reappearance of the two figures on the white plain, one hundred and fifty feet below; the cliff was difficult at any time, and now in this ice! The moments seemed very long, and, alarmed, I was on the point of arousing the garrison, when I spied the two dark figures on the snowy plain below, now clear in the moonlight, now lost in the shadow. I watched them for some distance; then a cloud came, and I lost them entirely.

Rodney did not return, although I sat late before the dying fire. Thinking over the evening, the idea came to me that perhaps, after all, he did admire my *protégée*, and, being a romantic old woman, I did not repel the fancy; it might go a certain distance without harm, and an idyl is always charming, doubly so to people cast away on a desert island. One falls into the habit of studying persons very closely in the limited circle of garrison life.

But, the next morning, the Major's wife gave me an account of the sociable. "It was very pleasant," she said. "Toward the last Dr. Prescott came in, quite unexpectedly. I had no idea he could be so agreeable. Augusta can tell you how charming he was!"

Augusta, a young lady cousin, of pale blond complexion, neutral opinions, and irreproachable manners, smiled primly. My idyl was crushed!

The days passed. The winds, the snows, and the high-up fort remained the same. Jeannette came and went, and the hour lengthened into two or three; not that we read much, but we talked more. Our surgeon did not again pass through the parlor; he had ordered a rickety stairway on the outside wall to be repaired, and we could hear him going up and down its icy steps as we sat by the hearth-fire. One day I said to him, "My *protégée* is improving wonderfully. If she could have a complete education, she might take her place with the best in the land."

"Do not deceive yourself, Mrs. Corlyne," he answered. "It is only the shallow French quickness."

"Why do you always judge the child so harshly, Doctor?"

"Do *you* take her part, Aunt Sarah?" (For sometimes he used the title which Archie had made so familiar.)

"Of course I do, Rodney. A poor, unfriended girl living in this remote place, against a United States surgeon with the best of Boston behind him."

"I wish you would tell me that every day, Aunt Sarah," was the reply I received. It set me musing, but I could make nothing of it. Troubled without knowing why, I suggested to Archie that he should endeavor to interest our surgeon in the fort gayety; there was something for every night in the merry little circle,—games, suppers, tableaux, music, theatricals, readings, and the like.

"Why, he 's in the thick of it already, Aunt Sarah," said my nephew. "He 's devoting himself to Miss Augusta; she sings 'The Harp that once—' to him every night."

("The Harp that once through Tara's Halls" was Miss Augusta's dress-parade song. The Major's quarters not being as large as the halls aforesaid, the melody was somewhat overpowering.)

"O, does she?" I thought, not without a shade of vexation. But the vague anxiety vanished.

The real spring came at last,—the rapid, vivid spring of Mackinac. Almost in a day the ice moved out, the snows melted, and the northern wild-flowers appeared in the sheltered glens. Lessons were at an end, for my scholar was away in the green woods. Sometimes she brought me a bunch of flowers; but I seldom saw her; my wild bird had flown back to the forest. When the ground was dry and the pine droppings warmed by the sun, I, too, ventured abroad. One day, wandering as far as the Arched Rock, I found the surgeon there, and together we sat down to rest under the trees, looking off over the blue water flecked with white caps. The Arch is a natural bridge over a chasm one hundred and fifty feet above the lake,—a fissure in the cliff which has fallen away in a hollow, leaving the bridge by itself far out over the water. This bridge springs upward in the shape of an arch; it is fifty feet long, and its width is in some places two feet, in others only a few inches,—a narrow, dizzy pathway hanging between sky and water.

"People have crossed it," I said.

"Only fools," answered our surgeon, who despised foolhardiness. "Has a man nothing better to do with his life than risk it for the sake of a silly feat like that? I would not so much as raise my eyes to see any one cross."

"O yes, you would, Monsieur Rodenai," cried a voice behind us. We both turned and caught a glimpse of Jeannette as she bounded through the bushes and out to the very centre of the Arch, where she stood balancing herself and laughing gayly. Her form was outlined against the sky; the breeze swayed her skirt; she seemed hovering over the chasm. I watched her, mute with fear; a word might cause her to lose her balance; but I could not turn my eyes away, I was fascinated with the sight. I was not aware that Rodney had left me until he, too, appeared on the Arch, slowly finding a foothold for himself and advancing toward the centre. A fragment of the rock broke off under his foot and fell into the abyss below.

"Go back, Monsieur Rodenai," cried Jeannette, seeing his danger.

"Will *you* come back too, Jeannette?"

"*Moi? C'est aut' chose,*" answered the girl, gayly tossing her pretty head.

"Then I shall come out and carry you back, wilful child," said the surgeon.

A peal of laughter broke from Jeannette as he spoke, and then she began to dance on her point of rock, swinging herself from side to side, marking the time with a song. I held my breath; her dance seemed unearthly; it was as though she belonged to the Prince of the Powers of the Air.

At length the surgeon reached the centre and caught the mocking creature in his arms: neither spoke, but I could see the flash of their eyes as they stood for an instant motionless. Then they struggled on the narrow foothold and swayed over so far that I buried my face in my trembling hands, unable to look at the dreadful end. When I opened my eyes again all was still; the Arch was tenantless, and no sound came from below. Were they, then, so soon dead? Without a cry? I forced myself to the brink to look down over the precipice; but while I stood there, fearing to look, I heard a sound behind me in the woods. It was Jeannette singing a gay French song. I called to her to stop. "How could you?" I said severely, for I was still trembling with agitation.

"*Ce n'est rien*, madame. I cross l'Arche when I had five year. *Mais*, Monsieur Rodenai le Grand, he raise his eye to look *this* time, I think," said Jeannette, laughing triumphantly.

"Where is he?"

"On the far side, gone on to Scott's Pic [Peak]. *Féroce, O féroce, comme un loupgarou! Ah! c'est joli, ça!*" And, overflowing with the wildest glee, the girl danced along through the woods in front of me, now pausing to look at something in her hand, now laughing, now shouting like a wild creature, until I lost sight of her. I went back to the fort alone.

For several days I saw nothing of Rodney. When at last we met, I said, "That was a wild freak of Jeannette's at the Arch."

"Planned, to get a few shillings out of us."

"O Doctor! I do not think she had any such motive," I replied, looking up deprecatingly into his cold, scornful eyes.

"Are you not a little sentimental over that ignorant, half-wild creature, Aunt Sarah?"

"Well," I said to myself, "perhaps I am!"

The summer came, sails whitened the blue straits again, steamers stopped for an hour or two at the island docks, and the summer travellers rushed ashore to buy "Indian curiosities," made by the nuns in Montreal, or to climb breathlessly up the steep fort-hill to see the pride and panoply of war. Proud was the little white fort in those summer days; the sentinels held themselves stiffly erect, the officers gave up lying on the parapet half asleep, the best flag was hoisted daily, and there was much bugle-playing and ceremony connected with the evening gun, fired from the ramparts at sunset; the hotels were full, the boarding-house keepers were in their annual state of wonder over the singular taste of these people from "below," who actually preferred a miserable white-fish to the best of beef brought up on ice all the way from Buffalo! There were picnics and walks, and much confusion of historical dates respecting Father Marquette and the irrepressible, omnipresent Pontiac. The fort officers did much escort duty; their buttons gilded every scene. Our quiet surgeon was foremost in everything.

"I am surprised! I had no idea Dr. Prescott was so gay," said the major's wife.

"I should not think of calling him gay," I answered.

"Why, my dear Mrs. Corlyne! He is going all the time. Just ask Augusta."

Augusta thereupon remarked that society, to a certain extent, was beneficial; that she considered Dr. Prescott much improved; really, he was now very "nice."

I silently protested against the word. But then I was not a Bostonian.

One bright afternoon I went through the village, round the point into the French quarter, in search of a laundress. The fishermen's cottages faced the west; they were low and wide, not unlike scows drifted ashore and moored on the beach for houses. The little windows had gay curtains fluttering in the breeze, and the rooms within looked clean and cheery; the rough walls were adorned with the spoils of the fresh-water seas, shells, green stones, agates, spar, and curiously shaped pebbles; occasionally there was a stuffed water-bird, or a bright-colored print, and always a violin. Black-eyed children played in the water which bordered their narrow beach-gardens; and slender women, with shining black hair, stood in their doorways knitting. I found my laundress, and then went on to Jeannette's home, the last house in the row. From the mother, a Chippewa woman, I learned that Jeannette was with her French father at the fishing-grounds off Drummond's Island.

"How long has she been away?" I asked.

"Veeks four," replied the mother, whose knowledge of English was confined to the price-list of white-fish and blueberries, the two articles of her traffic with the boarding-house keepers.

"When will she return?"

"*Je n' sais.*"

She knitted on, sitting in the sunshine on her little doorstep, looking out over the western water with tranquil content in her beautiful, gentle eyes. As I walked up the beach I glanced back several times to see if she had the curiosity to watch me; but no, she still looked out over the western water. What was I to her? Less than nothing. A white-fish was more.

A week or two later I strolled out to the Giant's Stairway and sat down in the little rock chapel. There was a picnic at the Lovers' Leap, and I had that side of the island to myself. I was leaning back, half asleep, in the deep shadow, when the sound of voices roused me; a birch-bark canoe was passing close in shore, and two were in it,—Jeannette and our surgeon. I could not hear their words, but I noticed Rodney's expression as he leaned forward. Jeannette was paddling slowly; her cheeks were flushed, and her eyes brilliant. Another moment, and a point hid them from my view. I went home troubled.

"Did you enjoy the picnic, Miss Augusta?" I said, with assumed carelessness, that evening. "Dr. Prescott was there, as usual, I suppose?"

"He was not present, but the picnic was highly enjoyable," replied Miss Augusta, in her even voice and impartial manner.

"The Doctor has not been with us for some days," said the major's wife, archly; "I suspect he does not like Mr. Piper."

Mr. Piper was a portly widower, of sanguine complexion, a Chicago produce-dealer, who was supposed to admire Miss Augusta, and was now going through a course of "The Harp that once."

The last days of summer flew swiftly by; the surgeon held himself aloof; we scarcely saw him in the garrison circles, and I no longer met him in my rambles.

"Jealousy!" said the major's wife.

September came. The summer visitors fled away homeward; the remaining "Indian curiosities" were stored away for another season; the hotels were closed, and the forests deserted; the bluebells swung unmolested on their heights, and the plump Indian-pipes grew in peace in their dark corners. The little white fort, too, began to assume its winter manners; the storm-flag was hoisted; there were evening fires upon the broad hearth-stones; the chaplain, having finished everything about Balak, his seven altars and seven rams, was ready for chess-problems; books and papers were ordered; stores laid in, and anxious inquiries made as to the "habits" of the new mail-carrier,—for the mail-carrier was the hero of the winter, and if his "habits" led him to whiskey, there was danger that our precious letters might be dropped all along the northern curve of Lake Huron.

Upon this quiet matter-of-course preparation, suddenly, like a thunderbolt from a clear sky, came orders to leave. The whole garrison, officers and men, were ordered to Florida.

In a moment all was desolation. It was like being ordered

into the Valley of the Shadow of Death. Dense everglades, swamp-fevers, malaria in the air, poisonous underbrush, and venomous reptiles and insects, and now and then a wily unseen foe picking off the men, one by one, as they painfully cut out roads through the thickets,—these were the features of military life in Florida at that period. Men who would have marched boldly to the cannon's mouth, officers who would have headed a forlorn hope, shrank from the deadly swamps.

Families must be broken up, also; no women, no children, could go to Florida. There were tears and the sound of sobbing in the little white fort, as the poor wives, all young mothers, hastily packed their few possessions to go back to their fathers' houses, fortunate if they had fathers to receive them. The husbands went about in silence, too sad for words. Archie kept up the best courage; but he was young, and had no one to leave save me.

The evening of the fatal day—for the orders had come in the early dawn—I was alone in my little parlor, already bare and desolate with packing-cases. The wind had been rising since morning, and now blew furiously from the west. Suddenly the door burst open and the surgeon entered. I was shocked at his appearance, as, pale, haggard, with disordered hair and clothing, he sank into a chair, and looked at me in silence.

"Rodney, what is it?" I said.

He did not answer, but still looked at me with that strange gaze. Alarmed, I rose and went toward him, laying my hand on his shoulder with a motherly touch. I loved the quiet, gray-eyed youth next after Archie.

"What is it, my poor boy? Can I help you?"

"O Aunt Sarah, perhaps you can, for *you* know her."

"Her?" I repeated, with sinking heart.

"Yes. Jeannette."

I sat down and folded my hands; trouble had come, but it was not what I apprehended,—the old story of military life, love, and desertion; the ever-present ballad of the "gay young knight who loves and rides away." This was something different.

"I love her,—I love her madly, in spite of myself," said Rodney, pouring forth his words with feverish rapidity. "I know it is an infatuation, I know it is utterly unreasonable, and yet—I love her. I have striven against it, I have fought with myself, I have written out elaborate arguments wherein I have clearly demonstrated the folly of such an affection, and I have compelled myself to read them over slowly, word for word, when alone in my own room, and yet—I love her! Ignorant, I know she would shame me; shallow, I know she could not satisfy me; as a wife she would inevitably drag me down to misery, and yet —I love her! I had not been on the island a week before I saw her, and marked her beauty. Months before you invited her to the fort I had become infatuated with her singular loveliness; but, in some respects, a race of the blood-royal could not be prouder than these French fishermen. They will accept your money, they will cheat you, they will tell you lies for an extra shilling; but make one step toward a simple acquaintance, and the door will be shut in your face. They will bow down before you as a customer, but they will not have you for a friend. Thus I found it impossible to reach Jeannette. I do not say that I tried, for all the time I was fighting myself; but I went far enough to see the barriers. It seemed a fatality that you should take a fancy to her, have her here, and ask me to admire her,— admire the face that haunted me by day and by night, driving me mad with its beauty.

"I realized my danger, and called to my aid all the pride of my race. I said to my heart, 'You shall not love this ignorant half-breed girl to your ruin.' I reasoned with myself, and said, 'It is only because you are isolated on this far-away island. Could you present this girl to your mother? Could she be a companion for your sisters?' I was beginning to gain a firmer control over myself, in spite of her presence, when you unfolded your plan of education. Fatality again. Instantly a crowd of hopes surged up. The education you began, could I not finish? She was but young; a few years of careful teaching might work wonders. Could I not train this forest flower so that it could take its place in the garden? But, when I actually saw this full-grown woman unable to add the simplest sum or write her name correctly, I was again ashamed of my infatuation. It is one thing to talk of ignorance, it is another to come face to face with it. Thus I wavered, at one moment ready to give up all for pride, at another to give up all for love.

"Then came the malicious suggestion of negro blood. Could it be proved, I was free; that taint I could not pardon. (And here, even as the surgeon spoke, I noticed this as the peculiarity of the New England Abolitionist. Theoretically he believed in the equality of the enslaved race, and stood ready to maintain the belief with his life, but practically he held himself entirely aloof from them; the Southern creed and practice were the exact reverse.) I made inquiries of Father Piret, who knows the mixed genealogy of the little French colony as far back as the first voyageurs of the fur trade, and found—as I, shall I say hoped or feared?—that the insinuation was utterly false. Thus I was thrown back into the old tumult.

"Then came that evening in this parlor when Jeannette made the coffee and baked little cakes over the coals. Do you remember the pathos with which she chanted *File, file, pauvre Marie; File, file, pour le prisonnier?* Do you remember how she looked when she repeated 'Ivry'? Did that tender pity, that ringing inspiration, come from a dull mind and shallow heart? I was avenged of my enforced disdain, my love gave itself up to delicious hope. She was capable of education, and then—! I made a pretext of old Antoine's cough in order to gain an opportunity of speaking to her alone; but she was like a thing possessed, she broke from me and sprang over the icy cliff, her laugh coming back on the wind as I followed her down the dangerous slope. On she rushed, jumping from rock to rock, waving her hand in wild glee when the moon shone out, singing and shouting with merry scorn at my desperate efforts to reach her. It was a mad chase, but only on the plain below could I come up with her. There, breathless and eager, I unfolded to her my plan of education. I only went so far as this: I was willing to send her to school, to give her opportunities of seeing the world, to provide for her whole future. I left the story of my love to come afterward. She laughed me to scorn. As well talk of education to the bird of the wilderness! She rejected my offers, picked up snow to throw in my face, covered me with her French sarcasms, danced around me in circles, laughed, and mocked, until I was at a loss to know whether she was human. Finally, as a shadow darkened the moon, she fled away; and when it passed she was gone, and I was alone on the snowy plain.

"Angry, fierce, filled with scorn for myself, I determined resolutely to crush out my senseless infatuation. I threw myself into such society as we had; I assumed an interest in that inane Miss Augusta; I read and studied far into the night; I walked until sheer fatigue gave me tranquillity; but all I gained was lost in that encounter at the Arch: you remember it? When I saw her on that narrow bridge, my love burst its bonds again, and, senseless as ever, rushed to save her,—to save her, poised on her native rocks, where every inch was familiar from childhood! To save her,—sure-footed and light as a bird! I caught her. She struggled in my arms, angrily, as an imprisoned animal might struggle, but—so beautiful! The impulse came to me to spring with her into the gulf below, and so end the contest forever. I might have done it,—I cannot tell,—but, suddenly, she wrenched herself out of my arms and fled over the Arch, to the farther side. I followed, trembling, blinded, with the violence of my emotion. At that moment I was ready to give up my life, my soul, into her hands.

"In the woods beyond she paused, glanced over her shoulder toward me, then turned eagerly. '*Voilà*,' she said, pointing. I looked down and saw several silver pieces that had dropped from my pocket as I sprang over the rocks, and, with an impatient gesture, I thrust them aside with my foot.

"'*Non*,' she cried, turning toward me and stooping eagerly, —'so much! O, so much! See! four shillings!' Her eyes glistened with longing as she held the money in her hand and fingered each piece lovingly.

"The sudden revulsion of feeling produced by her words and gesture filled me with fury. 'Keep it, and buy yourself a soul if you can!' I cried; and turning away, I left her with her gains.

"'*Merci, monsieur*,' she answered gayly, all unmindful of my scorn; and off she ran, holding her treasure tightly clasped in both hands. I could hear her singing far down the path.

"It is a bitter thing to feel a scorn for yourself! Did I love this girl who stooped to gather a few shillings from under my feet? Was it, then, impossible for me to conquer this ignoble passion? No; it could not and it should not be! I plunged again into all the gayety; I left myself not one free moment; if sleep came not, I forced it to come with opiates; Jeannette had gone to the fishing-grounds, the weeks passed, I did not see her. I had made the hardest struggle of all, and was beginning to recover my self-respect when, one day, I met her in the woods with some children; she had returned to gather blueberries. I looked at her. She was more gentle than usual, and smiled. Suddenly, as an embankment which has withstood the storms of many winters gives way at last in a calm summer night, I yielded. Without one outward sign, I laid down my arms. Myself knew that the contest was over, and my other self rushed to her feet.

"Since then I have often seen her; I have made plan after plan to meet her; I have—O degrading thought!—paid her to take me out in her canoe, under the pretence of fishing. I no longer looked forward; I lived only in the present, and thought only of when and where I could see her. Thus it has been until this morning, when the orders came. Now, I am brought face to face with reality; I must go; can I leave her behind? For hours I have been wandering in the woods. Aunt Sarah,—it is of no use,—I cannot live without her; I must marry her."

"Marry Jeannette!" I exclaimed.

"Even so."

"An ignorant half-breed?"

"As you say, an ignorant half-breed."

"You are mad, Rodney."

"I know it."

I will not repeat all I said; but, at last, silenced, if not convinced, by the power of this great love, I started with him out into the wild night to seek Jeannette. We went through the village and round the point, where the wind met us, and the waves broke at our feet with a roar. Passing the row of cabins, with their twinkling lights, we reached the home of Jeannette and knocked at the low door. The Indian mother opened it. I entered, without a word, and took a seat near the hearth, where a drift-wood fire was burning. Jeannette came forward with a surprised look. "You little think what good fortune is coming to you, child," I thought, as I noted her coarse dress and the poor furniture of the little room.

Rodney burst at once into his subject.

"Jeannette," he said, going toward her, "I have come to take you away with me. You need not go to school; I have given up that idea,—I accept you as you are. You shall have silk dresses and ribbons, like the ladies at the Mission-House this summer. You shall see all the great cities, you shall hear beautiful music. You shall have everything you want,—money, bright shillings, as many as you wish. See! Mrs. Corlyne has come with me to show you that it is true. This morning we had orders to leave Mackinac; in a few days we must go. But —listen, Jeannette; I will marry you. You shall be my wife. Do not look so startled. I mean it; it is really true."

"*Qu'est-ce-que-c'est?*" said the girl, bewildered by the rapid, eager words.

"Dr. Prescott wishes to marry you, child," I explained, some-what sadly, for never had the disparity between them seemed so great. The presence of the Indian mother, the common room, were like silent protests.

"Marry!" ejaculated Jeannette.

"Yes, love," said the surgeon, ardently. "It is quite true; you shall be my wife. Father Piret shall marry us. I will exchange into another regiment, or, if necessary, I will resign. Do you understand what I am saying, Jeannette? See! I give you my hand, in token that it is true."

But, with a quick bound, the girl was across the room. "What!" she cried. "You think I marry *you*? Have you not heard of Baptiste? Know, then, that I love one finger of him more than all you, ten times, hundred times."

"Baptiste?" repeated Rodney.

"*Oui, mon cousin*, Baptiste, the fisherman. We marry soon —*tenez—la fête de Saint André.*"

Rodney looked bewildered a moment, then his face cleared. "Oh! a child engagement? That is one of your customs, I know. But never fear; Father Piret will absolve you from all that. Baptiste shall have a fine new boat; he will let you off for a handful of silver-pieces. Do not think of that, Jeannette, but come to me—"

"*Je vous abhorre; je vous déteste,*" cried the girl with fury as he approached. "Baptiste not love me? He love me more than boat and silver dollar,—more than all the world! And I love him; I die for him! *Allez-vous-en, traître!*"

Rodney had grown white; he stood before her, motionless, with fixed eyes.

"Jeannette," I said in French, "perhaps you do not under-stand. Dr. Prescott asks you to marry him; Father Piret shall marry you, and all your friends shall come. Dr. Prescott will take you away from this hard life; he will make you rich; he will support your father and mother in comfort. My child, it is wonderful good fortune. He is an educated gentleman, and loves you truly."

"What is that to me?" replied Jeannette, proudly. "Let him go, I care not." She paused a moment. Then, with flashing eyes, she cried, "Let him go with his fine new boat and silver dollars! He does not believe me? See, then, how I despise him!" And, rushing forward, she struck him on the cheek.

Rodney did not stir, but stood gazing at her while the red mark glowed on his white face.

"You know not what love is," said Jeannette, with indescribable scorn. "You! *You! Ah, mon Baptiste, où es-tu?* But thou wilt kill him,—kill him for his boats and silver dollars!"

"Child!" I said, startled by her fury.

"I am not a child. *Je suis femme, moi!*" replied Jeannette, folding her arms with haughty grace. "*Allez!*" she said, pointing toward the door. We were dismissed. A queen could not have made a more royal gesture.

Throughout the scene the Indian mother had not stopped her knitting.

In four days we were afloat, and the little white fort was deserted. It was a dark afternoon, and we sat clustered on the stern of the steamer, watching the flag come slowly down from its staff in token of the departure of the commanding officer. "Isle of Beauty, fare thee well," sang the major's fair young wife, with the sound of tears in her sweet voice.

"We shall return," said the officers. But not one of them ever saw the beautiful island again.

Rodney Prescott served a month or two in Florida, "taciturn and stiff as ever," Archie wrote. Then he resigned suddenly, and went abroad. He has never returned, and I have lost all trace of him, so that I cannot say, from any knowledge of my own, how long the feeling lived,—the feeling that swept me along in its train down to the beach-cottage that wild night.

Each man who reads this can decide for himself.

Each woman has decided already.

*

Last year I met an islander on the cars, going eastward. It was the first time he had ever been "below"; but he saw nothing to admire, that dignified citizen of Mackinac!

"What has become of Jeannette Leblanc?" I asked.

"Jeannette? O, she married that Baptiste, a lazy, good-for-nothing fellow! They live in the same little cabin round the point, and pick up a living most anyhow for their tribe of young ones."

"Are they happy?"

"Happy?" repeated my islander, with a slow stare. "Well, I suppose they are, after their fashion; I don't know much about them. In my opinion, they are a shiftless set, those French half-breeds round the point."

# *Solomon*

M IDWAY in the eastern part of Ohio lies the coal country; round-topped hills there begin to show themselves in the level plain, trending back from Lake Erie; afterwards rising higher and higher, they stretch away into Pennsylvania and are dignified by the name of Alleghany Mountains. But no names have they in their Ohio birthplace, and little do the people care for them, save as storehouses for fuel. The roads lie along the slow-moving streams, and the farmers ride slowly over them in their broad-wheeled wagons, now and then passing dark holes in the bank from whence come little carts into the sunshine, and men, like *silhouettes,* walking behind them, with glow-worm lamps fastened in their hat-bands. Neither farmers nor miners glance up towards the hilltops; no doubt they consider them useless mounds, and, were it not for the coal, they would envy their neighbors of the grain-country, whose broad, level fields stretch unbroken through Central Ohio; as, however, the canal-boats go away full, and long lines of coal-cars go away full, and every man's coal-shed is full, and money comes back from the great iron-mills of Pittsburgh, Cincinnati, and Cleveland, the coal country, though unknown in a picturesque point of view, continues to grow rich and prosperous.

Yet picturesque it is, and no part more so than the valley where stands the village of the quaint German Community on the banks of the slow-moving Tuscarawas River. One October day we left the lake behind us and journeyed inland, following the water-courses and looking forward for the first glimpse of rising ground; blue are the waters of Erie on a summer day, red and golden are its autumn sunsets, but so level, so deadly level are its shores that, at times, there comes a longing for the sight of distant hills. Hence our journey. Night found us still in the "Western Reserve." Ohio has some queer names of her own for portions of her territory, the "Fire Lands," the "Donation Grant," the "Salt Section," the "Refugee's Tract," and the "Western Reserve" are names well known, although not found on the maps. Two days more and we came into the coal country; near by were the "Moravian Lands," and at the end of the last day's ride we crossed a yellow bridge over a stream called the "One-Leg Creek."

"I have tried in vain to discover the origin of this name," I said, as we leaned out of the carriage to watch the red leaves float down the slow tide.

"Create one, then. A one-legged soldier, a farmer's pretty daughter, an elopement in a flat-bottomed boat, and a home upon this stream which yields its stores of catfish for their support," suggested Erminia.

"The original legend would be better than that if we could only find it, for real life is always better than fiction," I answered.

"In real life we are all masked; but in fiction the author shows the faces as they are, Dora."

"I do not believe we are all masked, Erminia. I can read my friends like a printed page."

"O, the wonderful faith of youth!" said Erminia, retiring upon her seniority.

Presently the little church on the hill came into view through a vista in the trees. We passed the mill and its flowing race, the blacksmith's shop, the great grass meadow, and drew up in front of the quaint hotel where the trustees allowed the world's people, if uninquisitive and decorous, to remain in the Community for short periods of time, on the payment of three dollars per week for each person. This village was our favorite retreat, our little hiding-place in the hill-country; at that time it was almost as isolated as a solitary island, for the Community owned thousands of outlying acres and held no intercourse with the surrounding townships. Content with their own, unmindful of the rest of the world, these Germans grew steadily richer and richer, solving quietly the problem of co-operative labor, while the French and Americans worked at it in vain with newspapers, orators, and even cannon to aid them. The members of the Community were no ascetic anchorites; each tiled roof covered a home with a thrifty mother and train of grave little children, the girls in short-waisted gowns, kerchiefs, and frilled caps, and the boys in tailed coats, long-flapped vests, and trousers, as soon as they were able to toddle. We liked them all, we liked the life; we liked the mountain-high beds, the coarse snowy linen, and the remarkable counterpanes; we liked the cream-stewed chicken, the

Käse-lab, and fresh butter, but, best of all, the hot bretzels for breakfast. And let not the hasty city imagination turn to the hard, salty, sawdust cake in the shape of a broken-down figure eight which is served with lager-beer in saloons and gardens. The Community bretzel was of a delicate flaky white in the inside, shading away into a golden-brown crust of crisp involutions, light as a feather, and flanked by little pats of fresh, unsalted butter, and a deep-blue cup wherein the coffee was hot, the cream yellow, and the sugar broken lumps from the old-fashioned loaf, now alas! obsolete.

We stayed among the simple people and played at shepherdesses and pastorellas; we adopted the hours of the birds, we went to church on Sunday and sang German chorals as old as Luther. We even played at work to the extent of helping gather apples, eating the best, and riding home on top of the loaded four-horse wains. But one day we heard of a new diversion, a sulphur-spring over the hills about two miles from the hotel on land belonging to the Community; and, obeying the fascination which earth's native medicines exercise over all earth's children, we immediately started in search of the nauseous spring. The road wound over the hill, past one of the apple-orchards, where the girls were gathering the red fruit, and then down a little declivity where the track branched off to the Community coal-mine; then a solitary stretch through the thick woods, a long hill with a curve, and at the foot a little dell with a patch of meadow, a brook, and a log-house with overhanging roof, a forlorn house unpainted and desolate. There was not even the blue door which enlivened many of the Community dwellings. "This looks like the huts of the Black Forest," said Erminia. "Who would have supposed that we should find such an antique in Ohio!"

"I am confident it was built by the M. B.'s," I replied. "They tramped, you know, extensively through the State, burying axes and leaving every now and then a mastodon behind them."

"Well, if the Mound-Builders selected this site they showed good taste," said Erminia, refusing, in her afternoon indolence, the argumentum nonsensicum with which we were accustomed to enliven our conversation. It was, indeed, a lovely spot,—the little meadow, smooth and bright as green velvet, the brook chattering over the pebbles, and the hills, gay in red and yellow foliage, rising abruptly on all sides. After some labor we swung open the great gate and entered the yard, crossed the brook on a mossy plank, and followed the path through the grass towards the lonely house. An old shepherd-dog lay at the door of a dilapidated shed, like a block-house, which had once been a stable; he did not bark, but, rising slowly, came along beside us,—a large, gaunt animal that looked at us with such melancholy eyes that Erminia stooped to pat him. Ermine had a weakness for dogs; she herself owned a wild beast of the dog kind that went by the name of the "Emperor Trajan"; and, accompanied by this dignitary, she was accustomed to stroll up the avenues of C——, lost in maiden meditations.

We drew near the house and stepped up on the sunken piazza, but no signs of life appeared. The little loophole windows were pasted over with paper, and the plank door had no latch or handle. I knocked, but no one came. "Apparently it is a haunted house, and that dog is the spectre," I said, stepping back.

"Knock three times," suggested Ermine; "that is what they always do in ghost-stories."

"Try it yourself. My knuckles are not cast-iron."

Ermine picked up a stone and began tapping on the door. "Open sesame," she said, and it opened.

Instantly the dog slunk away to his block-house and a woman confronted us, her dull face lighting up as her eyes ran rapidly over our attire from head to foot. "Is there a sulphur-spring here?" I asked. "We would like to try the water."

"Yes, it's here fast enough in the back hall. Come in, ladies; I'm right proud to see you. From the city, I suppose?"

"From C——," I answered; "we are spending a few days in the Community."

Our hostess led the way through the little hall, and throwing open a back door pulled up a trap in the floor, and there we saw the spring,—a shallow well set in stones, with a jar of butter cooling in its white water. She brought a cup, and we drank. "Delicious," said Ermine. "The true, spoiled-egg flavor! Four cups is the minimum allowance, Dora."

"I reckon it's good for the insides," said the woman, standing with arms akimbo and staring at us. She was a singular creature, with large black eyes, Roman nose, and a mass of black hair tightly knotted on the top of her head, but pinched and gaunt; her yellow forehead was wrinkled with a fixed frown, and her thin lips drawn down in permanent discontent. Her dress was a shapeless linsey-woolsey gown, and home-made list slippers covered her long, lank feet. "Be that the fashion?" she asked, pointing to my short, closely fitting walking-dress.

"Yes," I answered; "do you like it?"

"Well, it does for you, sis, because you 're so little and peaked-like, but it would n't do for me. The other lady, now, don't wear nothing like that; is she even with the style, too?"

"There is such a thing as being above the style, madam," replied Ermine, bending to dip up glass number two.

"Our figgers is a good deal alike," pursued the woman; "I reckon that fashion ud suit me best."

Willowy Erminia glanced at the stick-like hostess. "You do me honor," she said, suavely. "I shall consider myself fortunate, madam, if you will allow me to send you patterns from C——. What are we if not well dressed?"

"You have a fine dog," I began hastily, fearing lest the great, black eyes should penetrate the sarcasm; "what is his name?"

"A stupid beast! He 's none of mine; belongs to my man."

"Your husband?"

"Yes, my man. He works in the coal-mine over the hill."

"You have no children?"

"Not a brat. Glad of it, too."

"You must be lonely," I said, glancing around the desolate house. To my surprise, suddenly the woman burst into a flood of tears, and sinking down on the floor she rocked from side to side, sobbing, and covering her face with her bony hands.

"What can be the matter with her?" I said in alarm; and, in my agitation, I dipped up some sulphur-water and held it to her lips.

"Take away the smelling stuff,—I hate it!" she cried, pushing the cup angrily from her.

Ermine looked on in silence for a moment or two, then she took off her neck-tie, a bright-colored Roman scarf, and threw it across the trap into the woman's lap. "Do me the favor to accept that trifle, madam," she said, in her soft voice.

The woman's sobs ceased as she saw the ribbon; she fingered it with one hand in silent admiration, wiped her wet face with the skirt of her gown, and then suddenly disappeared into an adjoining room, closing the door behind her.

"Do you think she is crazy?" I whispered.

"O no; merely pensive."

"Nonsense, Ermine! But why did you give her that ribbon?"

"To develop her æsthetic taste," replied my cousin, finishing her last glass, and beginning to draw on her delicate gloves.

Immediately I began gulping down my neglected dose; but so vile was the odor that some time was required for the operation, and in the midst of my struggles our hostess reappeared. She had thrown on an old dress of plaid delaine, a faded red ribbon was tied over her head, and around her sinewed throat reposed the Roman scarf pinned with a glass brooch.

"Really, madam, you honor us," said Ermine, gravely.

"Thankee, marm. It 's so long since I 've had on anything but that old bag, and so long since I 've seen anything but them Dutch girls over to the Community, with their wooden shapes and wooden shoes, that it sorter come over me all 't onct what a miserable life I 've had. You see, I ain't what I looked like; now I 've dressed up a bit I feel more like telling you that I come of good Ohio stock, without a drop of Dutch blood. My father, he kep' a store in Sandy, and I had everything I wanted until I must needs get crazy over Painting Sol at the Community. Father, he would n't hear to it, and so I ran away; Sol, he turned out good for nothing to work, and so here I am, yer see, in spite of all his pictures making me out the Queen of Sheby."

"Is your husband an artist?" I asked.

"No, miss. He 's a coal-miner, he is. But he used to like to paint me all sorts of ways. Wait, I 'll show yer." Going up the rough stairs that led into the attic, the woman came back after a moment with a number of sheets of drawing-paper which she hung up along the walls with pins for our inspection. They were all portraits of the same face, with brick-red cheeks, enormous black eyes, and a profusion of shining black hair hanging down over plump white shoulders; the costumes were various, but the faces were the same. I gazed in silence, seeing no likeness to anything earthly. Erminia took out her glasses and scanned the pictures slowly.

"Yourself, madam, I perceive," she said, much to my surprise.

"Yes, 'm, that 's me," replied our hostess, complacently. "I never was like those yellow-haired girls over to the Community. Sol allers said my face was real rental."

"Rental?" I repeated, inquiringly.

"Oriental, of course," said Ermine. "Mr.—Mr. Solomon is quite right. May I ask the names of these characters, madam?"

"Queen of Sheby, Judy, Ruth, Esthy, Po-co-hon-tus, Goddessaliberty, Sunset, and eight Octobers, them with the grapes. Sunset 's the one with the red paint behind it like clouds."

"Truly a remarkable collection," said Ermine. "Does Mr. Solomon devote much time to his art?"

"No, not now. He could n't make a cent out of it, so he 's took to digging coal. He painted all them when we was first married, and he went a journey all the way to Cincinnati to sell 'em. First he was going to buy me a silk dress and some earrings, and, after that, a farm. But pretty soon home he come on a canal-boat, without a shilling, and a bringing all the pictures back with him! Well, then he tried most everything, but he never could keep to any one trade, for he 'd just as lief quit work in the middle of the forenoon and go to painting; no boss 'll stand that, you know. We kep' a going down, and I had to sell the few things my father give me when he found I was married whether or no,—my chany, my feather-beds, and my nice clothes, piece by piece. I held on to the big looking-glass for four years, but at last it had to go, and then I just gave up and put on a linsey-woolsey gown. When a girl's spirit 's once broke, she don't care for nothing, you know; so, when the Community offered to take Sol back as coal-digger, I just said, 'Go,' and we come." Here she tried to smear the tears away with her bony hands, and gave a low groan.

"Groaning probably relieves you," observed Ermine.

"Yes, 'm. It 's kinder company like, when I 'm all alone. But you see it 's hard on the prettiest girl in Sandy to have to live in this lone lorn place. Why, ladies, you might n't believe it, but I had open-work stockings, and feathers in my winter bunnets before I was married!" And the tears broke forth afresh.

"Accept my handkerchief," said Ermine; "it will serve your purpose better than fingers."

The woman took the dainty cambric and surveyed it curiously, held at arm's length. "Reg'lar thistle-down, now, ain't it?" she said; "and smells like a locust-tree blossom."

"Mr. Solomon, then, belonged to the Community?" I asked, trying to gather up the threads of the story.

"No, he did n't either; he 's no Dutchman, I reckon, he 's a Lake County man, born near Painesville, he is."

"I thought you spoke as though he had been in the Community."

"So he had; he did n't belong, but he worked for 'em since he was a boy, did middling well, in spite of the painting, until one day, when he come over to Sandy on a load of wood and seen me standing at the door. That was the end of him," continued the woman, with an air of girlish pride; "he could n't work no more for thinking of me."

"*Où la vanité va-t-elle se nicher?*" murmured Ermine, rising. "Come, Dora; it is time to return."

As I hastily finished my last cup of sulphur-water, our hostess followed Ermine towards the door. "Will you have your handkercher back, marm?" she said, holding it out reluctantly.

"It was a free gift, madam," replied my cousin; "I wish you a good afternoon."

"Say, will yer be coming again to-morrow?" asked the woman as I took my departure.

"Very likely; good by."

The door closed, and then, but not till then, the melancholy dog joined us and stalked behind until we had crossed the meadow and reached the gate. We passed out and turned up the hill; but looking back we saw the outline of the woman's head at the upper window, and the dog's head at the bars, both watching us out of sight.

In the evening there came a cold wind down from the north, and the parlor, with its primitive ventilators, square openings in the side of the house, grew chilly. So a great fire of soft coal was built in the broad Franklin stove, and before its blaze we made good cheer, nor needed the one candle which flickered on the table behind us. Cider fresh from the mill, carded gingerbread, and new cheese crowned the scene, and during the evening came a band of singers, the young people of the Community, and sang for us the song of the Lorelei, accompanied by home-made violins and flageolets. At length we were left alone, the candle had burned out, the house door was barred, and the peaceful Community was asleep; still we two sat together with our feet upon the hearth, looking down into the glowing coals.

> "Ich weisz nicht was soll es bedeuten
> Dasz ich so traurig bin,"

I said, repeating the opening lines of the Lorelei; "I feel absolutely blue to-night."

"The memory of the sulphur-woman," suggested Ermine.

"Sulphur-woman! What a name!"

"Entirely appropriate, in my opinion."

"Poor thing! How she longed with a great longing for the finery of her youth in Sandy."

"I suppose from those barbarous pictures that she was originally in the flesh," mused Ermine; "at present she is but a bony outline."

"Such as she is, however, she has had her romance," I answered. "She is quite sure that there was one to love her; then let come what may, she has had her day."

"Misquoting Tennyson on such a subject!" said Ermine, with disdain.

"A man 's a man for all that and a woman 's a woman too," I retorted. "You are blind, cousin, blinded with pride. That woman has had her tragedy, as real and bitter as any that can come to us."

"What have you to say for the poor man, then?" exclaimed Ermine, rousing to the contest. "If there is a tragedy at the sulphur-house, it belongs to the sulphur-man, not to the sulphur-woman."

"He is not a sulphur-man, he is a coal-man; keep to your bearings, Ermine."

"I tell you," pursued my cousin, earnestly, "that I pitied that unknown man with inward tears all the while I sat by that trap-door. Depend upon it, he had his dream, his ideal; and this country girl with her great eyes and wealth of hair represented the beautiful to his hungry soul. He gave his whole life and hope into her hands, and woke to find his goddess a common wooden image."

"Waste sympathy upon a coal-miner!" I said, imitating my cousin's former tone.

"If any one is blind, it is you," she answered, with gleaming eyes. "That man's whole history stood revealed in the selfish complainings of that creature. He had been in the Community from boyhood, therefore of course he had no chance to learn life, to see its art-treasures. He has been shipwrecked, poor soul, hopelessly shipwrecked."

"She too, Ermine."

"She!"

"Yes. If he loved pictures, she loved her chany and her feather-beds, not to speak of the big looking-glass. No doubt she had other lovers, and might have lived in a red brick farm-house with ten unopened front windows and a blistered front door. The wives of men of genius are always to be pitied; they do not soar into the crowd of feminine admirers who circle round the husband, and they are therefore called 'grubs,' 'worms of the earth,' 'drudges,' and other sweet titles."

"Nonsense," said Ermine, tumbling the arched coals into chaos with the poker; "it 's after midnight, let us go up stairs." I knew very well that my beautiful cousin enjoyed the society of several poets, painters, musicians, and others of that ilk, without concerning herself about their stay-at-home wives.

The next day the winds were out in battle array, howling over the Strasburg hills, raging up and down the river, and whirling the colored leaves wildly along the lovely road to the One-Leg Creek. Evidently there could be no rambling in the painted woods that day, so we went over to old Fritz's shop, played on his home-made piano, inspected the woolly horse who turned his crank patiently in an underground den, and set in motion all the curious little images which the carpenter's deft fingers had wrought. Fritz belonged to the Community, and knew nothing of the outside world; he had a taste for mechanism, which showed itself in many labor-saving devices, and with it all he was the roundest, kindest little man, with bright eyes like a canary-bird.

"Do you know Solomon the coal-miner?" asked Ermine, in her correct, well-learned German.

"Sol Bangs? Yes, I know him," replied Fritz, in his Würtemberg dialect.

"What kind of a man is he?"

"Good for nothing," replied Fritz, placidly.

"Why?"

"Wrong here"; tapping his forehead.

"Do you know his wife?" I asked.

"Yes."

"What kind of a woman is she?"

"Too much tongue. Women must not talk much."

"Old Fritz touched us both there," I said, as we ran back laughing to the hotel through the blustering wind. "In his opinion, I suppose, we have the popular verdict of the township upon our two *protégés*, the sulphur-woman and her husband."

The next day opened calm, hazy, and warm, the perfection of Indian summer; the breezy hill was outlined in purple, and the trees glowed in rich colors. In the afternoon we started for the sulphur-spring without shawls or wraps, for the heat was almost oppressive; we loitered on the way through the still woods, gathering the tinted leaves, and wondering why no poet has yet arisen to celebrate in fit words the glories of the American autumn. At last we reached the turn whence the lonely house came into view, and at the bars we saw the dog awaiting us.

"Evidently the sulphur-woman does not like that melancholy animal," I said, as we applied our united strength to the gate.

"Did you ever know a woman of limited mind who liked a large dog?" replied Ermine. "Occasionally such a woman will fancy a small cur; but to appreciate a large, noble dog requires a large, noble mind."

"Nonsense with your dogs and minds," I said, laughing. "Wonderful! There is a curtain."

It was true. The paper had been removed from one of the windows, and in its place hung some white drapery, probably part of a sheet rigged as a curtain.

Before we reached the piazza the door opened, and our hostess appeared. "Glad to see yer, ladies," she said. "Walk right in this way to the keeping-room."

The dog went away to his block-house, and we followed the woman into a room on the right of the hall; there were three rooms, beside the attic above. An Old-World German stove of brick-work occupied a large portion of the space, and over it hung a few tins, and a clock whose pendulum swung outside; a table, a settle, and some stools completed the furniture; but on the plastered walls were two rude brackets, one holding a cup and saucer of figured china, and the other surmounted by a large bunch of autumn leaves, so beautiful in themselves and so exquisitely arranged that we crossed the room to admire them.

"Sol fixed 'em, he did," said the sulphur-woman; "he seen me setting things to rights, and he would do it. I told him they was trash, but he made me promise to leave 'em alone in case you should call again."

"Madam Bangs, they would adorn a palace," said Ermine, severely.

"The cup is pretty too," I observed, seeing the woman's eyes turn that way.

"It 's the last of my chany," she answered, with pathos in her voice,—"the very last piece."

As we took our places on the settle we noticed the brave attire of our hostess. The delaine was there; but how altered! Flounces it had, skimped, but still flounces, and at the top was a collar of crochet cotton reaching nearly to the shoulders; the hair, too, was braided in imitation of Ermine's sunny coronet, and the Roman scarf did duty as a belt around the large flat waist.

"You see she tries to improve," I whispered, as Mrs. Bangs went into the hall to get some sulphur-water for us.

"Vanity," answered Ermine.

We drank our dose slowly, and our hostess talked on and on. Even I, her champion, began to weary of her complainings. "How dark it is!" said Ermine at last, rising and drawing aside the curtain. "See, Dora, a storm is close upon us."

We hurried to the door, but one look at the black cloud was enough to convince us that we could not reach the Community hotel before it would break, and somewhat drearily we returned to the keeping-room, which grew darker and darker, until our hostess was obliged to light a candle. "Reckon you 'll have to stay all night; I 'd like to have you, ladies," she said. "The Community ain't got nothing covered to send after you, except the old king's coach, and I misdoubt they won't let that out in such a storm, steps and all. When it begins to rain in this valley, it do rain, I can tell you; and from the way it 's begun, 't won't stop 'fore morning. You just let me send the Roarer over to the mine, he 'll tell Sol; Sol can tell the Community folks, so they 'll know where you be."

I looked somewhat aghast at this proposal, but Ermine listened to the rain upon the roof a moment, and then quietly accepted; she remembered the long hills of tenacious red clay, and her kid boots were dear to her.

"The Roarer, I presume, is some faithful kobold who bears your message to and from the mine," she said, making herself as comfortable as the wooden settle would allow.

The sulphur-woman stared. "Roarer 's Sol's old dog," she answered, opening the door; "perhaps one of you will write a bit of a note for him to carry in his basket.—Roarer, Roarer!"

The melancholy dog came slowly in, and stood still while she tied a small covered basket around his neck.

Ermine took a leaf from her tablets and wrote a line or two with the gold pencil attached to her watch-chain.

"Well now, you do have everything handy, I do declare," said the woman, admiringly.

I glanced at the paper.

"MR. SOLOMON BANGS: My cousin Theodora Wentworth and myself have accepted the hospitality of your house for the night. Will you be so good as to send tidings of our safety to the Community, and oblige,

ERMINIA STUART."

The Roarer started obediently out into the rain-storm with his little basket; he did not run, but walked slowly, as if the storm was nothing compared to his settled melancholy.

"What a note to send to a coal-miner!" I said, during a momentary absence of our hostess.

"Never fear; it will be appreciated," replied Ermine.

"What is this king's carriage of which you spoke?" I asked, during the next hour's conversation.

"O, when they first come over from Germany, they had a sort of a king; he knew more than the rest, and he lived in that big brick house with dormel-winders and a cuperler, that stands next the garden. The carriage was hisn, and it had steps to let down, and curtains and all; they don't use it much now he 's dead. They 're a queer set anyhow! The women look like meal-sacks. After Sol seen me, he could n't abide to look at 'em."

Soon after six we heard the great gate creak.

"That 's Sol," said the woman, "and now of course Roarer 'll come in and track all over my floor." The hall door opened and a shadow passed into the opposite room, two shadows,—a man and a dog.

"He 's going to wash himself now," continued the wife; "he 's always washing himself, just like a horse."

"New fact in natural history, Dora love," observed Ermine.

After some moments the miner appeared,—a tall, stooping figure with high forehead, large blue eyes, and long thin yellow hair; there was a singularly lifeless expression in his face, and a far-off look in his eyes. He gazed about the room in an absent way, as though he scarcely saw us. Behind him stalked the Roarer, wagging his tail slowly from side to side.

"Now, then, don't yer see the ladies, Sol? Where 's yer manners?" said his wife, sharply.

"Ah,—yes,—good evening," he said, vaguely. Then his wandering eyes fell upon Ermine's beautiful face, and fixed themselves there with strange intentness.

"You received my note, Mr. Bangs?" said my cousin in her soft voice.

"Yes, surely. You are Erminia," replied the man, still standing in the centre of the room with fixed eyes. The Roarer laid himself down behind his master, and his tail, still wagging, sounded upon the floor with a regular tap.

"Now then, Sol, since you 've come home, perhaps you 'll entertain the ladies while I get supper," quoth Mrs. Bangs; and forthwith began a clatter of pans.

The man passed his long hand abstractedly over his forehead. "Eh," he said with long-drawn utterance,—"eh-h? Yes, my rose of Sharon, certainly, certainly."

"Then why don't you do it?" said the woman, lighting the fire in the brick stove.

"And what will the ladies please to do?" he answered, his eyes going back to Ermine.

"We will look over your pictures, sir," said my cousin, rising; "they are in the upper room, I believe."

A great flush rose in the painter's thin cheeks. "Will you," he said eagerly,—"will you? Come!"

"It 's a broken-down old hole, ladies; Sol will never let me sweep it out. Reckon you 'll be more comfortable here," said Mrs. Bangs, with her arms in the flour.

"No, no, my lily of the valley. The ladies will come with me; they will not scorn the poor room."

"A studio is always interesting," said Ermine, sweeping up the rough stairs behind Solomon's candle. The dog followed us, and laid himself down on an old mat, as though well accustomed to the place. "Eh-h, boy, you came bravely through the storm with the lady's note," said his master, beginning to light candle after candle. "See him laugh!"

"Can a dog laugh?" I asked.

"Certainly; look at him now. What is that but a grin of happy contentment? Don't the Bible say, 'grin like a dog'?"

"You seem much attached to the Roarer."

"Tuscarora, lady, Tuscarora. Yes, I love him well. He has been with me through all, and he has watched the making of all my pictures; he always lies there when I paint."

By this time a dozen candles were burning on shelves and brackets, and we could see all parts of the attic studio. It was but a poor place, unfloored in the corners where the roof slanted down, and having no ceiling but the dark beams and thatch; hung upon the walls were the pictures we had seen, and many others, all crude and high colored, and all representing the same face,—the sulphur-woman in her youth, the poor artist's only ideal. He showed us these one by one, handling them tenderly, and telling us, in his quaint language, all they symbolized. "This is Ruth, and denoteth the power of hope," he said. "Behold Judith, the queen of revenge. And this dear one is Rachel, for whom Jacob served seven years, and they seemed unto him but a day, so well he loved her." The light shone on his pale face, and we noticed the far-off look in his eyes, and the long, tapering fingers coming out from the hard-worked, broad palm. To me it was a melancholy scene, the poor artist with his daubs and the dreary attic.

But Ermine seemed eagerly interested; she looked at the staring pictures, listened to the explanations, and at last she said gently, "Let me show you something of perspective, and the part that shadows play in a pictured face. Have you any crayons?"

No; the man had only his coarse paints and lumps of char-coal; taking a piece of the coal in her delicate hand, my cousin began to work upon a sheet of drawing-paper attached to the rough easel. Solomon watched her intently, as she explained and demonstrated some of the rules of drawing, the lights and shades, and the manner of representing the different features and curves. All his pictures were full faces, flat and unshaded; Ermine showed him the power of the profile and the three-quarter view. I grew weary of watching them, and pressing my face against the little window gazed out into the night; steadily the rain came down and the hills shut us in like a well. I thought of our home in C——, and its bright lights, warmth, company, and life. Why should we come masquerading out among the Ohio hills at this late season? And then I remem-bered that it was because Ermine would come; she liked such expeditions, and from childhood I had always followed her lead. "*Dux nascitur*, etc., etc." Turning away from the gloomy night, I looked towards the easel again; Solomon's cheeks were deeply flushed, and his eyes shone like stars. The lesson went on, the merely mechanical hand explaining its art to the igno-rant fingers of genius. Ermine had taken lessons all her life, but she had never produced an original picture, only copies.

At last the lesson was interrupted by a voice from below, "Sol, Sol, supper 's ready!" No one stirred until, feeling some sympathy for the amount of work which my ears told me had been going on below, I woke up the two enthusiasts and took them away from the easel down stairs into the keeping-room, where a loaded table and a scarlet hostess bore witness to the truth of my surmise. Strange things we ate that night, dishes unheard of in towns, but not unpalatable. Ermine had the one china cup for her corn-coffee; her grand air always secured her such favors. Tuscarora was there and ate of the best, now and then laying his shaggy head on the table, and, as his master said, "smiling at us"; evidently the evening was his gala time. It was nearly nine when the feast was ended, and I immediately proposed retiring to bed, for, having but little art enthusiasm, I dreaded a vigil in that dreary attic. Solomon looked disap-pointed, but I ruthlessly carried off Ermine to the opposite

room, which we afterwards suspected was the apartment of our
hosts, freshened and set in order in our honor. The sound of
the rain on the piazza roof lulled us soon to sleep, in spite of
the strange surroundings; but more than once I woke and wondered where I was, suddenly remembering the lonely house in
its lonely valley with a shiver of discomfort. The next morning
we woke at our usual hour, but some time after the miner's
departure; breakfast was awaiting us in the keeping-room, and
our hostess said that an ox-team from the Community would
come for us before nine. She seemed sorry to part with us,
and refused any remuneration for our stay; but none the less
did we promise ourselves to send some dresses and even ornaments from C——, to feed that poor, starving love of finery. As
we rode away in the ox-cart, the Roarer looked wistfully after
us through the bars; but his melancholy mood was upon him
again, and he had not the heart even to wag his tail.

As we were sitting in the hotel parlor, in front of our soft-
coal fire in the evening of the following day, and discussing
whether or no we should return to the city within the week,
the old landlord entered without his broad-brimmed hat,—an
unusual attention, since he was a trustee and a man of note in
the Community, and removed his hat for no one or nothing;
we even suspected that he slept in it.

"You know Zolomon Barngs," he said, slowly.

"Yes," we answered.

"Well, he 's dead. Kilt in de mine." And putting on the hat,
removed, we now saw, in respect for death, he left the room
as suddenly as he had entered it. As it happened, we had been
discussing the couple, I, as usual, contending for the wife, and
Ermine, as usual, advocating the cause of the husband.

"Let us go out there immediately to see her, poor woman!"
I said, rising.

"Yes, poor man, we will go to him!" said Ermine.

"But the man is dead, cousin."

"Then he shall at least have one kind, friendly glance before
he is carried to his grave," answered Ermine, quietly.

In a short time we set out in the darkness, and dearly did we
have to pay for the night-ride; no one could understand the
motive of our going, but money was money, and we could pay
for all peculiarities. It was a dark night, and the ride seemed

endless as the oxen moved slowly on through the red-clay
mire. At last we reached the turn and saw the little lonely house
with its upper room brightly lighted.

"He is in the studio," said Ermine; and so it proved. He was
not dead, but dying; not maimed, but poisoned by the gas of
the mine, and rescued too late for recovery. They had placed
him upon the floor on a couch of blankets, and the dull-eyed
Community doctor stood at his side. "No good, no good," he
said; "he must die." And then, hearing of the returning cart, he
left us, and we could hear the tramp of the oxen over the little
bridge, on their way back to the village.

The dying man's head lay upon his wife's breast, and her
arms supported him; she did not speak, but gazed at us with
a dumb agony in her large eyes. Ermine knelt down and took
the lifeless hand streaked with coal-dust in both her own. "Solomon," she said, in her soft, clear voice, "do you know me?"

The closed eyes opened slowly, and fixed themselves upon
her face a moment: then they turned towards the window, as if
seeking something.

"It 's the picter he means," said the wife. "He sat up most all
last night a doing it."

I lighted all the candles, and Ermine brought forward the
easel; upon it stood a sketch in charcoal wonderful to behold,
—the same face, the face of the faded wife, but so noble in its
idealized beauty that it might have been a portrait of her glorified face in Paradise. It was a profile, with the eyes upturned,
—a mere outline, but grand in conception and expression. I
gazed in silent astonishment.

Ermine said, "Yes, I knew you could do it, Solomon. It is
perfect of its kind." The shadow of a smile stole over the pallid
face, and then the husband's fading gaze turned upward to
meet the wild, dark eyes of the wife.

"It 's you, Dorcas," he murmured; "that 's how you looked
to me, but I never could get it right before." She bent over
him, and silently we watched the coming of the shadow of
death; he spoke only once, "My rose of Sharon—" And then in
a moment he was gone, the poor artist was dead.

Wild, wild was the grief of the ungoverned heart left behind; she was like a mad-woman, and our united strength was
needed to keep her from injuring herself in her frenzy. I was

frightened, but Ermine's strong little hands and lithe arms kept her down until, exhausted, she lay motionless near her dead husband. Then we carried her down stairs and I watched by the bedside, while my cousin went back to the studio. She was absent some time, and then she came back to keep the vigil with me through the long, still night. At dawn the woman woke, and her face looked aged in the gray light. She was quiet, and took without a word the food we had prepared, awkwardly enough, in the keeping-room.

"I must go to him, I must go to him," she murmured, as we led her back.

"Yes," said Ermine, "but first let me make you tidy. He loved to see you neat." And with deft, gentle touch she dressed the poor creature, arranging the heavy hair so artistically that, for the first time, I saw what she might have been, and understood the husband's dream.

"What is that?" I said, as a peculiar sound startled us.

"It 's Roarer. He was tied up last night, but I suppose he 's gnawed the rope," said the woman. I opened the hall door, and in stalked the great dog, smelling his way directly up the stairs.

"O, he must not go!" I exclaimed.

"Yes, let him go, he loved his master," said Ermine; "we will go too." So silently we all went up into the chamber of death.

The pictures had been taken down from the walls, but the wonderful sketch remained on the easel, which had been moved to the head of the couch where Solomon lay. His long, light hair was smooth, his face peacefully quiet, and on his breast lay the beautiful bunch of autumn leaves which he had arranged in our honor. It was a striking picture,—the noble face of the sketch above, and the dead face of the artist below. It brought to my mind a design I had once seen, where Fame with her laurels came at last to the door of the poor artist and gently knocked; but he had died the night before!

The dog lay at his master's feet, nor stirred until Solomon was carried out to his grave.

The Community buried the miner in one corner of the lonely little meadow. No service had they and no mound was raised to mark the spot, for such was their custom; but in the early spring we went down again into the valley, and placed a block of granite over the grave. It bore the inscription:—

SOLOMON.
He will finish his work in Heaven.

Strange as it may seem, the wife pined for her artist husband. We found her in the Community trying to work, but so aged and bent that we hardly knew her. Her large eyes had lost their peevish discontent, and a great sadness had taken the place.

"Seems like I could n't get on without Sol," she said, sitting with us in the hotel parlor after work-hours. "I kinder miss his voice, and all them names he used to call me; he got 'em out of the Bible, so they must have been good, you know. He always thought everything I did was right, and he thought no end of my good looks, too; I suppose I 've lost 'em all now. He was mighty fond of me; nobody in all the world cares a straw for me now. Even Roarer would n't stay with me, for all I petted him; he kep' a going out to that meader and a lying by Sol, until, one day, we found him there dead. He just died of sheer loneliness, I reckon. I sha' n't have to stop long I know, because I keep a dreaming of Sol, and he always looks at me like he did when I first knew him. He was a beautiful boy when I first saw him on that load of wood coming into Sandy. Well, ladies, I must go. Thank you kindly for all you 've done for me. And say, Miss Stuart, when I die you shall have that coal picter; no one else 'ud vally it so much."

Three months after, while we were at the sea-shore, Ermine received a long tin case, directed in a peculiar handwriting; it had been forwarded from C——, and contained the sketch and a note from the Community.

"E. Stuart: The woman Dorcas Bangs died this day. She will be put away by the side of her husband, Solomon Bangs. She left the enclosed picture, which we hereby send, and which please acknowledge by return of mail.

Jacob Boll, *Trustee*."

I unfolded the wrappings and looked at the sketch. "It is indeed striking," I said. "She must have been beautiful once, poor woman!"

"Let us hope that at least she is beautiful now, for her husband's sake, poor man!" replied Ermine.

Even then we could not give up our preferences.

# *Wilhelmina*

"And so, Mina, you will not marry the baker?"

"No; I waits for Gustav."

"How long is it since you have seen him?"

"Three year; it was a three-year regi-mènt."

"Then he will soon be home?"

"I not know," answered the girl, with a wistful look in her dark eyes, as if asking information from the superior being who sat in the skiff,—a being from the outside world where news-papers, the modern Tree of Knowledge, were not forbidden.

"Perhaps he will re-enlist, and stay three years longer," I said.

"Ah, lady,—six year! It breaks the heart," answered Wil-helmina.

She was the gardener's daughter, a member of the Commu-nity of German Separatists who live secluded in one of Ohio's rich valleys, separated by their own broad acres and orchard-covered hills from the busy world outside; down the valley flows the tranquil Tuscarawas on its way to the Muskingum, its slow tide rolling through the fertile bottom-lands between stone dikes, and utilized to the utmost extent of carefulness by the thrifty brothers, now working a saw-mill on the bank, now sending a tributary to the flour-mill across the canal, and now branching off in a sparkling race across the valley to turn wheels for two or three factories, watering the great grass-meadow on the way. We were floating on this river in a skiff named by myself Der Fliegende Holländer, much to the slow wonder of the Zoarites, who did not understand how a Dutchman could, nor why he should, fly. Wilhelmina sat before me, her oars idly trailing in the water. She showed a Nubian head above her white kerchief: large-lidded soft brown eyes, heavy braids of dark hair, a creamy skin with purple tints in the lips and brown shadows under the eyes, and a far-off dreamy expression which even the steady, monotonous toil of Community life had not been able to efface. She wore the blue dress and white ker-chief of the society, the quaint little calico bonnet lying beside her; she was a small maiden; her slender form swayed in the stiff, short-waisted gown, her feet slipped about in the broad shoes, and her hands, roughened and browned with garden-work, were yet narrow and graceful. From the first we felt sure she was grafted, and not a shoot from the Community stalk. But we could learn nothing of her origin; the Zoarites are not communicative; they fill each day with twelve good hours of labor, and look neither forward nor back. "She is a daughter," said the old gardener in answer to our questions. "Adopted?" I suggested; but he vouchsafed no answer. I liked the little daughter's dreamy face, but she was pale and undeveloped, like a Southern flower growing in Northern soil; the rosy-cheeked, flaxen-haired Rosines, Salomes, and Dorotys, with their broad shoulders and ponderous tread, thought this brown change-ling ugly, and pitied her in their slow, good-natured way.

"It breaks the heart," said Wilhelmina again, softly, as if to herself.

I repented me of my thoughtlessness. "In any case he can come back for a few days," I hastened to say. "What regiment was it?"

"The One Hundred and Seventh, lady."

I had a Cleveland paper in my basket, and taking it out I glanced over the war-news column, carelessly, as one who does not expect to find what he seeks. But chance was with us, and gave this item: "The One Hundred and Seventh Regiment, O. V. I., is expected home next week. The men will be paid off at Camp Chase."

"Ah!" said Wilhelmina, catching her breath with a half-sob under her tightly drawn kerchief,—"ah, mein Gustav!"

"Yes, you will soon see him," I answered, bending forward to take the rough little hand in mine; for I was a romantic wife, and my heart went out to all lovers. But the girl did not notice my words or my touch; silently she sat, absorbed in her own emotion, her eyes fixed on the hilltops far away, as though she saw the regiment marching home through the blue June sky.

I took the oars and rowed up as far as the island, letting the skiff float back with the current. Other boats were out, filled with fresh-faced boys in their high-crowned hats, long-waisted, wide-flapped vests of calico, and funny little swallow-tailed coats with buttons up under the shoulder-blades; they appeared unaccountably long in front and short behind, these young Zoar brethren. On the vine-covered dike were groups of mothers and grave little children, and up in the hill-orchards were moving figures, young and old; the whole village was abroad in the lovely afternoon, according to their Sunday custom, which gave the morning to chorals and a long sermon in the little church, and the afternoon to nature, even old Christian, the pastor, taking his imposing white fur hat and tasselled cane for a walk through the Community fields, with the remark, "Thus is cheered the heart of man, and his countenance refreshed."

As the sun sank in the warm western sky, homeward came the villagers from the river, the orchards, and the meadows, men, women, and children, a hardy, simple-minded band, whose fathers, for religion's sake, had taken the long journey from Würtemberg across the ocean to this distant valley, and made it a garden of rest in the wilderness. We, too, landed, and walked up the apple-tree lane towards the hotel.

"The cows come," said Wilhelmina as we heard a distant tinkling; "I must go." But still she lingered. "Der regi-mènt, it come soon, you say?" she asked in a low voice, as though she wanted to hear the good news again and again.

"They will be paid off next week; they cannot be later than ten days from now."

"Ten day! Ah, mein Gustav," murmured the little maiden; she turned away and tied on her stiff bonnet, furtively wiping off a tear with her prim handkerchief folded in a square.

"Why, my child," I said, following her and stooping to look in her face, "what is this?"

"It is nothing; it is for glad,—for very glad," said Wilhelmina. Away she ran as the first solemn cow came into view, heading the long procession meandering slowly towards the stalls. They knew nothing of haste, these dignified Community cows; from stall to pasture, from pasture to stall, in a plethora of comfort, this was their life. The silver-haired shepherd came last with his staff and scrip, and the nervous shepherd-dog ran hither and thither in the hope of finding some cow to bark at; but the comfortable cows moved on in orderly ranks, and he was obliged to dart off on a tangent every now and then, and bark at nothing, to relieve his feelings. Reaching the paved court-yard each cow walked into her own stall, and the milking began. All the girls took part in this work, sitting on little stools and singing together as the milk frothed up in the tin pails; the pails were emptied into tubs, and when the tubs were full the girls bore them on their heads to the dairy, where the milk was poured into a huge strainer, a constant procession of girls with tubs above and the old milk-mother ladling out as fast as she could below. With the bee-hives near by, it was a realization of the Scriptural phrase, "A land flowing with milk and honey."

The next morning, after breakfast, I strolled up the still street, leaving the Wirthshaus with its pointed roof behind me. On the right were some ancient cottages built of crossed timbers filled in with plaster; sundials hung on the walls, and each house had its piazza, where, when the work of the day was over, the families assembled, often singing folk-songs to the music of their home-made flutes and pipes. On the left stood the residence of the first pastor, the reverend man who had led these sheep to their refuge in the wilds of the New World. It was a wide-spreading brick mansion, with a broad-side of white-curtained windows, an enclosed glass porch, iron railings, and gilded eaves; a building so stately among the surrounding cottages that it had gained from outsiders the name of the King's Palace, although the good man whose grave remains unmarked in the quiet God's Acre, according to the Separatist custom, was a father to his people, not a king.

Beyond the palace began the Community garden, a large square in the centre of the village filled with flowers and fruit, adorned with arbors and cedar-trees clipped in the form of birds, and enriched with an old-style greenhouse whose sliding glasses were viewed with admiration by the visitors of thirty years ago, who sent their choice plants thither from far and near to be tended through the long, cold lake-country winters. The garden, the cedars, and the greenhouse were all antiquated, but to me none the less charming. The spring that gushed up in one corner, the old-fashioned flowers in their box-bordered beds, larkspur, lady slippers, bachelor's buttons, peonies, aromatic pinks, and all varieties of roses, the arbors with red honeysuckle overhead and tan bark under foot, were all delightful; and I knew, also, that I should find the garden-er's daughter at her never-ending task of weeding. This time it was the strawberry bed. "I have come to sit in your pleasant garden, Mina," I said, taking a seat on a shaded bench near the bending figure.

"So?" said Wilhelmina in long-drawn interrogation, glancing up shyly with a smile. She was a child of the sun, this little maiden, and while her blond companions wore always their bonnets or broad-brimmed hats over their precise caps, Wilhelmina, as now, constantly discarded these coverings and sat in the sun basking like a bird of the tropics. In truth, it did not redden her; she was one of those whose coloring comes not from without, but within.

"Do you like this work, Mina?"

"O—so. Good as any."

"Do you like work?"

"Folks must work." This was said gravely, as part of the Community creed.

"Would n't you like to go with me to the city?"

"No; I 's better here."

"But you can see the great world, Mina. You need not work, I will take care of you. You shall have pretty dresses; would n't you like that?" I asked, curious to discover the secret of the Separatist indifference to everything outside.

"Nein," answered the little maiden, tranquilly; "nein, fräulein. Ich bin zufrieden."

Those three words were the key. "I am contented." So were they taught from childhood, and—I was about to say—they knew no better; but, after all, is there anything better to know?

We talked on, for Mina understood English, although many of her mates could chatter only in their Würtemberg dialect, whose provincialisms confused my carefully learned German; I was grounded in Goethe, well read in Schiller, and struggling with Jean Paul, who, fortunately, is "der Einzige," the only; another such would destroy life. At length a bell sounded, and forthwith work was laid aside in the fields, the workshops, and the houses, while all partook of a light repast, one of the five meals with which the long summer day of toil is broken. Flagons of beer had the men afield, with bread and cheese; the women took bread and apple-butter. But Mina did not care for the thick slice which the thrifty house-mother had provided; she had not the steady unfanciful appetite of the Community which eats the same food day after day, as the cow eats its grass, desiring no change.

"And the gardener really wishes you to marry Jacob?" I said as she sat on the grass near me, enjoying the rest.

"Yes. Jacob is good,—always the same."

"And Gustav?"

"Ah, mein Gustav! Lady, *he* is young, tall,—so tall as tree; he run, he sing, his eyes like veilchen there, his hair like gold. If I see him not soon, lady, I die! The year so long,—*so* long they are. Three year without Gustav!" The brown eyes grew dim, and out came the square-folded handkerchief, of colored calico for week-days.

"But it will not be long now, Mina."

"Yes; I hope."

"He writes to you, I suppose?"

"No. Gustav knows not to write, he not like school. But he speak through the other boys, Ernst the verliebte of Rosine, and Peter of Doroty."

"The Zoar soldiers were all young men?"

"Yes; all verliebte. Some are not; they have gone to the Next Country" (died).

"Killed in battle?"

"Yes; on the berge that looks,—what you call, I not know—"

"Lookout Mountain?"

"Yes."

"Were the boys volunteers?" I asked, remembering the Community theory of non-resistance.

"O yes; they volunteer, Gustav the first. *They* not drafted," said Wilhelmina, proudly. For these two words, so prominent during the war, had penetrated even into this quiet little valley.

"But did the trustees approve?"

"Apperouve?"

"I mean, did they like it?"

"Ah! they like it not. They talk, they preach in church, they say 'No.' Zoar must give soldiers? So. Then they take money and pay for der substitute; but the boys, they must not go."

"But they went, in spite of the trustees?"

"Yes; Gustav first. They go in night, they walk in woods, over the hills to Brownville, where is der recruiter. The morning come, they gone!"

"They have been away three years, you say? They have seen the world in that time," I remarked half to myself, as I thought of the strange mind-opening and knowledge-gaining of those years to youths brought up in the strict seclusion of the Community.

"Yes; Gustav have seen the wide world," answered Wilhelmina with pride.

"But will they be content to step back into the dull routine of Zoar life?" I thought; and a doubt came that made me scan more closely the face of the girl at my side. To me it was attractive because of its possibilities; I was always fancying some excitement that would bring the color to the cheeks and full lips, and light up the heavy-lidded eyes with soft brilliancy. But would this Gustav see these might-be beauties? And how far would the singularly ugly costume offend eyes grown accustomed to fanciful finery and gay colors?

"You fully expect to marry Gustav?" I asked.

"We are verlobt," answered Mina, not without a little air of dignity.

"Yes, I know. But that was long ago."

"Verlobt once, verlobt always," said the little maiden, confidently.

"But why, then, does the gardener speak of Jacob, if you are engaged to this Gustav?"

"O, fader he like the old, and Jacob is old, thirty year! His wife is gone to the Next Country. Jacob is a brother, too; he write his name in the book. But Gustav he not do so; he is free."

"You mean that the baker has signed the articles, and is a member of the Community?"

"Yes; but the baker is old, very old; thirty year! Gustav not twenty and three yet; he come home, then he sign."

"And have you signed these articles, Wilhelmina?"

"Yes; all the womens signs."

"What does the paper say?"

"Da ich Unterzeichneter,"—began the girl.

"I cannot understand that. Tell me in English."

"Well; you wants to join the Zoar Community of Separatists; you writes your name and says, 'Give me house, victual, and clothes for my work and I join; and I never ferner Forderung an besagte Gesellschaft machen kann, oder will.'"

"Will never make further demand upon said society," I repeated, translating slowly.

"Yes; that is it."

"But who takes charge of all the money?"

"The trustees."

"Don't they give you any?"

"No; for what? It 's no good," answered Wilhelmina.

I knew that all the necessaries of life were dealt out to the members of the Community according to their need, and, as they never went outside of their valley, they could scarcely have spent money even if they had possessed it. But, nevertheless, it was startling in this nineteenth century to come upon a sincere belief in the worthlessness of the green-tinted paper we cherish so fondly. "Gustav will have learned its value," I thought, as Mina, having finished the strawberry-bed, started away towards the dairy to assist in the butter-making.

I strolled on up the little hill, past the picturesque bakery, where through the open window I caught a glimpse of the "old, very old Jacob," a serious young man of thirty, drawing out his large loaves of bread from the brick oven with a long-handled rake. It was gingerbread-day also, and a spicy odor met me at the window; so I put in my head and asked for a piece, receiving a card about a foot square, laid on fresh grape-leaves.

"But I cannot eat all this," I said, breaking off a corner.

"O, dat 's noding!" answered Jacob, beginning to knead fresh dough in a long white trough, the village supply for the next day.

"I have been sitting with Wilhelmina," I remarked, as I leaned on the casement, impelled by a desire to see the effect of the name.

"So?" said Jacob, interrogatively.

"Yes; she is a sweet girl."

"So?" (doubtfully.)

"Don't you think so, Jacob?"

"Ye-es. So-so. A leetle black," answered this impassive lover.

"But you wish to marry her?"

"O, ye-es. She young and strong; her fader say she good to work. I have children five; I must have some one in the house."

"O Jacob! Is that the way to talk?" I exclaimed.

"Warum nicht?" replied the baker, pausing in his kneading, and regarding me with wide-open, candid eyes.

"Why not, indeed?" I thought, as I turned away from the window. "He is at least honest, and no doubt in his way he would be a kind husband to little Mina. But what a way!"

I walked on up the street, passing the pleasant house where all the infirm old women of the Community were lodged together, carefully tended by appointed nurses. The aged sisters were out on the piazza sunning themselves, like so many old cats. They were bent with hard, out-door labor, for they belonged to the early days when the wild forest covered the fields now so rich, and only a few log-cabins stood on the site of the tidy cottages and gardens of the present village. Some of them had taken the long journey on foot from Philadelphia westward, four hundred and fifty miles, in the depths of winter. Well might they rest from their labors and sit in the sunshine, poor old souls!

A few days later, my friendly newspaper mentioned the arrival of the German regiment at Camp Chase. "They will probably be paid off in a day or two," I thought, "and another day may bring them here." Eager to be the first to tell the good news to my little favorite, I hastened up to the garden, and found her engaged, as usual, in weeding.

"Mina," I said, "I have something to tell you. The regiment is at Camp Chase; you will see Gustav soon, perhaps this week."

And there, before my eyes, the transformation I had often fancied took place; the color rushed to the brown surface, the cheeks and lips glowed in vivid red, and the heavy eyes opened wide and shone like stars, with a brilliancy that astonished and even disturbed me. The statue had a soul at last; the beauty dormant had awakened. But for the fire of that soul would this expected Pygmalion suffice? Would the real prince fill his place in the long-cherished dreams of this beauty of the wood?

The girl had risen as I spoke, and now she stood erect, trembling with excitement, her hands clasped on her breast, breathing quickly and heavily as though an overweight of joy was pressing down her heart; her eyes were fixed upon my face, but she saw me not. Strange was her gaze, like the gaze of one walking in sleep. Her sloping shoulders seemed to expand and chafe against the stuff gown as though they would burst their bonds; the blood glowed in her face and throat, and her lips quivered, not as though tears were coming, but from the fulness of unuttered speech. Her emotion resembled the intensest fire of fever, and yet it seemed natural; like noon in the tropics when the gorgeous flowers flame in the white, shadowless heat. Thus stood Wilhelmina, looking up into the sky with eyes that challenged the sun.

"Come here, child," I said; "come here and sit by me. We will talk about it."

But she neither saw nor heard me. I drew her down on the bench at my side; she yielded unconsciously; her slender form throbbed, and pulses were beating under my hands wherever I touched her. "Mina!" I said again. But she did not answer. Like an unfolding rose, she revealed her hidden, beautiful heart, as though a spirit had breathed upon the bud; silenced in the presence of this great love, I ceased speaking, and left her to herself. After a time single words fell from her lips, broken utterances of happiness. I was as nothing; she was absorbed in the One. "Gustav! mein Gustav!" It was like the bird's note, oft repeated, ever the same. So isolated, so intense was her joy, that, as often happens, my mind took refuge in the opposite extreme of commonplace, and I found myself wondering whether she would be able to eat boiled beef and cabbage for dinner, or fill the soft-soap barrel for the laundry-women, later in the day.

All the morning I sat under the trees with Wilhelmina, who had forgotten her life-long tasks as completely as though they had never existed. I hated to leave her to the leather-colored wife of the old gardener, and lingered until the sharp voice came from the distant house-door, calling, "Veel-hel-*meeny*," as the twelve-o'clock bell summoned the Community to dinner. But as Mina rose and swept back the heavy braids that had fallen from the little ivory stick which confined them, I saw that she was armed *cap-à-pie* in that full happiness from which all weapons glance off harmless.

All the rest of the day she was like a thing possessed. I followed her to the hill-pasture, whither she had gone to mind

the cows, and found her coiled up on the grass in the blaze of
the afternoon sun, like a little salamander. She was lost in day-
dreams, and the decorous cows had a holiday for once in their
sober lives, wandering beyond bounds at will, and even tasting
the dissipations of the marsh, standing unheeded in the bog up
to their sleek knees. Wilhelmina had not many words to give
me; her English vocabulary was limited; she had never read a
line of romance nor a verse of poetry. The nearest approach to
either was the Community hymn-book, containing the Separatist hymns, of which the following lines are a specimen,

> "Ruhe ist das beste Gut
> Dasz man haben kann,"—

> "Rest is the best good
> That man can have,"—

and which embody the religious doctrine of the Zoar Brethren,
although they think, apparently, that the labor of twelve hours
each day is necessary to its enjoyment. The "Ruhe," however,
refers more especially to their quiet seclusion away from the
turmoil of the wicked world outside.

The second morning after this it was evident that an unusual
excitement was abroad in the phlegmatic village. All the daily
duties were fulfilled as usual at the Wirthshaus: Pauline went
up to the bakery with her board, and returned with her load
of bread and bretzels balanced on her head; Jacobina served
our coffee with her slow precision; and the broad-shouldered,
young-faced Lydia patted and puffed up our mountain-high
feather-beds with due care. The men went afield at the blast
of the horn, the workshops were full and the mills running.
But, nevertheless, all was not the same; the air seemed full of
mystery; there were whisperings when two met, furtive signals,
and an inward excitement glowing in the faces of men, women,
and children, hitherto placid as their own sheep. "They have
heard the news," I said, after watching the tailor's Gretchen
and the blacksmith's Barbara stop to exchange a whisper behind the wood-house. Later in the day we learned that several letters from the absent soldier-boys had been received that
morning, announcing their arrival on the evening train. The
news had flown from one end of the village to the other; and
although the well-drilled hands were all at work, hearts were

stirring with the greatest excitement of a lifetime, since there
was hardly a house where there was not one expected. Each
large house often held a number of families, stowed away in
little sets of chambers, with one dining-room in common.

Several times during the day we saw the three trustees con-
ferring apart with anxious faces. The war had been a sore
trouble to them, owing to their conscientious scruples against
rendering military service. They had hoped to remain non-
combatants. But the country was on fire with patriotism, and
nothing less than a *bona fide* Separatist in United States uniform would quiet the surrounding towns, long jealous of the
wealth of this foreign community, misunderstanding its ten-
ets, and glowing with that zeal against "sympathizers" which
kept star-spangled banners flying over every suspected house.
"Hang out the flag!" was their cry, and they demanded that
Zoar should hang out its soldiers, giving them to understand
that if not voluntarily hung out, they would soon be involuntarily hung up! A draft was ordered, and then the young men
of the society, who had long chafed against their bonds, broke
loose, volunteered, and marched away, principles or no principles, trustees or no trustees. These bold hearts once gone, the
village sank into quietude again. Their letters, however, were
a source of anxiety, coming as they did from the vain outside
world; and the old postmaster, autocrat though he was, hardly
dared to suppress them. But he said, shaking his head, that
they "had fallen upon troublous times," and handed each dangerous envelope out with a groan. But the soldiers were not
skilled penmen; their letters, few and far between, at length
stopped entirely. Time passed, and the very existence of the
runaways had become a far-off problem to the wise men
of the Community, absorbed in their slow calculations and
cautious agriculture, when now, suddenly, it forced itself upon
them face to face, and they were required to solve it in the
twinkling of an eye. The bold hearts were coming back, full
of knowledge of the outside world; almost every house would
hold one, and the bands of law and order would be broken.
Before this prospect the trustees quailed. Twenty years before they would have forbidden the entrance of these unruly
sons within their borders; but now they dared not, since even
into Zoar had penetrated the knowledge that America was a
free country. The younger generation were not as their fathers

were; objections had been openly made to the cut of the Sunday coats, and the girls had spoken together of ribbons!

The shadows of twilight seemed very long in falling that night, but at last there was no further excuse for delaying the evening bell, and home came the laborers to their evening meal. There was no moon, a soft mist obscured the stars, and the night was darkened with the excess of richness which rose from the ripening valley-fields and fat bottom-lands along the river. The Community store opposite the Wirthshaus was closed early in the evening, the houses of the trustees were dark, and indeed the village was almost unlighted, as if to hide its own excitement. The entire population was abroad in the night, and one by one the men and boys stole away down the station road, a lovely, winding track on the hillside, following the river on its way down the valley to the little station on the grass-grown railroad, a branch from the main track. As ten o'clock came, the women and girls, grown bold with excitement, gathered in the open space in front of the Wirthshaus, where the lights from the windows illumined their faces. There I saw the broad-shouldered Lydia, Rosine, Doroty, and all the rest, in their Sunday clothes, flushed, laughing, and chattering; but no Wilhelmina.

"Where can she be?" I said.

If she was there, the larger girls concealed her with their buxom breadth; I looked for the slender little maiden in vain.

"Shu!" cried the girls, "de bugle!"

Far down the station road we heard the bugle and saw the glimmering of lights among the trees. On it came, a will-o'-the-wisp procession: first a detachment of village boys each with a lantern or torch, next the returned soldiers winding their bugles,—for, German-like, they all had musical instruments, —then an excited crowd of brothers and cousins loaded with knapsacks, guns, and military accoutrements of all kinds; each man had something, were it only a tin cup, and proudly they marched in the footsteps of their glorious relatives, bearing the spoils of war. The girls set up a shrill cry of welcome as the procession approached, but the ranks continued unbroken until the open space in front of the Wirthshaus was reached; then, at a signal, the soldiers gave three cheers, the villagers joining in with all their hearts and lungs, but wildly and out of time, like the scattering fire of an awkward squad. The sound had never been heard in Zoar before. The soldiers gave a final "Tiger-r-r!" and then broke ranks, mingling with the excited crowd, exchanging greetings and embraces. All talked at once; some wept, some laughed; and through it all silently stood the three trustees on the dark porch in front of the store, looking down upon their wild flock, their sober faces visible in the glare of the torches and lanterns below. The entire population was present; even the babies were held up on the outskirts of the crowd, stolid and staring.

"Where can Wilhelmina be?" I said again.

"Here, under the window; I saw her long ago," replied one of the women.

Leaning against a piazza-pillar, close under my eyes, stood the little maiden, pale and still. I could not disguise from myself that she looked almost ugly among those florid, laughing girls, for her color was gone, and her eyes so fixed that they looked unnaturally large; her somewhat heavy Egyptian features stood out in the bright light, but her small form was lost among the group of broad, white-kerchiefed shoulders, adorned with breast-knots of gay flowers. And had Wilhelmina no flower? She, so fond of blossoms? I looked again; yes, a little white rose, drooping and pale as herself.

But where was Gustav? The soldiers came and went in the crowd, and all spoke to Mina; but where was the One? I caught the landlord's little son as he passed, and asked the question.

"Gustav? Dat 's him," he answered, pointing out a tall, rollicking soldier who seemed to be embracing the whole population in his gleeful welcome. That very soldier had passed Mina a dozen times, flinging a gay greeting to her each time; but nothing more.

After half an hour of general rejoicing, the crowd dispersed, each household bearing off in triumph the hero that fell to its lot. Then the tiled domiciles, where usually all were asleep an hour after twilight, blazed forth with unaccustomed light from every little window; and within we could see the circles, with flagons of beer and various dainties manufactured in secret during the day, sitting and talking together in a manner which, for Zoar, was a wild revel, since it was nearly eleven o'clock! We were not the only outside spectators of this unwonted gayety; several times we met the three trustees stealing along in the shadow from house to house, like anxious spectres in broad-brimmed hats. No doubt they said to each other, "How, how will this end!"

The merry Gustav had gone off by Mina's side, which gave me some comfort; but when in our rounds we came to the gardener's house and gazed through the open door, the little maiden sat apart, and the soldier, in the centre of an admiring circle, was telling stories of the war.

I felt a foreboding of sorrow as I gazed out through the little window before climbing up into my high bed. Lights still twinkled in some of the houses, but a white mist was rising from the river, and the drowsy, long-drawn chant of the summer night invited me to dreamless sleep.

The next morning I could not resist questioning Jacobina, who also had her lover among the soldiers, if all was well.

"O yes. They stay,—all but two. We 's married next mont."

"And the two?"

"Karl and Gustav."

"And Wilhelmina!" I exclaimed.

"O, she let him go," answered Jacobina, bringing fresh coffee.

"Poor child! How does she bear it?"

"O, so. She cannot help. She say noding."

"But the trustees, will they allow these young men to leave the Community?"

"They cannot help," said Jacobina. "Gustav and Karl write not in the book; they free to go. Wilhelmina marry Jacob; it 's joost the same; all r-r-ight," added Jacobina, who prided herself upon her English, caught from visitors at the Wirthshaus table.

"Ah! but it is not just the same," I thought as I went up to the garden to find my little maiden. She was not there; the leathery mother said she was out on the hills with the cows.

"So Gustav is going to leave the Community," I said in German.

"Yes, better so. He is an idle, wild boy. Now, Veelhelmeeny can marry the baker, a good steady man."

"But Mina does not like him," I suggested.

"Das macht nichts," answered the leathery mother.

Wilhelmina was not in the pasture; I sought for her everywhere, and called her name. The poor child had hidden herself, and whether she heard me or not, she did not respond. All day she kept herself aloof; I almost feared she would never return; but in the late twilight a little figure slipped through the garden-gate and took refuge in the house before I could speak; for I was watching for the child, apparently the only one, though a stranger, to care for her sorrow.

"Can I not see her?" I said to the leathery mother, following to the door.

"Eh, no; she 's foolish; she will not speak a word; she has gone off to bed," was the answer.

For three days I did not see Mina, so early did she flee away to the hills and so late return. I followed her to the pasture once or twice, but she would not show herself, and I could not discover her hiding-place. The fourth day I learned that Gustav and Karl were to leave the village in the afternoon, probably forever. The other soldiers had signed the articles presented by the anxious trustees, and settled down into the old routine, going afield with the rest, although still heroes of the hour; they were all to be married in August. No doubt the hardships of their campaigns among the Tennessee mountains had taught them that the rich valley was a home not to be despised; nevertheless, it was evident that the flowers of the flock were those who were about departing, and that in Gustav and Karl the Community lost its brightest spirits. Evident to us; but, possibly, the Community cared not for bright spirits.

I had made several attempts to speak to Gustav; this morning I at last succeeded. I found him polishing his bugle on the garden bench.

"Why are you going away, Gustav?" I asked. "Zoar is a pleasant little village."

"Too slow for me, miss."

"The life is easy, however; you will find the world a hard place."

"I don't mind work, ma'am, but I do like to be free. I feel all cramped up here, with these rules and bells; and, besides, I could n't stand those trustees; they never let a fellow alone."

"And Wilhelmina? If you do go, I hope you will take her with you, or come for her when you have found work."

"Oh no, miss. All that was long ago. It 's all over now."

"But you like her, Gustav?"

"O, so. She 's a good little thing, but too quiet for me."

"But she likes you," I said desperately, for I saw no other way to loosen this Gordian knot.

"O no, miss. She got used to it, and has thought of it all these years; that 's all. She 'll forget about it and marry the baker."

"But she does not like the baker."

"Why not? He 's a good fellow enough. She 'll like him in time. It 's all the same. I declare it 's too bad to see all these girls going on in the same old way, in their ugly gowns and big shoes! Why, ma'am, I could n't take Mina outside, even if I wanted to; she 's too old to learn new ways, and everybody would laugh at her. She could n't get along a day. Besides," said the young soldier, coloring up to his eyes, "I don't mind telling you that—that there 's some one else. Look here, ma'am." And he put into my hand a card photograph representing a pretty girl, over-dressed, and adorned with curls and gilt jewelry. "That 's Miss Martin," said Gustav with pride; "Miss Emmeline Martin, of Cincinnati. I 'm going to marry Miss Martin."

As I held the pretty, flashy picture in my hand, all my castles fell to the ground. My plan for taking Mina home with me, accustoming her gradually to other clothes and ways, teaching her enough of the world to enable her to hold her place without pain, my hope that my husband might find a situation for Gustav in some of the iron-mills near Cleveland, in short, all the idyl I had woven, was destroyed. If it had not been for this red-cheeked Miss Martin in her gilt beads! "Why is it that men will be such fools?" I thought. Up sprung a memory of the curls and ponderous jet necklace I sported at a certain period of my existence, when John— I was silenced, gave Gustav his picture, and walked away without a word.

At noon the villagers, on their way back to work, paused at the Wirthshaus to say good by; Karl and Gustav were there, and the old woolly horse had already gone to the station with their boxes. Among the others came Christine, Karl's former affianced, heart-whole and smiling, already betrothed to a new lover; but no Wilhelmina. Good wishes and farewells were exchanged, and at last the two soldiers started away, falling into the marching step, and watched with furtive satisfaction by the three trustees, who stood together in the shadow of the smithy, apparently deeply absorbed in a broken-down cask.

It was a lovely afternoon, and I, too, strolled down the station road embowered in shade. The two soldiers were not far in advance. I had passed the flour-mill on the outskirts of the village and was approaching the old quarry, when a sound startled me; out from the rocks in front rushed a little figure, and crying, "Gustav, mein Gustav!" fell at the soldier's feet. It was Wilhelmina.

I ran forward and took her from the young men; she lay in my arms as if dead. The poor child was sadly changed; always slender and swaying, she now looked thin and shrunken, her skin had a strange, dark pallor, and her lips were drawn in as if from pain. I could see her eyes through the large-orbed thin lids, and the brown shadows beneath extended down into the cheeks.

"Was ist's?" said Gustav, looking bewildered. "Is she sick?"

I answered "Yes," but nothing more. I could see that he had no suspicion of the truth, believing as he did that the "good fellow" of a baker would do very well for this "good little thing" who was "too quiet" for him. The memory of Miss Martin sealed my lips. But if it had not been for that pretty, flashy picture, would I not have spoken!

"You must go; you will miss the train," I said, after a few minutes. "I will see to Mina."

But Gustav lingered. Perhaps he was really troubled to see the little sweetheart of his boyhood in such desolate plight; perhaps a touch of the old feeling came back; and perhaps, also, it was nothing of the kind, and, as usual, my romantic imagination was carrying me away. At any rate, whatever it was, he stooped over the fainting girl.

"She looks bad," he said, "very bad. I wish— But she 'll get well and marry the baker. Good by, Mina." And bending his tall form, he kissed her colorless cheek, and then hastened away to join the impatient Karl; a curve in the road soon hid them from view.

Wilhelmina had stirred at his touch; after a moment her large eyes opened slowly; she looked around as if dazed, but all at once memory came back, and she started up with the same cry, "Gustav, mein Gustav!" I drew her head down on my shoulder to stifle the sound; it was better the soldier should not hear it, and its anguish thrilled my own heart also. She had not the strength to resist me, and in a few minutes I knew that the young men were out of hearing as they strode on towards the station and out into the wide world.

The forest was solitary, we were beyond the village; all the afternoon I sat under the trees with the stricken girl. Again, as in her joy, her words were few; again, as in her joy, her whole being was involved. Her little rough hands were cold, a film had gathered over her eyes; she did not weep, but moaned to herself, and all her senses seemed blunted. At nightfall I took her home, and the leathery mother received her with a frown; but the child was beyond caring, and crept away, dumbly, to her room.

The next morning she was off to the hills again, nor could I find her for several days. Evidently, in spite of my sympathy, I was no more to her than I should have been to a wounded fawn. She was a mixture of the wild, shy creature of the woods and the deep-loving woman of the tropics; in either case I could be but small comfort. When at last I did see her, she was apathetic and dull; her feelings, her senses, and her intelligence seemed to have gone within, as if preying upon her heart. She scarcely listened to my proposal to take her with me; for, in my pity, I had suggested it, in spite of its difficulties.

"No," she said, mechanically, "I 's better here"; and fell into silence again.

A month later a friend went down to spend a few days in the valley, and upon her return described to us the weddings of the whilom soldiers. "It was really a pretty sight," she said, "the quaint peasant dresses and the flowers. Afterwards, the band went round the village playing their odd tunes, and all had a holiday. There were two civilians married also; I mean two young men who had not been to the war. It seems that two of the soldiers turned their backs upon the Community and their allotted brides, and marched away; but the Zoar maidens are not romantic, I fancy, for these two deserted ones were be-trothed again and married, all in the short space of four weeks."

"Was not one Wilhelmina, the gardener's daughter, a short, dark girl?" I asked.

"Yes."

"And she married Jacob the baker?"

"Yes."

The next year, weary of the cold lake-winds, we left the icy shore and went down to the valley to meet the coming spring, finding her already there, decked with vines and flowers. A new waitress brought us our coffee.

"How is Wilhelmina?" I asked.

"Eh,—Wilhelmina? O, she not here now; she gone to the Next Country," answered the girl in a matter-of-fact way. "She die last October, and Jacob he haf anoder wife now."

In the late afternoon I asked a little girl to show me Wilhelmina's grave in the quiet God's Acre on the hill. Innovation was creeping in, even here; the later graves had mounds raised over them, and one had a little head-board with an inscription in ink.

Wilhelmina lay apart, and some one, probably the old gardener, who had loved the little maiden in his silent way, had planted a rose-bush at the head of the mound. I dismissed my guide and sat there alone in the sunset, thinking of many things, but chiefly of this: "Why should this great wealth of love have been allowed to waste itself? Why is it that the greatest of power, unquestionably, of this mortal life should so often seem a useless gift?"

No answer came from the sunset clouds, and as twilight sank down on the earth I rose to go. "I fully believe," I said, as though repeating a creed, "that this poor, loving heart, whose earthly body lies under this mound, is happy now in its own loving way. It has not been changed, but the happiness it longed for has come. How, we know not; but the God who made Wilhelmina understands her. He has given unto her not rest, not peace, but an active, living joy."

I walked away through the wild meadow, under whose turf, unmarked by stone or mound, lay the first pioneers of the Community, and out into the forest road, untravelled save when the dead passed over it to their last earthly home. The evening was still and breathless, and the shadows lay thick on the grass as I looked back. But I could still distinguish the little mound with the rose-bush at its head, and, not without tears, I said, "Farewell, poor Wilhelmina; farewell."

# St. Clair Flats

I N September, 1855, I first saw the St. Clair Flats. Owing to
Raymond's determination, we stopped there.

"Why go on?" he asked. "Why cross another long, rough
lake, when here is all we want?"

"But no one ever stops here," I said.

"So much the better; we shall have it all to ourselves."

"But we must at least have a roof over our heads."

"I presume we can find one."

The captain of the steamer, however, knew of no roof save
that covering a little lighthouse set on spiles, which the boat
would pass within the half-hour; we decided to get off there,
and throw ourselves upon the charity of the lighthouse-man.
In the mean time, we sat on the bow with Captain Kidd, our
four-legged companion, who had often accompanied us on
hunting expeditions, but never before so far westward. It had
been rough on Lake Erie,—very rough. We, who had sailed
the ocean with composure, found ourselves most inhumanly
tossed on the short, chopping waves of this fresh-water sea; we,
who alone of all the cabin-list had eaten our four courses and
dessert every day on the ocean-steamer, found ourselves here
reduced to the depressing diet of a herring and pilot-bread.
Captain Kidd, too, had suffered dumbly; even now he could
not find comfort, but tried every plank in the deck, one after
the other, circling round and round after his tail, dog-fashion,
before lying down, and no sooner down than up again for another melancholy wandering about the deck, another choice
of planks, another circling, and another failure. We were sailing
across a small lake whose smooth waters were like clear green
oil; as we drew near the outlet, the low, green shores curved
inward and came together, and the steamer entered a narrow,
green river.

"Here we are," said Raymond. "Now we can soon land."

"But there is n't any land," I answered.

"What is that, then?" asked my near-sighted companion,
pointing toward what seemed a shore.

"Reeds."

"And what do they run back to?"

"Nothing."

"But there must be solid ground beyond?"

"Nothing but reeds, flags, lily-pads, grass, and water, as far as I can see."

"A marsh?"

"Yes, a marsh."

The word "marsh" does not bring up a beautiful picture to the mind, and yet the reality was as beautiful as anything I have ever seen,—an enchanted land, whose memory haunts me as an idea unwritten, a melody unsung, a picture unpainted, haunts the artist, and will not away. On each side and in front, as far as the eye could reach, stretched the low green land which was yet no land, intersected by hundreds of channels, narrow and broad, whose waters were green as their shores. In and out, now running into each other for a moment, now setting off each for himself again, these many channels flowed along with a rippling current; zigzag as they were, they never seemed to loiter, but, as if knowing just where they were going and what they had to do, they found time to take their own pleasant roundabout way, visiting the secluded households of their friends the flags, who, poor souls, must always stay at home. These currents were as clear as crystal, and green as the water-grasses that fringed their miniature shores. The bristling reeds, like companies of free-lances, rode boldly out here and there into the deeps, trying to conquer more territory for the grasses, but the currents were hard to conquer; they dismounted the free-lances, and flowed over their submerged heads; they beat them down with assaulting ripples; they broke their backs so effectually that the bravest had no spirit left, but trailed along, limp and bedraggled. And, if by chance the lances succeeded in stretching their forces across from one little shore to another, then the unconquered currents forced their way between the closely serried ranks of the enemy, and flowed on as gayly as ever, leaving the grasses sitting hopeless on the bank; for they needed solid ground for their delicate feet, these graceful ladies in green.

You might call it a marsh; but there was no mud, no dark slimy water, no stagnant scum; there were no rank yellow lilies, no gormandizing frogs, no swinish mud-turtles. The clear waters of the channels ran over golden sands, and hurtled among the stiff reeds so swiftly that only in a bay, or where protected by a crescent point, could the fair white lilies float in the quiet their serene beauty requires. The flags, who brandished their swords proudly, were martinets down to their very heels, keeping themselves as clean under the water as above, and harboring not a speck of mud on their bright green uniforms. For inhabitants, there were small fish roving about here and there in the clear tide, keeping an eye out for the herons, who, watery as to legs, but venerable and wise of aspect, stood on promontories musing, apparently, on the secrets of the ages.

The steamer's route was a constant curve; through the larger channels of the archipelago she wound, as if following the clew of a labyrinth. By turns she headed toward all the points of the compass, finding a channel where, to our uninitiated eyes, there was no channel, doubling upon her own track, going broadside foremost, floundering and backing, like a whale caught in a shallow. Here, landlocked, she would choose what seemed the narrowest channel of all, and dash recklessly through, with the reeds almost brushing her sides; there she crept gingerly along a broad expanse of water, her paddle-wheels scarcely revolving, in the excess of her caution. Saplings, with their heads of foliage on, and branches adorned with fluttering rags, served as finger-posts to show the way through the watery defiles, and there were many other hieroglyphics legible only to the pilot. "This time, surely, we shall run ashore," we thought again and again, as the steamer glided, head-on, toward an islet; but at the last there was always a quick turn into some unseen strait opening like a secret passage in a castle-wall, and we found ourselves in a new lakelet, heading in the opposite direction. Once we met another steamer, and the two great hulls floated slowly past each other, with engines motionless, so near that the passengers could have shaken hands with each other had they been so disposed. Not that they were so disposed, however; far from it. They gathered on their respective decks and gazed at each other gravely; not a smile was seen, not a word spoken, not the shadow of a salutation given. It was not pride, it was not suspicion; it was the universal listlessness of the travelling American bereft of his business, Othello with his occupation gone. What can such a man do on a steamer? Generally, nothing. Certainly he would never think of any such light-hearted nonsense as a smile or passing bow.

But the ships were, *par excellence*, the bewitched craft, the Flying Dutchmen of the Flats. A brig, with lofty, sky-scraping sails, bound south, came into view of our steamer, bound north, and passed, we hugging the shore to give her room; five minutes afterward the sky-scraping sails we had left behind veered around in front of us again; another five minutes, and there they were far distant on the right; another, and there they were again close by us on the left. For half an hour those sails circled around us, and yet all the time we were pushing steadily forward; this seemed witching work indeed. Again, the numerous schooners thought nothing of sailing overland; we saw them on all sides gliding before the wind, or beating up against it over the meadows as easily as over the water; sailing on grass was a mere trifle to these spirit-barks. All this we saw, as I said before, apparently. But in that adverb is hidden the magic of the St. Clair Flats.

"It is beautiful,—beautiful," I said, looking off over the vivid green expanse.

"Beautiful?" echoed the captain, who had himself taken charge of the steering when the steamer entered the labyrinth, —"I don't see anything beautiful in it!—Port your helm up there; port!"

"Port it is, sir," came back from the pilot-house above.

"These Flats give us more trouble than any other spot on the lakes; vessels are all the time getting aground and blocking up the way, which is narrow enough at best. There 's some talk of Uncle Sam's cutting a canal right through,—a straight canal; but he 's so slow, Uncle Sam is, and I 'm afraid I 'll be off the waters before the job is done."

"A straight canal!" I repeated, thinking with dismay of an ugly utilitarian ditch invading this beautiful winding waste of green.

"Yes, you can see for yourself what a saving it would be," replied the captain. "We could run right through in no time, day or night; whereas, now, we have to turn and twist and watch every inch of the whole everlasting marsh." Such was the captain's opinion. But we, albeit neither romantic nor artistic, were captivated with his "everlasting marsh," and eager to penetrate far within its green fastnesses.

"I suppose there are other families living about here, besides the family at the lighthouse?" I said.

"Never heard of any. They 'd have to live on a raft if they did."

"But there must be some solid ground."

"Don't believe it; it 's nothing but one great sponge for miles.—Steady up there; steady!"

"Very well," said Raymond, "so be it. If there is only the lighthouse, at the lighthouse we 'll get off, and take our chances."

"You 're surveyors, I suppose?" said the captain.

Surveyors are the pioneers of the lake-country, understood by the people to be a set of harmless monomaniacs, given to building little observatories along-shore, where there is nothing to observe; mild madmen, whose vagaries and instruments are equally singular. As surveyors, therefore, the captain saw nothing surprising in our determination to get off at the lighthouse; if we had proposed going ashore on a plank in the middle of Lake Huron, he would have made no objection.

At length the lighthouse came into view, a little fortress perched on spiles, with a ladder for entrance; as usual in small houses, much time seemed devoted to washing, for a large crane, swung to and fro by a rope, extended out over the water, covered with fluttering garments hung out to dry. The steamer lay to, our row-boat was launched, our traps handed out, Captain Kidd took his place in the bow, and we pushed off into the shallows; then the great paddle-wheels revolved again, and the steamer sailed away, leaving us astern, rocking on her waves, and watched listlessly by the passengers until a turn hid us from their view. In the mean time numerous flaxen-haired children had appeared at the little windows of the lighthouse, —too many of them, indeed, for our hopes of comfort.

"Ten," said Raymond, counting heads.

The ten, moved by curiosity as we approached, hung out of the windows so far that they held on merely by their ankles.

"We cannot possibly save them all," I remarked, looking up at the dangling gazers.

"O, they 're amphibious," said Raymond; "web-footed, I presume."

We rowed up under the fortress, and demanded parley with the keeper in the following language:—

"Is your father here?"

"No; but ma is," answered the chorus.—"Ma! ma!"

Ma appeared, a portly female, who held converse with us from the top of the ladder. The sum and substance of the dialogue was that she had not a corner to give us, and recommended us to find Liakim, and have him show us the way to Waiting Samuel's.

"Waiting Samuel's?" we repeated.

"Yes; he 's a kind of crazy man living away over there in the Flats. But there 's no harm in him, and his wife is a tidy housekeeper. You be surveyors, I suppose?"

We accepted the imputation in order to avoid a broadside of questions, and asked the whereabouts of Liakim.

"O, he 's round the point, somewhere there, fishing!"

We rowed on and found him, a little, round-shouldered man, in an old flat-bottomed boat, who had not taken a fish, and looked as though he never would. We explained our errand.

"Did Rosabel Lee tell ye to come to me?" he asked.

"The woman in the lighthouse told us," I said.

"That 's Rosabel Lee, that 's my wife; I 'm Liakim Lee," said the little man, gathering together his forlorn old rods and tackle, and pulling up his anchor.

> "In the kingdom down by the sea
> Lived the beautiful Annabel Lee,"

I quoted, *sotto voce.*

"And what very remarkable feet had she!" added Raymond, improvising under the inspiration of certain shoes, scow-like in shape, gigantic in length and breadth, which had made themselves visible at the top round of the ladder.

At length the shabby old boat got under way, and we followed in its path, turning off to the right through a network of channels, now pulling ourselves along by the reeds, now paddling over a raft of lily-pads, now poling through a winding labyrinth, and now rowing with broad sweeps across the little lake. The sun was sinking, and the western sky grew bright at his coming; there was not a cloud to make mountain-peaks on the horizon, nothing but the level earth below meeting the curved sky above, so evenly and clearly that it seemed as though we could go out there and touch it with our hands. Soon we lost sight of the little lighthouse; then one by one the distant sails sank down and disappeared, and we were left alone on the grassy sea, rowing toward the sunset.

"We must have come a mile or two, and there is no sign of a house," I called out to our guide.

"Well, I don't pretend to know how far it is, exactly," replied Liakim; "we don't know how far anything is here in the Flats, we don't."

"But are you sure you know the way?"

"O my, yes! We 've got most to the boy. There it is!"

The "boy" was a buoy, a fragment of plank painted white, part of the cabin-work of some wrecked steamer.

"Now, then," said Liakim, pausing, "you jest go straight on in this here channel till you come to the ninth run from this boy, on the right; take that, and it will lead you right up to Waiting Samuel's door."

"Are n't you coming with us?"

"Well, no. In the first place, Rosabel Lee will be waiting supper for me, and she don't like to wait; and, besides, Samuel can't abide to see none of us round his part of the Flats."

"But—" I began.

"Let him go," interposed Raymond; "we can find the house without trouble." And he tossed a silver dollar to the little man, who was already turning his boat.

"Thank you," said Liakim. "Be sure you take the ninth run and no other,—the ninth run from this boy. If you make any mistake, you 'll find yourselves miles away."

With this cheerful statement, he began to row back. I did not altogether fancy being left on the watery waste without a guide; the name, too, of our mythic host did not bring up a certainty of supper and beds. "Waiting Samuel," I repeated, doubtfully. "What is he waiting for?" I called back over my shoulder; for Raymond was rowing.

"The judgment-day!" answered Liakim, in a shrill key. The boats were now far apart; another turn, and we were alone.

We glided on, counting the runs on the right: some were wide, promising rivers; others wee little rivulets; the eighth was far away; and, when we had passed it, we could hardly decide whether we had reached the ninth or not, so small was the opening, so choked with weeds, showing scarcely a gleam of water beyond when we stood up to inspect it.

"It is certainly the ninth, and I vote that we try it. It will do as well as another, and I, for one, am in no hurry to arrive anywhere," said Raymond, pushing the boat in among the reeds.

"Do you want to lose yourself in this wilderness?" I asked, making a flag of my handkerchief to mark the spot where we had left the main stream.

"I think we are lost already," was the calm reply. I began to fear we were.

For some distance the "run," as Liakim called it, continued choked with aquatic vegetation, which acted like so many devil-fish catching our oars; at length it widened and gradually gave us a clear channel, albeit so winding and erratic that the glow of the sunset, our only beacon, seemed to be executing a waltz all round the horizon. At length we saw a dark spot on the left, and distinguished the outline of a low house. "There it is," I said, plying my oars with renewed strength. But the run turned short off in the opposite direction, and the house disappeared. After some time it rose again, this time on our right, but once more the run turned its back and shot off on a tangent. The sun had gone, and the rapid twilight of September was falling around us; the air, however, was singularly clear, and, as there was absolutely nothing to make a shadow, the darkness came on evenly over the level green. I was growing anxious, when a third time the house appeared, but the wilful run passed by it, although so near that we could distinguish its open windows and door. "Why not get out and wade across?" I suggested.

"According to Liakim, it is the duty of this run to take us to the very door of Waiting Samuel's mansion, and it shall take us," said Raymond, rowing on. It did.

Doubling upon itself in the most unexpected manner, it brought us back to a little island, where the tall grass had given way to a vegetable-garden. We landed, secured our boat, and walked up the pathway toward the house. In the dusk it seemed to be a low, square structure, built of planks covered with plaster; the roof was flat, the windows unusually broad, the door stood open,—but no one appeared. We knocked. A voice from within called out, "Who are you, and what do you want with Waiting Samuel?"

"Pilgrims, asking for food and shelter," replied Raymond.

"Do you know the ways of righteousness?"

"We can learn them."

"Will you conform to the rules of this household without murmuring?"

"We will."

"Enter then, and peace be with you!" said the voice, drawing nearer. We stepped cautiously through the dark passage into a room, whose open windows let in sufficient twilight to show us a shadowy figure. "Seat yourselves," it said. We found a bench, and sat down.

"What seek ye here?" continued the shadow.

"Rest!" replied Raymond.

"Hunting and fishing!" I added.

"Ye will find more than rest," said the voice, ignoring me altogether (I am often ignored in this way),—"more than rest, if ye stay long enough, and learn of the hidden treasures. Are you willing to seek for them?"

"Certainly!" said Raymond. "Where shall we dig?"

"I speak not of earthly digging, young man. Will you give me the charge of your souls?"

"Certainly, if you will also take charge of our bodies."

"Supper, for instance," I said, again coming to the front; "and beds."

The shadow groaned; then it called out wearily, "Roxana!"

"Yes, Samuel," replied an answering voice, and a second shadow became dimly visible on the threshold. "The woman will attend to your earthly concerns," said Waiting Samuel. —"Roxana, take them hence." The second shadow came forward, and, without a word, took our hands and led us along the dark passage like two children, warning us now of a step, now of a turn, then of two steps, and finally opening a door and ushering us into a fire-lighted room. Peat was burning upon the wide hearth, and a singing kettle hung above it on a crane; the red glow shone on a rough table, chairs cushioned in bright calico, a loud-ticking clock, a few gayly flowered plates and cups on a shelf, shining tins against the plastered wall, and a cat dozing on a bit of carpet in one corner. The cheery domestic scene, coming after the wide, dusky Flats, the silence, the darkness, and the mystical words of the shadowy Samuel, seemed so real and pleasant that my heart grew light within me.

"What a bright fire!" I said. "This is your domain, I suppose, Mrs.—Mrs.—"

"I am not Mrs.; I am called Roxana," replied the woman, busying herself at the hearth.

"Ah, you are then the sister of Waiting Samuel, I presume?"

"No, I am his wife, fast enough; we were married by the minister twenty years ago. But that was before Samuel had seen any visions."

"Does he see visions?"

"Yes, almost every day."

"Do you see them, also?"

"O no; I 'm not like Samuel. He has great gifts, Samuel has! The visions told us to come here; we used to live away down in Maine."

"Indeed! That was a long journey!"

"Yes! And we did n't come straight either. We 'd get to one place and stop, and I 'd think we were going to stay, and just get things comfortable, when Samuel would see another vision, and we 'd have to start on. We wandered in that way two or three years, but at last we got here, and something in the Flats seemed to suit the spirits, and they let us stay."

At this moment, through the half-open door, came a voice.

"An evil beast is in this house. Let him depart."

"Do you mean me?" said Raymond, who had made himself comfortable in a rocking-chair.

"Nay; I refer to the four-legged beast," continued the voice. "Come forth, Apollyon!"

Poor Captain Kidd seemed to feel that he was the person in question, for he hastened under the table with drooping tail and mortified aspect.

"Roxana, send forth the beast," said the voice.

The woman put down her dishes and went toward the table; but I interposed.

"If he must go, I will take him," I said, rising.

"Yes; he must go," replied Roxana, holding open the door. So I ordered out the unwilling Captain, and led him into the passageway.

"Out of the house, out of the house," said Waiting Samuel. "His feet may not rest upon this sacred ground. I must take him hence in the boat."

"But where?"

"Across the channel there is an islet large enough for him; he shall have food and shelter, but here he cannot abide," said the man, leading the way down to the boat.

The Captain was therefore ferried across, a tent was made for him out of some old mats, food was provided, and, lest he should swim back, he was tethered by a long rope, which allowed him to prowl around his domain and take his choice of three runs for drinking-water. With all these advantages, the ungrateful animal persisted in howling dismally as we rowed away. It was company he wanted, and not a "dear little isle of his own"; but then, he was not by nature poetical.

"You do not like dogs?" I said, as we reached our strand again.

"St. Paul wrote, 'Beware of dogs,'" replied Samuel.

"But did he mean—"

"I argue not with unbelievers; his meaning is clear to me, let that suffice," said my strange host, turning away and leaving me to find my way back alone. A delicious repast was awaiting me. Years have gone by, the world and all its delicacies have been unrolled before me, but the memory of the meals I ate in that little kitchen in the Flats haunts me still. That night it was only fish, potatoes, biscuits, butter, stewed fruit, and coffee; but the fish was fresh, and done to the turn of a perfect broil, not burn; the potatoes were fried to a rare crisp, yet tender perfection, not chippy brittleness; the biscuits were light, flaked creamily, and brown on the bottom; the butter freshly churned, without salt; the fruit, great pears, with their cores extracted, standing whole on their dish, ready to melt, but not melted; and the coffee clear and strong, with yellow cream and the old-fashioned, unadulterated loaf-sugar. We ate. That does not express it; we devoured. Roxana waited on us, and warmed up into something like excitement under our praises.

"I *do* like good cooking," she confessed. "It 's about all I have left of my old life. I go over to the mainland for supplies, and in the winter I try all kinds of new things to pass away the time. But Samuel is a poor eater, he is; and so there is n't much comfort in it. I 'm mighty glad you 've come, and I hope you 'll stay as long as you find it pleasant." This we promised to do, as we finished the potatoes and attacked the great jellied pears. "There 's one thing, though," continued Roxana; "you 'll have to come to our service on the roof at sunrise."

"What service?" I asked.

"The invocation. Dawn is a holy time, Samuel says, and we always wait for it; 'before the morning watch,' you know,—it says so in the Bible. Why, my name means 'the dawn,' Samuel says; that 's the reason he gave it to me. My real name, down in Maine, was Maria,—Maria Ann."

"But I may not wake in time," I said.

"Samuel will call you."

"And if, in spite of that, I should sleep over?"

"You would not do that; it would vex him," replied Roxana, calmly.

"Do you believe in these visions, madam?" asked Raymond, as we left the table, and seated ourselves in front of the dying fire.

"Yes," said Roxana; emphasis was unnecessary,—of course she believed.

"How often do they come?"

"Almost every day there is a spiritual presence, but it does not always speak. They come and hold long conversations in the winter, when there is nothing else to do; that, I think, is very kind of them, for in the summer Samuel can fish, and his time is more occupied. There were fishermen in the Bible, you know; it is a holy calling."

"Does Samuel ever go over to the mainland?"

"No, he never leaves the Flats. I do all the business; take over the fish, and buy the supplies. I bought all our cattle," said Roxana, with pride. "I poled them away over here on a raft, one by one, when they were little things."

"Where do you pasture them?"

"Here, on the island; there are only a few acres, to be sure; but I can cut boat-loads of the best feed within a stone's throw. If we only had a little more solid ground! But this island is almost the only solid piece in the Flats."

"Your butter is certainly delicious."

"Yes, I do my best. It is sold to the steamers and vessels as fast as I make it."

"You keep yourself busy, I see."

"O, I like to work; I could n't get on without it."

"And Samuel?"

"He is not like me," replied Roxana. "He has great gifts, Samuel has. I often think how strange it is that I should be the wife of such a holy man! He is very kind to me, too; he tells me about the visions, and all the other things."

"What things?" said Raymond.

"The spirits, and the sacred influence of the sun; the fiery triangle, and the thousand years of joy. The great day is coming, you know; Samuel is waiting for it."

"Nine of the night. Take thou thy rest. I will lay me down in peace, and sleep, for it is thou, Lord, only, that makest me dwell in safety," chanted a voice in the hall; the tone was deep and not without melody, and the words singularly impressive in that still, remote place.

"Go," said Roxana, instantly pushing aside her half-washed dishes. "Samuel will take you to your room."

"Do you leave your work unfinished?" I said, with some curiosity, noticing that she had folded her hands without even hanging up her towels.

"We do nothing after the evening chant," she said. "Pray go; he is waiting."

"Can we have candles?"

"Waiting Samuel allows no false lights in his house; as imitations of the glorious sun, they are abominable to him. Go, I beg."

She opened the door, and we went into the passage; it was entirely dark, but the man led us across to our room, showed us the position of our beds by sense of feeling, and left us without a word. After he had gone, we struck matches, one by one, and, with the aid of their uncertain light, managed to get into our respective mounds in safety; they were shake-downs on the floor, made of fragrant hay instead of straw, covered with clean sheets and patchwork coverlids, and provided with large, luxurious pillows. O pillow! Has any one sung thy praises? When tired or sick, when discouraged or sad, what gives so much comfort as a pillow? Not your curled-hair brickbats; not your stiff, fluted, rasping covers, or limp cotton cases; but a good, generous, soft pillow, deftly cased in smooth, cool, untrimmed linen! There 's a friend for you, a friend who changes not, a friend who soothes all your troubles with a soft caress, a mesmeric touch of balmy forgetfulness.

I slept a dreamless sleep. Then I heard a voice borne toward me as if coming from far over a sea, the waves bringing it nearer and nearer.

"Awake!" it cried; "awake! The night is far spent; the day is at hand. Awake!"

I wondered vaguely over this voice as to what manner of voice it might be, but it came again, and again, and finally I awoke to find it at my side. The gray light of dawn came through the open windows, and Raymond was already up, engaged with a tub of water and crash towels. Again the chant sounded in my ears.

"Very well, very well," I said, testily. "But if you sing before breakfast you 'll cry before night, Waiting Samuel."

Our host had disappeared, however, without hearing my flippant speech, and slowly I rose from my fragrant couch; the room was empty save for our two mounds, two tubs of water, and a number of towels hanging on nails. "Not overcrowded with furniture," I remarked.

"From Maine to Florida, from Massachusetts to Missouri, have I travelled, and never before found water enough," said Raymond. "If waiting for the judgment-day raises such liberal ideas of tubs and towels, I would that all the hotel-keepers in the land could be convened here to take a lesson."

Our green hunting-clothes were soon donned, and we went out into the hall; a flight of broad steps led up to the roof; Roxana appeared at the top and beckoned us thither. We ascended, and found ourselves on the flat roof. Samuel stood with his face toward the east and his arms outstretched, watching the horizon; behind was Roxana, with her hands clasped on her breast and her head bowed: thus they waited. The eastern sky was bright with golden light; rays shot upward toward the zenith, where the rose-lights of dawn were retreating down to the west, which still lay in the shadow of night; there was not a sound; the Flats stretched out dusky and still. Two or three minutes passed, and then a dazzling rim appeared above

the horizon, and the first gleam of sunshine was shed over the
level earth; simultaneously the two began a chant, simple as
a Gregorian, but rendered in correct full tones. The words,
apparently, had been collected from the Bible:—

> "The heavens declare the glory of God—
> Joy cometh in the morning!
> In them is laid out the path of the sun—
> Joy cometh in the morning!
> As a bridegroom goeth he forth;
> As a strong man runneth his race.
> The outgoings of the morning
> Praise thee, O Lord!
> Like a pelican in the wilderness,
> Like a sparrow upon the house-top,
> I wait for the Lord.
> It is good that we hope and wait,
> Wait—wait."

The chant over, the two stood a moment silently, as if in
contemplation, and then descended, passing us without a word
or sign, with their hands clasped before them as though forming part of an unseen procession. Raymond and I were left
alone upon the house-top.

"After all, it is not such a bad opening for a day; and there is
the pelican of the wilderness to emphasize it," I said, as a heron
flew up from the water, and, slowly flapping his great wings,
sailed across to another channel. As the sun rose higher, the
birds began to sing; first a single note here and there, then a
little trilling solo, and finally an outpouring of melody on all
sides,—land-birds and water-birds, birds that lived in the Flats,
and birds that had flown thither for breakfast,—the whole
waste was awake and rejoicing in the sunshine.

"What a wild place it is!" said Raymond. "How boundless
it looks! One hill in the distance, one dark line of forest, even
one tree, would break its charm. I have seen the ocean, I have
seen the prairies, I have seen the great desert, but this is like a
mixture of the three. It is an ocean full of land,—a prairie full
of water,—a desert full of verdure."

"Whatever it is, we shall find in it fishing and aquatic hunting to our hearts' content," I answered.

And we did. After a breakfast delicious as the supper, we took our boat and a lunch-basket, and set out. "But how shall we ever find our way back?" I said, pausing as I recalled the network of runs, and the will-o'-the-wisp aspect of the house, the previous evening.

"There is no other way but to take a large ball of cord with you, fasten one end on shore, and let it run out over the stern of the boat," said Roxana. "Let it run out loosely, and it will float on the water. When you want to come back you can turn around and wind it in as you come. *I* can read the Flats like a book, but they 're very blinding to most people; and you might keep going round in a circle. You will do better not to go far, anyway. I 'll wind the bugle on the roof an hour before sunset; you can start back when you hear it; for it 's awkward getting supper after dark." With this musical promise we took the clew of twine which Roxana rigged for us in the stern of our boat, and started away, first releasing Captain Kidd, who was pacing his islet in sullen majesty, like another Napoleon on St. Helena. We took a new channel and passed behind the house, where the imported cattle were feeding in their little pasture; but the winding stream soon bore us away, the house sank out of sight, and we were left alone.

We had fine sport that morning among the ducks,—wood, teal, and canvas-back,—shooting from behind our screens woven of rushes; later in the day we took to fishing. The sun shone down, but there was a cool September breeze, and the freshness of the verdure was like early spring. At noon we took our lunch and a *siesta* among the water-lilies. When we awoke we found that a bittern had taken up his position near by, and was surveying us gravely:—

> "'The moping bittern, motionless and stiff,
>   That on a stone so silently and stilly
>   Stands, an apparent sentinel, as if
>       To guard the water-lily,'"

quoted Raymond. The solemn bird, in his dark uniform, seemed quite undisturbed by our presence; yellow-throats and swamp-sparrows also came in numbers to have a look at us; and the fish swam up to the surface and eyed us curiously. Lying at ease in the boat, we in our turn looked down into the water. There is a singular fascination in looking down into a clear stream as the boat floats above; the mosses and twining water-plants seem to have arbors and grottos in their recesses, where delicate marine creatures might live, naiads and mermaids of miniature size; at least we are always looking for them. There is a fancy, too, that one may find something,— a ring dropped from fair fingers idly trailing in the water; a book which the fishes have read thoroughly; a scarf caught among the lilies; a spoon with unknown initials; a drenched ribbon, or an embroidered handkerchief. None of these things did we find, but we did discover an old brass breastpin, whose probable glass stone was gone. It was a paltry trinket at best, but I fished it out with superstitious care,—a treasure-trove of the Flats. "'Drowned,'" I said, pathetically, "'drowned in her white robes—'"

"And brass breastpin," added Raymond, who objected to sentiment, true or false.

"You Philistine! Is nothing sacred to you?"

"Not brass jewelry, certainly."

"Take some lilies and consider them," I said, plucking several of the queenly blossoms floating alongside.

> "Cleopatra art thou, regal blossom,
>     Floating in thy galley down the Nile,—
> All my soul does homage to thy splendor,
>     All my heart grows warmer in thy smile;
> Yet thou smilest for thine own grand pleasure,
>     Caring not for all the world beside,
> As in insolence of perfect beauty,
>     Sailest thou in silence down the tide.
>
> "Loving, humble rivers all pursue thee,
>     Wasted are their kisses at thy feet;
> Fiery sun himself cannot subdue thee,
>     Calm thou smilest through his raging heat;
> Naught to thee the earth's great crowd of blossoms,
>     Naught to thee the rose-queen on her throne;
> Haughty empress of the summer waters,
>     Livest thou, and diest, all alone."

This from Raymond.

"Where did you find that?" I asked.

"It is my own."

"Of course! I might have known it. There is a certain rawness of style and versification which—"

"That 's right," interrupted Raymond; "I know just what you are going to say. The whole matter of opinion is a game of 'follow-my-leader'; not one of you dares admire anything unless the critics say so. If I had told you the verses were by somebody instead of a nobody, you would have found wonderful beauties in them."

"Exactly. My motto is, 'Never read anything unless it is by a somebody.' For, don't you see, that a nobody, if he is worth anything, will soon grow into a somebody, and, if he is n't worth anything, you will have saved your time!"

"But it is not merely a question of growing," said Raymond; "it is a question of critics."

"No; there you are mistaken. All the critics in the world can neither make nor crush a true poet."

"What is poetry?" said Raymond, gloomily.

At this comprehensive question, the bittern gave a hollow croak, and flew away with his long legs trailing behind him. Probably he was not of an æsthetic turn of mind, and dreaded lest I should give a ramified answer.

Through the afternoon we fished when the fancy struck us, but most of the time we floated idly, enjoying the wild freedom of the watery waste. We watched the infinite varieties of the grasses, feathery, lance-leaved, tufted, drooping, banner-like, the deer's tongue, the wild-celery, and the so-called wild-rice, besides many unknown beauties delicately fringed, as difficult to catch and hold as thistle-down. There were plants journeying to and fro on the water like nomadic tribes of the desert; there were fleets of green leaves floating down the current; and now and then we saw a wonderful flower with scarlet bells, but could never approach near enough to touch it.

At length, the distant sound of the bugle came to us on the breeze, and I slowly wound in the clew, directing Raymond as he pushed the boat along, backing water with the oars. The sound seemed to come from every direction. There was nothing for it to echo against, but, in place of the echo, we heard a long, dying cadence, which sounded on over the Flats fainter and fainter in a sweet, slender note, until a new tone broke forth. The music floated around us, now on one side, now on the other; if it had been our only guide, we should have been completely bewildered. But I wound the cord steadily; and at last suddenly, there before us, appeared the house with Roxana on the roof, her figure outlined against the sky. Seeing us, she played a final salute, and then descended, carrying the imprisoned music with her.

That night we had our supper at sunset. Waiting Samuel had his meals by himself in the front room. "So that in case the spirits come, I shall not be there to hinder them," explained Roxana. "I am not holy, like Samuel; they will not speak before me."

"Do you have your meals apart in the winter, also?" asked Raymond.

"Yes."

"That is not very sociable," I said.

"Samuel never was sociable," replied Roxana. "Only common folks are sociable; but he is different. He has great gifts, Samuel has."

The meal over, we went up on the roof to smoke our cigars in the open air; when the sun had disappeared and his glory had darkened into twilight, our host joined us. He was a tall man, wasted and gaunt, with piercing dark eyes and dark hair, tinged with gray, hanging down upon his shoulders. (Why is it that long hair on the outside is almost always the sign of something wrong in the inside of a man's head?) He wore a black robe like a priest's cassock, and on his head a black skull-cap like the *Faust* of the operatic stage.

"Why were the Flats called St. Clair?" I said; for there is something fascinating to me in the unknown history of the West. "There is n't any," do you say? you, I mean, who are strong in the Punic wars! you, too, who are so well up in Grecian mythology. But there is history, only we don't know it. The story of Lake Huron in the times of the Pharaohs, the story of the Mississippi during the reign of Belshazzar, would be worth hearing. But it is lost! All we can do is to gather together the details of our era,—the era when Columbus came to this New World, which was, nevertheless, as old as the world he left behind.

"It was in 1679," began Waiting Samuel, "that La Salle sailed up the Detroit River in his little vessel of sixty tons burden, called the Griffin. He was accompanied by thirty-four men, mostly fur-traders; but there were among them two holy monks, and Father Louis Hennepin, a friar of the Franciscan order. They passed up the river and entered the little lake just south of us, crossing it and these Flats on the 12th of August, which is St. Clair's day. Struck with the gentle beauty of the scene, they named the waters after their saint, and at sunset sang a *Te Deum* in her honor."

"And who was Saint Clair?"

"Saint Clair, virgin and abbess, born in Italy, in 1193, made superior of a convent by the great Francis, and canonized for her distinguished virtues," said Samuel, as though reading from an encyclopædia.

"Are you a Roman Catholic?" asked Raymond.

"I am everything; all sincere faith is sacred to me," replied the man. "It is but a question of names."

"Tell us of your religion," said Raymond, thoughtfully; for in religions Raymond was something of a polyglot.

"You would hear of my faith? Well, so be it. Your question is the work of spirit influence. Listen, then. The great Creator has sowed immensity with innumerable systems of suns. In one of these systems a spirit forgot that he was a limited, subordinate being, and misused his freedom; how, we know not. He fell, and with him all his kind. A new race was then created for the vacant world, and, according to the fixed purpose of the Creator, each was left free to act for himself; he loves not mere machines. The fallen spirit, envying the new creature called man, tempted him to sin. What was his sin? Simply the giving up of his birthright, the divine soul-sparkle, for a promise of earthly pleasure. The triune divine deep, the mysterious fiery triangle, which, to our finite minds, best represents the Deity, now withdrew his personal presence; the elements, their balance broken, stormed upon man; his body, which was once ethereal, moving by mere volition, now grew heavy; and it was also appointed unto him to die. The race thus darkened, crippled, and degenerate, sank almost to the level of the brutes, the mind-fire alone remaining of all their spiritual gifts. They lived on blindly, and as blindly died. The sun, however, was left to them, a type of what they had lost.

"At length, in the fulness of time, the world-day of four thousand years, which was appointed by the council in heaven for the regiving of the divine and forfeited soul-sparkle, as on the fourth day of creation the great sun was given, there came to earth the earth's compassionate Saviour, who took upon himself our degenerate body, and revivified it with the divine soul-sparkle, who overcame all our temptations, and finally allowed the tinder of our sins to perish in his own painful death upon the cross. Through him our paradise body was restored, it waits for us on the other side of the grave. He showed us what it was like on Mount Tabor, with it he passed through closed doors, walked upon the water, and ruled the elements; so will it be with us. Paradise will come again; this world will, for a thousand years, see its first estate; it will be again the Garden of Eden. America is the great escaping-place; here will the change begin. As it is written, 'Those who escape to my utmost borders.' As the time draws near, the spirits who watch above are permitted to speak to those souls who listen. Of these listening, waiting souls am I; therefore have I withdrawn myself. The sun himself speaks to me, the greatest spirit of all; each morning I watch for his coming; each morning I ask, 'Is it to-day?' Thus do I wait."

"And how long have you been waiting?" I asked.

"I know not; time is nothing to me."

"Is the great day near at hand?" said Raymond.

"Almost at its dawning; the last days are passing."

"How do you know this?"

"The spirits tell me. Abide here, and perhaps they will speak to you also," replied Waiting Samuel.

We made no answer. Twilight had darkened into night, and the Flats had sunk into silence below us. After some moments I turned to speak to our host; but, noiselessly as one of his own spirits, he had departed.

"A strange mixture of Jacob Bœhmen, chiliastic dreams, Christianity, sun-worship, and modern spiritualism," I said. "Much learning hath made the Maine farmer mad."

"Is he mad?" said Raymond. "Sometimes I think we are all mad."

"We should certainly become so if we spent our time in speculations upon subjects clearly beyond our reach. The whole race of philosophers from Plato down are all the time going round in a circle. As long as we are in the world, I for one propose to keep my feet on solid ground; especially as we have no wings. 'Abide here, and perhaps the spirits will speak to you,' did he say? I think very likely they will, and to such good purpose that you won't have any mind left."

"After all, why should not spirits speak to us?" said Raymond, in a musing tone.

As he uttered these words the mocking laugh of a loon came across the dark waste.

"The very loons are laughing at you," I said, rising. "Come down; there is a chill in the air, composed in equal parts of the Flats, the night, and Waiting Samuel. Come down, man; come down to the warm kitchen and common-sense."

We found Roxana alone by the fire, whose glow was refreshingly real and warm; it was like the touch of a flesh-and-blood hand, after vague dreamings of spirit-companions, cold and intangible at best, with the added suspicion that, after all, they are but creations of our own fancy, and even their spirit-nature fictitious. Prime, the graceful *raconteur* who goes a-fishing, says, "firelight is as much of a polisher in-doors as moonlight outside." It is; but with a different result. The moonlight polishes everything into romance, the firelight into comfort. We brought up two remarkably easy old chairs in front of the hearth and sat down, Raymond still adrift with his wandering thoughts, I, as usual, making talk out of the present. Roxana sat opposite, knitting in hand, the cat purring at her feet. She was a slender woman, with faded light hair, insignificant features, small dull blue eyes, and a general aspect which, with every desire to state at its best, I can only call commonplace. Her gown was limp, her hands roughened with work, and there was no collar around her yellow throat. O magic rim of white, great is thy power! With thee, man is civilized; without thee, he becomes at once a savage.

"I am out of pork," remarked Roxana, casually; "I must go over to the mainland to-morrow and get some."

If it had been anything but pork! In truth, the word did not chime with the mystic conversation of Waiting Samuel.

Yes; there was no doubt about it. Roxana's mind was sadly commonplace.

"See what I have found," I said, after a while, taking out the old breastpin. "The stone is gone; but who knows? It might have been a diamond dropped by some French duchess, exiled, and fleeing for life across these far Western waters; or perhaps that German Princess of Brunswick-Wolfen-something-or-other, who, about one hundred years ago, was dead and buried in Russia, and travelling in America at the same time, a sort of a female wandering Jew, who has been done up in stories ever since."

(The other day, in Bret Harte's "Melons," I saw the following: "The singular conflicting conditions of John Brown's body and soul were, at that time, beginning to attract the attention of American youth." That is good, is n't it? Well, at the time I visited the Flats, the singular conflicting conditions of the Princess of Brunswick-Wolfen-something-or-other had, for a long time, haunted me.)

Roxana's small eyes were near-sighted; she peered at the empty setting, but said nothing.

"It is water-logged," I continued, holding it up in the fire-light, "and it hath a brassy odor; nevertheless, I feel convinced that it belonged to the princess."

Roxana leaned forward and took the trinket; I lifted up my arms and gave a mighty stretch, one of those enjoyable lengthenings-out which belong only to the healthy fatigue of country life. When I drew myself in again, I was surprised to see Roxana's features working, and her rough hands trembling, as she held the battered setting.

"It was mine," she said; "my dear old cameo breastpin that Abby gave me when I was married. I saved it and saved it, and would n't sell it, no matter how low we got, for someway it seemed to tie me to home and baby's grave. I used to wear it when I had baby—I had neck-ribbons then; we had things like other folks, and on Sundays we went to the old meeting-house on the green. Baby is buried there—O baby, baby!" and the voice broke into sobs.

"You lost a child?" I said, pitying the sorrow which was, which must be, so lonely, so unshared.

"Yes. O baby! baby!" cried the woman, in a wailing tone. "It was a little boy, gentlemen, and it had curly hair, and could just talk a word or two; its name was Ethan, after father, but we all called it Robin. Father was mighty proud of Robin, and mother, too. It died, gentlemen, my baby died, and I buried it in the old churchyard near the thorn-tree. But still I thought to stay there always along with mother and the girls; I never supposed anything else, until Samuel began to see visions. Then, everything was different, and everybody against us; for, you see, I would marry Samuel, and when he left off working, and began to talk to the spirits, the folks all said, 'I told yer so, Maria Ann!' Samuel was n't of Maine stock exactly: his father was a sailor, and 't was suspected that his mother was some kind of an East-Injia woman, but no one knew. His father died and left the boy on the town, so he lived round from house to house until he got old enough to hire out. Then he came to our farm, and there he stayed. He had wonderful eyes, Samuel had, and he had a way with him—well, the long and short of it was, that I got to thinking about him, and could n't think of anything else. The folks did n't like it at all, for, you see, there was Adam Rand, who had a farm of his own over the hill; but I never could bear Adam Rand. The worst of it was, though, that Samuel never so much as looked at me, hardly. Well, it got to be the second year, and Susan, my younger sister, married Adam Rand. Adam, he thought he 'd break up my nonsense, that 's what they called it, and so he got a good place for Samuel away down in Connecticut, and Samuel said he 'd go, for he was always restless, Samuel was. When I heard it, I was ready to lie down and die. I ran out into the pasture and threw myself down by the fence like a crazy woman. Samuel happened to come by along the lane, and saw me; he was always kind to all the dumb creatures, and stopped to see what was the matter, just as he would have stopped to help a calf. It all came out then, and he was awful sorry for me. He sat down on the top bar of the fence and looked at me, and I sat on the ground a-crying with my hair down, and my face all red and swollen.

"'I never thought to marry, Maria Ann,' says he.

"'O, please do, Samuel,' says I, 'I 'm a real good housekeeper, I am, and we can have a little land of our own, and everything nice—'

"'But I wanted to go away. My father was a sailor,' he began, a-looking off toward the ocean.

"'O, I can't stand it,—I can't stand it,' says I, beginning to cry again. Well, after that he 'greed to stay at home and marry me, and the folks they had to give in to it when they saw how I felt. We were married on Thanksgiving day, and I wore a pink delaine, purple neck-ribbon, and this very breastpin that sister Abby gave me,—it cost four dollars, and came 'way from Boston. Mother kissed me, and said she hoped I 'd be happy.

"'Of course I shall, mother,' says I. 'Samuel has great gifts; he is n't like common folks.'

"'But common folks is a deal comfortabler,' says mother. The folks never understood Samuel.

"Well, we had a chirk little house and bit of land, and baby came, and was so cunning and pretty. The visions had begun to appear then, and Samuel said he must go.

"'Where?' says I.

"'Anywhere the spirits lead me,' says he.

"But baby could n't travel, and so it hung along; Samuel left off work, and everything ran down to loose ends; I did the best I could, but it was n't much. Then baby died, and I buried him under the thorn-tree, and the visions came thicker and thicker, and Samuel told me as how this time he must go. The folks wanted me to stay behind without him; but they never understood me nor him. I could no more leave him than I could fly; I was just wrapped up in him. So we went away; I cried dreadfully when it came to leaving the folks and Robin's little grave, but I had so much to do after we got started, that there was n't time for anything but work. We thought to settle in ever so many places, but after a while there would always come a vision, and I 'd have to sell out and start on. The little money we had was soon gone, and then I went out for days' work, and picked up any work I could get. But many 's the time we were cold, and many 's the time we were hungry, gentlemen. The visions kept coming, and by and by I got to like 'em too. Samuel he told me all they said when I came home nights, and it was nice to hear all about the thousand years of joy, when there 'd be no more trouble, and when Robin would come back to us again. Only I told Samuel that I hoped the world would n't alter much, because I wanted to go back to Maine for a few days, and see all the old places. Father and mother are dead, I suppose," said Roxana, looking up at us with a pathetic expression in her small dull eyes. Beautiful eyes are doubly beautiful in sorrow; but there is something peculiarly pathetic in small dull eyes looking up at you, struggling to express the grief that lies within, like a prisoner behind the bars of his small dull window.

"And how did you lose your breastpin?" I said, coming back to the original subject.

"Samuel found I had it, and threw it away soon after we came to the Flats; he said it was vanity."

"Have you been here long?"

"O yes, years. I hope we shall stay here always now,—at least, I mean until the thousand years of joy begin,—for it 's quiet, and Samuel 's more easy here than in any other place. I 've got used to the lonely feeling, and don't mind it much now. There 's no one near us for miles, except Rosabel Lee and Liakim; they don't come here, for Samuel can't abide 'em, but sometimes I stop there on my way over from the mainland, and have a little chat about the children. Rosabel Lee has got lovely children, she has! They don't stay there in the winter, though; the winters *are* long, I don't deny it."

"What do you do then?"

"Well, I knit and cook, and Samuel reads to me, and has a great many visions."

"He has books, then?"

"Yes, all kinds; he 's a great reader, and he has boxes of books about the spirits, and such things."

"Nine of the night. Take thou thy rest. I will lay me down in peace and sleep; for it is thou, Lord, only, that makest me dwell in safety," chanted the voice in the hall; and our evening was over.

At dawn we attended the service on the roof; then, after breakfast, we released Captain Kidd, and started out for another day's sport. We had not rowed far when Roxana passed us, poling her flat-boat rapidly along; she had a load of fish and butter, and was bound for the mainland village. "Bring us back a Detroit paper," I said. She nodded and passed on, stolid and homely in the morning light. Yes, I was obliged to confess to myself that she *was* commonplace.

A glorious day we had on the moors in the rushing September wind. Everything rustled and waved and danced, and the grass undulated in long billows as far as the eye could see. The wind enjoyed himself like a mad creature; he had no forests to oppose him, no heavy water to roll up,—nothing but merry, swaying grasses. It was the west wind,—"of all the winds, the best wind." The east wind was given us for our sins; I have long suspected that the east wind was the angel that drove Adam out of Paradise. We did nothing that day,—nothing but enjoy the rushing breeze. We felt like Bedouins of the desert, with our boat for a steed. "He came flying upon the wings of the wind," is the grandest image of the Hebrew poet.

Late in the afternoon we heard the bugle and returned, following our clew as before. Roxana had brought a late paper, and, opening it, I saw the account of an accident,—a yacht run down on the Sound and five drowned; five, all near and dear to us. Hastily and sadly we gathered our possessions together; the hunting, the fishing, were nothing now; all we thought of was to get away, to go home to the sorrowing ones around the new-made graves. Roxana went with us in her boat to guide us back to the little lighthouse. Waiting Samuel bade us no farewell, but as we rowed away we saw him standing on the house-top gazing after us. We bowed; he waved his hand; and then turned away to look at the sunset. What were our little affairs to a man who held converse with the spirits!

We rowed in silence. How long, how weary seemed the way! The grasses, the lilies, the silver channels,—we no longer even saw them. At length the forward boat stopped. "There 's the lighthouse yonder," said Roxana. "I won't go over there to-night. Mayhap you 'd rather not talk, and Rosabel Lee will be sure to talk to me. Good by." We shook hands, and I laid in the boat a sum of money to help the little household through the winter; then we rowed on toward the lighthouse. At the turn I looked back; Roxana was sitting motionless in her boat; the dark clouds were rolling up behind her; and the Flats looked wild and desolate. "God help her!" I said.

A steamer passed the lighthouse and took us off within the hour.

Years rolled away, and I often thought of the grassy sea, and intended to go there; but the intention never grew into reality. In 1870, however, I was travelling westward, and, finding myself at Detroit, a sudden impulse took me up to the Flats. The steamer sailed up the beautiful river and crossed the little lake, both unchanged. But, alas! the canal predicted by the captain fifteen years before had been cut, and, in all its unmitigated ugliness, stretched straight through the enchanted land. I got off at the new and prosaic brick lighthouse, half expecting to see Liakim and his Rosabel Lee; but they were not there, and no one knew anything about them. And Waiting Samuel? No one knew anything about him, either. I took a skiff, and, at the risk of losing myself, I rowed away into the wilderness, spending the day among the silvery channels, which were as beautiful as ever. There were fewer birds; I saw no grave herons, no sombre bitterns, and the fish had grown shy. But the water-lilies were beautiful as of old, and the grasses as delicate and luxuriant. I had scarcely a hope of finding the old house on the island, but late in the afternoon, by a mere chance, I rowed up unexpectedly to its little landing-place. The walls stood firm and the roof was unbroken; I landed and walked up the overgrown path. Opening the door, I found the few old chairs and tables in their places, weather-beaten and decayed, the storms had forced a way within, and the floor was insecure; but the gay crockery was on its shelf, the old tins against the wall, and all looked so natural that I almost feared to find the mortal remains of the husband and wife as I went from room to room. They were not there, however, and the place looked as if it had been uninhabited for years. I lingered in the doorway. What had become of them? Were they dead? Or had a new vision sent them farther toward the setting sun? I never knew, although I made many inquiries. If dead, they were probably lying somewhere under the shining waters; if alive, they must have "folded their tents, like the Arabs, and silently stolen away."

I rowed back in the glow of the evening across the grassy sea. "It is beautiful, beautiful," I thought, "but it is passing away. Already commerce has invaded its borders; a few more years and its loveliness will be but a legend of the past. The bittern has vanished; the loon has fled away. Waiting Samuel was the prophet of the waste; he has gone, and the barriers are broken down. Farewell, beautiful grass-water! No artist has painted, no poet has sung your wild, vanishing charm; but in one heart, at least, you have a place, O lovely land of St. Clair!"

# The Lady of Little Fishing

IT was an island in Lake Superior.

I beached my canoe there about four o'clock in the afternoon, for the wind was against me and a high sea running. The late summer of 1850, and I was coasting along the south shore of the great lake, hunting, fishing, and camping on the beach, under the delusion that in that way I was living "close to the great heart of nature,"—whatever that may mean. Lord Bacon got up the phrase; I suppose he knew. Pulling the boat high and dry on the sand with the comfortable reflection that here were no tides to disturb her with their goings-out and comings-in, I strolled through the woods on a tour of exploration, expecting to find bluebells, Indian pipes, juniper rings, perhaps a few agates along-shore, possibly a bird or two for company. I found a town.

It was deserted; but none the less a town, with three streets, residences, a meeting-house, gardens, a little park, and an attempt at a fountain. Ruins are rare in the New World; I took off my hat. "Hail, homes of the past!" I said. (I cultivated the habit of thinking aloud when I was living close to the great heart of nature.) "A human voice resounds through your arches" (there were no arches,—logs won't arch; but never mind) "once more, a human hand touches your venerable walls, a human foot presses your deserted hearth-stones." I then selected the best half of the meeting-house for my camp, knocked down one of the homes for fuel, and kindled a glorious bonfire in the park. "Now that you are illuminated with joy, O Ruin," I remarked, "I will go down to the beach and bring up my supplies. It is long since I have had a roof over my head; I promise you to stay until your last residence is well burned; then I will make a final cup of coffee with the meeting-house itself, and depart in peace, leaving your poor old bones buried in decent ashes."

The ruin made no objection, and I took up my abode there; the roof of the meeting-house was still water-tight (which is an advantage when the great heart of nature grows wet). I kindled a fire on the sacerdotal hearth, cooked my supper, ate it in leisurely comfort, and then stretched myself on a blanket to enjoy an evening pipe of peace, listening meanwhile to the sounding of the wind through the great pine-trees. There was no door to my sanctuary, but I had the cosey far end; the island was uninhabited, there was not a boat in sight at sunset, nothing could disturb me unless it might be a ghost. Presently a ghost came in.

It did not wear the traditional gray tarlatan armor of Hamlet's father, the only ghost with whom I am well acquainted; this spectre was clad in substantial deer-skin garments, and carried a gun and loaded game-bag. It came forward to my hearth, hung up its gun, opened its game-bag, took out some birds, and inspected them gravely.

"Fat?" I inquired.

"They 'll do," replied the spectre, and forthwith set to work preparing them for the coals. I smoked on in silence. The spectre seemed to be a skilled cook, and after deftly broiling its supper, it offered me a share; I accepted. It swallowed a huge mouthful and crunched with its teeth; the spell was broken, and I knew it for a man of flesh and blood.

He gave his name as Reuben, and proved himself an excellent camping companion; in fact, he shot all the game, caught all the fish, made all the fires, and cooked all the food for us both. I proposed to him to stay and help me burn up the ruin, with the condition that when the last timber of the meeting-house was consumed, we should shake hands and depart, one to the east, one to the west, without a backward glance. "In that way we shall not infringe upon each other's personality," I said.

"Agreed," replied Reuben.

He was a man of between fifty and sixty years, while I was on the sunny side of thirty; he was reserved, I was always generously affable; he was an excellent cook, while I—well, I was n't; he was taciturn, and so, in payment for the work he did, I entertained him with conversation, or rather monologue, in my most brilliant style. It took only two weeks to burn up the town, burned we never so slowly; at last it came the turn of the meeting-house, which now stood by itself in the vacant clearing. It was a cool September day; we cooked breakfast with the roof, dinner with the sides, supper with the odds and ends, and then applied a torch to the frame-work. Our last camp-fire was a glorious one. We lay stretched on our blankets, smoking and watching the glow. "I wonder, now, who built the old shanty," I said in a musing tone.

"Well," replied Reuben, slowly, "if you really want to know, I will tell you. I did."

"You!"

"Yes."

"You did n't do it alone?"

"No; there were about forty of us."

"Here?"

"Yes; here at Little Fishing."

"Little Fishing?"

"Yes; Little Fishing Island. That is the name of the place."

"How long ago was this?"

"Thirty years."

"Hunting and trapping, I suppose?"

"Yes; for the Northwest and Hudson Bay Companies."

"Was n't a meeting-house an unusual accompaniment?"

"Most unusual."

"Accounted for in this case by—"

"A woman."

"Ah!" I said in a tone of relish; "then of course there is a story?"

"There is."

"Out with it, comrade. I scarcely expected to find the woman and her story up here; but since the irrepressible creature would come, out with her by all means. She shall grace our last pipe together, the last timber of our meeting-house, our last night on Little Fishing. The dawn will see us far from each other, to meet no more this side heaven. Speak then, O comrade mine! I am in one of my rare listening moods!"

I stretched myself at ease and waited. Reuben was a long time beginning, but I was too indolent to urge him. At length he spoke.

"They were a rough set here at Little Fishing, all the worse for being all white men; most of the other camps were full of half-breeds and Indians. The island had been a station away back in the early days of the Hudson Bay Company; it was a station for the Northwest Company while that lasted; then it went back to the Hudson, and stayed there until the company moved its forces farther to the north. It was not at any time a regular post; only a camp for the hunters. The post was farther down the lake. O, but those were wild days! You think you know the wilderness, boy; but you know nothing, absolutely nothing. It makes me laugh to see the airs of you city gentlemen with your fine guns, improved fishing-tackle, elaborate paraphernalia, as though you were going to wed the whole forest, floating up and down the lake for a month or two in the summer! You should have seen the hunters of Little Fishing going out gayly when the mercury was down twenty degrees below zero, for a week in the woods. You should have seen the trappers wading through the hard snow, breast high, in the gray dawn, visiting the traps and hauling home the prey. There were all kinds of men here, Scotch, French, English, and American; all classes, the high and the low, the educated and the ignorant; all sorts, the lazy and the hard-working. One thing only they all had in common,—badness. Some had fled to the wilderness to escape the law, others to escape order; some had chosen the wild life because of its wildness, others had drifted into it from sheer lethargy. This far northern border did not attract the plodding emigrant, the respectable settler. Little Fishing held none of that trash; only a reckless set of fellows who carried their lives in their hands, and tossed them up, if need be, without a second thought."

"And other people's lives without a third," I suggested.

"Yes; if they deserved it. But nobody whined; there was n't any nonsense here. The men went hunting and trapping, got the furs ready for the bateaux, ate when they were hungry, drank when they were thirsty, slept when they were sleepy, played cards when they felt like it, and got angry and knocked each other down whenever they chose. As I said before, there was n't any nonsense at Little Fishing,—until *she* came."

"Ah! the she!"

"Yes, the Lady,—our Lady, as we called her. Thirty-one years ago; how long it seems!"

"And well it may," I said. "Why, comrade, I was n't born then!"

This stupendous fact seemed to strike me more than my companion; he went on with his story as though I had not spoken.

"One October evening, four of the boys had got into a row over the cards; the rest of us had come out of our wigwams to see the fun, and were sitting around on the stumps, chaffing them, and laughing; the camp-fire was burning in front, lighting up the woods with a red glow for a short distance, and making the rest doubly black all around. There we all were, as I said before, quite easy and comfortable, when suddenly there appeared among us, as though she had dropped from heaven, a woman!

"She was tall and slender, the firelight shone full on her pale face and dove-colored dress, her golden hair was folded back under a little white cap, and a white kerchief lay over her shoulders; she looked spotless. I stared; I could scarcely believe my eyes; none of us could. There was not a white woman west of the Sault Ste. Marie. The four fellows at the table sat as if transfixed; one had his partner by the throat, the other two were disputing over a point in the game. The lily lady glided up to their table, gathered the cards in her white hands, slowly, steadily, without pause or trepidation before their astonished eyes, and then, coming back, she threw the cards into the centre of the glowing fire. 'Ye shall not play away your souls,' she said in a clear, sweet voice. 'Is not the game sin? And its reward death?' And then, immediately, she gave us a sermon, the like of which was never heard before; no argument, no doctrine, just simple, pure entreaty. 'For the love of God,' she ended, stretching out her hands towards our silent, gazing group,—'for the love of God, my brothers, try to do better.'

"We did try; but it was not for the love of God. Neither did any of us feel like brothers.

"She did not give any name; we called her simply our Lady, and she accepted the title. A bundle carefully packed in birch-bark was found on the beach. 'Is this yours?' asked black Andy.

"'It is,' replied the Lady; and removing his hat, the black-haired giant carried the package reverently inside her lodge. For we had given her our best wigwam, and fenced it off with pine saplings so that it looked like a miniature fortress. The

Lady did not suggest this stockade; it was our own idea, and with one accord we worked at it like beavers, and hung up a gate with a ponderous bolt inside.

"'Mais, ze can nevare farsen eet wiz her leetle fingares,' said Frenchy, a sallow little wretch with a turn for handicraft; so he contrived a small spring which shot the bolt into place with a touch. The Lady lived in her fortress; three times a day the men carried food to her door, and, after tapping gently, withdrew again, stumbling over each other in their haste. The Flying Dutchman, a stolid Holland-born sailor, was our best cook, and the pans and kettles were generally left to him; but now all wanted to try their skill, and the results were extraordinary.

"'She 's never touched that pudding, now,' said Nightingale Jack, discontentedly, as his concoction of berries and paste came back from the fortress door.

"'She will starve soon, I think,' remarked the Doctor, calmly; 'to my certain knowledge she has not had an eatable meal for four days.' And he lighted a fresh pipe. This was an aside, and the men pretended not to hear it; but the pans were relinquished to the Dutchman from that time forth.

"The Lady wore always her dove-colored robe, and little white cap, through whose muslin we could see the glimmer of her golden hair. She came and went among us like a spirit; she knew no fear; she turned our life inside out, nor shrank from its vileness. It seemed as though she was not of earth, so utterly impersonal was her interest in us, so heavenly her pity. She took up our sins, one by one, as an angel might; she pleaded with us for our own lost souls, she spared us not, she held not back one grain of denunciation, one iota of future punishment. Sometimes, for days, we would not see her; then, at twilight, she would glide out among us, and, standing in the light of the camp-fire, she would preach to us as though inspired. We listened to her; I do not mean that we were one whit better at heart, but still we listened to her, always. It was a wonderful sight, that lily face under the pine-trees, that spotless woman standing alone in the glare of the fire, while around her lay forty evil-minded, lawless men, not one of whom but would have killed his neighbor for so much as a disrespectful thought of her.

"So strange was her coming, so almost supernatural her

appearance in this far forest, that we never wondered over its cause, but simply accepted it as a sort of miracle; your thoroughly irreligious men are always superstitious. Not one of us would have asked a question, and we should never have known her story had she not herself told it to us; not immediately, not as though it was of any importance, but quietly, briefly, and candidly as a child. She came, she said, from Scotland, with a band of God's people. She had always been in one house, a religious institution of some kind, sewing for the poor when her strength allowed it, but generally ill, and suffering much from pain in her head; often kept under the influence of soothing medicines for days together. She had no father or mother, she was only one of this band; and when they decided to send out missionaries to America, she begged to go, although but a burden; the sea voyage restored her health; she grew, she said, in strength and in grace, and her heart was as the heart of a lion. Word came to her from on high that she should come up into the northern lake-country and preach the gospel there; the band were going to the verdant prairies. She left them in the night, taking nothing but her clothing; a friendly vessel carried her north; she had preached the gospel everywhere. At the Sault the priests had driven her out, but nothing fearing, she went on into the wilderness, and so, coming part of the way in canoes, part of the way along-shore, she had reached our far island. Marvellous kindness had she met with, she said; the Indians, the half-breeds, the hunters, and the trappers had all received her, and helped her on her way from camp to camp. They had listened to her words also. At Portage they had begged her to stay through the winter, and offered to build her a little church for Sunday services. Our men looked at each other. Portage was the worst camp on the lake, notorious for its fights; it was a mining settlement.

"'But I told them I must journey on towards the west,' continued our Lady. 'I am called to visit every camp on this shore before the winter sets in; I must soon leave you also.'

"The men looked at each other again; the Doctor was spokesman. 'But, my Lady,' he said, 'the next post is Fort William, two hundred and thirty-five miles away on the north shore.'

"'It is almost November; the snow will soon be six and ten feet deep. The Lady could never travel through it,—could she, now?' said Black Andy, who had begun eagerly, but in his embarrassment at the sound of his own voice, now turned to Frenchy and kicked him covertly into answering.

"'Nevare!' replied the Frenchman; he had intended to place his hand upon his heart to give emphasis to his word, but the Lady turned her calm eyes that way, and his grimy paw fell, its gallantry wilted.

"'I thought there was one more camp,—at Burnt-Wood River,' said our Lady in a musing tone. The men looked at each other a third time; there was a camp there, and they all knew it. But the Doctor was equal to the emergency.

"'That camp, my Lady,' he said gravely,—'that camp no longer exists!' Then he whispered hurriedly to the rest of us, 'It will be an easy job to clean it out, boys. We 'll send over a party to-night; it 's only thirty-five miles.'

"We recognized superior genius; the Doctor was our oldest and deepest sinner. But what struck us most was his anxiety to make good his lie. Had it then come to this,—that the Doctor told the truth?

"The next day we all went to work to build our Lady a church; in a week it was completed. There goes its last cross-beam now into the fire; it was a solid piece of work, was n't it? It has stood this climate thirty years. I remember the first Sunday service: we all washed, and dressed ourselves in the best we had; we scarcely knew each other, we were so fine. The Lady was pleased with the church, but yet she had not said she would stay all winter; we were still anxious. How she preached to us that day! We had made a screen of young spruces set in boxes, and her figure stood out against the dark green background like a thing of light. Her silvery voice rang through the log-temple, her face seemed to us like a star. She had no color in her cheeks at any time; her dress, too, was colorless. Although gentle, there was an iron inflexibility about her slight, erect form. We felt, as we saw her standing there, that if need be she would walk up to the lion's jaws, the cannon's mouth, with a smile. She took a little book from her pocket and read to us a hymn,—'O come, all ye faithful,' the old 'Adeste Fideles.' Some of us knew it; she sang, and gradually, shame-facedly, voices joined in. It was a sight to see Nightingale Jack solemnly singing away about 'choirs of angels'; but it was a treat to hear him, too,—what a voice he had! Then our Lady prayed, kneeling down on the little platform in front of the evergreens, clasping her hands, and lifting her eyes to heaven. We did not know what to do at first, but the Doctor gave us a severe look and bent his head, and we all followed his lead.

"When service was over and the door opened, we found that it had been snowing; we could not see out through the windows because white cloth was nailed over them in place of glass.

"'Now, my Lady, you will have to stay with us,' said the Doctor. We all gathered around with eager faces.

"'Do you really believe that it will be for the good of your souls?' asked the sweet voice.

"The Doctor believed—for us all.

"'Do you really hope?'

"The Doctor hoped.

"'Will you try to do your best?'

"The Doctor was sure he would.

"'I will,' answered the Flying Dutchman, earnestly. 'I moost not fry de meat any more; I moost broil!'

"For we had begged him for months to broil, and he had obstinately refused; broil represented the good, and fry the evil, to his mind; he came out for the good according to his light; but none the less did we fall upon him behind the Lady's back, and cuff him into silence.

"She stayed with us all winter. You don't know what the winters are up here; steady, bitter cold for seven months, thermometer always below, the snow dry as dust, the air like a knife. We built a compact chimney for our Lady, and we cut cords of wood into small, light sticks, easy for her to lift, and stacked them in her shed; we lined her lodge with skins, and we made oil from bear's fat and rigged up a kind of lamp for her. We tried to make candles, I remember, but they would not run straight; they came out hump-backed and sidling, and burned themselves to wick in no time. Then we took to improving the town. We had lived in all kinds of huts and lean-to shanties; now nothing would do but regular log-houses. If it had been summer, I don't know what we might not have run to in the way of piazzas and fancy steps; but with the snow five feet deep, all we could accomplish was a plain, square log-house, and even that took our whole force. The only way to keep the peace was to have all the houses exactly alike; we laid out the three streets, and built the houses, all facing the meeting-house, just as you found them."

"And where was the Lady's lodge?" I asked, for I recalled no stockaded fortress, large or small.

My companion hesitated a moment. Then he said abruptly, "It was torn down."

"Torn down!" I repeated. "Why, what—"

Reuben waved his hand with a gesture that silenced me, and went on with his story. It came to me then for the first time, that he was pursuing the current of his own thoughts rather than entertaining me. I turned to look at him with a new interest. I had talked to him for two weeks, in rather a patronizing way; could it be that affairs were now, at this last moment, reversed?

"It took us almost all winter to build those houses," pursued Reuben. "At one time we neglected the hunting and trapping to such a degree, that the Doctor called a meeting and expressed his opinion. Ours was a voluntary camp, in a measure, but still we had formally agreed to get a certain amount of skins ready for the bateaux by early spring; this agreement was about the only real bond of union between us. Those whose houses were not completed scowled at the Doctor.

"'Do you suppose I'm going to live like an Injun when the other fellows has regular houses?' inquired Black Andy, with a menacing air.

"'By no means,' replied the Doctor, blandly. 'My plan is this: build at night.'

"'At night?'

"'Yes; by the light of pine fires.'

"We did. After that, we faithfully went out hunting and trapping as long as daylight lasted, and then, after supper, we built up huge fires of pine logs, and went to work on the next house. It was a strange picture: the forest deep in snow, black with night, the red glow of the great fires, and our moving figures working on as complacently as though daylight, balmy air, and the best of tools were ours.

"The Lady liked our industry. She said our new houses showed that the 'new cleanliness of our inner man required a cleaner tabernacle for the outer.' I don't know about our inner man, but our outer was certainly much cleaner.

"One day the Flying Dutchman made one of his unfortunate remarks. 'De boys t'inks you 'll like dem better in nize houses,' he announced when, happening to pass the fortress, he found the Lady standing at her gate gazing at the work of the preceding night. Several of the men were near enough to hear him, but too far off to kick him into silence as usual; but they glared at him instead. The Lady looked at the speaker with her dreamy, far-off eyes.

"'De boys t'inks you like dem,' began the Dutchman again, thinking she did not comprehend; but at that instant he caught the combined glare of the six eyes, and stopped abruptly, not at all knowing what was wrong, but sure there was something.

"'Like them,' repeated the Lady, dreamily; 'yea, I do like them. Nay, more, I love them. Their souls are as dear to me as the souls of brothers.'

"'Say, Frenchy, have you got a sister?' said Nightingale Jack, confidentially, that evening.

"'Mais oui,' said Frenchy.

"'You think all creation of her, I suppose?'

"'We fight like four cats and one dog; *she* is the cats,' said the Frenchman concisely.

"'You don't say so!' replied Jack. 'Now, I never had a sister, —but I thought perhaps—' He paused, and the sentence remained unfinished.

"The Nightingale and I were house-mates. We sat late over our fire not long after that; I gave a gigantic yawn. 'This lifting logs half the night is enough to kill one,' I said, getting out my jug. 'Sing something, Jack. It 's a long time since I 've heard anything but hymns.'

"Jack always went off as easily as a music-box: you had only to wind him up; the jug was the key. I soon had him in full blast. He was giving out

'The minute gun at sea,—the minute gun at sea,'

with all the pathos of his tenor voice, when the door burst open and the whole population rushed in upon us.

"'What do you mean by shouting this way, in the middle of the night?'

"'Shut up your howling, Jack.'

"'How do you suppose any one can sleep?'

"'It 's a disgrace to the camp!'

"'Now then, gentlemen,' I replied, for my blood was up (whiskey, perhaps), 'is this my house, or is n't it? If I want music, I 'll have it. Time was when you were not so particular.'

"It was the first word of rebellion. The men looked at each other, then at me.

"'I 'll go and ask her if she objects,' I continued, boldly.

"'No, no. You shall not.'

"'Let him go,' said the Doctor, who stood smoking his pipe on the outskirts of the crowd. 'It is just as well to have that point settled now. The Minute Gun at Sea is a good moral song in its way,—a sort of marine missionary affair.'

"So I started, the others followed; we all knew that the Lady watched late; we often saw the glimmer of her lamp far on towards morning. It was burning now. The gate was fastened, I knocked; no answer. I knocked again, and yet a third time; still, silence. The men stood off at a little distance and waited. 'She shall answer,' I said angrily, and going around to the side where the stockade came nearer to the wall of the lodge, I knocked loudly on the close-set saplings. For answer I thought I heard a low moan; I listened, it came again. My anger vanished, and with a mighty bound I swung myself up to the top of the stockade, sprung down inside, ran around, and tried the door. It was fastened; I burst it open and entered. There, by the light of the hanging lamp, I saw the Lady on the floor, apparently dead. I raised her in my arms; her heart was beating faintly, but she was unconscious. I had seen many fainting fits; this was something different; the limbs were rigid. I laid her on the low couch, loosened her dress, bathed her head and face in cold water, and wrenched up one of the warm hearth-stones to apply to her feet. I did not hesitate; I saw that it was a dangerous case, something like a trance or an 'ecstasis.' Somebody must attend to her, and there were only men to choose from. Then why not I?

"I heard the others talking outside; they could not understand the delay; but I never heeded, and kept on my work. To tell the truth, I had studied medicine, and felt a genuine enthusiasm over a rare case. Once my patient opened her eyes and looked at me, then she lapsed away again into unconsciousness in spite of all my efforts. At last the men outside came in, angry and suspicious; they had broken down the gate. There we all stood, the whole forty of us, around the deathlike form of our Lady.

"What a night it was! To give her air, the men camped outside in the snow with a line of pickets in whispering distance from each other from the bed to their anxious group. Two were detailed to help me,—the Doctor (whose title was a sarcastic D. D.) and Jimmy, a gentle little man, excellent at bandaging broken limbs. Every vial in the camp was brought in, —astonishing lotions, drops, and balms; each man produced something; they did their best, poor fellows, and wore out the night with their anxiety. At dawn our Lady revived suddenly, thanked us all, and assured us that she felt quite well again; the trance was over. 'It was my old enemy,' she said, 'the old illness of Scotland, which I hoped had left me forever. But I am thankful that it is no worse; I have come out of it with a clear brain. Sing a hymn of thankfulness for me, dear friends, before you go.'

"Now, we sang on Sunday in the church; but then she led us, and we had a kind of an idea that after all she did not hear us. But now, who was to lead us? We stood awkwardly around the bed, and shuffled our hats in our uneasy fingers. The Doctor fixed his eyes upon the Nightingale; Jack saw it and cowered. 'Begin,' said the Doctor in a soft voice; but gripping him in the back at the same time with an ominous clutch.

"'I don't know the words,' faltered the unhappy Nightingale.

"'Now thank we all our God,
     With hearts and hands and voices,'

began the Doctor, and repeated Luther's hymn with perfect accuracy from beginning to end. 'What will happen next? The Doctor knows hymns!' we thought in profound astonishment. But the Nightingale had begun, and gradually our singers joined in; I doubt whether the grand old choral was ever sung by such a company before or since. There was never any further question, by the way, about that minute gun at sea; it stayed at sea as far as we were concerned.

"Spring came, the faltering spring of Lake Superior. I won't go into my own story, but such as it was, the spring brought it back to me with new force. I wanted to go,—and yet I did n't. 'Where,' do you ask? To see her, of course,—a woman, the most beautiful,—well, never mind all that. To be brief, I loved her; she scorned me; I thought I had learned to hate her—but —I was n't sure about it now. I kept myself aloof from the others and gave up my heart to the old sweet, bitter memories; I did not even go to church on Sundays. But all the rest went; our Lady's influence was as great as ever. I could hear them singing; they sang better now that they could have the door open; the pent-up feeling used to stifle them. The time for the bateaux drew near, and I noticed that several of the men were hard at work packing the furs in bales, a job usually left to the *voyageurs* who came with the boats. 'What 's that for?' I asked.

"'You don't suppose we 're going to have those bateaux rascals camping on Little Fishing, do you?' said Black Andy, scornfully. 'Where are your wits, Reub?'

"And they packed every skin, rafted them all over to the mainland, and waited there patiently for days, until the train of slow boats came along and took off the bales; then they came back in triumph. 'Now we 're secure for another six months,' they said, and began to lay out a park, and gardens for every house. The Lady was fond of flowers; the whole town burst into blossom. The Lady liked green grass; all the clearing was soon turfed over like a lawn. The men tried the ice-cold lake every day, waiting anxiously for the time when they could bathe. There was no end to their cleanliness; Black Andy had grown almost white again, and Frenchy's hair shone like oiled silk.

"The Lady stayed on, and all went well. But, gradually, there came a discovery. The Lady was changing,—had changed! Gradually, slowly, but none the less distinctly to the eyes that knew her every eyelash. A little more hair was visible over the white brow, there was a faint color in the cheeks, a quicker step; the clear eyes were sometimes downcast now, the steady voice softer, the words at times faltering. In the early summer the white cap vanished, and she stood among us crowned only with her golden hair; one day she was seen through her open door sewing on a white robe! The men noted all these things silently; they were even a little troubled as at something they did not understand, something beyond their reach. Was she planning to leave them?

"'It 's my belief she 's getting ready to ascend right up into heaven,' said Salem.

"Salem was a little 'wanting,' as it is called, and the men knew it; still, his words made an impression. They watched the Lady with an awe which was almost superstitious; they were troubled, and knew not why. But the Lady bloomed on. I did not pay much attention to all this; but I could not help hearing it. My heart was moody, full of its own sorrows; I secluded myself more and more. Gradually I took to going off into the mainland forests for days on solitary hunting expeditions. The camp went on its way rejoicing; the men succeeded, after a world of trouble, in making a fountain which actually played, and they glorified themselves exceedingly. The life grew quite pastoral. There was talk of importing a cow from the East, and a messenger was sent to the Sault for certain choice supplies against the coming winter. But, in the late summer, the whisper went round again that the Lady had changed, this time for the worse. She looked ill, she drooped from day to day; the new life that had come to her vanished, but her former life was not restored. She grew silent and sad, she strayed away by herself through the woods, she scarcely noticed the men who followed her with anxious eyes. Time passed, and brought with it an undercurrent of trouble, suspicion, and anger. Everything went on as before; not one habit, not one custom was altered; both sides seemed to shrink from the first change, however slight. The daily life of the camp was outwardly the same, but brooding trouble filled every heart. There was no open discussion, men talked apart in twos and threes; a gloom rested over everything, but no one said, 'What is the matter?'

"There was a man among us,—I have not said much of the individual characters of our party, but this man was one of the least esteemed, or rather liked; there was not much esteem of any kind at Little Fishing. Little was known about him; although the youngest man in the camp, he was a mooning, brooding creature, with brown hair and eyes and a melancholy face. He was n't hearty and whole-souled, and yet he was n't an out-and-out rascal; he was n't a leader, and yet he was n't follower either. He would n't be; he was like a third horse, always. There was no goodness about him; don't go to fancying that that was the reason the men did not like him; he was as bad as they were, every inch! He never shirked his work, and they could n't get a handle on him anywhere; but he was just—unpopular. The why and the wherefore are of no consequence now. Well, do you know what was the suspicion that hovered over the camp? It was this: our Lady loved that man!

"It took three months for all to see it, and yet never a word was spoken. All saw, all heard; but they might have been blind and deaf for any sign they gave. And the Lady drooped more and more.

"September came, the fifteenth; the Lady lay on her couch, pale and thin; the door was open and a bell stood beside her, but there was no line of pickets whispering tidings of her state to an anxious group outside. The turf in the three streets had grown yellow for want of water, the flowers in the little gardens had drooped and died, the fountain was choked with weeds, and the interiors of the houses were all untidy. It was Sunday, and near the hour for service; but the men lounged about, dingy and unwashed.

"'A'n't you going to church?' said Salem, stopping at the door of one of the houses; he was dressed in his best, with a flower in his button-hole.

"'See him now! See the fool,' said Black Andy. 'He 's going to church, he is! And where 's the minister, Salem? Answer me that!'

"'Why,—in the church, I suppose,' replied Salem, vacantly.

"'No, she a'n't; not she! She 's at home, a-weeping, and a-wailing, and a-ger-nashing of her teeth,' replied Andy with bitter scorn.

"'What for?' said Salem.

"'What for? Why, that 's the joke! Hear him, boys; he wants to know what for!'

"The loungers laughed,—a loud, reckless laugh.

"'Well, I 'm going any way,' said Salem, looking wonderingly from one to the other; he passed on and entered the church.

"'I say, boys, let 's have a high old time,' cried Andy, savagely. 'Let 's go back to the old way and have a jolly Sunday. Let 's have out the jugs and the cards and be free again!'

"The men hesitated; ten months and more of law and order held them back.

"'What are you afraid of?' said Andy. 'Not of a canting hypocrite, I hope. She 's fooled us long enough, I say. Come on!' He brought out a table and stools, and produced the long-unused cards and a jug of whiskey. 'Strike up, Jack,' he cried; 'give us old Fiery-Eyes.'

"The Nightingale hesitated. Fiery-Eyes was a rollicking drinking song; but Andy put the glass to his lips and his scruples vanished in the tempting aroma. He began at the top of his voice, partners were chosen, and, trembling with excitement and impatience, like prisoners unexpectedly set free, the men gathered around, and made their bets.

"'What born fools we 've been,' said Black Andy, laying down a card.

"'Yes,' replied the Flying Dutchman, 'porn fools!' And he followed suit.

"But a thin white hand came down on the bits of colored pasteboard. It was our Lady. With her hair disordered, and the spots of fever in her cheeks, she stood among us again; but not as of old. Angry eyes confronted her, and Andy wrenched the cards from her grasp. 'No, my Lady,' he said, sternly; 'never again!'

"The Lady gazed from one face to the next, and so all around the circle; all were dark and sullen. Then she bowed her head upon her hands and wept aloud.

"There was a sudden shrinking away on all sides, the players rose, the cards were dropped. But the Lady glided away, weeping as she went; she entered the church door and the men could see her taking her accustomed place on the platform. One by one they followed; Black Andy lingered till the last, but he came. The service began, and went on falteringly, without spirit, with palpable fears of a total breaking down which never quite came; the Nightingale sang almost alone, and made sad work with the words; Salem joined in confidently, but did not improve the sense of the hymn. The Lady was silent. But when the time for the sermon came she rose and her voice burst forth.

"'Men, brothers, what have I done? A change has come over the town, a change has come over your hearts. You shun me! What have I done?'

"There was a grim silence; then the Doctor rose in his place and answered,—

"'Only this, madam. You have shown yourself to be a woman.'

"'And what did you think me?'

"'A saint.'

"'God forbid!' said the Lady, earnestly. 'I never thought myself one.'

"'I know that well. But you were a saint to us; hence your influence. It is gone.'

"'Is it all gone?' asked the Lady, sadly.

"'Yes. Do not deceive yourself; we have never been one whit better save through our love for you. We held you as something high above ourselves; we were content to worship you.'

"'O no, not me!' said the Lady, shuddering.

"'Yes, you, you alone! But—our idol came down among us and showed herself to be but common flesh and blood! What wonder that we stand aghast? What wonder that our hearts are bitter? What wonder (worse than all!) that when the awe has quite vanished, there is strife for the beautiful image fallen from its niche?'

"The Doctor ceased, and turned away. The Lady stretched out her hands towards the others; her face was deadly pale, and there was a bewildered expression in her eyes.

"'O, ye for whom I have prayed, for whom I have struggled to obtain a blessing,—ye whom I have loved so,—do *ye* desert me thus?' she cried.

"'*You* have deserted us,' answered a voice.

"'I have not.'

"'You have,' cried Black Andy, pushing to the front. 'You love that Mitchell! Deny it if you dare!'

"There was an irrepressible murmur, then a sudden hush. The angry suspicion, the numbing certainty had found voice at last; the secret was out. All eyes, which had at first closed with the shock, were now fixed upon the solitary woman before them; they burned like coals.

"'Do I?' murmured the Lady, with a strange questioning look that turned from face to face,—'do I?—Great God! I do.' She sank upon her knees and buried her face in her trembling hands. 'The truth has come to me at last,—I do!'

"Her voice was a mere whisper, but every ear heard it, and

every eye saw the crimson rise to the forehead and redden the white throat.

"For a moment there was silence, broken only by the hard breathing of the men. Then the Doctor spoke.

"'Go out and bring him in,' he cried. 'Bring in this Mitchell! It seems he has other things to do,—the blockhead!'

"Two of the men hurried out.

"'He shall not have her,' shouted Black Andy. 'My knife shall see to that!' And he pressed close to the platform. A great tumult arose, men talked angrily and clinched their fists, voices rose and fell together. 'He shall not have her,—Mitchell! Mitchell!'

"'The truth is, each one of you wants her himself,' said the Doctor.

"There was a sudden silence, but every man eyed his neighbor jealously. Black Andy stood in front, knife in hand, and kept guard. The Lady had not moved; she was kneeling, with her face buried in her hands.

"'I wish to speak to her,' said the Doctor, advancing.

"'You shall not,' cried Andy, fiercely interposing.

"'You fool! I love her this moment ten thousand times more than you do. But do you suppose I would so much as touch a woman who loved another man?'

"The knife dropped; the Doctor passed on and took his place on the platform by the Lady's side. The tumult began again, for Mitchell was seen coming in the door between his two keepers.

"'Mitchell! Mitchell!' rang angrily through the church.

"'Look, woman!' said the Doctor, bending over the kneeling figure at his side. She raised her head and saw the wolfish faces below.

"'They have had ten months of your religion,' he said.

"It was his revenge. Bitter, indeed; but he loved her.

"In the mean time the man Mitchell was hauled and pushed and tossed forward to the platform by rough hands that longed to throttle him on the way. At last, angry himself, but full of wonder, he confronted them, this crowd of comrades suddenly turned madmen! 'What does this mean?' he asked.

"'Mean! mean!' shouted the men; 'a likely story! He asks what this means!' And they laughed boisterously.

"The Doctor advanced. 'You see this woman,' he said.

"'I see our Lady.'

"'Our Lady no longer; only a woman like any other,—weak and fickle. Take her,—but begone.'

"'Take her!' repeated Mitchell, bewildered,—'take our Lady! And where?'

"'Fool! Liar! Blockhead!' shouted the crowd below.

"'The truth is simply this, Mitchell,' continued the Doctor, quietly. 'We herewith give you up our Lady,—ours no longer; for she has just confessed, openly confessed, that she loves you.'

"Mitchell started back. 'Loves me!'

"'Yes.'

"Black Andy felt the blade of his knife. 'He 'll never have her alive,' he muttered.

"'But,' said Mitchell, bluntly confronting the Doctor, 'I don't want her.'

"'You don't want her?'

"'I don't love her.'

"'You don't love her?'

"'Not in the least,' he replied, growing angry, perhaps at himself. 'What is she to me? Nothing. A very good missionary, no doubt; but *I* don't fancy woman-preachers. You may remember that *I* never gave in to her influence; *I* was never under her thumb. *I* was the only man in Little Fishing who cared nothing for her!'

"'And that is the secret of *her* liking,' murmured the Doctor. 'O woman! woman! the same the world over!'

"In the mean time the crowd had stood stupefied.

"'He does not love her!' they said to each other; 'he does not want her!'

"Andy's black eyes gleamed with joy; he swung himself up on to the platform. Mitchell stood there with face dark and disturbed, but he did not flinch. Whatever his faults, he was no hypocrite. 'I must leave this to-night,' he said to himself, and turned to go. But quick as a flash our Lady sprang from her knees and threw herself at his feet. 'You are going,' she cried. 'I heard what you said,—you do not love me! But take me with you,—oh, take me with you! Let me be your servant—your slave—anything—anything, so that I am not parted from you, my lord and master, my only, only love!'

"She clasped his ankles with her thin, white hands, and laid her face on his dusty shoes.

"The whole audience stood dumb before this manifestation of a great love. Enraged, bitter, jealous as was each heart, there was not a man but would at that moment have sacrificed his own love that she might be blessed. Even Mitchell, in one of those rare spirit-flashes when the soul is shown bare in the lightning, asked himself, 'Can I not love her?' But the soul answered, 'No.' He stooped, unclasped the clinging hands, and turned resolutely away.

"'You are a fool,' said the Doctor. 'No other woman will ever love you as she does.'

"'I know it,' replied Mitchell.

"He stepped down from the platform and crossed the church, the silent crowd making a way for him as he passed along; he went out into the sunshine, through the village, down towards the beach,—they saw him no more.

"The Lady had fainted. The men bore her back to the lodge and tended her with gentle care one week,—two weeks,—three weeks. Then she died.

"They were all around her; she smiled upon them all, and called them all by name, bidding them farewell. 'Forgive me,' she whispered to the Doctor. The Nightingale sang a hymn, sang as he had never sung before. Black Andy knelt at her feet. For some minutes she lay scarcely breathing; then suddenly she opened her fading eyes. 'Friends,' she murmured, 'I am well punished. I thought myself holy,—I held myself above my kind,—but God has shown me I am the weakest of them all.'

"The next moment she was gone.

"The men buried her with tender hands. Then, in a kind of blind fury against Fate, they tore down her empty lodge and destroyed its every fragment; in their grim determination they even smoothed over the ground and planted shrubs and bushes, so that the very location might be lost. But they did not stay to see the change. In a month the camp broke up of itself, the town was abandoned, and the island deserted for good and all; I doubt whether any of the men ever came back or even stopped when passing by. Probably I am the only one. Thirty years ago,—thirty years ago!"

"That Mitchell was a great fool," I said, after a long pause.

"The Doctor was worth twenty of him; for that matter, so was Black Andy. I only hope the fellow was well punished for his stupidity."

"He was."

"O, you kept track of him, did you?"

"Yes. He went back into the world, and the woman he loved repulsed him a second time, and with even more scorn than before."

"Served him right."

"Perhaps so; but after all, what could he do? Love is not made to order. He loved one, not the other; that was his crime. Yet,—so strange a creature is man,—he came back after thirty years, just to see our Lady's grave."

"What! Are you—"

"I am Mitchell,—Reuben Mitchell."

# RODMAN THE KEEPER: SOUTHERN SKETCHES

# Contents

# Rodman the Keeper

The long years come and go,
        And the Past,
The sorrowful, splendid Past,
With its glory and its woe,
        Seems never to have been.
——Seems never to have been?
        O somber days and grand,
        How ye crowd back once more,
Seeing our heroes' graves are green
By the Potomac and the Cumberland,
And in the valley of the Shenandoah!

When we remember how they died,—
In dark ravine and on the mountain-side,
In leaguered fort and fire-encircled town,
And where the iron ships went down,—
How their dear lives were spent
In the weary hospital-tent,
In the cockpit's crowded hive,
                        ——it seems
Ignoble to be alive!

Thomas Bailey Aldrich

"Keeper of what? Keeper of the dead. Well, it is easier to keep the dead than the living; and as for the gloom of the thing, the living among whom I have been lately were not a hilarious set."

John Rodman sat in the doorway and looked out over his domain. The little cottage behind him was empty of life save himself alone. In one room the slender appointments provided by Government for the keeper, who being still alive must sleep and eat, made the bareness doubly bare; in the other the desk and the great ledgers, the ink and pens, the register, the loud-ticking clock on the wall, and the flag folded on a shelf, were all for the kept, whose names, in hastily written, blotted rolls of manuscript, were waiting to be transcribed in the new red-bound ledgers in the keeper's best handwriting day by day, while the clock was to tell him the hour when the flag must rise over the mounds where reposed the bodies of fourteen thousand United States soldiers—who had languished where once stood the prison-pens, on the opposite slopes, now fair and peaceful in the sunset; who had fallen by the way in long marches to and fro under the burning sun; who had fought and died on the many battle-fields that reddened the beautiful State, stretching from the peaks of the marble mountains in the smoky west down to the sea-islands of the ocean border. The last rim of the sun's red ball had sunk below the horizon line, and the western sky glowed with deep rose-color, which faded away above into pink, into the salmon-tint, into shades of that far-away heavenly emerald which the brush of the earthly artist can never reproduce, but which is found sometimes in the iridescent heart of the opal. The small town, a mile distant, stood turning its back on the cemetery; but the keeper could see the pleasant, rambling old mansions, each with its rose-garden and neglected outlying fields, the empty negro quarters falling into ruin, and everything just as it stood when on that April morning the first gun was fired on Sumter; apparently not a nail added, not a brushful of paint applied, not a fallen brick replaced, or latch or lock repaired. The keeper had noted these things as he strolled through the town, but not with surprise; for he had seen the South in its first estate, when, fresh, strong, and fired with enthusiasm, he, too, had marched away from his village home with the colors flying above and the girls waving their handkerchiefs behind, as the regiment, a thousand strong, filed down the dusty road. That regiment, a weak, scarred two hundred, came back a year later with lagging step and colors tattered and scorched, and the girls could not wave their handkerchiefs, wet and sodden with tears. But the keeper, his wound healed, had gone again; and he had seen with his New England eyes the magnificence and the carelessness of the South, her splendor and negligence, her wealth and thriftlessness, as through Virginia and the fair Carolinas, across Georgia and into sunny Florida, he had marched month by month, first a lieutenant, then captain, and finally major and colonel, as death mowed down those above him, and he and his good conduct were left. Everywhere magnificence went hand in hand with neglect, and he had said so as chance now and then threw a conversation in his path.

"We have no such shiftless ways," he would remark, after he had furtively supplied a prisoner with hard-tack and coffee.

"And no such grand ones either," Johnny Reb would reply, if he was a man of spirit; and generally he was.

The Yankee, forced to acknowledge the truth of this statement, qualified it by observing that he would rather have more thrift with a little less grandeur; whereupon the other answered that *he* would not; and there the conversation rested. So now ex-Colonel Rodman, keeper of the national cemetery, viewed the little town in its second estate with philosophic eyes. "It is part of a great problem now working itself out; I am not here to tend the living, but the dead," he said.

Whereupon, as he walked among the long mounds, a voice seemed to rise from the still ranks below: "While ye have time, do good to men," it said. "Behold, we are beyond your care." But the keeper did not heed.

This still evening in early February he looked out over the level waste. The little town stood in the lowlands; there were no hills from whence cometh help—calm heights that lift the soul above earth and its cares; no river to lead the aspirations of the children outward toward the great sea. Everything was monotonous, and the only spirit that rose above the waste was a bitterness for the gained and sorrow for the lost cause. The keeper was the only man whose presence personated the former in their sight, and upon him therefore, as representative, the bitterness fell, not in words, but in averted looks, in sudden silences when he approached, in withdrawals and avoidance, until he lived and moved in a vacuum; wherever he went there was presently no one save himself; the very shop-keeper who sold him sugar seemed turned into a man of wood, and took his money reluctantly, although the shilling gained stood perhaps for that day's dinner. So Rodman withdrew himself, and came and went among them no more; the broad acres of his domain gave him as much exercise as his shattered ankle could bear; he ordered his few supplies by the quantity, and began the life of a solitary, his island marked out by the massive granite wall with which the United States Government has carefully surrounded those sad Southern cemeteries of hers; sad, not so much from the number of the mounds representing youth and strength cut off in their bloom, for that is but the fortune of war, as for the complete isolation which marks them. "Strangers in a strange land" is the thought of all who, coming and going to and from Florida, turn aside here and there to stand for a moment among the closely ranged graves which seem already a part of the past, that near past which in our hurrying American life is even now so far away. The Government work was completed before the keeper came; the lines of the trenches were defined by low granite copings, and the comparatively few single mounds were headed by trim little white boards bearing generally the word "Unknown," but here and there a name and an age, in most cases a boy from some far-away Northern State; "twenty-one," "twenty-two," said the inscriptions; the dates were those dark years among the sixties, measured now more than by anything else in the number of maidens widowed in heart, and women widowed indeed, who sit still and remember, while the world rushes by. At sunrise the keeper ran up the stars and stripes; and so precise were his ideas of the accessories belonging to the place, that from his own small store of money he had taken enough, by stinting himself, to buy a second flag for stormy weather, so that, rain or not, the colors should float over the dead. This was not patriotism so called, or rather miscalled, it was not sentimental fancy, it was not zeal or triumph; it was simply a sense of the fitness of things, a conscientiousness which had in it nothing of religion, unless indeed a man's endeavor to live up to his own ideal of his duty be a religion. The same feeling led the keeper to spend hours in copying the rolls. "John Andrew Warren, Company G, Eighth New Hampshire Infantry," he repeated, as he slowly wrote the name, giving "John Andrew" clear, bold capitals and a lettering impossible to mistake; "died August 15, 1863, aged twenty-two years. He came from the prison-pen yonder, and lies somewhere in those trenches, I suppose. Now then, John Andrew, don't fancy I am sorrowing for you; no doubt you are better off than I am at this very moment. But none the less, John Andrew, shall pen, ink, and hand do their duty to you. For that I am here."

Infinite pains and labor went into these records of the dead; one hair's-breadth error, and the whole page was replaced by a new one. The same spirit kept the grass carefully away from the low coping of the trenches, kept the graveled paths smooth and the mounds green, and the bare little cottage neat as a man-of-war. When the keeper cooked his dinner, the door toward the east, where the dead lay, was scrupulously closed, nor was it opened until everything was in perfect order again. At sunset the flag was lowered, and then it was the keeper's habit to walk slowly up and down the path until the shadows veiled the mounds on each side, and there was nothing save the peaceful green of earth. "So time will efface our little lives and sorrows," he mused, "and we shall be as nothing in the indistinguishable past." Yet none the less did he fulfill the duties of every day and hour with exactness. "At least they shall not say that I was lacking," he murmured to himself as he thought vaguely of the future beyond these graves. Who "they" were, it would have troubled him to formulate, since he was one of the many sons whom New England in this generation sends forth with a belief composed entirely of negatives. As the season advanced, he worked all day in the sunshine. "My garden looks well," he said. "I like this cemetery because it is the original resting-place of the dead who lie beneath. They were not brought here from distant places, gathered up by contract, numbered, and described like so much merchandise; their first repose has not been broken, their peace has been undisturbed. Hasty burials the prison authorities gave them; the thin bodies were tumbled into the trenches by men almost as thin, for the whole State went hungry in those dark days. There were not many prayers, no tears, as the dead-carts went the rounds. But the prayers had been said, and the tears had fallen, while the poor fellows were still alive in the pens yonder; and when at last death came, it was like a release. They suffered long; and I for one believe that therefore shall their rest be long—long and sweet."

After a time began the rain, the soft, persistent, gray rain of the Southern lowlands, and he staid within and copied another thousand names into the ledger. He would not allow himself the companionship of a dog lest the creature should bark at night and disturb the quiet. There was no one to hear save himself, and it would have been a friendly sound as he lay awake on his narrow iron bed, but it seemed to him against the spirit of the place. He would not smoke, although he had the soldier's fondness for a pipe. Many a dreary evening, beneath a hastily built shelter of boughs, when the rain poured down

and everything was comfortless, he had found solace in the
curling smoke; but now it seemed to him that it would be incongruous, and at times he almost felt as if it would be selfish
too. "*They* can not smoke, you know, down there under the
wet grass," he thought, as standing at the window he looked
toward the ranks of the mounds stretching across the eastern
end from side to side—"my parade-ground," he called it. And
then he would smile at his own fancies, draw the curtain, shut
out the rain and the night, light his lamp, and go to work on
the ledgers again. Some of the names lingered in his memory; he felt as if he had known the men who bore them, as if
they had been boys together, and were friends even now although separated for a time. "James Marvin, Company B, Fifth
Maine. The Fifth Maine was in the seven days' battle. I say,
do you remember that retreat down the Quaker church road,
and the way Phil Kearney held the rear-guard firm?" And over
the whole seven days he wandered with his mute friend, who
remembered everything and everybody in the most satisfactory way. One of the little head-boards in the parade-ground
attracted him peculiarly because the name inscribed was his
own: "——Rodman, Company A, One Hundred and Sixth
New York."

"I remember that regiment; it came from the extreme northern part of the State. Blank Rodman must have melted down
here, coming as he did from the half-arctic region along the St.
Lawrence. I wonder what he thought of the first hot day, say in
South Carolina, along those simmering rice-fields?" He grew
into the habit of pausing for a moment by the side of this grave
every morning and evening. "Blank Rodman. It might easily
have been John. And then, where should *I* be?"

But Blank Rodman remained silent, and the keeper, after
pulling up a weed or two and trimming the grass over his relative, went off to his duties again. "I am convinced that Blank
is a relative," he said to himself; "distant, perhaps, but still a
kinsman."

One April day the heat was almost insupportable; but
the sun's rays were not those brazen beams that sometimes
in Northern cities burn the air and scorch the pavements to
a white heat; rather were they soft and still; the moist earth
exhaled her richness, not a leaf stirred, and the whole level

country seemed sitting in a hot vapor-bath. In the early dawn the keeper had performed his outdoor tasks, but all day he remained almost without stirring in his chair between two windows, striving to exist. At high noon out came a little black bringing his supplies from the town, whistling and shuffling along, gay as a lark. The keeper watched him coming slowly down the white road, loitering by the way in the hot blaze, stopping to turn a somersault or two, to dangle over a bridge rail, to execute various impromptu capers all by himself. He reached the gate at last, entered, and, having come all the way up the path in a hornpipe step, he set down his basket at the door to indulge in one long and final double-shuffle before knocking. "Stop that!" said the keeper through the closed blinds. The little darkey darted back; but as nothing further came out of the window—a boot, for instance, or some other stray missile—he took courage, showed his ivories, and drew near again. "Do you suppose I am going to have you stirring up the heat in that way?" demanded the keeper.

The little black grinned, but made no reply, unless smoothing the hot white sand with his black toes could be construed as such; he now removed his rimless hat and made a bow.

"Is it, or is it not warm?" asked the keeper, as a naturalist might inquire of a salamander, not referring to his own so much as to the salamander's ideas on the subject.

"Dunno, mars'," replied the little black.

"How do *you* feel?"

"'Spects I feel all right, mars'."

The keeper gave up the investigation, and presented to the salamander a nickel cent. "I suppose there is no such thing as a cool spring in all this melting country," he said.

But the salamander indicated with his thumb a clump of trees on the green plain north of the cemetery. "Ole Mars' Ward's place—cole spring dah." He then departed, breaking into a run after he had passed the gate, his ample mouth watering at the thought of a certain chunk of taffy at the mercantile establishment kept by Aunt Dinah in a corner of her one-roomed cabin. At sunset the keeper went thirstily out with a tin pail on his arm, in search of the cold spring. "If it could only be like the spring down under the rocks where I used to drink when I was a boy!" he thought. He had never walked in that direction

before. Indeed, now that he had abandoned the town, he
seldom went beyond the walls of the cemetery. An old road
led across to the clump of trees, through fields run to waste,
and following it he came to the place, a deserted house with
tumble-down fences and overgrown garden, the out-buildings
indicating that once upon a time there were many servants
and a prosperous master. The house was of wood, large on the
ground, with encircling piazzas; across the front door rough
bars had been nailed, and the closed blinds were protected in
the same manner; from long want of paint the clapboards were
gray and mossy, and the floor of the piazza had fallen in here
and there from decay. The keeper decided that his cemetery
was a much more cheerful place than this, and then he looked
around for the spring. Behind the house the ground sloped
down; it must be there. He went around and came suddenly
upon a man lying on an old rug outside of a back door. "Excuse me. I thought nobody lived here," he said.

"Nobody does," replied the man; "I am not much of a body,
am I?"

His left arm was gone, and his face was thin and worn with
long illness; he closed his eyes after speaking, as though the few
words had exhausted him.

"I came for water from a cold spring you have here, somewhere," pursued the keeper, contemplating the wreck before
him with the interest of one who has himself been severely
wounded and knows the long, weary pain. The man waved his
hand toward the slope without unclosing his eyes, and Rodman went off with his pail and found a little shady hollow, once
curbed and paved with white pebbles, but now neglected, like
all the place. The water was cold, however, deliciously cold. He
filled his pail and thought that perhaps after all he would exert
himself to make coffee, now that the sun was down; it would
taste better made of this cold water. When he came up the
slope the man's eyes were open.

"Have some water?" asked Rodman.

"Yes; there's a gourd inside."

The keeper entered, and found himself in a large, bare room;
in one corner was some straw covered with an old counter-
pane, in another a table and chair; a kettle hung in the deep
fireplace, and a few dishes stood on a shelf; by the door on a

nail hung a gourd; he filled it and gave it to the host of this desolate abode. The man drank with eagerness.

"Pomp has gone to town," he said, "and I could not get down to the spring to-day, I have had so much pain."

"And when will Pomp return?"

"He should be here now; he is very late to-night."

"Can I get you anything?"

"No, thank you; he will soon be here."

The keeper looked out over the waste; there was no one in sight. He was not a man of any especial kindliness—he had himself been too hardly treated in life for that—but he could not find it in his heart to leave this helpless creature all alone with night so near. So he sat down on the door-step. "I will rest awhile," he said, not asking but announcing it. The man had turned away and closed his eyes again, and they both remained silent, busy with their own thoughts; for each had recognized the ex-soldier, Northern and Southern, in portions of the old uniforms, and in the accent. The war and its memories were still very near to the maimed, poverty-stricken Confederate; and the other knew that they were, and did not obtrude himself.

Twilight fell, and no one came.

"Let me get you something," said Rodman; for the face looked ghastly as the fever abated. The other refused. Darkness came; still, no one.

"Look here," said Rodman, rising, "I have been wounded myself, was in hospital for months; I know how you feel. You must have food—a cup of tea, now, and a slice of toast, brown and thin."

"I have not tasted tea or wheaten bread for weeks," answered the man; his voice died off into a wail, as though feebleness and pain had drawn the cry from him in spite of himself. Rodman lighted a match; there was no candle, only a piece of pitch-pine stuck in an iron socket on the wall; he set fire to this primitive torch and looked around.

"There is nothing there," said the man outside, making an effort to speak carelessly; "my servant went to town for supplies. Do not trouble yourself to wait; he will come presently, and—and I want nothing."

But Rodman saw through proud poverty's lie; he knew that

irregular quavering of the voice, and that trembling of the hand; the poor fellow had but one to tremble. He continued his search; but the bare room gave back nothing, not a crumb.

"Well, if you are not hungry," he said, briskly, "I am, hungry as a bear; and I'll tell you what I am going to do. I live not far from here, and I live all alone too; I haven't a servant as you have. Let me take supper here with you, just for a change; and, if your servant comes, so much the better, he can wait upon us. I'll run over and bring back the things."

He was gone without waiting for reply; the shattered ankle made good time over the waste, and soon returned, limping a little, but bravely hasting, while on a tray came the keeper's best supplies, Irish potatoes, corned beef, wheaten bread, butter, and coffee; for he would not eat the hot biscuits, the corn-cake, the bacon and hominy of the country, and constantly made little New England meals for himself in his prejudiced little kitchen. The pine-torch flared in the doorway; a breeze had come down from the far mountains and cooled the air. Rodman kindled a fire on the cavernous hearth, filled the kettle, found a saucepan, and commenced operations, while the other lay outside and watched every movement in the lighted room.

"All ready; let me help you in. Here we are now; fried potatoes, cold beef, mustard, toast, butter, and tea. Eat, man; and the next time I am laid up you shall come over and cook for me."

Hunger conquered, and the other ate, ate as he had not eaten for months. As he was finishing a second cup of tea, a slow step came around the house; it was the missing Pomp, an old negro, bent and shriveled, who carried a bag of meal and some bacon in his basket. "That is what they live on," thought the keeper.

He took leave without more words. "I suppose now I can be allowed to go home in peace," he grumbled to conscience. The negro followed him across what was once the lawn. "Fin' Mars' Ward mighty low," he said apologetically, as he swung open the gate which still hung between its posts, although the fence was down, "but I hurred and hurred as fas' as I could; it's mighty fur to de town. Proud to see you, sah; hope you'll come again. Fine fambly, de Wards, sah, befo' de war."

"How long has he been in this state?" asked the keeper.

"Ever sence one ob de las' battles, sah; but he's worse sence we come yer, 'bout a mont' back."

"Who owns the house? Is there no one to see to him? has he no friends?"

"House b'long to Mars' Ward's uncle; fine place once, befo' de war; he's dead now, and dah's nobuddy but Miss Bettina, an' she's gone off somewhuz. Propah place, sah, fur Mars' Ward—own uncle's house," said the old slave, loyally striving to maintain the family dignity even then.

"Are there no better rooms—no furniture?"

"Sartin; but—but Miss Bettina, she took de keys; she didn't know we was comin'—"

"You had better send for Miss Bettina, I think," said the keeper, starting homeward with his tray, washing his hands, as it were, of any future responsibility in the affair.

The next day he worked in his garden, for clouds veiled the sun and exercise was possible; but, nevertheless, he could not forget the white face on the old rug. "Pshaw!" he said to himself, "haven't I seen tumble-down old houses and battered human beings before this?"

At evening came a violent thunderstorm, and the splendor of the heavens was terrible. "We have chained you, mighty spirit," thought the keeper as he watched the lightning, "and some time we shall learn the laws of the winds and foretell the storms; then, prayers will no more be offered in churches to alter the weather than they would be offered now to alter an eclipse. Yet back of the lightning and the wind lies the power of the great Creator, just the same."

But still into his musings crept, with shadowy persistence, the white face on the rug.

"Nonsense!" he exclaimed; "if white faces are going around as ghosts, how about the fourteen thousand white faces that went under the sod down yonder? If they could arise and walk, the whole State would be filled and no more carpet-baggers needed." So, having balanced the one with the fourteen thousand, he went to bed.

Daylight brought rain—still, soft, gray rain; the next morning showed the same, and the third likewise, the nights keeping up their part with low-down clouds and steady pattering on the roof. "If there was a river here, we should have a flood," thought the keeper, drumming idly on his window-pane. Memory brought back the steep New England hillsides shedding their rain into the brooks, which grew in a night to torrents and filled the rivers so that they overflowed their banks; then, suddenly, an old house in a sunken corner of a waste rose before his eyes, and he seemed to see the rain dropping from a moldy ceiling on the straw where a white face lay.

"Really, I have nothing else to do to-day, you know," he remarked in an apologetic way to himself, as he and his umbrella went along the old road; and he repeated the remark as he entered the room where the man lay, just as he had fancied, on the damp straw.

"The weather *is* unpleasant," said the man. "Pomp, bring a chair."

Pomp brought one, the only one, and the visitor sat down. A fire smoldered on the hearth and puffed out acrid smoke now and then, as if the rain had clogged the soot in the long-neglected chimney; from the streaked ceiling oozing drops fell with a dull splash into little pools on the decayed floor; the door would not close; the broken panes were stopped with rags, as if the old servant had tried to keep out the damp; in the ashes a corn-cake was baking.

"I am afraid you have not been so well during these long rainy days," said the keeper, scanning the face on the straw.

"My old enemy, rheumatism," answered the man; "the first sunshine will drive it away."

They talked awhile, or rather the keeper talked, for the other seemed hardly able to speak, as the waves of pain swept over him; then the visitor went outside and called Pomp out. "*Is* there any one to help him, or not?" he asked impatiently.

"Fine fambly, befo' de war," began Pomp.

"Never mind all that; is there any one to help him now—yes or no?"

"No," said the old black with a burst of despairing truthfulness. "Miss Bettina, she's as poor as Mars' Ward, an' dere's no one else. He's had noth'n but hard corn-cake for three days, an' he can't swaller it no more."

The next morning saw Ward De Rosset lying on the white pallet in the keeper's cottage, and old Pomp, marveling at the cleanliness all around him, installed as nurse. A strange asylum for a Confederate soldier, was it not? But he knew nothing of the change, which he would have fought with his last breath if consciousness had remained; returning fever, however, had absorbed his senses, and then it was that the keeper and the slave had borne him slowly across the waste, resting many times, but accomplishing the journey at last.

That evening John Rodman, strolling to and fro in the dusky twilight, paused alongside of the other Rodman. "I do not want him here, and that is the plain truth," he said, pursuing the current of his thoughts. "He fills the house; he and Pomp together disturb all my ways. He'll be ready to fling a brick at me too, when his senses come back; small thanks shall I have for lying on the floor, giving up all my comforts, and, what is more, riding over the spirit of the place with a vengeance!" He threw himself down on the grass beside the mound and lay looking up toward the stars, which were coming out, one by one, in the deep blue of the Southern night. "With a vengeance, did I say? That is it exactly—the vengeance of kindness. The poor fellow has suffered horribly in body and in estate, and now ironical Fortune throws him in my way, as if saying, 'Let us see how far your selfishness will yield.' This is not a question of magnanimity; there is no magnanimity about it, for the war is over, and you Northerners have gained every point for which you fought. This is merely a question between man and man; it would be the same if the sufferer was a poor Federal, one of the carpet-baggers, whom you despise so, for instance, or a pagan Chinaman. And Fortune is right; don't you think so, Blank Rodman? I put it to you, now, to one who has suffered the extreme rigor of the other side—those prison-pens yonder."

Whereupon Blank Rodman answered that he had fought for a great cause, and that he knew it, although a plain man and not given to speech-making; he was not one of those who had sat safely at home all through the war, and now belittled it and made light of its issues. (Here a murmur came up from the long line of the trenches, as though all the dead had cried out.) But now the points for which he had fought being gained, and strife ended, it was the plain duty of every man to encourage peace. For his part he bore no malice; he was glad the poor Confederate was up in the cottage, and he did not think any

the less of the keeper for bringing him there. He would like
to add that he thought more of him; but he was sorry to say
that he was well aware what an effort it was, and how almost
grudgingly the charity began.

If Blank Rodman did not say this, at least the keeper imagined that he did. "That is what he would have said," he thought.
"I am glad you do not object," he added, pretending to himself
that he had not noticed the rest of the remark.

"We do not object to the brave soldier who honestly fought
for his cause, even though he fought on the other side," answered Blank Rodman for the whole fourteen thousand. "But
never let a coward, a double-face, or a flippant-tongued idler
walk over our heads. It would make us rise in our graves!"

And the keeper seemed to see a shadowy pageant sweep
by—gaunt soldiers with white faces, arming anew against the
subtle product of peace: men who said, "It was nothing! Behold, we saw it with our eyes!"—stay-at-home eyes.

The third day the fever abated, and Ward De Rosset noticed his surroundings. Old Pomp acknowledged that he had
been moved, but veiled the locality: "To a frien's house, Mars'
Ward."

"But I have no friends now, Pomp," said the weak voice.

Pomp was very much amused at the absurdity of this. "No
frien's! Mars' Ward, no frien's!" He was obliged to go out of
the room to hide his laughter. The sick man lay feebly thinking
that the bed was cool and fresh, and the closed green blinds
pleasant; his thin fingers stroked the linen sheet, and his eyes
wandered from object to object. The only thing that broke the
rule of bare utility in the simple room was a square of white
drawing-paper on the wall, upon which was inscribed in ornamental text the following verse:

> "Toujours femme varie,
>   Bien fou qui s'y fie;
>   Une femme souvent
>   N'est qu'une plume au vent."

With the persistency of illness the eyes and mind of Ward De
Rosset went over and over this distich; he knew something
of French, but was unequal to the effort of translating; the

rhymes alone caught his vagrant fancy. "Toujours femme varie," he said to himself over and over again; and when the keeper entered, he said it to him.

"Certainly," answered the keeper; "bien fou qui s'y fie. How do you find yourself this morning?"

"I have not found myself at all, so far. Is this your house?"

"Yes."

"Pomp told me I was in a friend's house," observed the sick man, vaguely.

"Well, it isn't an enemy's. Had any breakfast? No? Better not talk, then."

He went to the detached shed which served for a kitchen, upset all Pomp's clumsy arrangements, and ordered him outside; then he set to work and prepared a delicate breakfast with his best skill. The sick man eagerly eyed the tray as he entered. "Better have your hands and face sponged off, I think," said Rodman; and then he propped him up skillfully, and left him to his repast. The grass needed mowing on the parade-ground; he shouldered his scythe and started down the path, viciously kicking the gravel aside as he walked. "Wasn't solitude your principal idea, John Rodman, when you applied for this place?" he demanded of himself. "How much of it are you likely to have with sick men, and sick men's servants, and so forth?"

The "and so forth," thrown in as a rhetorical climax, turned into reality and arrived bodily upon the scene—a climax indeed. One afternoon, returning late to the cottage, he found a girl sitting by the pallet—a girl young and dimpled and dewy; one of the creamy roses of the South that, even in the bud, are richer in color and luxuriance than any Northern flower. He saw her through the door, and paused; distressed old Pomp met him and beckoned him cautiously outside. "Miss Bettina," he whispered gutturally; "she's come back from somewhuz, an' she's awful mad 'cause Mars' Ward's here. I tole her all 'bout 'em—de leaks an' de rheumatiz an' de hard corn-cake, but she done gone scole me; and Mars' Ward, he know now whar he is, an' he mad too."

"Is the girl a fool?" said Rodman. He was just beginning to rally a little. He stalked into the room and confronted her. "I have the honor of addressing—"

"Miss Ward."

"And I am John Rodman, keeper of the national cemetery."

This she ignored entirely; it was as though he had said, "I am John Jones, the coachman." Coachmen were useful in their way; but their names were unimportant.

The keeper sat down and looked at his new visitor. The little creature fairly radiated scorn; her pretty head was thrown back, her eyes, dark brown fringed with long dark lashes, hardly deigned a glance; she spoke to him as though he was something to be paid and dismissed like any other mechanic.

"We are indebted to you for some days' board, I believe, keeper—medicines, I presume, and general attendance. My cousin will be removed to-day to our own residence; I wish to pay now what he owes."

The keeper saw that her dress was old and faded; the small black shawl had evidently been washed and many times mended; the old-fashioned knitted purse she held in her hand was lank with long famine.

"Very well," he said; "if you choose to treat a kindness in that way, I consider five dollars a day none too much for the annoyance, expense, and trouble I have suffered. Let me see: five days—or is it six? Yes. Thirty dollars, Miss Ward."

He looked at her steadily; she flushed. "The money will be sent to you," she began haughtily; then, hesitatingly, "I must ask a little time—"

"O Betty, Betty, you know you can not pay it. Why try to disguise— But that does not excuse *you* for bringing me here," said the sick man, turning toward his host with an attempt to speak fiercely, which ended in a faltering quaver.

All this time the old slave stood anxiously outside of the door; in the pauses they could hear his feet shuffling as he waited for the decision of his superiors. The keeper rose and threw open the blinds of the window that looked out on the distant parade-ground. "Bringing you here," he repeated—"*here*; that is my offense, is it? There they lie, fourteen thousand brave men and true. Could they come back to earth they would be the first to pity and aid you, now that you are down. So would it be with you if the case were reversed; for a soldier is generous to a soldier. It was not your own heart that spoke then; it was the small venom of a woman, that here, as everywhere through the South, is playing its rancorous part."

The sick man gazed out through the window, seeing for the first time the far-spreading ranks of the dead. He was very weak, and the keeper's words had touched him; his eyes were suffused with tears. But Miss Ward rose with a flashing glance. She turned her back full upon the keeper and ignored his very existence. "I will take you home immediately, Ward—this very evening," she said.

"A nice, comfortable place for a sick man," commented the keeper, scornfully. "I am going out now, De Rosset, to prepare your supper; you had better have one good meal before you go."

He disappeared, but as he went he heard the sick man say, deprecatingly: "It isn't very comfortable over at the old house now, indeed it isn't, Betty; I suffered"—and the girl's passionate outburst in reply. Then he closed his door and set to work.

When he returned, half an hour later, Ward was lying back exhausted on the pillows, and his cousin sat leaning her head upon her hand; she had been weeping, and she looked very desolate, he noticed, sitting there in what was to her an enemy's country. Hunger is a strong master, however, especially when allied to weakness; and the sick man ate with eagerness.

"I must go back," said the girl, rising. "A wagon will be sent out for you, Ward; Pomp will help you."

But Ward had gained a little strength as well as obstinacy with the nourishing food. "Not to-night," he said.

"Yes, to-night."

"But I can not go to-night; you are unreasonable, Bettina. To-morrow will do as well, if go I must."

"If go you must! You do not want to go, then—to go to our own home—and with me"— Her voice broke; she turned toward the door.

The keeper stepped forward. "This is all nonsense, Miss Ward," he said, "and you know it. Your cousin is in no state to be moved. Wait a week or two, and he can go in safety. But do not dare to offer me your money again; my kindness was to the soldier, not to the man, and as such he can accept it. Come out and see him as often as you please. I shall not intrude upon you. Pomp, take the lady home."

And the lady went.

Then began a remarkable existence for the four: a Confederate soldier lying ill in the keeper's cottage of a national cemetery; a rampant little rebel coming out daily to a place which was to her anathema-maranatha; a cynical, misanthropic keeper sleeping on the floor and enduring every variety of discomfort for a man he never saw before—a man belonging to an idle, arrogant class he detested; and an old black freedman allowing himself to be taught the alphabet in order to gain permission to wait on his master—master no longer in law—with all the devotion of his loving old heart. For the keeper had announced to Pomp that he must learn his alphabet or go; after all these years of theory, he, as a New-Englander, could not stand by and see precious knowledge shut from the black man. So he opened it, and mighty dull work he found it.

Ward De Rosset did not rally as rapidly as they expected. The white-haired doctor from the town rode out on horseback, pacing slowly up the graveled roadway with a scowl on his brow, casting, as he dismounted, a furtive glance down toward the parade-ground. His horse and his coat were alike old and worn, and his broad shoulders were bent with long service in the miserably provided Confederate hospitals, where he had striven to do his duty through every day and every night of those shadowed years. Cursing the incompetency in high places, cursing the mismanagement of the entire medical department of the Confederate army, cursing the recklessness and indifference which left the men suffering for want of proper hospitals and hospital stores, he yet went on resolutely doing his best with the poor means in his control until the last. Then he came home, he and his old horse, and went the rounds again, he prescribing for whooping-cough or measles, and Dobbin waiting outside; the only difference was that fees were small and good meals scarce for both, not only for the man but for the beast. The doctor sat down and chatted awhile kindly with De Rosset, whose father and uncle had been dear friends of his in the bright, prosperous days; then he left a few harmless medicines and rose to go, his gaze resting a moment on Miss Ward, then on Pomp, as if he were hesitating. But he said nothing until on the walk outside he met the keeper, and recognized a person to whom he could tell the truth. "There is nothing to be done; he may recover, he may not; it is a question of strength merely. He needs no medicines, only nourishing food, rest, and careful tendance."

"He shall have them," answered the keeper briefly. And then the old gentleman mounted his horse and rode away, his first and last visit to a national cemetery.

"National!" he said to himself—"national!"

All talk of moving De Rosset ceased, but Miss Ward moved into the old house. There was not much to move: herself, her one trunk, and Marí, a black attendant, whose name probably began life as Maria, since the accent still dwelt on the curtailed last syllable. The keeper went there once, and once only, and then it was an errand for the sick man, whose fancies came sometimes at inconvenient hours—when Pomp had gone to town, for instance. On this occasion the keeper entered the mockery of a gate and knocked at the front door, from which the bars had been removed; the piazza still showed its decaying planks, but quick-growing summer vines had been planted, and were now encircling the old pillars and veiling all defects with their greenery. It was a woman's pathetic effort to cover up what can not be covered—poverty. The blinds on one side were open, and white curtains waved to and fro in the breeze; into this room he was ushered by Marí. Matting lay on the floor, streaked here and there ominously by the dampness from the near ground. The furniture was of dark mahogany, handsome in its day: chairs, a heavy pier-table with low-down glass, into which no one by any possibility could look unless he had eyes in his ankles, a sofa with a stiff round pillow of haircloth under each curved end, and a mirror with a compartment framed off at the top, containing a picture of shepherds and shepherdesses, and lambs with blue ribbons around their necks, all enjoying themselves in the most natural and life-like manner. Flowers stood on the high mantelpiece, but their fragrance could not overcome the faint odor of the damp strawmatting. On a table were books—a life of General Lee, and three or four shabby little volumes printed at the South during the war, waifs of prose and poetry of that highly wrought, richly colored style which seems indigenous to Southern soil.

"Some way, the whole thing reminds me of a funeral," thought the keeper.

Miss Ward entered, and the room bloomed at once; at least that is what a lover would have said. Rodman, however, merely noticed that she bloomed, and not the room, and he said to himself that she would not bloom long if she continued to live in such a moldy place. Their conversation in these days was excessively polite, shortened to the extreme minimum possible, and conducted without the aid of the eyes, at least on one side. Rodman had discovered that Miss Ward never looked at him, and so he did not look at her—that is, not often; he was human, however, and she was delightfully pretty. On this occasion they exchanged exactly five sentences, and then he departed, but not before his quick eyes had discovered that the rest of the house was in even worse condition than this parlor, which, by the way, Miss Ward considered quite a grand apartment; she had been down near the coast, trying to teach school, and there the desolation was far greater than here, both armies having passed back and forward over the ground, foragers out, and the torch at work more than once.

"Will there ever come a change for the better?" thought the keeper, as he walked homeward. "What an enormous stone has got to be rolled up hill! But at least, John Rodman, *you* need not go to work at it; *you* are not called upon to lend your shoulder."

None the less, however, did he call out Pomp that very afternoon and sternly teach him "E" and "F," using the smooth white sand for a blackboard, and a stick for chalk. Pomp's primer was a Government placard hanging on the wall of the office. It read as follows:

IN THIS CEMETERY REPOSE THE REMAINS
OF
FOURTEEN THOUSAND THREE HUNDRED AND TWENTY-ONE
UNITED STATES SOLDIERS.

"Tell me not in mournful numbers
     Life is but an empty dream;
For the soul is dead that slumbers,
     And things are not what they seem.

"Life is real! Life is earnest!
     And the grave is not its goal;
Dust thou art, to dust returnest,
     Was not written of the soul!"

"The only known instance of the Government's condescending to poetry," the keeper had thought, when he first read this placard. It was placed there for the instruction and edification of visitors; but, no visitors coming, he took the liberty of using it as a primer for Pomp. The large letters served the purpose admirably, and Pomp learned the entire quotation; what he thought of it has not transpired. Miss Ward came over daily to see her cousin. At first she brought him soups and various concoctions from her own kitchen—the leaky cavern, once the dining-room, where the soldier had taken refuge after his last dismissal from hospital; but the keeper's soups were richer, and free from the taint of smoke; his martial laws of neatness even disorderly old Pomp dared not disobey, and the sick man soon learned the difference. He thanked the girl, who came bringing the dishes over carefully in her own dimpled hands, and then, when she was gone, he sent them untasted away. By chance Miss Ward learned this, and wept bitter tears over it; she continued to come, but her poor little soups and jellies she brought no more.

One morning in May the keeper was working near the flagstaff, when his eyes fell upon a procession coming down the road which led from the town and turning toward the cemetery. No one ever came that way: what could it mean? It drew near, entered the gate, and showed itself to be negroes walking two and two—old uncles and aunties, young men and girls, and even little children, all dressed in their best; a very poor best, sometimes gravely ludicrous imitations of "ole mars'" or "ole miss'," sometimes mere rags bravely patched together and adorned with a strip of black calico or rosette of black ribbon; not one was without a badge of mourning. All carried flowers, common blossoms from the little gardens behind the cabins that stretched around the town on the outskirts—the new forlorn cabins with their chimneys of piled stones and ragged patches of corn; each little darkey had his bouquet and marched solemnly along, rolling his eyes around, but without even the beginning of a smile, while the elders moved forward with gravity, the bubbling, irrepressible gayety of the negro subdued by the new-born dignity of the freedman.

"Memorial Day," thought the keeper; "I had forgotten it."

"Will you do us de hono', sah, to take de head ob de pro-cessio', sah?" said the leader, with a ceremonious bow. Now, the keeper had not much sympathy with the strewing of flow-ers, North or South; he had seen the beautiful ceremony more than once turned into a political demonstration. Here, how-ever, in this small, isolated, interior town, there was nothing of that kind; the whole population of white faces laid their roses and wept true tears on the graves of their lost ones in the village churchyard when the Southern Memorial Day came round, and just as naturally the whole population of black faces went out to the national cemetery with their flowers on the day when, throughout the North, spring blossoms were laid on the graves of the soldiers, from the little Maine village to the stretching ranks of Arlington, from Greenwood to the far Western burial-places of San Francisco. The keeper joined the procession and led the way to the parade-ground. As they ap-proached the trenches, the leader began singing and all joined. "Swing low, sweet chariot," sang the freedmen, and their hymn rose and fell with strange, sweet harmony—one of those wild, unwritten melodies which the North heard with surprise and marveling when, after the war, bands of singers came to their cities and sang the songs of slavery, in order to gain for their children the coveted education. "Swing low, sweet chariot," sang the freedmen, and two by two they passed along, strewing the graves with flowers till all the green was dotted with color. It was a pathetic sight to see some of the old men and women, ignorant field-hands, bent, dull-eyed, and past the possibility of education even in its simplest forms, carefully placing their poor flowers to the best advantage. They knew dimly that the men who lay beneath those mounds had done something won-derful for them and for their children; and so they came bring-ing their blossoms, with little intelligence but with much love.

The ceremony over, they retired. As he turned, the keeper caught a glimpse of Miss Ward's face at the window.

"Hope we 's not makin' too free, sah," said the leader, as the procession, with many a bow and scrape, took leave, "but we 's kep' de day now two years, sah, befo' you came, sah, an we 's teachin' de chil'en to keep it, sah."

The keeper returned to the cottage. "Not a white face," he said.

"Certainly not," replied Miss Ward, crisply.

"I know some graves at the North, Miss Ward, graves of Southern soldiers, and I know some Northern women who do not scorn to lay a few flowers on the lonely mounds as they pass by with their blossoms on our Memorial Day."

"You are fortunate. They must be angels. We have no angels here."

"I am inclined to believe you are right," said the keeper.

That night old Pomp, who had remained invisible in the kitchen during the ceremony, stole away in the twilight and came back with a few flowers. Rodman saw him going down toward the parade-ground, and watched. The old man had but a few blossoms; he arranged them hastily on the mounds with many a furtive glance toward the house, and then stole back, satisfied; he had performed his part.

Ward De Rosset lay on his pallet, apparently unchanged; he seemed neither stronger nor weaker. He had grown childishly dependent upon his host, and wearied for him, as the Scotch say; but Rodman withstood his fancies, and gave him only the evenings, when Miss Bettina was not there. One afternoon, however, it rained so violently that he was forced to seek shelter; he set himself to work on the ledgers; he was on the ninth thousand now. But the sick man heard his step in the outer room, and called in his weak voice, "Rodman, Rodman." After a time he went in, and it ended in his staying; for the patient was nervous and irritable, and he pitied the nurse, who seemed able to please him in nothing. De Rosset turned with a sigh of relief toward the strong hands that lifted him readily, toward the composed manner, toward the man's voice that seemed to bring a breeze from outside into the close room; animated, cheered, he talked volubly. The keeper listened, answered once in a while, and quietly took the rest of the afternoon into his own hands. Miss Ward yielded to the silent change, leaned back, and closed her eyes. She looked exhausted and for the first time pallid; the loosened dark hair curled in little rings about her temples, and her lips were parted as though she was too tired to close them; for hers were not the thin, straight lips that shut tight naturally, like the straight line of a closed box. The sick man talked on. "Come, Rodman," he said, after a while, "I have read that lying verse of yours over at least ten

thousand and fifty-nine times; please tell me its history; I want
to have something definite to think of when I read it for the
ten thousand and sixtieth."

> "Toujours femme varie,
>   Bien fou qui s'y fie;
>   Une femme souvent
>   N'est qu'une plume au vent,"

read the keeper slowly, with his execrable English accent.
"Well, I don't know that I have any objection to telling the
story. I am not sure but that it will do me good to hear it all
over myself in plain language again."

"Then it concerns yourself," said De Rosset; "so much the
better. I hope it will be, as the children say, the truth, and
long."

"It will be the truth, but not long. When the war broke out
I was twenty-eight years old, living with my mother on our
farm in New England. My father and two brothers had died
and left me the homestead; otherwise I should have broken
away and sought fortune farther westward, where the lands
are better and life is more free. But mother loved the house,
the fields, and every crooked tree. She was alone, and so I staid
with her. In the center of the village green stood the square,
white meeting-house, and near by the small cottage where the
pastor lived; the minister's daughter, Mary, was my promised
wife. Mary was a slender little creature with a profusion of pale
flaxen hair, large, serious blue eyes, and small, delicate features;
she was timid almost to a fault; her voice was low and gentle. She was not eighteen, and we were to wait a year. The
war came, and I volunteered, of course, and marched away;
we wrote to each other often; my letters were full of the camp
and skirmishes; hers told of the village, how the widow Brown
had fallen ill, and how it was feared that Squire Stafford's boys
were lapsing into evil ways. Then came the day when my regiment marched to the field of its slaughter, and soon after our
shattered remnant went home. Mary cried over me, and came
out every day to the farmhouse with her bunches of violets;
she read aloud to me from her good little books, and I used to
lie and watch her profile bending over the page, with the light

falling on her flaxen hair low down against the small, white throat. Then my wound healed, and I went again, this time for three years; and Mary's father blessed me, and said that when peace came he would call me son, but not before, for these were no times for marrying or giving in marriage. He was a good man, a red-hot abolitionist, and a roaring lion as regards temperance; but nature had made him so small in body that no one was much frightened when he roared. I said that I went for three years; but eight years have passed and I have never been back to the village. First, mother died. Then Mary turned false. I sold the farm by letter and lost the money three months afterwards in an unfortunate investment; my health failed. Like many another Northern soldier, I remembered the healing climate of the South; its soft airs came back to me when the snow lay deep on the fields and the sharp wind whistled around the poor tavern where the moneyless, half-crippled volunteer sat coughing by the fire. I applied for this place and obtained it. That is all."

"But it is not all," said the sick man, raising himself on his elbow; "you have not told half yet, nor anything at all about the French verse."

"Oh—that? There was a little Frenchman staying at the hotel; he had formerly been a dancing-master, and was full of dry, withered conceits, although he looked like a thin and bilious old ape dressed as a man. He taught me, or tried to teach me, various wise sayings, among them this one, which pleased my fancy so much that I gave him twenty-five cents to write it out in large text for me."

"Toujours femme varie," repeated De Rosset; "but you don't really think so, do you, Rodman?"

"I do. But they can not help it; it is their nature.—I beg your pardon, Miss Ward. I was speaking as though you were not here."

Miss Ward's eyelids barely acknowledged his existence; that was all. But some time after she remarked to her cousin that it was only in New England that one found that pale flaxen hair.

June was waning, when suddenly the summons came. Ward De Rosset died. He was unconscious toward the last, and death, in the guise of sleep, bore away his soul. They carried him home to the old house, and from there the funeral started, a few family carriages, dingy and battered, following the hearse, for death revived the old neighborhood feeling; that honor at least they could pay—the sonless mothers and the widows who lived shut up in the old houses with everything falling into ruin around them, brooding over the past. The keeper watched the small procession as it passed his gate on its way to the church-yard in the village. "There he goes, poor fellow, his sufferings over at last," he said; and then he set the cottage in order and began the old solitary life again.

He saw Miss Ward but once.

It was a breathless evening in August, when the moonlight flooded the level country. He had started out to stroll across the waste; but the mood changed, and climbing over the east-ern wall he had walked back to the flag-staff, and now lay at its foot gazing up into the infinite sky. A step sounded on the gravel-walk; he turned his face that way, and recognized Miss Ward. With confident step she passed the dark cottage, and brushed his arm with her robe as he lay unseen in the shadow. She went down toward the parade-ground, and his eyes fol-lowed her. Softly outlined in the moonlight, she moved to and fro among the mounds, pausing often, and once he thought she knelt. Then slowly she returned, and he raised himself and waited; she saw him, started, then paused.

"I thought you were away," she said; "Pomp told me so."

"You set him to watch me?"

"Yes. I wished to come here once, and I did not wish to meet you."

"Why did you wish to come?"

"Because Ward was here—and because—because—never mind. It is enough that I wished to walk once among those mounds."

"And pray there?"

"Well—and if I did!" said the girl defiantly.

Rodman stood facing her, with his arms folded; his eyes rested on her face; he said nothing.

"I am going away to-morrow," began Miss Ward again, as-suming with an effort her old, pulseless manner. "I have sold the place, and I shall never return, I think; I am going far away."

"Where?"

"To Tennessee."

"That is not so very far," said the keeper, smiling.

"There I shall begin a new existence," pursued the voice, ignoring the comment.

"You have scarcely begun the old; you are hardly more than a child, now. What are you going to do in Tennessee?"

"Teach."

"Have you relatives there?"

"No."

"A miserable life—a hard, lonely, loveless life," said Rodman. "God help the woman who must be that dreary thing, a teacher from necessity!"

Miss Ward turned swiftly, but the keeper kept by her side. He saw the tears glittering on her eyelashes, and his voice softened. "Do not leave me in anger," he said; "I should not have spoken so, although indeed it was the truth. Walk back with me to the cottage, and take your last look at the room where poor Ward died, and then I will go with you to your home."

"No; Pomp is waiting at the gate," said the girl, almost inarticulately.

"Very well; to the gate, then."

They went toward the cottage in silence; the keeper threw open the door. "Go in," he said. "I will wait outside."

The girl entered and went into the inner room, throwing herself down upon her knees at the bedside. "O Ward, Ward!" she sobbed; "I am all alone in the world now, Ward —all alone!" She buried her face in her hands and gave way to a passion of tears; and the keeper could not help but hear as he waited outside. Then the desolate little creature rose and came forth, putting on, as she did so, her poor armor of pride. The keeper had not moved from the door-step. Now he turned his face. "Before you go—go away for ever from this place—will you write your name in my register," he said—"the visitors' register? The Government had it prepared for the throngs who would visit these graves; but with the exception of the blacks, who can not write, no one has come, and the register is empty. Will you write your name? Yet do not write it unless you can think gently of the men who lie there under the grass. I believe you do think gently of them, else why have you come of your own accord to stand by the side of their graves?" As he said this, he looked fixedly at her.

Miss Ward did not answer; but neither did she write.

"Very well," said the keeper; "come away. You will not, I see."

"I can not! Shall I, Bettina Ward, set my name down in black and white as a visitor to this cemetery, where lie fourteen thousand of the soldiers who killed my father, my three brothers, my cousins; who brought desolation upon all our house, and ruin upon all our neighborhood, all our State, and all our country?—for the South *is* our country, and not your North. Shall I forget these things? Never! Sooner let my right hand wither by my side! I was but a child; yet I remember the tears of my mother, and the grief of all around us. There was not a house where there was not one dead."

"It is true," answered the keeper; "at the South, all went."

They walked down to the gate together in silence.

"Good-by," said John, holding out his hand; "you will give me yours or not as you choose, but I will not have it as a favor."

She gave it.

"I hope that life will grow brighter to you as the years pass. May God bless you!"

He dropped her hand; she turned, and passed through the gateway; then he sprang after her.

"Nothing can change you," he said; "I know it, I have known it all along; you are part of your country, part of the time, part of the bitter hour through which she is passing. Nothing can change you; if it could, you would not be what you are, and I should not— But you can not change. Good-by, Bettina, poor little child—good-by. Follow your path out into the world. Yet do not think, dear, that I have not seen—have not understood."

He bent and kissed her hand; then he was gone, and she went on alone.

A week later the keeper strolled over toward the old house. It was twilight, but the new owner was still at work. He was one of those sandy-haired, energetic Maine men, who, probably on the principle of extremes, were often found through the South, making new homes for themselves in the pleasant land.

"Pulling down the old house, are you?" said the keeper, leaning idly on the gate, which was already flanked by a new fence.

"Yes," replied the Maine man, pausing; "it was only an old shell, just ready to tumble on our heads. You're the keeper over yonder, an't you?" (He already knew everybody within a circle of five miles.)

"Yes. I think I should like those vines if you have no use for them," said Rodman, pointing to the uprooted greenery that once screened the old piazza.

"Wuth about twenty-five cents, I guess," said the Maine man, handing them over.

# Sister St. Luke

She lived shut in by flowers and trees,
And shade of gentle bigotries;
On this side lay the trackless sea,
On that the great world's mystery;
But, all unseen and all unguessed,
They could not break upon her rest.
The world's far glories flamed and flashed,
Afar the wild seas roared and dashed;
But in her small dull paradise,
Safe housed from rapture or surprise,
    Nor day nor night had power to fright
The peace of God within her eyes.

JOHN HAY

THEY found her there. "This is more than I expected," said Carrington as they landed—"seven pairs of Spanish eyes at once."

"Three pairs," answered Keith, fastening the statement to fact and the boat to a rock in his calm way; "and one if not two of the pairs are Minorcan."

The two friends crossed the broad white beach toward the little stone house of the light-keeper, who sat in the doorway, having spent the morning watching their sail cross over from Pelican reef, tacking lazily east and west—an event of more than enough importance in his isolated life to have kept him there, gazing and contented, all day. Behind the broad shoulders of swarthy Pedro stood a little figure clothed in black; and as the man lifted himself at last and came down to meet them, and his wife stepped briskly forward, they saw that the third person was a nun—a large-eyed, fragile little creature, promptly introduced by Melvyna, the keeper's wife, as "Sister St. Luke." For the keeper's wife, in spite of her black eyes, was not a Minorcan; not even a Southerner. Melvyna Sawyer was born in Vermont, and, by one of the strange chances of this vast, many-raced, motley country of ours, she had traveled south as nurse—and a very good, energetic nurse too, albeit somewhat sharp-voiced—to a delicate young wife, who had died in the sunny land, as so many of them die; the sun, with all his good will and with all his shining, not being able to undo in three months the work of long years of the snows and bleak east winds of New England.

The lady dead, and her poor thin frame sent northward again to lie in the hillside churchyard by the side of bleak Puritan ancestors, Melvyna looked about her. She hated the lazy tropical land, and had packed her calf-skin trunk to go, when Pedro Gonsalvez surprised her by proposing matrimony. At least that is what she wrote to her aunt Clemanthy, away in Vermont; and, although Pedro may not have used the words, he at least meant the fact, for they were married two weeks later by a justice of the peace, whom Melvyna's sharp eyes had unearthed, she of course deeming the padre of the little parish and one or two attendant priests as so much dust to be trampled energetically under her shoes, Protestant and number six and a half double-soled mediums. The justice of the peace, a good-natured old gentleman who had forgotten that he held the office at all, since there was no demand for justice and the peace was never broken, married them as well as he could in a surprised sort of way; and, instead of receiving a fee, gave one, which Melvyna, however, promptly rescued from the bridegroom's willing hand, and returned with the remark that there was no "call for alms" (pronounced as if rhymed with hams), and that two shilling, or mebbe three, she guessed, would be about right for the job. This sum she deposited on the table, and then took leave, walking off with a quick, enterprising step, followed by her acquiescent and admiring bridegroom. He had remained acquiescent and admiring ever since, and now, as lighthouse-keeper on Pelican Island, he admired and acquiesced more than ever; while Melvyna kept the house in order, cooked his dinners, and tended his light, which, although only third-class, shone and glittered under her daily care in the old square tower which was founded by the Spaniards, heightened by the English, and now finished and owned by the United States, whose Lighthouse Board said to each other every now and then that really they must put a first-class Fresnel on Pelican Island and a good substantial tower instead of that old-fashioned beacon. They did so a year or two later; and a hideous barber's pole it remains to the present day. But when Carrington and Keith landed there the square tower still stood in its gray old age at the very edge of the ocean, so that high tides swept the step of the keeper's house. It was originally a lookout where the Spanish soldier stood and fired his culverin when a vessel came in sight outside the reef; then the British occupied the land, added a story, and placed an iron grating on the top, where their coastguardsman lighted a fire of pitch-pine knots that flared up against the sky, with the tidings, "A sail! a sail!" Finally the United States came into possession, ran up a third story, and put in a revolving light, one flash for the land and two for the sea—a proportion unnecessarily generous now to the land, since nothing came in any more, and every-thing went by, the little harbor being of no importance since the indigo culture had failed. But ships still sailed by on their way to the Queen of the Antilles, and to the far Windward and Leeward Islands, and the old light went on revolving, pre-sumably for their benefit. The tower, gray and crumbling, and the keeper's house, were surrounded by a high stone wall with angles and loopholes—a small but regularly planned defensive fortification built by the Spaniards; and odd enough it looked there on that peaceful island, where there was nothing to de-fend. But it bore itself stoutly nevertheless, this ancient little fortress, and kept a sharp lookout still over the ocean for the damnable Huguenot sail of two centuries before.

The sea had encroached greatly on Pelican Island, and sooner or later it must sweep the keeper's house away; but now it was a not unpleasant sensation to hear the water wash against the step—to sit at the narrow little windows and watch the sea roll up, roll up, nearer and nearer, coming all the way landless in long surges from the distant African coast, only to never quite get at the foundations of that stubborn little dwelling, which held its own against them, and then triumphantly watched them roll back, roll back, departing inch by inch down the beach, until, behold! there was a magnificent parade-ground, broad enough for a thousand feet to tread—a floor more fresh and beautiful than the marble pavements of palaces. There were not a thousand feet to tread there, however; only six. For

Melvyna had more than enough to do within the house, and Pedro never walked save across the island to the inlet once in two weeks or so, when he managed to row over to the village, and return with supplies, by taking two entire days for it, even Melvyna having given up the point, tacitly submitting to loitering she could not prevent, but recompensing herself by a general cleaning on those days of the entire premises, from the top of the lantern in the tower to the last step in front of the house.

You could not argue with Pedro. He only smiled back upon you as sweetly and as softly as molasses. Melvyna, endeavoring to urge him to energy, found herself in the position of an active ant wading through the downy recesses of a feather bed, which well represented his mind.

Pedro was six feet two inches in height, and amiable as a dove. His wife sensibly accepted him as he was, and he had his two days in town—a very mild dissipation, however, since the Minorcans are too indolent to do anything more than smoke, lie in the sun, and eat salads heavily dressed in oil. They said, "The serene and august wife of our friend is well, we trust?" and, "The island—does it not remain lonely?" and then the salad was pressed upon him again. For they all considered Pedro a man of strange and varied experiences. Had he not married a woman of wonder—of an energy unfathomable? And he lived with her alone in a lighthouse, on an island; alone, mind you, without a friend or relation near!

The six feet that walked over the beautiful beach of the southern ocean were those of Keith, Carrington, and Sister St. Luke.

"Now go, Miss Luke," Melvyna had said, waving her energetically away with the skimmer as she stood irresolute at the kitchen door. "'Twill do you a power of good, and they're nice, quiet gentlemen who will see to you, and make things pleasant. Bless you, *I* know what they are. They ain't none of the miserable, good-for-nothing race about here! Your convent is fifty miles off, ain't it? And besides, you were brought over here half dead for me to cure up—now, warn't you?"

The Sister acknowledged that she was, and Melvyna went on:

"You see, things is different up North, and I understand 'em, but you don't. Now you jest go right along and hev a pleasant walk, and I'll hev a nice bowl of venison broth ready for you when you come back. Go right along now." The skimmer waved again, and the Sister went.

"Yes, she's taken the veil, and is a nun for good and all," explained Melvyna to her new guests the evening of their arrival, when the shy little Sister had retreated to her own room above. "They thought she was dying, and she was so long about it, and useless on their hands, that they sent her up here to the village for sea air, and to be red of her, I guess. 'Tany rate, there she was in one of them crowded, dirty old houses, and so—I jest brought her over here. To tell the truth, gentlemen —the real bottom of it—my baby died last year—and—and Miss Luke she was so good I'll never forget it. I ain't a Catholic —fur from it; I hate 'em. But she seen us coming up from the boat with our little coffin, and she came out and brought flowers to lay on it, and followed to the grave, feeble as she was; and she even put in her little black shawl, because the sand was wet—this miserable half-afloat land, you know—and I couldn't bear to see the coffin set down into it. And I said to myself then that I'd never hate a Catholic again, gentlemen. I don't love 'em yet, and don't know as I ever shell; but Miss Luke, she's different. Consumption? Well, I hardly know. She's a sight better than she was when she come. I'd like to make her well again, and, someway, I can't help a-trying to, for I was a nurse by trade once. But then what's the use? She'll only hev to go back to that old convent!" And Melvyna clashed her pans together in her vexation. "Is she a good Catholic, do you say? Heavens and earth, yes! She's *that* religious—my! I couldn't begin to tell! She believes every word of all that rubbish those old nuns have told her. She thinks it's beautiful to be the bride of heaven; and, as far as that goes, I don't know but she's right: 'tain't much the other kind is wuth," pursued Melvyna, with fine contempt for mankind in general. "As to freedom, they've as good as shoved her off their hands, haven't they? And I guess I can do as I like any way on my own island. There wasn't any man about their old convent, as I can learn, and so Miss Luke, she hain't been taught to run away from 'em like most nuns. Of course, if they knew, they would be sending over here after her; but they don't know, and them priests in the village are too fat and lazy to earn their salt, let alone caring what has become of her. I guess, if they think of her at all, they think that she died, and that they buried her in their crowded, sunken old graveyard. They're so slow and sleepy that they forget half the time who they're burying! But Miss Luke, she ought to go out in the air, and she is so afraid of everything that it don't do her no good to go alone. I haven't got the time to go; and so, if you will let her walk along the beach with you once in a while, it will do her a sight of good, and give her an appetite —although what I want her to hev an appetite for I am sure I don't know; for, ef she gets well, of course she'll go back to the convent. Want to go? *That* she does. She loves the place, and feels lost and strange anywhere else. She was taken there when she was a baby, and it is all the home she has. *She* doesn't know they wanted to be red of her, and she wouldn't believe it ef I was to tell her forty times. She loves them all dearly, and prays every day to go back there. Spanish? Yes, I suppose so; she don't know herself what she is exactly. She speaks English well though, don't she? Yes, Sister St. Luke is her name; and a hea-thenish name it is for a woman, in my opinion. *I* call her Miss Luke. Convert her? Couldn't any more convert her than you could convert a white gull, and make a land-bird of him. It's his nature to ride on the water and be wet all the time. Towels couldn't dry him—not if you fetched a thousand!"

"Our good hostess is a woman of discrimination, and sorely perplexed, therefore, over her *protégée*," said Keith, as the two young men sought their room, a loft under the peaked roof, which was to be their abode for some weeks, when they were not afloat. "As a nurse she feels a professional pride in curing, while as a Calvinist she would almost rather kill than cure, if her patient is to go back to the popish convent. But the lit-tle Sister looks very fragile. She will probably save trouble all round by fading away."

"She is about as faded now as a woman can be," answered Carrington.

The two friends, or rather companions, plunged into all the phases of the southern ocean with a broad, inhaling, expand-ing delight which only a physique naturally fine, or carefully trained, can feel. George Carrington was a vigorous young Saxon, tall and broad, feeling his life and strength in every vein and muscle. Each night he slept his eight hours dreamlessly, like a child, and each day he lived four hours in one, counting by the pallid hours of other men. Andrew Keith, on the other hand, represented the physique cultured and trained up to a high point by years of attention and care. He was a slight man, rather undersized, but his wiry strength was more than a match for Carrington's bulk, and his finely cut face, if you would but study it, stood out like a cameo by the side of a ruddy minia-ture in oils. The trouble is that but few people study cameos. He was older than his companion, and "one of those quiet fellows, you know," said the world. The two had never done or been anything remarkable in their lives. Keith had a little money, and lived as he pleased, while Carrington, off now on a vacation, was junior member of a firm in which family influ-ence had placed him. Both were city men.

"You absolutely do not know how to walk, señora," said Keith. "I will be doctor now, and you must obey me. Never mind the crabs, and never mind the jelly-fish, but throw back your head and walk off briskly. Let the wind blow in your face, and try to stand more erect."

"You are doctor? They told me, could I but see one, well would I be," said the Sister. "At the convent we have only Sister Inez, with her small and old medicines."

"Yes, I think I may call myself doctor," answered Keith gravely. "What do you say, Carrington?"

"Knows no end, Miss, Miss—Miss Luke—I should say, Miss St. Luke. I am sure I do not know why I should stumble over it when St. John is a common enough name," answered Car-rington, who generally did his thinking aloud.

"No end?" repeated the little Sister inquiringly. "But there is an end in this evil world to all things."

"Never mind what he says, señora," interrupted Keith, "but step out strongly and firmly, and throw back your head. There now, there are no crabs in sight, and the beach is hard as a floor. Try it with me: one, two; one, two."

So they treated her, partly as a child, partly as a gentle being of an inferior race. It was a new amusement, although a rather mild one Carrington said, to instruct this unformed, timid mind, to open the blinded eyes, and train the ignorant ears to listen to the melodies of nature.

"Do you not hear? It is like the roll of a grand organ," said

Keith as they sat on the door-step one evening at sunset. The sky was dark; the wind had blown all day from the north to the south, and frightened the little Sister as she toiled at her lace-work, made on a cushion in the Spanish fashion, her lips mechanically repeating prayers meanwhile; for never had they such winds at the inland convent, embowered in its orange-trees. Now, as the deep, low roll of the waves sounded on the shore, Keith, who was listening to it with silent enjoyment, happened to look up and catch the pale, repressed nervousness of her face.

"Oh, not like an organ," she murmured. "This is a fearful sound; but an organ is sweet—soft and sweet. When Sister Teresa plays the evening hymn it is like the sighing of angels."

"But your organ is probably small, señora."

"We have not thought it small. It remains in our chapel, by the window of arches, and below we walk, at the hour of meditation, from the lime-tree to the white-rose bush, and back again, while the music sounds above. We have not thought it small, but large—yes, very large."

"Four feet long, probably," said Carrington, who was smoking an evening pipe, now listening to the talk awhile, now watching the movements of two white heron who were promenading down the beach. "I saw the one over in the village church. It was about as long as this step."

"Yes," said the Sister, surveying the step, "it is about as long as that. It is a very large organ."

"Walk with me down to the point," said Keith—"just once and back again."

The docile little Sister obeyed; she always did immediately whatever they told her to do.

"I want you to listen now; stand still and listen—listen to the sea," said Keith, when they had turned the point and stood alone on the shore. "Try to think only of the pure, deep, blue water, and count how regularly the sound rolls up in long, low chords, dying away and then growing louder, dying away and then growing louder, as regular as your own breath. Do you not hear it?"

"Yes," said the little Sister timorously.

"Keep time, then, with your hand, and let me see whether you catch the measure."

So the small brown hand, nerveless and slender, tried to mark and measure the roar of the great ocean surges, and at last succeeded, urged on by the alternate praises and rebukes of Keith, who watched with some interest a faint color rise in the pale oval face, and an intent listening look come into the soft, unconscious eyes, as, for the first time, the mind caught the mighty rhythm of the sea. She listened, and listened, standing mute, with head slightly bent and parted lips.

"I want you to listen to it in that way every day," said Keith, as he led the way back. "It has different voices: sometimes a fresh, joyous song, sometimes a faint, loving whisper; but always something. You will learn in time to love it, and then it will sing to you all day long."

"Not at the dear convent; there is no ocean there."

"You want to go back to the convent?"

"Oh, could I go! could I go!" said the Sister, not impatiently, but with an intense yearning in her low voice. "Here, so lost, so strange am I, so wild is everything. But I must not murmur"; and she crossed her hands upon her breast and bowed her head.

The two young men led a riotous life; they rioted with the ocean, with the winds, with the level island, with the sunshine and the racing clouds. They sailed over to the reef daily and plunged into the surf; they walked for miles along the beach, and ran races over its white floor; they hunted down the center of the island, and brought back the little brown deer who lived in the low thicket on each side of the island's backbone. The island was twenty miles long and a mile or two broad, with a central ridge of shell-formed rock about twenty feet in height, that seemed like an Appalachian chain on the level waste; below, in the little hollows on each side, spread a low tangled thicket, a few yards wide; and all the rest was barren sand, with movable hills here and there—hills a few feet in height, blown up by the wind, and changed in a night. The only vegetation besides the thicket was a rope-like vine that crept over the sand, with few leaves far apart, and now and then a dull purple blossom—a solitary tenacious vine of the desert, satisfied with little, its growth slow, its life monotonous; yet try to tear it from the surface of the sand, where its barren length seems to lie loosely like an old brown rope thrown down at random, and behold, it resists you stubbornly. You find a mile or two of it on your hands, clinging and pulling as the strong ivy clings to a stone wall; a giant could not conquer it, this seemingly dull and half-dead thing; and so you leave it there to creep on in its own way, over the damp, shell-strewn waste. One day Carrington came home in great glory; he had found a salt marsh. "Something besides this sand, you know—a stretch of saw-grass away to the south, the very place for fat ducks. And somebody has been there before us, too, for I saw the mast of a sail-boat some distance down, tipped up against the sky."

"That old boat is ourn, I guess," said Melvyna. "She drifted down there one high tide, and Pedro he never would go for her. She was a mighty nice little boat, too, ef she *was* cranky."

Pedro smiled amiably back upon his spouse, and helped himself to another hemisphere of pie. He liked the pies, although she was obliged to make them, she said, of such outlandish things as figs, dried oranges, and pomegranates. "If you could only see a pumpkin, Pedro," she often remarked, shaking her head. Pedro shook his back in sympathy; but, in the mean time, found the pies very good as they were.

"Let us go down after the boat," said Carrington. "You have only that old tub over at the inlet, Pedro, and you really need another boat." (Carrington always liked to imagine that he was a constant and profound help to the world at large.) "Suppose anything should happen to the one you have?" Pedro had not thought of that; he slowly put down his knife and fork to consider the subject.

"We will go this afternoon," said Keith, issuing his orders, "and you shall go with us, señora."

"And Pedro, too, to help you," said Melvyna. "I've always wanted that boat back, she was such a pretty little thing: one sail, you know, and decked over in front; you sat on the bottom. I'd like right well to go along myself; but I suppose I'd better stay at home and cook a nice supper for you."

Pedro thought so, decidedly.

When the February sun had stopped blazing down directly overhead, and a few white afternoon clouds had floated over from the east to shade his shining, so that man could bear it, the four started inland toward the backbone ridge, on whose summit there ran an old trail southward, made by the fierce Creeks three centuries before. Right up into the dazzling light soared the great eagles—straight up, up to the sun, their unshrinking eyes fearlessly fixed full on his fiery ball.

"It would be grander if we did not know they had just stolen their dinners from the poor hungry fish-hawks over there on the inlet," said Carrington.

Sister St. Luke had learned to walk quite rapidly now. Her little black gown trailed lightly along the sand behind her, and she did her best to "step out boldly," as Keith directed; but it was not firmly, for she only succeeded in making a series of quick, uncertain little paces over the sand like bird-tracks. Once Keith had taken her back and made her look at her own uneven footsteps. "Look—no two the same distance apart," he said. The little Sister looked and was very much mortified. "Indeed, I *will* try with might to do better," she said. And she did try with might; they saw her counting noiselessly to herself as she walked, "One, two; one, two." But she had improved so much that Keith now devoted his energies to teaching her to throw back her head and look about her. "Do you not see those soft banks of clouds piled up in the west?" he said, constantly directing her attention to objects above her. But this was a harder task, for the timid eyes had been trained from childhood to look down, and the head was habitually bent, like a pendant flower on its stem. Melvyna had deliberately laid hands upon the heavy veil and white band that formerly encircled the small face. "You can not breathe in them," she said. But the Sister still wore a light veil over the short dark hair, which would curl in little rings upon her temples in spite of her efforts to prevent it; the cord and heavy beads and cross encircled her slight waist, while the wide sleeves of her nun's garb fell over her hands to the finger-tips.

"How do you suppose she would look dressed like other women?" said Carrington one day. The two men were drifting in their small yacht, lying at ease on the cushions, and smoking.

"Well," answered Keith slowly, "if she was well dressed—very well, I mean, say in the French style—and if she had any spirit of her own, any vivacity, you might, with that dark face of hers and those eyes—you *might* call her piquant."

"Spirit? She has not the spirit of a fly," said Carrington,

knocking the ashes out of his pipe and fumbling in an embroidered velvet pouch, one of many offerings at his shrine, for a fresh supply of the strong aromatic tobacco he affected, Keith meanwhile smoking nothing but the most delicate cigarettes. "The other day I heard a wild scream; and rushing down stairs I found her half fainting on the steps, all in a little heap. And what do you think it was? She had been sitting there, lost in a dream—mystic, I suppose, like St. Agnes—

> Deep on the convent roof the snows
> Are sparkling to the moon:
> My breath to heaven like vapor goes.
> May my soul follow soon—

and that sort of thing."

"No," said Keith, "there is nothing mystical about the Luke maiden; she has never even dreamed of the ideal ecstasies of deeper minds. She says her little prayers simply, almost mechanically, so many every day, and dwells as it were content in the lowly valleys of religion."

"Well, whatever she was doing," continued Carrington, "a great sea crab had crawled up and taken hold of the toe of her little shoe. Grand tableau—crab and Luke maiden! And the crab had decidedly the better of it."

"She *is* absurdly timid," admitted Keith.

And absurdly timid she was now, when, having crossed the stretch of sand and wound in and out among the low hillocks, they came to the hollow where grew the dark green thicket, through which they must pass to reach the Appalachian range, the backbone of the island, where the trail gave them an easier way than over the sands. Carrington went first and hacked out a path with his knife; Keith followed, and held back the branches; the whole distance was not more than twelve feet; but its recesses looked dark and shadowy to the little Sister, and she hesitated.

"Come," said Carrington; "we shall never reach the salt marsh at this rate."

"There is nothing dangerous here, señora," said Keith. "Look, you can see for yourself. And there are three of us to help you."

"Yes," said Pedro—"three of us." And he swung his broad bulk into the gap.

Still she hesitated.

"Of what are you afraid?" called out Carrington impatiently.

"I know not, indeed," she answered, almost in tears over her own behavior, yet unable to stir. Keith came back, and saw that she was trembling—not violently, but in a subdued, helpless sort of way which was pathetic in its very causelessness.

"Take her up, Pedro," he ordered; and, before she could object, the good-natured giant had borne her in three strides through the dreaded region, and set her down safely upon the ridge. She followed them humbly now, along the safe path, trying to step firmly, and walk with her head up, as Keith had directed. Carrington had already forgotten her again, and even Keith was eagerly looking ahead for the first glimpse of green.

"There is something singularly fascinating in the stretch of a salt marsh," he said. "Its level has such a far sweep as you stand and gaze across it, and you have a dreamy feeling that there is no end to it. The stiff, drenched grasses hold the salt which the tide brings in twice a day, and you inhale that fresh, strong, briny odor, the rank, salt, invigorating smell of the sea; the breeze that blows across has a tang to it like the snap of a whip-lash across your face, bringing the blood to the surface, and rousing you to a quicker pace."

"Ha!" said Carrington; "there it is. Don't you see the green? A little farther on, you will see the mast of the boat."

"That is all that is wanted," said Keith. "A salt marsh is not complete without a boat tilted up aground somewhere, with its slender dark mast outlined against the sky. A boat sailing along in a commonplace way would blight the whole thing; what we want is an abandoned craft, aged and deserted, aground down the marsh with only its mast rising above the waste."

"*Bien!* there it is," said Carrington; "and now the question is, how to get to it."

"You two giants will have to go," said Keith, finding a comfortable seat. "I see a mile or two of tall wading before us, and up to your shoulders is over my head. I went duck-shooting with that man last year, señora. 'Come on,' he cried—'splendid sport ahead, old fellow; come on.'

"'Is it deep?' I asked from behind. I was already up to my knees, and could not see bottom, the water was so dark.

"'Oh, no, not at all; just right,' he answered, striding ahead. 'Come on.'

"I came; and went in up to my eyes."

But the señora did not smile.

"You know Carrington is taller than I am," explained Keith, amused by the novelty of seeing his own stories fall flat.

"Is he?" said the Sister vaguely.

It was evident that she had not observed whether he was or not.

Carrington stopped short, and for an instant stared blankly at her. What every one noticed and admired all over the country wherever he went, this little silent creature had not even seen!

"He will never forgive you," said Keith laughing, as the two tall forms strode off into the marsh. Then, seeing that she did not comprehend in the least, he made a seat for her by spreading his light coat on the Appalachian chain, and, leaning back on his elbow, began talking to her about the marsh. "Breathe in the strong salt," he said, "and let your eyes rest on the green, reedy expanse. Supposing you were painting a picture, now—does any one paint pictures at your convent?"

"Ah, yes," said the little nun, rousing to animation at once. "Sister St. James paints pictures the most beautiful on earth. She painted for us Santa Inez with her lamb, and Santa Rufina of Sevilla, with her palms and earthen vases."

"And has she not taught you to paint also?"

"Me! Oh, no. I am only a Sister young and of no gifts. Sister St. James is a great saint, and of age she has seventy years."

"Not requisites for painting, either of them, that I am aware," said Keith. "However, if you were painting this marsh, do you not see how the mast of that boat makes the feature of the landscape the one human element; and yet, even that abandoned, merged as it were in the desolate wildness of the scene?"

The Sister looked over the green earnestly, as if trying to see all that he suggested. Keith talked on. He knew that he talked well, and he did not confuse her with more than one subject, but dwelt upon the marsh; stories of men who had been lost in them, of women who had floated down in boats and never returned; descriptions clear as etchings; studies of the monotone of hues before them—one subject pictured over and over again, as, wishing to instruct a child, he would have drawn with a chalk one letter of the alphabet a hundred times, until the wandering eyes had learned at last to recognize and know it.

"Do you see nothing at all, feel nothing at all?" he said. "Tell me exactly."

Thus urged, the Sister replied that she thought she did feel the salt breeze a little.

"Then take off that shroud and enjoy it," said Keith, extending his arm suddenly, and sweeping off the long veil by the corner that was nearest to him.

"Oh!" said the little Sister—"oh!" and distressfully she covered her head with her hands, as if trying to shield herself from the terrible light of day. But the veil had gone down into the thicket, whither she dared not follow. She stood irresolute.

"I will get it for you before the others come back," said Keith. "It is gone now, however, and, what is more, you could not help it; so sit down, like a sensible creature, and enjoy the breeze."

The little nun sat down, and confusedly tried to be a sensible creature. Her head, with its short rings of dark hair, rose childlike from the black gown she wore, and the breeze swept freshly over her; but her eyes were full of tears, and her face so pleading in its pale, silent distress, that at length Keith went down and brought back the veil.

"See the cranes flying home," he said, as the long line dotted the red of the west. "They always seem to be flying right into the sunset, sensible birds!"

The little Sister had heard that word twice now; evidently the cranes were more sensible than she. She sighed as she fastened on the veil; there were a great many hard things out in the world, then, she thought. At the dear convent it was not expected that one should be as a crane.

The other two came back at length, wet and triumphant, with their prize. They had stopped to bail it out, plug its cracks, mend the old sail after a fashion, and nothing would do but that the three should sail home in it, Pedro, for whom there was no room, returning by the way they had come. Carrington, having worked hard, was determined to carry out his plan; and said so.

"A fine plan to give us all a wetting," remarked Keith.

"You go down there and work an hour or two yourself, and see how *you* like it," answered the other, with the irrelevance produced by aching muscles and perspiration dripping from every pore.

This conversation had taken place at the edge of the marsh where they had brought the boat up through one of the numerous channels.

"Very well," said Keith. "But mind you, not a word about danger before the Sister. I shall have hard enough work to persuade her to come with us as it is."

He went back to the ridge, and carelessly suggested returning home by water.

"You will not have to go through the thicket then," he said.

Somewhat to his surprise, Sister St. Luke consented immediately, and followed without a word as he led the way. She was mortally afraid of the water, but, during his absence, she had been telling her beads, and thinking with contrition of two obstinacies in one day—that of the thicket and that of the veil —she could not, she would not have three. So, commending herself to all the saints, she embarked.

"Look here, Carrington, if ever you inveigle me into such danger again for a mere fool's fancy, I will show you what I think of it. You knew the condition of that boat, and I did not," said Keith, sternly, as the two men stood at last on the beach in front of the lighthouse. The Sister had gone within, glad to feel land underfoot once more. She had sat quietly in her place all the way, afraid of the water, of the wind, of everything, but entirely unconscious of the real danger that menaced them. For the little craft would not mind her helm; her mast slipped about erratically; the planking at the bow seemed about to give way altogether; and they were on a lee shore, with the tide coming in, and the surf beating roughly on the beach. They were both good sailors, but it had taken all they knew to bring the boat safely to the lighthouse.

"To tell the truth, I did not think she was so crippled," said Carrington. "She really is a good boat for her size."

"Very," said Keith sarcastically.

But the younger man clung to his opinion; and, in order to verify it, he set himself to work repairing the little craft. You would have supposed his daily bread depended upon her being made seaworthy, by the way he labored. She was made over from stem to stern: a new mast, a new sail; and, finally, scarlet and green paint were brought over from the village, and out she came as brilliant as a young paroquet. Then Carrington took to sailing in her. Proud of his handy work, he sailed up and down, over to the reef, and up the inlet, and even persuaded Melvyna to go with him once, accompanied by the meek little Sister.

"Why shouldn't you both learn how to manage her?" he said in his enthusiasm. "She's as easy to manage as a child—"

"And as easy to tip over," replied Melvyna, screwing up her lips tightly and shaking her head. "You don't catch me out in her again, sure's as my name's Sawyer."

For Melvyna always remained a Sawyer in her own mind, in spite of her spouse's name; she could not, indeed, be anything else—*noblesse oblige*. But the Sister, obedient as usual, bent her eyes in turn upon the ropes, the mast, the sail, and the helm, while Carrington, waxing eloquent over his favorite science, delivered a lecture upon their uses, and made her experiment a little to see if she comprehended. He used the simplest words for her benefit, words of one syllable, and unconsciously elevated his voice somewhat, as though that would make her understand better; her wits seemed to him always of the slowest. The Sister followed his directions, and imitated his motions with painstaking minuteness. She did very well until a large porpoise rolled up his dark, glistening back close alongside, when, dropping the sail-rope with a scream, she crouched down at Melvyna's feet and hid her face in her veil. Carrington from that day could get no more passengers for his paroquet boat. But he sailed up and down alone in his little craft, and, when that amusement palled, he took the remainder of the scarlet and green paint and adorned the shells of various sea-crabs and other crawling things, so that the little Sister was met one afternoon by a whole procession of unearthly creatures, strangely variegated, proceeding gravely in single file down the beach from the pen where they had been confined. Keith pointed out to her, however, the probability of their being much admired in their own circles as long as the hues lasted, and she was comforted.

They strolled down the beach now every afternoon, sometimes two, sometimes three, sometimes four when Melvyna had no cooking to watch, no bread to bake; for she rejected with scorn the omnipresent hot biscuit of the South, and kept her household supplied with light loaves in spite of the difficulties of yeast. Sister St. Luke had learned to endure the crabs, but she still fled from the fiddlers when they strayed over from their towns in the marsh; she still went carefully around the great jelly-fish sprawling on the beach, and regarded from a safe distance the beautiful blue Portuguese men-of-war, stranded unexpectedly on the dangerous shore, all their fair voyagings over. Keith collected for her the brilliant sea-weeds, little flecks of color on the white sand, and showed her their beauties; he made her notice all the varieties of shells, enormous conches for the tritons to blow, and beds of wee pink ovals and cornucopias, plates and cups for the little web-footed fairies. Once he came upon a sea-bean.

"It has drifted over from one of the West Indian islands," he said, polishing it with his handkerchief—"one of the islands —let us say Miraprovos—a palmy tropical name, bringing up visions of a volcanic mountain, vast cliffs, a tangled gorgeous forest, and the soft lapping wash of tropical seas. Is it not so, señora?"

But the señora had never heard of the West Indian Islands. Being told, she replied: "As you say it, it is so. There is, then, much land in the world?"

"If you keep the sea-bean for ever, good will come," said Keith, gravely presenting it; "but, if after having once accepted it you then lose it, evil will fall upon you."

The Sister received the amulet with believing reverence. "I will lay it up before the shrine of Our Lady," she said, carefully placing it in the little pocket over her heart, hidden among the folds of her gown, where she kept her most precious treasures —a bead of a rosary that had belonged to some saint who lived somewhere some time, a little faded prayer copied in the handwriting of a young nun who had died some years before and whom she had dearly loved, and a list of her own most vicious faults, to be read over and lamented daily; crying evils such as a perverse and insubordinate bearing, a heart froward and evil, gluttonous desires of the flesh, and a spirit of murderous rage. These were her own ideas of herself, written down at the convent. Had she not behaved herself perversely to the Sister Paula, with whom one should be always mild on account of the affliction which had sharpened her tongue? Had she not wrongfully coveted the cell of the novice Felipa, because it looked out upon the orange walk? Had she not gluttonously longed for more of the delectable marmalade made by the aged Sanchita? And, worse than all, had she not, in a spirit of murderous rage, beat the yellow cat with a palm-branch for carrying off the young doves, her especial charge? "Ah, my sins are great indeed," she sighed daily upon her knees, and smote her breast with tears.

Keith watched the sea-bean go into the little heart-pocket almost with compunction. Many of these amulets of the sea, gathered during his winter rambles, had he bestowed with formal warning of their magic powers, and many a fair hand had taken them, many a soft voice had promised to keep them "for ever." But he well knew they would be mislaid and forgotten in a day. The fair ones well knew it too, and each knew that the other knew, so no harm was done. But this sea-bean, he thought, would have a different fate—laid up in some little nook before the shrine, a witness to the daily prayers of the simple-hearted little Sister. "I hope they may do it good," he thought vaguely. Then, reflecting that even the most depraved bean would not probably be much affected by the prayers, he laughed off the fancy, yet did not quite like to think, after all, that the prayers were of no use. Keith's religion, however, was in the primary rocks.

Far down the beach they came upon a wreck, an old and long hidden relic of the past. The low sand-bluff had caved away suddenly and left a clean new side, where, imbedded in the lower part, they saw a ponderous mast. "An old Spanish galleon," said Keith, stooping to examine the remains. "I know it by the curious bolts. They ran ashore here, broadside on, in one of those sudden tornadoes they have along this coast once in a while, I presume. Singular! This was my very place for lying in the sun and letting the blaze scorch me with its clear scintillant splendor. I never imagined I was lying on the bones of this old Spaniard."

"God rest the souls of the sailors!" said the Sister, making the sign of the cross.

"They have been in—wherever they are, let us say, for about three centuries now," observed Keith, "and must be used to it, good or bad."

"Nay; but purgatory, señor."

"True. I had forgotten that," said Keith.

One morning there came up a dense, soft, southern-sea fog, "The kind you can cut with a knife," Carrington said. It lasted for days, sweeping out to sea at night on the land breeze, and lying in a gray bank low down on the horizon, and then rolling in again in the morning enveloping the water and the island in a thick white cloud which was not mist and did not seem damp even, so freshly, softly salt was the feeling it gave to the faces that went abroad in it. Carrington and Keith, of course, must needs be out in it every moment of the time. They walked down the beach for miles, hearing the muffled sound of the near waves, but not seeing them. They sailed in it not knowing whither they went, and they drifted out at sunset and watched the land breeze lift it, roll it up, and carry it out to sea, where distant ships on the horizon line, bound southward, and nearer ones, sailing northward with the Gulf Stream, found themselves enveloped and bothered by their old and baffling foe. They went over to the reef every morning, these two, and bathed in the fog, coming back by sense of feeling, as it were, and landing not infrequently a mile below or above the lighthouse; then what appetites they had for breakfast! And, if it was not ready, they roamed about, roaring like young lions. At least that is what Melvyna said one morning when Carrington had put his curly head into her kitchen door six times in the course of one half hour.

The Sister shrank from the sea fog; she had never seen one before, and she said it was like a great soft white creature that came in on wings, and brooded over the earth. "Yes, beautiful, perhaps," she said in reply to Keith, "but it is so strange—and —and—I know not how to say it—but it seems like a place for spirits to walk, and not of the mortal kind."

They were wandering down the beach, where Keith had

lured her to listen to the sound of the hidden waves. At that moment Carrington loomed into view coming toward them. He seemed of giant size as he appeared, passed them, and disappeared again into the cloud behind, his voice sounding muffled as he greeted them. The Sister shrank nearer to her companion as the figure had suddenly made itself visible. "Do you know it is a wonder to me how you have ever managed to live so far," said Keith smiling.

"But it was not far," said the little nun. "Nothing was ever far at the dear convent, but everything was near, and not of strangeness to make one afraid; the garden wall was the end. There we go not outside, but our walk is always from the lime-tree to the white rose-bush and back again. Everything we know there—not roar of waves, not strong wind, not the thick, white air comes to give us fear, but all is still and at peace. At night I dream of the organ, and of the orange-trees, and of the doves. I wake, and hear only the sound of the great water below."

"You will go back," said Keith.

He had begun to pity her lately, for her longing was deeper than he had supposed. It had its roots in her very being. He had studied her and found it so.

"She will die of pure homesickness if she stays here much longer," he said to Carrington. "What do you think of our writing down to that old convent and offering—of course unknown to her—to pay the little she costs them, if they will take her back?"

"All right," said Carrington. "Go ahead."

He was making a larger sail for his paroquet boat. "If none of you will go out in her, I might as well have all the sport I can," he said.

"Sport to consist in being swamped?" Keith asked.

"By no means, croaker. Sport to consist in shooting over the water like a rocket; I sitting on the tilted edge, watching the waves, the winds, and the clouds, and hearing the water sing as we rush along."

Keith took counsel with no one else, not even with Melvyna, but presently he wrote his letter and carried it himself over to the village to mail. He did good deeds like that once in a while, "to help humanity," he said. They were tangible always; like the primary rocks.

At length one evening the fog rolled out to sea for good and all, at least as far as that shore was concerned. In the morning there stood the lighthouse, and the island, and the reef, just the same as ever. They had almost expected to see them altered, melted a little.

"Let us go over to the reef, all of us, and spend the day," said Keith. "It will do us good to breathe the clear air, and feel the brilliant, dry, hot sunshine again."

"Hear the man!" said Melvyna laughing. "After trying to persuade us all those days that he liked that sticky fog too!"

"Mme. Gonsalvez, we like a lily; but is that any reason why we may not also like a rose?"

"Neither of 'em grows on this beach as I'm aware of," answered Melvyna dryly.

Then Carrington put in his voice, and carried the day. Women never resisted Carrington long, but yielded almost unconsciously to the influence of his height and his strength, and his strong, hearty will. A subtiler influence over them, however, would have waked resistance, and Carrington himself would have been conquered far sooner (and was conquered later) by one who remained unswayed by those influences, to which others paid involuntary obeisance.

Pedro had gone to the village for his supplies and his two days of mild Minorcan dissipation, and Melvyna, beguiled and cajoled by the chaffing of the two young men, at last consented, and not only packed the lunch-basket with careful hand, but even donned for the occasion her "best bonnet," a structure trimmed in Vermont seven years before by the experienced hand of Miss Althy Spears, the village milliner, who had adorned it with a durable green ribbon and a vigorous wreath of artificial flowers. Thus helmeted, Mme. Gonsalvez presided at the stern of the boat with great dignity. For they were in the safe, well-appointed little yacht belonging to the two gentlemen, the daring paroquet having been left at home tied to the last of a low heap of rocks that jutted out into the water in front of the lighthouse, the only remains of the old stone dock built by the Spaniards long before. Sister St. Luke was with them of course, gentle and frightened as usual. Her breath came quickly as they neared the reef, and Carrington with a sure hand guided the little craft outside into the surf, and, rounding a point, landed them safely in a miniature harbor he had noted there. Keith had counted the days, and felt sure that the answer from the convent would come soon. His offer—for he had made it his alone without Carrington's aid—had been liberal; there could be but one reply. The little Sister would soon go back to the lime-tree, the white rose-bush, the doves, the old organ that was "so large"—all the quiet routine of the life she loved so well; and they would see her small oval face and timid dark eyes no more. So he took her for a last walk down the reef, while Melvyna made coffee, and Carrington, having noticed a dark line floating on the water, immediately went out in his boat, of course, to see what it was.

The reef had its high backbone, like the island. Some day it would be the island, with another reef outside, and the lighthouse beach would belong to the mainland. Down the stretch of sand toward the sea the pelicans stood in rows, toeing a mark, solemn and heavy, by the hundreds—a countless number—for the reef was their gathering-place.

"They are holding a conclave," said Keith. "That old fellow has the floor. See him wag his head."

In and out among the pelicans, and paying no attention to them and their conclave, sped the sickle-bill curlews, actively probing everywhere with their long, grotesque, sickle-shaped bills; and woe be to the burrowing things that came in their way! The red-beaked oyster-bird flew by, and close down to the sea skimmed the razor-bill shear-water, with his head bent forward and his feet tilted up, just grazing the water with his open bill as he flew, and leaving a shining mark behind, as though he held a pencil in his mouth and was running a line. The lazy gulls, who had no work to do, and would not have done it if they had, rode at ease on the little wavelets close in shore. The Sister, being asked, confessed that she liked the lazy gulls best. Being pressed to say why, she thought it was because they were more like the white doves that sat on the old stone well-curb in the convent garden.

Keith had always maintained that he liked to talk to women. He said that the talk of any woman was more piquant than the conversation of the most brilliant men. There was only one obstacle: the absolute inability of the sex to be sincere, or to tell the truth, for ten consecutive minutes. Today, however, as he wandered to and fro whither he would on the reef, he also wandered to and fro whither he would in the mind, and the absolutely truthful mind too, of a woman. Yet he found it dull! He sighed to himself, but was obliged to acknowledge that it *was* dull. The lime-tree, the organ, the Sisters, the Sisters, the lime-tree, the organ; it grew monotonous after a while. Yet he held his post, for the sake of the old theory, until the high voice of Melvyna called them back to the little fire on the beach and the white cloth spread with her best dainties. They saw Carrington sailing in with an excited air, and presently he brought the boat into the cove and dragged ashore his prize, towed behind—nothing less than a large shark, wounded, dead, after a struggle with some other marine monster, a sword-fish probably. "A man-eater," announced the captor. "Look at him, will you? Look at him, Miss Luke!"

But Miss Luke went far away, and would not look. In truth he was an ugly creature; even Melvyna kept at a safe distance. But the two men noted all his points; they measured him carefully; they turned him over, and discussed him generally in that closely confined and exhaustive way which marks the masculine mind. Set two women to discussing a shark, or even the most lovely little brook-trout, if you please, and see how far off they will be in five minutes!

But the lunch was tempting, and finally its discussion called them away even from that of the shark. And then they all sailed homeward over the green and blue water, while the white sand-hills shone silvery before them, and then turned red in the sunset. That night the moon was at its full. Keith went out and strolled up and down on the beach. Carrington was playing fox-and-goose with Mme. Gonsalvez on a board he had good-naturedly constructed for her entertainment when she confessed one day to a youthful fondness for that exciting game. Up stairs gleamed the little Sister's light. "Saying her prayers with her lips, but thinking all the time of that old convent," said the stroller to himself, half scornfully. And he said the truth.

The sea was still and radiant; hardly more than a ripple

broke at his feet; the tide was out, and the broad beach silvery and fresh. "At home they are buried in snow," he thought, "and the wind is whistling around their double windows." And then he stretched himself on the sand, and lay looking upward into the deep blue of the night, bathed in the moonlight, and listening dreamily to the soft sound of the water as it returned slowly, slowly back from the African coast. He thought many thoughts, and deep ones too, and at last he was so far away on ideal heights, that, coming home after midnight, it was no wonder if, half unconsciously, he felt himself above the others; especially when he passed the little Sister's closed door, and thought, smiling not unkindly, how simple she was.

The next morning the two men went off in their boat again for the day, this time alone. There were still a few more questions to settle about that shark, and, to tell the truth, they both liked a good day of unencumbered sailing better than anything else.

About four o'clock in the afternoon Melvyna, happening to look out of the door, saw a cloud no bigger than a man's hand low down on the horizon line of the sea. Something made her stand and watch it for a few moments. Then, "Miss Luke! Miss Luke! Miss Luke! Miss Luke!" she called quickly. Down came the little Sister, startled at the cry, her lace-work still in her hand.

"Look!" said Melvyna.

The Sister looked, and this is what she saw: a line white as milk coming toward them on the water, and behind it a blackness.

"What is it?" she asked.

"A tornader," said Melvyna with white lips. "I've only seen one, and then I was over in the town; but it's awful! We must run back to the thicket." Seizing her companion's arm, the strong Northern woman hurried her across the sand, through the belt of sand-hills, and into the thicket, where they crouched on its far side close down under the projecting backbone. "The bushes will break the sand, and the ridge will keep us from being buried in it," she said. "I dursn't stay on the shore, for the water'll rise."

The words were hardly spoken before the tornado was upon

them, and the air was filled with the flying sand, so that they could hardly breathe. Half choked, they beat with their hands before them to catch a breath. Then came a roar, and for an instant, distant as they were, they caught a glimpse of the crest of the great wave that followed the whirlwind. It seemed to them mountain-high, and ready to ingulf the entire land. With a rushing sound it plunged over the keeper's house, broke against the lower story of the tower, hissed across the sand, swallowed the sand-hills, and swept to their very feet, then sullenly receded with slow, angry muttering. A gale of wind came next, singularly enough from another direction, as if to restore the equipoise of the atmosphere. But the tornado had gone on inland, where there were trees to uproot, and houses to destroy, and much finer entertainment generally.

As soon as they could speak, "Where are the two out in the sail-boat?" asked the Sister.

"God knows!" answered Melvyna. "The last time I noticed their sail they were about a mile outside of the reef."

"I will go and see."

"Go and see! Are you crazy? You can never get through that water."

"The saints would help me, I think," said the little Sister.

She had risen, and now stood regarding the watery waste with the usual timid look in her gentle eyes. Then she stepped forward with her uncertain tread, and before the woman by her side comprehended her purpose she was gone, ankle-deep in the tide, knee-deep, and finally wading across the sand up to her waist in water toward the lighthouse. The great wave was no deeper, however, even there. She waded to the door of the tower, opened it with difficulty, climbed the stairway, and gained the light-room, where the glass of the windows was all shattered, and the little chamber half full of the dead bodies of birds, swept along by the whirlwind and dashed against the tower, none of them falling to the ground or losing an inch of their level in the air as they sped onward, until they struck against some high object, which broke their mad and awful journey. Holding on by the shattered casement, Sister St. Luke gazed out to sea. The wind was blowing fiercely, and the waves were lashed to fury. The sky was inky black. The reef was under water, save one high knob of its backbone, and

to that two dark objects were clinging. Farther down she saw
the wreck of the boat driving before the gale. Pedro was over
in the village; the tide was coming in over the high sea, and
night was approaching. She walked quickly down the rough
stone stairs, stepped into the water again, and waded across
where the paroquet boat had been driven against the wall of
the house, bailed it out with one of Melvyna's pans, and then,
climbing in from the window of the sitting-room, she hoisted
the sail, and in a moment was out on the dark sea.

Melvyna had ascended to the top of the ridge, and when
the sail came into view beyond the house she fell down on
her knees and began to pray aloud: "O Lord, save her; save
the lamb! She don't know what's she is doing, Lord. She's as
simple as a baby. Oh, save her, out on that roaring sea! Good
Lord, good Lord, deliver her!" Fragments of prayers she had
heard in her prayer-meeting days came confusedly back into
her mind, and she repeated them all again and again, wringing
her hands as she saw the little craft tilt far over under its all too
large sail, so that several times, in the hollows of the waves, she
thought it was gone. The wind was blowing hard but steadily,
and in a direction that carried the boat straight toward the reef;
no tacks were necessary, no change of course; the black-robed
little figure simply held the sail-rope, and the paroquet drove
on. The two clinging to the rock, bruised, exhausted, with the
waves rising and falling around them, did not see the boat until
it was close upon them.

"By the great heavens!" said Keith.

His face was pallid and rigid, and there was a ghastly cut
across his forehead, the work of the sharp-edged rock. The
next moment he was on board, brought the boat round just in
time, and helped in Carrington, whose right arm was injured.

"You have saved our lives, señora," he said abruptly.

"By Jove, yes," said Carrington. "We could not have stood
it long, and night was coming." Then they gave all their attention to the hazardous start.

Sister St. Luke remained unconscious of the fact that she
had done anything remarkable. Her black gown was spoiled,
which was a pity, and she knew of a balm which was easily com-
pounded and which would heal their bruises. Did they think

Melvyna had come back to the house yet? And did they know that all her dishes were broken—yes, even the cups with the red flowers on the border? Then she grew timorous again, and hid her face from the sight of the waves.

Keith said not a word, but sailed the boat, and it was a wild and dangerous voyage they made, tacking up and down in the gayly painted little craft, that seemed like a toy on that angry water. Once Carrington took the little Sister's hand in his, and pressed his lips fervently upon it. She had never had her hand kissed before, and looked at him, then at the place, with a vague surprise, which soon faded, however, into the old fear of the wind. It was night when at last they reached the lighthouse; but during the last two tacks they had a light from the window to guide them; and when nearly in they saw the lantern shining out from the shattered windows of the tower in a fitful, surprised sort of way, for Melvyna had returned, and, with the true spirit of a Yankee, had immediately gone to work at the ruins.

The only sign of emotion she gave was to Keith. "I saw it all," she said. "That child went right out after you, in that terrible wind, as natural and as quiet as if she was only going across the room. And she so timid a fly could frighten her! Mark my words, Mr. Keith, the good Lord helped her to do it! And I'll go to that new mission chapel over in the town every Sunday after this, as sure's my name is Sawyer!" She ceased abruptly, and, going into her kitchen, slammed the door behind her. Emotion with Melvyna took the form of roughness.

Sister St. Luke went joyfully back to her convent the next day, for Pedro, when he returned, brought the letter, written, as Keith had directed, in the style of an affectionate invitation. The little nun wept for happiness when she read it. "You see how they love me—love me as I love them," she repeated with innocent triumph again and again.

"It is all we can do," said Keith. "She could not be happy anywhere else, and with the money behind her she will not be neglected. Besides, I really believe they do love her. The sending her up here was probably the result of some outside dictation."

Carrington, however, was dissatisfied. "A pretty return

we make for our saved lives!" he said. "I hate ingratitude."
For Carrington was half disposed now to fall in love with his
preserver.

But Keith stood firm.

"Adios," said the little Sister, as Pedro's boat received her.
Her face had lighted so with joy and glad anticipation that they
hardly knew her. "I wish you could to the convent go with
me," she said earnestly to the two young men. "I am sure you
would like it." Then, as the boat turned the point, "I am sure
you would like it," she called back, crossing her hands on her
breast. "It is very heavenly there—very heavenly."

That was the last they saw of her.

Carrington sent down the next winter from New York a
large silver crucifix, superbly embossed and ornamented. It
was placed on the high altar of the convent, and much admired and reverenced by all the nuns. Sister St. Luke admired
it too. She spoke of the island occasionally, but she did not tell
the story of the rescue. She never thought of it. Therefore, in
the matter of the crucifix, the belief was that a special grace
had touched the young man's heart. And prayers were ordered
for him. Sister St. Luke tended her doves, and at the hour of
meditation paced to and fro between the lime-tree and the
bush of white roses. When she was thirty years old her cup was
full, for then she was permitted to take lessons and play a little
upon the old organ.

Melvyna went every Sunday to the bare, struggling little
Presbyterian mission over in the town, and she remains to this
day a Sawyer.

But Keith remembered. He bares his head silently in reverence to all womanhood, and curbs his cynicism as best he can,
for the sake of the little Sister—the sweet little Sister St. Luke.

# Miss Elisabetha

In yonder homestead, wreathed with bounteous vines,
A lonely woman dwells, whose wandering feet
Pause oft amid one chamber's calm retreat,
Where an old mirror from its quaint frame shines.
And here, soft wrought in memory's vague designs,
Dim semblances her wistful gaze will greet
Of lost ones that inthrall phantasmally sweet
The mirror's luminous quietude enshrines.

But unto her these dubious forms that pass
With shadowy majesty or dreamy grace,
Wear nothing of ghostliness in mien or guise.
The only ghost that haunts this glimmering glass
Carries the sad reality in its face
Of her own haggard cheeks and desolate eyes!

EDGAR FAWCETT

OVERLOOKING the tide-water river stands an old house, gleaming white in the soft moonlight; the fragrance of tropic flowers floats out to sea on the land-breeze, coming at sunset over the pine-barrens to take the place of the ocean winds that have blown all day long, bringing in the salt freshness to do battle with the hot shafts of the sun and conquer them. The side of the house toward the river shows stone arches, doorless, opening into a hall; beyond is a large room, lighted by two candles placed on an old-fashioned piano; and full in their yellow radiance sits Miss Elisabetha, playing, with clear, measured touch, an old-time minuet. The light falls upon her face, with its sharp, high-curved features, pale-blue eyes, and the three thin curls of blonde hair on each side. She is not young, our Elisabetha: the tall, spare form, stiffly erect, the little wisp of hair behind ceremoniously braided and adorned with a high comb, the long, thin hands, with the tell-tale wrist-bones prominent as she plays, and the fine network of wrinkles over her pellucid, colorless cheeks, tell this. But the boy who listens sees it not; to him she is a St. Cecilia, and the gates of heaven open as she plays. He leans his head against the piano, and his thoughts are lost in melody; they do not take the form of words, but sway to and fro with the swell and the ebb of the music. If you should ask him, he could not express what he feels, for his is no analytical mind; attempt to explain it to him, and very likely he would fall asleep before your eyes. Miss Elisabetha plays well—in a prim, old-fashioned way, but yet well; the ancient piano has lost its strength, but its tones are still sweet, and the mistress humors its failings. She tunes it herself, protects its strings from the sea-damps, dusts it carefully, and has embroidered for it a cover in cross-stitch, yellow tulips growing in straight rows out of a blue ground—an heirloom pattern brought from Holland. Yet entire happiness can not be ours in this world, and Miss Elisabetha sometimes catches herself thinking how delightful it would be to use E flat once more; but the piano's E flat is hopelessly gone.

"Is not that enough for this evening, Theodore?" said Miss Elisabetha, closing the manuscript music-book, whose delicate little pen-and-ink notes were fading away with age.

"Oh, no, dear aunt; sing for me, please, 'The Proud Ladye.'"

And so the piano sounded forth again in a prim melody, and the thin voice began the ballad of the knight, who, scorned by his lady-love, went to the wars with her veil bound on his heart; he dies on the field, but a dove bears back the veil to the Proud Ladye, who straightway falls "a-weeping and a-weeping till she weeps her life away." The boy who listens is a slender stripling, with brown eyes, and a mass of brown curls tossed back from a broad, low forehead; he has the outlines of a Greek, and a dark, silken fringe just borders his boyish mouth. He is dressed in a simple suit of dark-blue cotton jacket and trousers, the broad white collar turned down, revealing his round young throat; on his slender feet he wears snowy stockings, knitted by Miss Elisabetha's own hands, and over them a low slipper of untanned leather. His brown hands are clasped over one knee, the taper fingers and almond-shaped nails betraying the artistic temperament—a sign which is confirmed by the unusually long, slender line of the eyebrows, curving down almost to the cheeks.

"A-weeping and a-weeping till she weeps her life away," sang Miss Elisabetha, her voice in soft *diminuendo* to express the

mournful end of the Proud Ladye. Then, closing the piano
carefully, and adjusting the tulip-bordered cover, she extinguished the candles, and the two went out under the open
arches, where chairs stood ready for them nightly. The tide-
water river—the Warra—flowed by, the moon-path shining
goldenly across it; up in the north palmettos stood in little
groups alongshore, with the single feathery pine-trees of the
barrens coming down to meet them; in the south shone the
long lagoon, with its low islands, while opposite lay the slender
point of the mainland, fifteen miles in length, the Warra on one
side, and on the other the ocean; its white sand-ridges gleamed
in the moonlight, and the two could hear the sound of the
waves on its outer beach.

"It is so beautiful," said the boy, his dreamy eyes following
the silver line of the lagoon.

"Yes," replied Miss Elisabetha, "but we have no time to
waste, Theodore. Bring your guitar and let me hear you sing
that *romanza* again; remember the pauses—three beats to the
measure."

Then sweetly sounded forth the soft tenor voice, singing
an old French *romanza*, full of little quavers, and falls, and
turns, which the boy involuntarily slurred into something like
naturalness, or gave *staccato* as the mocking-bird throws out
his shower of short, round notes. But Miss Elisabetha allowed
no such license: had she not learned that very *romanza* from
Monsieur Vocard himself forty years before? and had he not
carefully taught her every one of those little turns and quavers?
Taking the guitar from Theodore's hand, she executed all the
flourishes slowly and precisely, making him follow her, note
for note. Then he must sing it all over again while she beat the
time with her long, slender foot, incased in a black-silk slipper
of her own making. The ladies of the Daarg family always wore
slippers—the heavy-sounding modern boot they considered a
structure suitable only for persons of plebeian origin. A lady
should not even step perceptibly; she should glide.

"Miss 'Lisabeet, de toas' is ready. Bress de chile, how sweet
he sings to-night! Mos' like de mock-bird's self, Mass' Doro."

So spoke old Viny, the one servant of the house, a broad-
shouldered, jet-black, comfortable creature, with her gray
wool peeping from beneath a gay turban. She had belonged

to Doro's Spanish mother, but, when Miss Elisabetha came South to take the house and care for the orphan-boy, she had purchased the old woman, and set her free immediately.

"It don't make naw difference as I can see, Miss 'Lisabeet," said Viny, when the new mistress carefully explained to her that she was a free agent from that time forth. "'Pears harnsome in you to do it, but it arn't likely I'll leabe my chile, my Doro-boy, long as I lib—is it, now? When I die, he'll have ole Viny burred nice, wid de priests, an' de candles, an' de singing, an' all."

"Replace your guitar, Theodore," said Miss Elisabetha, rising, "and then walk to and fro between here and the gate ten times. Walk briskly, and keep your mouth shut; after singing you should always guard against the damps."

The boy obeyed in his dreamy way, pacing down the white path, made hard with pounded oyster-shells, to the high stone wall. The old iron-clamped gate, which once hung between the two pomegranate-topped pillars, was gone; for years it had leaned tottering half across the entrance-way, threatening to brain every comer, but Miss Elisabetha had ordered its removal in the twinkling of her Northern eye, and in its place now hung a neat, incongruous little wicket, whose latch was a standing bone of contention between the mistress and the entire colored population of the small village.

"Go back and latch the gate," was her constantly repeated order; "the cows might enter and injure the garden."

"But th' arn't no cows, Miss 'Lisabeet."

"There should be, then," the ancient maiden would reply, severely. "Grass would grow with a little care and labor; look at our pasture. You are much too indolent, good people!"

Theodore stood leaning over the little gate, his eyes fixed on the white sand-hills across the Warra; he was listening to the waves on the outer beach.

"Theodore, Theodore!" called Miss Elisabetha's voice, "do not stand, but pace to and fro; and be sure and keep your mouth closed."

Mechanically the boy obeyed, but his thoughts were following the sound of the water. Following a sound? Yes. Sounds were to him a language, and he held converse with the surf, the winds, the rustling marsh-grass, and the sighing pines of the barrens. The tale of the steps completed, he reentered the house, and, following the light, went into a long, narrow room, one of three which, built out behind the main body of the house, formed with its back-wall a square, surrounding a little courtyard, in whose center stood the well, a ruined fountain, rose- and myrtle-bushes, and two ancient fig-trees, dwarfed and gnarled. Miss Elisabetha was standing at the head of the table; before her was a plate containing three small slices of dry toast, crisp and brown, and a decanter of orange-wine, made by her own hands. One slice of the toast was for herself, two were for the boy, who was still supposed to be growing; a Northerner would have said that he was over twenty, but Spanish blood hastens life, and Teodoro in years was actually not yet eighteen. In mind he was still younger, thanks to Miss Elisabetha's care and strict control. It had never even occurred to him that he need not so absolutely obey her; and, to tell the truth, neither had it occurred to her. Doro ate his simple supper standing—the Daarg family never sat down gluttonously to supper, but browsed lightly on some delicate fragments, moving about and chatting meanwhile as though half forgetting they were eating at all. Then Miss Elisabetha refilled his little glass, watched him drink the clear amber liquid to the last drop, and bade him good night in her even voice. He turned at the door and made her a formal bow, not without grace; she had carefully taught him this salutation, and required it of him every night.

"I wish you a blessed rest, Theodore," she said, courtesying in reply; "do not keep the light burning."

Half an hour later, when the ancient maiden glided out of her chamber, clad in a long frilled wrapper, the three curls in papers on each side of her head, she saw no gleam from under the low door of the little room across the hall; she listened, but there was no sound, and, satisfied, she retired to her high couch and closed the gayly flowered curtains around her. But, out on the small balcony which hung like a cage from his eastern window, Doro stood, leaning over the iron railing and listening, listening to the far sound of the sea.

Such had been the life down in the old house for sixteen long, winterless years, the only changes being more difficult music and more toast, longer lessons in French, longer legs to the little blue trousers, increased attention to sea-baths and deportment, and always and ever a careful saving of every copper penny and battered shilling. What became of these coins old Viny did not know; she only knew how patiently they were collected, and how scrupulously saved. Miss Elisabetha attended to the orange-grove in person; not one orange was lost, and the annual waste of the other proprietors, an ancient and matter-of-course waste, handed down from father to son, represented in her purse not a few silver pieces. Pedro, the Minorcan, who brought her fish and sea-food, she had drilled from boyhood in his own art by sheer force of will, paying him by the day, and sending him into the town to sell from door to door all she did not need herself, to the very last clam. The lazy housewives soon grew into the habit of expecting Pedro and his basket, and stood in their doorways chatting in the sun and waiting for him, while the husbands let their black dugouts lie idle, and lounged on the sea-wall, smoking and discussing the last alligator they had shot, or the last ship, a coasting-schooner out of water, which had sailed up their crooked harbor six months before. Miss Elisabetha had learned also to braid palmetto, and her long fingers, once accustomed to the work, accomplished as much in a week as Zanita Perez and both her apprentices accomplished in two; she brought to the task also original ideas, original at least in Beata, where the rude hats and baskets were fac-similes of those braided there two hundred years before by the Spanish women, who had learned the art from the Indians. Thus Miss Elisabetha's wares found ready sale at increased prices, little enough to Northern ideas—sixpence for a hat—one shilling for a basket; but all down the coast, and inland toward the great river, there was a demand for her work, and the lines hung in the garden were almost constantly covered with the drying palmetto. Then she taught music. To whom, do you ask? To the black-eyed daughters of the richer townspeople, and to one or two demoiselles belonging to Spanish families down the coast, sent up to Beata to be educated by the nuns. The good Sisters did their best, but they knew little, poor things, and were glad to call in Miss Elisabetha with her trills and quavers; so the wiry organ in the little cathedral sounded out the ballads and *romanzas* of Monsieur Vocard, and the demoiselles learned to sing them in their broken French, no doubt greatly to the satisfaction of the golden-skinned old fathers and mothers on the plantations down the coast. The *padre* in charge of the parish had often importuned Miss Elisabetha to play this organ on Sundays, as the decorous celebration of high-mass suffered sadly, not to say ludicrously, from the blunders of poor Sister Paula. But Miss Elisabetha briefly refused; she must draw a line somewhere, and a pagan ceremonial she could not countenance. The Daarg family, while abhorring greatly the Puritanism of the New England colonies, had yet held themselves equally aloof from the image-worship of Rome; and they had always considered it one of the inscrutable mysteries of Providence that the French nation, so skilled in polite attitude, so versed in the singing of *romanzas*, should yet have been allowed to remain so long in ignorance of the correct religious mean.

The old house was managed with the nicest care. Its thick coquina-walls remained solid still, and the weak spots in the roof were mended with a thatch of palmetto and tar, applied monthly under the mistress's superintendence by Viny, who never ceased to regard the performance as a wonder of art, accustomed as she was to the Beata fashion of letting roofs leak when they wanted to, the family never interfering, but encamping on the far side of the flow with calm undisturbed. The few pieces of furniture were dusted and rubbed daily, and the kitchen department was under martial law; the three had enough to eat—indeed, an abundance—oysters, fish, and clams, sweet potatoes from the garden, and various Northern vegetables forced to grow under the vigilant nursing they received, but hating it, and coming up as spindling as they could. The one precious cow gave them milk and butter, the well-conducted hens gave them eggs; flour and meal, coffee and tea, hauled across the barrens from the great river, were paid for in palmetto-work. Yes, Miss Elisabetha's household, in fact, lived well, better perhaps than any in Beata; but so measured were her quantities, so exact her reckonings, so long her look ahead, that sometimes, when she was away, old Viny felt a sudden wild desire to toss up fritters in the middle of the afternoon, to throw away yesterday's tea-leaves, to hurl the soured milk into the road, or even to eat oranges without counting them, according to the fashions of the easy old days when Doro's Spanish grandmother held the reins, and everything

went to ruin comfortably. Every morning after breakfast Miss
Elisabetha went the rounds through the house and garden;
then English and French with Doro for two hours; next a sea-
bath for him, and sailing or walking as he pleased, when the
sun was not too hot. Luncheon at noon, followed by a *siesta*;
then came a music-lesson, long and charming to both; and,
after that, he had his choice from among her few books. Dinner at five, a stroll along the beach, music in the evenings—at
first the piano in the parlor, then the guitar under the arches;
last of all, the light supper, and good-night. Such was Doro's
day. But Miss Elisabetha, meanwhile, had a hundred other duties which she never neglected, in spite of her attention to his
welfare—first the boy, then his money, for it was earned and
destined for him. Thus the years had passed, without change,
without event, without misfortune; the orange-trees had not
failed, the palmetto-work had not waned, and the little store
of money grew apace. Doro, fully employed, indulged by
Viny, amused with his dogs, his parrot, his mocking-birds, and
young owls, all the variety of pets the tropical land afforded,
even to young alligators clandestinely kept in a sunken barrel up the marsh, knew no *ennui*. But, most of all, the music
filled his life, rounding out every empty moment, and making
an undercurrent, as it were, to all other occupations; so that
the French waltzed through his brain, the English went to
marches, the sailing made for itself *gondelieds*, and even his
plunges in the Warra were like crashes of fairy octaves, with
*arpeggios* of pearly notes in showers coming after.

These were the *ante-bellum* days, before the war had opened
the Southern country to winter visitors from the North; invalids
a few, tourists a few, came and went, but the great tide, which
now sweeps annually down the Atlantic coast to Florida, was
then unknown. Beata, lying by itself far down the peninsula, no
more looked for winter visitors than it looked for angels; but
one day an angel arrived unawares, and Doro saw her.

Too simple-hearted to conceal, excited, longing for sympathy, he poured out his story to Miss Elisabetha, who sat copying from her music-book a certain ballad for the Demoiselle
Xantez.

"It was over on the north beach, aunt, and I heard the music
and hastened thither. She was sitting on a tiger-skin thrown

down on the white sand; purple velvet flowed around her, and above, from embroideries like cream, rose her flower-face set on a throat so white, where gleamed a star of brilliancy; her hair was like gold—yellow gold—and it hung in curls over her shoulders, a mass of radiance; her eyes were blue as the deepest sky-color; and oh! so white her skin, I could scarcely believe her mortal. She was playing on a guitar, with her little hands so white, so soft, and singing—aunt, it was like what I have dreamed."

The boy stopped and covered his face with his hands. Miss Elisabetha had paused, pen in hand. What was this new talk of tiger-skins and golden hair? No one could sing in Beata save herself alone; the boy was dreaming!

"Theodore," she said, "fancy is permitted to us under certain restrictions, but no well-regulated mind will make to itself realities of fancies. I am sorry to be obliged to say it, but the romances must be immediately removed from the shelf."

These romances, three in number, selected and sanctioned by the governess of the Misses Daarg forty years before, still stood in Miss Elisabetha's mind as exemplars of the wildest flights of fancy.

"But this is not fancy, dear aunt," said Doro eagerly, his brown eyes velvet with moisture, and his brown cheeks flushed. "I saw it all this afternoon over on the beach; I could show you the very spot where the tiger-skin lay, and the print of her foot, which had a little shoe so odd—like this," and rapidly he drew the outline of a walking-boot in the extreme of the Paris fashion.

Miss Elisabetha put on her glasses.

"Heels," she said slowly; "I have heard of them."

"There is nothing in all the world like her," pursued the excited boy, "for her hair is of pure gold, not like the people here; and her eyes are so sweet, and her forehead so white! I never knew such people lived—why have you not told me all these years?"

"She is a blonde," replied Miss Elisabetha primly. "I, too, am a blonde, Theodore."

"But not like this, aunt. My lovely lady is like a rose."

"A subdued monotone of coloring has ever been a characteristic of our family, Theodore. But I do not quite understand your story. Who is this person, and was she alone on the beach?"

"There were others, but I did not notice them; I only looked at her."

"And she sang?"

"O aunt, so heavenly sweet—so strange, so new her song, that I was carried away up into the blue sky as if on strong wings—I seemed to float in melody. But I can not talk of it; it takes my breath away, even in thought!"

Miss Elisabetha sat perplexed.

"Was it one of our *romanzas*, Theodore, or a ballad?" she said, running over the list in her mind.

"It was something I never heard before," replied Doro, in a low voice; "it was not like anything else—not even the mocking-bird, for, though it went on and on, the same strain floated back into it again and again; and the mocking-bird, you know, has a light and fickle soul. Aunt, I can not tell you what it was like, but it seemed to tell me a new story of a new world."

"How many beats had it to the measure?" asked Miss Elisabetha, after a pause.

"I do not know," replied the boy dreamily.

"You do not know! All music is written in some set time, Theodore. At least, you can tell me about the words. Were they French?"

"No."

"Nor English?"

"No."

"What then?"

"I know not; angel-words, perhaps."

"Did she speak to you?"

"Yes," replied Doro, clasping his hands fervently. "She asked me if I liked the song, and I said, 'Lady, it is of the angels.' Then she smiled, and asked my name, and I told her, 'Doro'—"

"You should have said, 'Theodore,'" interrupted Miss Elisabetha; "do I not always call you so?"

"And she said it was a lovely name; and could I sing? I took her guitar, and sang to her—"

"And she praised your method, I doubt not?"

"She said, 'Oh, what a lovely voice!' and she touched my

hair with her little hands, and I—I thought I should die, aunt, but I only fell at her feet."

"And where—where is this person now?" said the perplexed maiden, catching at something definite.

"She has gone—gone! I stood and watched the little flag on the mast until I could see it no more. She has gone! Pity me, aunt, dear aunt. What shall I do? How shall I live?"

The boy broke into sobs, and would say no more. Miss Elisabetha was strangely stirred; here was a case beyond her rules; what should she do? Having no precedent to guide her, she fell back into her old beliefs gained from studies of the Daarg family, as developed in boys. Doro was excused from lessons, and the hours were made pleasant to him. She spent many a morning reading aloud to him; and old Viny stood amazed at the variety and extravagance of the dishes ordered for him.

"What! chickens ebery day, Miss 'Lisabeet? 'Pears like Mass' Doro hab eberyting now!"

"Theodore is ill, Lavinia," replied the mistress; and she really thought so.

Music, however, there was none; the old charmed after-noons and evenings were silent.

"I can not bear it," the boy had said, with trembling lips.

But one evening he did not return: the dinner waited for him in vain; the orange after-glow faded away over the pine-barrens; and in the pale green of the evening sky arose the star of the twilight; still he came not.

Miss Elisabetha could eat nothing.

"Keep up the fire, Lavinia," she said, rising from the table at last.

"Keep up de fire, Miss 'Lisabeet! Till when?"

"Till Theodore comes!" replied the mistress shortly.

"De worl' mus' be coming to de end," soliloquized the old black woman, carrying out the dishes; "sticks of wood no account!"

Late in the evening a light footstep sounded over the white path, and the strained, watching eyes under the stone arches saw at last the face of the missing one.

"O aunt, I have seen her—I have seen her! I thought her gone for ever. O aunt—dear, dear aunt, she has sung for me again!" said the boy, flinging himself down on the stones, and laying his flushed face on her knee. "This time it was over by the old lighthouse, aunt. I was sailing up and down in the very worst breakers I could find, half hoping they would swamp the boat, for I thought perhaps I could forget her down there under the water—when I saw figures moving over on the island-beach. Something in the outlines of one made me tremble; and I sailed over like the wind, the little boat tilted on its side within a hair's-breadth of the water, cutting it like a knife as it flew. It was she, aunt, and she smiled! 'What, my young Southern nightingale,' she said, 'is it you?' And she gave me her hand —her soft little hand."

The thin fingers, hardened by much braiding of palmetto, withdrew themselves instinctively from the boy's dark curls. He did not notice it, but rushed on with his story unheeding.

"She let me walk with her, aunt, and hold her parasol, decked with lace, and she took off her hat and hung it on my arm, and it had a long, curling plume. She gave me sweet things—oh, so delicious! See, I kept some," said Doro, bringing out a little package of bonbons. "Some are of sugar, you see, and some have nuts in them; those are chocolate. Are they not beautiful?"

"Candies, I think," said Miss Elisabetha, touching them doubtfully with the end of her quill.

"And she sang for me, aunt, the same angel's music; and then, when I was afar in heaven, she brought me back with a song about three fishermen who sailed out into the west; and I wept to hear her, for her voice then was like the sea when it feels cruel. She saw the tears, and, bidding me sit by her side, she struck a few chords on her guitar and sang to me of a miller's daughter who grew so dear, so dear. Do you know it, aunt?"

"A miller's daughter? No; I have no acquaintance with any such person," said Miss Elisabetha, considering.

"Wait, I will sing it to you," said Doro, running to bring his guitar; "she taught it to me herself!"

And then the tenor voice rose in the night air, bearing on the lovely melody the impassioned words of the poet. Doro sang them with all his soul, and the ancient maiden felt her heart disquieted within her—why, she knew not. It seemed as though her boy was drifting away whither she could not follow.

"Is it not beautiful, aunt? I sang it after her line by line until

I knew it all, and then I sang her all my songs; and she said I must come and see her the day after to-morrow, and she would give me her picture and something else. What do you suppose it is, aunt? She would not tell me, but she smiled and gave me her hand for good-by. And now I can live, for I am to see her at Martera's house, beyond the convent, the day after to-morrow, the day after to-morrow—oh, happy day, the day after to-morrow!"

"Come and eat your dinner, Theodore," said Miss Elisabetha, rising. Face to face with a new world, whose possibilities she but dimly understood, and whose language was to her an unknown tongue, she grasped blindly at the old anchors riveted in years of habit; the boy had always been something of an epicure in his fastidious way, and one of his favorite dishes was on the table.

"You may go, Lavinia," she said, as the old slave lingered to see if her darling enjoyed the dainties; she could not bear that even Viny's faithful eyes should notice the change, if change there was.

The boy ate nothing.

"I am not hungry, aunt," he said, "I had so many delicious things over on the beach. I do not know what they were, but they were not like our things at all." And, with a slight gesture of repugnance, he pushed aside his plate.

"You had better go to bed," said Miss Elisabetha, rising. In her perplexity this was the first thing which suggested itself to her; a good night's rest had been known to work wonders; she would say no more till morning. The boy went readily; but he must have taken his guitar with him, for long after Miss Elisabetha had retired to her couch she heard him softly singing again and again the romance of the miller's daughter. Several times she half rose as if to go and stop him; then a confused thought came to her that perhaps his unrest might work itself off in that way, and she sank back, listening meanwhile to the fanciful melody with feelings akin to horror. It seemed to have no regular time, and the harmony was new and strange to her old-fashioned ears. "Truly, it must be the work of a composer gone mad," said the poor old maid, after trying in vain for the fifth time to follow the wild air. There was not one trill or turn in all its length, and the accompaniment, instead of being the decorous one octave in the bass, followed by two or three chords according to the time, seemed to be but a general sweeping over the strings, with long pauses, and unexpected minor harmony introduced, turning the air suddenly upside down, and then back again before one had time to comprehend what was going on. "Heaven help me!" said Miss Elisabetha, as the melody began again for the sixth time, "but I fear I am sinful enough to hate that miller's daughter." And it was very remarkable, to say the least, that a person in her position "was possessed of a jewel to tremble in her ear," she added censoriously, "not even to speak of a necklace." But the comfort was cold, and, before she knew it, slow, troubled tears had dampened her pillow.

Early the next morning she was astir by candle-light, and, going into the detached kitchen, began preparing breakfast with her own hands, adding to the delicacies already ordered certain honey-cakes, an heirloom in the Daarg family. Viny could scarcely believe her eyes when, on coming down to her domain at the usual hour, she found the great fireplace glowing, and the air filled with the fragrance of spices; Christmas alone had heretofore seen these honey-cakes, and to-day was only a common day!

"I do not care for anything, aunt," said Doro, coming listlessly to the table when all was ready. He drank some coffee, broke a piece of bread, and then went back to his guitar; the honey-cakes he did not even notice.

One more effort remained. Going softly into the parlor during the morning, Miss Elisabetha opened the piano, and, playing over the prelude to "The Proud Ladye," began to sing in her very best style, giving the flourishes with elaborate art, scarcely a note without a little step down from the one next higher; these airy descents, like flights of fairy stairs, were considered very high art in the days of Monsieur Vocard. She was in the middle of "a-weeping and a-weeping," when Doro rushed into the room. "O aunt," he cried, "please, please do not sing! Indeed, I can not bear it. We have been all wrong about our music; I can not explain it, but I feel it—I know it. If you could only hear her! Come with me to-morrow and hear her, dear aunt, and then you will understand what I mean."

Left to herself again, Miss Elisabetha felt a great resolve

come to her. She herself would go and see this stranger, and grind her to powder! She murmured these words over several times, and derived much comfort from them.

With firm hands she unlocked the cedar chest which had come with her from the city seventeen years before; but the ladies of the Daarg family had not been wont to change their attire every passing fashion, and the robe she now drew forth was made in the style of full twenty-five years previous—a stiff drab brocade flowered in white, two narrow flounces around the bottom of the scant skirt, cut half low in the neck with a little bertha, the material wanting in the lower part standing out resplendent in the broad leg-of-mutton sleeves, stiffened with buckram. Never had the full daylight of Beata seen this precious robe, and Miss Elisabetha herself considered it for a moment with some misgivings as to its being too fine for such an occasion. But had not Doro spoken of "velvet" and "embroideries"? So, with solemnity, she arrayed herself, adding a certain Canton-crape scarf of a delicate salmon color, and a Leghorn bonnet with crown and cape, which loomed out beyond her face so that the three curls slanted forward over the full ruche to get outside, somewhat like blinders. Thus clad, with her slippers, her bag on her arm, and lace mitts on her hands, Miss Elisabetha surveyed herself in the glass. In the bag were her handkerchief, an ancient smelling-bottle, and a card, yellow indeed, but still a veritable engraved card, with these words upon it:

"Miss ELISABETHA DAARG,
DAARG'S BAY."

The survey was satisfactory. "Certainly I look the gentlewoman," she thought, with calm pride, "and this person, whoever she is, can not fail to at once recognize me as such. It has never been our custom to visit indiscriminately; but in this case I do it for the boy's sake." So she sallied forth, going out by a side-door to escape observation, and walked toward the town, revolving in her mind the words she should use when face to face with the person. "I shall request her—with courtesy, of course—still I shall feel obliged to request her to leave the neighborhood," she thought. "I shall express to her—with kindness, but also with dignity—my opinion of the meretricious music she has taught my boy, and I shall say to her frankly that I really can not permit her to see him again. Coming from me, these words will, of course, have weight, and—"

"Oh, see Miss 'Lisabeet!" sang out a child's voice. "Nita, do but come and see how fine she is!"

Nita came, saw, and followed, as did other children—girls carrying plump babies, olive-skinned boys keeping close together, little blacks of all ages, with go-carts made of turtleshells. It was not so much the splendor—though that was great, too—as it was the fact that Miss Elisabetha wore it. Had they not all known her two cotton gowns as far back as they could remember? Reaching the Martera house at last, her accustomed glide somewhat quickened by the presence of her escort (for, although she had often scolded them over her own gate, it was different now when they assumed the proportions of a body-guard), she gave her card to little Inez, a daughter of the household, and one of her pupils.

"Bear this card to the person you have staying with you, my child, and ask her if she will receive me."

"But there is more than one person, señora," replied Inez, lost in wonder over the brocade.

"The one who sings, then."

"They all sing, Miss 'Lisabeet."

"Well, then, I mean the person who—who wears purple velvet and—and embroideries," said the visitor, bringing out these items reluctantly.

"Ah! you mean the beautiful lady," cried Inez. "I run, I run, señora"; and in a few minutes Miss Elisabetha was ushered up the stairs, and found herself face to face with "the person."

"To whom have I the honor of speaking?" said a languid voice from the sofa.

"Madame, my card—"

"Oh, was that a card? Pray excuse me.—Lucille, my glasses." Then, as a French maid brought the little, gold-rimmed toy, the person scanned the name. "Ma'm'selle Dag?" she said inquiringly.

"Daarg, madame," replied Miss Elisabetha. "If you have resided in New York at all, you are probably familiar with the name"; and majestically she smoothed down the folds of the salmon-colored scarf.

"I have resided in New York, and I am not familiar with the name," said the person, throwing her head back indolently among the cushions.

She wore a long, full robe of sea-green silk, opening over a mist of lace-trimmed skirts, beneath whose filmy borders peeped little feet incased in green-silk slippers, with heels of grotesque height; a cord and tassels confined the robe to her round waist; the hanging sleeves, open to the shoulders, revealed superb white arms; and the mass of golden hair was gathered loosely up behind, with a mere *soupçon* of a cap perched on top, a knot of green ribbon contrasting with the low-down golden ripples over the forehead. Miss Elisabetha surveyed the attitude and the attire with disfavor; in her young days no lady in health wore a wrapper, or lolled on sofas. But the person, who was the pet prima donna of the day, English, with a world-wide experience and glory, knew nothing of such traditions.

"I have called, madame," began the visitor, ignoring the slight with calm dignity (after all, how should "a person" know anything of the name of Daarg?), "on account of my—my ward, Theodore Oesterand."

"Never heard of him," replied the diva. It was her hour for *siesta*, and any infringement of her rules told upon the carefully tended, luxuriant beauty.

"I beg your pardon," said Miss Elisabetha, with increased accentuation of her vowels. "Theodore has had the honor of seeing you twice, and he has also sung for you."

"What! you mean my little bird of the tropics, my Southern nightingale!" exclaimed the singer, raising herself from the cushions.—"Lucille, why have you not placed a chair for this lady?—I assure you, I take the greatest interest in the boy, Miss Dag."

"Daarg," replied Miss Elisabetha; and then, with dignity, she took the chair, and, seating herself, crossed one slipper over the other, in the attitude number one of her youth. Number one had signified "repose," but little repose felt she now; there was something in the attire of this person, something in her yellow hair and white arms, something in the very air of the room, heavy with perfumes, that seemed to hurt and confuse her.

"I have never heard a tenor of more promise, never in my life; and consider how much that implies, ma'm'selle! You probably know who I am?"

"I have not that pleasure."

"*Bien*, I will tell you. I am Kernadi."

Miss Elisabetha bowed, and inhaled salts from her smelling-bottle, her little finger elegantly separated from the others.

"You do not mean to say that you have never heard of Kernadi—Cécile Kernadi?" said the diva, sitting fairly erect now in her astonishment.

"Never," replied the maiden, not without a proud satisfaction in the plain truth of her statement.

"Where have you lived, ma'm'selle?"

"Here, Mistress Kernadi."

The singer gazed at the figure before her in its ancient dress, and gradually a smile broke over her beautiful face.

"Ma'm'selle," she said, dismissing herself and her fame with a wave of her white hand, "you have a treasure in Doro, a voice rare in a century; and, in the name of the world, I ask you for him."

Miss Elisabetha sat speechless; she was never quick with words, and now she was struck dumb.

"I will take him with me when I go in a few days," pursued Kernadi; "and I promise you he shall have the very best instructors. His method now is bad—insufferably bad. The poor boy has had, of course, no opportunities; but he is still young, and can unlearn as well as learn. Give him to me. I will relieve you of all expenses, so sure do I feel that he will do me credit in the end. I will even pass my word that he shall appear with me upon either the London or the Vienna stage before two years are out."

Miss Elisabetha had found her words at last.

"Madame," she said, "do you wish to make an opera-singer of the son of Petrus Oesterand?"

"I wish to make an opera-singer of this pretty Doro; and, if this good Petrus is his father, he will, no doubt, give his consent."

"Woman, he is dead."

"So much the better; he will not interfere with our plans, then," replied the diva, gayly.

Miss Elisabetha rose; her tall form shook perceptibly.

"I have the honor to bid you good day," she said, courtesying formally.

The woman on the sofa sprang to her feet.

"You are offended?" she asked; "and why?"

"That you, a person of no name, of no antecedents, a public singer, should presume to ask for my boy, an Oesterand—should dare to speak of degrading him to your level!"

Kernadi listened to these words in profound astonishment. Princes had bowed at her feet, blood-royal had watched for her smile. Who was this ancient creature, with her scarf and bag? Perhaps, poor thing! she did not comprehend! The diva was not bad-hearted, and so, gently enough, she went over her offer a second time, dwelling upon and explaining its advantages. "That he will succeed, I do not doubt," she said; "but in any case he shall not want."

Miss Elisabetha was still standing.

"Want?" she repeated; "Theodore want? I should think not."

"He shall have the best instructors," pursued Kernadi, all unheeding. To do her justice, she meant all she said. It is ever a fancy of singers to discover singers—provided they sing other *rôles*.

"Madame, I have the honor of instructing him myself."

"Ah, indeed. Very kind of you, I am sure; but—but no doubt you will be glad to give up the task. And he shall see all the great cities of Europe, and hear their music. I am down here merely for a short change—having taken cold in your miserable New York climate; but I have my usual engagements in London, St. Petersburg, Vienna, and Paris, you know."

"No, madame, I do not know," was the stiff reply.

Kernadi opened her fine eyes still wider. It was true, then, and not a pretense. People really lived—white people, too— who knew nothing of her and her movements! She thought, in her vague way, that she really must give something to the missionaries; and then she went back to Doro.

"It will be a great advantage to him to see artist-life abroad—" she began.

"I intend him to see it," replied Miss Elisabetha.

"But he should have the right companions—advisers—"

"*I* shall be with him, madame."

The diva surveyed the figure before her, and amusement shone in her eyes.

"But you will find it fatiguing," she said—"so much journeying, so much change! Nay, ma'm'selle, remain at home in your peaceful quiet, and trust the boy to me." She had sunk back upon her cushions, and, catching a glimpse of her face in the mirror, she added, smiling: "One thing more. You need not fear lest I should trifle with his young heart. I assure you I will not; I shall be to him like a sister."

"You could scarcely be anything else, unless it was an aunt," replied the ancient maiden; "I should judge you fifteen years his senior, madame."

Which was so nearly accurate that the beauty started, and for the first time turned really angry.

"Will you give me the boy?" she said, shortly. "If he were here I might show you how easily— But, *ciel!* you could never understand such things; let it pass. Will you give me the boy —yes or no?"

"No."

There was a silence. The diva lolled back on her cushions, and yawned.

"You must be a very selfish woman—I think the most selfish I have ever known," she said coolly, tapping the floor with her little slippered feet, as if keeping time to a waltz.

"I—selfish?"

"Yes, you—selfish. And, by the by, what right have you to keep the boy at all? Certainly, he resembles you in nothing. What relation does he hold to you?"

"He is—he is my ward," answered Miss Elisabetha, nervously rearranging her scarf. "I bid you, madame, good day."

"Ward!" pursued Kernadi; "that means nothing. Was his mother your sister?"

"Nay; his mother was a Spanish lady," replied the troubled one, who knew not how to evade or lie.

"And the father—you spoke of him—was he a relative?"

A sudden and painful blush dyed the thin old face, creeping up to the very temples.

"Ah," said the singer, with scornful amusement in her voice, "if that is all, I shall take the boy without more ado"; and, lift-ing her glasses, she fixed her eyes full on the poor face before her, as though it was some rare variety of animal.

"You shall not have him; I say you shall not!" cried the el-der woman, rousing to the contest like a tigress defending her young.

"Will you let him choose?" said Kernadi, with her mocking laugh. "See! I dare you to let him choose"; and, springing to her feet, she wheeled her visitor around suddenly, so that they stood side by side before the mirror. It was a cruel deed. Never before had the old eyes realized that their mild blue had faded; that the curls, once so soft, had grown gray and thin; that the figure, once sylph-like, was now but angles; and the throat, once so fair, yellow and sinewed. It came upon her suddenly—the face, the coloring, and the dress; a veil was torn away, and she saw it all. At the same instant gleamed the golden beauty of the other, the folds of her flowing robe, the mists of her laces. It was too much. With ashen face the stricken woman turned away, and sought the door-knob; she could not speak; a sob choked all utterance. Doro would choose.

But Cécile Kernadi rushed forward; her better nature was touched.

"No, no," she said impulsively, "you shall not go so. See! I will promise; you shall keep the boy, and I will let him go. He is all you have, perhaps, and I—I have so much! Do you not believe me? I will go away this very day and leave no trace be-hind. He will pine, but it will pass—a boy's first fancy. I prom-ised him my picture, but you shall take it. There! Now go, go, before I regret what I do. He has such a voice!—but never mind, you shall not be robbed by me. Farewell, poor lady; I, too, may grow old some day. But hear one little word of advice from my lips: The boy has waked up to life; he will never be again the child you have known. Though I go, another will come; take heed!"

That night, in the silence of her own room, Miss Elisabetha prayed a little prayer, and then, with firm hand, burned the bright picture to ashes.

Wild was the grief of the boy; but the fair enchantress was gone. He wept, he pined; but she was gone. He fell ill, and lay feverish upon his narrow bed; but she was none the less gone, and nothing brought her back. Miss Elisabetha tended him with a great patience, and spoke no word. When he raved of golden hair, she never said, "I have seen it"; when he cried, "Her voice, her angel-voice!" she never said, "I have heard it." But one day she dropped these words: "Was she not a false woman, Theodore, who went away not caring, although under promise to see you, and to give you her picture?" And then she walked quietly to her own room, and barred the door, and wept; for the first time in her pure life she had burdened her soul with falsehood—yet would she have done it ten times over to save the boy.

Time and youth work wonders; it is not that youth forgets so soon; but this—time is then so long. Doro recovered, almost in spite of himself, and the days grew calm again. Harder than ever worked Miss Elisabetha, giving herself hardly time to eat or sleep. Doro studied a little listlessly, but he no longer cared for his old amusements. He had freed his pets: the mocking-birds had flown back to the barrens, and the young alligators, who had lived in the sunken barrel, found themselves unexpectedly obliged to earn their own living along the marshes and lagoons. But of music he would have none; the piano stood silent, and his guitar had disappeared.

"It is wearing itself away," thought the old maid; "then he will come back to me." But nightly she counted her secret store, and, angered at its smallness, worked harder and harder, worked until her shoulders ached and her hands grew knotted. "One more year, only one more year," she thought; "then he shall go!" And through all the weary toil these words echoed like a chant—"One more year—only one more!"

Two months passed, and then the spring came to the winterless land—came with the yellow jasmine. "But four months now, and he shall go," said Miss Elisabetha, in her silent musings over the bag of coin. "I have shortened the time by double tasks." Lightly she stepped about the house, counted her orange-buds, and reckoned up the fish. She played the cathedral organ now on Sundays, making inward protest after every note, and sitting rigidly with her back toward the altar in the little high-up gallery during the sermon, as much as to say: "It is only my body which is here. Behold! I do not even bow down in the house of Rimmon." Thus laboring early and late, with heart, and hand, and strength, she saw but little of Doro, save at meals and through his one hour of listless study; but the hidden hope was a comforter, and she worked and trusted on. There was one little gleam of light: he had begun to play again on his guitar, softly, furtively, and as it were in secret. But she heard him, and was cheered.

One evening, toiling home through the white sand after a late music-lesson, laden with a bag of flour which she would not trust Viny to buy, she heard a girl's voice singing. It was a plaintive, monotonous air that she sang, simple as a Gregorian chant; but her voice was a velvet contralto, as full of rich tones as a peach is full of lusciousness. The contralto voice is like the violoncello.

"The voice is not bad," thought Miss Elisabetha, listening critically, "but there is a certain element of the *sauvage* in it. No lady, no person of culture, would permit herself to sing in that way; it must be one of the Minorcans."

Still, in spite of prejudices, the music in her turned her steps toward the voice; her slippers made no sound, and she found it. A young girl, a Minorcan, sat under a bower of jasmine, leaning back against her lover's breast; her dark eyes were fixed on the evening star, and she sang as the bird sings, naturally, unconsciously, for the pure pleasure of singing. She was a pretty child. Miss Elisabetha knew her well—Catalina, one of a thriftless, olive-skinned family down in the town. "Not fourteen, and a lover already," thought the old maid with horror. "Would it be of any use, I wonder, if I spoke to her mother?" Here the lover—the Paul of this Virginia—moved, and the shadows slid off his face; it was Doro!

Alone in her chamber sat Miss Elisabetha. Days had passed, but of no avail. Even now the boy was gone to the tumble-down house in the village where Catalina's little brothers and sisters swarmed out of doors and windows, and the brown, broad mother bade him welcome with a hearty slap on the shoulder. She had tried everything—argument, entreaty, anger, grief—and failed; there remained now only the secret, the secret of years, of much toil and many pains. The money was not yet sufficient for two; so be it. She would stay herself, and work on; but he should go. Before long she would hear his step, perhaps not until late, for those people had no settled hours (here a remembrance of all their ways made her shudder), but come he would in time; this was still his home. At midnight she heard the footfall, and opening the door called gently, "Theodore, Theodore." The youth came, but slowly. Many times had she called him lately, and he was weary of the strife. Had he not told her all—the girl singing as she passed, her voice haunting him, his search for her, and her smile; their meetings in the *chaparral*, where she sang to him by the hour, and then, naturally as the bud opens, their love? It seemed to him an all-sufficient story, and he could not understand the long debates.

"And the golden-haired woman," Miss Elisabetha had said; "she sang to you too, Theodore."

"I had forgotten her, aunt," replied the youth simply.

So he came but slowly. This time, however, the voice was gentle, and there was no anger in the waiting eyes. She told him all as he sat there: the story of his father, who was once her friend, she said with a little quiver in her voice, the death of the young widowed mother, her own coming to this far Southern land, and her long labors for him. Then she drew a picture of the bright future opening before him, and bringing forth the bag showed him its contents, the savings and earnings of seventeen years, tied in packages with the contents noted on their labels. "All is for you, dear child," she said, "for you are still but a child. Take it and go. I had planned to accompany you, but I give that up for the present. I will remain and see to the sale of everything here, and then I will join you—that is, if you wish it, dear. Perhaps you will enjoy traveling alone, and—and I have plenty of friends to whom I can go, and shall be quite content, dear—quite content."

"Where is it that you wish me to go, aunt?" asked Doro coldly. They were going over the same ground, then, after all.

"Abroad, dear—abroad, to all the great cities of the world," said the aunt, faltering a little as she met his eyes. "You are well educated, Theodore; I have taught you myself. You are a gentleman's son, and I have planned for you a life suited to your descent. I have written to my cousins in Amsterdam; they have never seen me, but for the sake of the name they will—O my boy, my darling, tell me that you will go!" she burst forth, breaking into entreaty as she read his face.

But Doro shook off her hands. "Aunt," he said, rising, "why will you distress yourself thus? I shall marry Catalina, and you know it; have I not told you so? Let us speak no more on the subject. As to the money, I care not for it; keep it." And he turned toward the door as if to end the discussion. But Miss Elisabetha followed and threw herself on her knees before him.

"Child!" she cried, "give me, give yourself a little delay; only that, a little delay. Take the money—go; and if at the end of the year your mind is still the same, I will say not one word, no, not one, against it. She is but young, too young to marry. O my boy, for whom I have labored, for whom I have planned, for whom I have prayed, will you too forsake me?"

"Of course not, aunt," replied Doro; "I mean you to live with us always"; and with his strong young arms he half led, half carried her back to her arm-chair. She sat speechless. To live with them always—with *them*! Words surged to her lips in a flood—then, as she met his gaze, surged back to her heart again. There was that in the expression of his face which told her all words were vain; the placid, far-away look, unmoved in spite of her trouble, silenced argument and killed hope. As well attack a creamy summer cloud with axes; as well attempt to dip up the ocean with a cup. She saw it all in a flash, as one sees years of past life in the moment before drowning; and she was drowning, poor soul! Yet Doro saw nothing, felt nothing, save that his aunt was growing into an old woman with foolish fancies, and that he himself was sleepy. And then he fell to thinking of his love, and all her enchanting ways—her little angers and quick repentances, the shoulder turned away in pretended scorn, and the sudden waves of tenderness that swept him into paradise. So he stood dreaming, while tearless, silent Miss Elisabetha sat before her broken hopes. At last Doro, coming back to reality, murmured, "Aunt, you will like her when you know her better, and she will take good care of you."

But the aunt only shuddered.

"Theodore, Theodore!" she cried, "will you break my heart? Shall the son of Petrus Oesterand marry so?"

"I do not know what you mean by 'so,' aunt. All men marry, and why not I? I never knew my father; but, if he were here, I feel sure he would see Catalina with my eyes. Certainly, in all my life, I have never seen a face so fair, or eyes so lustrous."

"Child, you have seen nothing—nothing. But I intended, Heaven knows I intended—"

"It makes no difference now, aunt; do not distress yourself about it."

"Theodore, I have loved you long—your youth has not been an unhappy one; will you, for my sake, go for this one year?" she pleaded, with quivering lips.

The young man shook his head with a half smile.

"Dear aunt," he said gently, "pray say no more. I do not care to see the world; I am satisfied here. As to Catalina, I love her. Is not that enough?" He bent and kissed her cold forehead, and then went away to his happy dreams; and, if he thought of her at all as he lingered in the soft twilight that comes before sleep, it was only to wonder over her distress—a wonder soon indolently comforted by the belief that she would be calm and reasonable in the morning. But, across the hall, a gray old woman sat, her money beside her, and the hands that had earned it idle in her lap. God keep us from such a vigil!

And did she leave him? No; not even when the "him" became "them."

The careless young wife, knowing nothing save how to love, queened it right royally over the old house, and the little brown brothers and sisters ran riot through every room. The piano was soon broken by the ignorant hands that sounded its chords at random; but only Doro played on it now, and nothing pleased him so well as to improvise melodies from the plaintive Minorcan songs the little wife sang in her velvet voice. Years passed; the money was all spent, and the house full —a careless, idle, ignorant, happy brood, asking for nothing, planning not at all, working not at all, but loving each other in their own way, contented to sit in the sunshine, and laugh, and eat, and sing, all the day long. The tall, gaunt figure that came and went among them, laboring ceaselessly, striving always against the current, they regarded with tolerating eyes as a species differing from theirs, but good in its way, especially for work. The children loved the still silent old woman, and generously allowed her to take care of them until she tried to teach them; then away they flew like wild birds of the forest, and not one learned more than the alphabet.

Doro died first, a middle-aged man; gently he passed away without pain, without a care. "You have been very good to me, aunt; my life has been a happy one; I have had nothing to wish for," he murmured, as she bent to catch the last look from his dying eyes.

He was gone; and she bore on the burden he had left to her. I saw her last year—an old, old woman, but working still.

# Old Gardiston

One by one they died—
   Last of all their race;
Nothing left but pride,
   Lace and buckled hose;
Their quietus made,
   On their dwelling-place
Ruthless hands are laid:
   Down the old house goes!

Many a bride has stood
   In yon spacious room;
Here her hand was wooed
   Underneath the rose;
O'er that sill the dead
   Reached the family tomb;
All that were have fled—
   Down the old house goes!

EDMUND CLARENCE STEDMAN

OLD GARDISTON was a manor-house down in the ricelands, six miles from a Southern seaport. It had been called Old Gardiston for sixty or seventy years, which showed that it must have belonged to colonial days, since no age under that of a century could have earned for it that honorable title in a neighborhood where the Declaration of Independence was still considered an event of comparatively modern times. The war was over, and the mistress of the house, Miss Margaretta Gardiston, lay buried in St. Mark's churchyard, near by. The little old church had long been closed; the very road to its low stone doorway was overgrown, and a second forest had grown up around it; but the churchyard was still open to those of the dead who had a right there; and certainly Miss Margaretta had this right, seeing that father, grandfather, and great-grandfather all lay buried there, and their memorial tablets, quaintly emblazoned, formed a principal part of the decorations of the ancient little sanctuary in the wilderness. There was no one left at Old Gardiston now save Cousin Copeland and Gardis Duke, a girl of seventeen years, Miss Margaretta's niece and heir. Poor little Gardis, having been born a girl when she should have been a boy, was christened with the family name—a practice not uncommon in some parts of the South, where English customs of two centuries ago still retain their hold with singular tenacity; but the three syllables were soon abbreviated to two for common use, and the child grew up with the quaint name of Gardis.

They were at breakfast now, the two remaining members of the family, in the marble-floored dining-room. The latticed windows were open; birds were singing outside, and roses blooming; a flood of sunshine lit up every corner of the apartment, showing its massive Chinese vases, its carved ivory ornaments, its hanging lamp of curious shape, and its spindle-legged sideboard, covered with dark-colored plates and platters ornamented with dark-blue dragons going out to walk, and crocodiles circling around fantastically roofed temples as though they were waiting for the worshipers to come out in order to make a meal of them. But, in spite of these accessories, the poor old room was but a forlorn place: the marble flooring was sunken and defaced, portions were broken into very traps for unwary feet, and its ancient enemy, the penetrating dampness, had finally conquered the last resisting mosaic, and climbed the walls, showing in blue and yellow streaks on the old-fashioned moldings. There had been no fire in the tiled fireplace for many years; Miss Margaretta did not approve of fires, and wood was costly: this last reason, however, was never mentioned; and Gardis had grown into a girl of sixteen before she knew the comfort of the sparkling little fires that shine on the hearths morning and evening during the short winters in well-appointed Southern homes. At that time she had spent a few days in the city with some family friends who had come out of the war with less impoverishment than their neighbors. Miss Margaretta did not approve of them exactly; it was understood that all Southerners of "our class" were "impoverished." She did not refuse the cordial invitation *in toto*, but she sent for Gardis sooner than was expected, and set about carefully removing from the girl's mind any wrong ideas that might have made a lodgment there. And Gardis, warmly loving her aunt, and imbued with all the family pride from her

birth, immediately cast from her the bright little comforts she
had met in the city as plebeian, and, going up stairs to the old
drawing-room, dusted the relics enshrined there with a new
reverence for them, glorifying herself in their undoubted antiquity. Fires, indeed! Certainly not.

The breakfast-table was spread with snowy damask, worn
thin almost to gossamer, and fairly embroidered with delicate
darning; the cups and plates belonged to the crocodile set, and
the meager repast was at least daintily served. Cousin Copeland had his egg, and Gardis satisfied her young appetite with
fish caught in the river behind the house by Pompey, and a fair
amount of Dinah's corn-bread. The two old slaves had refused
to leave Gardiston House. They had been trained all their lives
by Miss Margaretta; and now that she was gone, they took
pride in keeping the expenses of the table, as she had kept
them, reduced to as small a sum as possible, knowing better
than poor Gardis herself the pitiful smallness of the family income, derived solely from the rent of an old warehouse in the
city. For the war had not impoverished Gardiston House; it
was impoverished long before. Acre by acre the land had gone,
until nothing was left save a small corn-field and the flower-
garden; piece by piece the silver had vanished, until nothing
was left save three teaspoons, three tablespoons, and four forks.
The old warehouse had brought in little rent during those four
long years, and they had fared hardly at Gardiston. Still, in
their isolated situation away from the main roads, their well-
known poverty a safeguard, they had not so much as heard
a drum or seen a uniform, blue or gray, and this was a rare
and fortunate exemption in those troublous times; and when
the war was at last ended, Miss Margaretta found herself no
poorer than she was before, with this great advantage added,
that now everybody was poor, and, indeed, it was despicable to
be anything else. She bloomed out into a new cheerfulness under this congenial state of things, and even invited one or two
contemporaries still remaining on the old plantations in the
neighborhood to spend several days at Gardiston. Two ancient
dames accepted the invitation, and the state the three kept together in the old drawing-room under the family portraits, the
sweep of their narrow-skirted, old-fashioned silk gowns on the
inlaid staircase when they went down to dinner, the supreme

unconsciousness of the break-neck condition of the marble flooring and the mold-streaked walls, the airy way in which they drank their tea out of the crocodile cups, and told little stories of fifty years before, filled Gardis with admiring respect. She sat, as it were, in the shadow of their greatness, and obediently ate only of those dishes that required a fork, since the three spoons were, of course, in use. During this memorable visit Cousin Copeland was always "engaged in his study" at meal-times; but in the evening he appeared, radiant and smiling, and then the four played whist together on the Chinese table, and the ladies fanned themselves with stately grace, while Cousin Copeland dealt not only the cards, but compliments also—both equally old-fashioned and well preserved.

But within this first year of peace Miss Margaretta had died —an old lady of seventy-five, but bright and strong as a winter apple. Gardis and Cousin Copeland, left alone, moved on in the same way: it was the only way they knew. Cousin Copeland lived only in the past, Gardis in the present; and indeed the future, so anxiously considered always by the busy, restless Northern mind, has never been lifted into the place of supreme importance at the South.

When breakfast was over, Gardis went up stairs into the drawing-room. Cousin Copeland, remarking, in his busy little way, that he had important work awaiting him, retired to his study—a round room in the tower, where, at an old desk with high back full of pigeon-holes, he had been accustomed for years to labor during a portion of the day over family documents a century or two old, recopying them with minute care, adding foot-notes, and references leading back by means of red-ink stars to other documents, and appending elaborately phrased little comments neatly signed in flourishes with his initials and the date, such as "Truly a doughty deed. C. B. G. 1852."—"'Worthy,' quotha? Nay, it seemeth unto my poor comprehension a *marvelous* kindness! C. B. G. 1856."—"May we all profit by this! C. B. G. 1858."

This morning, as usual, Gardis donned her gloves, threw open the heavy wooden shutters, and, while the summer morning sunshine flooded the room, she moved from piece to piece of the old furniture, carefully dusting it all. The room was large and lofty; there was no carpet on the inlaid floor, but a tapestry rug lay under the table in the center of the apartment; everything was spindle-legged, chairs, tables, the old piano, two cabinets, a sofa, a card-table, and two little tabourets embroidered in Scriptural scenes, reduced now to shadows, Joseph and his wicked brethren having faded to the same dull yellow hue, which Gardis used to think was not the discrimination that should have been shown between the just and the unjust. The old cabinets were crowded with curious little Chinese images and vases, and on the high mantel were candelabra with more crocodiles on them, and a large mirror which had so long been veiled in gauze that Gardis had never fairly seen the fat, gilt cherubs that surrounded it. A few inches of wax-candle still remained in the candelabra, but they were never lighted, a tallow substitute on the table serving as a nucleus during the eight months of warm weather when the evenings were spent in the drawing-room. When it was really cold, a fire was kindled in the boudoir—a narrow chamber in the center of the large rambling old mansion, where, with closed doors and curtained windows, the three sat together, Cousin Copeland reading aloud, generally from the "Spectator," often pausing to jot down little notes as they occurred to him in his orderly memorandum-book—"mere outlines of phrases, but sufficiently full to recall the desired train of thought," he observed. The ladies embroidered, Miss Margaretta sitting before the large frame she had used when a girl. They did all the sewing for the household (very little new material, and much repairing of old), but these domestic labors were strictly confined to the privacy of their own apartments; in the drawing-room or boudoir they always embroidered. Gardis remembered this with sadness as she removed the cover from the large frame, and glanced at "Moses in the Bulrushes," which her inexperienced hand could never hope to finish; she was thinking of her aunt, but any one else would have thought of the bulrushes, which were now pink, now saffron, and now blue, after some mediæval system of floss-silk vegetation.

Having gone all around the apartment and dusted everything, Chinese images and all, Gardis opened the old piano and gently played a little tune. Miss Margaretta had been her only teacher, and the young girl's songs were old-fashioned; but the voice was sweet and full, and before she knew it she was filling the house with her melody.

"Little Cupid one day in a myrtle-bough strayed,
And among the sweet blossoms he playfully played,
Plucking many a sweet from the boughs of the tree,
Till he felt that his finger was stung by a bee,"

sang Gardis, and went on blithely through the whole, giving
Mother Venus's advice archly, and adding a shower of improvised trills at the end.

"Bravo!" said a voice from the garden below.

Rushing to the casement, Miss Duke beheld, first with astonishment, then dismay, two officers in the uniform of the
United States army standing at the front door. They bowed
courteously, and one of them said, "Can I see the lady of the
house?"

"I—I am the lady," replied Gardis, confusedly; then drawing
back, with the sudden remembrance that she should not have
shown herself at all, she ran swiftly up to the study for Cousin
Copeland. But Cousin Copeland was not there, and the little
mistress remembered with dismay that old Dinah was out in
the corn-field, and that Pompey had gone fishing. There was
nothing for it, then, but to go down and face the strangers.
Summoning all her self-possession, Miss Duke descended. She
would have preferred to hold parley from the window over the
doorway, like the ladies of olden time, but she feared it would
not be dignified, seeing that the times were no longer olden,
and therefore she went down to the entrance where the two
were awaiting her. "Shall I ask them in?" she thought. "What
would Aunt Margaretta have done?" The Gardiston spirit was
hospitable to the core; but these—these were the Vandals, the
despots, under whose presence the whole fair land was groaning. No; she would not ask them in.

The elder officer, a grave young man of thirty, was spokesman. "Do I address Miss Gardiston?" he said.

"I am Miss Duke. My aunt, Miss Gardiston, is not living,"
replied Gardis.

"Word having been received that the yellow fever has appeared on the coast, we have been ordered to take the troops
a few miles inland and go into camp immediately, Miss Duke.
The grove west of this house, on the bank of the river, having
been selected as camping-ground for a portion of the command, we have called to say that you need feel no alarm at the

proximity of the soldiers; they will be under strict orders not to trespass upon your grounds."

"Thanks," said Gardis mechanically; but she was alarmed; they both saw that.

"I assure you, Miss Duke, that there is not the slightest cause for nervousness," said the younger officer, bowing as he spoke.

"And your servants will not be enticed away, either," added the other.

"We have only two, and they—would not go," replied Gardis, not aggressively, but merely stating her facts.

The glimmer of a smile crossed the face of the younger officer, but the other remained unmoved.

"My name, madam, is Newell—David Newell, captain commanding the company that will be encamped here. I beg you to send me word immediately if anything occurs to disturb your quiet," he said.

Then the two saluted the little mistress with formal courtesy, and departed, walking down the path together with a quick step and soldierly bearing, as though they were on parade.

"Ought I to have asked them in?" thought Gardis; and she went slowly up to the drawing-room again and closed the piano. "I wonder who said 'bravo'? The younger one, I presume." And she presumed correctly.

At lunch (corn-bread and milk) Cousin Copeland's old-young face appeared promptly at the dining-room door. Cousin Copeland, Miss Margaretta's cousin, was a little old bachelor, whose thin dark hair had not turned gray, and whose small bright eyes needed no spectacles; he dressed always in black, with low shoes on his small feet, and his clothes seemed never to wear out, perhaps because his little frame hardly touched them anywhere; the cloth certainly was not strained. Everything he wore was so old-fashioned, however, that he looked like the pictures of the high-collared, solemn little men who, accompanied by ladies all bonnet, are depicted in English Sunday-school books following funeral processions, generally of the good children who die young.

"O Cousin Copeland, where were you this morning when I went up to your study?" began Gardis, full of the event of the morning.

"You may well ask where I was, my child," replied the

bachelor, cutting his toasted corn-bread into squares with mathematical precision. "A most interesting discovery—most interesting. Not being thoroughly satisfied as to the exact identity of the first wife of one of the second cousins of our grandfather, a lady who died young and left no descendants, yet none the less a Gardiston, at least by marriage, the happy idea occurred to me to investigate more fully the contents of the papers in barrel number two on the east side of the central garret—documents that I myself classified in 1849, as collateral merely, not relating to the main line. I assure you, my child, that I have spent there, over that barrel, a most delightful morning—most delightful. I had not realized that there was so much interesting matter in store for me when I shall have finished the main line, which will be, I think, in about a year and a half—a year and a half. And I have good hopes of finding there, too, valuable information respecting this first wife of one of the second cousins of our respected grandfather, a lady whose memory, by some strange neglect, has been suffered to fall into oblivion. I shall be proud to constitute myself the one to rescue it for the benefit of posterity," continued the little man, with chivalrous enthusiasm, as he took up his spoon. (There was one spoon to spare now; Gardis often thought of this with a saddened heart.) Miss Duke had not interrupted her cousin by so much as an impatient glance; trained to regard him with implicit respect, and to listen always to his gentle, busy little stream of talk, she waited until he had finished all he had to say about this "first wife of one of the second cousins of our grandfather" (who, according to the French phrase-books, she could not help thinking, should have inquired immediately for the green shoe of her aunt's brother-in-law's wife) before she told her story. Cousin Copeland shook his head many times during the recital. He had not the bitter feelings of Miss Margaretta concerning the late war; in fact, he had never come down much farther than the Revolution, having merely skirmished a little, as it were, with the war of 1812; but he knew his cousin's opinions, and respected their memory. So he "earnestly hoped" that some other site would be selected for the camp. Upon being told that the blue army-wagons had already arrived, he then "earnestly hoped" that the encampment would not be of long continuance. Cousin Copeland had

hoped a great many things during his life; his capacity for hoping was cheering and unlimited; a hope carefully worded and
delivered seemed to him almost the same thing as reality; he
made you a present of it, and rubbed his little hands cheerfully
afterward, as though now all had been said.

"Do you think I should have asked them in?" said Gardis,
hesitatingly.

"Most certainly, most certainly. Hospitality has ever been
one of our characteristics as a family," said Cousin Copeland,
finishing the last spoonful of milk, which had come out exactly
even with the last little square of corn-bread.

"But I did not ask them."

"Do I hear you aright? You did not ask them, Cousin Gardiston?" said the little bachelor, pausing gravely by the table,
one hand resting on its shining mahogany, the other extended
in the attitude of surprise.

"Yes, Cousin Copeland, you do. But these are officers of the
United States army, and you know Aunt Margaretta's feelings
regarding them."

"True," said Cousin Copeland, dropping his arm; "you
are right; I had forgotten. But it is a very sad state of things,
my dear—very sad. It was not so in the old days at Gardiston
House: then we should have invited them to dinner."

"We could not do that," said Gardis thoughtfully, "on account of forks and spoons; there would not be enough to go
— But I would not invite them anyway," she added, the color
rising in her cheeks, and her eyes flashing. "Are they not our
enemies, and the enemies of our country? Vandals? Despots?"

"Certainly," said Cousin Copeland, escaping from these signs
of feminine disturbance with gentle haste. Long before, he was
accustomed to remark to a bachelor friend that an atmosphere
of repose was best adapted to his constitution and to his work.
He therefore now retired to the first wife of the second cousin
of his grandfather, and speedily forgot all about the camp and
the officers. Not so Gardis. Putting on her straw hat, she went
out into the garden to attend to her flowers and work off her
annoyance. Was it annoyance, or excitement merely? She did
not know. But she did know that the grove was full of men and
tents, and she could see several of the blue-coats fishing in the
river. "Very well," she said to herself hotly; "we shall have no

dinner, then!" But the river was not hers, and so she went on
clipping the roses, and tying back the vines all the long bright
afternoon, until old Dinah came to call her to dinner. As she
went, the bugle sounded from the grove, and she seemed to
be obeying its summons; instantly she sat down on a bench to
wait until its last echo had died away. "I foresee that I shall hate
that bugle," she said to herself.

The blue-coats were encamped in the grove three long
months. Captain Newell and the lieutenant, Roger Saxton,
made no more visits at Gardiston House; but, when they
passed by and saw the little mistress in the garden or at the
window, they saluted her with formal courtesy. And the lieutenant looked back; yes, there was no doubt of that—the
lieutenant certainly looked back, Saxton was a handsome
youth; tall and finely formed, he looked well in his uniform,
and knew it. Captain Newell was not so tall—a gray-eyed, quiet
young man. "Commonplace," said Miss Gardis. The bugle still
gave forth its silvery summons. "It is insupportable," said the
little mistress daily; and daily Cousin Copeland replied, "Certainly." But the bugle sounded on all the same.

One day a deeper wrath came. Miss Duke discovered Dinah
in the act of taking cakes to the camp to sell to the soldiers!

"Well, Miss Gardis, dey pays me well for it, and we's next
to not'ing laid up for de winter," replied the old woman anxiously, as the irate little mistress forbade the sale of so much as
"one kernel of corn."

"Dey don't want de corn, but dey pays well for de cakes,
dearie Miss Gardis. Yer see, yer don't know not'ing about it;
it's only ole Dinah makin' a little money for herself and Pomp,"
pleaded the faithful creature, who would have given her last
crumb for the family, and died content. But Gardis sternly forbade all dealings with the camp from that time forth, and then
she went up to her room and cried like a child. "They knew
it, of course," she thought; "no doubt they have had many a
laugh over the bakery so quietly carried on at Gardiston House.
They are capable of supposing even that *I* sanctioned it." And
with angry tears she fell to planning how she could best inform
them of their mistake, and overwhelm them with her scorn.
She prepared several crushing little speeches, and held them
in reserve for use; but the officers never came to Gardiston

House, and of course she never went to the camp—no, nor so much as looked that way; so there was no good opportunity for delivering them. One night, however, the officers did come to Gardiston House—not only the officers, but all the men; and Miss Duke was very glad to see them.

It happened in this way. The unhappy State had fallen into the hands of double-faced, conscienceless whites, who used the newly enfranchised blacks as tools for their evil purposes. These leaders were sometimes emigrant Northerners, sometimes renegade Southerners, but always rascals. In the present case they had inflamed their ignorant followers to riotous proceedings in the city, and the poor blacks, fancying that the year of jubilee had come, when each man was to have a plantation, naturally began by ejecting the resident owners before the grand division of spoils. At least this was their idea. During the previous year, when the armies were still marching through the land, they had gone out now and then in a motiveless sort of way and burned the fine plantation residences near the city; and now, chance having brought Gardiston to their minds, out they came, inconsequent and reasonless as ever, to burn Gardiston. But they did not know the United States troops were there.

There was a siege of ten minutes, two or three volleys from the soldiers, and then a disorderly retreat; one or two wounded were left on the battle-field (Miss Duke's flower-garden), and the dining-room windows were broken. Beyond this there was no slaughter, and the victors drew off their forces in good order to the camp, leaving the officers to receive the thanks of the household—Cousin Copeland, enveloped in a mammoth dressing-gown that had belonged to his grandfather, and Gardis, looking distractingly pretty in a hastily donned short skirt and a little white sack (she had no dressing-gown), with her brown hair waving over her shoulders, and her cheeks scarlet from excitement. Roger Saxton fell into love on the spot: hitherto he had only hovered, as it were, on the border.

"Had you any idea she was so exquisitely beautiful?" he exclaimed, as they left the old house in the gray light of dawn.

"Miss Duke is not exquisitely beautiful; she is not even beautiful," replied the slow-voiced Newell. "She has the true Southern colorless, or rather cream-colored, complexion, and her features are quite irregular."

"Colorless! I never saw more beautiful coloring in my life than she had to-night," exclaimed Saxton.

"To-night, yes; I grant that. But it took a good-sized riot to bring it to the surface," replied the impassive captain.

A guard was placed around the house at night and pickets sent down the road for some time after this occurrence. Gardis, a prey to conflicting feelings, deserted her usual haunts and shut herself up in her own room, thinking, thinking what she ought to do. In the mean time, beyond a formal note of inquiry delivered daily by a wooden-faced son of Mars, the two officers made no effort toward a further acquaintance; the lieutenant was on fire to attempt it, but the captain held him back. "It is her place to make the advances now," he said. It was; and Gardis knew it.

One morning she emerged from her retreat, and with a decided step sought Cousin Copeland in his study. The little man had been disquieted by the night attack; it had come to him vaguely once or twice since then that perhaps there might be other things to do in the world besides copying family documents; but the nebula—it was not even a definite thought —had faded, and now he was at work again with more ardor than ever.

"Cousin Copeland," said Gardis, appearing at the door of the study, "I have decided at last to yield to your wishes, and —and invite the officers to dinner."

"By all means," said Cousin Copeland, putting down his pen and waving his hands with a hearty little air of acquiescence —"by all means." It was not until long afterward that he remembered he had never expressed any wish upon the subject whatever. But it suited Gardis to imagine that he had done so; so she imagined it.

"We have little to work with," continued the little mistress of the house; "but Dinah is an excellent cook, and—and—O cousin, I do not wish to do it; I can not bear the mere thought of it; but oh! we must, we must." Tears stood in her eyes as she concluded.

"They are going soon," suggested Cousin Copeland, hesitatingly, biting the end of his quill.

"That is the very reason. They are going soon, and we have done nothing to acknowledge their aid, their courtesy—we Gardistons, both of us. They have saved our home, perhaps our lives; and we—we let them go without a word! O cousin, it must not be. Something we must do; *noblesse oblige!* I have thought and thought, and really there is nothing but this: we must invite them to dinner," said Miss Duke, tragically.

"I—I always liked little dinners," said Cousin Copeland, in a gentle, assenting murmur.

Thus it happened that the officers received two formal little notes with the compliments of Miss Gardiston Duke inclosed, and an invitation to dinner. "Hurrah!" cried Saxton. "At last!"

The day appointed was at the end of the next week; Gardis had decided that that would be more ceremonious. "And they are to understand," she said proudly, "that it is a mere dinner of ceremony, and not of friendship."

"Certainly," said Cousin Copeland.

Old Dinah was delighted. Gardis brought out some of the half-year rent money, and a dinner was planned, of few dishes truly, but each would be a marvel of good cooking, as the old family servants of the South used to cook when time was nothing to them. It is not much to them now; but they have heard that it ought to be, and that troubles the perfection of their pie-crust. There was a little wine left in the wine-room—a queer little recess like a secret chamber; and there was always the crocodile china and the few pieces of cut glass. The four forks would be enough, and Gardis would take no jelly, so that the spoons would serve also; in fact, the dinner was planned to accommodate the silver. So far, so good. But now as to dress; here the poor little mistress was sadly pinched. She knew this; but she hoped to make use of a certain well-worn changeable silk that had belonged to Miss Margaretta, in hue a dull green and purple. But, alas! upon inspection she discovered that the faithful garment had given way at last, after years of patient service, and now there was nothing left but mildew and shreds. The invitation had been formally accepted; the dinner was in course of preparation: what should she do? She had absolutely nothing, poor child, save the two faded old lawns which she wore ordinarily, and the one shabby woolen dress for cooler weather. "If they were anything but what they are," she said to herself, after she had again and again turned over the contents of her three bureau drawers, "I would wear my every-day dress without a moment's thought or trouble. But I will not allow these men, belonging to the despot army of the North, these aliens forced upon us by a strong hand and a hard fate, to smile at the shabby attire of a Southern lady."

She crossed the hall to Miss Margaretta's closed room: she would search every corner; possibly there was something she did not at the moment recall. But, alas! only too well did she know the contents of the closet and the chest of drawers, the chest of drawers and the closet; had she not been famil-iar with every fold and hue from her earliest childhood? Was there nothing else? There was the cedar chamber, a little ce-dar cupboard in the wall, where Miss Margaretta kept several stately old satin bonnets, elaborate structures of a past age. Mechanically Gardis mounted the steps, and opened the lit-tle door half-way up the wall. The bonnets were there, and with them several packages; these she took down and opened. Among various useless relics of finery appeared, at last, one whole dress; narrow-skirted, short, with a scantily fashioned waist, it was still a complete robe of its kind, in color a delicate blue, the material clinging and soft like Canton crape. Folded with the dress were blue kid slippers and a silk belt with a broad buckle. The package bore a label with this inscription, "The gown within belonged to my respected mother, Pam-ela Gardiston," in the handwriting of Miss Margaretta; and Gardis remembered that she had seen the blue skirt once, long ago, in her childhood. But Miss Margaretta allowed no pry-ing, and her niece had been trained to ask permission always before entering her apartment, and to refrain from touching anything, unless asked to do so while there. Now the poverty-stricken little hostess carried the relics carefully across to her own room, and, locking the door, attired herself, and anx-iously surveyed the effect. The old-fashioned gown left her shoulders and arms bare, the broad belt could not lengthen the short waist, and the skirt hardly covered her ankles. "I can wear my old muslin cape, but my arms will have to show, and my feet too," she thought, with nervous distress. The creased blue kid slippers were full of little holes and somewhat mil-dewed, but the girl mended them bravely; she said to herself that she need only walk down to the dining-room and back; and, besides, the rooms would not be brightly lighted. If she had had anything to work with, even so much as one yard of material, she would have made over the old gown; but she had absolutely nothing, and so she determined to overcome her necessities by sheer force of will.

"How do I look, cousin?" she said, appearing at the study-door on the afternoon of the fatal day. She spoke nervously, and yet proudly, as though defying criticism. But Cousin Copeland had no thought of criticism.

"My child," he said, with pleased surprise, "you look charming. I am very glad you have a new gown, dear, very glad."

"Men are all alike," thought Gardis exultingly. "The others will think it is new also."

Cousin Copeland possessed but one suit of clothes; consequently he had not been able to honor the occasion by a change of costume; but he wore a ruffled shirt and a flower in his buttonhole, and his countenance was sedately illumined by the thought of the festal board below. He was not at work, but merely dabbling a little on the outer edges—making flourishes at the ends of the chapters, numbering pages, and so forth. Gardis had gone to the drawing-room; she longed to see herself from head to foot, but, with the exception of the glasses in two old pier-tables, there was no large mirror save the gauze-veiled one in the drawing-room. Should she do it? Eve listened to the tempter, and fell. Likewise Gardis. A scissors, a chair, a snip, and lo! it was done. There she was, a little figure in a quaint blue gown, the thick muslin cape hiding the neck, but the dimpled arms bare almost to the shoulder, since the sleeve was but a narrow puff; the brown hair of this little image was braided around the head like a coronet; the wistful face was colorless and sad; in truth, there seemed to be tears in the brown eyes. "I will not cry," said Gardis, jumping down from her chair, "but I *do* look odd; there is no doubt of that." Then she remembered that she should not have jumped, on account of the slippers, and looked anxiously down; but the kid still held its place over the little feet, and, going to the piano, the young mistress of the manor began playing a gay little love-song, as if to defy her own sadness. Before it was finished, old Pompey, his every-day attire made majestic by a large, stiffly starched collar, announced the guests, and the solemnities began.

Everything moved smoothly, however. Cousin Copeland's conversation was in its most flowing vein, the simple little dinner was well cooked and served, Pompey was statuesque, and the two guests agreeable. They remained at the table some time, according to the old Gardiston custom, and then, the ends of wax-candles having been lighted in the drawing-room, coffee was served there in the crocodile cups, and Miss Duke sang one or two songs. Soon after the officers took leave. Captain Newell bowed as he said farewell, but Roger Saxton, younger and more impulsive, extended his hand. Miss Duke made a stately courtesy, with downcast eyes, as though she had not observed it; but by her heightened color the elder guest suspected the truth, and smiled inwardly at the proud little reservation. "The *hand* of Douglas is his own," he said to himself.

The dreaded dinner was over, and the girl had judged correctly: the two visitors had no suspicion of the antiquity of the blue gown.

"Did you ever see such a sweet little picture, from the pink rose in the hair down to the blue slipper!" said Saxton enthusiastically.

"She looked well," replied Newell; "but as for cordiality—"

"I'll win that yet. I like her all the better for her little ways," said the lieutenant. "I suppose it is only natural that Southern girls should cherish bitterness against us; although, of course, *she* is far too young to have lost a lover in the war—far too young."

"Which is a comfort," said Newell dryly.

"A great comfort, old man. Don't be bearish, now, but just wait a while and see."

"Precisely what I intend to do," said Newell.

In the mean time Gardis, in the privacy of her own room, was making a solemn funeral pyre on the hearth, composed of the blue gown, the slippers, and the pink rose, and watching the flame as it did its work. "So perish also the enemies of my country!" she said to herself. (She did not mean exactly that they should be burned on funeral pyres, but merely consigned them on this, as on all occasions, to a general perdition.) The old dress was but a rag, and the slippers were worthless; but, had they been new and costly, she would have done the same. Had they not been desecrated? Let them die!

It was, of course, proper that the guests should call at Gardiston House within a day or two; and Roger Saxton, ignoring the coldness of his reception, came again and again. He even sought out Cousin Copeland in his study, and won the heart of the old bachelor by listening a whole morning to extracts from the documents. Gardis found that her reserve was of no avail against this bold young soldier, who followed her into all her little retreats, and paid no attention to her stinging little speeches. Emboldened and also angered by what she deemed his callousness, she every day grew more and more open in her tone, until you might have said that she, as a unit, poured out upon his head the whole bitterness of the South. Saxton made no answer until the time came for the camp to break up, the soldiers being ordered back to the city. Then he came to see her one afternoon, and sat for some time in silence; the conversation of the little mistress was the same as usual.

"I forgive this, and all the bitter things you have said to me, Gardis," he remarked abruptly.

"Forgive! And by what right, sir—"

"Only this: I love you, dear." And then he poured out all the tide of his young ardor, and laid his heart and his life at her feet.

But the young girl, drawing her slight figure up to its full height, dismissed him with haughty composure. She no longer spoke angrily, but simply said, "That you, a Northerner and a soldier, should presume to ask for the hand of a Southern lady, shows, sir, that you have not the least comprehension of us or of our country." Then she made him a courtesy and left the room. The transformation was complete; it was no longer the hot-tempered girl flashing out in biting little speeches, but the woman uttering the belief of her life. Saxton rode off into town that same night, dejected and forlorn.

Captain Newell took his leave a day later in a different fashion; he told Miss Duke that he would leave a guard on the premises if she wished it.

"I do not think it will be necessary," answered the lady.

"Nor do I; indeed, I feel sure that there will be no further trouble, for we have placed the whole district under military rule since the last disturbance. But I thought possibly you might feel timid."

"I am not timid, Captain Newell."

The grave captain stroked his mustache to conceal a smile, and then, as he rose to go, he said: "Miss Duke, I wish to say to you one thing. You know nothing of us, of course, but I trust you will accept my word when I say that Mr. Saxton is of good family, that he is well educated, and that he is heir to a fair fortune. What he is personally you have seen for yourself—a frank, kind-hearted, manly young fellow."

"Did you come here to plead his cause?" said the girl scornfully.

"No; I came here to offer you a guard, Miss Duke, for the protection of your property. But at the same time I thought it only my duty to make you aware of the real value of the gift laid at your feet."

"How did you know—" began Gardis.

"Roger tells me everything," replied the officer. "If it were not so, I—" Here he paused; and then, as though he had concluded to say no more, he bowed and took leave.

That night Gardiston House was left to itself in the forest stillness. "I am glad that bugle is silenced for ever," said Gardis.

"And yet it was a silvern sound," said Cousin Copeland.

The rains began, and there was no more walking abroad; the excitement of the summer and the camp gone, in its place came the old cares which had been half forgotten. (Care always waits for a cold or a rainy day.) Could the little household manage to live—live with their meager comforts—until the next payment of rent came in? That was the question.

Bitterly, bitterly poor was the whole Southern country in those dreary days after the war. The second year was worse than the first; for the hopes that had buoyed up the broken fortunes soon disappeared, and nothing was left. There was no one to help Gardis Duke, or the hundreds of other women in like desolate positions. Some of the furniture and ornaments of the old house might have been sold, could they have been properly brought forward in New York City, where there were people with purses to buy such things; but in the South no one wanted Chinese images, and there was nothing of intrinsic value. So the little household lived along, in a spare, pinched way, until, suddenly, final disaster overtook them: the tenant of the warehouse gave up his lease, declaring that the old building was too ruinous for use; and, as no one succeeded him, Gardiston House beheld itself face to face with starvation.

"If we wasn't so old, Pomp and me, Miss Gardis, we could

work for yer," said Dinah, with great tears rolling down her wrinkled cheeks; "but we's just good for not'ing now."

Cousin Copeland left his manuscripts and wandered aimlessly around the garden for a day or two; then the little man rose early one morning and walked into the city, with the hopeful idea of obtaining employment as a clerk. "My handwriting is more than ordinarily ornate, I think," he said to himself, with proud confidence.

Reaching the town at last, he walked past the stores several times and looked timidly within; he thought perhaps some one would see him, and come out. But no one came; and at last he ventured into a clothing-store, through a grove of ticketed coats and suspended trousers. The proprietor of the establishment, a Northern Hebrew whose venture had not paid very well, heard his modest request, and asked what he could do.

"I can write," said Cousin Copeland, with quiet pride; and in answer to a sign he climbed up on a tall stool and proceeded to cover half a sheet of paper in his best style. As he could not for the moment think of anything else, he wrote out several paragraphs from the last family document.

"Richard, the fourth of the name, a descendant on the maternal side from the most respected and valorous family—"

"Oh, we don't care for that kind of writing; it's old-fashioned," said Mr. Ottenheimer, throwing down the paper, and waving the applicant toward the door with his fat hand. "I don't want my books frescoed."

Cousin Copeland retired to the streets again with a new sensation in his heart. Old-fashioned? Was it old-fashioned? And even if so, was it any the less a rarely attained and delicately ornate style of writing? He could not understand it. Weary with the unaccustomed exercise, he sat down at last on the steps of a church—an old structure whose spire bore the marks of bomb-shells sent in from the blockading fleet outside the bar during those months of dreary siege—and thought he would refresh himself with some furtive mouthfuls of the corn-bread hidden in his pocket for lunch.

"Good morning, sir," said a voice, just as he had drawn forth his little parcel and was opening it behind the skirt of his coat. "When did you come in from Gardiston?"

It was Captain Newell. With the rare courtesy which comes

from a kind heart, he asked no questions regarding the fatigue and the dust-powdered clothes of the little bachelor, and took a seat beside him as though a church-step on a city street was a customary place of meeting.

"I was about to—to eat a portion of this corn-bread," said Cousin Copeland, hesitatingly; "will you taste it also?"

The young officer accepted a share of the repast gravely, and then Cousin Copeland told his story. He was a simple soul. Miss Margaretta would have made the soldier believe she had come to town merely for her own lofty amusement or to buy jewels. It ended, however, in the comfortable eating of a good dinner at the hotel, and a cigar in Captain Newell's own room, which was adorned with various personal appliances for comfort that astonished the eyes of the careful little bachelor, and left him in a maze of vague wonderings. Young men lived in that way, then, nowadays? They could do so, and yet not be persons of—of irregular habits?

David Newell persuaded his guest to abandon, for the present, all idea of obtaining employment in the city. "These shopkeepers are not capable of appreciating qualifications such as yours, sir," he said. "Would it not be better to set about obtaining a new tenant for the warehouse?"

Cousin Copeland thought it would; but repairs were needed, and—

"Will you give me the charge of it? I am in the city all the time, and I have acquaintances among the Northerners who are beginning to come down here with a view of engaging in business."

Cousin Copeland gladly relinquished the warehouse, and then, after an hour's rest, he rode gallantly back to Gardiston House on one of the captain's horses; he explained at some length that he had been quite a man of mettle in his youth as regards horse-flesh—"often riding, sir, ten and fifteen miles a day."

"I will go in for a moment, I think," said the young officer, as they arrived at the old gate.

"Most certainly," said Cousin Copeland cordially; "Gardis will be delighted to see you."

"Will she?" said the captain.

Clouds had gathered, a raw wind from the ocean swept over

the land, and fine rain was beginning to fall. The house seemed dark and damp as the two entered it. Gardis listened to Cousin Copeland's detailed little narrative in silence, and made no comments while he was present; but when he left the room for a moment she said abruptly:

"Sir, you will make no repairs, and you will take no steps toward procuring a tenant for our property in the city. I will not allow it."

"And why may I not do it as well as any other person?" said Captain Newell.

"You are not 'any other person,' and you know it," said Gardis, with flushed cheeks. "I do not choose to receive a favor from your hands."

"It is a mere business transaction, Miss Duke."

"It is not. You know you intend to make the repairs yourself," cried the girl passionately.

"And if I do so intend? It will only be advancing the money, and you can pay me interest if you like. The city will certainly regain her old position in time; my venture is a sure one. But I *wish* to assist you, Miss Duke; I do not deny it."

"And I—will not allow it!"

"What will you do, then?"

"God knows," said Gardis. "But I would rather starve than accept assistance from you." Her eyes were full of tears as she spoke, but she held her head proudly erect.

"And from Saxton? He has gone North, but he would be so proud to help you."

"From him least of all."

"Because of his love for you?"

Gardis was silent.

"Miss Duke, let me ask you one question. If you had loved Roger Saxton, would you have married him?"

"Never!"

"You would have sacrificed your whole life, then, for the sake of—"

"My country, sir."

"We have a common country, Gardis," answered the young man gravely. Then, as he rose, "Child," he said, "I shall not relinquish the charge of your property, given into my hands by Mr. Copeland Gardiston, and, for your own sake, I beg you to be more patient, more gentle, as becomes a woman. A few weeks will no doubt see you released from even your slight obligation to me: you will have but a short time to wait."

Poor Gardis! Her proud scorn went for nothing, then? She was overridden as though she had been a child, and even re-buked for want of gentleness. The drawing-room was cheerless and damp in the rainy twilight; the girl wore a faded lawn dress, and her cheeks were pale; the old house was chilly through and through, and even the soldier, strong as he was, felt himself shivering. At this instant enter Cousin Copeland. "Of course you will spend the night here," he said heartily. "It is raining, and I must insist upon your staying over until to-morrow— must really insist."

Gardis looked up quickly; her dismayed face said plainly, "Oh no, no." Thereupon the young officer immediately ac-cepted Cousin Copeland's invitation, and took his seat again with quiet deliberation. Gardis sank down upon the sofa. "Very well," she thought desperately, "this time it is hopeless. Nothing can be done."

And hopeless it was. Pompey brought in a candle, and placed it upon the table, where its dim light made the large apartment more dismal than before; the rain poured down outside, and the rising wind rattled the loose shutters. Dinner was announced—one small fish, potatoes, and corn-bread. Pale Gardis sat like a statue at the head of the table, and made no effort to entertain the guest; but Cousin Copeland threw him-self bravely into the breach, and, by way of diversion, related the whole story of the unchronicled "wife of one of our grand-father's second cousins," who had turned out to be a most re-markable personage of Welsh descent, her golden harp having once stood in the very room in which they were now seated.

"Do you not think, my child, that a—a little fire in your aunt Margaretta's boudoir would—would be conducive to our comfort?" suggested the little bachelor, as they rose from the table.

"As you please," said Gardis.

So the three repaired thither, and when the old red curtains were drawn, and the fire lighted, the little room had at least a semblance of comfort, whatever may have been in the hearts of its occupants. Gardis embroidered, Cousin Copeland chatted on in a steady little stream, and the guest listened. "I will step up stairs to my study, and bring down that file of documents," said the bachelor, rising. He was gone, and left only silence behind him. Gardis did not raise her head, but went steadily on with the embroidered robe of the Queen of Sheba.

"I am thinking," began David Newell, breaking the long pause at last, "how comfortable you would be, Miss Duke, as the wife of Roger Saxton. He would take you North, away from this old house, and he would be so proud and so fond of you."

No answer.

"The place could be put in order if you did not care to sell it, and your cousin Copeland could live on here as usual; indeed, I could scarcely imagine him in any other home."

"Nor myself."

"Oh yes, Miss Duke; I can easily imagine you in New York, Paris, or Vienna. I can easily imagine you at the opera, in the picture-galleries, or carrying out to the full your exquisite taste in dress."

Down went the embroidery. "Sir, do you mean to insult me?" said the pale, cotton-robed little hostess.

"By no means."

"Why do you come here? Why do you sneer at my poor clothes? Why—" Her voice trembled, and she stopped abruptly.

"I was not aware that they were poor or old, Miss Duke. I have never seen a more exquisite costume than yours on the evening when we dined here by invitation; it has been like a picture in my memory ever since."

"An old robe that belonged to my grandmother, and I burned it, every shred, as soon as you had gone," said Gardis hotly.

Far from being impressed as she had intended he should be, David Newell merely bowed; the girl saw that he set the act down as "temper."

"I suppose your Northern ladies never do such things?" she said bitterly.

"You are right; they do not," he answered.

"Why do you come here?" pursued Gardis. "Why do you speak to me of Mr. Saxton? Though he had the fortune of a prince, he is nothing to me."

"Roger's fortune is comfortable, but not princely, Miss Duke—by no means princely. We are not princely at the North," added Newell, with a slight smile, "and neither are we 'knightly.' We must, I fear, yield all claim to those prized words of yours."

"I am not aware that I have used the words," said Miss Duke, with lofty indifference.

"Oh, I did not mean you alone—you personally—but all Southern women. However, to return to our subject: Saxton loves you, and has gone away with a saddened heart."

This was said gravely. "As though," Miss Duke remarked to herself—"really as though a heart was of consequence!"

"I presume he will soon forget," she said carelessly, as she took up her embroidery again.

"Yes, no doubt," replied Captain Newell. "I remember once on Staten Island, and again out in Mississippi, when he was even more— Yes, as you say, he will soon forget."

"Then why do you so continually speak of him?" said Miss Duke sharply. Such prompt corroboration was not, after all, as agreeable as it should have been to a well-regulated mind.

"I speak of him, Miss Duke, because I wish to know whether it is only your Southern girlish pride that speaks, or whether you really, as would be most natural, love him as he loves you; for, in the latter case, you would be able, I think, to fix and retain his somewhat fickle fancy. He is a fine fellow, and, as I said before, it would be but natural, Miss Duke, that you should love him."

"I do not love him," said Gardis, quickly and angrily, putting in her stitches all wrong. Who was this person, daring to assume what would or would not be natural for her to do?

"Very well; I believe you. And now that I know the truth, I will tell you why I come here: you have asked me several times. I too love you, Miss Duke."

Gardis had risen. "You?" she said—"you?"

"Yes, I; I too."

He was standing also, and they gazed at each other a moment in silence.

"I will never marry you," said the girl at last—"never! never! You do not, can not, understand the hearts of Southern women, sir."

"I have not asked you to marry me, Miss Duke," said the young soldier composedly; "and the hearts of Southern women are much like those of other women, I presume." Then, as the girl opened the door to escape, "You may go away if you like, Gardis," he said, "but I shall love you all the same, dear."

She disappeared, and in a few moments Cousin Copeland reëntered, with apologies for his lengthened absence. "I found several other documents I thought you might like to see," he said eagerly. "They will occupy the remainder of our evening delightfully."

They did. But Gardis did not return; neither did she appear at the breakfast-table the next morning. Captain Newell rode back to the city without seeing her.

Not long afterward Cousin Copeland received a formal letter from a city lawyer. The warehouse had found a tenant, and he, the lawyer, acting for the agent, Captain Newell, had the honor to inclose the first installment of rent-money, and remained an obedient servant, and so forth. Cousin Copeland was exultant. Gardis said to herself, "He is taking advantage of our poverty," and, going to her room, she sat down to plan some way of release. "I might be a governess," she thought. But no one at the South wanted a governess now, and how could she go North? She was not aware how old-fashioned were her little accomplishments—her music, her embroidery, her ideas of literature, her prim drawings, and even her deportment. No one made courtesies at the North any more, save perhaps in the Lancers. As to chemistry, trigonometry, physiology, and geology, the ordinary studies of a Northern girl, she knew hardly more than their names. "We might sell the place," she thought at last, "and go away somewhere and live in the woods."

This, indeed, seemed the only way open to her. The house was an actual fact; it was there; it was also her own. A few days later an advertisement appeared in the city newspaper: "For sale, the residence known as Gardiston House, situated six miles from the city, on Green River. Apply by letter, or on the premises, to Miss Gardiston Duke." Three days passed, and no one came. The fourth day an applicant appeared, and was ushered into the dining-room. He sent up no name; but Miss

Duke descended hopefully to confer with him, and found—
Captain Newell.

"You!" she said, paling and flushing. Her voice faltered; she
was sorely disappointed.

"It will always be myself, Gardis," said the young man
gravely. "So you wish to sell the old house? I should not have
supposed it."

"I wish to sell it in order to be freed from obligations forced
upon us, sir."

"Very well. But if *I* buy it, then what?"

"You will not buy it, for the simple reason that I will not sell
it to you. You do not wish the place; you would only buy it to
assist us."

"That is true."

"Then there is nothing more to be said, I believe," said Miss
Duke, rising.

"*Is* there nothing more, Gardis?"

"Nothing, Captain Newell."

And then, without another word, the soldier bowed, and
rode back to town.

The dreary little advertisement remained in a corner of the
newspaper a month longer, but no purchaser appeared. The
winter was rainy, with raw east winds from the ocean, and
the old house leaked in many places. If they had lived in one or
two of the smaller rooms, which were in better condition and
warmer than the large apartments, they might have escaped;
but no habit was changed, and three times a day the table was
spread in the damp dining-room, where the atmosphere was
like that of a tomb, and where no fire was ever made. The long
evenings were spent in the somber drawing-room by the light
of the one candle, and the rain beat against the old shutters so
loudly that Cousin Copeland was obliged to elevate his gentle
little voice as he read aloud to his silent companion. But one
evening he found himself forced to pause; his voice had failed.
Four days afterward he died, gentle and placid to the last. He
was an old man, although no one had ever thought so.

The funeral notice appeared in the city paper, and a few old
family friends came out to Gardiston House to follow the last
Gardiston to his resting-place in St. Mark's forest churchyard.

They were all sad-faced people, clad in mourning much the worse for wear. Accustomed to sorrow, they followed to the grave quietly, not a heart there that had not its own dead. They all returned to Gardiston House, sat a while in the drawing-room, spoke a few words each in turn to the desolate little mistress, and then took leave. Gardis was left alone.

Captain Newell did not come to the funeral; he could not come into such a company in his uniform, and he would not come without it. He had his own ideas of duty, and his own pride. But he sent a wreath of beautiful flowers, which must have come from some city where there was a hot-house. Miss Duke would not place the wreath upon the coffin, neither would she leave it in the drawing-room; she stood a while with it in her hand, and then she stole up stairs and laid it on Cousin Copeland's open desk, where daily he had worked so patiently and steadily through so many long years. Uselessly? Who among us shall dare to say that?

A week later, at twilight, old Dinah brought up the young officer's card.

"Say that I see no one," replied Miss Duke.

A little note came back, written on a slip of paper: "I beg you to see me, if only for a moment; it is a business matter that has brought me here to-day." And certainly it was a very forlorn day for a pleasure ride: the wind howled through the trees, and the roads were almost impassable with deep mire. Miss Duke went down to the dining-room. She wore no mourning garments; she had none. She had not worn mourning for her aunt, and for the same reason. Pale and silent, she stood before the young officer waiting to hear his errand. It was this: some one wished to purchase Gardiston House—a real purchaser this time, a stranger. Captain Newell did not say that it was the wife of an army contractor, a Northern woman, who had taken a fancy for an old family residence, and intended to be herself an old family in future; he merely stated the price offered for the house and its furniture, and in a few words placed the business clearly before the listener.

Her face lighted with pleasure.

"At last!" she said.

"Yes, at last, Miss Duke." There was a shade of sadness in his tone, but he spoke no word of entreaty. "You accept?"

"I do," said Gardis.

"I must ride back to the city," said David Newell, taking up his cap, "before it is entirely dark, for the roads are very heavy. I came out as soon as I heard of the offer, Miss Duke, for I knew you would be glad, very glad."

"Yes," said Gardis, "I am glad; very glad." Her cheeks were flushed now, and she smiled as she returned the young officer's bow. "Some time, Captain Newell—some time I trust I shall feel like thanking you for what was undoubtedly intended, on your part, as kindness," she said.

"It was never intended for kindness at all," said Newell bluntly. "It was never but one thing, Gardis, and you know it; and that one thing is, and always will be, love. Not 'always will be,' though; I should not say that. A man can conquer an unworthy love if he chooses."

"Unworthy?" said Gardis involuntarily.

"Yes, unworthy; like this of mine for you. A woman should be gentle, should be loving; a woman should have a womanly nature. But you—you—you do not seem to have anything in you but a foolish pride. I verily believe, Gardis Duke, that, if you loved me enough to die for me, you would still let me go out of that door without a word, so deep, so deadly is that pride of yours. What do I want with such a wife? No. My wife must love me—love me ardently, as I shall love her. Farewell, Miss Duke; I shall not see you again, probably. I will send a lawyer out to complete the sale."

He was gone, and Gardis stood alone in the darkening room. Gardiston House, where she had spent her life—Gardiston House, full of the memories and associations of two centuries —Gardiston House, the living reminder and the constant support of that family pride in which she had been nurtured, her one possession in the land which she had so loved, the beautiful, desolate South—would soon be hers no longer. She began to sob, and then when the sound came back to her, echoing through the still room, she stopped suddenly, as though ashamed. "I will go abroad," she said; "there will be a great deal to amuse me over there." But the comfort was dreary; and, as if she must do something, she took a candle, and slowly visited every room in the old mansion, many of them long unused. From garret to cellar she went, touching every piece

of the antique furniture, folding back the old curtains, standing by the dismantled beds, and softly pausing by the empty
chairs; she was saying farewell. On Cousin Copeland's desk the
wreath still lay; in that room she cried from sheer desolation.
Then, going down to the dining-room, she found her solitary
repast awaiting her, and, not to distress old Dinah, sat down
in her accustomed place. Presently she perceived smoke, then a
sound, then a hiss and a roar. She flew up stairs; the house was
on fire. Somewhere her candle must have started the flame; she
remembered the loose papers in Cousin Copeland's study, and
the wind blowing through the broken window-pane; it was
there that she had cried so bitterly, forgetting everything save
her own loneliness.

Nothing could be done; there was no house within several
miles—no one to help. The old servants were infirm, and the
fire had obtained strong headway; then the high wind rushed
in, and sent the flames up through the roof and over the tops
of the trees. When the whole upper story was one sheet of red
and yellow, some one rode furiously up the road and into the
garden, where Gardis stood alone, her little figure illumined by
the glare; nearer the house the two old servants were at work,
trying to save some of the furniture from the lower rooms.

"I saw the light and hurried back, Miss Duke," began Captain Newell. Then, as he saw the wan desolation of the girl's
face: "O Gardis! why will you resist me longer?" he cried passionately. "You shall be anything you like, think anything you
like—only love me, dear, as I love you."

And Gardis burst into tears. "I can not help it," she sobbed;
"everything is against me. The very house is burning before
my eyes. O David, David! it is all wrong; everything is wrong.
But what can I do when—when you hold me so, and when—
Oh, do not ask me any more."

"But I shall," said Newell, his face flushing with deep happiness. "When what, dear?"

"When I—"

"Love me?" said Newell. He would have it spoken.

"Yes," whispered Gardis, hanging her head.

"And I have adored the very shoe-tie of my proud little love
ever since I first saw her sweet face at the drawing-room window," said Newell, holding her close and closer, and gazing

down into her eyes with the deep gaze of the quiet heart that loves but once.

And the old house burned on, burned as though it knew a contractor's wife was waiting for it. "I see our Gardis is provided for," said the old house. "She never was a real Gardiston —only a Duke; so it is just as well. As for that contractor's wife, she shall have nothing; not a Chinese image, not a spindle-legged chair, not one crocodile cup—no, not even one stone upon another."

It kept its word: in the morning there was nothing left. Old Gardiston was gone!

# The South Devil

The trees that lean'd in their love unto trees,
    That lock'd in their loves, and were made so strong,
Stronger than armies; ay, stronger than seas
    That rush from their caves in a storm of song.

The cockatoo swung in the vines below,
    And muttering hung on a golden thread,
Or moved on the moss'd bough to and fro,
    In plumes of gold and array'd in red.

The serpent that hung from the sycamore bough,
    And sway'd his head in a crescent above,
Had folded his head to the white limb now,
    And fondled it close like a great black love.

JOAQUIN MILLER

ON the afternoon of the 23d of December, the thermometer marked eighty-six degrees in the shade on the outside wall of Mark Deal's house. Mark Deal's brother, lying on the white sand, his head within the line of shadow cast by a live-oak, but all the remainder of his body full in the hot sunshine, basked liked a chameleon, and enjoyed the heat. Mark Deal's brother spent much of his time basking. He always took the live-oak for a head-protector; but gave himself variety by trying new radiations around the tree, his crossed legs and feet stretching from it in a slightly different direction each day, as the spokes of a wheel radiate from the hub. The live-oak was a symmetrical old tree, standing by itself; having always had sufficient space, its great arms were straight, stretching out evenly all around, densely covered with the small, dark, leathery leaves, unnotched and uncut, which are as unlike the Northern oak-leaf as the leaf of the willow is unlike that of the sycamore. Behind the live-oak, two tall, ruined chimneys and a heap of white stones marked where the mansion-house had been. The old tree had watched its foundations laid; had shaded its blank, white front and little hanging balcony above; had witnessed its destruction, fifty years before, by the Indians; and had mounted guard over its remains ever since, alone as far as man was concerned, until this year, when a tenant had arrived, Mark Deal, and, somewhat later, Mark Deal's brother.

The ancient tree was Spanish to the core; it would have resented the sacrilege to the tips of its small acorns, if the new-comer had laid hands upon the dignified old ruin it guarded. The new-comer, however, entertained no such intention; a small out-building, roofless, but otherwise in good condition, on the opposite side of the circular space, attracted his attention, and became mentally his residence, as soon as his eyes fell upon it, he meanwhile standing with his hands in his pockets, surveying the place critically. It was the old Monteano plantation, and he had taken it for a year.

The venerable little out-building was now firmly roofed with new, green boards; its square windows, destitute of sash or glass, possessed new wooden shutters hung by strips of deer's hide; new steps led up to its two rooms, elevated four feet above the ground. But for a door it had only a red cotton curtain, now drawn forward and thrown carelessly over a peg on the outside wall, a spot of vivid color on its white. Underneath the windows hung flimsy strips of bark covered with brightly-hued flowers.

"They won't live," said Mark Deal.

"Oh, I shall put in fresh ones every day or two," answered his brother. It was he who had wanted the red curtain.

As he basked, motionless, in the sunshine, it could be noted that this brother was a slender youth, with long, pale-yellow hair—hair fine, thin, and dry, the kind that crackles if the comb is passed rapidly through it. His face in sleep was pale and wizened, with deep purple shadows under the closed eyes; his long hands were stretched out on the white, hot sand in the blaze of the sunshine, which, however, could not alter their look of blue-white cold. The sunken chest and blanched temples told of illness; but, if cure were possible, it would be gained from this soft, balmy, fragrant air, now soothing his sore lungs. He slept on in peace; and an old green chameleon came down from the tree, climbed up on the sleeve of his brown sack-coat, occupied himself for a moment in changing his own miniature hide to match the cloth, swelled out his scarlet throat, caught a fly or two, and then, pleasantly established, went to sleep also in company. Butterflies, in troops of twenty or thirty, danced in the golden air; there was no sound. Everything was hot and soft and brightly colored. Winter? Who knew of winter here? Labor? What was labor? This was the land and the sky and the air of never-ending rest.

Yet one man was working there, and working hard, namely, Mark Deal. His little central plaza, embracing perhaps an acre, was surrounded when he first arrived by a wall of green, twenty feet high. The sweet orange-trees, crape-myrtles, oleanders, guavas, and limes planted by the Spaniards had been, during the fifty years, conquered and partially enslaved by a wilder growth—andromedas, dahoons, bayberries, and the old field loblollies, the whole bound together by the tangled vines of the jessamine and armed smilax, with bear-grass and the dwarf palmetto below. Climbing the central live-oak, Deal had found, as he expected, traces of the six paths which had once led from this little plaza to the various fields and the sugar plantation, their course still marked by the tops of the bitter-sweet orange-trees, which showed themselves glossily, in regular lines, amid the duller foliage around them. He took their bearings and cut them out slowly, one by one. Now the low-arched aisles, eighty feet in length, were clear, with the thick leaves interlacing overhead, and the daylight shining through at their far ends, golden against the green. Here, where the north path terminated, Deal was now working.

He was a man slightly below middle height, broad-shouldered, and muscular, with the outlines which are called thick-set. He appeared forty-five, and was not quite thirty-five. Although weather-beaten and bronzed, there was yet a pinched look in his face, which was peculiar. He was working in an old field, preparing it for sweet potatoes—those omnipresent, monotonous vegetables of Florida which will grow anywhere, and which at last, with their ugly, gray-mottled skins, are regarded with absolute aversion by the Northern visitor.

The furrows of half a century before were still visible in the field. No frost had disturbed the winterless earth; no atom had changed its place, save where the gopher had burrowed beneath, or the snake left its waving trail above in the sand which constitutes the strange, white, desolate soil, wherever there is what may be called by comparison solid ground, in the

lake-dotted, sieve-like land. There are many such traces of former cultivation in Florida: we come suddenly upon old tracks,
furrows, and drains in what we thought primeval forest; rose-
bushes run wild, and distorted old fig-trees meet us in a jungle
where we supposed no white man's foot had ever before penetrated; the ruins of a chimney gleam whitely through a waste
of thorny *chaparral*. It is all natural enough, if one stops to
remember that fifty years before the first settlement was made
in Virginia, and sixty-three before the Mayflower touched the
shores of the New World, there were flourishing Spanish plantations on this Southern coast—more flourishing, apparently,
than any the indolent peninsula has since known. But one
does not stop to remember it; the belief is imbedded in all our
Northern hearts that, because the narrow, sun-bathed State
is far away and wild and empty, it is also new and virgin, like
the lands of the West; whereas it is old—the only gray-haired
corner our country holds.

Mark Deal worked hard. Perspiration beaded his forehead
and cheeks, and rolled from his short, thick, red-brown hair.
He worked in this way every day from daylight until dusk, and
was probably the only white man in the State who did. When
his task was finished, he made a circuit around the belt of
thicket through which the six paths ran to his orange-grove on
the opposite side. On the way he skirted an edge of the sugar-
plantation, now a wide, empty waste, with the old elevated
causeway still running across it. On its far edge loomed the
great cypresses of South Devil, a swamp forty miles long; there
was a sister, West Devil, not far away, equally beautiful, dark,
and deadly. Beyond the sugar waste were the indigo-fields, still
fenced by their old ditches. Then came the orange-grove; luxuriant, shady word—the orange-grove!

It was a space of level white sand, sixty feet square, fertilized
a century before with pounded oyster-shells, in the Spanish
fashion. Planted in even rows across it, tied to stakes, were slips
of green stem, each with three leaves—forlorn little plants, five
or six inches in height. But the stakes were new and square and
strong, and rose to Deal's shoulder; they were excellent stakes,
and made quite a grove of themselves, firm, if somewhat bare.

Deal worked in his grove until sunset; then he shouldered
his tools and went homeward through one of the arched aisles

to the little plaza within, where stood his two-roomed house with its red cotton door. His brother was still sleeping on the sand, at least, his eyes were closed. Deal put his tools in a rack behind the house, and then crossed to where he lay.

"You should not sleep here after sunset, Carl," he said, somewhat roughly. "You know better; why do you do it?"

"I'm not asleep," answered the other, sitting up, and then slowly getting on his feet. "Heigh-ho! What are you going to have for dinner?"

"You are tired, Carl; and I see the reason. You have been in the swamp." Deal's eyes as he spoke were fixed upon the younger man's shoes, where traces of the ink-black soil of South Devil were plainly visible.

Carl laughed. "Can't keep anything from your Yankee eyes, can I, Mark?" he said. "But I only went a little way."

"It isn't the distance, it's the folly," said Mark, shortly, going toward the house.

"I never pretended to be wise," answered Carl, slouching along behind him, with his hands wrapped in his blue cotton handkerchief, arranged like a muff.

Although Deal worked hard in his fields all day, he did not cook. In a third out-building lived a gray-headed old negro with one eye, who cooked for the new tenant—and cooked well. His name was Scipio, but Carl called him Africanus; he said it was equally appropriate, and sounded more impressive. Scip's kitchen was out-of-doors—simply an old Spanish chimney. His kettle and few dishes, when not in use, hung on the sides of this chimney, which now, all alone in the white sand, like an obelisk, cooked solemnly the old negro's messes, as half a century before it had cooked the more dignified repasts of the dead hidalgos. The brothers ate in the open air also, sitting at a rough board table which Mark had made behind the house. They had breakfast soon after daylight, and at sunset dinner; in the middle of the day they took only fruit and bread.

"Day after to-morrow will be Christmas," said Carl, leaving the table and lighting his long pipe. "What are you going to do?"

"I had not thought of doing anything in particular."

"Well, at least don't work on Christmas day."

"What would you have me do?"

Carl took his pipe from his mouth, and gazed at his brother in silence for a moment. "Go into the swamp with me," he urged, with sudden vehemence. "Come—for the whole day!"

Deal was smoking, too, a short clay pipe, very different from the huge, fantastic, carved bowl with long stem which weighed down Carl's thin mouth. "I don't know what to do with you, boy. You are mad about the swamp," he said, smoking on calmly.

They were sitting in front of the house now, in two chairs tilted back against its wall. The dark, odorous earth looked up to the myriad stars, but was not lighted by them; a soft, languorous gloom lay over the land. Carl brushed away the ashes from his pipe impatiently.

"It's because you can't understand," he said. "The swamp haunts me. I *must* see it once; you will be wise to let me see it once. We might go through in a canoe together by the branch; the branch goes through."

"The water goes, no doubt, but a canoe couldn't."

"Yes, it could, with an axe. It has been done. They used to go up to San Miguel that way sometimes from here; it shortens the distance more than half."

"Who told you all this—Scip? What does he know about it?"

"Oh, Africanus has seen several centuries; the Spaniards were living here only fifty years ago, you know, and that's nothing to him. He remembers the Indian attack."

"Ponce de Leon, too, I suppose; or, to go back to the old country, Cleopatra. But you must give up the swamp, Carl. I positively forbid it. The air inside is thick and deadly, to say nothing of the other dangers. How do you suppose it gained its name?"

"Diabolus is common enough as a title among Spaniards and Italians; it don't mean anything. The prince of darkness never lives in the places called by his name; he likes baptized cities better."

"Death lives there, however; and I brought you down here to cure you."

"I'm all right. See how much stronger I am! I shall soon be quite well again, old man," answered Carl, with the strange, sanguine faith of the consumptive.

The next day Deal worked very hard. He had a curious, inflexible, possibly narrow kind of conscience, which required
him to do double duty to-day in order to make up for the
holiday granted to Carl to-morrow. There was no task-master
over him; even the seasons were not task-masters here. But so
immovable were his own rules for himself that nothing could
have induced him to abate one jot of the task he had laid out
in his own mind when he started afield at dawn.

When he returned home at sunset, somewhat later than
usual, Carl was absent. Old Scipio could give no information;
he had not seen "young marse" since early morning. Deal
put up his tools, ate something, and then, with a flask in his
pocket, a fagot of light-wood torches bound on his back, and
one of these brilliant, natural flambeaux in his hand, he started
away on his search, going down one of the orange-aisles, the
light gleaming back through the arch till he reached the far
end, when it disappeared. He crossed an old indigo-field, and
pushed his way through its hedge of Spanish-bayonets, while
the cacti sown along the hedge—small, flat green plates with
white spines, like hideous tufted insects—fastened themselves
viciously on the strong leather of his high boots. Then, reaching the sugar waste, he advanced a short distance on the old
causeway, knelt down, and in the light of the torch examined
its narrow, sandy level. Yes, there were the footprints he had
feared to find. Carl had gone again into the poisonous swamp
—the beautiful, deadly South Devil. And this time he had not
come back.

The elder brother rose, and with the torch held downward
slowly traced the footmarks. There was a path, or rather trail,
leading in a short distance. The footprints followed it as far as
it went, and the brother followed the footprints, the red glare
of the torch foreshortening each swollen, gray-white cypress-
trunk, and giving to the dark, hidden pools below bright
gleamings which they never had by day. He soon came to the
end of the trail; here he stopped and shouted loudly several
times, with pauses between for answer. No answer came.

"But I know the trick of this thick air," he said to himself.
"One can't hear anything in a cypress-swamp."

He was now obliged to search closely for the footprints,
pausing at each one, having no idea in which direction the next
would tend. The soil did not hold the impressions well; it was

not mud or mire, but wet, spongy, fibrous, black earth, thinly spread over the hard roots of trees, which protruded in distorted shapes in every direction. He traced what seemed footmarks across an open space, and then lost them on the brink of a dark pool. If Carl had kept on, he must have crossed this pool; but how? On the sharp cypress-knees standing sullenly in the claret-colored water? He went all around the open space again, seeking for footmarks elsewhere; but no, they ended at the edge of the pool. Cutting a long stick, he made his way across by its aid, stepping from knee-point to knee-point. On the other side he renewed his search for the trail, and after some labor found it, and went on again.

He toiled forward slowly in this way a long time, his course changing often; Carl's advance seemed to have been aimless. Then, suddenly, the footprints ceased. There was not another one visible anywhere, though he searched in all directions again and again. He looked at his watch; it was midnight. He hallooed; no reply. What could have become of the lad? He now began to feel his own fatigue; after the long day of toil in the hot sun, these hours of laboring over the ground in a bent position, examining it inch by inch, brought on pains in his shoulders and back. Planting the torch he was carrying in the soft soil of a little knoll, he placed another one near it, and sat down between the two flames to rest for a minute or two, pouring out for himself a little brandy in the bottom of the cup belonging to his flask. He kept strict watch as he did this. Venomous things, large and small, filled the vines above, and might drop at any moment upon him. But he had quick eyes and ears, and no intention of dying in the South Devil; so, while he watched keenly, he took the time to swallow the brandy. After a moment or two he was startled by a weak human voice saying, with faint decision, "*That's* brandy!"

"I should say it was," called Deal, springing to his feet. "Where are you, then?"

"Here."

The rescuer followed the sound, and, after one or two errors, came upon the body of his brother lying on a dank mat of water-leaves and ground-vines at the edge of a pool. In the red light of the torch he looked as though he was dead; his eyes only were alive.

"Brandy," he said again, faintly, as Deal appeared.

After he had swallowed a small quantity of the stimulant, he revived with unexpected swiftness.

"I have been shouting for you not fifty feet away," said Deal; "how is it that you did not hear?" Then in the same breath, in a soft undertone, he added, "Ah-h-h-h!" and without stirring a hair's breadth from where he stood, or making an unnecessary motion, he slowly drew forth his pistol, took careful aim, and fired. He was behind his brother, who lay with closed eyes, not noticing the action.

"What have you killed?" asked Carl languidly. "I've seen nothing but birds; and the most beautiful ones, too."

"A moccasin, that's all," said Deal, kicking the dead creature into the pool. He did not add that the snake was coiled for a spring. "Let us get back to the little knoll where I was, Carl; it's drier there."

"I don't think I can walk, old man. I fell from the vines up there, and something's the matter with my ankles."

"Well, I can carry you that distance," said Deal. "Put your arms around my neck, and raise yourself as I lift you—so."

The burning flambeau on the knoll served as a guide, and, after one or two pauses, owing to the treacherous footing, the elder brother succeeded in carrying the other thither. He then took off the light woolen coat he had put on before entering the swamp, spread it over the driest part of the little knoll, and laid Carl upon it.

"If you can not walk," he said, "we shall have to wait here until daylight. I could not carry you and the torch also; and the footing is bad—there are twenty pools to cross, or go around. Fortunately, we have light-wood enough to burn all night."

He lit fresh torches and arranged them at the four corners of their little knoll; then he began to pace slowly to and fro, like a picket walking his beat.

"What were you doing up among those vines?" he asked. He knew that it would be better for them both if they could keep themselves awake; those who fell asleep in the night air of South Devil generally awoke the next morning in another world.

"I climbed up a ladder of vines to gather some of the great red blossoms swinging in the air; and, once up, I went along on the mat to see what I could find. It's beautiful there

—fairy-land. You can't see anything down below, but above the long moss hangs in fine, silvery lines like spray from ever so high up, and mixed with it air-plants, sheafs, and bells of scarlet and cream-colored blossoms. I sat there a long time looking, and I suppose I must have dozed; for I don't know when I fell."

"You did not hear me shout?"

"No. The first consciousness I had was the odor of brandy."

"The odor reached you, and the sound did not; that is one of the tricks of such air as this! You must have climbed up, I suppose, at the place where I lost the trail. What time did you come in?"

"I don't know," murmured Carl drowsily.

"Look here! you *must* keep awake!"

"I can't," answered the other.

Deal shook him, but could not rouse him even to anger. He only opened his blue eyes and looked reproachfully at his brother, but as though he was a long distance off. Then Deal lifted him up, uncorked the flask, and put it to his lips.

"Drink!" he said, loudly and sternly; and mechanically Carl obeyed. Once or twice his head moved aside, as if refusing more; but Deal again said, "Drink!" and without pity made the sleeper swallow every drop the flask contained. Then he laid him down upon the coat again, and covered his face and head with his own broad-brimmed palmetto hat, Carl's hat having been lost. He had done all he could—changed the lethargy of the South Devil into the sleep of drunkenness, the last named at least a human slumber. He was now left to keep the watch alone.

During the first half hour a dozen red and green things, of the centipede and scorpion kind, stupefied by the glare of the torches, fell from the trees; and he dispatched them. Next, enormous grayish-white spiders, in color exactly like the bark, moved slowly one furred leg into view, and then another, on the trunks of the cypresses near by, gradually coming wholly into the light—creatures covering a circumference as large as that of a plate. At length the cypresses all around the knoll were covered with them; and they all seemed to be watching him. He was not watching the spiders, however; he cared very little for the spiders. His eyes were upon the ground all the time, moving along the borders of his little knoll-fort. It was bounded on two sides by pools, in whose dark depths he knew moccasins were awake, watching the light, too, with whatever of curiosity belongs to a snake's cold brain. His torches aroused them; and yet darkness would have been worse. In the light he could at least see them, if they glided forth and tried to ascend the brilliant knoll. After a while they began to rise to the surface; he could distinguish portions of their bodies in waving lines, moving noiselessly hither and thither, appearing and disappearing suddenly, until the pools around seemed alive with them. There was not a sound; the soaked forest stood motionless. The absolute stillness made the quick gliding motions of the moccasins even more horrible. Yet Deal had no instinctive dread of snakes. The terrible "coach-whip," the deadly and grotesque spread-adder, the rattlesnake of the barrens, and these great moccasins of the pools were endowed with no imaginary horrors in his eyes. He accepted them as nature made them, and not as man's fancy painted them; it was only their poison-fangs he feared.

"If the sea-crab could sting, how hideous we should think him! If the lobster had a deadly venom, how devilish his shape would seem to us!" he said.

But now no imagination was required to make the moccasins terrible. His revolver carried six balls; and he had already used one of them. Four hours must pass before dawn; there could be no unnecessary shooting. The creatures might even come out and move along the edge of his knoll; only when they showed an intention of coming up the slope must their gliding life be ended. The moccasin is not a timorous or quick-nerved snake; in a place like the South Devil, when a human foot or boat approaches, generally he does not stir. His great body, sometimes over six feet in length, and thick and fat in the middle, lies on a log or at the edge of a pool, seemingly too lazy to move. But none the less, when roused, is his coil sudden and his long spring sure; his venom is deadly. After a time one of the creatures did come out and glide along the edge of the knoll. He went back into the water; but a second came out on the other side. During the night Deal killed three; he was an excellent marksman, and picked them off easily as they crossed his dead-line.

"Fortunately they come one by one," he said to himself. "If

there was any concert of action among them, I couldn't hold the place a minute."

As the last hour began, the long hour before dawn, he felt the swamp lethargy stealing into his own brain; he saw the trees and torches doubled. He walked to and fro more quickly, and sang to keep himself awake. He knew only a few old-fashioned songs, and the South Devil heard that night, probably for the first time in its tropical life, the ancient Northern strains of "Gayly the Troubadour touched his Guitar." Deal was no troubadour, and he had no guitar. But he sang on bravely, touching that stringed instrument, vocally at least, and bringing himself "home from the war" over and over again, until at last faint dawn penetrated from above down to the knoll where the four torches were burning. They were the last torches, and Deal was going through his sixtieth rehearsal of the "Troubadour"; but, instead of "Lady-love, lady-lo-o-o-ve," whom he apostrophized, a large moccasin rose from the pool, as if in answer. She might have been the queen of the moccasins, and beautiful —to moccasin eyes; but to Deal she was simply the largest and most hideous of all the snake-visions of the night. He gave her his fifth ball, full in her mistaken brain; and, if she had admired him (or the "Troubadour"), she paid for it with her life.

This was the last. Daylight appeared. The watchman put out his torches and roused the sleeper. "Carl! Carl! It's daylight. Let us get out of this confounded crawling hole, and have a breath of fresh air."

Carl stirred, and opened his eyes; they were heavy and dull. His brother lifted him, told him to hold on tightly, and started with his burden toward home. The snakes had disappeared, the gray spiders had vanished; he could see his way now, and he followed his own trail, which he had taken care to make distinct when he came in the night before. But, loaded down as he was, and obliged to rest frequently, and also to go around all the pools, hours passed before he reached the last cypresses and came out on the old causeway across the sugar-waste.

It was Christmas morning; the thermometer stood at eighty-eight.

Carl slept off his enforced drunkenness in his hammock. Mark, having bandaged his brother's strained ankles, threw himself upon his rude couch, and fell into a heavy slumber also. He slept until sunset; then he rose, plunged his head into a tub of the limpid, pure, but never cold water of Florida, drawn from his shallow well, and went out to the chimney to see about dinner. The chimney was doing finely: a fiery plume of sparks waved from its white top, a red bed of coals glowed below. Scip moved about with as much equanimity as though he had a row of kitchen-tables upon which to arrange his pans and dishes, instead of ruined blocks of stone, under the open sky. The dinner was good. Carl, awake at last, was carried out to the table to enjoy it, and then brought back to his chair in front of the house to smoke his evening pipe.

"I must make you a pair of crutches," said Deal.

"One will do; my right ankle is not much hurt, I think."

The fall, the air of the swamp, and the inward drenching of brandy had left Carl looking much as usual; the tenacious disease that held him swallowed the lesser ills. But for the time, at least, his wandering footsteps were staid.

"I suppose there is no use in my asking, Carl, *why* you went in there?" said Deal, after a while.

"No, there isn't. I'm haunted—that's all."

"But what is it that haunts you?"

"Sounds. *You* couldn't understand, though, if I was to talk all night."

"Perhaps I could; perhaps I can understand more than you imagine. I'll tell you a story presently; but first you must explain to me, at least as well as you can, what it is that attracts you in South Devil."

"Oh—well," said Carl, with a long, impatient sigh, closing his eyes wearily. "I am a musician, you know, a musician *manqué*; a musician who can't play. Something's the matter; I *hear* music, but can not bring it out. And I know so well what it ought to be, ought to be and isn't, that I've broken my violin in pieces a dozen times in my rages about it. Now, other fellows in orchestras, who *don't* know, get along very well. But I couldn't. I've thought at times that, although I can not sound what I hear with my own hands, perhaps I could *write* it out so that other men could sound it. The idea has never come to anything definite yet—that is, what *you* would call definite; but it haunts me persistently, and *now* it has got into that swamp. The wish," here Carl laid down his great pipe, and pressed his hand eagerly upon his brother's knee—"the wish that haunts me—drives me—is to write out the beautiful music of the South Devil, the sounds one hears in there"—

"But there are no sounds."

"No sounds? You must be deaf! The air fairly reeks with sounds, with harmonies. But there—I told you you couldn't understand." He leaned back against the wall again, and took up the great pipe, which looked as though it must consume whatever small store of strength remained to him.

"Is it what is called an opera you want to write, like—like the 'Creation,' for instance?" asked Deal. The "Creation" was the only long piece of music he had ever heard.

Carl groaned. "Oh, *don't* talk of it!" he said; then added, irritably, "It's a song, that's all—the song of a Southern swamp."

"Call it by its real name, Devil," said the elder brother, grimly.

"I would, if I was rich enough to have a picture painted—the Spirit of the Swamp—a beautiful woman, falsely called a devil by cowards, dark, languorous, mystical, sleeping among the vines I saw up there, with the great red blossoms dropping around her."

"And the great mottled snakes coiling over her?"

"*I* didn't see any snakes."

"Well," said Mark, refilling his pipe, "now I'm going to tell you *my* story. When I met you on that windy pier at Exton, and proposed that you should come down here with me, I was coming myself, in any case, wasn't I? And why? I wanted to get to a place where I could be warm—warm, hot, baked; warm through and through; warm all the time. I wanted to get to a place where the very ground was warm. And *now*—I'll tell you why."

He rose from his seat, laid down his pipe, and, extending his hand, spoke for about fifteen minutes without pause. Then he turned, went back hastily to the old chimney, where red coals still lingered, and sat down close to the glow, leaving Carl wonder-struck in his tilted chair. The elder man leaned over the fire and held his hands close to the coals; Carl watched him. It was nine o'clock, and the thermometer marked eighty.

For nearly a month after Christmas, life on the old plantation went on without event or disaster. Carl, with his crutch and

cane, could not walk far; his fancy now was to limp through the
east orange-aisle to the place of tombs, and sit there for hours,
playing softly, what might be called crooning, on his violin.
The place of tombs was a small, circular space surrounded by
wild orange-trees in a close, even row, like a hedge; here were
four tombs, massive, oblong blocks of the white conglomerate
of the coast, too coarse-grained to hold inscription or mark
of any kind. Who the old Spaniards were whose bones lay beneath, and what names they bore in the flesh, no one knew;
all record was lost. Outside in the wild thicket was a tomb still
more ancient, and of different construction: four slabs of stone,
uncovered, about three feet high, rudely but firmly placed, as
though inclosing a coffin. In the earth between these low walls
grew a venerable cedar; but, old as it was, it must have been
planted by chance or by hand after the human body beneath
had been laid in its place.

"Why do you come here?" said Deal, pausing and looking into the place of tombs, one morning, on his way to the
orange-grove. "There are plenty of pleasanter spots about."

"No; I like this better," answered Carl, without stopping the
low chant of his violin. "Besides, they like it too."

"Who?"

"The old fellows down below. The chap outside there, who
must have been an Aztec, I suppose, and the original proprietor, catches a little of it; but I generally limp over and give
him a tune to himself before going home. I have to imagine
the Aztec style."

Mark gave a short laugh, and went on to his work. But he
knew the real reason for Carl's fancy for the place; between the
slim, clean trunks of the orange-trees, the long green line of
South Devil bounded the horizon, the flat tops of the cypresses
far above against the sky, and the vines and silver moss filling
the space below—a luxuriant wall across the broad, thinly-
treed expanses of the pine barrens.

One evening in January Deal came homeward as usual at
sunset, and found a visitor. Carl introduced him. "My friend
Schwartz," he said. Schwartz merited his name; he was dark in
complexion, hair, and eyes, and if he had any aims they were
dark also. He was full of anecdotes and jests, and Carl laughed

heartily; Mark had never heard him laugh in that way before. The elder brother ordered a good supper, and played the host as well as he could; but, in spite of the anecdotes, he did not altogether like friend Schwartz. Early the next morning, while the visitor was still asleep, he called Carl outside, and asked in an undertone who he was.

"Oh, I met him first in Berlin, and afterward I knew him in New York," said Carl. "All the orchestra fellows know Schwartz."

"Is he a musician, then?"

"Not exactly; but he used to be always around, you know."

"How comes he down here?"

"Just chance. He had an offer from a sort of a—of a restaurant, up in San Miguel, a new place recently opened. The other day he happened to find out that I was here, and so came down to see me."

"How did he find out?"

"I suppose you gave our names to the agent when you took the place, didn't you?"

"I gave mine; and—yes, I think I mentioned you."

"If you didn't, I mentioned myself. I was at San Miguel, two weeks you remember, while you were making ready down here; and I venture to say almost everybody remembers Carl Brenner."

Mark smiled. Carl's fixed, assured self-conceit in the face of the utter failure he had made of his life did not annoy, but rather amused him; it seemed part of the lad's nature.

"I don't want to grudge you your amusement, Carl," he said; "but I don't much like this Schwartz of yours."

"He won't stay; he has to go back to-day. He came in a cart with a man from San Miguel, who, by some rare chance, had an errand down this forgotten, God-forsaken, dead-alive old road. The man will pass by on his way home this afternoon, and Schwartz is to meet him at the edge of the barren."

"Have an early dinner, then; there are birds and venison, and there is lettuce enough for a salad. Scip can make you some coffee."

But, although he thus proffered his best, none the less did the elder brother take with him the key of the little chest which contained his small store of brandy and the two or three bottles of orange wine which he had brought down with him from San Miguel.

After he had gone, Schwartz and Carl strolled around the plantation in the sunshine. Schwartz did not care to sit down among Carl's tombs; he said they made him feel moldy. Carl argued the point with him in vain, and then gave it up, and took him around to the causeway across the sugar-waste, where they stretched themselves out in the shade cast by the ruined wall of the old mill.

"What brought this brother of yours away down here?" asked the visitor, watching a chameleon on the wall near by. "See that little beggar swelling out his neck!"

"He's catching flies. In a storm they will come and hang themselves by one paw on our windows, and the wind will blow them out like dead leaves, and rattle them about, and they'll never move. But, when the sun shines out, there they are all alive again."

"But about your brother?"

"He isn't my brother."

"What?"

"My mother, a widow, named Brenner, with one son, Carl, married his father, a widower, named Deal, with one son, Mark. There you have the whole."

"He is a great deal older than you. I suppose he has been in the habit of assisting you?"

"Never saw him in my life until this last October, when, one windy day, he found me coughing on the Exton pier; and, soon afterward, he brought me down here."

"Came, then, on your account?"

"By no means; he was coming himself. It's a queer story; I'll tell it to you. It seems he went with the Kenton Arctic expedition—you remember it? Two of the ships were lost; his was one. But I'll have to get up and say it as he did." Here Carl rose, put down his pipe, extended one hand stiffly in a fixed position, and went on speaking, his very voice, by force of the natural powers of mimicry he possessed, sounding like Mark's:

"We were a company of eight when we started away from the frozen hulk, which would never see clear water under her bows again. Once before we had started, thirty-five strong, and had come back thirteen. Five had died in the old ship, and now the last survivors were again starting forth. We drew a sledge behind us, carrying our provisions and the farcical records of the expedition which had ended in death, as they must all end. We soon lose sight of the vessel. It was our only shelter, and we look back; then, at each other. 'Cheer up!' says one. 'Take this extra skin, Mark; I am stronger than you.' It's Proctor's voice that speaks. Ten days go by. There are only five of us now, and we are walking on doggedly across the ice, the numbing ice, the killing ice, the never-ending, gleaming, taunting, devilish ice. We have left the sledge behind. No trouble now for each to carry his share of food, it is so light. Now we walk together for a while; now we separate, sick of seeing one another's pinched faces, but we keep within call. On the eleventh day a wind rises; bergs come sailing into view. One moves down upon us. Its peak shining in the sunshine far above is nothing to the great mass that moves on under the water. Our ice-field breaks into a thousand pieces. We leap from block to block; we cry aloud in our despair; we call to each other, and curse, and pray. But the strips of dark water widen between us; our ice-islands grow smaller; and a current bears us onward. We can no longer keep in motion, and freeze as we stand. Two float near each other as darkness falls; 'Cheer up, Mark, cheer up!' cries one, and throws his flask across the gap between. Again it is Proctor's voice that speaks.

"In the morning only one is left alive. The others are blocks of ice, and float around in the slow eddy, each solemnly staring, one foot advanced, as if still keeping up the poor cramped steps with which he had fought off death. The one who is still alive floats around and around, with these dead men standing stiffly on their islands, all day, sometimes so near them that the air about him is stirred by their icy forms as they pass. At evening his cake drifts away through an opening toward the south, and he sees them no more, save that after him follows his dead friend, Proctor, at some distance behind. As night comes, the figure seems to wave its rigid hand in the distance, and cry from its icy throat, 'Cheer up, Mark, and good-by!'"

Here Carl stopped, rubbed his hands, shivered, and looked to see how his visitor took the narrative.

"It's a pretty cold story," said Schwartz, "even in this broiling sun. So he came down here to get a good, full warm, did he? He's got the cash, I suppose, to pay for his fancies."

"I don't call that a fancy, exactly," said Carl, seating himself on the hot white sand in the sunshine, with his thin hands clasped around his knees. "As to cash—I don't know. He works very hard."

"He works because he likes it," said Schwartz, contemptuously; "he looks like that sort of a man. But, at any rate, he don't make *you* work much!"

"He *is* awfully good to me," admitted Carl.

"It isn't on account of your beauty."

"Oh, I'm good looking enough in my way," replied the youth. "I acknowledge it isn't a common way; like yours, for instance." As he spoke, he passed his hand through his thin light hair, drew the ends of the long locks forward, and examined them admiringly.

"As he never saw you before, it couldn't have been brotherly love," pursued the other. "I suppose it was pity."

"No, it wasn't pity, either, you old blockhead," said Carl, laughing. "He *likes* to have me with him; he *likes* me."

"I see that myself, and that's exactly the point. Why should he? You haven't any inheritance to will to him, have you?"

"My violin, and the clothes on my back. I believe that's all," answered Carl, lightly. He took off his palmetto hat, made a pillow of it, and stretched himself out at full length, closing his eyes.

"Well, give *me* a brother with cash, and I'll go to sleep, too," said Schwartz. When Deal came home at sunset, the dark-skinned visitor was gone.

But he came again; and this time stayed three days. Mark allowed it, for Carl's sake. All he said was, "He can not be of much use in the restaurant up there. What is he? Cook? Or waiter?"

"Oh, Schwartz isn't a servant, old fellow. He helps entertain the guests."

"Sings, I suppose."

Carl did not reply, and Deal set Schwartz down as a lager-beer-hall ballad-singer, borne southward on the tide of winter travel to Florida. One advantage at least was gained—when Schwartz was there, Carl was less tempted by the swamp.

And now, a third time, the guest came. During the first evening of this third visit, he was so good-tempered, so frankly lazy and amusing, that even Deal was disarmed. "He's a good-for-nothing, probably; but there's no active harm in him," he said to himself.

The second evening was a repetition of the first.

When he came home at sunset on the third evening, Carl was lying coiled up close to the wall of the house, his face hidden in his arms.

"What are you doing there?" said Deal, as he passed by, on his way to put up the tools.

No answer. But Carl had all kinds of whims, and Deal was used to them. He went across to Scip's chimney.

"Awful time, cap'en," said the old negro, in a low voice. "Soon's you's gone, dat man make young marse drink, and bot' begin to holler and fight."

"Drink? They had no liquor."

"Yes, dey hab. Mus' hab brought 'em 'long."

"Where is the man?"

"Oh, he gone long ago—gone at noon."

Deal went to his brother. "Carl," he said, "get up. Dinner is ready." But the coiled form did not stir.

"Don't be a fool," continued Deal. "I know you've been drinking; Scip told me. It's a pity. But no reason why you should not eat."

Carl did not move. Deal went off to his dinner, and sent some to Carl. But the food remained untasted. Then Deal passed into the house to get some tobacco for his pipe. Then a loud cry was heard. The hiding-place which his Yankee fingers had skillfully fashioned in the old wall had been rifled; all his money was gone. No one knew the secret of the spot but Carl.

"Did he overpower you and take it?" he asked, kneeling down and lifting Carl by force, so that he could see his face.

"No; I gave it to him," Carl answered, thickly and slowly.

"You *gave* it to him?"

"I lost it—at cards."

*"Cards!"*

Deal had never thought of that. All at once the whole flashed upon him: the gambler who was always "around" with the "orchestra fellows"; the "restaurant" at San Miguel where he helped "entertain" the guests; the probability that business was slack in the ancient little town, unaccustomed to such luxuries; and the treasure-trove of an old acquaintance within a day's journey—an old acquaintance like Carl, who had come also into happy possession of a rich brother. A rich brother! —probably that was what Schwartz called him!

At any rate, rich or poor, Schwartz had it all. With the exception of one hundred dollars which he had left at San Miguel as a deposit, he had now only five dollars in the world; Carl had gambled away his all.

It was a hard blow.

He lifted his brother in his arms and carried him in to his hammock. A few minutes later, staff in hand, he started down the live-oak avenue toward the old road which led northward to San Miguel. The moonlight was brilliant; he walked all night. At dawn he was searching the little city.

Yes, the man was known there. He frequented the Esmeralda Parlors. The Esmeralda Parlors, however, represented by an attendant, a Northern mulatto, with straight features, long, narrow eyes, and pale-golden skin, a bronze piece of insolence, who was also more faultlessly dressed than any one else in San Miguel, suavely replied that Schwartz was no longer one of their "guests"; he had severed his connection with the Parlors several days before. Where was he? The Parlors had no idea.

But the men about the docks knew. Schwartz had been seen the previous evening negotiating passage at the last moment on a coasting schooner bound South—one of those nondescript little craft engaged in smuggling and illegal trading, with which the waters of the West Indies are infested. The schooner had made her way out of the harbor by moonlight. Although ostensibly bound for Key West, no one could say with any certainty that she would touch there; bribed by Schwartz, with all the harbors, inlets, and lagoons of the West Indies open to her, pursuit would be worse than hopeless. Deal realized this. He ate the food he had brought with him, drank a cup of coffee, called for his deposit, and then walked back to the plantation.

When he came into the little plaza, Carl was sitting on the steps of their small house. His head was clear again; he looked pale and wasted.

"It's all right," said Deal. "I've traced him. In the mean time, don't worry, Carl. If I don't mind it, why should you?"

Without saying more, he went inside, changed his shoes, then came out, ordered dinner, talked to Scip, and when the meal was ready called Carl, and took his place at the table as though nothing had happened. Carl scarcely spoke; Deal approved his silence. He felt so intensely for the lad, realized so strongly what he must be feeling—suffering and feeling—that conversation on the subject would have been at that early moment unendurable. But waking during the night, and hearing him stirring, uneasy, and apparently feverish, he went across to the hammock.

"You are worrying about it, Carl, and you are not strong enough to stand worry. Look here—I have forgiven you; I would forgive you twice as much. Have you no idea why I brought you down here with me?"

"Because you're kind-hearted. And perhaps, too, you thought it would be lonely," answered Carl.

"No, I'm not kind-hearted, and I never was lonely in my life. I didn't intend to tell you, but—you *must not* worry. It is your name, Carl, and—and your blue eyes. I was fond of Eliza."

"Fond of Leeza—Leeza Brenner? Then why on earth didn't you marry her?" said Carl, sitting up in his hammock, and trying to see his step-brother's face in the moonlight that came through the chinks in the shutters.

Mark's face was in shadow. "She liked some one else better," he said.

"Who?"

"Never mind. But—yes, I will tell you—Graves."

"John Graves? That dunce? No, she didn't."

"As it happens, I know she did. But we won't talk about it. I only told you to show you why I cared for you."

"*I* wouldn't care about a girl that didn't care for me," said Carl, still peering curiously through the checkered darkness. The wizened young violin-player fancied himself an omnipotent power among women. But Deal had gone to his bed, and would say no more.

Carl had heard something now which deeply astonished him. He had not been much troubled about the lost money;

it was not in his nature to be much troubled about money at any time. He was sorry; but what was gone was gone; why waste thought upon it? This he called philosophy. Mark, out of regard for Carl's supposed distress, had forbidden conversation on the subject; but he was not shutting out, as he thought, torrents of shame, remorse, and self-condemnation. Carl kept silence willingly enough; but, even if the bar had been removed, he would have had little to say. During the night his head had ached, and he had had some fever; but it was more the effect of the fiery, rank liquor pressed upon him by Schwartz than of remorse. But *now* he had heard what really interested and aroused him. Mark in love!—hard-working, steady, dull old Mark, whom he had thought endowed with no fancies at all, save perhaps that of being thoroughly warmed after his arctic freezing. Old Mark fond of Leeza—in love with Leeza!

Leeza wasn't much. Carl did not even think his cousin pretty; his fancy was for something large and Oriental. But, pretty or not, she had evidently fascinated Mark Deal, coming, a poor little orphan maid, with her aunt, Carl's mother, to brighten old Abner Deal's farm-house, one mile from the windy Exton pier. Carl's mother could not hope to keep her German son in this new home; but she kept little Leeza, or Eliza, as the neighbors called her. And Mark, a shy, awkward boy, had learned to love the child, who had sweet blue eyes, and thick braids of flaxen hair fastened across the back of her head.

"To care all that for Leeza!" thought Carl, laughing silently in his hammock. "And then to fancy that she liked that Graves! And then to leave her, and come away off down here, just on the suspicion!"

But Carl was mistaken. A man, be he never so awkward and silent, will generally make at least one effort to get the woman he loves. Mark had made two, and failed. After his first, he had gone North; after his second, he had come South, bringing Leeza's cousin with him.

In the morning a new life began on the old plantation. First, Scipio was dismissed; then the hunter who had kept the open-air larder supplied with game, an old man of unknown, or rather mixed descent, having probably Spanish, African, and Seminole blood in his veins, was told that his services were required no more.

"But are you going to starve us, then?" asked Carl, with a comical grimace.

"I am a good shot, myself," replied Deal; "and a fair cook, too."

"But *why* do you do it?" pursued the other. He had forgotten all about the money.

The elder man looked at his brother. Could it be possible that he had forgotten? And, if he had, was it not necessary, in their altered circumstances, that the truth should be brought plainly before his careless eyes?

"I am obliged to do it," he answered, gravely. "We must be very saving, Carl. Things will be easier, I hope, when the fields begin to yield."

"Good heavens, you don't mean to say I took all you had!" said Carl, with an intonation showing that the fact that the abstracted sum was "all" was impressing him more than any agency of his own in the matter.

"I told you I did not mind it," answered Mark, going off with his gun and game-bag.

"But *I* do, by Jove!" said Carl to himself, watching him disappear.

Musicians, in this world's knowledge and wisdom, are often fools, or rather they remain always children. The beautiful gift, the divine gift, the gift which is the nearest to heaven, is accompanied by lacks of another sort. Carl Brenner, like a child, could not appreciate poverty unless his dinner was curtailed, his tobacco gone. The petty changes now made in the small routine of each day touched him acutely, and roused him at last to the effort of connected, almost practical thought. Old Mark was troubled—poor. The cook was going, the hunter discharged; the dinners would be good no longer. This was because he, Carl, had taken the money. There was no especial harm in the act *per se*; but, as the sum happened to be all old Mark had, it was unfortunate. Under the circumstances, what could he, Carl, do to help old Mark?

Mark loved that light-headed little Leeza. Mark had brought him down here and taken care of him on Leeza's account. Mark, therefore, should have Leeza. He, Carl, would bring it about. He set to work at once to be special providence in Mark's affairs. He sat down, wrote a long letter, sealed it with a stern air, and then laid it on the table, got up, and surveyed it with decision. There it was—done! Gone! But no; not "gone" yet. And how could it go? He was now confronted by the difficulty of mailing it without Mark's knowledge. San Miguel was the nearest post-office; and San Miguel was miles away. Africanus was half crippled; the old hunter would come no more; he himself could not walk half the distance. Then an idea came to him: Africanus, although dismissed, was not yet gone. He went out to find him.

Mark came home at night with a few birds. "They will last us over one day," he said, throwing down the spoil. "You still here, Scip? I thought I sent you off."

"He's going to-morrow," interposed Carl. Scip sat up all night cooking.

"What in the world has got into him?" said Deal, as the light from the old chimney made their sleeping-room bright.

"He wants to leave us well supplied, I suppose," said Carl, from his hammock. "Things keep better down here when they're cooked, you know." This was true; but it was unusual for Carl to interest himself in such matters.

The next morning Deal started on a hunting expedition, intending to be absent two days. Game was plenty in the high lands farther west. He had good luck, and came back at the end of the second day loaded, having left also several caches behind to be visited on the morrow. But there was no one in the house, or on the plantation; both Scip and Carl were gone.

A slip of paper was pinned to the red cotton door. It contained these words: "It's all right, old fellow. If I'm not back at the end of three days, counting this as one, come into South Devil after me. You'll find a trail."

"Confound the boy!" said Deal, in high vexation. "He's crazy." He took a torch, went to the causeway, and there saw from the foot-prints that two had crossed. "Scip went with him," he thought, somewhat comforted. "The old black rascal used to declare that he knew every inch of the swamp." He went back, cooked his supper, and slept. In the matter of provisions, there was little left save what he kept under lock and key. Scipio had started with a good supply. At dawn he rose, made a fire under the old chimney, cooked some venison, baked some corn-bread, and, placing them in his bag, started into South Devil, a bundle of torches slung on his back as before, his gun in his hand, his revolver and knife in his belt. "They have already been gone two days," he said to himself; "they must be coming toward home, now." He thought Carl was carrying out his cherished design of exploring the swamp. There was a trail—hatchet marks on the trees, and broken boughs. "That's old Scip. Carl would never have been so systematic," he thought.

He went on until noon, and then suddenly found himself on the bank of a sluggish stream. "The Branch," he said—"South Devil Branch. It joins West Devil, and the two make the San Juan Bautista (a queer origin for a saint!) three miles below Miguel. But where does the trail go now?" It went nowhere. He searched and searched, and could not find it. It ended at the Branch. Standing there in perplexity, he happened to raise his eyes. Small attention had he hitherto paid to the tangled vines and blossoms swinging above him. He hated the beauty of South Devil. But now he saw a slip of paper hanging from a vine, and, seizing it, he read as follows: "We take boat here; wait for me if not returned."

Mark stood, the paper in his hand, thinking. There was only one boat in the neighborhood, a canoe belonging to the mongrel old hunter, who occasionally went into the swamp. Carl must have obtained this in some way; probably the mongrel had brought it in by the Branch, or one of its tributaries, and this was the rendezvous. One comfort—the old hunter must then be of the party, too. But why should he, Mark, wait, if Carl had two persons with him? Still, the boy had asked. It ended in his waiting.

He began to prepare for the night. There was a knoll near by, and here he made a camp-fire, spending the time before sunset in gathering the wood by the slow process of climbing the trees and vines, and breaking off dead twigs and branches; everything near the ground was wet and sogged. He planted his four torches, ate his supper, examined his gun and revolver, and then, as darkness fell, having nothing else to do, he made a plot on the ground with twigs and long splinters of light-wood, and played, one hand against the other, a swamp game of fox-and-geese. He played standing (his fox-and-geese were two feet high), so that he could keep a lookout for every sort of creature. There were wild-cats and bears in the interior of South Devil, and in the Branch, alligators. He did not fear the large creatures, however; his especial guard, as before, was against the silent snakes. He lighted the fire and torches early, so that whatever uncanny inhabitants there might be in the near trees could have an opportunity of coming down and seeking night-quarters elsewhere. He played game after game of fox-and-geese; and this time he sang "Sweet Afton." He felt that he had exhausted the "Troubadour" on the previous occasion. He shot five snakes, and saw (or rather it seemed to him that he saw) five thousand others coiling and gliding over the roots of the cypresses all around. He made a rule not to look at them if he could help it, as long as they did not approach. "Otherwise," he thought, "I shall lose my senses, and think the very trees are squirming."

It was a long, long night. The knoll was dented all over with holes made by the long splinters representing his fox-and-geese. Dizziness was creeping over him at intervals. His voice, singing "Sweet Afton," had become hoarse and broken, and his steps uneven, as he moved to and fro, still playing the game dully, when at last dawn came. But, although the flat tops of the great cypresses far above were bathed in the golden sunshine, it was long before the radiance penetrated to the dark glades below. The dank, watery aisles were still in gray shadow, when the watcher heard a sound—a real sound now, not an imaginary one—and at the same moment his glazed eyes saw a boat coming up the Branch. It was a white canoe, and paddled by a wraith; at least, the creature who sat within looked so grayly pale, and its eyes in its still, white face so large and unearthly, that it seemed like a shade returned from the halls of death.

"Why, Carl!" said Mark, in a loud, unsteady voice, breaking through his own lethargy by main force. "It's you, Carl, isn't it?"

He tramped down to the water's edge, each step seeming to him a rod long, and now a valley, and now a hill. The canoe touched the bank, and Carl fell forward; not with violence, but softly, and without strength. What little consciousness he had kept was now gone.

Dawn was coming down from above; the air was slightly

stirred. The elder man's head grew more steady, as he lifted his step-brother, gave him brandy, rubbed his temples and chest, and then, as he came slowly back to life again, stood thinking what he should do. They were a half-day's journey from home, and Carl could not walk. If he attempted to carry him, he was fearful that they should not reach pure air outside before darkness fell again, and a second night in the thick air might be death for both of them; but there was the boat. It had come into South Devil in some way; by that way it should go out again. He laid Carl in one end, putting his own coat under his head for a pillow, and then stepped in himself, took the paddle, and moved off. Of course he must ascend the Branch; as long as there were no tributaries, he could not err. But presently he came to an everglade—a broadening of the stream with apparently twenty different outlets, all equally dark and tangled. He paddled around the border, looking first at one, then at another. The matted water-vines caught at his boat like hundreds of hands; the great lily-leaves slowly sank and let the light bow glide over them. Carl slept; there was no use trying to rouse him; but probably he would remember nothing, even if awake. The elder brother took out his compass, and had decided by it which outlet to take, when his eye rested upon the skin of a moccasin nailed to a cypress on the other side of the pond. It was the mongrel's way of making a guide-post. Without hesitation, although the direction was the exact opposite of the one he had selected, Deal pushed the canoe across and entered the stream thus indicated. At the next pool he found another snake-skin; and so on out of the swamp. Twenty-five snakes had died in the cause. He came to firm land at noon, two miles from the plantation. Carl was awake now, but weak and wandering. Deal lifted him on shore, built a fire, heated some meat, toasted corn-bread, and made him eat. Then, leaning upon his brother's arm, walking slowly, and often pausing to rest, the blue-eyed ghost reached home at sunset—two miles in five hours.

Ten days now passed; the mind of the young violin player did not regain its poise. He rose and dressed himself each morning, and slept in the sunshine as before. He went to the place of tombs, carrying his violin, but forgot to play. Instead, he sat looking dreamily at the swamp. He said little, and that little was disconnected. The only sentence which seemed to have meaning, and to be spoken earnestly, was, "It's all right, old fellow. Just you wait fifteen days—fifteen days!" But, when Mark questioned him, he could get no definite reply, only a repetition of the exhortation to "wait fifteen days."

Deal went over to one of the mongrel's haunts, and, by good luck, found him at home. The mongrel had a number of camps, which he occupied according to convenience. The old man acknowledged that he had lent his canoe, and that he had accompanied Carl and Scip part of the way through South Devil. But only part of the way; then he left them, and struck across to the west. Where were they going? Why, straight to San Miguel; the Branch brought them to the King's Road crossing, and the rest of the way they went on foot. What were they going to do in San Miguel? The mongrel had no idea; he had not many ideas. Scip was to stay up there; Brenner was to return alone in the canoe, they having made a trail all the way.

Deal returned to the plantation. He still thought that Carl's idea had been merely to explore the swamp.

Twelve days had passed, and had grown to fourteen; Carl was no stronger. He was very gentle now, like a sick child. Deal was seized with a fear that this soft quiet was the peace that often comes before the last to the poor racked frame of the consumptive. He gave up all but the necessary work, and stayed with Carl all day. The blue-eyed ghost smiled, but said little; into its clouded mind penetrated but one ray—"Wait fifteen days." Mark had decided that the sentence meant nothing but some wandering fancy. Spring in all her superb luxuriance was now wreathing Florida with flowers; the spring flowers met the old flowers, the spring leaves met the old leaves. The yellow jessamine climbed over miles of thicket; the myriad purple balls of the sensitive-plant starred the ground; the atamasco lilies grew whitely, each one shining all alone, in the wet woods; chocolate-hued orchids nodded, and the rose-colored ones rang their bells, at the edge of the barren. The old causeway across the sugar waste was blue with violets, and Mark carried Carl thither; he would lie there contentedly in the sunshine for hours, his pale fingers toying with the blue blossoms, his eyes lifted to the green line of South Devil across the sapphire sky.

One afternoon he fell asleep there, and Mark left him, to

cook their dinner. When he came back, his step-brother's eyes had reason in them once more, or rather remembrance.

"Old fellow," he said, as Mark, surprised and somewhat alarmed at the change, sat down beside him, "you got me out of the swamp, I suppose? I don't remember getting myself out. Now I want to ask something. I'm going to leave this world in a few days, and try it in another; better luck next time, you know. What I want to ask is that you'll take me up and bury me at San Miguel in a little old burying-ground they have there, on a knoll overlooking the ocean. I don't want to lie here with the Dons and the Aztecs; and, besides, I particularly want to be carried through the swamp. Take me through in the canoe, as I went the last time; it's the easiest way, and there's a trail. And I want to go. And do not cover my face, either; I want to see. Promise."

Mark promised, and Carl closed his eyes. Then he roused himself again.

"Inquire at the post-office in San Miguel for a letter," he said drowsily. "Promise." Again Mark promised. He seemed to sleep for some minutes; then he spoke again.

"I heard that music, you know—heard it all out plainly and clearly," he said, looking quietly at his brother. "I know the whole, and have sung it over to myself a thousand times since. I can not write it down *now*. But it will not be lost."

"Music is never lost, I suppose," answered Mark, somewhat at random.

"Certainly not," said Carl, with decision. "My song will be heard some time. I'm sure of that. And it will be much admired."

"I hope so."

"You try to be kind always, don't you, old fellow, whether you comprehend or not?" said the boy, with his old superior smile—the smile of the artist, who, although he be a failure and a pauper, yet always pities the wise. Then he slept again. At dawn, peacefully and with a smile, he died.

It should not have been expected, perhaps, that he could live. But in some way Mark had expected it.

A few hours later a canoe was floating down the Branch through South Devil. One man was paddling at the stern; another was stretched on a couch, with his head on a pillow placed at the bow, where he could see the blossoming network above through his closed eyes. As Carl had said, Scipio had left a trail all the way—a broken branch, a bent reed, or a shred of cloth tied to the lily-leaves. All through the still day they glided on, the canoe moving without a sound on the bosom of the dark stream. They passed under the gray and solemn cypresses, rising without branches to an enormous height, their far foliage hidden by the moss, which hung down thickly in long flakes, diffusing the sunshine and making it silvery like mist; in the silver swung the air-plants, great cream-colored disks, and wands of scarlet, crowded with little buds, blossoms that looked like butterflies, and blossoms that looked like humming-birds, and little dragon-heads with grinning faces. Then they came to the region of the palms; these shot up, slender and graceful, and leaned over the stream, the great aureum-ferns growing on their trunks high in the air. Beneath was a firmer soil than in the domain of the cypresses, and here grew a mat of little flowers, each less than a quarter of an inch wide, close together, pink, blue, scarlet, yellow, purple, but never white, producing a hue singularly rich, owing to the absence of that colorless color which man ever mingles with his floral combinations, and strangely makes sacred alike to the bridal and to death. Great vines ran up the palms, knotted themselves, and came down again, hand over hand, wreathed in little fresh leaves of exquisite green. Birds with plumage of blush-rose pink flew slowly by; also some with scarlet wings, and the jeweled paroquets. The great Savannah cranes stood on the shore, and did not stir as the boat moved by. And, as the spring was now in its prime, the alligators showed their horny heads above water, and climbed awkwardly out on the bank; or else, swimming by the side of the canoe, accompanied it long distances, no doubt moved by dull curiosity concerning its means of locomotion, and its ideas as to choice morsels of food. The air was absolutely still; no breeze reached these blossoming aisles; each leaf hung motionless. The atmosphere was hot, and heavy with perfumes. It was the heart of the swamp, a riot of intoxicating, steaming, swarming, fragrant, beautiful, tropical life, without man to make or mar it. All the world was once so, before man was made.

Did Deal appreciate this beauty? He looked at it, because

he could not get over the feeling that Carl was looking at it too; but he did not admire it. The old New England spirit was rising within him again at last, after the crushing palsy of the polar ice, and the icy looks of a certain blue-eyed woman.

He came out of the swamp an hour before sunset, and, landing, lifted his brother in his arms, and started northward toward San Miguel. The little city was near; but the weight of a dead body grown cold is strange and mighty, and it was late evening before he entered the gate, carrying his motionless burden. He crossed the little plaza, and went into the ancient cathedral, laying it down on the chancel-step before the high altar. It was the only place he could think of; and he was not repelled. A hanging lamp of silver burned dimly; in a few moments kind hands came to help him. And thus Carl, who never went to church in life, went there in death, and, with tapers burning at his head and feet, rested all night under the picture of the Madonna, with nuns keeping watch and murmuring their gentle prayers beside him.

The next morning he was buried in the dry little burial-ground on the knoll overlooking the blue Southern ocean.

When all was over, Deal, feeling strangely lonely, remembered his promise, and turned toward the post-office. He expected nothing; it was only one of the poor lad's fancies; still, he would keep his word. There was nothing for him.

He went out. Then an impulse made him turn back and ask if there was a letter for Carl. "For Carl Brenner," he said, and thought how strange it was that there was now no Carl. There was a letter; he put it into his pocket and left the town, going homeward by the King's Road on foot; the South Devil should see *him* no more. He slept part of the night by the roadside, and reached home the next morning; everything was as he had left it. He made a fire and boiled some coffee; then he set the little house in order, loaded his gun, and went out mechanically after game. The routine of daily life had begun again.

"It's a pleasant old place," he said to himself, as he went through one of the orange-aisles and saw the wild oranges dotting the ground with their golden color. "It's a pleasant old place," he repeated, as he went out into the hot, still sunshine beyond. He filled his game-bag, and sat down to rest a while before returning. Then for the first time he remembered the letter, and drew it forth. This was the letter Carl meant; Carl asked him to get it after he was dead; he must have intended, then, that he, Mark, should read it. He opened it, and looked at the small, slanting handwriting without recognizing it. Then from the inside a photograph fell out, and he took it up; it was Leeza. On the margin was written, "For Mark."

She had written; but, womanlike, not, as Carl expected, to Mark. Instead, she had written to Carl, and commissioned *him* to tell Mark—what? Oh, a long story, such as girls tell, but with the point that, after all, she "liked" (liked?) Mark best. Carl's letter had been blunt, worded with unflattering frankness. Leeza was tired of her own coquetries, lonely, and poor; she wrote her foolish little apologizing, confessing letter with tears in her blue eyes—those blue eyes that sober, reticent Mark Deal could not forget.

Carl had gone to San Miguel, then, to mail a letter—a letter which had brought this answer! Mark, with his face in his hands, thanked God that he had not spoken one harsh word to the boy for what had seemed obstinate disobedience, but had tended him gently to the last.

Then he rose, stretched his arms, drew a long breath, and looked around. Everything seemed altered. The sky was brassy, the air an oven. He remembered the uplands where the oats grew, near Exton; and his white sand-furrows seemed a ghastly mockery of fields. He went homeward and drew water from his well to quench his burning thirst; it was tepid, and he threw it away, recalling as he did so the spring under the cool, brown rocks where he drank when a boy. A sudden repugnance came over him when his eyes fell on the wild oranges lying on the ground, over-ripe with rich, pulpy decay; he spurned them aside with his foot, and thought of the firm apples in the old orchard, a fruit cool and reticent, a little hard, too, not giving itself to the first comer. Then there came over him the hue of Northern forests in spring, the late, reluctant spring of Exton; and the changeless olive-green of the pine barrens grew hideous in his eyes. But, most of all, there seized him a horror of the swamp—a horror of its hot steaming air, and its intoxicating perfume, which reached him faintly even where he stood; it seemed to him that if he staid long within their reach his brain would be affected as Carl's had been, and that he should wander within and die. For there would be no one to rescue *him*.

So strong was this new feeling, like a giant full armed, that he started that very night, carrying his gun and Carl's violin, and a knapsack of clothes on his back, and leaving his other possessions behind. Their value was not great, but they made a princely home for the mongrel, who came over after he had departed, looked around stealthily, stole several small articles, and hastened away; came back again after a day or two, and stole a little more; and finally, finding the place deserted, brought back all his spoil and established himself there permanently, knowing full well that it would be long before Monteano's would find another tenant from the North.

As Mark Deal passed across the King's Road Bridge over the Branch (now soon to be sainted), he paused, and looked down into the north border of South Devil. Then he laid aside his gun and the violin, went off that way, and gathered a large bunch of swamp blossoms. Coming into San Miguel, he passed through the town and out to the little burial-ground beyond. Here he found the new-made grave, and laid the flowers upon it.

"He will like them because they come from *there*," was his thought.

Then, with a buoyant step, he started up the long, low, white peninsula, set with its olive-woods in a sapphire sea; and his face was turned northward.

# In the Cotton Country

The loveliest land that smiles beneath the sky,
The coast-land of our western Italy.
I view the waters quivering; quaff the breeze,
Whose briny raciness keeps an under taste
Of flavorous tropic sweets, perchance swept home
From Cuba's perfumed groves and garden spiceries.

PAUL HAMILTON HAYNE

Call on thy children of the hill,
Wake swamp and river, coast and rill,
Rouse all thy strength, and all thy skill,
                    Carolina!
Tell how the patriot's soul was tried,
And what his dauntless breast defied;
How Rutledge ruled and Laurens died,
                    Carolina!

HENRY TIMROD

Do you know the cotton country—the country of broad levels open to the sun, where the ungainly, ragged bushes stand in long rows, bearing the clothing of a nation on their backs? Not on their backs either, for the white wool is scattered over the branches and twigs, looking, not as if it grew there, but as if it had been blown that way, and had caught and clung at random. When I first came to the cotton country, I used to stand with my chin on the top-rail of the fences, trying to rid my eyes of that first impression. I saw the fields only when the cotton was white, when there were no green leaves left, and the fleecy down did not seem to me a vegetable at all. Starved cows passed through the half-plucked rows untempted, and I said to myself: "Of course. Cows do not eat cotton any more than they eat wool; but what bush is there at the North that they would not nibble if starving?" Accustomed to the trim, soldierly ranks of the Western corn-fields, or the billowy grace of the wheat, I could think of nothing save a parade of sturdy beggarmen unwillingly drawn up in line, when I gazed upon the stubborn, uneven branches, and generally lop-sided appearance of these plants—plants, never-theless, of wealth, usefulness, and historic importance in the annals of our land. But after a while I grew accustomed to their contrary ways, and I even began to like their defiant wild-ness, as a contrast, perhaps, to the languorous sky above, the true sky of the cotton country, with its soft heat, its hazy air, and its divine twilight that lingers so long. I always walked abroad at sunset, and it is in the sunset-light that I always see the fields now when far away. No doubt there was plenty of busy, prosaic reality down there in the mornings, but I never saw it; I only saw the beauty and the fancies that come with the soft after-glow and the shadows of the night.

Down in the cotton country the sun shines steadily all day long, and the earth is hot under your feet. There are few birds, but at nightfall the crows begin to fly home in a long line, going down into the red west as though they had important messages to deliver to some imprisoned princess on the edge of the horizon. One day I followed the crows. I said to myself: "The princess is a *ruse*; they probably light not far from here, and I am going to find their place. The crows at home—that would be something worth seeing." Turning from the path, I went westward. "What!" said a country-woman, meeting Wordsworth on the road, "are ye stepping westward, sir?" I, too, stepped westward.

Field after field I crossed; at last the fences ceased, and only old half-filled ditches marked the boundary-lines. The land sloped downward slightly, and after a while the ridge be-hind me seemed like a line of heights, the old cotton-plants on its top standing out as distinctly as single pine-trees on a mountain-summit outlined against the sky; so comparative is height. The crows still flew westward as I came out upon a sec-ond level lower down than the first, and caught a golden gleam through the fringe of bushes in the middle of the plain. I had unwittingly found the river at last, that broad, brown river that I knew was down there somewhere, although I had not seen it with my bodily eyes. I had full knowledge of what it was, though, farther south toward the ocean; I knew the long tres-tles over the swamps and dark canebrakes that stretched out for miles on each side of the actual stream—trestles over which the trains passed cautiously every day, the Northern passengers looking nervously down at the quaking, spongy surface below, and prophesying accidents as certain some time—when they were not on board. Up here in the cotton country, however, the river was more docile; there were no tides to come up and destroy the banks, and with the exception of freshets the habits of the stream were orderly. The levels on each side might have been, should have been, rich with plenty. Instead, they were uncultivated and desolate. Here and there a wild, outlawed cotton-bush reared its head, and I could trace the old line of the cart-road and cross-tracks; but the soil was spongy and disintegrated, and for a long time evidently no care had been bestowed upon it. I crossed over to the river, and found that the earth-bank which had protected the field was broken down and washed away in many places; the low trees and bushes on shore still held the straws and driftwood that showed the last freshet's high-water mark.

The river made an irregular bend a short distance below, and I strolled that way, walking now on the thick masses of lespedeza that carpeted the old road-track, and now on the singularly porous soil of the level, a soil which even my inexperienced eyes recognized as worthless, all its good particles having been drained out of it and borne away on the triumphant tide of the freshets. The crows still evaded me, crossing the river in a straight line and flying on toward the west, and, in that arbitrary way in which solitary pedestrians make compacts with themselves, I said, "I will go to that tree at the exact turn of the bend, and not one step farther." I went to that tree at the exact turn of the bend, and then I went—farther; for I found there one solemn, lonely old house. Now, if there had been two, I should not have gone on; I should not have broken my compact. Two houses are sociable and commonplace; but one all alone on a desolate waste like that inspired me with—let us call it interest, and I went forward.

It was a lodge rather than a house; in its best day it could never have been more than a very plain abode, and now, in its worst, it seemed to have fallen into the hands of Giant Despair. "Forlorn" was written over its lintels, and "without hope" along its low roof-edge. Raised high above the ground, in the Southern fashion, on wooden supports, it seemed even more unstable than usual to Northern eyes, because the lattice-work, the valance, as it were, which generally conceals the bare, stilt-like underpinning, was gone, and a thin calf and some melancholy chickens were walking about underneath, as though the place was an arbor. There was a little patch of garden, but no grass, no flowers; everything was gray, the unpainted house, the sand of the garden-beds, and the barren waste stretching away on all sides. At first I thought the place was uninhabited, but as I drew nearer a thin smoke from one of the chimneys told of life within, and I said to myself that the life would be black-skinned life, of course. For I was quite accustomed now to finding the families of the freedmen crowded into just such old houses as this, hidden away in unexpected places; for the freedmen hardly ever live up on the even ground in the broad sunshine as though they had a right there, but down in the hollows or out into the fringes of wood, where their low-roofed cabins, numerous though they may be, are scarcely visible to the passer-by. There was no fence around this house; it stood at large on the waste as though it belonged there. Take away the fence from a house, and you take away its respectability; it becomes at once an outlaw. I ascended the crazy, sunken steps that led to the front door, and lifted the knocker that hung there as if in mockery; who ever knocked there now save perhaps a river-god with his wet fingers as he hurried by, mounted on the foaming freshet, to ravage and lay waste again the poor, desolate fields? But no spirit came to the door, neither came the swarm of funny little black faces I had expected; instead, I saw before me a white woman, tall, thin, and gray-haired. Silently she stood there, her great, dark eyes, still and sad, looking at me as much as to say, "By what right are you here?"

"Excuse me, madam," was my involuntary beginning; then I somewhat stupidly asked for a glass of water.

"I would not advise you to drink the water we have here; it is not good," replied the woman. I knew it was not; the water is never good down on the levels. But I was very stupid that day.

"I should like to rest a while," was my next attempt. It brought out a wooden chair, but no cordiality. I tried everything I could think of in the way of subjects for conversation, but elicited no replies beyond monosyllables. I could not very well say, "Who are you, and how came you here?" and yet that was exactly what I wanted to know. The woman's face baffled me, and I do not like to be baffled. It was a face that was old and at the same time young; it had deep lines, it was colorless, and the heavy hair was gray; and still I felt that it was not old in years, but that it was like the peaches we find sometimes on the ground, old, wrinkled, and withered, yet showing here and there traces of that evanescent bloom which comes before the ripeness. The eyes haunted me; they haunt me now, the dry, still eyes of immovable, hopeless grief. I thought, "Oh, if I could only help her!" but all I said was, "I fear I am keeping you standing"; for that is the senseless way we human creatures talk to each other.

Her answer was not encouraging.

"Yes," she replied, in her brief way, and said no more.

I felt myself obliged to go.

But the next afternoon I wandered that way again, and the next, and the next. I used to wait impatiently for the hour when I could enter into the presence of her great silence. How still she was! If she had wept, if she had raved, if she had worked with nervous energy, or been resolutely, doggedly idle, if she had seemed reckless, or callous, or even pious; but no, she was none of these. Her old-young face was ever the same, and she went about her few household tasks in a steady, nerveless manner, as though she could go on doing them for countless ages, and yet never with the least increase of energy. She swept the room, for instance, every day, never thoroughly, but in a gentle, incompetent sort of way peculiarly her own; yet she always swept it and never neglected it, and she took as much time to do it as though the task was to be performed with microscopic exactness.

She lived in her old house alone save for the presence of one child, a boy of six or seven years—a quiet, grave-eyed little fellow, who played all by himself hour after hour with two little wooden soldiers and an empty spool. He seldom went out of the house; he did not seem to care for the sunshine or the open air as other children care, but gravely amused himself in-doors in his own quiet way. He did not make his wooden soldiers talk or demolish each other triumphantly, according to the manner of boys; but he marshaled them to and fro with slow consideration, and the only sound was the click of their little muskets as he moved them about. He seemed never to speak of his own accord; he was strangely silent always. I used to wonder if the two ever talked together playfully as mother and child should talk; and one day, emboldened by a welcome, not warmer, for it was never warm, but not quite so cold perhaps, I said:

"Your little son is very quiet, madam."

"He is not my son."

"Ah!" I replied, somewhat disconcerted. "He is a pretty child; what is his name?"

"His name is John."

The child heard us in his barren corner, but did not look up or speak; he made his two soldiers advance solemnly upon the spool in silence, with a flank movement. I have called the corner barren, because it seemed doubly so when the boy sat there. The poorest place generally puts on something of a homelike air when a little child is in it; but the two bare walls and angle of bare floor remained hopelessly empty and desolate. The room was large, but there was nothing in it save the two wooden chairs and a table; there was no womanly attempt at a rag-carpet, curtains for the windows, or newspaper pictures for the walls—none of those little contrivances for comfort with which women generally adorn even the most miserable abiding-places, showing a kind of courage which is often pathetic in its hopefulness. Here, however, there was nothing. A back-room held a few dishes, some boxes and barrels, and showed on its cavernous hearth the ashes of a recent fire. "I suppose they sleep in a third bare room somewhere, with their two beds, no doubt, standing all alone in the center of the chamber; for it would be too human, of course, to put them up snugly against the wall, as anybody else would do," I said to myself.

In time I succeeded in building up a sort of friendship with this solitary woman of the waste, and in time she told me her story. Let me tell it to you. I have written stories of imagination, but this is a story of fact, and I want you to believe it. It is true, every word of it, save the names given, and, when you read it, you whose eyes are now upon these lines, stop and reflect that it is only one of many life-stories like unto it. "War is cruelty," said our great general. It is. It must be so. But shall

we not, we women, like Sisters of Charity, go over the field
when the battle is done, bearing balm and wine and oil for
those who suffer?

"Down here in the cotton country we were rich once,
madam; we were richer than Northerners ever are, for we toiled
not for our money, neither took thought for it; it came and we
spent it; that was all. My father was Clayton Cotesworth, and
our home was twenty miles from here, at the Sand Hills. Our
cotton-lands were down on these river-levels; this was one of
our fields, and this house was built for the overseer; the negro-
quarters that stood around it have been carried off piecemeal
by the freedmen." (Impossible to put on paper her accentuation of this title.) "My father was an old man; he could not go
to battle himself, but he gave first his eldest son, my brother
James. James went away from earth at Fredericksburg. It was
in the winter, and very cold. How often have I thought of that
passage, 'And pray ye that your flight be not in the winter,'
when picturing his sufferings before his spirit took flight! Yes,
it was very cold for our Southern boys; the river was full of
floating ice, and the raw wind swept over them as they tried to
throw up intrenchments on the heights. They had no spades,
only pointed sticks, and the ground was frozen hard. Their old
uniforms, worn thin by hard usage, hung in tatters, and many
of them had no shoes; the skin of their poor feet shone blue, or
glistening white, like a dead man's skin, through the coverings
of rags they made for themselves as best they could. They say
it was a pitiful sight to see the poor fellows sitting down in the
mornings, trying to adjust these rag-wrappings so that they
would stay in place, and fastening them elaborately with their
carefully saved bits of string. He was an honored man who
invented a new way. My brother was one of the shoeless; at the
last, too, it seems that he had no blanket, only a thin counter-
pane. When night came, hungry and tired as he was, he could
only wrap himself in that and lie down on the cold ground to
wait for morning. When we heard all this afterward, we said,
'Blessed be the bullet that put him out of his misery!' for poor
James was a delicate boy, and had been accustomed to loving,
watchful care all his life. Yet, oh, if I could only know that he
was warm once, just once, before he died! They told us he said
nothing after he was shot save 'How cold! How cold!' They

put his poor, stiff body hastily down under the sod, and then the brigade moved on; 'no man knoweth his sepulchre unto this day.'

"Next John went, my second brother. He said good-by, and marched away northward—northward, northward, always northward—to cold, corpse-strewed Virginia, who cried aloud to us continually, 'More! more!' Her roads are marked with death from her Peaks of Otter to the sea, and her great valley ran red. We went to her from all over the South, from Alabama, Florida, and Georgia, and from our own Carolina. We died there by thousands, and by tens of thousands. O Virginia, our dead lie thick in thy tidewater plains, in thy tangled Wilderness, and along thy river-shores, with faces upturned, and hearts still for ever.

"John came back to us once, and wedded the fair girl to whom he was betrothed. It was a sad bridal, although we made it as gay as we could; for we had come to the times of determined gayety then. The tone of society was like the determinedly gay quicksteps which the regimental bands play when returning from a funeral, as much as to say, 'Le roi est mort, vive le roi!' So we turned our old silk dresses, and made a brave appearance; if our shoes were shabby, we hid them under our skirts as well as we could, and held our heads the higher. Maum Sally made a big wedding-cake, as of old, and we went without meat to pay for the spices in it; such luxuries we obtained from the blockade-runners now and then, but they were worth almost their weight in gold. Then John, too, left us. In four months he also was taken—killed by guerrillas, it is supposed, as he rode through a lonely mountain-defile. He was not found for weeks; the snow fell and covered him, mercifully giving the burial the frozen earth denied. After a while the tidings came to us, and poor Mabel slowly wept herself into the grave. She was a loving-hearted little creature, and her life was crushed. She looked at her baby once, called his name John, and then died. The child, that boy yonder, seems to have inherited her grief. He sheds no tears, however; his girl-mother shed them all, both for him and for herself, before ever he saw the light. My turn came next.

"You have been married, madam? Did you love, too? I do not mean regard, or even calm affection; I do not mean sense of duty, self-sacrifice, or religious goodness. I mean love—love that absorbs the entire being. Some women love so; I do not say they are the happiest women. I do not say they are the best. I am one of them. But God made us all; he gave us our hearts —we did not choose them. Let no woman take credit to herself for her even life, simply because it has been even. Doubtless, if he had put her out in the breakers, she would have swayed too. Perhaps she would have drifted from her moorings also, as I have drifted. I go to no church; I can not pray. But do not think I am defiant; no, I am only dead. I seek not the old friends, few and ruined, who remain still above-ground; I have no hope, I might almost say no wish. Torpidly I draw my breath through day and night, nor care if the rain falls or the sun shines. You Northern women would work; I can not. Neither have I the courage to take the child and die. I live on as the palsied animal lives, and if some day the spring fails, and the few herbs within his reach, he dies. Nor do I think he grieves much about it; he only eats from habit. So I.

"It was in the third year of the war that I met Ralph Kinsolving. I was just eighteen. Our courtship was short; indeed, I hardly knew that I loved him until he spoke and asked me to give him myself. 'Marry me, Judith,' he pleaded ardently; 'marry me before I go; let it be my wife I leave behind me, and not my sweetheart. For sweethearts, dear, can not come to us in camp when we send, as we shall surely send soon, that you may all see our last grand review.' So spoke Rafe, and with all his heart he believed it. We all believed it. Never for a moment did we doubt the final triumph of our arms. We were so sure we were right!

"'Our last grand review,' said Rafe; but he did not dream of that last review at Appomattox, when eight thousand hungry, exhausted men stacked their muskets in the presence of the enemy, whose glittering ranks, eighty thousand strong, were drawn up in line before them, while in the rear their well-filled wagons stood—wagons whose generous plenty brought tears to the eyes of many a poor fellow that day, thinking, even while he eagerly ate, of his desolated land, and his own empty fields at home.

"I did marry my soldier, and, although it was in haste, I had my wedding-dress, my snowy veil; lace and gauze were not needed at the hospitals! But we went without the wedding-cake this time, and my satin slippers were made at home, looking very like a pair of white moccasins when finished.

"In the middle of the ceremony there was an alarm; the slaves had risen at Latto's down the river, and were coming to the village armed with clubs, and, worse still, infuriated with liquor they had found. Even our good old rector paused. There were but few white men at home. It seemed indeed a time for pausing. But Rafe said, quietly, 'Go on!' and, unsheathing his sword, he laid it ready on the chancel-rail. 'To have and to hold, from this day forward, for better for worse, for richer for poorer, in sickness and in health, to love and to cherish, till death us do part,' repeated Rafe, holding my hand in his firm clasp, and looking down into my frightened face so tenderly that I forgot my alarm—everything, indeed, save his love. But when the last word was spoken, and the blessing pronounced over our bowed heads, the shining sword seeming a silent witness, Rafe left me like a flash. The little church was empty when I rose from my knees; the women had hurried home with blanched faces to bar their doors and barricade their windows, and the men had gone for their horses and guns; only my old father waited to give me his blessing, and then we, too, hastened homeward. Our little band of defenders assembled in the main street, and rode gallantly out to meet the negroes, who were as fifty to their one. Rafe was the leader, by virtue of his uniform, and he waved his hand to me as he rode by. 'Cheer up, Judith,' he cried; 'I will soon return.'

"I never saw him again.

"They dispersed the negroes without much difficulty; Latto's slaves had been badly treated for months, they had not the strength to fight long. But Rafe rode to the next town with the prisoners under his charge, and there he met an imploring summons to the coast; the Federal ships had appeared unexpectedly off the harbor, and the little coast-city lay exposed and helpless at the mouth of the river. All good men and true within reach were summoned to the defense. So my soldier went, sending back word to me a second time, 'I will soon return.' But the siege was long, long—one of those bitterly contested little sieges of minor importance, with but small forces engaged on each side, which were so numerous during the middle times of the war—those middle times after the first high hopes had been disappointed, and before the policy of concentration had been adopted by the North—that slow, dogged North of yours that kept going back and beginning over again, until at last it found out how to do it. This little siege was long and weary, and when at last the Federal vessels went suddenly out beyond the bar again, and the town, unconquered, but crippled and suffering, lay exhausted on the shore, there was not much cause for rejoicing. Still I rejoiced; for I thought that Rafe would come. I did not know that his precious furlough had expired while he was shut up in the beleaguered city, and that his colonel had sent an imperative summons, twice repeated. Honor, loyalty, commanded him to go, and go immediately. He went.

"The next tidings that came to me brought word that he loved me and was well; the next, that he loved me and was well; the next, that he loved me and was—dead. Madam, my husband, Ralph Kinsolving, was shot—as a spy!

"You start—you question—you doubt. But spies were shot in those days, were they not? That is a matter of history. Very well; you are face to face now with the wife of one of them.

"You did not expect such an ending, did you? You have always thought of spies as outcasts, degraded wretches, and, if you remembered their wives at all, it was with the idea that they had not much feeling, probably, being so low down in the scale of humanity. But, madam, in those bitter, hurrying days men were shot as spies who were no spies. Nay, let me finish; I know quite well that the shooting was not confined to one side; I acknowledge that; but it was done, and mistakes were made. Now and then chance brings a case to light, so unmistakable in its proof that those who hear it shudder—as now and then also chance brings a coffin to light whose occupant was buried alive, and came to himself when it was too late. But what of the cases that chance does *not* bring to light?

"My husband was no spy; but it had been a trying time for the Northern commanders: suspicion lurked everywhere; the whole North clamored to them to advance, and yet their plans, as fast as they made them, were betrayed in some way to the enemy. An example was needed—my husband fell in the way.

"He explained the suspicious circumstances of his case, but a cloud of witnesses rose up against him, and he proudly closed his lips. They gave him short shrift; that same day he was led out and met his death in the presence of thousands. They told me that he was quite calm, and held himself proudly; at the last he turned his face to the south, as if he were gazing down, down, into the very heart of that land for whose sake he was about to die. I think he saw the cotton-fields then, and our home; I think he saw me, also, for the last time.

"By the end of that year, madam, my black hair was gray, as you see it now; I was an old woman at nineteen.

"My father and I and that grave-eyed baby lived on in the old house. Our servants had left us, all save one, old Cassy, who had been my nurse or 'maumee,' as we called her. We suffered, of course. We lived as very poor people live. The poorest slaves in the old time had more than we had then. But we did not murmur; the greater griefs had swallowed up the less. I said, 'Is there any sorrow like unto my sorrow?' But the end was not yet.

"You have heard the story of the great march, the march to the sea? But there was another march after that, a march of which your own writers have said that its route was marked by a pillar of smoke by day and of flame by night—the march through South Carolina. The Northern soldiers shouted when they came to the yellow tide of the Savannah, and looked across and knew that the other shore was South Carolina soil. They crossed, and Carolina was bowed to the dust. Those were the days we cried in the morning, 'O God, that it were night!' and in the night, 'O God, that it were morning!' Retribution, do you say? It may be so. But love for our State seemed loyalty to us; and slavery was the sin of our fathers, not ours. Surely we have expiated it now.

"'Chile, chile, dey is come!' cried old Cassy, bursting into my room one afternoon, her withered black face grayly pale with fear. I went out. Cavalrymen were sweeping the village of all it contained, the meager little that was left to us in our penury. My father was asleep; how I prayed that he might not waken! Although an old man, he was fiery as a boy, and proudly, passionately rebellious against the fate which had come upon us. Our house was some distance back from the road, and broad grounds separated us from the neighboring residences. Cassy and I softly piled our pillows and cushions against the doors and windows that opened from his room to the piazza, hoping to deaden the sounds outside, for some of our people were resisting, and now and then I heard shouts and oaths. But it was of no use. My dear old father woke, heard the sounds, and rushed out into the street sword in hand; for he had been a soldier too, serving with honor through the Mexican War. Made desperate by my fears for him, I followed. There was a *mêlée* in the road before our house; a high wind blew the thick dust in my eyes and half blinded me, so that I only saw struggling forms on foot and on horseback, and could not distinguish friend or foe. Into this group my father rushed. I never knew the cause of the contest; probably it was an ill-advised attack by some of our people, fiery and reasonless always. But, whatever it was, at length there came one, two, three shots, and then the group broke apart. I rushed forward and received my old father in my arms, dying—dead. His head lay on my shoulder as I knelt in the white road, and his silver hair was dabbled with blood; he had been shot through the head and breast, and lived but a moment.

"We carried him back to the house, old Cassy and I, slowly, and with little regard for the bullets which now whistled through the air; for the first shots had brought together the scattered cavalrymen, who now rode through the streets firing right and left, more at random, I think, than with direct aim, yet still determined to 'frighten the rebels,' and avenge the soldier, one of their number, who had been killed at the beginning of the fray. We laid my father down in the center of the hall, and prepared him for his long sleep. No one came to help us; no one came to sorrow with us; each household gathered its own together and waited with bated breath for what was still to come. I watched alone beside my dead that night, the house-doors stood wide open, and lights burned at the head and foot of the couch. I said to myself, 'Let them come now and take their fill.' But no one disturbed me, and I kept my vigil from midnight until dawn; then there came a sound of many feet, and when the sun rose our streets were full of blue-coated soldiers, thousands upon thousands; one wing of the great army was marching through. There was still hot anger against us for our resistance, and when the commanding officers arrived they ordered guards to be stationed at every house, with orders to shoot any man or boy who showed himself outside of his doorway. All day and night the Federal soldiers would be passing through, and the guards gave notice that if another man was injured twenty rebel lives should answer for it.

"'We must bury my father, you and I together, Cassy,' I said; 'there is no one to help us. Come!'

"The old woman followed me without a word. Had I bidden her go alone, even as far as the door-step, she would have cowered at my feet in abject terror; but, following me, she would have gone unquestioning to the world's end. The family burial-place was on our own grounds, according to the common custom of the South; thither we turned our steps, and in silence hollowed out a grave as best we could. The guard near by watched us with curiosity for some time; at last he approached:

"'What are you two women doing there?'

"'Digging a grave.'

"'For whom?'

"'For my father, who lies dead in the house.'

"He withdrew a short distance, but still watched us closely, and when all was ready, and we returned to the house for our burden, I saw him signal the next guard. 'They will not interrupt us,' I said; 'we are only two women and a dead man.'

"I wrapped my dear father in his cloak, and covered his face; then we bore the lounge on which he lay out into the sunshine down toward the open grave. The weight of this poor frame of ours when dead is marvelous, and we moved slowly; but at length we reached the spot. I had lined the grave with coverlids and a fine linen sheet, and now, with the aid of blankets, we lowered the clay to its last resting-place. Then, opening my prayer-book, I read aloud the service for the burial of the dead, slowly, and without tears, for I was thinking of the meeting above of the old father and his two boys: 'Lord, thou hast been our refuge from one generation to another. Before the mountains were brought forth, or ever the earth and the world were made, thou art God from everlasting.' I took a clod and cast it upon the shrouded breast below. 'Earth to earth, ashes to ashes, dust to dust,' I said, and old Cassy, kneeling opposite, broke forth into low wailing, and rocked her body to and fro.

Then we filled the grave. I remember that I worked with feverish strength; if it was not done quickly, I knew I could never do it at all. Can you realize what it would be to stand and shovel the earth with your own hands upon your dead?—to hear the gravel fall and strike?—to see the last shrouded outline disappear under the stifling, heavy clods? All this it was mine to do. When it was over I turned to go, and for the first time lifted my eyes. There at the fence-corner stood a row of Federal soldiers, silent, attentive, and with bared heads; my father was buried with military honors after all.

"During all that day and night the blue-coated ranks marched by; there seemed to be no end to the line of glittering muskets. I watched them passively, holding the orphan-boy on my knee; I felt as though I should never move or speak again. But after the army came the army-followers and stragglers, carrion-birds who flew behind the conquerors and devoured what they had left. They swept the town clean of food and raiment; many houses they wantonly burned; what they could not carry with them they destroyed. My own home did not escape: rude men ransacked every closet and drawer, and cut in ribbons the old portraits on the wall. A German, coming in from the smokehouse, dripping with bacon-juice, wiped his hands upon my wedding-veil, which had been discovered and taken from its box by a former intruder. It was a little thing; but, oh, how it hurt me! At length the last straggler left us, and we remained in the ashes. We could not sit down and weep for ourselves and for our dead; the care of finding wherewithal to eat thrust its coarse necessity upon us, and forced us to our feet. I had thought that all the rest of my life would be but a bowed figure at the door of a sepulchre; but the camp-followers came by, took the bowed figure by the arm, and forced it back to everyday life. We could no longer taste the luxury of tears. For days our people lived on the refuse left by the army, the bits of meat and bread they had thrown aside from their plenty; we picked up the corn with which they had fed their horses, kernel by kernel, and boiled it for our dinner; we groped in the ashes of their camp-fires; little children learned the sagacity of dogs seeking for bones, and quarreled over their findings. The fortune of war, do you say? Yes, the fortune of war! But it is one thing to say, and another thing to feel!

"We came away, madam, for our home was in ashes—old Cassy, the child, and I; we came on foot to this place, and here we have staid. No, the fields are never cultivated now. The dike has been broken down in too many places, and freshets have drained all the good out of the soil; the land is worthless. It was once my father's richest field. Yes, Cassy is dead. She was buried by her own people, who forgave her at the last for having been so spiritless as to stay with 'young missis,' when she might have tasted the glories of freedom over in the crowded hollow where the blacks were enjoying themselves and dying by the score. In six months half of them were gone. They had their freedom—oh, yes, plenty of it; they were quite free— to die! For, you see, madam, their masters, those villainous old masters of theirs, were no longer there to feed and clothe them. Oh! it was a great deliverance for the enfranchised people! Bitter, am I? Put yourself in my place.

"What am I going to do? Nothing. The boy? He must take his chances. Let him grow up under the new *régime*; I have told him nothing of the old. It may be that he will prosper; people do prosper, they tell me. It seems we were wrong, all wrong; then we must be very right now, for the blacks are our judges, councilors, postmasters, representatives, and law-makers. That is as it should be, isn't it? What! not so? But how can it be otherwise? Ah, you think that a new king will arise who knows not Joseph—that is, that a new generation will come to whom these questions will be things of the past. It may be so; I do not know. I do not know anything certainly any more, for my world has been torn asunder, and I am uprooted and lost. No, you can not help me, no one can help me. I can not adjust myself to the new order of things; I can not fit myself in new soil; the fibers are broken. Leave me alone, and give your help to the young; they can profit by it. The child? Well, if—if you really wish it, I will not oppose you. Take him, and bring him up in your rich, prosperous North; the South has no place for him. Go, and God speed you! But, as for me, I will abide in mine own country. It will not be until such as I have gone from earth that the new blood can come to her. Let us alone; we will watch the old life out with her, and when her new dawning comes we shall have joined our dead, and all of us, our errors, our sins, and our sufferings will be forgotten."

# *Felipa*

Glooms of the live-oaks, beautiful-braided and woven
With intricate shades of the vines that, myriad cloven,
Clamber the forks of the multiform boughs.
        . . . . Green colonnades
Of the dim sweet woods, of the dear dark woods,
Of the heavenly woods and glades,
That run to the radiant marginal sand-beach within
        The wide sea-marshes of Glynn.
        . . . . Free
By a world of marsh that borders a world of sea.
Sinuous southward and sinuous northward the shimmering band
Of the sand-beach fastens the fringe of the marsh to the folds of
    the land.

Inward and outward to northward and southward the beach-
    lines linger and curl
As a silver-wrought garment that clings to and follows the firm,
    sweet limbs of a girl.
A league and a league of marsh-grass, waist-high, broad in the
    blade,
Green, and all of a height, and unflecked with a light or a shade.

SIDNEY LANIER

CHRISTINE and I found her there. She was a small, dark-skinned, yellow-eyed child, the offspring of the ocean and the heats, tawny, lithe and wild, shy yet fearless—not unlike one of the little brown deer that bounded through the open reaches of the pine-barren behind the house. She did not come to us —we came to her; we loomed into her life like genii from another world, and she was partly afraid and partly proud of us. For were we not her guests? proud thought! and, better still, were we not women? "I have only seen three women in all my life," said Felipa, inspecting us gravely, "and I like women. I am a woman too, although these clothes of the son of Pedro make me appear as a boy; I wear them on account of the boat and the hauling in of the fish. The son of Pedro being dead at a convenient age, and his clothes fitting me, what would you

308

have? It was a chance not to be despised. But when I am grown I shall wear robes long and beautiful like the señora's." The little creature was dressed in a boy's suit of dark-blue linen, much the worse for wear, and torn.

"If you are a girl, why do you not mend your clothes?" I said.

"Do you mend, señora?"

"Certainly: all women sew and mend."

"The other lady?"

Christine laughed as she lay at ease upon the brown carpet of pine-needles, warm and aromatic after the tropic day's sunshine. "The child has divined me already, Catherine," she said.

Christine was a tall, lissome maid, with an unusually long stretch of arm, long sloping shoulders, and a long fair throat; her straight hair fell to her knees when unbound, and its clear flaxen hue had not one shade of gold, as her clear gray eyes had not one shade of blue. Her small, straight, rose-leaf lips parted over small, dazzlingly white teeth, and the outline of her face in profile reminded you of an etching in its distinctness, although it was by no means perfect according to the rules of art. Still, what a comfort it was, after the blurred outlines and smudged profiles many of us possess—seen to best advantage, I think, in church on Sundays, crowned with flower-decked bonnets, listening calmly serene to favorite ministers, unconscious of noses! When Christine had finished her laugh—and she never hurried anything—she stretched out her arm carelessly and patted Felipa's curly head. The child caught the descending hand and kissed the long white fingers.

It was a wild place where we were, yet not new or crude— the coast of Florida, that old-new land, with its deserted plantations, its skies of Paradise, and its broad wastes open to the changeless sunshine. The old house stood on the edge of the dry land, where the pine-barren ended and the salt-marsh began; in front curved the tide-water river that seemed ever trying to come up close to the barren and make its acquaintance, but could not quite succeed, since it must always turn and flee at a fixed hour, like Cinderella at the ball, leaving not a silver slipper behind, but purple driftwood and bright seaweeds, brought in from the Gulf Stream outside. A planked platform ran out into the marsh from the edge of the barren, and at its end the boats were moored; for, although at high tide the river was at our feet, at low tide it was far away out in the green waste somewhere, and if we wanted it we must go and seek it. We did not want it, however; we let it glide up to us twice a day with its fresh salt odors and flotsam of the ocean, and the rest of the time we wandered over the barrens or lay under the trees looking up into the wonderful blue above, listening to the winds as they rushed across from sea to sea. I was an artist, poor and painstaking. Christine was my kind friend. She had brought me South because my cough was troublesome, and here because Edward Bowne recommended the place. He and three fellow sportsmen were down at the Madre Lagoon, farther south; I thought it probable we should see him, without his three fellow sportsmen, before very long.

"Who were the three women you have seen, Felipa?" said Christine.

"The grandmother, an Indian woman of the Seminoles who comes sometimes with baskets, and the wife of Miguel of the island. But they are all old, and their skins are curled: I like better the silver skin of the señora."

Poor little Felipa lived on the edge of the great salt-marsh alone with her grandparents, for her mother was dead. The yellow old couple were slow-witted Minorcans, part pagan, part Catholic, and wholly ignorant; their minds rarely rose above the level of their orange-trees and their fish-nets. Felipa's father was a Spanish sailor, and, as he had died only the year before, the child's Spanish was fairly correct, and we could converse with her readily, although we were slow to comprehend the patois of the old people, which seemed to borrow as much from the Italian tongue and the Greek as from its mother Spanish. "I know a great deal," Felipa remarked confidently, "for my father taught me. He had sailed on the ocean out of sight of land, and he knew many things. These he taught to me. Do the gracious ladies think there is anything else to know?"

One of the gracious ladies thought not, decidedly. In answer to my remonstrance, expressed in English, she said, "Teach a child like that, and you ruin her."

"Ruin her?"

"Ruin her happiness—the same thing."

Felipa had a dog, a second self—a great gaunt yellow creature of unknown breed, with crooked legs, big feet, and the
name Drollo. What Drollo meant, or whether it was an abbre-
viation, we never knew; but there was a certain satisfaction in
it, for the dog was droll: the fact that the Minorcan title, whatever it was, meant nothing of that sort, made it all the better.
We never saw Felipa without Drollo. "They look a good deal
alike," observed Christine—"the same coloring."

"For shame!" I said.

But it was true. The child's bronzed yellow skin and soft
eyes were not unlike the dog's, but her head was crowned
with a mass of short black curls, while Drollo had only his
two great flapping ears and his low smooth head. Give him an
inch or two more of skull, and what a creature a dog would
be! For love and faithfulness even now what man can match
him? But, although ugly, Felipa was a picturesque little object
always, whether attired in boy's clothes or in her own forlorn
bodice and skirt. Olive-hued and meager-faced, lithe and thin,
she flew over the pine-barrens like a creature of air, laughing
to feel her short curls toss and her thin childish arms buoyed
up on the breeze as she ran, with Drollo barking behind. For
she loved the winds, and always knew when they were coming
—whether down from the north, in from the ocean, or across
from the Gulf of Mexico: she watched for them, sitting in the
doorway, where she could feel their first breath, and she taught
us the signs of the clouds. She was a queer little thing: we used
to find her sometimes dancing alone out on the barren in a
circle she had marked out with pine-cones, and once she confided to us that she talked to the trees. "They hear," she said in
a whisper; "you should see how knowing they look, and how
their leaves listen."

Once we came upon her most secret lair in a dense thicket
of thorn-myrtle and wild smilax—a little bower she had made,
where was hidden a horrible-looking image formed of the
rough pieces of saw-palmetto grubbed up by old Bartolo from
his garden. She must have dragged these fragments thither one
by one, and with infinite pains bound them together with her
rude withes of strong marsh-grass, until at last she had formed
a rough trunk with crooked arms and a sort of a head, the red
hairy surface of the palmetto looking not unlike the skin of

some beast, and making the creature all the more grotesque. This fetich was kept crowned with flowers, and after this we often saw the child stealing away with Drollo to carry to it portions of her meals or a new-found treasure—a sea-shell, a broken saucer, or a fragment of ribbon. The food always mysteriously disappeared, and my suspicion is that Drollo used to go back secretly in the night and devour it, asking no questions and telling no lies: it fitted in nicely, however, Drollo merely performing the ancient part of the priests of Jupiter, men who have been much admired. "What a little pagan she is!" I said.

"Oh, no, it is only her doll," replied Christine.

I tried several times to paint Felipa during these first weeks, but those eyes of hers always evaded me. They were, as I have said before, yellow—that is, they were brown with yellow lights —and they stared at you with the most inflexible openness. The child had the full-curved, half-open mouth of the tropics, and a low Greek forehead. "Why isn't she pretty?" I said.

"She is hideous," replied Christine; "look at her elbows."

Now Felipa's arms *were* unpleasant: they were brown and lean, scratched and stained, and they terminated in a pair of determined little paws that could hold on like grim Death. I shall never forget coming upon a tableau one day out on the barren—a little Florida cow and Felipa, she holding on by the horns, and the beast with its small fore feet stubbornly set in the sand; girl pulling one way, cow the other; both silent and determined. It was a hard contest, but the girl won.

"And if you pass over her elbows, there are her feet," continued Christine languidly. For she was a sybaritic lover of the fine linens of life, that friend of mine—a pre-Raphaelite lady with clinging draperies and a mediæval clasp on her belt. Her whole being rebelled against ugliness, and the mere sight of a sharp-nosed, light-eyed woman on a cold day made her uncomfortable.

"Have we not feet too?" I replied sharply.

But I knew what she meant. Bare feet are not pleasant to the eye nowadays, whatever they may have been in the days of the ancient Greeks; and Felipa's little brown insteps were half the time torn or bruised by the thorns of the chaparral. Besides, there was always the disagreeable idea that she might step upon something cold and squirming when she prowled through the thickets knee-deep in the matted grasses. Snakes abounded, although we never saw them; but Felipa went up to their very doors, as it were, and rang the bell defiantly.

One day old Grandfather Bartolo took the child with him down to the coast: she was always wild to go to the beach, where she could gather shells and sea-beans, and chase the little ocean-birds that ran along close to the waves with that swift gliding motion of theirs, and where she could listen to the roar of the breakers. We were several miles up the salt-marsh, and to go down to the ocean was quite a voyage to Felipa. She bade us good-by joyously; then ran back to hug Christine a second time, then to the boat again; then back.

"I thought you wanted to go, child?" I said, a little impatiently; for I was reading aloud, and these small irruptions were disturbing.

"Yes," said Felipa, "I want to go; and still— Perhaps if the gracious señora would kiss me again—"

Christine only patted her cheek and told her to run away: she obeyed, but there was a wistful look in her eyes, and, even after the boat had started, her face, watching us from the stern, haunted me.

"Now that the little monkey has gone, I may be able at last to catch and fix a likeness of her," I said; "in this case a recollection is better than the changing quicksilver reality."

"You take it as a study of ugliness?"

"Do not be hard upon the child, Christine."

"Hard? Why, she adores me," said my friend, going off to her hammock under the tree.

Several days passed, and the boat returned not. I accomplished a fine amount of work, and Christine a fine amount of swinging in the hammock and dreaming. At length one afternoon I gave my final touch, and carried my sketch over to the pre-Raphaelite lady for criticism. "What do you see?" I said.

"I see a wild-looking child with yellow eyes, a mat of curly black hair, a lank little bodice, her two thin brown arms embracing a gaunt old dog with crooked legs, big feet, and turned-in toes."

"Is that all?"

"All."

"You do not see latent beauty, courage, and a possible great gulf of love in that poor wild little face?"

"Nothing of the kind," replied Christine decidedly. "I see an ugly little girl; that is all."

The next day the boat returned, and brought back five persons, the old grandfather, Felipa, Drollo, Miguel of the island, and—Edward Bowne.

"Already?" I said.

"Tired of the Madre, Kitty; thought I would come up here and see you for a while. I knew you must be pining for me."

"Certainly," I replied; "do you not see how I have wasted away?"

He drew my arm through his and raced me down the plank-walk toward the shore, where I arrived laughing and out of breath.

"Where is Christine?" he asked.

I came back into the traces at once. "Over there in the hammock. You wish to go to the house first, I suppose?"

"Of course not."

"But she did not come to meet you, Edward, although she knew you had landed."

"Of course not, also."

"I do not understand you two."

"And of course not, a third time," said Edward, looking down at me with a smile. "What do peaceful little artists know about war?"

"Is it war?"

"Something very like it, Kitty. What is that you are carrying?"

"Oh! my new sketch. What do you think of it?"

"Good, very good. Some little girl about here, I suppose?"

"Why, it is Felipa!"

"And who is Felipa? Seems to me I have seen that old dog, though."

"Of course you have; he was in the boat with you, and so was Felipa; but she was dressed in boy's clothes, and that gives her a different look."

"Oh! that boy? I remember him. His name is Philip. He is a funny little fellow," said Edward calmly.

"Her name is Felipa, and she is not a boy or a funny little fellow at all," I replied.

"Isn't she? I thought she was both," replied Ned carelessly; and then he went off toward the hammock. I turned away, after noting Christine's cool greeting, and went back to the boat.

Felipa came bounding to meet me. "What is his name?" she demanded.

"Bowne."

"Buon—Buona; I can not say it."

"Bowne, child—Edward Bowne."

"Oh! Eduardo; I know that. Eduardo—Eduardo—a name of honey."

She flew off singing the name, followed by Drollo carrying his mistress's palmetto basket in his big patient mouth; but when I passed the house a few moments afterward she was singing, or rather talking volubly of, another name—"Miguel," and "the wife of Miguel," who were apparently important personages on the canvas of her life. As it happened, I never really saw that wife of Miguel, who seemingly had no name of her own; but I imagined her. She lived on a sand-bar in the ocean not far from the mouth of our salt-marsh; she drove pelicans like ducks with a long switch, and she had a tame eagle; she had an old horse also, who dragged the driftwood across the sand on a sledge, and this old horse seemed like a giant horse always, outlined as he was against the flat bar and the sky. She went out at dawn, and she went out at sunset, but during the middle of the burning day she sat at home and polished sea-beans, for which she obtained untold sums; she was very tall, she was very yellow, and she had but one eye. These items, one by one, had been dropped by Felipa at various times, and it was with curiosity that I gazed upon the original Miguel, the possessor of this remarkable spouse. He was a grave-eyed, yellow man, who said little and thought less, applying *cui bono?* to mental much as the city man applies it to bodily exertion, and therefore achieving, I think, a finer degree of inanition. The tame eagle, the pelicans, were nothing to him; and, when I saw his lethargic, gentle countenance, my own curiosity about them seemed to die away in haze, as though I had breathed in an invisible opiate. He came, he went, and that was all; exit Miguel.

Felipa was constantly with us now. She and Drollo followed the three of us wherever we went—followed the two also whenever I staid behind to sketch, as I often staid, for in those days I was trying to catch the secret of the salt-marsh; a hopeless effort—I know it now. "Stay with me, Felipa," I said; for it was natural to suppose that the lovers might like to be alone. (I call them lovers for want of a better name, but they were more like haters; however, in such cases it is nearly the same thing.) And then Christine, hearing this, would immediately call "Felipa!" and the child would dart after them, happy as a bird. She wore her boy's suit now all the time, because the señora had said she "looked well in it." What the señora really said was, that in boy's clothes she looked less like a grasshopper. But this had been translated as above by Edward Bowne when Felipa suddenly descended upon him one day and demanded to be instantly told what the gracious lady was saying about her; for she seemed to know by intuition when we spoke of her, although we talked in English and mentioned no names. When told, her small face beamed, and she kissed Christine's hand joyfully and bounded away. Christine took out her handkerchief and wiped the spot.

"Christine," I said, "do you remember the fate of the proud girl who walked upon bread?"

"You think that I may starve for kisses some time?" said my friend, going on with the wiping.

"Not while I am alive," called out Edward from behind. His style of courtship *was* of the sledge-hammer sort sometimes. But he did not get much for it on that day; only lofty tolerance, which seemed to amuse him greatly.

Edward played with Felipa very much as if she was a rubber toy or a little trapeze performer. He held her out at arm's length in mid-air, he poised her on his shoulder, he tossed her up into the low myrtle-trees, and dangled her by her little belt over the claret-colored pools on the barren; but he could not frighten her; she only laughed and grew wilder and wilder, like a squirrel. "She has muscles and nerves of steel," he said admiringly.

"Do put her down; she is too excitable for such games," I said in French, for Felipa seemed to divine our English now. "See the color she has."

For there was a trail of dark red over the child's thin oval cheeks which made her look unlike herself. As she caught our eyes fixed upon her, she suddenly stopped her climbing and came and sat at Christine's feet. "Some day I shall wear robes like the señora's," she said, passing her hand over the soft fabric; "and I think," she added after some slow consideration, "that my face will be like the señora's too."

Edward burst out laughing. The little creature stopped abruptly and scanned his face.

"Do not tease her," I said.

Quick as a flash she veered around upon me. "He does not tease me," she said angrily in Spanish; "and, besides, what if he does? I like it." She looked at me with gleaming eyes and stamped her foot.

"What a little tempest!" said Christine.

Then Edward, man-like, began to explain. "You could not look much like this lady, Felipa," he said, "because you are so dark, you know."

"Am I dark?"

"Very dark; but many people are dark, of course; and for my part I always liked dark eyes," said this mendacious person.

"Do you like my eyes?" asked Felipa anxiously.

"Indeed I do: they are like the eyes of a dear little calf I once owned when I was a boy."

The child was satisfied, and went back to her place beside Christine. "Yes, I shall wear robes like this," she said dreamily, drawing the flowing drapery over her knees clad in the little linen trousers, and scanning the effect; "they would trail behind me—so." Her bare feet peeped out below the hem, and again we all laughed, the little brown toes looked so comical coming out from the silk and the snowy embroideries. She came down to reality again, looked at us, looked at herself, and for the first time seemed to comprehend the difference. Then suddenly she threw herself down on the ground like a little animal, and buried her head in her arms. She would not speak, she would not look up: she only relaxed one arm a little to take in Drollo, and then lay motionless. Drollo looked at us out of one eye solemnly from his uncomfortable position, as much as to say: "No use; leave her to me." So after a while we went away and left them there.

That evening I heard a low knock at my door. "Come in," I said, and Felipa entered. I hardly knew her. She was dressed in a flowered muslin gown which had probably belonged to her mother, and she wore her grandmother's stockings and large baggy slippers; on her mat of curly hair was perched a high-crowned, stiff white cap adorned with a ribbon streamer; and her lank little neck, coming out of the big gown, was decked with a chain of large sea-beans, like exaggerated lockets. She carried a Cuban fan in her hand which was as large as a parasol, and Drollo, walking behind, fairly clanked with the chain of sea-shells which she had wound around him from head to tail. The droll tableau and the supreme pride on Felipa's countenance overcame me, and I laughed aloud. A sudden cloud of rage and disappointment came over the poor child's face: she threw her cap on the floor and stamped on it; she tore off her necklace and writhed herself out of her big flowered gown, and, running to Drollo, nearly strangled him in her fierce efforts to drag off his shell chains. Then, a half-dressed, wild little phantom, she seized me by the skirts and dragged me toward the looking-glass. "You are not pretty either," she cried. "Look at yourself! look at yourself!"

"I did not mean to laugh at you, Felipa," I said gently; "I would not laugh at any one; and it is true I am not pretty, as you say. I can never be pretty, child; but, if you will try to be more gentle, I could teach you how to dress yourself so that no one would laugh at you again. I could make you a little bright-barred skirt and a scarlet bodice: you could help, and that would teach you to sew. But a little girl who wants all this done for her must be quiet and good."

"I am good," said Felipa; "as good as everything."

The tears still stood in her eyes, but her anger was forgotten: she improvised a sort of dance around my room, followed by Drollo dragging his twisted chain, stepping on it with his big feet, and finally winding himself up into a knot around the chair-legs.

"Couldn't we make Drollo something too? dear old Drollo!" said Felipa, going to him and squeezing him in an enthusiastic embrace. I used to wonder how his poor ribs stood it: Felipa used him as a safety-valve for her impetuous feelings.

She kissed me good night, and then asked for "the other lady."

"Go to bed, child," I said; "I will give her your good night."

"But I want to kiss her too," said Felipa.

She lingered at the door and would not go; she played with the latch, and made me nervous with its clicking; at last I ordered her out. But on opening my door half an hour afterward there she was sitting on the floor outside in the darkness, she and Drollo, patiently waiting. Annoyed, but unable to reprove her, I wrapped the child in my shawl and carried her out into the moonlight, where Christine and Edward were strolling to and fro under the pines. "She will not go to bed, Christine, without kissing you," I explained.

"Funny little monkey!" said my friend, passively allowing the embrace.

"Me too," said Edward, bending down. Then I carried my bundle back satisfied.

The next day Felipa and I in secret began our labors; hers consisted in worrying me out of my life and spoiling material —mine in keeping my temper and trying to sew. The result, however, was satisfactory, never mind how we got there. I led Christine out one afternoon: Edward followed. "Do you like tableaux?" I said. "There is one I have arranged for you."

Felipa sat on the edge of the low, square-curbed Spanish well, and Drollo stood behind her, his great yellow body and solemn head serving as a background. She wore a brown petticoat barred with bright colors, and a little scarlet bodice fitting her slender waist closely; a chemisette of soft cream-color with loose sleeves covered her neck and arms, and set off the dark hues of her cheeks and eyes; and around her curly hair a red scarf was twisted, its fringed edges forming a drapery at the back of the head, which, more than anything else, seemed to bring out the latent character of her face. Brown moccasins, red stockings, and a quantity of bright beads completed her costume.

"By Jove!" cried Edward, "the little thing is almost pretty."

Felipa understood this, and a great light came into her face: forgetting her pose, she bounded forward to Christine's side. "I am pretty, then?" she said with exultation; "I *am* pretty, then, after all? For now you yourself have said it—have said it."

"No, Felipa," I interposed, "the gentleman said it." For the child had a curious habit of confounding the two identities which puzzled me then as now. But this afternoon, this happy afternoon, she was content, for she was allowed to sit at Christine's feet and look up into her fair face unmolested. I was forgotten, as usual.

"It is always so," I said to myself. But cynicism, as Mr. Aldrich says, is a small brass field-piece that eventually bursts and kills the artilleryman. I knew this, having been blown up myself more than once; so I went back to my painting and forgot the world. Our world down there on the edge of the salt-marsh, however, was a small one: when two persons went out of it there was a vacuum.

One morning Felipa came sadly to my side. "They have gone away," she said.

"Yes, child."

"Down to the beach to spend all the day."

"Yes, I know it."

"And without me!"

This was the climax. I looked up. Her eyes were dry, but there was a hollow look of disappointment in her face that made her seem old; it was as though for an instant you caught what her old-woman face would be half a century on.

"Why did they not take me?" she said. "I am pretty now: she herself said it."

"They can not always take you, Felipa," I replied, giving up the point as to who had said it.

"Why not? I am pretty now: she herself said it," persisted the child. "In these clothes, you know: she herself said it. The clothes of the son of Pedro you will never see more: they are burned."

"Burned?"

"Yes, burned," replied Felipa composedly. "I carried them out on the barren and burned them. Drollo singed his paw. They burned quite nicely. But they are gone, and I am pretty now, and yet they did not take me! What shall I do?"

"Take these colors and make me a picture," I suggested. Generally, this was a prized privilege, but to-day it did not attract; she turned away, and a few moments after I saw her going down to the end of the plank-walk, where she stood gazing wistfully toward the ocean. There she staid all day, going into camp with Drollo, and refusing to come to dinner in spite of old Dominga's calls and beckonings. At last the patient old grandmother went down herself to the end of the long walk where they were, with some bread and venison on a plate. Felipa ate but little, but Drollo, after waiting politely until she had finished, devoured everything that was left in his calmly hungry way, and then sat back on his haunches with one paw on the plate, as though for the sake of memory. Drollo's hunger was of the chronic kind; it seemed impossible either to assuage it or to fill him. There was a gaunt leanness about him which I am satisfied no amount of food could ever fatten. I think he knew it too, and that accounted for his resignation. At length, just before sunset, the boat returned, floating up the marsh with the tide, old Bartolo steering and managing the brown sails. Felipa sprang up joyfully; I thought she would spring into the boat in her eagerness. What did she receive for her long vigil? A short word or two; that was all. Christine and Edward had quarreled.

How do lovers quarrel ordinarily? But I should not ask that, for these were no ordinary lovers: they were extraordinary.

"You should not submit to her caprices so readily," I said the next day while strolling on the barren with Edward. (He was not so much cast down, however, as he might have been.)

"I adore the very ground her foot touches, Kitty."

"I know it. But how will it end?"

"I will tell you: some of these days I shall win her, and then —she will adore me."

Here Felipa came running after us, and Edward immediately challenged her to a race: a game of romps began. If Christine had been looking from her window she might have thought he was not especially disconsolate over her absence; but she was not looking. She was never looking out of anything or for anybody. She was always serenely content where she was. Edward and Felipa strayed off among the pine-trees, and gradually I lost sight of them. But as I sat sketching an hour afterward Edward came into view, carrying the child in his arms. I hurried to meet them.

"I shall never forgive myself," he said; "the little thing has fallen and injured her foot badly, I fear."

"I do not care at all," said Felipa; "I like to have it hurt. It is *my* foot, isn't it?"

These remarks she threw at me defiantly, as though I had laid claim to the member in question. I could not help laughing.

"The other lady will not laugh," said the child proudly. And in truth Christine, most unexpectedly, took up the *rôle* of nurse. She carried Felipa to her own room—for we each had a little cell opening out of the main apartment—and as white-robed Charity she shone with new radiance. "Shone" is the proper word; for through the open door of the dim cell, with the dark little face of Felipa on her shoulder, her white robe and skin seemed fairly to shine, as white lilies shine on a dark night. The old grandmother left the child in our care and watched our proceedings wistfully, very much as a dog watches the human hands that extract the thorn from the swollen foot of her puppy. She was grateful and asked no questions; in fact, thought was not one of her mental processes. She did not think much; she felt. As for Felipa, the child lived in rapture during those days in spite of her suffering. She scarcely slept at all—she was too happy: I heard her voice rippling on through the night, and Christine's low replies. She adored her beautiful nurse.

The fourth day came: Edward Bowne walked into the cell. "Go out and breathe the fresh air for an hour or two," he said in the tone more of a command than a request.

"The child will never consent," replied Christine sweetly.

"Oh, yes, she will; I will stay with her," said the young man, lifting the feverish little head on his arm and passing his hand softly over the bright eyes.

"Felipa, do you not want me?" said Christine, bending down.

"He stays; it is all the same," murmured the child.

"So it is.—Go, Christine," said Edward with a little smile of triumph.

Without a word Christine left the cell. But she did not go to walk; she came to my room, and, throwing herself on my bed, fell in a moment into a deep sleep, the reaction after her three nights of wakefulness. When she awoke it was long after dark, and I had relieved Edward in his watch.

"You will have to give it up," he said as our lily came forth at last with sleep-flushed cheeks and starry eyes shielded from the light. "The spell is broken; we have all been taking care of Felipa, and she likes one as well as the other."

Which was not true, in my case at least, since Felipa had openly derided my small strength when I lifted her, and beat off the sponge with which I attempted to bathe her hot face. "They" used no sponges, she said, only their nice cool hands; and she wished "they" would come and take care of her again. But Christine had resigned *in toto*. If Felipa did not prefer her to all others, then Felipa should not have her; she was not a common nurse. And indeed she was not. Her fair face, ideal grace, cooing voice, and the strength of her long arms and flexible hands, were like magic to the sick, and—distraction to the well; the well in this case being Edward Bowne looking in at the door.

"You love them very much, do you not, Felipa?" I said one day when the child was sitting up for the first time in a cushioned chair.

"Ah, yes; it is so strong when they carry me," she replied. But it was Edward who carried her.

"He is very strong," I said.

"Yes; and their long soft hair, with the smell of roses in it too," said Felipa dreamily. But the hair was Christine's.

"I shall love them for ever, and they will love me for ever," continued the child. "Drollo too." She patted the dog's head as she spoke, and then concluded to kiss him on his little inch of forehead; next she offered him all her medicines and lotions in turn, and he smelled at them grimly. "He likes to know what I am taking," she explained.

I went on: "You love them, Felipa, and they are fond of you. They will always remember you, no doubt."

"Remember!" cried Felipa, starting up from her cushions like a Jack-in-the-box. "They are not going away? Never! never!"

"But of course they must go some time, for—"

But Felipa was gone. Before I could divine her intent she had flung herself out of her chair down on the floor, and was crawling on her hands and knees toward the outer room. I ran after her, but she reached the door before me, and, dragging her bandaged foot behind her, drew herself toward Christine. "You are *not* going away! You are not! you are not!" she sobbed, clinging to her skirts.

Christine was reading tranquilly; Edward stood at the outer door mending his fishing-tackle. The coolness between them remained, unwarmed by so much as a breath. "Run away, child; you disturb me," said Christine, turning over a leaf. She did not even look at the pathetic little bundle at her feet. Pathetic little bundles must be taught some time what ingratitude deserves.

"How can she run, lame as she is?" said Edward from the doorway.

"You are not going away, are you? Tell me you are not," sobbed Felipa in a passion of tears, beating on the floor with one hand, and with the other clinging to Christine.

"I am not going," said Edward. "Do not sob so, you poor little thing!"

She crawled to him, and he took her up in his arms and soothed her into stillness again; then he carried her out on the barren for a breath of fresh air.

"It is a most extraordinary thing how that child confounds you two," I said. "It is a case of color-blindness, as it were—supposing you two were colors."

"Which we are not," replied Christine carelessly. "Do not stray off into mysticism, Catherine."

"It is not mysticism; it is a study of character—"

"Where there is no character," replied my friend.

I gave it up, but I said to myself: "Fate, in the next world make me one of those long, lithe, light-haired women, will you? I want to see how it feels."

Felipa's foot was well again, and spring had come. Soon we must leave our lodge on the edge of the pine-barren, our outlook over the salt-marsh, with the river sweeping up twice a day, bringing in the briny odors of the ocean; soon we should see no more the eagles far above us or hear the night-cry of the great owls, and we must go without the little fairy flowers of the barren, so small that a hundred of them scarcely made a tangible bouquet, yet what beauty! what sweetness! In my portfolio were sketches and studies of the salt-marsh, and in my heart were hopes. Somebody says somewhere: "Hope is more than a blessing; it is a duty and a virtue." But I fail to appreciate preserved hope—hope put up in cans and served out in seasons of depression. I like it fresh from the tree. And so when I hope it *is* hope, and not that well-dried, monotonous cheerfulness which makes one long to throw the persistent smilers out of the window. Felipa danced no more on the barrens; her illness had toned her down; she seemed content to sit at our feet while we talked, looking up dreamily into our faces, but no longer eagerly endeavoring to comprehend. We were there; that was enough.

"She is growing like a reed," I said; "her illness has left her weak."

"-Minded," suggested Christine.

At this moment Felipa stroked the lady's white hand tenderly and laid her brown cheek against it.

"Do you not feel reproached?" I said.

"Why? Must we give our love to whoever loves us? A fine parcel of paupers we should all be, wasting our inheritance in pitiful small change! Shall I give a thousand beggars a half hour's happiness, or shall I make one soul rich his whole life long?"

"The latter," remarked Edward, who had come up unobserved.

They gazed at each other unflinchingly. They had come to open battle during those last days, and I knew that the end was near. Their words had been cold as ice, cutting as steel, and I said to myself, "At any moment." There would be a deadly struggle, and then Christine would yield. Even I comprehended something of what that yielding would be.

"Why do they hate each other so?" Felipa said to me sadly.

"Do they hate each other?"

"Yes, for I feel it here," she answered, touching her breast with a dramatic little gesture.

"Nonsense! Go and play with your doll, child." For I had made her a respectable, orderly doll to take the place of the ungainly fetich out on the barren.

Felipa gave me a look and walked away. A moment afterward she brought the doll out of the house before my very eyes, and, going down to the end of the dock, deliberately threw it into the water; the tide was flowing out, and away went my toy-woman out of sight, out to sea.

"Well!" I said to myself. "What next?"

I had not told Felipa we were going; I thought it best to let it take her by surprise. I had various small articles of finery ready as farewell gifts, which should act as sponges to absorb her tears. But Fate took the whole matter out of my hands. This is how it happened: One evening in the jasmine arbor, in the fragrant darkness of the warm spring night, the end came; Christine was won. She glided in like a wraith, and I, divining at once what had happened, followed her into her little room, where I found her lying on her bed, her hands clasped on her breast, her eyes open and veiled in soft shadows, her white robe drenched with dew. I kissed her fondly—I never could help loving her then or now—and next I went out to find Edward. He had been kind to me all my poor gray life; should I not go to him now? He was still in the arbor, and I sat down by his side quietly; I knew that the words would come in time. They came; what a flood! English was not enough for him. He poured forth his love in the rich-voweled Spanish tongue also; it has sounded doubly sweet to me ever since.

> "Have you felt the wool of the beaver?
>   Or swan's down ever?
>   Or have smelt the bud o' the brier?
>   Or the nard in the fire?
>   Or ha' tasted the bag o' the bee?
>   Oh so white, oh so soft, oh so sweet is she!"

said the young lover; and I, listening there in the dark fragrant night, with the dew heavy upon me, felt glad that the old simple-hearted love was not entirely gone from our tired metallic world.

It was late when we returned to the house. After reaching my room I found that I had left my cloak in the arbor. It was a strong fabric; the dew could not hurt it, but it could hurt my sketching materials and various trifles in the wide inside pockets—*objets de luxe* to me, souvenirs of happy times, little artistic properties that I hang on the walls of my poor studio when in the city. I went softly out into the darkness again and sought the arbor; groping on the ground I found, not the cloak, but—Felipa! She was crouched under the foliage, face downward; she would not move or answer.

"What is the matter, child?" I said, but she would not speak. I tried to draw her from her lair, but she tangled herself stubbornly still farther among the thorny vines, and I could not move her. I touched her neck; it was cold. Frightened, I ran back to the house for a candle.

"Go away," she said in a low hoarse voice when I flashed the light over her. "I know all, and I am going to die. I have eaten the poison things in your box, and just now a snake came on my neck and I let him. He has bitten me, and I am glad. Go away; I am going to die."

I looked around; there was my color-case rifled and empty, and the other articles were scattered on the ground. "Good Heavens, child!" I cried, "what have you eaten?"

"Enough," replied Felipa gloomily. "I knew they were poisons; you told me so. And I let the snake stay."

By this time the household, aroused by my hurried exit with the candle, came toward the arbor. The moment Edward appeared Felipa rolled herself up like a hedgehog again and refused to speak. But the old grandmother knelt down and drew the little crouching figure into her arms with gentle tenderness, smoothing its hair and murmuring loving words in her soft dialect.

"What is it?" said Edward; but even then his eyes were devouring Christine, who stood in the dark vine-wreathed doorway like a picture in a frame. I explained.

Christine smiled. "Jealousy," she said in a low voice. "I am not surprised."

But at the first sound of her voice Felipa had started up, and, wrenching herself free from old Dominga's arms, threw herself at Christine's feet. "Look at *me* so," she cried—"me too; do not look at him. He has forgotten poor Felipa; he does not love her any more. But *you* do not forget, señora; *you* love me —*you* love me. Say you do, or I shall die!"

We were all shocked by the pallor and the wild, hungry look of her uplifted face. Edward bent down and tried to lift her in his arms; but when she saw him a sudden fierceness came into her eyes; they shot out yellow light and seemed to narrow to a point of flame. Before we knew it she had turned, seized something, and plunged it into his encircling arm. It was my little Venetian dagger.

We sprang forward; our dresses were spotted with the fast-flowing blood; but Edward did not relax his hold on the writhing, wild little body he held until it lay exhausted in his arms. "I am glad I did it," said the child, looking up into his face with her inflexible eyes. "Put me down—put me down, I say, by the gracious señora, that I may die with the trailing of her white robe over me." And the old grandmother with trembling hands received her and laid her down mutely at Christine's feet.

Ah, well! Felipa did not die. The poisons racked but did not kill her, and the snake must have spared the little thin brown neck so despairingly offered to him. We went away; there was nothing for us to do but to go away as quickly as possible and leave her to her kind. To the silent old grandfather I said: "It will pass; she is but a child."

"She is nearly twelve, señora. Her mother was married at thirteen."

"But she loved them both alike, Bartolo. It is nothing; she does not know."

"You are right, lady; she does not know," replied the old man slowly; "but *I* know. It was two loves, and the stronger thrust the knife."

# King David

I met a traveler on the road;
His face was wan, his feet were weary;
Yet he unresting went with such
A strange, still, patient mien—a look
Set forward in the empty air,
As he were reading an unseen book.

RICHARD WATSON GILDER

THE scholars were dismissed. Out they trooped—big boys, little boys, and full-grown men. Then what antics—what linked lines of scuffling; what double shuffles, leaps, and somersaults; what rolling laughter, interspersed with short yelps and guttural cries, as wild and free as the sounds the mustangs make, gamboling on the plains! For King David's scholars were black —black as the ace of spades. He did not say that; he knew very little about the ace. He said simply that his scholars were "colored"; and sometimes he called them "the Children of Ham." But so many mistakes were made over this title, in spite of his careful explanations (the Children having an undoubted taste for bacon), that he finally abandoned it, and fell back upon the national name of "freedmen," a title both good and true. He even tried to make it noble, speaking to them often of their wonderful lot as the emancipated teachers and helpers of their race; laying before them their mission in the future, which was to go over to Africa, and wake out of their long sloth and slumber the thousands of souls there. But Cassius and Pompey had only a mythic idea of Africa; they looked at the globe as it was turned around, they saw it there on the other side, and then their attention wandered off to an adventurous ant who was making the tour of Soodan and crossing the mountains of Kong as though they were nothing.

Lessons over, the scholars went home. The schoolmaster went home too, wiping his forehead as he went. He was a grave young man, tall and thin, somewhat narrow-chested, with the diffident air of a country student. And yet this country student was here, far down in the South, hundreds of miles

329

away from the New Hampshire village where he had thought
to spend his life as teacher of the district school. Extreme near-
sightedness and an inherited delicacy of constitution which he
bore silently had kept him out of the field during the days of
the war. "I should be only an encumbrance," he thought. But,
when the war was over, the fire which had burned within burst
forth in the thought, "The freedmen!" There was work fitted
to his hand; that one thing he could do. "My turn has come at
last," he said. "I feel the call to go." Nobody cared much because he was leaving. "Going down to teach the blacks?" said
the farmers. "I don't see as you're called, David. We've paid
dear enough to set 'em free, goodness knows, and now they
ought to look out for themselves."

"But they must first be taught," said the schoolmaster. "Our
responsibility is great; our task is only just begun."

"Stuff!" said the farmers. What with the graves down in the
South, and the taxes up in the North, they were not prepared
to hear any talk about beginning. Beginning, indeed! They
called it ending. The slaves were freed, and it was right they
should be freed; but Ethan and Abner were gone, and their
households were left unto them desolate. Let the blacks take
care of themselves.

So, all alone, down came David King, with such aid and
instruction as the Freedman's Bureau could give him, to this
little settlement among the pines, where the freedmen had
built some cabins in a careless way, and then seated themselves to wait for fortune. Freedmen! Yes; a glorious idea!
But how will it work its way out into practical life? What are
you going to do with tens of thousands of ignorant, childish,
irresponsible souls thrown suddenly upon your hands; souls
that will not long stay childish, and that have in them also
all the capacities for evil that you yourselves have—you with
your safeguards of generations of conscious responsibility and
self-government, and yet—so many lapses! This is what David
King thought. He did not see his way exactly; no, nor the
nation's way. But he said to himself: "I can at least begin; if
I am wrong, I shall find it out in time. But now it seems to
me that our first duty is to educate them." So he began at "a,
b, and c"; "You must not steal"; "You must not fight"; "You
must wash your faces"; which may be called, I think, the first
working out of the emancipation problem.

Jubilee Town was the name of the settlement; and when the schoolmaster announced his own, David King, the title struck the imitative minds of the scholars, and, turning it around, they made "King David" of it, and kept it so. Delighted with the novelty, the Jubilee freedmen came to school in such numbers that the master was obliged to classify them; boys and men in the mornings and afternoons; the old people in the evenings; the young women and girls by themselves for an hour in the early morning. "I can not do full justice to all," he thought, "and in the men lies the danger, in the boys the hope; the women can not vote. Would to God the men could not either, until they have learned to read and to write, and to maintain themselves respectably!" For, abolitionist as he was, David King would have given years of his life for the power to restrict the suffrage. Not having this power, however, he worked at the problem in the only way left open: "Take two apples from four apples, Julius—how many will be left?" "What is this I hear, Cæsar, about stolen bacon?"

On this day the master went home, tired and dispirited; the novelty was over on both sides. He had been five months at Jubilee, and his scholars were more of a puzzle to him than ever. They learned, some of them, readily; but they forgot as readily. They had a vast capacity for parrot-like repetition, and caught his long words so quickly, and repeated them so volubly, with but slight comprehension of their meaning, that his sensitive conscience shrank from using them, and he was forced back upon a rude plainness of speech which was a pain to his pedagogic ears. Where he had once said, "Demean yourselves with sobriety," he now said, "Don't get drunk." He would have fared better if he had learned to say "uncle" and "aunty," or "maumer," in the familiar Southern fashion. But he had no knowledge of the customs; how could he have? He could only blunder on in his slow Northern way.

His cabin stood in the pine forest, at a little distance from the settlement; he had allowed himself that grace. There was a garden around it, where Northern flowers came up after a while—a little pale, perhaps, like English ladies in India, but doubly beautiful and dear to exiled eyes. The schoolmaster had cherished from the first a wish for a cotton-field—a cotton-field of his own. To him a cotton-field represented the South—a cotton-field in the hot sunshine, with a gang of slaves toiling under the lash of an overseer. This might have been a fancy picture, and it might not. At any rate, it was real to him. There was, however, no overseer now, and no lash; no slaves and very little toil. The negroes would work only when they pleased, and that was generally not at all. There was no doubt but that they were almost hopelessly improvident and lazy. "Entirely so," said the planters. "Not quite," said the Northern school-master. And therein lay the difference between them.

David lighted his fire of pitch-pine, spread his little table, and began to cook his supper carefully. When it was nearly ready, he heard a knock at his gate. Two representative speci-mens of his scholars were waiting without—Jim, a field-hand, and a woman named Esther, who had been a house-servant in a planter's family. Jim had come "to borry an axe," and Esther to ask for medicine for a sick child.

"Where is your own axe, Jim?" said the schoolmaster.

"Somehow et's rusty, sah. Dey gets rusty mighty quick."

"Of course, because you always leave them out in the rain. When will you learn to take care of your axes?"

"Don' know, mars."

"I have told you not to call me master," said David. "I am not your master."

"You's schoolmars, I reckon," answered Jim, grinning at his repartee.

"Well, Jim," said the schoolmaster, relaxing into a smile, "you have the best of it this time; but you know quite well what I mean. You can take the axe; but bring it back to-night. And you must see about getting a new one immediately; there is something to begin with.—Now, Esther, what is it? Your boy sick? Probably it is because you let him drink the water out of that swampy pool. I warned you."

"Yes, sah," said the woman impassively.

She was a slow, dull-witted creature, who had executed her tasks marvelously well in the planter's family, never varying by a hair's breadth either in time or method during long years. Freed, she was lost at once; if she had not been swept along by her companions, she would have sat down dumbly by the wayside, and died. The schoolmaster offered supper to both of his guests. Jim took a seat at the table at once, nothing loath, and ate and drank, talking all the time with occasional flashes of wit, and an unconscious suggestion of ferocity in the way he hacked and tore the meat with his clasp-knife and his strong white teeth. Esther stood; nothing could induce her to sit in the master's presence. She ate and drank quietly, and dropped a courtesy whenever he spoke to her, not from any especial respect or gratitude, however, but from habit. "I may possibly teach the man something," thought the schoolmaster; "but what a terrible creature to turn loose in the world, with power in his hand! Hundreds of these men will die, nay, must die violent deaths before their people can learn what freedom means, and what it does not mean. As for the woman, it is hopeless; she can not learn. But her child can. In truth, our hope is in the children."

And then he threw away every atom of the food, washed his dishes, made up the fire, and went back to the beginning again and cooked a second supper. For he still shrank from personal contact with the other race. A Southerner would have found it impossible to comprehend the fortitude it required for the New-Englander to go through his daily rounds among them. He did his best; but it was duty, not liking. Supper over, he went to the schoolhouse again: in the evenings he taught the old people. It was an odd sight to note them as they followed the letters with a big, crooked forefinger, slowly spelling out words of three letters. They spelled with their whole bodies, stooping over the books which lay before them until their old grizzled heads and gay turbans looked as if they were set on the table by the chins in a long row. Patiently the master taught them; they had gone no further than "cat" in five long months. He made the letters for them on the blackboard again and again, but the treat of the evening was the making of these letters on the board by the different scholars in turn. "Now, Dinah—B." And old Dinah would hobble up proudly, and, with much screwing of her mouth and tongue, and many long hesitations, produce something which looked like a figure eight gone mad. Joe had his turn next, and he would make, perhaps, an H for a D. The master would go back and explain to him carefully the difference, only to find at the end of ten minutes that the whole class was hopelessly confused: Joe's mistake had routed them all. There was one pair of spectacles among the old people: these were passed from hand to hand as the turn came, not from necessity always, but as an adjunct to the dignity of reading.

"Never mind the glasses, Tom. Surely you can spell 'bag' without them."

"Dey helps, Mars King David," replied old Tom with solemn importance. He then adorned himself with the spectacles, and spelled it—"g, a, b."

But the old people enjoyed their lesson immensely; no laughter, no joking broke the solemnity of the scene, and they never failed to make an especial toilet—much shirt-collar for the old men, and clean turbans for the old women. They seemed to be generally half-crippled, poor old creatures; slow in their movements as tortoises, and often unwieldy; their shoes were curiosities of patches, rags, strings, and carpeting. But sometimes a fine old black face was lifted from the slow-moving bulk, and from under wrinkled eyelids keen sharp eyes met the master's, as intelligent as his own.

There was no church proper in Jubilee. On Sundays, the people, who were generally Baptists, assembled in the schoolroom, where services were conducted by a brother who had "de gif' ob preachin'," and who poured forth a flood of Scripture phrases with a volubility, incoherence, and earnestness alike extraordinary. Presbyterian David attended these services, not only for the sake of example, but also because he steadfastly believed in "the public assembling of ourselves together for the worship of Almighty God."

"Perhaps they understand him," he thought, noting the rapt black faces, "and I, at least, have no right to judge them—I, who, with all the lights I have had, still find myself unable to grasp the great doctrine of Election." For David had been bred in Calvinism, and many a night, when younger and more hopeful of arriving at finalities, had he wrestled with its problems. He was not so sure, now, of arriving at finalities either in belief or in daily life; but he thought the fault lay with himself, and deplored it.

The Yankee schoolmaster was, of course, debarred from intercourse with those of his own color in the neighborhood. There were no "poor whites" there; he was spared the sight of their long, clay-colored faces, lank yellow hair, and half-open mouths; he was not brought into contact with the ignorance and dense self-conceit of this singular class. The whites of the neighborhood were planters, and they regarded the school-master as an interloper, a fanatic, a knave, or a fool, according to their various degrees of bitterness. The phantom of a cotton-field still haunted the master, and he often walked by the abandoned fields of these planters, and noted them carefully. In addition to his fancy, there was now another motive. Things were not going well at Jubilee, and he was anxious to try whether the men would not work for good wages, paid regularly, and for their Northern teacher and friend. Thus it happened that Harnett Ammerton, retired planter, one afternoon perceived a stranger walking up the avenue that led to his dilapidated mansion; and as he was near-sighted, and as any visitor was, besides, a welcome interruption in his dull day, he went out upon the piazza to meet him; and not until he had offered a chair did he recognize his guest. He said nothing; for he was in his own house; but a gentleman can freeze the atmosphere around him even in his own house, and this he did. The schoolmaster stated his errand simply: he wished to rent one of the abandoned cotton-fields for a year. The planter could have answered with satisfaction that his fields might lie for ever untilled before Yankee hands should touch them; but he was a poor man now, and money was money. He endured his visitor, and he rented his field; and, with the perplexed feelings of his class, he asked himself how it was, how it could be, that a man like that—yes, like that—had money, while he himself had none! David had but little money—a mere handful to throw away in a day, the planter would have thought in the lavish old times; but David had the New England thrift.

"I am hoping that the unemployed hands over at Jubilee will cultivate this field for me," he said—"for fair wages, of course. I know nothing of cotton myself."

"You will be disappointed," said the planter.

"But they must live; they must lay up something for the winter."

"They do not know enough to live. They might exist, perhaps, in Africa, as the rest of their race exists; but here, in this colder climate, they must be taken care of, worked, and fed, as we work and feed our horses—precisely in the same way."

"I can not agree with you," replied David, a color rising in his thin face. "They are idle and shiftless, I acknowledge that; but is it not the natural result of generations of servitude and ignorance?"

"They have not capacity for anything save ignorance."

"You do not know then, perhaps, that I—that I am trying to educate those who are over at Jubilee," said David. There was no aggressive confidence in his voice; he knew that he had accomplished little as yet. He looked wistfully at his host as he spoke.

Harnett Ammerton was a born patrician. Poor, homely, awkward David felt this in every nerve as he sat there; for he loved beauty in spite of himself, and in spite of his belief that it was a tendency of the old Adam. (Old Adam has such nice things to bother his descendants with; almost a monopoly, if we are to believe some creeds.) So now David tried not to be influenced by the fine face before him, and steadfastly went on to sow a little seed, if possible, even upon this prejudiced ground.

"I have a school over there," he said.

"I have heard something of the kind, I believe," replied the old planter, as though Jubilee Town were a thousand miles away, instead of a blot upon his own border. "May I ask how you are succeeding?"

There was a fine irony in the question. David felt it, but replied courageously that success, he hoped, would come in time.

"And I, young man, hope that it will never come! The negro with power in his hand, which you have given him, with a little smattering of knowledge in his shallow, crafty brain—a knowledge which you and your kind are now striving to give him—will become an element of more danger in this land than it has ever known before. You Northerners do not understand the blacks. They are an inferior race by nature; God made them so. And God forgive those (although I never can) who have placed them over us—yes, virtually over us, their former masters—poor ignorant creatures!"

At this instant an old negro came up the steps with an armful of wood, and the eye of the Northerner noted (was forced to note) the contrast. There sat the planter, his head crowned with silver hair, his finely chiseled face glowing with the warmth of his indignant words; and there passed the old slave, bent and black, his low forehead and broad animal features seeming to typify scarcely more intelligence than that of the dog that followed him. The planter spoke to the servant in his kindly way as he passed, and the old black face lighted with pleasure. This, too, the schoolmaster's sensitive mind noted: none of his pupils looked at him with anything like that affection. "But it *is* right they should be freed—it *is* right," he said to himself as he walked back to Jubilee; "and to that belief will I cling as long as I have my being. It *is* right." And then he came into Jubilee, and found three of his freedmen drunk and quarreling in the street.

Heretofore the settlement, poor and forlorn as it was, had escaped the curse of drunkenness. No liquor was sold in the vicinity, and David had succeeded in keeping his scholars from wandering aimlessly about the country from place to place— often the first use the blacks made of their freedom. Jubilee did not go to the liquor; but, at last, the liquor had come to Jubilee. Shall they not have all rights and privileges, these new-born citizens of ours? The bringer of these doctrines, and of the fluids to moisten them, was a white man, one of that class which has gone down on the page of American history, knighted with the initials C. B. "The Captain" the negroes called him; and he was highly popular already, three hours of the Captain being worth three weeks of David, as far as familiarity went. The man was a glib-tongued, smartly dressed fellow, well supplied with money; and his errand was, of course, to influence the votes at the next election. David, meanwhile, had so carefully kept all talk of politics from his scholars that they hardly knew that an election was near. It became now a contest between the two higher intelligences. If the schoolmaster had but won the easily won and strong affections of his pupils! But, in all those months, he had gained only a dutiful attention. They did not even respect him as they had respected their old masters, and the cause (poor David!) was that very thrift and industry which he relied upon as an example.

"Ole Mars Ammerton wouldn't wash his dishes ef dey was nebber washed," confided Maum June to Elsy, as they caught sight of David's shining pans.

The schoolmaster could have had a retinue of servants for a small price, or no price at all; but, to tell a truth which he never told, he could not endure them about him.

"I must have one spot to myself," he said feverishly, after he had labored all day among them, teaching, correcting untidy ways, administering simple medicines, or binding up a bruised foot. But he never dreamed that this very isolation of his personality, this very thrift, were daily robbing him of the influence which he so earnestly longed to possess. In New England every man's house was his castle, and every man's hands were thrifty. He forgot the easy familiarity, the lordly ways, the crowded households, and the royal carelessness to which the slaves had always been accustomed in their old masters' homes.

At first the Captain attempted intimacy.

"No reason why you and me shouldn't work together," he said with a confidential wink. "This thing's being done all over the South, and easy done, too. Now's the time for smart chaps like us—'transition,' you know. The old Southerners are mad, and won't come forward, so we'll just sail in and have a few years of it. When they're ready to come back—why, we'll give 'em up the place again, of course, if our pockets are well lined. Come, now, just acknowledge that the negroes have got to have somebody to lead 'em."

"It shall not be such as you," said David indignantly. "See those two men quarreling; that is the work of the liquor you have given them!"

"They've as good a right to their liquor as other men have," replied the Captain carelessly; "and that's what I tell 'em; they ain't slaves now—they're free. Well, boss, sorry you don't like my ideas, but can't help it; must go ahead. Remember, I offered you a chance, and you would not take it. Morning."

The five months had grown into six and seven, and Jubilee Town was known far and wide as a dangerous and disorderly neighborhood. The old people and the children still came to school, but the young men and boys had deserted in a body. The schoolmaster's cotton-field was neglected; he did a little there himself every day, but the work was novel, and his attempts were awkward and slow. One afternoon Harnett Ammerton rode by on horseback; the road passed near the angle of the field where the schoolmaster was at work.

"How is your experiment succeeding?" said the planter, with a little smile of amused scorn as he saw the lonely figure.

"Not very well," replied David.

He paused and looked up earnestly into the planter's face. Here was a man who had lived among the blacks all his life, and knew them: if he would but give honest advice! The schoolmaster was sorely troubled that afternoon. Should he speak? He would at least try.

"Mr. Ammerton," he said, "do you intend to vote at the approaching election?"

"No," replied the planter; "nor any person of my acquaintance."

"Then incompetent, and, I fear, evil-minded men will be put into office."

"Of course—the certain result of negro voting."

"But if you, sir, and the class to which you belong, would exert yourselves, I am inclined to think much might be done. The breach will only grow broader every year; act now, while you still have influence left."

"Then you think that we have influence?" said the planter.

He was curious concerning the ideas of this man, who, although not like the typical Yankee exactly, was yet plainly a fanatic; while as to dress and air—why, Zip, his old valet, had more polish.

"I know at least that I have none," said David. Then he came a step nearer. "Do you think, sir," he began slowly, "that I have gone to work in the wrong way? Would it have been wiser to have obtained some post of authority over them—the office of justice of the peace, for instance, with power of arrest?"

"I know nothing about it," said the planter curtly, touching his horse with his whip and riding on. He had no intention of stopping to discuss ways and means with an abolition schoolmaster!

Things grew from bad to worse at Jubilee. Most of the men had been field-hands; there was but little intelligence among them. The few bright minds among David's pupils caught the specious arguments of the Captain, and repeated them to the others. The Captain explained how much power they held; the Captain laid before them glittering plans; the Captain said that by good rights each family ought to have a plantation to repay them for their years of enforced labor; the Captain promised them a four-story brick college for their boys, which was more than King David had ever promised, teacher though he was. They found out that they were tired of King David and his narrow talk; and they went over to Hildore Corners, where a new store had been opened, which contained, among other novelties, a bar. This was one of the Captain's benefactions. "If you pay your money for it, you've as good a right to your liquor as any one, I guess," he observed. "Not that it's anything to me, of course; but I allow I like to see fair play!"

It was something to him, however: the new store had a silent partner; and this was but one of many small and silent enterprises in which he was engaged throughout the neighborhood.

The women of Jubilee, more faithful than the men, still sent their children to school; but they did it with discouraged hearts, poor things! Often now they were seen with bandaged heads and bruised bodies, the result of drunken blows from husband or brother; and, left alone, they were obliged to labor all day to get the poor food they ate, and to keep clothes on their children. Patient by nature, they lived along as best they could, and toiled in their small fields like horses; but the little prides, the vague, grotesque aspirations and hopes that had come to them with their freedom, gradually faded away. "A blue-painted front do'," "a black-silk apron with red ribbons," "to make a minister of little Job," and "a real crock'ry pitcher," were wishes unspoken now. The thing was only how to live from day to day, and keep the patched clothes together. In the mean while trashy finery was sold at the new store, and the younger girls wore gilt ear-rings.

The master, toiling on at his vain task, was at his wit's end. "They will not work; before long they must steal," he said. He brooded and thought, and at last one morning he came to a decision. The same day in the afternoon he set out for Hildore Corners. He had thought of a plan. As he was walking rapidly through the pine-woods Harnett Ammerton on horseback passed him. This time the Northerner had no questions to ask—nay, he almost hung his head, so ashamed was he of the reputation that had attached itself to the field of his labors. But the planter reined in his horse when he saw who it was: he was the questioner now.

"Schoolmaster," he began, "in the name of all the white families about here, I really must ask if you can do nothing to keep in order those miserable, drinking, ruffianly negroes of yours over at Jubilee? Why, we shall all be murdered in our beds before long! Are you aware of the dangerous spirit they have manifested lately?"

"Only too well," said David.

"What are you going to do? How will it end?"

"God knows."

"God knows! Is that all you have to say? Of course he knows; but the question is, Do you know? You have brought the whole trouble down upon our heads by your confounded insurrectionary school! Just as I told you, your negroes, with the little smattering of knowledge you have given them, are now the most dangerous, riotous, thieving, murdering rascals in the district."

"They are bad; but it is not the work of the school, I hope."

"Yes, it is," said the planter angrily.

"They have been led astray lately, Mr. Ammerton; a person has come among them—"

"Another Northerner."

"Yes," said David, a flush rising in his cheek; "but not all Northerners are like this man, I trust."

"Pretty much all we see are. Look at the State."

"Yes, I know it; I suppose time alone can help matters," said the troubled teacher.

"Give up your school, and come and join us," said the planter abruptly. "You, at least, are honest in your mistakes. We are going to form an association for our own protection; join with us. You can teach my grandsons if you like, provided you do not put any of your—your fanaticism into them."

This was an enormous concession for Harnett Ammerton to make; something in the schoolmaster's worn face had drawn it out.

"Thank you," said David slowly; "it is kindly meant, sir. But I can not give up my work. I came down to help the freedmen, and—"

"Then stay with them," said the planter, doubly angry for the very kindness of the moment before. "I thought you were a decent-living white man, according to your fashion, but I see

I was mistaken. Dark days are coming, and you turn your back upon those of your own color and side with the slaves! Go and herd with your negroes. But, look you, sir, we are prepared. We will shoot down any one found upon our premises after dark—shoot him down like a dog. It has come to that, and, by Heaven! we shall protect ourselves."

He rode on. David sat down on a fallen tree for a moment, and leaned his head upon his hand. Dark days were coming, as the planter had said; nay, were already there. Was he in any way responsible for them? He tried to think. "I know not," he said at last; "but I must still go on and do the best I can. I must carry out my plan." He rose and went forward to the Corners.

A number of Jubilee men were lounging near the new store, and one of them was reading aloud from a newspaper which the Captain had given him. He had been David's brightest scholar, and he could read readily; but what he read was inflammable matter of the worst kind, a speech which had been written for just such purposes, and which was now being circulated through the district. Mephistopheles in the form of Harnett Ammerton seemed to whisper in the schoolmaster's ears, "Do you take pride to yourself that you taught that man to read?"

The reader stopped; he had discovered the new auditor. The men stared; they had never seen the master at the Corners before. They drew together and waited. He approached them, and paused a moment; then he began to speak.

"I have come, friends," he said, "to make a proposition to you. You, on your side, have nothing laid up for the winter, and I, on my side, am anxious to have your work. I have a field, you know, a cotton-field; what do you say to going to work there, all of you, for a month? I will agree to pay you more than any man about here pays, and you shall have the cash every Monday morning regularly. We will hold a meeting over at Jubilee, and you shall choose your own overseer; for I am very ignorant about cotton-fields; I must trust to you. What do you say?"

The men looked at each other, but no one spoke.

"Think of your little children without clothes."

Still silence.

"I have not succeeded among you," continued the teacher,

"as well as I hoped to succeed. You do not come to school any more, and I suppose it is because you do not like me."

Something like a murmur of dissent came from the group. The voice went on:

"I have thought of something I can do, however. I can write to the North for another teacher to take my place, and he shall be a man of your own race; one who is educated, and, if possible, also a clergyman of your own faith. You can have a little church then, and Sabbath services. As soon as he comes, I will yield my place to him; but, in the mean time, will you not cultivate that field for me? I ask it as a favor. It will be but for a little while, for, when the new teacher comes, I shall go—unless, indeed," he added, looking around with a smile that was almost pathetic in its appeal, "you should wish me to stay."

There was no answer. He had thrown out this last little test question suddenly. It had failed.

"I am sorry I have not succeeded better at Jubilee," he said after a short pause—and his voice had altered in spite of his self-control—"but at least you will believe, I hope, that I have tried."

"Dat's so"; "Dat's de trouf," said one or two; the rest stood irresolute. But at this moment a new speaker came forward; it was the Captain, who had been listening in ambush.

"All gammon, boys, all gammon," he began, seating himself familiarly among them on the fence-rail. "The season for planting's over, and your work would be thrown away in that field of his. He knows it, too; he only wants to see you marching around to his whistling. And he pays you double wages, does he? Double wages for perfectly useless work! Doesn't that show, clear as daylight, what he's up to? If he hankers so after your future—your next winter, and all that—why don't he give yer the money right out, if he's so flush? But no; he wants to put you to work, and that's all there is of it. He can't deny a word I've said, either."

"I do not deny that I wish you to work, friends," began David—

"There! he tells yer so himself," said the Captain; "he wants yer back in yer old places again. *I* seen him talking to old Ammerton the other day. Give 'em a chance, them two classes, and they'll have you slaves a second time before you know it."

"Never!" cried David. "Friends, it is not possible that you can believe this man! We have given our lives to make you free," he added passionately; "we came down among you, bearing your freedom in our hands—"

"Come, now—I'm a Northerner too, ain't I?" interrupted the Captain. "There's two kinds of Northerners, boys. *I* was in the army, and that's more than he can say. Much freedom *he* brought down in *his* hands, safe at home in his narrer-minded, penny-scraping village! He wasn't in the army at all, boys, and he can't tell you he was."

This was true; the schoolmaster could not. Neither could he tell them what was also true, namely, that the Captain had been an *attaché* of a sutler's tent, and nothing more. But the sharp-witted Captain had the whole history of his opponent at his fingers' ends.

"Come along, boys," said this jovial leader; "we'll have suthin' to drink the health of this tremenjous soldier in—this fellow as fought so hard for you and for your freedom. I always thought he looked like a fighting man, with them fine broad shoulders of his!" He laughed loudly, and the men trooped into the store after him. The schoolmaster, alone outside, knew that his chance was gone. He turned away and took the homeward road. One of his plans had failed; there remained now nothing save to carry out the other.

Prompt as usual, he wrote his letter as soon as he reached his cabin, asking that another teacher, a colored man if possible, should be sent down to take his place.

"I fear I am not fitted for the work," he wrote. "I take shame to myself that this is so; yet, being so, I must not hinder by any disappointed strivings the progress of the great mission. I will go back among my own kind; it may be that some whom I shall teach may yet succeed where I have failed." The letter could not go until the next morning. He went out and walked up and down in the forest. A sudden impulse came to him; he crossed over to the schoolhouse and rang the little tinkling belfry-bell. His evening class had disbanded some time before; the poor old aunties and uncles crept off to bed very early now, in order to be safely out of the way when their disorderly sons and grandsons came home. But something moved the master to see them all together once more. They came across the green, wondering, and entered the schoolroom; some of the younger wives came too, and the children. The master waited, letter in hand. When they were all seated—

"Friends," he said, "I have called you together to speak to you of a matter which lies very near my own heart. Things are not going on well at Jubilee. The men drink; the children go in rags. Is this true?"

Groans and slow assenting nods answered him. One old woman shrieked out shrilly, "It is de Lord's will," and rocked her body to and fro.

"No, it is not the Lord's will," answered the schoolmaster gently; "you must not think so. You must strive to reclaim those who have gone astray; you must endeavor to inspire them with renewed aspirations toward a higher plane of life; you must—I mean," he said, correcting himself, "you must try to keep the men from going over to the Corners and getting drunk."

"But dey will do it, sah; what can we do?" said Uncle Scipio, who sat leaning his chin upon his crutch and peering at the teacher with sharp intelligence in his old eyes. "If dey won't stay fo' you, sah, will dey stay fo' us?"

"That is what I was coming to," said the master. (They had opened the subject even before he could get to it! They saw it too, then—his utter lack of influence.) "I have not succeeded here as I hoped to succeed, friends; I have not the influence I ought to have." Then he paused. "Perhaps the best thing I can do will be to go away," he added, looking quickly from face to face to catch the expression. But there was nothing visible. The children stared stolidly back, and the old people sat unmoved; he even fancied that he could detect relief in the eyes of one or two, quickly suppressed, however, by the innate politeness of the race. A sudden mist came over his eyes; he had thought that perhaps some of them would care a little. He hurried on: "I have written to the North for a new teacher for you, a man of your own people, who will not only teach you, but also, as a minister, hold services on the Sabbath; you can have a little church of your own then. Such a man will do better for you than I have done, and I hope you will like him"—he was going to say, "better than you have liked me," but putting down all thought of self, he added, "and that his work among you will be abundantly blessed."

"Glory! glory!" cried an old aunty. "A color'd preacher ob our own! Glory! glory!"

Then Uncle Scipio rose slowly, with the aid of his crutches, and, as orator of the occasion, addressed the master.

"You see, sah, how it is; you see, Mars King David," he said, waving his hand apologetically, "a color'd man will unnerstan us, 'specially ef he hab lib'd at de Souf; we don't want no Nordern free niggahs hyar. But a 'spectable color'd preacher, now, would be de makin' ob Jubilee, fo' dis worl' an' de nex'."

"Fo' dis worl' and de nex'," echoed the old woman.

"Our service to you, sah, all de same," continued Scipio, with a grand bow of ceremony; "but you hab nebber *quite* unnerstan us, sah, nebber quite; an' you can nebber do much fo' us, sah, on 'count ob dat fack—ef you'll scuse my saying so. But it is de trouf. We give you our t'anks and our congratturrurlations, an' we hopes you'll go j'yful back to your own people, an' be a shining light to 'em for ebbermore."

"A shinin' light for ebbermore," echoed the rest. One old woman, inspired apparently by the similarity of words, began a hymn about "the shining shore," and the whole assembly, thinking no doubt that it was an appropriate and complimentary termination to the proceedings, joined in with all their might, and sang the whole six verses through with fervor.

"I should like to shake hands with you all as you go out," said the master, when at last the song was ended, "and—and I wish, my friends, that you would all remember me in your prayers to-night before you sleep."

What a sight was that when the pale Caucasian, with the intelligence of generations on his brow, asked for the prayers of these sons of Africa, and gently, nay, almost humbly, received the pressure of their black, toil-hardened hands as they passed out! They had taught him a great lesson, the lesson of a failure.

The schoolmaster went home, and sat far into the night, with his head bowed upon his hands. "Poor worm!" he thought—"poor worm! who even went so far as to dream of saying, 'Here am I, Lord, and these brethren whom thou hast given me!'"

The day came for him to go; he shouldered his bag and started away. At a turn in the road, some one was waiting for him; it was dull-faced Esther with a bunch of flowers, the common flowers of her small garden-bed. "Good-by, Esther," said the master, touched almost to tears by the sight of the solitary little offering.

"Good-by, mars," said Esther. But she was not moved; she had come out into the woods from a sort of instinct, as a dog follows a little way down the road to look after a departing carriage.

"David King has come back home again, and taken the district school," said one village gossip to another.

"Has he, now? Didn't find the blacks what he expected, I guess."

FROM

# THE FRONT YARD AND
# OTHER ITALIAN STORIES

# Contents

# The Front Yard

"WELL, now, with Gooster at work in the per-dairy, and Bepper settled at last as help in a good family, and Parlo and Squawly gone to Perugia, and Soonter taken by the nuns, and Jo Vanny learning the carpenter's trade, and only Nounce left for me to see to (let alone Granmar, of course, and Pipper and old Patro), it doos seem, it really doos, as if I might get it done *sometime*; say next Fourth of July, now; that's only ten months off. 'Twould be something to celebrate the day with, that would; something like!"

The woman through whose mind these thoughts were passing was sitting on a low stone-wall, a bundle of herbs, a fagot of twigs, and a sickle laid carefully beside her. On her back was strapped a large deep basket, almost as long as herself; she had loosened the straps so that she could sit down. This basket was heavy; one could tell that from the relaxed droop of her shoulders relieved from its weight for the moment, as its end rested on a fallen block on the other side of the wall. Her feet were bare, her dress a narrow cotton gown, covered in front to the hem by a dark cotton apron; on her head was a straw bonnet, which had behind a little cape of brown ribbon three inches deep, and in front broad strings of the same brown, carefully tied in a bow, with the loops pulled out to their full width and pinned on each side of her chin. This bonnet, very clean and decent (the ribbons had evidently been washed more than once), was of old-fashioned shape, projecting beyond the wearer's forehead and cheeks. Within its tube her face could be seen, with its deeply browned skin, its large irregular features, smooth, thin white hair, and blue eyes, still bright, set amid a bed of wrinkles. She was sixty years old, tall and broad-shouldered. She had once been remarkably erect and strong. This strength had been consumed more by constant toil than by the approach of old age; it was not all gone yet; the great basket showed that. In addition, her eyes spoke a language which told of energy that would last as long as her breath.

These eyes were fixed now upon a low building that stood at a little distance directly across the path. It was small and ancient, built of stone, with a sloping roof and black door. There were no windows; through this door entered the only light and air. Outside were two large heaps of refuse, one of which had been there so long that thick matted herbage was growing vigorously over its top. Bars guarded the entrance; it was impossible to see what was within. But the woman knew without seeing; she always knew. It had been a cow; it had been goats; it had been pigs, and then goats again; for the past two years it had been pigs steadily—always pigs. Her eyes were fixed upon this door as if held there by a magnet; her mouth fell open a little as she gazed; her hands lay loose in her lap. There was nothing new in the picture, certainly. But the intensity of her feeling made it in one way always new. If love wakes freshly every morning, so does hate, and Prudence Wilkin had hated that cow-shed for years.

The bells down in the town began to ring the Angelus. She woke from her reverie, rebuckled the straps of the basket, and adjusting it by a jerk of her shoulders in its place on her back, she took the fagot in one hand, the bundle of herbs in the other, and carrying the sickle under her arm, toiled slowly up the ascent, going round the cow-shed, as the interrupted path too went round it, in an unpaved, provisional sort of way (which had, however, lasted fifty years), and giving a wave of her herbs towards the offending black door as she passed— a gesture that was almost triumphant. "Jest you wait till next Fourth of July, you indecent old Antiquity, you!" This is what she was thinking.

Prudence Wilkin's idea of Antiquity was everything that was old and dirty; indecent Antiquity meant the same qualities increased to a degree that was monstrous, a degree that the most profligate imagination of Ledham (New Hampshire) would never have been able to conceive. There was naturally a good deal of this sort of Antiquity in Assisi, her present abode; it was all she saw when she descended to that picturesque town; the great triple church of St. Francis she never entered; the magnificent view of the valley, the serene vast Umbrian plain, she never noticed; but the steep, narrow streets, with garbage here and there, the crowding stone houses, centuries old, from whose court-yard doors issued odors indescribable—these she knew well, and detested with all her soul. Her deepest degree of loathing, however, was reserved for the especial Antiquity that blocked her own front path, that elbowed her own front door, this noisome stable or sty—for it was now one, now the other—which she had hated and abhorred for sixteen long years.

For it was just sixteen years ago this month since she had first entered the hill town of St. Francis. She had not entered it alone, but in the company of a handsome bridegroom, Antonio Guadagni by name, and so happy was she that everything had seemed to her enchanting—these same steep streets with their ancient dwellings, the same dirt, the same yellowness, the same continuous leisure and causeless beatitude. And when her Tonio took her through the town and up this second ascent to the squalid little house, where, staring and laughing and crowding nearer to look at her, she found his family assembled, innumerable children (they seemed innumerable then), a bedridden grandam, a disreputable old uncle (who began to compliment her), even this did not appear a burden, though of course it was a surprise. For Tonio had told her, sadly, that he was "all alone in the world." It had been one of the reasons why she had wished to marry him—that she might make a home for so desolate a man.

The home was already made, and it was somewhat full. Desolate Tonio explained, with shouts of laughter, in which all the assemblage joined, that seven of the children were his, the eighth being an orphan nephew left to his care; his wife had died eight months before, and this was her grandmother—on the bed there; this her good old uncle, a very accomplished man, who had written sonnets. Mrs. Guadagni number two had excellent powers of vision, but she was never able to discover the goodness of this accomplished uncle; it was a quality which, like the beneficence of angels, one is obliged to take on trust.

She was forty-five, a New England woman, with some small savings, who had come to Italy as companion and attendant to a distant cousin, an invalid with money. The cousin had died suddenly at Perugia, and Prudence had allowed the chance of returning to Ledham with her effects to pass by unnoticed— a remarkable lapse of the quality of which her first name was the exponent, regarding which her whole life hitherto had been one sharply outlined example. This lapse was due to her having already become the captive of this handsome, this irresistible, this wholly unexpected Tonio, who was serving as waiter in the Perugian inn. Divining her savings, and seeing with his own eyes her wonderful strength and energy, this good-natured reprobate had made love to her a little in the facile Italian way, and the poor plain simple-hearted spinster, to whom no one had ever spoken a word of gallantry in all her life before, had been completely swept off her balance by the novelty of it, and by the thronging new sensations which his few English words, his speaking dark eyes, and ardent entreaties roused in her maiden breast. It was her one moment of madness (who has not had one?). She married him, marvelling a little inwardly when he required her to walk to Assisi, but content to walk to China if that should be his pleasure. When she reached the squalid house on the height and saw its crowd of occupants, when her own money was demanded to send down to Assisi to purchase the wedding dinner, then she understood—why they had walked.

But she never understood anything else. She never permitted herself to understand. Tonio, plump and idle, enjoyed a year of paradisiacal opulence under her ministrations (and in spite of some of them); he was eighteen years younger than she was; it was natural that he should wish to enjoy on a larger scale than hers—so he told her. At the end of twelve months a fever carried him off, and his widow, who mourned for him with all her heart, was left to face the world with the eight children, the grandmother, the good old uncle, and whatever courage she was able to muster after counting over and over the eighty-five dollars that alone remained to her of the six hundred she had brought him.

Of course she could have gone back to her own country. But that idea never once occurred to her; she had married Tonio for better or worse; she could not in honor desert the worst now that it had come. It had come in force; on the very day of the funeral she had been obliged to work eight hours; on every day that had followed through all these years, the hours had been on an average fourteen; sometimes more.

Bent under her basket, the widow now arrived at the back door of her home. It was a small narrow house, built of rough stones plastered over and painted bright yellow. But though thus gay without, it was dark within; the few windows were very small, and their four little panes of thick glass were covered with an iron grating; there was no elevation above the ground, the brick floor inside being of the same level as the flagging of the path without, so that there was always a sense of groping when one entered the low door. There were but four rooms, the kitchen, with a bedroom opening from it, and two chambers above under the sloping roof.

Prudence unstrapped her basket and placed it in a woodshed which she had constructed with her own hands. For she could not comprehend a house without a wood-shed; she called it a wood-shed, though there was very little wood to put in it: in Assisi no one made a fire for warmth; for cooking they burned twigs. She hung up the fagot (it was a fagot of twigs), the herbs, and the sickle; then, after giving her narrow skirts a shake, she entered the kitchen.

There was a bed in this room. Granmar would not allow it to be moved elsewhere; her bed had always been in the kitchen, and in the kitchen it should remain; no one but Denza, indeed, would wish to shove her off; Annunziata had liked to have her dear old granmar there, where she could see for herself that she was having everything she needed; but Annunziata had been an angel of goodness, as well as of the dearest beauty; whereas Denza—but any one could see what Denza was! As Granmar's tongue was decidedly a thing to be reckoned with, her bed remained where it always had been; from its comfortable cleanliness the old creature could overlook and criticise to her heart's content the entire household economy of Annunziata's successor. Not only the kitchen, but the whole house and garden, had been vigorously purified by this successor; single-handed she had attacked and carried away accumulations which had been there since Columbus discovered America. Even Granmar was rescued from her squalor and coaxed to wear a clean cap and neat little shawl, her withered brown hands reposing meanwhile upon a sheet which, though coarse, was spotless.

Granmar was a very terrible old woman; she had a beak-like nose, round glittering black eyes set in broad circles of yellow wrinkles, no mouth to speak of, and a receding chin; her voice was now a gruff bass, now a shrill yell.

"How late you are! you do it on purpose," she said as Prudence entered. "And me—as haven't had a thing I've wanted since you went away hours upon hours ago. Nunziata there has been as stupid as a stone—behold her!"

She spoke in peasant Italian, a tongue which Mrs. Guadagni the second (called Denza by the family, from Prudenza, the Italian form of her first name) now spoke readily enough, though after a fashion of her own. She remained always convinced that Italian was simply lunatic English, English spoiled. One of the children, named Pasquale, she called Squawly, and she always believed that the title came from the strength of his infant lungs; many other words impressed her in the same way.

She now made no reply to Granmar's complaints save to give one business-like look towards the bed to see whether the pillows were properly adjusted for the old creature's comfort; then she crossed the room towards the stove, a large ancient construction of bricks, with two or three small depressions over which an iron pot could be set.

"Well, Nounce," she said to a girl who was sitting there on a little bench. The tone of her voice was kindly; she looked to see if a fire had been made. A few coals smouldered in one of the holes. "Good girl," said Prudence, commendingly.

"Oh, very good!" cried Granmar from the bed—"very good, when I told her forty times, and fifty, to make me an omelet, a wee fat one with a drop of fig in it, and I so faint, and she wouldn't, the snake! she wouldn't, the toad!—toadest of toads!"

The dark eyes of the girl turned slowly towards Prudence. Prudence, as she busied herself with the coals, gave her a little nod of approbation, which Granmar could not see. The girl looked pleased for a moment; then her face sank into immobility again. She was not an idiot, but wanting, as it was called; a delicate, pretty young creature, who, with her cousin Pippo, had been only a year old when the second wife came to Assisi. It was impossible for any one to be fond of Pippo, who even at that age had been selfish and gluttonous to an abnormal degree; but Prudence had learned to love the helpless little girl committed to her care, as she had also learned to love very dearly the child's brother Giovanni, who was but a year older; they had been but babies, both of them. The girl was now seventeen. Her name was Annunziata, but Prudence called her Nounce. "If it means 'Announce,' Nounce is near enough, I guess," she said to herself, aggressively. The truth was that she hated the name; it had belonged to Tonio's first wife, and of the memory of that comely young mother, poor Prudence, with her sixty years, her white hair, and wrinkled skin, was burningly jealous even now. Giovanni's name she pronounced as though it were two words—Jo Vanny; she really thought there were two. Jo she knew well, of course; it was a good New England name; Vanny was probably some senseless Italian addition. The name of the eldest son, Augusto, became on her lips Gooster; Paolo was Parlo, Assunta was Soonter.

The nuns had finally taken Soonter. The step-mother had been unable to conceal from herself her own profound relief. True, the girl had gone to a "papish" convent; but she had always been a mystery in the house, and the constant presence of a mystery is particularly trying to the New England mind. Soonter spent hours in meditation; she was very quiet; she believed that she saw angels; her face wore often a far-away smile.

On this September evening she prepared a heavily abundant supper for Granmar, and a simple one for Nounce, who ate at any time hardly more than a bird; Granmar, on the contrary, was gifted with an appetite of extraordinary capacities, the amount of food which was necessary to keep her, not in good-humor (she was never in good-humor), but in passable bodily tranquillity, through the twenty-four hours being equal to that which would have been required (so Prudence often thought) for three hearty New England harvesters at home. Not that Granmar would touch New England food; none of the family would eat the home dishes which Prudence in the earlier years had hopefully tried to prepare from such materials as seemed to her the least "onreasonable"; Granmar, indeed, had declared each and all fit only for the hogs. Prudence never tried them now, and she had learned the art of Italian cooking; for she felt that she could not afford to make anything that was to be for herself alone; the handful of precious twigs must serve for the family as a whole. But every now and then, in spite of her natural abstemiousness, she would be haunted by a vision of a "boiled dinner," the boiled corned-beef, the boiled cabbage, turnips, and potatoes, and the boiled Indian pudding of her youth. She should never taste these dainties on earth again. More than once she caught herself hoping that at least the aroma of them would be given to her some time in heaven.

When Granmar was gorged she became temporarily more tranquil. Prudence took this time to speak of a plan which she had had in her mind for several days. "Now that Gooster and the other boys are doing for themselves, Granmar, and Bepper too at last, and Jo Vanny only needing a trifle of help now and then (he's so young yet, you know), I feel as though I might be earning more money," she began.

"Money's a very good thing; we've never had half enough since my sainted Annunziata joined the angels," responded Granmar, with a pious air.

"Well, it seems a good time to try and earn some more. Soonter's gone to the convent; and as it's a long while since Pipper's been here, I really begin to think he has gone off to get work somewhere, as he always said he was going to."

"Don't you be too sure of Pippo," said Granmar, shaking her owl-like head ominously.

"'Tany rate he hasn't been here, and I always try to hope the best about him—"

"And *that's* what you call the best?" interrupted Granmar, with one of her sudden flank movements, "to have him gone away off no one knows where—Annunziata's own precious little nephew—taken by the pirates—yam! Sold as a slave—yam! Killed in the war! Oh, Pippo! poor Pippo! poor little Pipp, Pipp, Pipp!"

"And so I thought I'd try to go to the shop by the day," Prudence went on, when this yell had ceased; "they want me to come and cut out. I shouldn't go until after your breakfast, of course; and I could leave cold things out, and Nounce would cook you something hot at noon; then I should be home myself every night in time to get your supper."

"And so that's the plan—I'm to be left alone here with an idiot while you go flouncing your heels round Assisi! Flounce, cat! It's a wonder the dead don't rise in their graves to hear it. But we buried my Annunziata too deep for that—yam! —otherwise she'd 'a been here to tear your eyes out. An old woman left to starve alone, her own precious grandmother, growing weaker and weaker, and pining and pining. Blessed stomach, do you hear—do you hear, my holy, blessed stomach, always asking for so little, and now not even to get that? It's turned all a mumble of cold just thinking of it—yam! I, poor sufferer, who have had to stand your ugly face so long—I *so* fond of beauty! You haven't got but twenty-four hairs now; you know you haven't—yam! I've got more than you twenty times over—hey! *that* I have." And Granmar, tearing off her cap, pulled loose her coarse white hair, and grasping the ends of the long locks with her crooked fingers, threw them aloft with a series of shrill halloos.

"I won't go to the shop," said Prudence. "Mercy on us, what a noise! I say I won't go to the shop. There! do you hear?"

"Will you be here every day of your life at twelve o'clock to cook me something that won't poison me?" demanded Granmar, still hallooing.

"Yes, yes, I promise you."

Even Granmar believed Prudence's yes; her yea was yea and her nay nay to all the family. "You cook me something this very minute," she said, sullenly, putting on her cap askew.

"Why, you've only just got through your supper!" exclaimed Prudence, astonished, used though she was to Granmar's abdominal capacities, by this sudden demand.

"You won't? Then I'll yell again," said Granmar. And yell she did.

"Hold up—do; I believe you now," said Prudence. She fanned the dying coals with a straw fan, made up the fire, and prepared some griddle-cakes. Granmar demanded fig syrup to eat with them; and devoured six. Filled to repletion, she then suffered Prudence to change her day cap for a nightcap, falling asleep almost before her head touched the pillow.

During this scene Nounce had sat quietly in her corner. Prudence now went to her to see if she was frightened, for the girl was sometimes much terrified by Granmar's outcries; she stroked her soft hair. She was always looking for signs of intelligence in Nounce, and fancying that she discovered them. Taking the girl's hand, she went with her to the next room, where were their two narrow pallet beds. "You were very smart to save the eggs for me to-day when Granmar wanted that omerlet," she whispered, as she helped her to undress.

Memory came back to Nounce; she smiled comprehendingly.

Prudence waited until she was in bed; then she kissed her good-night, and put out the candle.

Her two charges asleep, Mrs. Guadagni the second opened the back door softly and went out. It was not yet nine o'clock, a warm dark night; though still September, the odors of autumn were already in the air, coming from the September flowers, which have a pungency mingled with their perfume, from the rank ripeness of the vegetables, from the aroma of the ground after the first rains.

"I could have made thirty cents a week more at the shop," she said to herself, regretfully (she always translated the Italian money into American or French). "In a month that would have been a dollar and twenty cents! Well, there's no use thinking about it sence I can't go." She bent over her vegetables, feeling of their leaves, and estimating anew how many she could afford to sell, now that the family was so much reduced in size. Then she paid a visit to her fig-trees. She had planted these trees herself, and watched over their infancy with anxious care; at the present moment they were loaded with fruit, and it seemed as if she knew the position of each fig, so many times had she stood under the boughs looking up at the slowly swelling bulbs. She had never before been able to sell the fruit. But now she should be able, and the sale would add a good many cents to the store of savings kept in her work-box. This work-box, a possession of her youth, was lined with vivid green paper, and had a colored lithograph of the Honorable Mrs. Norton (taken as a Muse) on the inside of the cover; it held already three francs and a half, that is seventy cents—an excellent sum when one considered that only three weeks had passed since the happy day when she had at last beheld the way open to saving regularly, laying by regularly; many times had she begun to save, but she had never been able to continue it. Now, with this small household, she should be able to continue. The sale of the figs would probably double the savings already in the work-box; she might even get eighty cents for them; and that would make a dollar and fifty cents in all! A fig fell to the ground. "They're ripe," she thought; "they must be picked to-morrow." She felt for the fallen fig in the darkness, and carrying it to the garden wall, placed it in a dry niche where it would keep its freshness until she could send it to town with the rest. Then she went to the hen-house. "Smart of Nounce to save the eggs for me," she thought, laughing delightedly to herself over this proof of the girl's intelligence. "Granmar didn't need that omerlet one bit; I left out two tremenjous lunches for her." She peered in; but could not see the hens in the darkness. "If Granmar 'd only eat the things we do!" her thoughts went on. "But she's always possessed after everything that takes eggs. And then she wants the very best coffee, and white sugar, and the best wine, and fine flour and meal and oil—my! how much oil! But I wonder if *I* couldn't stop eating something or other, steader pestering myself about her? Let's see. I don't take wine nor coffee, so I can't stop them; but I could stop soup meat, just for myself; and I will." Thus meditating, she went slowly round to the open space before the house.

To call it a space was a misnomer. The house stood at the apex of the hill, and its garden by right extended as far down the descent in front as it extended down the opposite descent behind, where Prudence had planted her long rows of vegetables. But in this front space, not ten feet distant from the house door, planted directly across the paved path which came up from below, was the cow-shed, the intruding offensive neighbor whose odors, gruntings (for it was now a pig-sty), and refuse were constantly making themselves perceptible to one sense and another through the open windows of the dwelling behind. For the house had no back windows; the small apertures which passed for windows were all in front; in that climate it was impossible that they should be always closed. How those odors choked Prudence Wilkin! It seemed as if she could not respect herself while obliged to breathe them, as if she had not respected herself (in the true Ledham way) since the pig-sty became her neighbor.

For fifty francs the owners would take it away; for another twenty or thirty she could have "a front yard." But though she had made many beginnings, she had never been able to save a tenth of the sum. None of the family shared her feelings in the least; to spend precious money for such a whim as that—only an American could be capable of it; but then, as everybody knew, most Americans were mad. And why should Denza object to pigs?

Prudence therefore had been obliged to keep her longings to herself. But this had only intensified them. And now when at last, after thinking of it for sixteen years, she was free to begin to save daily and regularly, she saw as in a vision her front yard completed as she would like to have it: the cowshed gone; "a nice straight path going down to the front gate, set in a new paling fence; along the sides currant bushes; and in the open spaces to the right and left a big flowerin' shrub —snowballs, or Missouri currant; near the house a clump of matrimony, perhaps; and in the flower beds on each side of the path bachelor's-buttons, Chiny-asters, lady's-slippers, and pinks; the edges bordered with box." She heaved a sigh of deep satisfaction as she finished her mental review. But it was hardly mental after all; she saw the gate, she saw the straight path, she saw the currant bushes and the box-bordered flower beds as distinctly as though they had really been there.

Cheered, almost joyous, she went within, locking the door behind her; then, after softly placing the usual store of provisions beside Granmar's bed (for Granmar had a habit of waking in the night to eat), she sought her own couch. It was hard, but she stretched herself upon it luxuriously. "The figs 'll double the money," she thought, "and by this time to-morrow I shall have a dollar and forty cents; mebby a dollar fifty!" She fell asleep happily.

Her contentment made her sleep soundly. Still it was not long after dawn when she hurried down the hill to the town to get her supply of work from the shop. Hastening back with it, she found Granmar clamoring for her coffee, and Nounce, neatly dressed and clean (for so much Prudence had succeeded in teaching her), sitting patiently in her corner. Prudence's mind was full of a sale she had made; but she prepared the coffee and Nounce's broth with her usual care; she washed her dishes, and made Granmar tidy for the day; finally she arranged all her sewing implements on the table by the window beside her pile of work. Now she could give herself the luxury of one last look, one last estimate; for she had made a miracle of a bargain for her figs. By ten o'clock the men would be up to gather them.

It was a hazy morning; butterflies danced before her as she hastened towards the loaded trees. Reaching them, she looked up. The boughs were bare. All the figs had been gathered in the night, or at earliest dawn.

"Pipper!" she murmured to herself.

The ground under the trees was trampled.

Seven weeks later, on the 16th of November, this same Prudence was adding to her secreted store the fifteen cents needed to make the sum ten francs exactly—that is, two dollars. "Ten francs, a fifth of the whole! It seems 'most too lucky that I've got on so well, spite of Pipper's taking the figs. If I can keep along this way, it 'll *all* be done by the Fourth of July; not just the cow-shed taken away, but the front yard done too. My!" She sat down on a fagot to think it over. The thought was rapture; she laughed to herself and at herself for being so happy.

Some one called, "Mamma." She came out, and found Jo Vanny looking for her. Nounce and Jo Vanny were the only ones among the children who had ever called her mother.

"Oh, you're up there in the shed, are you?" said Jo Vanny. "Somehow, mamma, you look very gay."

"Yes, I'm gay," answered Prudence. "Perhaps some of these days I'll tell you why." In her heart she thought: "Jo Vanny, now, *he'd* understand; he'd feel as I do if I should explain it to him. A nice front yard he has never seen in all his life, for they don't have 'em *here*. But once he knew what it was, he'd care about it as much as I do; I know he would. He's sort of American, anyhow." It was the highest praise she could give. The boy had his cap off; she smoothed his hair. "'Pears to me you must have lost your comb," she said.

"I'm going to have it all cut off as short as can be," announced Jo Vanny, with a resolute air.

"Oh no."

"Yes, I am. Some of the other fellows have had theirs cut that way, and I'm going to, too," pursued the young stoic.

He was eighteen, rather undersized and slender, handsome as to his face, with large dark long-lashed eyes, well-cut features, white teeth, and the curly hair which Prudence had smoothed. Though he had vowed them to destruction, these love-locks were for the present arranged in the style most approved in Assisi, one thick glossy flake being brought down low over the forehead, so that it showed under his cap in a sentimental wave. He did not look much like a hard-working carpenter as he stood there dressed in dark clothes made in that singular exaggeration of the fashions which one sees only in Italy. His trousers, small at the knee, were large and wing-like at the ankle, half covering the tight shabby shoes run down at the heel and absurdly short, which, however, as they were made of patent-leather and sharply pointed at the toes, Jo Vanny considered shoes of gala aspect. His low flaring collar was surrounded by a red-satin cravat ornamented by a gilt horseshoe. He wore a ring on the little finger of each hand. In his own eyes his attire was splendid.

In the eyes of some one else also. To Prudence, as he stood there, he looked absolutely beautiful; she felt all a mother's pride rise in her heart as she surveyed him. But she must not let him see it, and she must scold him for wearing his best clothes every day.

"I didn't know it was a festa," she began.

"'Tain't. But one of the fellows has had a sister married, and they've invited us all to a big supper to-night."

"To-night isn't to-day, that I know of."

"Do you wish me to go all covered with sawdust?" said the little dandy, with a disdainful air. "Besides, I wanted to come up here."

"It *is* a good while sence we've seen you," Prudence admitted. In her heart she was delighted that he had wished to come. "Have you had your dinner, Jo Vanny?"

"All I want. I'll take a bit of bread and some wine by-and-by. But you needn't go to cooking for me, mamma. I say, tell me what it was that made you look so glad?" said the boy, curiously.

"Never you mind *now*," said Prudence, the gleam of content coming again into her eyes, and lighting up her brown, wrinkled face. She was glad that she had the ten francs; she was glad to see the boy; she was touched by his unselfishness in declining her offer of a second dinner. No other member of the family would have declined or waited to decline; the others would have demanded some freshly cooked dish immediately upon entering; Uncle Patro would have demanded three or four.

"I've brought my mandolin," Jo Vanny went on. "I've got to take it to the supper, of course, because they always want me to sing—I never can get rid of 'em! And so you can hear me, if you like. I know the new songs, and one of them I composed myself. Well, it's rather heavenly."

All Tonio's children sang like birds. Poor Prudence, who had no ear for music, had never been able to comprehend either the pleasure or the profit of the hours they gave to their carollings. But when, in his turn, her little Jo Vanny began his pipings, then she listened, or tried to listen. "Real purty, Jo Vanny," she would say, when the silence of a moment or two had assured her that his song was ended; it was her only way of knowing—the silence.

So now she brought her work out to the garden, and sewed busily while Jo Vanny sang and thrummed. Nounce, too, came out, and sat on the wall near by, listening.

At length the little singer took himself off—took himself off with his red-satin cravat, his horseshoe pin, and his mandolin under his arm. Nounce went back to the house, but Prudence sat awhile longer, using, as she always did, the very last rays of the sunset light for her sewing.

After a while she heard a step, and looked up. "Why, Gooster! —anything the matter?" she said, in surprise.

Unlike the slender little Jo Vanny, Gooster was a large, stoutly built young man, as slow in his motions as Jo Vanny was quick. He was a lethargic fellow with sombre eyes, eyes which sometimes had a gleam in them.

"There's nothing especial the matter," he answered, dully. "I think I'll go for a soldier, Denza."

"Go for a soldier? And the per-dairy?"

"I can't never go back to the podere. *She's* there, and she has taken up with Matteo. I've had my heart trampled upon, and so I've got a big hankering either to kill somebody or get killed myself; and I'll either do it here, or I'll go for a soldier and get knifed in the war."

"Mercy on us! there isn't any war now," said Prudence, dazed by these sanguinary suggestions.

"There's always a war. What else are there soldiers for? And there's lots of soldiers. But I could get knifed here easy enough; Matteo and I—already we've had one tussle; I gave him a pretty big cut, you may depend."

Seventeen years earlier Prudence Wilkin would have laughed at the idea of being frightened by such words as these. But

Mrs. Tonio Guadagni had heard of wild deeds in Assisi, and wilder ones still among the peasants of the hill country round-about; these singing, indolent Umbrians dealt sometimes in revenges that were very direct and primitive.

"You let Matteo alone, Gooster," she said, putting her hand on his arm; "you go straight over to Perugia and stay there. Perhaps you can get work where Parlo and Squawly are."

"I shall have it out with Matteo here, or else go for a soldier to-morrow," answered Gooster, in his lethargic tone.

"Well, go for a soldier, then."

"It don't make much difference to me which I do," Gooster went on, as if only half awake. "If I go for a soldier, I shall have to get to Florence somehow, I suppose; I shall have to have ten francs for the railroad."

"Is it ten exactly?" said Prudence. Her mind flew to her work-box, which held just that sum.

"It's ten."

"Haven't you got any money at all, Gooster?" She meant to help him on his way; but she thought that she should like to keep, if possible, a nest-egg to begin with again—say twenty cents, or ten.

Gooster felt in his pockets. "Three soldi," he replied, producing some copper coins and counting them over.

"And there's nothing due you at the per-dairy?"

There was no necessity for answering such a foolish question as this, and Gooster did not answer it.

"Well, I will give you the money," said Prudence. "But to-morrow 'll do, won't it? Stay here a day or two, and we'll talk it over."

While she was speaking, Gooster had turned and walked towards the garden wall. The sight of his back going from her —as though she should never see it again—threw her into a sudden panic; she ran after him and seized his arm. "I'll give you the money, Gooster; I told you I would; I've got it all ready, and it won't take a minute; promise me that you won't leave this garden till I come back."

Gooster had had no thought of leaving the garden; he had espied a last bunch of grapes still hanging on the vine, and was going to get it; that was all. "All right," he said.

Prudence disappeared. He gathered the grapes and began

to eat them, turning over the bunch to see which were best. Before he had finished, Prudence came back, breathless with the haste she had made. "Here," she said; "and now you'll go straight to Florence, won't you? There's a train to-night, very soon now; you must hurry down and take that."

He let her put the money in his coat-pocket while he finished the grapes. Then he threw the stem carefully over the garden wall.

"And no doubt you'll be a brave soldier," Prudence went on, trying to speak hopefully. "Brave soldiers are thought a heap of everywhere."

"I don't know as I care what's thought," answered Gooster, indifferently. He took up his cap and put it on. "Well, good-bye, Denza. Best wishes to you. Every happiness." He shook hands with her.

Prudence stood waiting where she was for five minutes; then she followed him. It was already dark; she went down the hill rapidly, and turned into the narrow main street. A few lamps were lighted. She hastened onward, hoping every minute to distinguish somewhere in front a tall figure with slouching gait. At last, where the road turns to begin the long descent to the plain, she did distinguish it. Yes, that was certainly Gooster; he was going down the hill towards the railway station. All was well, then; she could dismiss her anxiety. She returned through the town. Stopping for a moment at an open space, she gazed down upon the vast valley, now darkening into night; here suddenly a fear came over her—he might have turned round and come back! She hurried through the town a second time, and not meeting him, started down the hill. The road went down in long zigzags. As she turned each angle she expected to see him; but she did not see him, and finally she reached the plain: there were the lights of the station facing her. She drew near cautiously, nearer and nearer, until, herself unseen in the darkness, she could peer through the window into the lighted waiting-room. If he was there, she could see him; but if he was on the platform on the other side— No; he was there. She drew a long breath of relief, and stole away.

A short distance up the hill a wheelbarrow loaded with stones had been left by the side of the road; she sat down on the stones to rest, for the first time realizing how tired she was.

The train came rushing along; stopped; went on again. She watched it as long as she could see its lights. Then she rose and turned slowly up the hill, beginning her long walk home. "My," she thought, "won't Granmar be in a tantrum, though!"

When she reached the house she made a circuit, and came through the garden behind towards the back door. "I don't want to see the front yard *to-night*!" she thought.

But she was rather ashamed of this egotism.

"And they say they'll put me in prison—oh—ow!—an old man, a good old man, a suffering son of humanity like me!" moaned Uncle Pietro.

"An old man, a good old man, a suffering son of humanity like *him*," repeated Granmar, shrilly, proud of this fine language.

Suddenly she brandished her lean arms. "You Denza there, with your stored-up money made from *my* starvation—yam!—mine, how dare you be so silent, figure of a mule? Starvation! yes, indeed. Wait and I'll show you my arms, Pietro; wait and I'll show you my ribs—yam!"

"You keep yourself covered up, Granmar," said Prudence, tucking her in; "you'll do yourself a mischief in this cold weather."

"Ahi!" said Granmar, "and do I care? If I could live to see you drowned, I'd freeze and be glad. Stored-up money! stored-up money!"

"What do you know of my money?" said Prudence. Her voice trembled a little.

"She confesses it!" announced Granmar, triumphantly.

"An old ma—an," said Pietro, crouching over Nounce's scaldino. "A good old ma—an. But—accommodate yourself."

Prudence sat down and took up her sewing. "I don't believe they'll put you in jail at all, Patro," she said; "'twon't do 'em any good, and what they want is their money. You just go to 'em and say that you'll do day's work for 'em till it's made up, and they'll let you off, I'll bet. Nine francs, is it? Well, at half a franc a day you can make it up full in eighteen days; or call it twenty-four with the festas."

"The Americans are all mercenary," remarked old Pietro, waving his hand in scorn. "Being themselves always influenced by gain, they cannot understand lofty motives nor the cold, glittering anger of the nobility. The Leoncinis are noble; they are of the old Count's blood. They do not want their money; they want revenge—they want to rack my bones."

Granmar gave a long howl.

"Favor me, my niece, with no more of your mistakes," concluded Pietro, with dignity.

"I don't believe they'd refuse," said Prudence, unmoved. "I'll go and ask 'em myself, if you like; that 'll be the best way. I'll go right away now." She began to fold up her work.

At this Pietro, after putting the scaldino safely on the stove, fell down in a round heap on the floor. Never were limbs so suddenly contorted and tangled; he clawed the bricks so fiercely with his fingers that Nounce, frightened, left her bench and ran into the next room.

"What's the matter with you? I never saw such a man," said Prudence, trying to raise him.

"Let be! let be!" called out Granmar; "it's a stroke; and you've brought it on, talking to him about working, working all day long like a horse—a good old man like that."

"I don't believe it's a stroke," said Prudence, still trying to get him up.

"My opinion is," said Granmar, sinking into sudden calm, "that he will die in ten minutes—exactly ten."

His face had indeed turned very red.

"Dear me! I suppose I shall have to run down for the doctor," said Prudence, desisting. "Perhaps he'd ought to be bled."

"You leave the doctor alone, and ease his mind," directed Granmar; "that's what he needs, sensitive as he is, and poetical too, poor fellow. You just shout in his ear that you'll pay that money, and you'll be surprised to see how it 'll loosen his joints."

Mrs. Guadagni surveyed the good old uncle for a moment. Then she bent over him and shouted in his ear, "I'll make you a hot fig-tart right away now, Patro, if you'll set up."

As she finished these words Granmar threw her scaldino suddenly into the centre of the kitchen, where it broke with a crash upon the bricks.

"He's going to get up," announced Prudence, triumphantly.

"He isn't any such thing; 'twas the scaldino shook him,"

responded Granmar, in a loud, admonitory tone. "He'll never get up again in *this* world unless you shout in his ear that you'll pay that money."

And in truth Pietro was now more knotted than ever.

At this moment the door opened and Jo Vanny came in. "Why, what's the matter with uncle?" he said, seeing the figure on the floor. He bent over him and tried to ease his position.

"It's a stroke," said Granmar, in a soft voice. "It 'll soon be over. Hush! leave him in peace. He's dying; Denza there, she did it."

"They want me to pay the nine francs he has—lost," said Prudence. "Perhaps you have heard, Jo Vanny, that he has—lost nine francs that belonged to the Leoncinis? Nine whole francs." She looked at the lad, and he understood the look; for only the day before she had confided to him at last her long-cherished dream, and (as she had been sure he would) he had sympathized with it warmly.

"I declare I wish I had even a franc!" he said, searching his pockets desperately; "but I've only got a cigarette. Will you try a cigarette, uncle?" he shouted in the heap's ear.

"Don't you mock him," ordered Granmar (but Jo Vanny had been entirely in earnest). "He'll die soon, and Denza will be rid of him; that's what she wants. 'Twill be murder, of course; and he'll haunt us—he's always said he'd haunt somebody. But *I* ain't long for this world, so I ain't disturbed. Heaven's waiting wide open for *me*."

Jo Vanny looked a little frightened. He hesitated a moment, surveying the motionless Pietro; then he drew Prudence aside. "He's an awful wicked old man, and might really do it," he whispered; "'specially as you ain't a Catholic, mamma. I think you'd better give him the money if it 'll stop him off; *I* don't mind, but it would be bad for you if he should come rapping on your windows and showing corpse-lights in the garden by-and-by."

Prudence brought her hands together sharply—a gesture of exasperation. "He ain't going to die any more than I am," she said. But she knew what life would be in that house with such a threat hanging over it, even though the execution were deferred to some vague future time. Angrily she left the room.

Jo Vanny followed her. "Come along, if you want to," she said, half impatient, half glad. She felt a sudden desire that some one besides herself should see the sacrifice, see the actual despoiling of the little box she had labored to fill. She went to the wood-shed. It was a gloomy December day, and the vegetables hanging on the walls had a dreary, stone-like look; she climbed up on a barrel, and removed the hay which filled a rough shelf; in a niche behind was her work-box; with it in her hand she climbed down again.

She gave him the box to hold while she counted out the money—nine francs. "There are twelve in all," she said.

"Then you'll have three left," said Jo Vanny.

"Yes, three." She could not help a sigh of retrospect, the outgoing nine represented so many long hours of toil.

"Let me put the box back," said the boy. It was quickly and deftly done. "Never mind about it, mamma," he said, as he jumped down. "*I'll* help you to make it up again. I want that front yard as much as you do, now you've told me about it; I think it will be beautiful."

"Well," said Prudence, "when the flower-beds are all fixed up, and the new front path and swing gate, it *will* be kind of nice, I reckon."

"Nice?" said Jo Vanny. "That's not the word. 'Twill be an ecstasy! a smile! a dream!"

"Bless the boy, what nonsense he talks!" said the step-mother. But she loved to hear his romantic phrases all the same.

They went back to the kitchen. The sacrifice had now become a cheerful one. She bent over the heap. "Here's your nine francs, Patro," she shouted. "Come, now, come!"

Pietro felt the money in his hand. He rose quietly. "I'm nearly killed with all your yelling," he said. Then he took his hat and left the house.

"We did yell," said Prudence, picking up the fragments of the broken scaldino. "I don't quite know why we did."

"Never mind why-ing, but get supper," said Granmar. "Then go down on your knees and thank the Virgin for giving us such a merciful, mild old man as Pietro. You brought on his stroke; but what did he do? He just took what you gave him, and went away *so* forgivingly—the soul of a dove, the spice-cake soul!"

*

In January, the short, sharp winter of Italy had possession of Assisi.

One day towards the last of the month a bitter wind was driving through the bleak, stony little street, sending clouds of gritty, frozen dust before it. The dark, fireless dwellings were colder than the outside air, and the people, swathed in heavy layers of clothing, to which all sorts of old cloaks and shawls and mufflers had been added, were standing about near the open doors of their shops and dwellings, various prominences under apron or coat betraying the hidden scaldino, the earthen dish which Italians tightly hug in winter with the hope that the few coals it contains will keep their benumbed fingers warm. All faces were reddened and frost-bitten. The hands of the children who were too young to hold a scaldino were purple-black.

Prudence Guadagni, with her great basket strapped on her back, came along, receiving but two or three greetings as she passed. Few knew her; fewer still liked her, for was she not a foreigner and a pagan? Besides, what could you do with a woman who drank water, simple water, like a toad, and never touched wine—a woman who did not like oil, good, sweet, wholesome oil! Tonio's children were much commiserated for having fallen into such hands.

Prudence was dressed as she had been in September, save that she now wore woollen stockings and coarse shoes, and tightly pinned round her spare person a large shawl. This shawl (she called it "my Highland shawl") had come with her from America; it was green in hue, plaided; she thought it still very handsome. Her step was not as light as it had been; rheumatism had crippled her sorely.

As she left the town and turned up the hill towards home, some one who had been waiting there joined her. "Is that you, Bepper? Were you coming up to the house?" she said.

"Yes," answered Beppa, showing her white teeth in a smile. "I'm bringing you some news, Denza."

"Well, what is it? I hope you're not going to leave your place?"

"I'm going to leave it, and that's my news: I'm going to be married."

"My! it's sudden, isn't it?" said Prudence, stopping.

"Giuseppe doesn't think it's sudden," said Beppa, laughing

and tossing her head; "he thinks I've been ages making up my mind. Come on, Denza, do; it's so cold!"

"I don't know Giuseppe, do I?" said Prudence, trudging on again; "I don't remember the name."

"No; I've never brought him up to the house. But the boys know him—Paolo and Pasquale; Augusto, too. He's well off, Giuseppe is; he's got beautiful furniture. He's a first-rate mason, and gets good wages, so I sha'n't have to work any more —I mean go out to work as I do now."

"Bepper, do you *like* him?" said Prudence, stopping again. She took hold of the girl's wrist and held it tightly.

"Of course I like him," said Beppa, freeing herself. "How cold your hands are, Denza—ugh!"

"You ain't marrying him for his furniture? You love him for himself—and better than any one else in the whole world?" Prudence went on, solemnly.

"Oh, how comical you do look, standing there talking about love, with your white hair and your great big basket!" said Beppa, breaking into irrepressible laughter. The cold had not made her hideous, as it makes so many Italians hideous; her face was not empurpled, her fine features were not swollen. She looked handsome. What was even more attractive on such a day, she looked warm. As her merriment ceased, a sudden change came over her. "Sainted Maria! she doubts whether I love him! Love him? Why, you poor old woman, I'd die for him to-morrow. I'd cut myself in pieces for him this minute." Her great black eyes gleamed; the color flamed in her oval cheeks; she gave a rich, angry laugh.

It was impossible to doubt her, and Prudence did not doubt. "Well, I'm right down glad, Bepper," she said, in a softened tone—"right down glad, my dear." She was thinking of her own love for the girl's father.

"I was coming up," continued Beppa, "because I thought I'd better talk it over with you."

"Of course," said Prudence, cordially. "A girl can't get married all alone; nobody ever heard of that."

"I sha'n't be much alone, for Giuseppe's family's a very big one; too big, I tell him—ten brothers and sisters. But they're all well off, that's one comfort. Of course I don't want to shame 'em."

"Of course not," said Prudence, assenting again. Then, with the awakened memories still stirring in her heart: "It's a pity your father isn't here now," she said, in a moved tone; "he'd have graced a wedding, Bepper, he was so handsome." She seldom spoke of Tonio; the subject was too sacred; but it seemed to her as if she might venture a few words to this his daughter on the eve of her own marriage.

"Yes, it's a pity, I suppose," answered Beppa. "Still, he would have been an old man now. And 'tain't likely he would have had a good coat either—that is, not such a one as I should call good."

"Yes, he would; I'd have made him one," responded Prudence, with a spark of anger. "This whole basket's full of coats now."

"I know you're wonderful clever with your needle," said the girl, glancing carelessly at the basket that weighed down her step-mother's shoulders. "I can't think how you can sew so steadily, year in, year out; I never could."

"Well, I've had to get stronger spectacles," Prudence confessed. "And they wouldn't take my old ones in exchange, neither, though they were perfectly good."

"They're robbers, all of them, at that shop," commented Beppa, agreeingly.

"Now, about your clothes, Bepper—when are you going to begin? I suppose you'll come home for a while, so as to have time to do 'em; I can help you some, and Nounce too; Nounce can sew a little."

"No, I don't think I'll come home; 'twouldn't pay me. About the clothes—I'm going to buy 'em."

"They won't be half so good," Prudence began. Then she stopped. "I'm very glad you've got the money laid up, my dear," she said, commendingly.

"Oh, but I haven't," answered Beppa, laughing. "I want to borrow it of you; that is what I came up for to-day—to tell you about it."

Prudence, her heart still softened, looked at the handsome girl with gentle eyes. "Why, of course I'll lend it to you, Bepper," she said. "How much do you want?"

"All you've got won't be any too much, I reckon," answered Beppa, with pride. "I shall have to have things nice, you know; I don't want to shame 'em."

"I've got twenty-five francs," said Prudence; "I mean I've got that amount saved and put away; 'twas for—for a purpose —something I was going to do; but 'tain't important; you can have it and welcome." Her old face, as she said this, looked almost young again. "You see, I'm so glad to have you happy," she went on. "And I can't help thinking—if your father had only lived—the first wedding in his family! However, *I'll* come —just as though I was your real mother, dear; you sha'n't miss that. I've got my Sunday gown, and five francs will buy me a pair of new shoes; I can earn 'em before the day comes, I guess."

"I'm afraid you can't," said Beppa, laughing.

"Why, when's the wedding? Not for two or three weeks, I suppose?"

"It's day after to-morrow," answered Beppa. "Everything's bought, and all I want is the money to pay for 'em; I knew I could get it of you."

"Dear me! how quick! And these shoes are really too bad; they're clear wore out, and all the cleaning in the world won't make 'em decent."

"Well, Denza, why do you want to come? You don't know any of Giuseppe's family. To tell the truth, I never supposed you'd care about coming, and the table's all planned out for (at Giuseppe's sister's), and there ain't no place for you."

"And you didn't have one saved?"

"I never thought you'd care to come. You see they're different, they're all well off, and you don't like people who are well off—who wear nice clothes. You never wanted *us* to have nice clothes, and you like to go barefoot."

"No, I don't!" said Prudence.

"'Tany rate, one would think you did; you always go so in summer. But even if you had new shoes, none of your clothes would be good enough; that bonnet, now—"

"My bonnet? Surely my *bonnet's* good?" said the New England woman; her voice faltered, she was struck on a tender point.

"Well, people laugh at it," answered Beppa, composedly.

They had now reached the house. "You go in," said Prudence; "I'll come presently."

She went round to the wood-shed, unstrapped her basket, and set it down; then she climbed up on the barrel, removed the hay, and took out her work-box. Emptying its contents into her handkerchief, she descended, and, standing there, counted the sum—twenty-seven francs, thirty centimes. "'Twon't be any too much; she don't want to shame 'em." She made a package of the money with a piece of brown paper, and, entering the kitchen, she slipped it unobserved into Beppa's hand.

"Seems to me," announced Granmar from the bed, "that when a girl comes to tell her own precious Granmar of her *wedding*, she ought in decency to be offered a bite of something to eat. Any one but Denza would think so. Not that it's anything to me."

"Very well, what will you have?" asked Prudence, wearily. Freed from her bonnet and shawl, it could be seen that her once strong figure was much bent; her fingers had grown knotted, enlarged at the joints, and clumsy; years of toil had not aged her so much as these recent nights—such long nights! —of cruel rheumatic pain.

Granmar, in a loud voice, immediately named a succulent dish; Prudence began to prepare it. Before it was ready, Jo Vanny came in.

"You knew I was up here, and you've come mousing up for an invitation," said Beppa, in high good-humor. "I was going to stop and invite you on my way back, Giovanni; there's a nice place saved for you at the supper."

"Yes, I knew you were up here, and I've brought you a wedding-present," answered the boy. "I've brought one for mamma, too." And he produced two silk handkerchiefs, one of bright colors, the other of darker hue.

"Is the widow going to be married, too?" said Beppa. "Who under heaven's the man?"

In spite of the jesting, Prudence's face showed that she was pleased; she passed her toil-worn hand over the handkerchief softly, almost as though its silk were the cheek of a little child. The improvised feast was turned into a festival now, and of her own accord she added a second dish; the party, Granmar at the head, devoured unknown quantities. When at last there was nothing left, Beppa, carrying her money, departed.

"You know, Jo Vanny, you hadn't ought to leave your work so often," said Prudence, following the boy into the garden when he took leave; she spoke in an expostulating tone.

"Oh, I've got money," said Jo Vanny, loftily; "*I* needn't crawl." And carelessly he showed her a gold piece.

But this sudden opulence only alarmed the step-mother. "Why, where did you get that?" she said, anxiously.

"How frightened you look! Your doubts offend me," pursued Jo Vanny, still with his grand air. "Haven't I capacities? —hasn't Heaven sent me a swarming genius? Wasn't I the acclaimed, even to laurel crowns, of my entire class?"

This was true: Jo Vanny was the only one of Tonio's children who had profited by the new public schools.

"And now what shall I get for you, mamma?" the boy went on, his tone changing to coaxing; "I want to get you something real nice; what will you have? A new dress to go to Beppa's wedding in?"

For an instant Prudence's eyes were suffused. "I ain't going, Jo Vanny; they don't want me."

"They *shall* want you!" declared Jo Vanny, fiercely.

"I didn't mean that; I don't want to go anyhow; I've got too much rheumatism. You don't know," she went on, drawn out of herself for a moment by the need of sympathy—"you don't know how it does grip me at night sometimes, Jo Vanny! No; you go to the supper, and tell me all about it afterwards; I like to hear you tell about things just as well as to go myself."

Jo Vanny passed his hand through his curly locks with an air of desperation. "There it is again—my gift of relating, of narrative; it follows me wherever I go. What will become of me with such talents? I shall never die in my bed; nor have my old age in peace."

"You go 'long!" said Prudence (or its Italian equivalent). She gave him a push, laughing.

Jo Vanny drew down his cap, put his hands deep in his pockets, and thus close-reefed scudded down the hill in the freezing wind to the shelter of the streets below.

By seven o'clock Nounce and Granmar were both asleep; it was the most comfortable condition in such weather. Prudence adjusted her lamp, put on her strong spectacles, and sat down to sew. The great brick stove gave out no warmth; it was not intended to heat the room; its three yards of length and one yard of breadth had apparently been constructed for the purpose of holding and heating one iron pot. The scaldino at her feet did not keep her warm; she put on her Highland shawl. After a while, as her head (scantily covered with thin white hair) felt the cold also, she went to get her bonnet. As she took it from the box she remembered Beppa's speech, and the pang came back; in her own mind that bonnet had been the one link that still united her with her old Ledham respectability, the one possession that distinguished her from all these "papish" peasants, with their bare heads and frowzy hair. It was not new, of course, as it had come with her from home. But what signified an old-fashioned shape in a community where there were no shapes of any kind, new or old? At least it was always a bonnet. She put it on, even now from habit pulling out the strings carefully, and pinning the loops on each side of her chin. Then she went back and sat down to her work again.

At eleven o'clock Granmar woke. "Yam! how cold my legs are! Denza, are you there? You give me that green shawl of yours directly; precisely, I am dying."

Prudence came out from behind her screen, lamp in hand. "I've got it on, Granmar; it's so cold setting up sewing. I'll get you the blanket from my bed."

"I don't want it; it's as hard as a brick. You give me that shawl; if you've got it on, it 'll be so much the warmer."

"I'll give you my other flannel petticoat," suggested Prudence.

"And I'll tear it into a thousand pieces," responded Granmar, viciously. "You give me that shawl, or the next time you leave Nounce alone here, *she* shall pay for it."

Granmar was capable of frightening poor little Nounce into spasms. Prudence took off the shawl and spread it over the bed, while Granmar grinned silently.

Carrying the lamp, Prudence went into the bedroom to see what else she could find to put on. She first tried the blanket from her bed; but as it was a very poor one, partly cotton, it was stiff (as Granmar had said), and would not stay pinned; the motion of her arms in sewing would constantly loosen it. In the way of wraps, except her shawl, she possessed almost nothing; so she put on another gown over the one she wore, pinned her second flannel petticoat round her shoulders, and over that a little cloak that belonged to Nounce; then she tied a woollen stocking round her throat, and crowned with her bonnet, and carrying the blanket to put over her knees, she returned to her work.

"I declare I'm clean tired out," she said to herself; "my feet are like ice. I wouldn't sew any longer such a bitter night if it warn't that that work-box ain't got a thing in it. I can't bear to think of it empty. But as soon as I've got a franc or two to begin with again, I'll stop these extry hours."

But they lasted on this occasion until two o'clock.

"It don't seem as if I'd ever known it *quite* so baking as it is to-night." It was Prudence who spoke; she spoke to Nounce; she must speak to some one.

Nounce answered with one of her patient smiles. She often smiled patiently, as though it were something which she was expected to do.

Prudence was sitting in the wood-shed resting; she had been down to town to carry home some work. Now the narrow streets there, thrown into shade by the high buildings on each side, were a refuge from the heat; now the dark houses, like burrows, gave relief to eyes blinded by the yellow glare. It was the 30th of August. From the first day of April the broad valley and this brown hill had simmered in the hot light, which filled the heavens and lay over the earth day after day, without a change, without a cloud, relentless, splendid; each month the ground had grown warmer and drier, the roads more white, more deep in dust; insect life, myriad legged and winged, had been everywhere; under the stones lurked the scorpions.

In former summers here this never-ending light, the long days of burning sunshine, the nights with the persistent moon, the importunate nightingales, and the magnificent procession of the stars had sometimes driven the New England woman almost mad; she had felt as if she must bury her head in the earth somewhere to find the blessed darkness again, to feel its cool pressure against her tired eyes. But this year these things had not troubled her; the possibility of realizing her long-cherished hope at last had made the time seem short, had made the heat nothing, the light forgotten; each day, after fifteen hours of toil, she had been sorry that she could not accomplish more.

But she had accomplished much; the hope was now almost a reality. "Nounce," she said, "do you know I'm 'most too happy to live. I shall have to tell you: I've got *all* the money saved up at last, and the men are coming to-morrow to take away the cow-shed. Think of that!"

Nounce thought of it; she nodded appreciatively.

Prudence took the girl's slender hand in hers and went on: "Yes, to-morrow. And it 'll cost forty-eight francs. But with the two francs for wine-money it will come to fifty in all. By this time to-morrow night it will be gone!" She drew in her breath with a satisfied sound. "I've got seventy-five francs in all, Nounce. When Bepper married, of course I knew I couldn't get it done for Fourth of July. And so I thought I'd try for Thanksgiving—that is, Thanksgiving *time*; I never know the exact day now. Well, here it's only the last day of August, and the cow-shed will be gone to-morrow. Then will come the new fence; and then the fun, the real fun, Nounce, of laying out our front yard! It 'll have a nice straight path down to the gate, currant bushes in neat rows along the sides, two big flowerin' shrubs, and little flower beds bordered with box. I tell you you won't know your own house when you come in a decent gate and up a nice path to the front door; all these years we've been slinking in and out of a back door, just as though we didn't have no front one. I don't believe myself in tramping in and out of a front door *every* day; but on Sundays, now, when we have on our best clothes, we shall come in and out respectably. You'll feel like another person, Nounce; and I'm sure *I* shall —I shall feel like Ledham again—my!" And Prudence actually laughed.

Still holding Nounce's hand, she went round to the front of the house.

The cow-shed was shedding forth its usual odors; Prudence took a stone and struck a great resounding blow on its side. She struck with so much force that she hurt her hand. "Never mind—it done me good!" she said, laughing again.

She took little Nounce by the arm and led her down the descent. "I shall have to make the front walk all over," she explained. "And here 'll be the gate, down here—a swing one. And the path will go from here straight up to the door. Then the fence will go along here—palings, you know, painted white; a good clean American white, with none of these yellows in it, you may depend. And over there—and there—along the sides, the fence will be just plain boards, notched at the top; the currant bushes will run along there. In the middle, here—and here —will be the big flowerin' shrubs. And then the little flower-beds bordered with box. Oh, Nounce, I can't hardly believe it—it will be so beautiful! I really can't!"

Nounce waited a moment. Then she came closer to her step-mother, and after looking quickly all about her, whispered, "You needn't if you don't want to; there's here yet to believe."

"It's just as good as here," answered Prudence, almost indignantly. "I've got the money, and the bargain's all made; nothing could be surer than that."

The next morning Nounce was awakened by the touch of a hand on her shoulder. It was her step-mother. "I've got to go down to town," she said, in a low tone. "You must try to get Granmar's breakfast yourself, Nounce; do it as well as you can. And—and I've changed my mind about the front yard; it 'll be done some time, but not now. And we won't talk any more about it for the present, Nounce; that 'll please me most; and you're a good girl, and always want to please me, I know."

She kissed her, and went out softly.

In October three Americans came to Assisi. Two came to sketch the Giotto frescos in the church of St. Francis; the third came for her own entertainment; she read Symonds, and wandered about exploring the ancient town.

One day her wanderings led her to the little Guadagni house on the height. The back gate was open, and through it she saw an old woman staggering, then falling, under the weight of a sack of potatoes which she was trying to carry on her back.

The American rushed in to help her. "It's much too heavy for you," she said, indignantly, after she had given her assistance. "Oh dear—I mean, *è troppo grave*," she added, elevating her voice.

"Are you English?" said the old woman. "I'm an American myself; but I ain't deaf. The sack warn't too heavy; it's only that I ain't so strong as I used to be—it's perfectly redeculous!"

"You're not strong at all," responded the stranger, still indignantly, looking at the wasted old face and trembling hands.

A week later Prudence was in bed, and an American nurse was in charge.

This nurse, whose name was Baily, was a calm woman with long strong arms, monotonous voice, and distinct New England pronunciation; her Italian (which was grammatically correct) was delivered in the vowels of Vermont.

One day, soon after her arrival, she remarked to Granmar, "That yell of yours, now—that yam—is a very unusual thing."

"My sufferings draw it from me," answered Granmar, flattered by the adjective used. "I'm a very pious woman; I don't want to swear."

"I think I have never heard it equalled, except possibly in lunatic asylums," Marilla Baily went on. "I have had a great deal to do with lunatic asylums; I am what is called an expert; that is, I find out people who are troublesome, and send them there; I never say much about it, but just make my observations; then, when I've got the papers out, whiff!—off they go."

Granmar put her hand over her mouth apprehensively, and surveyed her in silence. From that time the atmosphere of the kitchen was remarkably quiet.

Marilla Baily had come from Florence at the bidding of the American who had helped to carry the potatoes. This American was staying at the Albergo del Subasio with her friends who were sketching Giotto; but she spent most of her time with Prudence Wilkin.

"You see, I minded it because it was *him*," Prudence explained to her one day, at the close of a long conversation. "For I'd always been so fond of the boy; I had him first when he warn't but two years old—just a baby—and *so* purty and cunning! He always called me mamma—the only one of the children, 'cept poor Nounce there, that really seemed to care for me. And I cared everything for him. I went straight down to town and hunted all over. But he warn't to be found. I tried it the next day, and the next, not saying what I wanted, of course; but nobody knew where he was, and at last I made up my mind that he'd gone away. For three weeks I waited; I was almost dead; I couldn't do nothing; I felt as if I was broke in two, and only the skin held me together. Every morning I'd say to myself, 'There'll certainly come a letter to-day, and he'll tell me all about it.' But the letter didn't come, and didn't come. From the beginning, of course, I knew it was him—I couldn't help but know; Jo Vanny was the only person in the whole world that knew where it was. For I'd showed it to him one day—the work-box, I mean—and let him put it back in the hole behind the hay—'twas the time I took the money out for Patro. At last I did get a letter, and he said as how he'd meant to put it back the very next morning, sure. But something had happened, so he couldn't, and so he'd gone away. And now he was working just as hard as he could, he said, so as to be able to pay it back soon; he hardly played on his mandolin at all now, he said, he was working so hard. You see, he wasn't bad himself, poor little fellow, but he was led away by bad men; gambling's an awful thing, once you get started in it, and he was sort of *drove* to take that money, meaning all the while to pay it back. Well, of course I felt ever so much better just as soon as I got that letter. And I began to work again. But I didn't get on as well as I'd oughter; I can't understand why. That day, now, when I first saw you—when you ran in to help me—I hadn't been feeling sick at all; there warn't no sense in my tumbling down that way all of a sudden."

One lovely afternoon in November Prudence's bed was carried out to the front of the dark little house.

The cow-shed was gone. A straight path, freshly paved, led down to a swing gate set in a new paling fence, flower beds bordered the path, and in the centre of the open spaces on each side there was a large rose bush. The fence was painted a glittering white; there had been an attempt at grass; currant bushes in straight rows bordered the two sides.

Prudence lay looking at it all in peaceful silence. "It's mighty purty," she said at last, with grateful emphasis. "It's everything I planned to have, and a great deal nicer than I could have done it myself, though I thought about it goodness knows how many years!"

"I'm not surprised that you thought about it," the American answered. "It was the view you were longing for—fancy its having been cut off so long by that miserable stable! But now you have it in perfection."

"You mean the view of the garden," said Prudence. "There wasn't much to look at before; but now it's real sweet."

"No; I mean the great landscape all about us here," responded the American, surprised. She paused. Then seeing that Prudence did not lift her eyes, she began to enumerate its features, to point them out with her folded parasol. "That broad Umbrian plain, Prudence, with those tall slender trees; the other towns shining on their hills, like Perugia over there; the gleam of the river; the velvety blue of the mountains; the color of it all—I do believe it is the very loveliest view in the whole world!"

"I don't know as I've ever noticed it much—the view," Prudence answered. She turned her eyes towards the horizon for a moment. "You see I was always thinking about my front yard."

"The front yard is very nice now," said the American. "I am so glad you are pleased; we couldn't get snowballs or Missouri currant, so we had to take roses." She paused; but she could not give up the subject without one more attempt. "You have probably noticed the view without being aware of it," she went on; "it is so beautiful that you must have noticed it. If you should leave it you would find yourself missing it very much, I dare say."

"Mebbe," responded Prudence. "Still, I ain't so sure. The truth is, I don't care much for these Eyetalian views; it seems to me a poor sort of country, and always did." Then, wishing to be more responsive to the tastes of this new friend, if she could be so honestly, she added, "But I like views, as a general thing; there was a very purty view from Sage's Hill, I remember."

"Sage's Hill?"

"Yes; the hill near Ledham. You told me you knew Ledham. You could see all the fields and medders of Josiah Strong's farm, and Deacon Mayberry's too; perfectly level, and not a stone in 'em. And the turnpike for miles and miles, with three toll-gates in sight. Then, on the other side, there were the factories to make it lively. It was a sweet view."

A few days afterwards she said: "People tell us that we never get what we want in this world, don't they? But I'm fortunate. I think I've always been purty fortunate. I got my front yard, after all."

A week later, when they told her that death was near, "My! I'd no idea I was so sick as that," she whispered. Then, looking at them anxiously, "What 'll become of Nounce?"

They assured her that Nounce should be provided for. "You

know you have to be sorter patient with her," she explained; "but she's growing quicker-witted every day."

Later, "I should like so much to see Jo Vanny," she murmured, longingly; "but of course I can't. You must get Bepper to send him my love, my dearest, dearest love."

Last of all, as her dulled eyes turned from the little window and rested upon her friend: "It seems a pity—But perhaps I shall find—"

# A Pink Villa

"YES, of the three, I liked Pierre best," said Mrs. Churchill. "Yet it was hard to choose. I have lived so long in Italy that I confess it would have been a pleasure to see Eva at court; it's a very pretty little court they have now at Rome, I assure you, with that lovely Queen Margherita at the head. The old Marchese is to resign his post this month, and the King has already signified his intention of giving it to Gino. Eva, as the Marchesa Lamberti, living in that ideal old Lamberti palace, you know—Eva, I flatter myself, would have shone in her small way as brightly as Queen Margherita in hers. You may think I am assuming a good deal, Philip. But you have no idea how much pains has been taken with that child; she literally is fitted for a court or for any other high position. Yet at the same time she is very childlike. I have kept her so purposely; she has almost never been out of my sight. The Lambertis are one of the best among the old Roman families, and there could not be a more striking proof of Gino's devotion than his having persuaded his father to say (as he did to me two months ago) that he should be proud to welcome Eva 'as she is,' which meant that her very small dowry would not be considered an objection. As to Eva herself, of course the Lambertis, or any other family, would be proud to receive her," pursued Mrs. Churchill, with the quiet pride which in its unruffled serenity became her well. "But not to hesitate over her mere pittance of a portion, that is very remarkable; for the marriage-portion is considered a sacred point by all Italians; they are brought up to respect it—as we respect the Constitution."

"It's a very pretty picture," answered Philip Dallas—"the court and Queen Margherita, the handsome Gino and the old Lamberti palace. But I'm a little bewildered, Fanny; you speak of it all so appreciatively, yet Gino was certainly not the name you mentioned; Pierre, wasn't it?"

"Yes, Pierre," answered Mrs. Churchill, laughing and sighing with the same breath. "I've strayed far. But the truth is, I did like Gino, and I wanted to tell you about him. No, Eva will not be the Marchesa Lamberti, and live in the old palace;

I have declined that offer. Well, then, the next was Thornton Stanley."

"Thornton Stanley? Has he turned up here? I used to know him very well."

"I thought perhaps you might."

"He is a capital fellow—when he can forget his first editions."

Mrs. Churchill folded her arms, placing one hand on each elbow, and slightly hugging herself. "He has forgotten them more than once in *this* house," she said, triumphantly.

"He is not only a capital fellow, but he has a large fortune —ten times as large, I venture to say, as your Lambertis have."

"I know that. But—"

"But you prefer an old palace. I am afraid Stanley could not build Eva an old castle. Couldn't you manage to jog on with half a dozen new ones?"

"The trouble with Thornton Stanley was his own uncertainty," said Fanny; "he was not in the least firm about staying over here, though he pretended he was. I could see that he would be always going home. More than that, I should not be at all surprised if at the end of five years—three even—he should have bought or built a house in New York, and settled down there forever."

"And you don't want that for your American daughter, renegade?"

Mrs. Churchill unfolded her arms. "No one can be a warmer American than I am, Philip—no one. During the war I nearly cried my eyes out; have you forgotten that? I scraped lint; I wanted to go to the front as nurse—everything. What days they were! We *lived* then. I sometimes think we have never lived since."

Dallas felt a little bored. He was of the same age as Fanny Churchill; but the school-girl, whose feelings were already those of a woman, had had her nature stirred to its depths by events which the lad had been too young to take seriously to heart. His heart had never caught up with them, though, of course, his reason had.

"Yes, I know you are flamingly patriotic," he said. "All the same, you don't want Eva to live in Fiftieth Street."

"In Fiftieth Street?"

"I chose the name at random. In New York."

"I don't see why you should be sarcastic," said Fanny. "Of course I expect to go back myself some time; I could not be content without that. But Eva—Eva is different; she has been brought up over here entirely; she was only three when I came abroad. It seems such a pity that all that should be wasted."

"And why should it be wasted in Fiftieth Street?"

"The very qualities that are admired here would be a drawback to her there," replied Mrs. Churchill. "A shy girl who cannot laugh and talk with everybody, who has never been out alone a step in her life, where would she be in New York?— I ask you that. While here, as you see, before she is eighteen—"

"Isn't the poor child eighteen yet? Why in the world do you want to marry her to any one for five years more at least?"

Mrs. Churchill threw up her pretty hands. "How little you have learned about some things, Philip, in spite of your winters on the Nile and your Scotch shooting-box! I suppose it is because you have had no daughters to consider."

"Daughters?—I should think not!" was Dallas's mental exclamation. Fanny, then, with all her sense, was going to make that same old mistake of supposing that a bachelor of thirty-seven and a mother of thirty-seven were of the same age.

"Why, it's infinitely better in every way that a nice girl like Eva should be married as soon as possible after her school-books are closed, Philip," Mrs. Churchill went on; "for then, don't you see, she can enter society—which is always so dangerous —safely; well protected, and yet quite at liberty as well. I mean, of course, in case she has a good husband. That is the mother's business, the mother's responsibility, and I think a mother who does not give her heart to it, her whole soul and energy, and choose *well*—I think such a mother an infamous woman. In this case I am sure I have chosen well; I am sure Eva will be happy with Pierre de Verneuil. They have the same ideas; they have congenial tastes, both being fond of music and art. And Pierre is a very lovable fellow; you will think so yourself when you see him."

"And you say she likes him?"

"Very much. I should not have gone on with it, of course, if there had been any dislike. They are not formally betrothed as yet; that is to come soon; but the old Count (Pierre's father) has been to see me, and everything is virtually arranged—

a delightful man, the old Count. They are to make handsome settlements; not only are they rich, but they are not in the least narrow—as even the best Italians are, I am sorry to say. The Verneuils are cosmopolitans; they have been everywhere; their estate is near Brussels, but they spend most of their time in Paris. They will never tie Eva down in any small way. In addition, both father and son are extremely nice to *me*."

"Ah!" said Dallas, approvingly.

"Yes; they have the French ideas about mothers; you know that in France the mother is and remains the most important person in the family." As she said this, Mrs. Churchill unconsciously lifted herself and threw back her shoulders. Ordinarily the line from the knot of her hair behind to her waist was long and somewhat convex, while correspondingly the distance between her chin and her belt in front was surprisingly short: she was a plump woman, and she had fallen into the habit of leaning upon a certain beguiling steel board, which leads a happy existence in wrappings of white kid and perfumed lace.

"Not only will they never wish to separate me from Eva," she went on, still abnormally erect, "but such a thought would never enter their minds; they think it an honor and a pleasure to have me with them; the old Count assured me of it in those very words."

"And now we have the secret of the Belgian success," said Dallas.

"Yes. But I have not been selfish; I have tried to consider everything; I have investigated carefully. If you will stay half an hour longer you can see Pierre for yourself; and then I know that you will agree with me."

In less than half an hour the Belgian appeared—a slender, handsome young man of twenty-two, with an ease of manner and grace in movement which no American of that age ever had. With all his grace, however, and his air of being a man of the world, there was such a charming expression of kindliness and purity in his still boyish eyes that any mother, with her young daughter's happiness at heart, might have been pardoned for coveting him as a son-in-law. This Dallas immediately comprehended. "You have chosen well," he said to Fanny, when they were left for a moment alone; "the boy's a jewel."

Before the arrival of Pierre, Eva Churchill, followed by her governess, had come out to join her mother on the terrace; Eva's daily lessons were at an end, save that the music went on; Mlle. Legrand was retained as a useful companion.

Following Pierre, two more visitors appeared, not together; one was an Englishman of fifty, small, meagre, plain in face; the other an American, somewhat younger, a short, ruddy man, dressed like an Englishman. Mrs. Churchill mentioned their names to Dallas: "Mr. Gordon-Gray." "Mr. Ferguson."

It soon appeared that Mr. Gordon-Gray and Mr. Ferguson were in the habit of looking in every afternoon, at about that hour, for a cup of tea. Dallas, who hated tea, leaned back in his chair and watched the scene, watched Fanny especially, with the amused eyes of a contemporary who remembers a different past. Fanny was looking dimpled and young; her tea was excellent, her tea-service elaborate (there was a samovar); her daughter was docile, her future son-in-law a Count and a pearl; in addition, her terrace was an enchanting place for lounging, attached as it was to a pink-faced villa that overlooked the sea.

Nor were there wanting other soft pleasures. "Dear Mrs. Murray-Churchill, how delicious is this nest of yours!" said the Englishman, with quiet ardor; "I never come here without admiring it."

Fanny answered him in a steady voice, though there was a certain flatness in its tone: "Yes, it's very pretty indeed." Her face was red; she knew that Dallas was laughing; she would not look in his direction. Dallas, however, had taken himself off to the parapet, where he could have his laugh out at ease: to be called Mrs. Murray-Churchill as a matter of course in that way —what joy for Fanny!

Eva was listening to the busy Mark Ferguson; he was showing her a little silver statuette which he had unearthed that morning in Naples, "in a dusty out-of-the-way shop, if you will believe it, where there was nothing else but rubbish—literally nothing. From the chasing I am inclined to think it's fifteenth century. But you will need glasses to see it well; I can lend you a pair of mine."

"I can see it perfectly—thanks," said Eva. "It is very pretty, I suppose."

"Pretty, Miss Churchill? Surely it's a miracle!" Ferguson protested.

Pierre, who was sitting near the mother, glanced across and smiled. Eva did not smile in reply; she was looking vaguely at the blackened silver; but when he came over to see for himself the miracle, then she smiled very pleasantly.

Pierre was evidently deeply in love; he took no pains to conceal it; but during the two hours he spent there he made no effort to lure the young girl into the drawing-room, or even as far as the parapet. He was very well bred. At present he stood beside her and beside Mark Ferguson, and talked about the statuette. "It seems to me old Vienna," he said.

"Signor Bartalama," announced Angelo, Mrs. Churchill's man-servant, appearing at the long window of the drawing-room which served as one of the terrace doors; he held the lace curtains apart eagerly, with the smiling Italian welcome.

Fanny had looked up, puzzled. But when her eyes fell upon the figure emerging from the lace she recognized it instantly. "Horace Bartholomew! Now from what quarter of the heavens do you drop *this* time?"

"So glad you call it heaven," said the new-comer, as she gave him her hand. "But from heaven indeed this time, Mrs. Churchill—I say so emphatically; from our own great, grand country—with the permission of the present company be it spoken." And he bowed slightly to the Englishman and Pierre, his discriminating glance including even the little French governess, who smiled (though non-comprehendingly) in reply. "May I present to you a compatriot, Mrs. Churchill?" he went on. "I have taken the liberty of bringing him without waiting for formal permission; he is, in fact, in your drawing-room now. His credentials, however, are small and puny; they consist entirely of the one item—that I like him."

"That will do perfectly," said Fanny, smiling.

Bartholomew went back to the window and parted the curtains. "Come," he said. A tall man appeared. "Mrs. Churchill, let me present to you Mr. David Rod."

Mrs. Churchill was gracious to the stranger; she offered him a chair near hers, which he accepted; a cup of tea, which he declined; and the usual small questions of a first meeting, which only very original minds are bold enough to jump over. The stranger answered the questions promptly; he was evidently not original. He had arrived two days before; this was his first visit to Italy; the Bay of Naples was beautiful; he had not been up Vesuvius; he had not visited Pompeii; he was not afraid of fever; and he had met Horace Bartholomew in Florida the year before.

"I am told they are beginning to go a great deal to Florida," remarked Fanny.

"I don't go there; I live there," Rod answered.

"Indeed! in what part?" (She brought forward the only names she knew.) "St. Augustine, perhaps? Or Tallahassee?"

"No; I live on the southern coast; at Punta Palmas?"

"How Spanish that is! Perhaps you have one of those old Spanish plantations?" She had now exhausted all her knowledge of the State save a vague memory of her school geography: "Where are the Everglades?" "They are in the southern part of Florida. They are shallow lakes filled with trees." But the stranger could hardly live in such a place as that.

"No," answered Rod; "my plantation isn't old and it isn't Spanish; it's a farm, and quite new. I am over here now to get hands for it."

"Hands?"

"Yes, laborers—Italians. They work very well in Florida."

Eva and Mademoiselle Legrand had turned with Pierre to look at the magnificent sunset. "Did you receive the flowers I sent this morning?" said Pierre, bending his head so that if Eva should glance up when she answered, he should be able to look into her eyes.

"Yes; they were beautiful," said Eva, giving the hoped-for glance.

"Yet they are not in the drawing-room."

"You noticed that?" she said, smiling. "They are in the music-room; Mademoiselle put them there."

"They are the flowers for Mozart, are they not?" said Mademoiselle—"heliotrope and white lilies; and we have been studying Mozart this morning. The drawing-room, as you know, Monsieur le Comte, is always full of roses."

"And how do you come on with Mozart?" asked Pierre.

"As usual," answered Eva. "Not very well, I suppose."

Mademoiselle twisted her handkerchief round her fingers. She was passionately fond of music; it seemed to her that her pupil, who played accurately, was not. Pierre also was fond of music, and played with taste. He had not perceived Eva's coldness in this respect simply because he saw no fault in her.

"I want to make up a party for the Deserto," he went on, "to lunch there. Do you think Madame Churchill will consent?"

"Probably," said Eva.

"I hope she will. For when we are abroad together, under the open sky, then it sometimes happens I can stay longer by your side."

"Yes; we never have very long talks, do we?" remarked Eva, reflectively.

"Do you desire them?" said Pierre, with ardor. "Ah, if you could know how I do! With me it is one long thirst. Say that you share the feeling, even if only a little; give me that pleasure."

"No," said Eva laughing, "I don't share it at all. Because, if we should have longer talks, you would find out too clearly that I am not clever."

"Not clever!" said Pierre, with all his heart in his eyes. Then, with his unfailing politeness, he included Mademoiselle. "She is clever, Mademoiselle?"

"She is good," answered Mademoiselle, gravely. "Her heart has a depth—but a depth!"

"I shall fill it all," murmured Pierre to Eva. "It is not that I myself am anything, but my love is so great, so vast; it holds you as the sea holds Capri. Some time—some time, you must let me try to tell you!"

Eva glanced at him. Her eyes had for the moment a vague expression of curiosity.

This little conversation had been carried on in French; Mademoiselle spoke no English, and Pierre would have been incapable of the rudeness of excluding her by means of a foreign tongue.

II

The pink villa was indeed a delicious nest, to use the Englishman's phrase. It crowned one of the perpendicular cliffs of Sorrento, its rosy façade overlooking what is perhaps the most beautiful expanse of water in the world—the Bay of Naples. The broad terrace stretched from the drawing room windows to the verge of the precipice; leaning against its strong stone parapet, with one's elbows comfortably supported on the flat top (which supported also several battered goddesses of marble), enjoying the shade of a lemon-tree set in a great vase of tawny terra-cotta—leaning thus, one could let one's idle gaze drop straight down into the deep blue water below, or turn it to the white line of Naples opposite, shining under castled heights, to Vesuvius with its plume of smoke, or to beautiful dark Ischia rising from the waves in the west, guarding the entrance to the sea. On each side, close at hand, the cliffs of Sorrento stretched away, tipped with their villas, with their crowded orange and lemon groves. Each villa had its private stairway leading to the beach below; strange dark passages, for the most part cut in the solid rock, winding down close to the face of the cliff, so that every now and then a little rock-window can let in a gleam of light to keep up the spirits of those who are descending. For every one does descend: to sit and read among the rocks; to bathe from the bathing-house on the fringe of beach; to embark for a row to the grottos or a sail to Capri.

The afternoon which followed the first visit of Philip Dallas to the pink villa found him there a second time; again he was on the terrace with Fanny. The plunging sea-birds of the terrace's mosaic floor were partially covered by a large Persian rug, and it was upon this rich surface that the easy-chairs were assembled, and also the low tea-table, which was of a construction so solid that no one could possibly knock it over. A keen observer had once said that that table was in itself a sufficient indication that Fanny's house was furnished to attract masculine, not feminine, visitors (a remark which was perfectly true).

"You are the sun of a system of masculine planets, Fanny," said Dallas. "After long years, that is how I find you."

"Oh, Philip—we who live so quietly!"

"So is the sun quiet, I suppose; I have never heard that he howled. Mr. Gordon-Gray, Mark Ferguson, Pierre de Verneuil, Horace Bartholomew, unknown Americans. Do they come to see Eva or you?"

"They come to see the view—as you do; to sit in the shade and talk. I give very good dinners too," Fanny added, with simplicity.

"O romance! good dinners on the Bay of Naples!"

"Well, you may laugh; but nothing draws men of a certain age—of a certain kind, I mean; the most satisfactory men, in short—nothing draws them so surely as a good dinner delicately served," announced Fanny, with decision. "Please go and ring for the tea."

"I don't wonder that they all hang about you," remarked Dallas as he came back, his eyes turning from the view to his hostess in her easy-chair. "Your villa is admirable, and you yourself, as you sit there, are the personification of comfort, the personification, too, of gentle, sweet, undemonstrative affectionateness. Do you know that, Fanny?"

Fanny, with a very pink blush, busied herself in arranging the table for the coming cups.

Dallas smiled inwardly. "She thinks I am in love with her because I said that about affectionateness," he thought. "Oh, the fatuity of women!"

At this moment Eva came out, and presently appeared Mr. Gordon-Gray and Mark Ferguson. A little later came Horace Bartholomew. The tea had been brought; Eva handed the cups. Dallas, looking at her, was again struck by something in the manner and bearing of Fanny's daughter. Or rather he was not struck by it; it was an impression that made itself felt by degrees, as it had done the day before—a slow discovery that the girl was unusual.

She was tall, dressed very simply in white. Her thick smooth flaxen hair was braided in two long flat tresses behind, which were doubled and gathered up with a ribbon, so that they only reached her shoulders. This school-girl coiffure became her young face well. Yes, it was a very young face. Yet it was a serious face too. "Our American girls are often serious, and when they are brought up under the foreign system it really makes them too quiet," thought Dallas. Eva had a pair of large gray eyes under dark lashes: these eyes were thoughtful; sometimes they were dull. Her smooth complexion was rather brown. The oval of her face was perfect. Though her dress was so child-like, her figure was womanly; the poise of her head was noble, her step light and free. Nothing could be more unlike the dimpled, smiling mother than was this tall, serious daughter who followed in her train. Dallas tried to recall Edward Churchill (Edward Murray Churchill), but could not; he had only seen him once. "He must have been an obstinate sort of fellow," he said to himself. The idea had come to him suddenly from something in Eva's expression. Yet it was a sweet expression; the curve of the lips was sweet.

"She isn't such a very pretty girl, after all," he reflected, summing her up finally before he dismissed her. "Fanny is a clever woman to have made it appear that she is."

At this moment Eva, having finished her duties as cupbearer, walked across the terrace and stood by the parapet, outlined against the light.

"By Jove she's beautiful!" thought Dallas.

Fanny's father had not liked Edward Churchill; he had therefore left his money tied up in such a way that neither Churchill nor any children whom he might have should be much benefited by it; Fanny herself, though she had a comfortable income for life, could not dispose of it. This accounted for the very small sum belonging to Eva: she had only the few hundreds that came to her from her father.

But she had been brought up as though she had many thousands; studiedly quiet as her life had been, studiedly simple as her attire always was, in every other respect her existence had been arranged as though a large fortune certainly awaited her. This had been the mother's idea; she had been sure from the beginning that a large fortune did await her daughter. It now appeared that she had been right.

"I don't know what you thought of me for bringing a fellow-countryman down upon you yesterday in that unceremonious way, Mrs. Churchill," Bartholomew was saying. "But I wanted to do something for him—I met him at the top of your lane by accident; it was an impulse."

"Oh, I'm sure—any friend of yours—" said Fanny, looking into the teapot.

Bartholomew glanced round the little circle on the rug, with an expression of dry humor in his brown eyes. "You didn't any of you like him—I see that," he said.

There was a moment's silence.

"Well, he is rather a commonplace individual, isn't he?" said Dallas, unconsciously assuming the leadership of this purely feminine household.

"I don't know what you mean by commonplace; but yes, I do, coming from *you*, Dallas. Rod has never been abroad in his life until now; and he's a man with convictions."

"Oh, come, don't take that tone," said Mark Ferguson; "I've got convictions too; I'm as obstinate about them as an Englishman."

"What did your convictions tell you about Rod, then, may I ask?" pursued Bartholomew.

"I didn't have much conversation with him, you may re-member; I thought he had plenty of intelligence. His clothes were—were a little peculiar, weren't they?"

"Made in Tampa, probably. And I've no doubt but that he took pains with them—wanted to have them appropriate."

"That is where he disappointed me," said Gordon-Gray—"that very appearance of having taken pains. When I learned that he came from that—that place in the States you have just named—a wild part of the country, is it not?—I thought he would be more—more interesting. But he might as well have come from Clerkenwell."

"You thought he would be more wild, you mean; trousers in his boots; long hair; knives."

All the Americans laughed.

"Yes. I dare say you cannot at all comprehend our penchant for that sort of thing," said the Englishman, composedly. "And —er—I am afraid there would be little use in attempting to explain it to you. But this Mr. Rod seemed to me painfully unconscious of his opportunities; he told me (when I asked) that there was plenty of game there—deer, and even bears and panthers—royal game; yet he never hunts."

"He never hunts, because he has something better to do," retorted Bartholomew.

"Ah, better?" murmured the Englishman, doubtfully.

Bartholomew got up and took a chair which was nearer Fanny. "No—no tea," he said, as she made a motion towards a cup; then, without further explaining his change of position, he gave her a little smile. Dallas, who caught this smile on the wing, learned from it unexpectedly that there was a closer intimacy between his hostess and Bartholomew than he had suspected. "Bartholomew!" he thought, contemptuously. "Gray —spectacles—stout." Then suddenly recollecting the increasing plumpness of his own person, he drew in his out-stretched legs, and determined, from that instant, to walk fifteen miles a day.

"Rod knows how to shoot, even though he doesn't hunt," said Bartholomew, addressing the Englishman. "I saw him once bring down a mad bull, who was charging directly upon an old man—the neatest sort of a hit."

"He himself being in a safe place meanwhile," said Dallas.

"On the contrary, he had to rush forward into an open field. If he had missed his aim by an eighth of an inch, the beast— a terrible creature—would have made an end of him."

"And the poor old man?" said Eva.

"He was saved, of course; he was a rather disreputable old darky. Another time Rod went out in a howling gale—the kind they have down there—to rescue two men whose boat had capsized in the bay. They were clinging to the bottom; no one else would stir; they said it was certain death; but Rod went out—he's a capital sailor—and got them in. I didn't see that myself, as I saw the bull episode; I was told about it."

"By Rod?" said Dallas.

"By one of the men he saved. As you've never been saved yourself, Dallas, you probably don't know how it feels."

"He seems to be a modern Chevalier Bayard, doesn't he?" said good-natured Mark Ferguson.

"He's modern, but no Bayard. He's a modern and a model pioneer—"

"Pioneers! oh, pioneers!" murmured Gordon-Gray, half chanting it.

None of the Americans recognized his quotation.

"He's the son of a Methodist minister," Bartholomew went on. "His father, a missionary, wandered down to Florida in the early days, and died there, leaving a sickly wife and seven children. You know the sort of man—a linen duster for a coat, prunella shoes, always smiling and hopeful—a great deal about 'Brethren.' Fortunately they could at least be warm in that climate, and fish were to be had for the catching; but I suspect it was a struggle for existence while the boys were small. David was the youngest; his five brothers, who had come up almost laborers, were determined to give this lad a chance if they could; together they managed to send him to school, and later to a forlorn little Methodist college somewhere in Georgia. David doesn't call it forlorn, mind you; he still thinks it an important institution. For nine years now—he is thirty—he has taken care of himself; he and a partner have cleared this large farm, and have already done well with it. Their hope is to put it all into sugar in time, and a Northern man with capital has advanced them the money for this Italian colonization scheme: it has been tried before in Florida, and has worked well. They have been very enterprising, David and his partner; they have a saw-mill running, and two school-houses already—one for whites, one for blacks. You ought to see the little darkies, with their wool twisted into twenty tails, going proudly in when the bell rings," he added, turning to Fanny.

"And the white children, do they go too?" said Eva.

"Yes, to their own school-house—lank girls, in immense sun-bonnets, stalking on long bare feet. He has got a brisk little Yankee school-mistress for them. In ten years more I declare he will have civilized that entire neighborhood."

"You are evidently the Northern man with capital," said Dallas.

"I don't care in the least for your sneers, Dallas; I'm not the Northern man, but I should like to be. If I admire Rod, with his constant driving action, his indomitable pluck, his simple but tremendous belief in the importance of what he has undertaken to do, that's my own affair. I do admire him just as he stands, clothes and all; I admire his creaking saw-mill; I admire his groaning dredge; I even admire his two hideously ugly new school-houses, set staring among the stumps."

"Tell me one thing, does he preach in the school-houses on Sundays and Friday evenings, say?" asked Ferguson. "Because if he does he will make no money, whatever else he may make. They never do if they preach."

"It's his father who was the minister, not he," said Bartholomew. "David never preached in his life; he wouldn't in the least know how. In fact, he's no talker at all; he says very little at any time; he's a doer—David is; he *does* things. I declare it used to make me sick of myself to see how much that fellow accomplished every day of his life down there, and thought nothing of it at all."

"And what were you doing 'down there,' besides making yourself sick, if I may ask?" said Ferguson.

"Oh, I went down for the hunting, of course. What else does one go to such a place for?"

"Tell me a little about that, if you don't mind," said the Englishman, interested for the first time.

"M. de Verneuil wants us all to go to the Deserto some day soon," said Fanny; "a lunch party. We shall be sure to enjoy it; M. de Verneuil's parties are always delightful."

### III

The end of the week had been appointed for Pierre's excursion.

The morning opened fair and warm, with the veiled blue that belongs to the Bay of Naples, the soft hazy blue which is so different from the dry glittering clearness of the Riviera.

Fanny was mounted on a donkey; Eva preferred to walk, and Mademoiselle accompanied her. Pierre had included in his invitation the usual afternoon assemblage at the villa—Dallas, Mark Ferguson, Bartholomew, Gordon-Gray, and David Rod.

For Fanny had, as Dallas expressed it, "taken up" Rod; she had invited him twice to dinner. The superfluous courtesy had annoyed Dallas, for of course, as Rod himself was nothing, less than nothing, the explanation must lie in the fact that Horace Bartholomew had suggested it. "Bartholomew was always wrong-headed; always picking up some perfectly impossible creature, and ramming him down people's throats," he thought, with vexation.

Bartholomew was walking now beside Fanny's donkey.

Mark Ferguson led the party, as it moved slowly along the narrow paved road that winds in zigzags up the mountain; Eva, Mademoiselle, Pierre, Dallas, and Rod came next. Fanny and Bartholomew were behind; and behind still, walking alone and meditatively, came Gordon-Gray, who looked at life (save for the hunting) from the standpoint of the Italian Renaissance. Gordon-Gray knew a great deal about the Malatesta family; he had made a collection of Renaissance cloak clasps; he had written an essay on the colors of the long hose worn in the battling, leg-displaying days which had aroused his admiration, aroused it rather singularly, since he himself was as far as possible from having been qualified by nature to shine in such vigorous society.

Pierre went back to give some directions to one of the men in the rear of their small procession.

When he returned, "So the bears sometimes get among the canes?" Eva was saying.

"But then, how very convenient," said Pierre; "for they can take the canes and chastise them punctually." He spoke in his careful English.

"They're sugar-canes," said Rod.

"It's his plantation we are talking about," said Eva. "Once it was a military post, he says. Perhaps like Ehrenbreitstein."

"Exactly," said Dallas, from behind; "the same massive frowning stone walls."

"There were four one-story wooden barracks once," said Rod; "whitewashed; flag-pole in the centre. There's nothing now but a chimney; we've taken the boards for our mill."

"See the cyclamen, good folk," called out Gordon-Gray.

On a small plateau near by a thousand cyclamen, white and pink, had lifted their wings as if to fly away. Off went Pierre to get them for Eva.

"Have you ever seen the bears in the canes yourself?" pursued Eva.

"I've seen them in many places besides canes," answered Rod, grimly.

"I too have seen bears," Eva went on. "At Berne, you know."

"The Punta Palmas bears are quite the same," commented Dallas. "When they see Mr. Rod coming they sit up on their hind legs politely. And he throws them apples."

"No apples; they won't grow there," said Rod, regretfully. "Only oranges."

"Do you make the saw-mill go yourself—with your own hands?" pursued Eva.

"Not now. I did once."

"Wasn't it very hard work?"

"That? Nothing at all. You should have seen us grubbing up the stumps—Tipp and I!"

"Mr. Tipp is perhaps your partner?" said Dallas.

"Yes; Jim Tipp. Tipp and Rod is the name of the firm."

"Tipp—and Rod," repeated Dallas, slowly. Then with quick utterance, as if trying it, "Tippandrod."

Pierre was now returning with his flowers. As he joined them, round the corner of their zigzag, from a pasture above came a troop of ponies that had escaped from their driver, and were galloping down to Sorrento; two and two they came rushing on, too rapidly to stop, and everybody pressed to one side to give them room to pass on the narrow causeway.

Pierre jumped up on the low stone wall and extended his hand to Eva. "Come!" he said, hastily.

Rod put out his arm and pushed each outside pony, as he passed Eva, forcibly against his mate who had the inside place; a broad space was thus left beside her, and she had no need to leave the causeway. She had given one hand to Pierre as a beginning; he held it tightly. Mademoiselle meanwhile had climbed the wall like a cat. There were twenty of the galloping little nags; they took a minute or two to pass. Rod's outstretched hands, as he warded them off, were seen to be large and brown.

Eva imagined them "grubbing up" the stumps. "What is grubbing?" she said.

"It is writing for the newspapers in a street in London," said Pierre, jumping down. "And you must wear a torn coat, I believe." Pierre was proud of his English.

He presented his flowers.

Mademoiselle admired them volubly. "They are like souls just ready to wing their way to another world," she said, sentimentally, with her head on one side. She put her well-gloved hand in Eva's arm, summoned Pierre with an amiable gesture to the vacant place at Eva's left hand, and the three walked on together.

The Deserto, though disestablished and dismantled, like many another monastery, by the rising young kingdom, held still a few monks; their brown-robed brethren had aided Pierre's servant in arranging the table in the high room which commands the wonderful view of the sea both to the north and the south of the Sorrento peninsula, with Capri lying at its point too fair to be real—like an island in a dream.

"O la douce folie—
Aimable Capri!"

said Mark Ferguson. No one knew what he meant; he did not know himself. It was a poetical inspiration—so he said.

The lunch was delicate, exquisite; everything save the coffee (which the monks wished to provide: coffee, black-bread, and grapes which were half raisins was the monks' idea of a lunch) had been sent up from Sorrento. Dallas, who was seated beside Fanny, gave her a congratulatory nod.

"Yes, all Pierre does is well done," she answered, in a low tone, unable to deny herself this expression of maternal content.

Pierre was certainly a charming host. He gave them a toast; he gave them two; he gave them a song: he had a tenor voice which had been admirably cultivated, and his song was gay and sweet. He looked very handsome; he wore one of the cyclamen in his button-hole; Eva wore the rest, arranged by the deft fingers of Mademoiselle in a knot at her belt. But at the little feast Fanny was much more prominent than her daughter: this was Pierre's idea of what was proper; he asked her opinion, he referred everything to her with a smile which was homage in itself. Dallas, after a while, was seized with a malicious desire to take down for a moment this too prosperous companion of his boyhood. It was after Pierre had finished his little song. "Do you ever sing now, Fanny?" he asked, during a silence. "I remember how you used to sing Trancadillo."

"I am sure I don't know what you refer to," answered Fanny, coldly.

Another week passed. They sailed to Capri; they sailed to Ischia; they visited Pompeii. Bartholomew suggested these excursions. Eva too showed an almost passionate desire for constant movement, constant action. "Where shall we go to-day, mamma?" she asked every morning.

One afternoon they were strolling through an orange grove on the outskirts of Sorrento. Under the trees the ground was ploughed and rough; low stone copings, from whose interstices innumerable violets swung, ran hither and thither, and the paths followed the copings. The fruit hung thickly on the trees. Above the high wall which surrounded the place loomed the campanile of an old church. While they were strolling the bells rang the Angelus, swinging far out against the blue.

Rod, who was of the party, was absent-minded; he looked a little at the trees, but said nothing, and after a while he became absent-bodied as well, for he fell behind the others, and pursued his meditations, whatever they were, in solitude.

"He is bothered about his Italians," said Bartholomew; "he has only secured twenty so far."

Pierre joined Fanny; he had not talked with her that afternoon, and he now came to fulfil the pleasant duty. Eva, who had been left with Mademoiselle, turned round, and walking rapidly across the ploughed ground, joined Rod, who was sitting on one of the low stone walls at some distance from the party. Mademoiselle followed her, putting on her glasses as she went, in order to see her way over the heaped ridges. She held up her skirts, and gave ineffectual little leaps, always landing in the wrong spot, and tumbling up hill, as Dallas called it. "Blue," he remarked, meditatively. Every one glanced in that direction, and it was perceived that the adjective described the hue of Mademoiselle's birdlike ankles.

"For shame!" said Fanny.

But Dallas continued his observations. "Do look across," he said, after a while; "it's too funny. The French woman evidently thinks that Rod should rise, or else that Eva should be seated also. But her pantomime passes unheeded; neither Eva nor the backwoodsman is conscious of her existence."

"Eva is so fond of standing," explained Fanny. "I often say to her, 'Do sit down, child; it tires me to see you.' But Eva is never tired."

Pierre, who had a spray of orange buds in his hand, pressed it to his lips, and waved it imperceptibly towards his betrothed. "In everything she is perfect—perfect," he murmured to the pretty mother.

"Rod doesn't in the least mean to be rude," began Bartholomew.

"Oh, don't explain that importation of yours at this late day," interposed Dallas; "it isn't necessary. He is accustomed to sitting on fences probably; he belongs to the era of the singing-school."

This made Fanny angry. For as to singing-schools, there had

been a time—a remote time long ago—and Dallas knew it. She had smiled in answer to Pierre's murmured rapture; she now took his arm. To punish Dallas she turned her steps—on her plump little feet in their delicate kid boots—towards the still seated Rod, with the intention of asking him (for the fifth time) to dinner. This would not only exasperate Dallas, but it would please Bartholomew at the same stroke. Two birds, etc.

When they came up to the distant three, Mademoiselle glanced at Mrs. Churchill anxiously. But in the presence of the mistress of the villa, Rod did at last lift his long length from the wall.

This seemed, however, to be because he supposed they were about to leave the grove. "Is the walk over?" he said.

Pierre looked at Eva adoringly. He gave her the spray of orange buds.

IV

A week later Fanny's daughter entered the bedroom which she shared with her mother.

From the girl's babyhood the mother had had her small white-curtained couch placed close beside her own. She could not have slept unless able at any moment to stretch out her hand and touch her sleeping child.

Fanny was in the dressing-room; hearing Eva's step, she spoke. "Do you want me, Eva?"

"Yes, please."

Fanny appeared, a vision of white arms, lace, and embroidery.

"I thought that Rosine would not be here yet," said Eva. Rosine was their maid; her principal occupation was the elaborate arrangement of Fanny's brown hair.

"No, she isn't there—if you mean in the dressing-room," answered Fanny, nodding her head towards the open door.

"I wanted to see you alone, mamma, for a moment. I wanted to tell you that I shall not marry Pierre."

Fanny, who had sunk into an easy-chair, at these words sprang up. "What is the matter? Are you ill?"

"Not in the least, mamma; I am only telling you that I cannot marry Pierre."

"You *must* be ill," pursued Fanny. "You have fever. Don't

deny it." And anxiously she took the girl's hands. But Eva's hands were cooler than her own.

"I don't think I have any fever," replied Eva. She had been taught to answer all her mother's questions in fullest detail. "I sleep and eat as usual; I have no headache."

Fanny still looked at her anxiously. "Then if you are not ill, what can be the matter with you?"

"I have only told you, mamma, that I could not marry Pierre; it seems to me very simple."

She was so quiet that Fanny began at last to realize that she was in earnest. "My dearest, you know you like Pierre. You have told me so yourself."

"I don't like him now."

"What has he done—poor Pierre? He will explain, apologize; you may be sure of that."

"He has done nothing; I don't want him to apologize. He is as he always is. It is I who have changed."

"Oh, it is you who have changed," repeated Fanny, bewildered.

"Yes," answered Eva.

"Come and sit down and tell mamma all about it. You are tired of poor Pierre—is that it? It is very natural, he has been here so often, and stayed so long. But I will tell him that he must go away—leave Sorrento. And he shall stay away as long as you like, Eva; just as long as you like."

"Then he will stay away forever," the girl answered, calmly.

Fanny waited a moment. "Did you like Gino better? Is that it?" she said, softly, watching Eva's face.

"No."

"Thornton Stanley?"

"Oh no!"

"Dear child, explain this a little to your mother. You know I think only of your happiness," said Fanny, with tender solicitude.

Eva evidently tried to obey. "It was this morning. It came over me suddenly that I could not possibly marry him. Now or a year from now. Never." She spoke tranquilly; she even seemed indifferent. But this one decision was made.

"You know that I have given my word to the old Count," began Fanny, in perplexity.

Eva was silent.

"And everything was arranged."

Eva still said nothing. She looked about the room with wandering attention, as though this did not concern her.

"Of course I would never force you into anything," Fanny went on. "But I thought Pierre would be so congenial." In her heart she was asking herself what the young Belgian could have done. "Well, dear," she continued, with a little sigh, "you must always tell mamma everything." And she kissed her.

"Of course," Eva answered. And then she went away.

Fanny immediately rang the bell, and asked for Mademoiselle. But Mademoiselle knew nothing about it. She was overwhelmed with surprise and dismay. She greatly admired Pierre; even more she admired the old Count, whom she thought the most distinguished of men. Fanny dismissed the afflicted little woman, and sat pondering. While she was thinking, Eva re-entered.

"Mamma, I forgot to say that I should like to have you tell Pierre immediately. To-day."

Fanny was almost irritated. "You have never taken that tone before, my daughter. Have you no longer confidence in my judgment?"

"If you do not want to tell him this afternoon, it can be easily arranged, mamma; I will not come to the dinner-table; that is all. I do not wish to see him until he knows."

Pierre was to dine at the villa that evening.

"What can he have done?" thought Fanny again.

She rang for Rosine; half an hour later she was in the drawing-room. "Excuse me to every one but M. de Verneuil," she said to Angelo. She was very nervous, but she had decided upon her course: Pierre must leave Sorrento, and remain away until she herself should call him back.

"At the end of a month, perhaps even at the end of a week, she will miss you so much that I shall have to issue the summons," she said, speaking as gayly as she could, as if to make it a sort of joke. It was very hard for her, at best, to send away the frank, handsome boy.

Poor Pierre could not understand it at all. He declared over and over again that nothing he had said, nothing he had done, could possibly have offended his betrothed. "But surely you

know yourself that it is impossible!" he added, clasping his
hands beseechingly.

"It is a girlish freak," explained the mother. "She is so young,
you know."

"But that is the very reason. I thought it was only older
women who say what they wish to do in that decided way;
who have freaks, as you call it," said the Belgian, his voice for
a moment much older, more like the voice of a man who has
spent half his life in Paris.

This was so true that Fanny was driven to a defence that
scarcely anything else would have made her use. "Eva is different from the young girls here," she said. "You must not forget
that she is an American."

At last Pierre went away; he had tried to bear himself as a
gentleman should; but the whole affair was a mystery to him,
and he was very unhappy. He went as far as Rome, and there
he waited, writing to Fanny an anxious letter almost every
day.

In the meanwhile life at the villa went on; there were many
excursions. Fanny's thought was that Eva would miss Pierre
more during these expeditions than at other times, for Pierre
had always arranged them, and he had enjoyed them so much
himself that his gay spirits and his gay wit had made all the
party gay. Eva, however, seemed very happy, and at length
the mother could not help being touched to see how light-
hearted her serious child had become, now that she was entirely free. And yet how slight the yoke had been, and how
pleasant! thought Fanny. At the end of two weeks there were
still no signs of the "missing" upon which she had counted.
She thought that she would try the effect of briefly mentioning
the banished man. "I hear from Pierre almost every day, poor
fellow. He is in Rome."

"Why does he stay in Rome?" said Eva. "Why doesn't he
return home?"

"I suppose he doesn't want to go so far away," answered
Fanny, vaguely.

"Far away from what? Home should always be the first
place," responded the young moralist. "Of course you have
told him, mamma, that I shall never be his wife? That it is

forever?" And she turned her gray eyes towards her mother, for the first time with a shade of suspicion in them.

"Never is a long word, Eva."

"Oh, mamma!" The girl rose. "I shall write to him myself, then."

"How you speak! Do you wish to disobey me, my own little girl?"

"No; but it is so dishonest; it is like a lie."

"My dear, trust your mother. You have changed once; you may change again."

"Not about this, mamma. Will you please write this very hour, and make an end of it?"

"You are hard, Eva. You do not think of poor Pierre at all."

"No, I do not think of Pierre."

"And is there any one else you think of? I must ask you that once more," said Fanny, drawing her daughter down beside her caressingly. Her thoughts could not help turning again towards Gino, and in her supreme love for her child she now accomplished the mental somerset of believing that on the whole she preferred the young Italian to all the liberty, all the personal consideration for herself, which had been embodied in the name of Verneuil.

"Yes, there is some one else I think of," Eva replied, in a low voice.

"In Rome?" said Fanny.

Eva made a gesture of denial that was fairly contemptuous.

Fanny's mind flew wildly from Bartholomew to Dallas, from Ferguson to Gordon-Gray: Eva had no acquaintances save those which were her mother's also.

"It is David Rod," Eva went on, in the same low tone. Then, with sudden exaltation, her eyes gleaming, "I have never seen any one like him."

It was a shock so unexpected that Mrs. Churchill drew her breath under it audibly, as one does under an actual blow. But instantly she rallied. She said to herself that she had got a romantic idealist for a daughter—that was all. She had not suspected it; she had thought of Eva as a lovely child who would develop into what she herself had been. Fanny, though far-seeing and intelligent, had not been endowed with imagination. But now that she did realize it, she should know how to deal with it. A disposition like that, full of visionary fancies, was not so uncommon as some people supposed. Horace Bartholomew should take the Floridian away out of Eva's sight forever, and the girl would soon forget him; in the meanwhile not one word that was harsh should be spoken on the subject, for that would be the worst policy of all.

This train of thought had passed through her mind like a flash. "My dear," she began, as soon as she had got her breath back, "you are right to be so honest with me. Mr. Rod has not —has not said anything to you on the subject, has he?"

"No. Didn't I tell you that he cares nothing for me? I think he despises me—I am so useless!" And then suddenly the girl began to sob; a passion of tears.

Fanny was at her wits' end; Eva had not wept since the day of her baby ills, for life had been happy to her, loved, caressed, and protected as she had been always, like a hot-house flower.

"My darling," said the mother, taking her in her arms.

But Eva wept on and on, as if her heart would break. It ended in Fanny's crying too.

V

Early the next morning her letter to Bartholomew was sent. Bartholomew had gone to Munich for a week. The letter begged, commanded, that he should make some pretext that would call David Rod from Sorrento at the earliest possible moment. She counted upon her fingers; four days for the letter to go and the answer to return. Those four days she would spend at Capri.

Eva went with her quietly. There had been no more conversation between mother and daughter about Rod; Fanny thought that this was best.

On the fourth day there came a letter from Bartholomew. Fanny returned to Sorrento almost gayly: the man would be gone.

But he was not gone. Tranquillized, glad to be at home again, Mrs. Churchill was enjoying her terrace and her view, when Angelo appeared at the window: "Signor Ra."

Angelo's mistress made him a peremptory sign. "Ask the gentleman to wait in the drawing-room," she said. Then crossing to Eva, who had risen, "Go round by the other door to our own room, Eva," she whispered.

The girl did not move; her face had an excited look. "But why—"

"Go, child; go."

Still Eva stood there, her eyes fixed upon the long window veiled in lace; she scarcely seemed to breathe.

Her mother was driven to stronger measures. "You told me yourself that he cared nothing for you."

A deep red rose in Eva's cheeks; she turned and left the terrace by the distant door.

The mother crossed slowly to the long window and parted the curtains. "Mr. Rod, are you there? Won't you come out? Or stay—I will join you." She entered the drawing-room and took a seat.

Rod explained that he was about to leave Sorrento; Bartholomew had summoned him so urgently that he did not like to refuse, though it was very inconvenient to go at such short notice.

"Then you leave to-morrow?" said Fanny; "perhaps to-night?"

"No; on Monday. I could not arrange my business before."

"Three days more," Fanny thought.

She talked of various matters; she hoped that some one else would come in; but, by a chance, no one appeared that day, neither Dallas, nor Ferguson, nor Gordon-Gray. "What can have become of them?" she thought, with irritation. After a while she gave an inward start; she had become conscious of a foot-fall passing to and fro behind the half-open door near her—a door which led into the dining-room. It was a very soft foot-fall upon a thick carpet, but she recognized it: it was Eva. She was there—why? The mother could think of no good reason. Her heart began to beat more quickly; for the first time in her life she did not know her child. This person walking up and down behind that door so insistently, this was not Eva. Eva was docile; this person was not docile. What would be done next? She felt strangely frightened. It was a proof of her terror that she did not dare to close the door lest it should be instantly reopened. She began to watch every word she said to Rod, who had not perceived the foot-fall. She began to be extraordinarily polite to him; she stumbled through the most irrelevant complimentary sentences. Her dread was, every minute, lest Eva should appear.

But Eva did not appear; and at last, after long lingering, Rod went away. Fanny, who had hoped to bid him a final farewell, had not dared to go through that ceremony. He said that he should come again.

When at last he was gone the mother pushed open the half-closed door. "Eva," she began. She had intended to be severe, as severe as she possibly could be; but the sight of Eva stopped her. The girl had flung herself down upon the floor, her bowed head resting upon her arms on a chair. Her attitude expressed a hopeless desolation.

"What is it?" said Fanny, rushing to her.

Eva raised her head. "He never once spoke of me—asked for me," she murmured, looking at her mother with eyes so dreary with grief that any one must have pitied her.

Her mother pitied her, though it was an angry pity, too —a non-comprehending, jealous, exasperated feeling. She sat down and gathered her child to her breast with a gesture that was almost fierce. That Eva should suffer so cruelly when she, Fanny, would have made any sacrifice to save her from it, would have died for her gladly, were it not that she was the girl's only protector—oh, what fate had come over their happy life together! She had not the heart to be stern. All she said was, "We will go away, dear; we will go away."

"No," said Eva, rising; "let me stay here. You need not be afraid."

"Of course I am not afraid," answered Fanny, gravely. "My daughter will never do anything unseemly; she has too much pride."

"I am afraid I have no pride—that is, not as you have it, mamma. Pride doesn't seem to me at all important compared with— But of course I know that there is nothing I can do. He is perfectly indifferent. Only do not take me away again—do not."

"Why do you wish to stay?"

"Because then I can think—for three days more—that he is at least as near me as that." She trembled as she said this; there was a spot of sombre red in each cheek; her fair face looked strange amid her disordered hair.

Her mother watched her helplessly. All her beliefs, all her creed, all her precedents, the experience of her own life and her own nature even, failed to explain such a phenomenon as this. And it was her own child who was saying these things.

The next day Eva was passive. She wandered about the terrace, or sat for hours motionless staring blankly at the sea. Her mother left her to herself. She had comprehended that words were useless. She pretended to be embroidering, but in reality as she drew her stitches she was counting the hours as they passed: seventy-two hours; forty-eight hours. Would he ever be gone?

On the second day, in the afternoon, she discovered that Eva had disappeared. The girl had been on the terrace with Mademoiselle; Mademoiselle had gone to her room for a moment, and when she returned her pupil could not be found. She had not passed through the drawing-room, where Fanny was sitting with her pretended industry; nor through the other door, for Rosine was at work there, and had seen nothing of her. There remained only the rock stairway to the beach. Mademoiselle ran down it swiftly: no one. But there was a small boat not far off, she said. Fanny, who was near-sighted, got the glass. In a little boat with a broad sail there were two figures; one was certainly David Rod, and the other —yes, the other was Eva. There was a breeze, the boat was rapidly going westward round the cliffs; in two minutes more it was out of sight.

Fanny wrung her hands. The French woman, to whom the event wore a much darker hue than it did to the American mother, turned yellowly pale.

At this moment Horace Bartholomew came out on the terrace; uneasy, for Fanny's missive had explained nothing, he had followed his letter himself. "What is it?" he said, as he saw the agitation of the two women.

"Your friend—*yours*—the man you brought here, has Eva with him at this moment out on the bay!" said Fanny, vehemently.

"Well, what of that? You must look at it with Punta Palmas eyes, Fanny; at Punta Palmas it would be an ordinary event."

"But my Eva is not a Punta Palmas girl, Horace Bartholomew!"

"She is as innocent as one, and I'll answer for Rod. Come, be sensible, Fanny. They will be back before sunset, and no one in Sorrento—if that is what is troubling you so—need be any the wiser."

"You do not know all," said Fanny. "Oh, Horace—I must tell somebody—she fancies she cares for that man!" She wrung her hands again. "Couldn't we follow them? Get a boat."

"It would take an hour. And it would be a very conspicuous thing to do. Leave them alone—it's much better; I tell you I'll answer for Rod. Fancies she cares for him, does she? Well, he is a fine fellow; on the whole, the finest I know."

The mother's eyes flashed through her tears. "This from *you*?"

"I can't help it; he is. Of course you do not think so. He has got no money; he has never been anywhere that you call anywhere; he doesn't know anything about the only life you care for nor the things you think important. All the same, he is a man in a million. He is a man—not a puppet."

Gentle Mrs. Churchill appeared for the moment transformed. She looked as though she could strike him. "Never mind your Quixotic ideas. Tell me whether he is in love with Eva; it all depends upon that."

"I don't know, I am sure," answered Bartholomew. He began to think. "I can't say at all; he would conceal it from me."

"Because he felt his inferiority. I am glad he has that grace."

"He wouldn't be conscious of any inferiority save that he is poor. It would be that, probably, if anything; of course he supposes that Eva is rich."

"Would to Heaven she were!" said the mother. "Added to every other horror of it, poverty, miserable poverty, for my poor child!" She sat down and hid her face.

"It may not be as bad as you fear, nor anything like it. Do cheer up a little, Fanny. When Eva comes back, ten to one you will find that nothing at all has happened—that it has been a mere ordinary excursion. And I promise you I will take Rod away with me to-morrow."

Mrs. Churchill rose and began to pace to and fro, biting her lips, and watching the water. Mademoiselle, who was still hovering near, she waved impatiently away. "Let no one in," she called to her.

There seemed, indeed, to be nothing else to do, as Bartholomew had said, save to wait. He sat down and discussed the matter a little.

Fanny paid no attention to what he was saying. Every now and then broken phrases of her own burst from her: "How much good will her perfect French and Italian, her German, Spanish, and even Russian, do her down in that barbarous wilderness?"—"In her life she has never even buttoned her boots. Do they think she can make bread?"—"And there was Gino. And poor Pierre." Then, suddenly, "But it *shall* not be!"

"I have been wondering why you did not take that tone from the first," said Bartholomew. "She is very young. She has been brought up to obey you implicitly. It would be easy enough, I should fancy, if you could once make up your mind to it."

"Make up my mind to save her, you mean," said the mother, bitterly. She did not tell him that she was afraid of her daughter. "Should you expect *me* to live at Punta Palmas?" she demanded, contemptuously, of her companion.

"That would depend upon Rod, wouldn't it?" answered Bartholomew, rather unamiably. He was tired—he had been there an hour—of being treated like a door-mat.

At this Fanny broke down again, and completely. For it was only too true; it would depend upon that stranger, that farmer, that unknown David Rod, whether she, the mother, should or should not be with her own child.

A little before sunset the boat came into sight again round the western cliffs. Fanny dried her eyes. She was very pale. Little Mademoiselle, rigid with anxiety, watched from an upper window. Bartholomew rose to go down to the beach to receive the returning fugitives. "No," said Fanny, catching his arm, "don't go; no one must know before I do—no one." So they waited in silence.

Down below, the little boat had rapidly approached. Eva had jumped out, and was now running up the rock stairway; she was always light-footed, but to her mother it seemed that the ascent took an endless time. At length there was the vision of a young, happy, rushing figure—rushing straight to Fanny's arms. "Oh, mamma, mamma," the girl whispered, seeing that there was no one there but Bartholomew, "he loves me! He has told me so! he has told me so!"

For an instant the mother drew herself away. Eva, left alone, and mindful of nothing but her own bliss, looked so radiant with happiness that Bartholomew (being a man) could not help sympathizing with her. "You will have to give it up," he said to Fanny, significantly. Then he took his hat and went away.

Fifteen minutes later his place was filled by David Rod.

"Ah! you have come. I must have a few words of conversation with you, Mr. Rod," said Fanny, in an icy tone. "Eva, leave us now."

"Oh no, mamma, not now; never again, I hope," answered the girl. She spoke with secure confidence; her eyes were fixed upon her lover's face.

"Do you call this honorable behavior, Mr. Rod?" Fanny began. She saw that Eva would not go.

"Why, I hope so," answered Rod, surprised. "I have come at once, as soon as I possibly could, Mrs. Churchill (I had to take the boat back first, you know), to tell you that we are engaged; it isn't an hour old yet—is it, Eva?" He looked at Eva smilingly, his eyes as happy as her own.

"It is the custom to ask permission," said Fanny, stiffly.

"I have never heard of the custom, then; that is all I can say," answered Rod, with good-natured tranquillity, still looking at the girl's face, with its rapt expression, its enchanting joy.

"Please to pay attention; I decline to consent, Mr. Rod; you cannot have my daughter."

"Mamma—" said Eva, coming up to her.

"No, Eva; if you will remain here—which is most improper —you will have to hear it all. You are so much my daughter's inferior, Mr. Rod, that I cannot, and I shall not, consent."

At the word "inferior," a slight shock passed over Eva from head to foot. She went swiftly to her lover, knelt down and pressed her lips to his brown hand, hiding her face upon it.

He raised her tenderly in his arms, and thus embraced, they stood there together, confronting the mother—confronting the world.

Fanny put out her hands with a bitter cry. "Eva!"

The girl ran to her, clung to her. "Oh, mamma, I love you dearly. But you must not try to separate me from David. I could not leave him—I never will."

"Let us go in, to our own room," said the mother, in a broken voice.

"Yes; but speak to David first, mamma."

Rod came forward and offered his arm. He was sorry for the mother's grief, which, however, in such intensity as this, he could not at all understand. But though he was sorry, he was resolute, he was even stern; in his dark beauty, his height and strength, he looked indeed, as Bartholomew had said, a man.

At the sight of his offered arm Mrs. Churchill recoiled; she glanced all round the terrace as though to get away from it; she even glanced at the water; it almost seemed as if she would have liked to take her child and plunge with her to the depths below. But one miserable look at Eva's happy, trustful eyes still watching her lover's face cowed her; she took the offered arm. And then Rod went with her, supporting her gently into the house, and through it to her own room, where he left her with her daughter. That night the mother rose from her sleepless couch, lit a shaded taper, and leaving it on a distant table, stole softly to Eva's side. The girl was in a deep slumber, her head pillowed on her arm. Fanny, swallowing her tears, gazed at her sleeping child. She still saw in the face the baby outlines of years before, her mother's eye could still distinguish in the motionless hand the dimpled fingers of the child. The fair hair, lying on the pillow, recalled to her the short flossy curls of the little girl who had clung to her skirts, who had had but one thought—"mamma."

"What will her life be now? What must she go through, perhaps—what pain, privation—my darling, my own little child!"

The wedding was to take place within the month; Rod said that he could not be absent longer from his farm. Fanny, breaking her silence, suggested to Bartholomew that the farm might be given up; there were other occupations.

"I advise you not to say a word of that sort to Rod," Bartholomew answered. "His whole heart is in that farm, that colony he has built up down there. You must remember that he was brought up there himself, or rather came up. It's all he knows, and he thinks it the most important thing in life; I was going to say it's all he cares for, but of course now he has added Eva."

Pierre came once. He saw only the mother.

When he left her he went round by way of the main street of Sorrento in order to pass a certain small inn. His carriage was waiting to take him back to Castellamare, but there was some one he wished to look at first. It was after dark; he could see into the lighted house through the low uncurtained windows, and he soon came upon the tall outline of the young farmer seated at a table, his eyes bent upon a column of figures. The Belgian surveyed him from head to foot slowly. He stood there gazing for five minutes. Then he turned away. "*That*, for Americans!" he murmured in French, snapping his fingers in the darkness. But there was a mist in his boyish eyes all the same.

The pink villa witnessed the wedding. Fanny never knew how she got through that day. She was calm; she did not once lose her self-control.

They were to sail directly for New York from Naples, and thence to Florida; the Italian colonists were to go at the same time.

"Mamma comes next year," Eva said to everybody. She looked indescribably beautiful; it was the radiance of a complete happiness, like a halo.

By three o'clock they were gone, they were crossing the bay in the little Naples steamer. No one was left at the villa with Fanny—it was her own arrangement—save Horace Bartholomew.

"She won't mind being poor," he said, consolingly, "she won't mind anything—with *him*. It is one of those sudden, overwhelming loves that one sometimes sees; and after all, Fanny, it is the sweetest thing life offers."

"And the mother?" said Fanny.

# The Street of the Hyacinth

Iᴛ was a street in Rome—narrow, winding, not over-clean. Two vehicles meeting there could pass only by grazing the doors and windows on either side, after the usual excited whip-cracking and shouts which make the new-comer imagine, for his first day or two, that he is proceeding at a perilous speed through the sacred city of the soul.

But two vehicles did not often meet in the street of the Hyacinth. It was not a thoroughfare, not even a convenient connecting link; it skirted the back of the Pantheon, the old buildings on either side rising so high against the blue that the sun never came down lower than the fifth line of windows, and looking up from the pavement was like looking up from the bottom of a well. There was no foot-walk, of course; even if there had been one no one would have used it, owing to the easy custom of throwing from the windows a few ashes and other light trifles for the city refuse-carts, instead of carrying them down the long stairs to the door below. They must be in the street at an appointed hour, must they not? Very well, then—there they were; no one but an unreasonable foreigner would dream of objecting.

But unreasonable foreigners seldom entered the street of the Hyacinth. There were, however, two who lived there one winter not long ago, and upon a certain morning in the January of that winter a third came to see these two. At least he asked for them, and gave two cards to the Italian maid who answered his ring; but when, before he had time to even seat himself, the little curtain over the parlor door was raised again, and Miss Macks entered, she came alone. Her mother did not appear. The visitor was not disturbed by being obliged to begin conversation immediately; he was an old Roman sojourner, and had stopped fully three minutes at the end of the fourth flight of stairs to regain his breath before he mounted the fifth and last to ring Miss Macks's bell. Her card was tacked upon the door: "Miss Ettie F. Macks." He surveyed it with disfavor, while the little, loose-hung bell rang a small but exceedingly shrill and ill-tempered peal, like the barking of a small cur.

"Why in the world doesn't she put her mother's card here instead of her own?" he said to himself. "Or, if her own, why not simply 'Miss Macks,' without that nickname?"

But Miss Macks's mother had never possessed a visiting-card in her life. Miss Macks was the visiting member of the family; and this was so well understood at home, that she had forgotten that it might not be the same abroad. As to the "Ettie," having been called so always, it had not occurred to her to make a change. Her name was Ethelinda Faith, Mrs. Macks having thus combined euphony and filial respect—the first title being her tribute to æsthetics, the second her tribute to the memory of her mother.

"I am so very glad to see you, Mr. Noel," said Miss Macks, greeting her visitor with much cordial directness of voice and eyes. "I have been expecting you. But you have waited so long —three days!"

Raymond Noel, who thought that under the circumstances he had been unusually courteous and prompt, was rather surprised to find himself thus put at once upon the defensive.

"We are not always able to carry out our wishes immediately, Miss Macks," he replied, smiling a little. "I was hampered by several previously made engagements."

"Yes; but this was a little different, wasn't it? This was something important—not like an invitation to lunch or dinner, or the usual idle society talk."

He looked at her; she was quite in earnest.

"I suppose it to be different," he answered. "You must remember how little you have told me."

"I thought I told you a good deal! However, the atmosphere of a reception is no place for such subjects, and I can understand that you did not take it in. That is the reason I asked you to come and see me here. Shall I begin at once? It seems rather abrupt."

"I enjoy abruptness; I have not heard any for a long time."

"That I can understand, too; I suppose the society here is all finished off—there are no rough ends."

"There are ends. If not rough, they are often sharp."

But Miss Macks did not stop to analyze this; she was too much occupied with her own subject.

"I will begin immediately, then," she said. "It will be rather long; but if you are to understand me you ought, of course, to know the whole."

"My chair is very comfortable," replied Noel, placing his hat and gloves on the sofa near him, and taking an easy position with his head back.

Miss Macks thought that he ought to have said, "The longer it is, the more interesting," or something of that sort. She had already described him to her mother as "not over-polite. Not rude in the least, you know—as far as possible from that; wonderfully smooth-spoken; but yet, somehow—awfully indifferent." However, he was Raymond Noel; and that, not his politeness or impoliteness, was her point.

"To begin with, then, Mr. Noel, a year ago I had never read one word you have written; I had never even heard of you. I suppose you think it strange that I should tell you this so frankly; but, in the first place, it will give you a better idea of my point of view; and, in the second, I feel a friendly interest in your taking measures to introduce your writings into the community where I lived. It is a very intelligent community. Naturally, a writer wants his articles read. What else does he write them for?"

"Perhaps a little for his own entertainment," suggested her listener.

"Oh no! He would never take so much trouble just for that."

"On the contrary, many would take any amount just for that. Successfully to entertain one's self—that is one of the great successes of life."

Miss Macks gazed at him; she had a very direct gaze.

"This is just mere talk," she said, not impatiently, but in a business-like tone. "We shall never get anywhere if you take me up so. It is not that your remarks are not very cultivated and interesting, and all that, but simply that I have so much to tell you."

"Perhaps I can be cultivated and interesting dumbly. I will try."

"You are afraid I am going to be diffuse; I see that. So many women are diffuse! But I shall not be, because I have been thinking for six months just what I should say to you. It was very lucky that I went with Mrs. Lawrence to that reception where I met you. But if it had not happened as it did I should have found you out all the same. I should have looked for your address at all the bankers', and if it was not there I should have inquired at all the hotels. But it was delightful luck getting hold of you in this way almost the very minute I enter Rome!"

She spoke so simply and earnestly that Noel did not say that he was immensely honored, and so forth, but merely bowed his acknowledgments.

"To go back. I shall give you simply heads," pursued Miss Macks. "If you want details, ask, and I will fill them in. I come from the West. Tuscolee Falls is the name of our town. We had a farm there, but we did not do well with it after Mr. Spurr's death, so we rented it out. That is how I come to have so much leisure. I have always had a great deal of ambition; by that I mean that I did not see why things that had once been done could not be done again. It seemed to me that the point was—just determination. And then, of course, I always had the talent. I made pictures when I was a very little girl. Mother has them still, and I can show them to you. It is just like all the biographies, you know. They always begin in childhood, and astonish the family. Well, I had my first lessons from a drawing-teacher who spent a summer in Tuscolee. I can show you what I did while with him. Then I attended, for four years, the Young Ladies' Seminary in the county-town, and took lessons while there. I may as well be perfectly frank and tell the whole, which is that everybody was astonished at my progress, and that I was myself. All sorts of things are prophesied out there about my future. You see, the neighborhood is a very generous-spirited one, and they like to think they have discovered a genius at their own doors. My telling you all this sounds, I know, rather conceited, Mr. Noel. But if you could see my motive, and how entirely without conceit my idea of myself really is, you would hold me free from that charge. It is only that I want you to know absolutely the whole."

"I quite understand," answered her visitor.

"Well, I hope you do. I went on at home after that by myself, and I did a good deal. I work pretty rapidly, you see. Then came my last lessons, from a third teacher. He was a young man from New York. He had consumption, poor fellow! and cannot last long. He wasn't of much use to me in actual work. His ideas were completely different from those of my other teachers, and, indeed, from my own. He was unreliable, too, and his temper was uneven. However, I had a good deal of respect for his opinion, and *he* told me to get your art-articles and read them. It wasn't easy. Some of them are scattered about in the magazines and papers, you know. However, I am pretty determined, and I kept at it until I got them all. Well, they made a great impression upon me. You see, they were new." She paused. "But I doubt, Mr. Noel, whether we should ever entirely agree," she added, looking at him reflectively.

"That is very probable, Miss Macks."

Miss Macks thought this an odd reply. "He is so queer, with all his smoothness!" she said to her mother afterwards. "He never says what you think he will say. Now, any one would suppose that he would have answered that he would try to make me agree, or something like that. Instead, he just gave it right up without trying! But I expect he sees how independent I am, and that I don't intend to *reflect any* one.

"Well, they made a great impression," she resumed. "And as you seemed to think, Mr. Noel, that no one could do well in painting who had not seen and studied the old pictures over here, I made up my mind to come over at any cost, if it was a possible thing to bring it about. It wasn't easy, but—here we are. In the lives of all—almost all—artists, I have noticed —haven't you?—that there comes a time when they have to live on hope and their own pluck more than upon anything tangible that the present has to offer. They have to take that risk. Well, I have taken it; I took it when we left America. And now I will tell you what it is I want from *you*. I haven't any hesitation in asking, because I am sure you will feel interested in a case like mine, and because it was your writings really that brought me here, you know. And so, then, first: I would like your opinion of all that I have done so far. I have brought everything with me to show you. Second: I want your advice as to the best teacher; I suppose there is a great choice in Rome. Third: I should be glad if you would give a general oversight to all I do for the next year. And last, if you would be so kind, I should much enjoy making visits with you to all the galleries and hearing your opinions again by word of mouth, because that is always so much more vivid, you know, than the printed page."

"My dear Miss Macks! you altogether over-estimate my powers," said Noel, astounded by these far-reaching demands, so calmly and confidently made.

"Yes, I know. Of course it strikes you so—strikes you as a great compliment that I should wish to put myself so entirely in your hands," answered Miss Macks, smiling. "But you must give up thinking of me as the usual young lady; you must not think of me in that way any more than I shall think of you as the usual young gentleman. You will never meet me at a reception again; now that I have found *you*, I shall devote myself entirely to my work."

"An alarming girl!" said Noel to himself. But, even as he said it, he knew that, in the ordinary acceptation of the term at least, Miss Macks was not alarming.

She was twenty-two; in some respects she looked older, in others much younger, than most girls of that age. She was tall, slender, erect, but not especially graceful. Her hands were small and finely shaped, but thin. Her features were well cut; her face oval. Her gray eyes had a clear directness in their glance, which, combined with the other expressions of her face, told the experienced observer at once that she knew little of what is called "the world." For, although calm, it was a deeply confident glance; it showed that the girl was sure that she could take care of herself, and even several others also, through any contingencies that might arise. She had little color; but her smooth complexion was not pale—it was slightly brown. Her mouth was small, her teeth small and very white. Her light-brown hair was drawn back smoothly from her forehead, and drawn up smoothly behind, its thickness braided in a close knot on the top of her head. This compact coiffure, at a time when most feminine foreheads in Rome and elsewhere were shaded almost to the eyebrows by curling locks, and when the arched outline of the head was left unbroken, the hair being coiled in a low knot behind, made Miss Macks look somewhat peculiar. But she was not observant of fashion's changes. That had been the mode in Tuscolee; she had grown accustomed to it; and, as her mind was full of other things, she had not considered this one. One or two persons, who noticed her on the voyage over, said to themselves, "If that girl had more color, and if she was graceful, and if she was a little more womanly—that is, if she would not look at everything in such a direct, calm, impartial, impersonal sort of way—she would be almost pretty."

But Miss Macks continued without color and without grace, and went on looking at things as impersonally and impartially as ever.

"I shall be most happy, of course, to do anything that I can," Noel had answered. Then to make a diversion, "Shall I not have the pleasure of seeing Mrs. Macks?" he asked.

"Mrs. Macks? Oh, you mean mother. My mother's name is Spurr—Mrs. Spurr. My father died when I was a baby, and some years afterwards she married Mr. Spurr. She is now again a widow. Her health is not good, and she sees almost no one, thank you."

"I suppose you are much pleased with the picturesqueness of Roman life, and—ah—your apartment?" he went on.

"Pleased?" said Miss Macks, looking at him in wonder. "With our apartment? We get along with it because we must; there seems to be no other way to live in Rome. The idea of having only a story of a house, and not a whole house to ourselves, is dreadful to mother; she cannot get used to it. And with so many families below us—we have a clock-mender, a dress-maker, an engraver, a print-seller, and a cobbler—and only one pair of stairs, it does seem to me dreadfully public."

"You must look upon the stairway as a street," said Noel. "You have established yourselves in a very short time."

"Oh yes. I got an agent, and looked at thirty places the very first day. I speak Italian a little, so I can manage the housekeeping; I began to study it as soon as we thought of coming, and I studied hard. But all this is of secondary importance; the real thing is to get to work. Will you look at my paintings now?" she said, rising as if to go for them.

"Thanks; I fear I have hardly time to-day," said Noel. He was thinking whether it would be better to decline clearly and in so many words the office she had thrust upon him, or trust to time to effect the same without an open refusal. He decided upon the latter course; it seemed the easier, and also the kinder to her.

"Well, another day, then," said Miss Macks, cheerfully, taking her seat again. "But about a teacher?"

"I hardly know—"

"Oh, Mr. Noel! you *must* know."

And, in truth, he did know. It came into his mind to give her the name of a good teacher, and then put all further responsibilities upon him.

Miss Macks wrote down the name in a clear, ornamental handwriting.

"I am glad it isn't a foreigner," she said. "I don't believe I should get on with a foreigner."

"But it is a foreigner."

"Why, it's an English name, isn't it?—Jackson."

"Yes, he is an Englishman. But isn't an Englishman a foreigner in Rome?"

"Oh, you take that view? Now, to me, America and—well, yes, perhaps England, too, are the nations. Everything else is foreign."

"The English would be very much obliged to you," said Noel, laughing.

"Yes, I know I am more liberal than most Americans; I really like the English," said Miss Macks, calmly. "But we keep getting off the track. Let me see— Oh yes. As I shall go to see this Mr. Jackson this afternoon, and as it is not likely that he will be ready to begin to-morrow, will you come then and look at my pictures? Or would you rather commence with a visit to one of the galleries?"

Raymond Noel was beginning to be amused. If she had shown the faintest indication of knowing how much she was asking, if she had betrayed the smallest sign of a desire to secure his attention as Raymond Noel personally, and not simply the art authority upon whom she had pinned her faith, his disrelish for various other things about her would have been heightened into utter dislike, and it is probable that he would never have entered the street of the Hyacinth again. But she was so unaware of any intrusion, or any exorbitance in her demands, probably so ignorant of—certainly so indifferent to —the degree of perfection (perfection of the most quiet kind, however) visible in the general appearance and manner of the gentleman before her, that (he said to himself) he might as well have been one of her own Tuscolee farmers, for all she knew to the contrary. The whole affair was unusual; and Noel rather liked the unusual, if it was not loud—and Miss Macks was, at least, not loud; she was dressed plainly in black, and she had the gift of a sweet voice, which, although very clear, was low-toned. Noel was an observer of voices, and he had noticed hers the first time he heard her speak. While these thoughts were passing through his mind, he was answering that he feared his engagements for the next day would, unfortunately, keep him from putting himself at her service.

Her face fell; she looked much disappointed.

"Is it going to be like this all the time?" she asked, anxiously. "Are you always engaged?"

"In Rome, in the winter, one generally has small leisure. It will be the same with you, Miss Macks, when you have been here a while longer; you will see. As to the galleries, Mr. Jackson has a class, I think, and probably the pupils will visit them all under his charge; you will find that very satisfactory."

"But I don't want Mr. Jackson for the galleries; I want *you*," said Miss Macks. "I have studied your art criticisms until I know them by heart, and I have a thousand questions to ask about every picture you have mentioned. Why, Mr. Noel, I came to Europe to see you!"

Raymond Noel was rather at a loss what to answer to this statement, made by a girl who looked at him so soberly and earnestly with clear gray eyes. It would be of no avail again to assure her that his opinions would be of small use to her; as she had said herself, she was very determined, and she had made up her mind that they would be of great use instead of small. Her idea must wear itself out by degrees. He would try to make the degrees easy. He decided that he would have a little private talk with Jackson, who was a very honest fellow; and, for the present, he would simply take leave.

"You are very kind," he said, rising. "I appreciate it, I assure you. It has made me stay an unconscionable time. I hope you will find Rome all you expected, and I am sure you will; all people of imagination like Rome. As to the galleries, yes, certainly; a—ah—little later. You must not forget the various small precautions necessary here as regards the fever, you know."

"Rome will not be at all what I expected if *you* desert me," answered Miss Macks, paying no attention to his other phrases.

She had risen, also, and was now confronting him at a distance of less than two feet; as she was tall, her eyes were not much below the level of his own.

"How can a man desert when he has never enlisted?" thought Noel, humorously. But he kept his thought to himself, and merely replied, as he took his hat: "Probably you will desert me; you will find out how useless I am. You must not be too hard upon us, Miss Macks; we Americans lose much of our native energy if we stay long over here."

"Hard?" she answered—"hard? Why, Mr. Noel, I am absolutely at your feet!"

He looked at her, slightly startled, although his face showed nothing of it; was she, after all, going to— But no; her sentence had been as impersonal as those which had preceded it.

"All I said about having contrary opinions, and all that, amounts to nothing," she went on, thereby relieving him from the necessity of making reply. "I desire but one thing, and that is to have you guide me. And I don't believe you are really going to refuse. You haven't an unkind face, although you *have* got such a cold way! Why, think of it: here I have come all this long distance, bringing mother, too, just to study, and to see you. I shall study hard; I have a good deal of perseverance. It took a good deal to get here in the first place, for we are poor. But I don't mind that at all; the only thing I should mind, the only thing that would take my courage away, would be to have you desert me. In all the troubles that I thought might happen, I assure you, I never once thought of *that*, Mr. Noel. I thought, of course, you would be interested. Why, in your books you are all interest. Are you different from your books?"

"I fear, Miss Macks, that writers are seldom good illustrations of their own doctrines," replied Noel.

"That would make them hypocrites. I don't believe you are a hypocrite. I expect you have a habit of running yourself down. Many gentlemen do that, and then they think they will be cried up. I don't believe you are going to be unkind; you *will* look at the pictures I have brought with me, won't you?"

"Mr. Jackson's opinion is worth a hundred of mine, Miss Macks; my knowledge is not technical. But, of course, if you wish it, I shall take pleasure in obeying." He added several conventional remarks as filling-up, and then, leaving his compliments for "your mother"—he could not recall the name she had given—he went towards the little curtained door.

She had brightened over his promise.

"You will come Monday, then, to see them, won't you?—as you cannot come to-morrow," she said, smiling happily.

When she smiled (and she did not smile often), showing her little white, child-like teeth, she looked very young. He was fairly caught, and answered, "Yes." But he immediately qualified it with a "That is, if it is possible."

"Oh, *make* it possible," she answered, still smiling and going with him herself to the outer door instead of summoning the maid. The last he saw of her she was standing in the open doorway, her face bright and contented, watching him as he went down. He did not go to see her pictures on the following Monday; he sent a note of excuse.

Some days later he met her.

"Ah, you are taking one of the delightful walks?" he said. "I envy you your first impressions of Rome."

"I am not taking a walk—that is, for pleasure," she answered. "I am trying to find some vegetables that mother can eat; the vegetables here are so foreign! You don't know how disappointed I was, Mr. Noel, when I got your note. It was such a setback! Why couldn't you come right home with me now —that is, after I have got the vegetables—and see the pictures? It wouldn't take you fifteen minutes."

It was only nine o'clock, and a beautiful morning. He thought her such a novelty, with her urgent invitations, her earnest eyes, and her basket on her arm, that he felt the impulse to walk beside her a while through the old streets of Rome; he was very fond of the old streets, and was curious to see whether she would notice the colors and outlines that made their picturesqueness. She noticed nothing but the vegetable-stalls, and talked of nothing but her pictures.

He still went on with her, however, amused by the questions she put to the vegetable-dealers (questions compiled from the phrase-books), and the calm contempt with which she surveyed the Roman artichokes they offered. At last she secured some beans, but of sadly Italian aspect, and Noel took the basket. He was much entertained by the prospect of carrying it home. He remarked to himself that of all the various things he had done in Rome this was the freshest. They reached the street of the Hyacinth and walked down its dark centre.

"I see you have the sun," he said, looking up.

"Yes; that is the reason we took the top floor. We will go right up. Everything is ready."

He excused himself.

"Some other time."

They had entered the dusky hallway. She looked at him without replying; then held out her hand for the basket. He gave it to her.

"I suppose you have seen Mr. Jackson?" he said, before taking leave.

She nodded, but did not speak. Then he saw two tears rise in her eyes.

"My dear young lady, you have been doing too much! You are tired. Don't you know that that is very dangerous in Rome?"

"It is nothing. Mother has been sick, and I have been up with her two nights. Then, as she did not like our servant, I dismissed her, and as we have not got any one else yet, I have had a good deal to do. But I don't mind that at all, beyond being a little tired; it was only your refusing to come up, when it seemed so easy. But never mind; you will come another day." And, repressing the tears, she smiled faintly, and held out her hand for good-bye.

"I will come now," said Noel. He took the basket again, and went up the stairs. He was touched by the two tears, but, at the same time, vexed with himself for being there at all. There was not one chance in five hundred that her work was worth anything; and, in the four hundred and ninety-nine, pray what was he to say?

She brought him everything. They were all in the four hundred and ninety-nine. In his opinion they were all extremely and essentially bad.

It was one of Raymond Noel's beliefs that, where women were concerned, a certain amount of falsity was sometimes indispensable. There were occasions when a man could no more tell the bare truth to a woman than he could strike her; the effect would be the same as a blow. He was an excellent evader when he chose to exert himself, and he finally got away from the little high-up apartment without disheartening or offending its young mistress, and without any very black record of direct untruth—what is more, without any positive promise as to the exact date of his next visit. But all this was a good deal of trouble to take for a girl he did not know or care for.

Soon afterwards he met, at a small party, Mrs. Lawrence.

"Tell me a little, please, about the young lady to whom you presented me at Mrs. Dudley's reception—Miss Macks," he said, after some conversation.

"A little is all I can tell," replied Mrs. Lawrence. "She brought a letter of introduction to me from a faraway cousin of mine, who lives out West somewhere, and whom I have not seen for twenty years; my home, you know, is in New Jersey. How they learned I was in Rome I cannot imagine; but, knowing it, I suppose they thought that Miss Macks and I would meet, as necessarily as we should if together in their own village. The letter assures me that the girl is a great genius; that all she needs is an opportunity. They even take the ground that it will be a privilege for me to know her! But I am mortally tired of young geniuses; we have so many here in Rome! So I told her at once that I knew nothing of modern art—in fact, detested it —but that in any other way I should be delighted to be of use. And I took her to Mrs. Dudley's *omnium gatherum*."

"Then you have not been to see her?"

"No; she came to see me. I sent cards, of course; I seldom call. What did you think of her?"

"I thought her charming," replied Noel, remembering the night-vigils, the vegetables, the dismissed servant, and the two tears of the young stranger—remembering, also, her extremely bad pictures.

"I am glad she has found a friend in you," replied Mrs. Lawrence. "She was very anxious to meet you; she looks upon you as a great authority. If she really has talent—of course *you* would know—you must tell me. It is not talent I am so tired of, but the pretence of it. She struck me, although wofully unformed and awkward, of course, as rather intelligent."

"She is intelligence personified," replied Noel, qualifying it mentally with "intelligence without cultivation." He perceived that the young stranger would have no help from Mrs. Lawrence, and he added to himself: "And totally inexperienced purity alone in Rome." To be sure, there was the mother; but he had a presentiment that this lady, as guardian, would not be of much avail.

The next day he went down to Naples for a week with some friends. Upon his return he stopped at Horace Jackson's studio one afternoon as he happened to be passing. His time was really much occupied; he was a favorite in Rome. To his surprise, Jackson seemed to think that Miss Macks had talent. Her work was very crude, of course; she had been brutally taught; teachers of that sort should simply be put out of existence with the bowstring. He had turned her back to the alphabet; and, in time, in time, they—would see what she could do.

Horace Jackson was English by birth, but he had lived in Italy almost all his life. He was a man of forty-five—short, muscular, his thick, rather shaggy, beard and hair mixed with gray; there was a permanent frown over his keen eyes, and his rugged face had marked lines. He was a man of strong individuality. He had the reputation of being the most incorruptibly honest teacher in Rome. Noel had known him a long time, and liked him, ill-tempered though he was. Jackson, however, had not shown any especial signs of a liking for Noel in return. Perhaps he thought that, in the nature of things, there could not be much in common between a middle-aged, morose teacher, who worked hard, who knew nothing of society, and did not want to know, and a man like Raymond Noel. True, Noel was also an artist—that is, a literary one. But he had been highly successful in his own field, and it was understood, also, that he had an income of his own by inheritance, which, if not opulence, was yet sufficiently large to lift him quite above the usual *res angusta* of his brethren in the craft. In addition, Jackson considered Noel a fashionable man; and that would have been a barrier, even if there had been no other.

As the Englishman seemed to have some belief in Miss Macks, Noel did not say all he had intended to say; he did, however, mention that the young lady had a mistaken idea regarding any use he could be to her; he should be glad if she could be undeceived.

"I think she will be," said Jackson, with a grim smile, giving his guest a glance of general survey that took him in from head to foot; "she isn't dull."

Noel understood the glance, and smiled at Jackson's idea of him.

"She is not dull, certainly," he answered. "But she is rather—inexperienced." He dismissed the subject, went home, dressed, and went out to dinner.

One morning, a week later, he was strolling through the Doria gallery. He was in a bad humor. There were many people in the gallery that day, but he was not noticing them; he detested a crowd. After a while some one touched his coat-sleeve from behind. He turned, with his calmest expression upon his face; when he was in an ill-humor he was impassively calm. It was Miss Macks, her eyes eager, her face flushed with pleasure.

"Oh, what good luck!" she said. "And to think that I almost went to the Borghese, and might have missed you! I am so delighted that I don't know what to do. I am actually trembling." And she was. "I have so longed to see these pictures with you," she went on. "I have had a real aching disappointment about it, Mr. Noel."

Again Noel felt himself slightly touched by her earnestness. She looked prettier than usual, too, on account of the color.

"I always feel a self-reproach when with you, Miss Macks," he answered—"you so entirely over-estimate me."

"Well, if I do, live up to it," she said, brightly.

"Only an archangel could do that."

"An archangel who knows about Art! I have been looking at the Caraccis; what do you think of them?"

"Never mind the Caraccis; there are better things to look at here." And then he made the circuit of the gallery with her slowly, pointing out the best pictures. During this circuit he talked to her as he would have talked to an intelligent child who had been put in his charge in order to learn something of the paintings; he used the simplest terms, mentioned the marked characteristics, and those only of the different schools, and spoke a few words of unshaded condemnation here and there. All he said was in broad, plain outlines. His companion listened earnestly. She gave him a close attention, almost always a comprehension, but seldom agreement. Her disagreement she did not express in words, but he could read it in her eyes. When they had seen everything—and it took some time—

"Now," he said, "I want you to tell me frankly, and without

reference to anything I have said, your real opinion of several pictures I shall name—that is, if you can remember?"

"I remember everything. I always remember."

"Very well. What do you think, then, of the Raphael double portrait?"

"I think it very ugly."

"And the portrait of Andrea Doria, by Sebastiano del Piombo?"

"Uglier still."

"And the Velasquez?"

"Ugliest of all."

"And the two large Claude Lorraines?"

"Rather pretty; but insipid. There isn't any reality or meaning in them."

"The Memling?"

"Oh, *that* is absolutely hideous, Mr. Noel; it hasn't a redeeming point."

Raymond Noel laughed with real amusement, and almost forgot his ill-humor.

"When you have found anything you really admire in the galleries here, Miss Macks, will you tell me?"

"Of course I will. I should wish to do so in any case, because, if you are to help me, you ought to thoroughly understand me. There is one thing more I should like to ask," she added, as they turned towards the door, "and that is that you would not call me Miss Macks. I am not used to it, and it sounds strangely; no one ever called me that in Tuscolee."

"What did they call you in Tuscolee?"

"They called me Miss Ettie; my name is Ethelinda Faith. But my friends and older people called me just 'Ettie'; I wish you would, too."

"I am certainly older," replied Noel, gravely (he was thirty-three); "but I do not like Ettie. With your permission, I will call you Faith."

"Do you like it? It's so old-fashioned! It was my grandmother's name."

"I like it immensely," he answered, leading the way downstairs.

"You can't think how I've enjoyed it," she said, warmly, at the door.

"Yet you do not agree with my opinions?"

"Not yet. But all the same it was perfectly delightful. Good-bye."

He had signalled for a carriage, as he had, as usual, an engagement. She preferred to walk. He drove off, and did not see her for ten days.

Then he came upon her again and again in the Doria gallery. He was fond of the Doria, and often went there, but he had no expectation of meeting Miss Macks this time; he fancied that she followed a system, going through her list of galleries in regular order, one by one, and in that case she would hardly have reached the Doria on a second round. Her list was a liberal one; it included twenty. Noel had supposed that there were but nine in Rome.

This time she did not see him; she had some sheets of manuscript in her hand, and was alternately reading from them and looking at one of the pictures. She was much absorbed. After a while he went up.

"Good-morning, Miss Macks."

She started; her face changed, and the color rose. She was as delighted as before. She immediately showed him her manuscript. There he beheld, written out in her clear handwriting, all he had said of the Doria pictures, page after page of it; she had actually reproduced from memory his entire discourse of an hour.

There were two blank spaces left.

"There, I could not exactly remember," said Miss Macks, apologetically. "If you would tell me, I should be so glad; then it would be quite complete."

"I shall never speak again. I am frightened," said Noel. He had taken the manuscript, and was looking it over with inward wonder.

"Oh, please do."

"Why do you care for my opinions, Miss Macks, when you do not agree with them?" he asked, his eyes still on the pages.

"You said you would call me Faith. Why do I care? Because they are yours, of course."

"Then you think I know?"

"I am sure you do."

"But it follows, then, that you do not."

"Yes; and there is where my work comes in; I have got to study up to you. I am afraid it will take a long time, won't it?"

"That depends upon you. It would take very little if you would simply accept noncombatively."

"Without being convinced? That I could never do."

"You want to be convinced against your will?"

"No; my will itself must be convinced to its lowest depths."

"This manuscript won't help you."

"Indeed, it has helped me greatly already. I have been here twice with it. I wrote it out the evening after I saw you. I only wish I had one for each of the galleries! But I feel differently now about asking you to go."

"I told you you would desert me."

"No, it is not that. But Mr. Jackson says you are much taken up with the fashionable society here, and that I must not expect you to give me so much of your time as I had hoped for. He says, too, that your art articles will do me quite as much good as you yourself, and more; because you have a way, he says, like all society men, of talking as if you had no real convictions at all, and that would unsettle me."

"Jackson is an excellent fellow," replied Noel; "I like him extremely. And when would you like to go to the Borghese?"

"Oh, will you take me?" she said, joyfully. "Any time. To-morrow."

"Perhaps Mrs.—your mother, will go, also," he suggested, still unable to recall the name; he could think of nothing but "stirrup," and of course it was not that.

"I don't believe she would care about it," answered the daughter.

"She might. You know we make more of mothers here than we do in America," he ventured to remark.

"That is impossible," said Miss Macks, calmly. Evidently she thought his remark frivolous.

He abandoned the subject, and did not take it up again. It was not his duty to instruct Miss Macks in foreign customs. In addition, she was not only not "in society," but she was an art student, and art students had, or took, privileges of their own in Rome.

"At what hour shall I come for you?" he said.

"It will be out of your way to come for me; I will meet you at the gallery," she answered, radiant at the prospect.

He hesitated, then accepted her arrangement of things. He would take her way, not his own. The next morning he went to the Borghese Palace ten minutes before the appointed time. But she was already there.

"Mother thought she would not come out—the galleries tire her so," she said; "but she was pleased to be remembered."

They spent an hour and a half among the pictures. She listened to all he said with the same earnest attention.

Within the next five weeks Raymond Noel met Miss Macks at other galleries. It was always very business-like—they talked of nothing but the pictures; in truth, her systematic industry kept him strictly down to the subject in hand. He learned that she made the same manuscript copies of all he said, and, when he was not with her, she went alone, armed with these documents, and worked hard. Her memory was remarkable; she soon knew the names and the order of all the pictures in all the galleries, and had made herself acquainted with an outline, at least, of the lives of all the artists who had painted them. During this time she was, of course, going on with her lessons; but as he had not been again to see Jackson, or to the street of the Hyacinth, he knew nothing of her progress. He did not want to know; she was in Jackson's hands, and Jackson was quite competent to attend to her.

In these five weeks he gave to Miss Macks only the odd hours of his leisure. He made her no promises; but when he found that he should have a morning or half-morning unoccupied, he sent a note to the street of the Hyacinth, naming a gallery and an hour. She was always promptly there, and so pleased, that there was a sort of fresh aroma floating through the time he spent with her, after all—but a mild one.

To give the proper position to the place the young art student's light figure occupied on the canvas of Raymond Noel's winter, it should be mentioned that he was much interested in a French lady who was spending some months in Rome. He had known her and admired her for a long time; but this winter he was seeing more of her, some barriers which had heretofore stood in the way being down. Madame B—— was a charming product of the effects of finished cultivation and fashionable life upon a natural foundation of grace, wit, and beauty of the French kind. She was not artificial, because she was art itself. Real art is as real as real nature is natural. Raymond Noel had a highly artistic nature. He admired art. This did not prevent him from taking up occasionally, as a contrast to this lady, the society of the young girl he called "Faith." Most men of imagination, artistic or not, do the same thing once in a while; it seems a necessity. With Noel it was not the contrast alone. The French lady led him an uneasy life, and now and then he took an hour of Faith, as a gentle soothing draught of safe quality. She believed in him so perfectly! Now Madame appeared to believe in him not at all.

It must be added that, in his conversations with Miss Macks, he had dropped entirely even the very small amount of conventional gallantry that he had bestowed upon her in the beginning. He talked to her not as though she was a boy exactly, or an old woman, but as though he himself was a relative of mature age—say an uncle of benevolent disposition and a taste for art.

February gave way to March. And now, owing to a new position of his own affairs, Noel saw no more of Faith Macks. She had been a contrast, and he did not now wish for a contrast or a soothing draught, and a soothing draught was not at present required. He simply forgot all about her.

In April he decided rather suddenly to leave Rome. This was because Madame B—— had gone to Paris, and had not forbidden her American suitor to follow her a few days later. He made his preparations for departure, and these, of course, included farewell calls. Then he remembered Faith Macks; he had not seen her for six weeks. He drove to the street of the Hyacinth, and went up the dark stairs. Miss Macks was at home, and came in without delay; apparently, in her trim neatness, she was always ready for visitors.

She was very glad to see him; but did not, as he expected, ask why he had not come before. This he thought a great advance; evidently she was learning. When she heard that he had come to say good-bye her face fell.

"I am so very sorry; please sit as long as you can, then," she said, simply. "I suppose it will be six months before I see you again; you will hardly return to Rome before October." That he would come at that time she did not question.

"My plans are uncertain," replied Noel. "But probably I shall come back. One always comes back to Rome. And you —where do you go? To Switzerland?"

"Why—we go nowhere, of course; we stay here. That is what we came for, and we are all settled."

He made some allusion to the heat and unhealthiness.

"I am not afraid," replied Miss Macks. "Plenty of people stay; Mr. Jackson says so. It is only the rich who go away, and we are not rich. We have been through hot summers in Tuscolee, I can tell you!" Then, without asking leave this time, as if she was determined to have an opinion from him before he departed, she took from a portfolio some of the work she had done under Mr. Jackson's instruction.

Noel saw at once that the Englishman had not kept his word. He had not put her back upon the alphabet, or, if he had done so, he had soon released her, and allowed her to pursue her own way again. The original faults were as marked as ever. In his opinion all was essentially bad.

He looked in silence. But she talked on hopefully, explaining, comparing, pointing out.

"What does Mr. Jackson think of this?" he said, selecting the one he thought the worst.

"He admires the idea greatly; he thinks it very original. He says that my strongest point is originality," she answered, with her confident frankness.

"He means—ah—originality of subject?"

"Oh yes; my execution is not much yet. But that will come in time. Of course, the subject, the idea, is the important thing; the execution is secondary." Here she paused; something seemed to come into her mind. "I know *you* do not think so," she added, thoughtfully, "because, you know, you said"—and here she quoted a page from one of his art articles with her clear accuracy. "I have never understood what you meant by that, Mr. Noel; or why you wrote it."

She looked at him questioningly. He did not reply; his eyes were upon one of the sketches.

"It would be dreadful for me if you were right!" she added, with slow conviction.

"I thought you believed that I was always right," he said, smiling, as he placed the sketches on the table.

But she remained very serious.

"You are—in everything but that."

He made some unimportant reply, and turned the conversation. But she came back to it.

"It would be dreadful," she repeated, earnestly, with the utmost gravity in her gray eyes.

"I hope the long summer will not tire you," he answered, irrelevantly. "Shall I not have the pleasure of saying good-bye —although that, of course, is not a pleasure—to Mrs.—to your mother?"

He should have made the speech in any case, as it was the proper one to make; but as he sat there he had thought that he really would like to have a look at the one guardian this young girl was to have during her long, lonely summer in Rome.

"I will tell her. Perhaps when she hears that you are going away she will feel like coming in," said Miss Macks.

She came back after some delay, and with her appeared a matron of noticeable aspect.

"My mother," she said, introducing her (evidently Noel was never to get the name); "this is Mr. Noel, mother."

"And very glad I am to see you, sir, I'm sure," said Mrs. Spurr, extending her hand with much cordiality. "I said to Ettie that I'd come in, seeing as 'twas you, though I don't often see strangers nowadays on account of poor health for a long time past; rheumatism and asthma. But I feel beholden to you, Mr. No-ul, because you've been so good to Ettie. You've been real kind."

Ettie's mother was a very portly matron of fifty-five, with a broad face, indistinct features, very high color, and a breathless, panting voice. Her high color—it really was her most noticeable feature—was surmounted by an imposing cap, adorned with large bows of scarlet ribbon; a worsted shawl, of the hue known as "solferino," decked her shoulders; under her low-necked collar reposed a bright blue necktie, its ends embroidered in red and yellow; and her gown was of a vivid dark green. But although her colors swore at each other, she seemed amiable. She was also voluble.

Noel, while shaking hands, was considering, mentally, with

some retrospective amusement, his condition of mind if this lady had accepted his invitations to visit the galleries.

"You must sit down, mother," said Miss Macks, bringing forward an easy-chair. "She has not been so well as usual, lately," she said, explanatorily, to Noel, as she stood for a moment beside her mother's chair.

"It's this queer Eye-talian air," said Mrs. Spurr. "You see I ain't used to it. Not but what I ain't glad to be here on Ettie's account—real glad. It's just what she needs and oughter have."

The girl put her hand on her mother's shoulder with a little caressing touch. Then she left the room.

"Yes, I do feel beholden to you, Mr. No-ul. But, then, she'll be a credit to you, to whatever you've done for her," said Mrs. Spurr, when they were left alone. "Her talunts are very remarkable. She was the head scholar of the Young Ladies' Seminary through four whole years, and all the teachers took a lot of pride in her. And then her paintings, too! I'm sorry you're going off so soon. You see, she sorter depends upon your opinion."

Noel felt a little stir at the edges of his conscience; he knew perfectly that his opinion was that Miss Macks, as an artist, would never do anything worth the materials she used.

"I leave her in good hands," he said.

After all, it was Jackson's responsibility, not his.

"Yes, Mr. Jackson thinks a deal of her. I can see that plain!" answered Mrs. Spurr, proudly.

Here the daughter returned, bringing a little notebook and pencil.

"Do you know what these are for?" she said. "I want you to write down a list of the best books for me to read this summer, while you are gone. I am going to work hard; but if I have books, too, the time won't seem so long."

Noel considered a moment. In one way her affairs were certainly none of his business; in another way they were, because she had thrust them upon him.

"I will not give you a list, Miss Macks; probably you would not be able to find the books here. But I will send you, from Paris or London, some things that are rather good, if you will permit me to do so."

She said he was very kind. Her face brightened.

"If she has appreciation enough to comprehend what I send her," he thought, "perhaps in the end she will have a different opinion about my 'kindness'!"

Soon afterwards he took leave. The next day he went to Paris.

II

The events of Raymond Noel's life, after he left Rome that spring, were various. Some were pleasant, some unpleasant; several were quite unexpected. Their combinations and results kept him from returning to Italy the following winter, and the winter after that he spent in Egypt. When he again beheld the dome of St. Peter's he remembered that it lacked but a month of two full years since he had said good-bye to it; it was then April, and now it was March. He established himself in some pleasant rooms, looked about him, and then began to take up, one by one, the old threads of his Roman life—such, at least, as remained unbroken. He found a good many. Threads do not break in Rome. He had once said himself that the air was so soft and historic that nothing broke there—not even hearts. But this was only one of his little speeches. In reality he did not believe much in the breaking of hearts; he had seen them stretch so!

It may be said with truth that Noel had not thought of Miss Macks for months. This was because he had had other things to think of. He had sent her the books from Paris, with an accompanying note, a charming little note—which gave no address for reply. Since then his mind had been otherwise occupied. But as he never entirely forgot anything that had once interested him, even although but slightly (this was in reality a system of his; it gave him many holds on life, and kept stored up a large supply of resources ready for use when wanted), he came, after a while, on the canvas of his Roman impressions, to the figure of Miss Macks. When he came to it he went to see her; that is, he went to the street of the Hyacinth.

Of course, she might not be there; a hundred things might have happened to her. He could have hunted up Horace Jackson; but, on the whole, he rather preferred to see the girl herself first—that is, if she was there. Mrs. Lawrence, the only person among his acquaintances who had known her, was not in Rome. Reaching the street of the Hyacinth, he interrogated the old woman who acted as portress at the lower door, keeping up at the same time a small commerce in fritters; yes, the Americans were still on the fourth floor. He ascended the dark stairway. The confiding little "Ettie" card was no longer upon the door. In its place was a small framed sign: "Miss Macks' School."

This told a story!

However, he rang. It was the same shrill, ill-tempered little bell, and when the door opened it was Miss Macks herself who opened it. She was much changed.

The parlor had been turned into a school-room—at present empty of pupils. But even as a school-room it was more attractive than it had been before. He took a seat, and spoke the usual phrases of a renewal of acquaintance with his accustomed ease and courtesy; Miss Macks responded briefly. She said that her mother was not very well; she herself quite well. No, they had not left Italy, nor indeed the neighborhood of Rome; they had been a while at Albano.

The expression of her face had greatly altered. The old direct, wide glance was gone; gone also what he had called her over-confidence; she looked much older. On the other hand, there was more grace in her bearing, more comprehension of life in her voice and eyes. She was dressed as plainly as before; but everything, including the arrangement of her hair, was in the prevalent style.

She did not speak of her school, and therefore he did not. But after a while he asked how the painting came on. Her face changed a little; but it was more in the direction of a greater calm than hesitation or emotion.

"I am not painting now," she answered.

"You have given it up temporarily?"

"Permanently."

"Ah—isn't that rather a pity?"

She looked at him, and a gleam of scorn filtered into the glance.

"You know it is not a pity," she said.

He was a little disgusted at the scorn. Of course, the only ground for him to take was the ground upon which she stood

when he last saw her; at that time she proposed to pass her life
in painting, and it was but good manners for him to accept her
intentions as she had presented them.

"I never assumed to be a judge, you know," he answered.
"When I last had the pleasure of seeing you, painting was, you
remember, your cherished occupation!"

"When you last had the pleasure of seeing me, Mr. Noel,"
said Miss Macks, still with unmoved calm, "I was a fool."

Did she wish to go into the subject at length? Or was that
merely an exclamation?

"When I last had the pleasure of seeing you, you were taking
lessons of Mr. Jackson," he said, to give a practical turn to the
conversation. "Is he still here? How is he?"

"He is very well, now. He is dead."

(She was going to be dramatic then, in any case.)

He expressed his regret, and it was a sincere one; he had always liked and respected the honest, morose Englishman. He
asked a question or two. Miss Macks replied that he had died
here in the street of the Hyacinth—in the next room. He had
fallen ill during the autumn following Noel's departure, and
when his illness grew serious, they—her mother and herself
—had persuaded him to come to them. He had lived a month
longer, and died peacefully on Christmas Eve.

"He was one of the most honest men I ever knew," said
Noel. Then, as she did not reply, he ventured this: "That was
the reason I recommended him when you asked me to select a
teacher for you."

"Your plan was made useless by an unfortunate circumstance," she answered, with an evident effort.

"A circumstance?"

"Yes; he fell in love with me. If I did not consider his pure,
deep, and devoted affection the greatest honor of my life I
would not mention it. I tell you because it will explain to you
his course."

"Yes, it explains," said Noel. As he spoke there came across
him a realization of the whole of the strength of the love such
a man as Horace Jackson would feel, and the way in which it
would influence him. Of course, he saw to the full the imper-
fection of her work, the utter lack of the artist's conception,

the artist's eye and touch; but probably he had loved her from the beginning, and had gone on hoping to win her love in return. She was not removed from him by any distance; she was young, but she was also poor, friendless, and alone. When she was his wife he would tell her the truth, and in the greatness of his love the revelation would be naught. "He was a good man," he said. "He was always lonely. I am glad that at last he was with your mother and you."

"His goodness was simply unbounded. If he had lived he would have remained always a faithful, kind, and respectful son to my dear mother. That, of course, would have been everything to me." She said this quietly, yet her tone seemed to hold intention.

For a moment he thought that perhaps she had married the Englishman, and was now his widow. The sign on the door bore her maiden name, but that might have been an earlier venture.

"Had you opened your school at that time?" he asked. "I may speak of it, since, of course, I saw the sign upon the door."

"Not until two months later; I had the sign made then. But it was of little use; day-schools do not prosper in Rome; they are not the custom. I have a small class twice a week, but I live by going out as day-governess. I have a number of pupils of that kind; I have been very successful. The old Roman families have a fancy for English-speaking governesses, you know. Last summer I was with the Princess C——, at Albano; her children are my pupils."

"Her villa is a delightful one," said Noel; "you must have enjoyed that."

"I don't know that I enjoyed, but I learned. I have learned a great deal in many ways since I saw you last, Mr. Noel. I have grown very old."

"As you were especially young when you saw me last it does not matter much," he answered, smiling.

"Yes, I was especially young." She looked at him soberly. "I do not feel bitterly towards you," she continued. "Strange! I thought I should. But now that I see you in person it comes over me that, probably, you did not intend to deceive me; that not only you tried to set me right by selecting Mr. Jackson as my teacher, but again you tried when you sent me those books. It was not much to do! But knowing the world as I now know it, I see that it was all that could have been expected. At first, however, I did not see this. After I went to Mr. Bellot, and, later, to Mr. Salviati, there were months when I felt very bitterly towards you. My hopes were false ones, and had been so from the beginning; you knew that they were, yet you did not set me right."

"I might have done more than I did," answered Noel. "I have a habit of not assuming responsibility; I suppose I have grown selfish. But if you went to Bellot, then it was not Jackson who told you?"

"He intimated something when he asked me to marry him; after that his illness came on, and we did not speak of it again. But I did not believe him. I was very obstinate. I went to Mr. Bellot the 1st of January; I wished him to take me as pupil. In answer he told me that I had not a particle of talent; that all my work was insufferably bad; that I better throw away my brushes and take in sewing."

"Bellot is always a brute!" said Noel.

"If he told the truth brutally, it was still the truth; and it was the truth I needed. But even then I was not convinced, and I went to Mr. Salviati. He was more gentle; he explained to me my lacks; but his judgment was the same. I came home; it was the 10th of January, a beautiful Roman winter day. I left my pictures, went over to St. Peter's, and walked there under its bright mosaics all the afternoon. The next day I had advertisements of a day-school placed at the bankers' and in the newspapers. I thought that I could teach better than I could sew." All this she said with perfect calm.

"I greatly admire your bravery, Miss Macks. Permit me to add that I admire, even more, the clear, strong, good sense which has carried you through."

"I had my mother to think of; my—good sense might not have been so faithful otherwise."

"You do not think of returning to America?"

"Probably not; I doubt if my mother could bear the voyage now. We have no one to call us back but my brother, and he has not been with us for years, and would not be if we should return; he lives in California. We sold the farm, too, before we came. No; for the present, at least, it is better for us to remain here."

"There is one more question I should like to ask," said Noel, later. "But I have no possible right to do so."

"I will give you the right. When I remember the things I asked you to do for me, the demands I made upon your time, I can well answer a few questions in return. I was a miracle of ignorance."

"I always did you justice in those respects, Miss Macks; all that I understood at once. My question refers to Horace Jackson: I see you appreciated his worth—which was rare—yet you would not marry him."

"I did not love him."

"Did any of his relatives come out from England?" he said, after a moment of silence.

"After his death a cousin came."

"As heir to what was left?"

"Yes."

"He should have left it to you."

"He wished to do so. Of course, I would not accept it."

"I thank you for answering. My curiosity was not an idle one." He paused. "If you will permit me to express it, your course has been very brave and true. I greatly admire it."

"You are kind," said Miss Macks.

There was not in her voice any indication of sarcasm. Yet the fact that he immediately thought of it made him suspect that it was there. He took leave soon afterwards. He was smarting a little under the sarcasm he had divined, and, as he was, it was like him to request permission to come again.

For Raymond Noel lived up with a good deal of determination to his own standard of what was manly; if his standard was not set on any very fine elevation of self-sacrifice or heroism, it was at least firmly established where it did stand, and he kept himself fairly near it. If Miss Macks was sarcastic, he had been at fault somewhere; he would try to atone.

He saw her four times during the five weeks of his stay in Rome; upon three other occasions when he went to the street of the Hyacinth she was not at home. The third week in April he decided to go to Venice. Before going he asked if there was not something he could do for her; but she said there was nothing, and he himself could think of nothing. She was well established in her new life and occupations, and needed nothing—at least, nothing that he could bestow.

The next winter he came back to Rome early in the season, before Christmas. By chance one of the first persons he encountered was Mrs. Lawrence. She began immediately to tell him a piece of American news, in which he, as an American, would of course be interested; the news was that "the brother of the Princess C—— —that is Count L——, you know—is determined to marry Ettie Macks. You remember her, don't you? I introduced you to her at the Dudley reception, three years ago."

Noel thought that probably he remembered her better than Mrs. Lawrence did, seeing that that lady had never troubled herself to enter the street of the Hyacinth. But he did her injustice. Mrs. Lawrence had troubled herself—lately.

"It seems that she has been out at Albano for two summers, as governess to his sister's children; it was there that he saw her. He has announced his determination to the family, and they are immensely disturbed and frightened; they had it all arranged for him to marry a second cousin down at Naples, who is rich—these Italians are so worldly, you know! But he is very determined, they say, and will do as he pleases in spite of them. He hasn't much money, but of course it's a great match for Ettie Macks. She will be a countess, and now, I suppose, more American girls will come over than ever before! Of course, as soon as I heard of it, I went to see her. I felt that she would need advice about a hundred things. In the beginning she brought a letter of introduction to me from a dear cousin of mine, and, naturally, she would rely upon me as her chief friend now. She is very much improved. She was rather silent; but, of course, I shall go again. The count is willing to take the mother, too, and that, under the circumstances, is not a small matter; she is a good deal to take. Until the other day I had not seen Mrs. Spurr! However, I suppose that her deficiencies are not apparent in a language she cannot speak. If her daughter would only insist upon her dressing in black! But the old lady told me herself, in the most cheerful way, that she liked 'a sprinkling of color.' And at the moment, I assure you, she had on five different shades of red!"

Noel had intended to present himself immediately at the street of the Hyacinth; but a little attack of illness kept him in for a while, and ten days had passed before he went up the dark stairway. The maid said that Miss Macks was at home; presently she came in. They had ten minutes of conversation upon ordinary topics, and then he took up the especial one.

"I am told that you are soon to be a countess," he said, "and I have come to give you my best good wishes. My congratulations I reserve for Count L——, with whom I have a slight acquaintance; he is, in my opinion, a very fortunate man."

"Yes, I think he is fortunate; fortunate in my refusal. I shall not marry Count L——."

"He is not a bad fellow."

"Isn't your praise somewhat faint?" This time the sarcasm was visible.

"Oh, I am by no means his advocate! All I meant was that, as these modern Romans go, he was not among the worst. Of course I should have expressed myself very differently if you had said you were to marry him."

"Yes; you would then have honored me with your finest compliments."

He did not deny this.

"Shall you continue to live in Rome?" he asked.

"Certainly. I shall have more pupils and patronage now than I know what to do with; the whole family connection is deeply obliged to me."

They talked awhile longer.

"We have always been unusually frank with each other, Miss Macks," he said, towards the end of his visit. "We have never stopped at conventionalities. I wonder if you will tell me why you refused him?"

"You are too curious. As to frankness, I have been frank with you; not you with me. And there was no conventionality, simply because I did not know what it was."

"I believe you are in love with some one in America," he said, laughing.

"Perhaps I am," answered Miss Macks. She had certainly gained greatly in self-possession during the past year.

He saw her quite frequently after this. Her life was no longer solitary. As she had said, she was overwhelmed with pupils and patronage from the friends of the Princess C——; in addition, the American girl who had refused a fairly-indorsed and well-appearing count was now something of a celebrity among the American visitors in Rome. That they knew of her refusal was not her fault; the relatives of Count L—— had announced their objections as loud and widely as the count had announced his determination. Apparently neither side had thought of a non-acceptance. Cards, not a few, were sent to the street of the Hyacinth; some persons even climbed the five flights of stairs. Mrs. Spurr saw a good deal of company—and enjoyed it.

Noel was very fond of riding; when in Rome he always rode on the Campagna. He had acted as escort to various ladies, and one day he invited Miss Macks to accompany him—that is, if she were fond of riding. She had ridden in America, and enjoyed it; she would like to go once, if he would not be troubled by an improvised habit. They went once. Then a second time, an interval of three weeks between. Then, after a while, a third time.

Upon this occasion an accident happened, the first of Noel's life; his horse became frightened, and, skilled rider though he was, he was thrown. He was dragged, too, for a short distance. His head came against some stones, and he lost consciousness. When it came back it did not come wholly. He seemed to himself to be far away, and the girl who was weeping and calling his name to be upon the other side of a wide space like an ocean, over which, without volition of his own, he was being slowly wafted. As he came nearer, still slowly, he perceived that in some mysterious way she was holding in her arms something that seemed to be himself, although he had not yet reached her. Then, gradually, spirit and body were reunited, he heard what she was saying, and felt her touch. Even then it was only after several minutes that he was able to move and unclose his heavy eyes.

When she saw that he was not dead, her wild grief was at once merged in the thought of saving him. She had jumped from her horse, she knew not how; but he had not strayed far; a shepherd had seen him, and was now coming towards them. He signalled to another, and the two carried Noel to a house which was not far distant. A messenger was sent to the city; aid came, and before night Noel was in his own rooms at the head of the Via Sistina, near the Spanish steps.

His injuries proved to be not serious; he had lost consciousness from the shock, and this, with his pallor and the blood from the cuts made by the stones, had given him the look of death. The cuts, however, were not deep; the effect of the shock passed away. He kept his bed for a week under his physician's advice; he had a good deal of time to think during that week. Later his friends were admitted. As has been said before, Noel was a favorite in Rome, and he had friends not a few. Those who could not come in person sent little notes and baskets of flowers. Among these Miss Macks was not numbered. But then she was not fashionable.

At the end of two weeks the patient was allowed to go out. He took a short walk to try his strength, and, finding that it held out well, he went to the street of the Hyacinth.

Miss Macks was at home. She was "so glad" to see him out again; and was he "really strong enough;" and he "should be very prudent for a while;" and so forth and so forth. She talked more than usual, and, for her, quite rapidly.

He let her go on for a time. Then he took the conversation into his own hands. With few preliminaries, and with much feeling in his voice and eyes, he asked her to be his wife.

She was overwhelmed with astonishment; she turned very white, and did not answer. He thought she was going to burst into tears. But she did not; she only sat gazing at him, while her lips trembled. He urged his point; he spoke strongly.

"You are worth a hundred of me," he said. "You are true and sincere; I am a dilettante in everything. But, dilettante as I am, in one way I have always appreciated you, and, lately, all other ways have become merged in that one. I am much in earnest; I know what I am doing; I have thought of it searchingly and seriously, and I beg you to say yes."

He paused. Still she did not speak.

"Of course I do not ask you to separate yourself from your mother," he went on, his eyes dropping for the moment to the brim of his hat, which he held in his hand; "I shall be glad if she will always make her home with us."

Then she did speak. And as her words came forth, the red rose in her face until it was deeply colored.

"With what an effort you said that! But you will not be tried. One gray hair in my mother's head is worth more to me, Mr. Noel, than anything you can offer."

"I knew before I began that this would be the point of trouble between us, Faith," he answered. "I can only assure you that she will find in me always a most respectful son."

"And when you were thinking so searchingly and seriously, it was *this* that you thought of—whether you could endure her! Do you suppose that I do not see the effort? Do you suppose I would ever place my mother in such a position? Do you suppose that you are of any consequence beside her, or that anything in this world weighs in my mind for one moment compared with her happiness?"

"We can make her happy; I suppose that. And I suppose another thing, and that is that we could be very happy ourselves if we were married."

"The Western girl, the girl from Tuscolee! The girl who thought she could paint, and could not! The girl who knew so little of social rules that she made a fool of herself every time she saw you!"

"All this is of no consequence, since it is the girl I love," answered Noel.

"You do not. It is a lie. Oh, of course, a very unselfish and noble one; but a lie, all the same. You have thought of it seriously and searchingly? Yes, but only for the last fourteen days! I understand it all now. At first I did not, I was confused; but now I see the whole. You were not unconscious out there on the Campagna; you heard what I said when I thought you were dying, or dead. And so you come—come very generously and self-sacrificingly, I acknowledge that—and ask me to be your wife." She rose; her eyes were brilliant as she faced him. "I might tell you that it was only the excitement, that I did not know or mean what I was saying; I might tell you that I did not know that I had said anything. But I am not afraid. I will not, like you, tell a lie, even for a good purpose. I did love you; there, you have it! I have loved you for a long time, to my sorrow and shame. For I do not respect you or admire you; you have been completely spoiled, and will always remain so. I shall make it the one purpose of my life from this moment to overcome the feeling I have had for you; and I shall succeed. Nothing could make me marry you, though you should ask me a thousand times."

"I shall ask but once," said Noel. He had risen also; and, as he did, he remembered the time when they had stood in the same place and position, facing each other, and she had told him that she was at his feet. "I did hear what you said. And it is of that I have been seriously thinking during the days of my confinement to the house. It is also true that it is what you said which has brought me here to-day. But the reason is that it has become precious to me—this knowledge that you love me. As I said before, in one way I have always done you justice, and it is that way which makes me realize to the full now what such a love as yours would be to me. If it is true that I am spoiled, as you say I am, a love like yours would make me better, if anything can." He paused. "I have not said much about my own feelings," he added; "I know you will not credit me with having any. But I think I have. I think that I love you."

"It is of little moment to me whether you do or not."

"You are making a mistake," he said, after a pause, during which their eyes had met in silence.

"The mistake would be to consent."

She had now recovered her self-possession. She even smiled a little.

"Imagine Mr. Raymond Noel in the street of the Hyacinth!" she said.

"Ah, I should hardly wish to live here; and my wife would naturally be with me."

"I hope so. And I hope she will be very charming and obedient and sweet." Then she dropped her sarcasms, and held out her hand in farewell. "There is no use in prolonging this, Mr. Noel. Do not think, however, that I do not appreciate your action; I do appreciate it. I said that I did not respect you, and I have not until now; but now I do. You will understand, of course, that I would rather not see you again, and refrain from seeking me. Go your way, and forget me; you can do so now with a clear conscience, for you have behaved well."

"It is not very likely that I shall forget you," answered Noel, "although I go my way. I see you are firmly resolved. For the present, therefore, all I can do is to go."

They shook hands, and he left her. As he passed through the small hall on his way to the outer door he met Mrs. Spurr; she was attired as opulently, in respect to colors, as ever, and she returned his greeting with much cordiality. He glanced back;

Miss Macks had witnessed the meeting through the parlor door. Her color had faded; she looked sad and pale.

She kept her word; she did not see him again. If he went to the street of the Hyacinth, as he did two or three times, the little maid presented him with the Italian equivalent of "begs to be excused," which was evidently a standing order. If he wrote to her, as he did more than two or three times, she returned what he wrote, not unread, but without answer. He thought perhaps he should meet her, and was at some pains to find out her various engagements. But all was in vain; the days passed, and she remained invisible. Towards the last of May he left Rome. After leaving, he continued to write to her, but he gave no address for reply; she would now be obliged either to burn his letters or keep them, since she could no longer send them back. They could not have been called love-letters; they were friendly epistles, not long—pleasant, easy, sometimes amusing, like his own conversation. They came once a week. In addition he sent new books, and occasionally some other small remembrance.

In early September of that year there came to the street of the Hyacinth a letter from America. It was from one of Mrs. Spurr's old neighbors at Tuscolee, and she wrote to say that John Macks had come home—had come home broken in health and spirits, and, as he himself said, to die. He did not wish his mother to know; she could not come to him, and it would only distress her. He had money enough for the short time that was left him, and when she heard it would be only that he had passed away; he had passed from her life in reality years before. In this John Macks was sincere. He had been a ne'er-do-well, a rolling stone; he had not been a dutiful son. The only good that could be said of him, as far as his mother was concerned, was contained in the fact that he had not made demands upon her small purse since the sum he took from her when he first went away. He had written to her at intervals, briefly. His last letter had come eight months before.

But the Tuscolee neighbor was a mother herself, and, doing as she would be done by, she wrote to Rome. When her letter came Mrs. Spurr was overwhelmed with grief; but she was also stirred to an energy and determination which she had never shown before. For the first time in years she took the leadership, put her daughter decisively back into a subordinate place, and assumed the control. She would go to America. She must see her boy (the dearest child of the two, as the prodigal always is) again. But even while she was planning her journey illness seized her—her old rheumatic troubles, only more serious than before; it was plain that she could not go. She then required that her daughter should go in her place—go and bring her boy to Rome; this soft Italian air would give new life to his lungs. Oh, she should not die! Ettie need not be afraid of that. She would live for years just to get one look at him! And so it ended in the daughter's departure, an efficient nurse being left in charge; the physician said that although Mrs. Spurr would probably be crippled, she was in no danger otherwise.

Miss Macks left Rome on the 15th of September. On the 2d of December she again beheld the dome of St. Peter's rising in the blue sky. She saw it alone. John Macks had lived three weeks after her arrival at Tuscolee, and those three weeks were the calmest and the happiest of his unsuccessful—unworthy it may be—but also bitterly unhappy life. His sister did not judge him. She kissed him good-bye as he lost consciousness, and soon afterwards closed his eyes tenderly, with tears in her own. Although he was her brother, she had never known him; he went away when she was a child. She sat beside him a long time after he was dead, watching the strange, youthful peace come back to his worn face.

When she reached the street of the Hyacinth a carriage was before the door; carriages of that sort were not often required by the dwellers on the floors below their own, and she was rather surprised. She had heard from her mother in London, the nurse acting as amanuensis; at that time Mrs. Spurr was comfortable, although still confined to her bed most of the day. As she was paying her driver she heard steps on the stairway within. Then she beheld this: The nurse, carrying a pillow and shawls; next, her mother, in an invalid-chair, borne by two men; and last, Raymond Noel.

When Mrs. Spurr saw her daughter she began to cry. She had not expected her until the next day. Her emotion was so great that the drive was given up, and she was carried back to her room. Noel did not follow her; he shook hands with the new-comer, said that he would not detain her, and then, lifting his hat, he stepped into the carriage which was waiting and was driven away.

For two days Mrs. Spurr wished for nothing but to hear, over and over again, every detail of her boy's last hours. Then the excitement and renewed grief made her dangerously ill. After ten days she began to improve; but two weeks passed before she came back to the present sufficiently to describe to her daughter all "Mr. No-ul's kind attentions." He had returned to Rome the first of October, and had come at once to the street of the Hyacinth. Learning what had happened, he had devoted himself to her "most as if he was my real son, Ettie, I do declare! Of course, he couldn't never be like my own darling boy," continued the poor mother, overlooking entirely, with a mother's sublime forgetfulness, the small amount of devotion her boy had ever bestowed; "but he's just done everything he could, and there's no denying that."

"He has not been mentioned in your letters, mother."

"Well, child, I just told Mrs. Bowler not to. For he said himself, frankly, that you might not like it; but that he'd make his peace with you when you come back. I let him have his way about it, and I *have* enjoyed seeing him. He's the only person I've seen but Mrs. Bowler and the doctor, and I'm mortal tired of both."

During Mrs. Spurr's second illness Noel had not come in person to the street of the Hyacinth; he had sent to inquire, and fruits and flowers came in his name. Miss Macks learned that these had come from the beginning.

When three weeks had passed Mrs. Spurr was back in her former place as regarded health. One of her first requests was to be taken out to drive; during her daughter's absence Mr. Noel had taken her five times, and she had greatly enjoyed the change. It was not so simple a matter for the daughter as it had been for Mr. Noel; her purse was almost empty; the long journeys and her mother's illness had exhausted her store. Still she did it. Mrs. Spurr wished to go to the Pincio. Her daughter thought the crowd there would be an objection.

"It didn't tire me one bit when Mr. No-ul took me," said Mrs. Spurr, in an aggrieved tone; "and we went there every single time—just as soon as he found out that I liked it. What a lot of folks he does know, to be sure! They kept him a-bowing every minute."

The day after this drive Mr. Noel came to the street of the Hyacinth. He saw Miss Macks. Her manner was quiet, a little distant; but she thanked him, with careful acknowledgment of every item, for his kind attentions to her mother. He said little. After learning that Mrs. Spurr was much better he spoke of her own health.

"You have had two long, fatiguing journeys, and you have been acting as nurse; it would be well for you to give yourself entire rest for several weeks at least."

She replied, coldly, that she was perfectly well, and turned the conversation to subjects less personal. He did not stay long. As he rose to take leave, he said:

"You will let me come again, I hope? You will not repeat the 'not at home' of last spring?"

"I would really much rather not see you, Mr. Noel," she answered, after hesitating.

"I am sorry. But of course I must submit." Then he went away.

Miss Macks now resumed her burdens. She was obliged to take more pupils than she had ever accepted before, and to work harder. She had not only to support their little household, but there were now debts to pay. She was out almost the whole of every day.

After she had entered upon her winter's work Raymond Noel began to come again to the street of the Hyacinth. But he did not come to see her; his visits were to her mother. He came two or three times a week, and always during the hours when the daughter was absent. He sat and talked to Mrs. Spurr, or rather listened to her, in a way that greatly cheered that lady's monotonous days. She told him her whole history; she minutely described Tuscolee and its society; and, finally, he heard the whole story of "John." In addition, he sent her various little delicacies, taking pains to find something she had not had.

Miss Macks would have put an end to this if she had known how. But certainly Mr. Noel was not troubling *her*, and Mrs. Spurr resented any attempt at interference.

"I don't see why you should object, Ettie. He seems to like

to come, and there's but few pleasures left to me, I'm sure! You oughtn't to grudge them!"

In this way two months passed, Noel continuing his visits, and Miss Macks continuing her lessons. She was working very hard. She now looked not only pale, but much worn. Count L——, who had been long absent, returned to Rome about this time. He saw her one day, although she did not see him. The result of this vision of her was that he went down to Naples, and, before long, the desirable second cousin with the fortune was the sister of the Princess C——.

One afternoon in March Miss Macks was coming home from the broad, new, tiresome piazza Indipendenza; the distance was long, and she walked with weariness. As she drew near the dome of the Pantheon she met Raymond Noel. He stopped, turned, and accompanied her homeward. She had three books.

"Give them to me," he said, briefly, taking them from her.

"Do you know what I have heard to-day?" he went on. "They are going to tear down your street of the Hyacinth. The Government has at last awakened to the shame of allowing all those modern accretions to disfigure longer the magnificent old Pagan temple. All the streets in the rear, up to a certain point, are to be destroyed. And the street of the Hyacinth goes first. You will be driven out."

"I presume we can find another like it."

He went on talking about the Pantheon until they entered the doomed street; it was as obstinately narrow and dark as ever. Then he dropped his Pagan temple.

"How much longer are you going to treat me in this way, Faith?" he said. "You make me very unhappy. You are wearing yourself out, and it troubles me greatly. If you should fall ill I think that would be the end. I should then take matters into my own hands, and I don't believe you would be able to keep me off. But why should we wait for illness? It is too great a risk."

They were approaching her door. She said nothing, only hastened her steps.

"I have been doing my best to convince you, without annoying you, that you were mistaken about me. And the reason I have been doing it is that I am convinced myself. If I was not entirely sure last spring that I loved you, I certainly am sure now. I spent the summer thinking of it. I know now, beyond the possibility of a doubt, that I love you above all and everything. There is no 'duty' or 'generosity' in this, but simply my own feelings. I could perfectly well have let the matter drop; you gave me every opportunity to do so. That I have not done it should show you—a good deal. For I am not of the stuff of which heroes are made. I should not be here unless I wanted to; my motive is the selfish one of my own happiness."

They had entered the dark hallway.

"Do you remember the morning when you stood here, with two tears in your eyes, saying 'Never mind; you will come another time'?" (Here the cobbler came down the stairs.) "Why not let the demolition of the street of the Hyacinth be the crisis of our fate?" he went on, returning the cobbler's bow. (Here the cobbler departed.) "If you refuse, I shall not give you up; I shall go on in the same way. But—haven't I been tried long enough?"

"You have not," she answered. "But, unless you will leave Rome, and—me, I cannot bear it longer."

It was a great downfall, of course; Noel always maintained that it was.

"But the heights upon which you had placed yourself, my dear, were too superhuman," he said, excusingly.

The street of the Hyacinth experienced a great downfall, also. During the summer it was demolished.

Before its demolition Mrs. Lawrence, after three long breaths of astonishment, had come to offer her congratulations—in a new direction this time.

"It is the most fortunate thing in the world," she said to everybody, "that Mrs. Spurr is now confined to her bed for life, and is obliged to wear mourning."

But Mrs. Spurr is not confined to her bed; she drives out with her daughter whenever the weather is favorable. She wears black, but is now beginning to vary it with purple and lavender.

# DOROTHY AND OTHER ITALIAN STORIES

# Contents

# *Dorothy*

As it was Saturday, many visitors came to the villa, Giuseppe receiving them at the open door, and waving them across the court or up the stone stairway, according to their apparent inclination, murmuring as he did so: "To the garden; the Signora North!" "To the salon; the Signora Tracy!" with his most inviting smiles. Dorothy probably was with Mrs. North in the garden. And everybody knew that the tea and the comfortable chairs were up-stairs. The company therefore divided itself, the young people as far as possible, the men who like to appear young, and the mothers who have heavier cares than the effects of open-air light on a middle-aged complexion, crossing the paved quadrangle to the north hall, while the old ladies and the ladies (not so old) who detest gardens ascended the stairs, accompanied by, first, the contented husbands; second, the well-trained husbands; third, other men, bond or free, who cherish no fondness for damp belvederes, for grassy mounds, or for poising themselves on a parapet which has a yawning abyss below.

Giuseppe was the gardener; he became a footman once a week, that is, on Saturday afternoons, when the American ladies of the Villa Dorio received those of their friends who cared to come to their hill-top above the Roman Gate of Florence —a hill-top bearing the appropriate name of Bellosguardo. For fair indeed is the outlook from that supremely blessed plateau, whether towards the north, south, east, or west, with perhaps an especial loveliness towards the west, where the Arno winds down to the sea. Enchanting as is this Occidental landscape, Mrs. Tracy had ended by escaping from it.

"When each new person begins: 'Oh, what lovely shadows!' 'Oh, the Carrara Mountains!' we cannot look at each other, Laura and I," she explained; "it's like the two Roman what-do-you-call-ems—augurs. I'm incapable of saying another word about the Carrara Mountains, Laura; and so, after this, I shall leave them to you."

This was the cause of Giuseppe's indicating the drawing-room, and not the garden, as Mrs. Tracy's domain.

It was not difficult for Giuseppe to turn himself into a footman; Raffaello, the butler (or cameriere), could have turned himself into a coachman, a cook, a laundress, a gardener, or even a parlor-maid, if occasion had so required; for Italian servants can do anything. And if Mrs. Sebright sighed, "Ah, but so badly!" (which was partly true from the English point of view) the Americans at least could respond, "Yes, but so easily!" In truth, it was not precisely in accordance with the English standard to be welcomed by smiles of personal recognition from the footman at the door, nor to have the tea offered by the butler with an urgent hospitality which was almost tender. But Italy is not England; radiant smiles from the servants accord perhaps with radiant sunshine from the sky, both things being unknown at home. As for the American standard, it does not exist, save as a vacillating pennon.

The Villa Dorio is a large, ancient structure of pale yellow hue; as is often the case in Tuscany, its façade rises directly from the roadway, so that any one can drive to the door, and knock by simply leaning from the carriage. But privacy is preserved all the same by the massive thickness of the stone walls, by the stern iron cages over the lofty lower windows, and by an entrance portal which resembles the gateway of a fortress. The villa, which, in the shape of a parallelogram, extends round an open court within, is large enough for five or six families; for in the old days, according to the patriarchal Italian custom, the married sons of the house, with their wives and children, were all gathered under its roof. In these later years its tenants have been foreigners, for the most part people of English and American birth—members of that band of pilgrims from the land of fog and the land of haste, who, having once fallen under the spell of Italy, the sorcery of that loveliest of countries, return thither again and yet again, sometimes unconscious of their thraldom, sometimes calling it staying for the education of the children, but seldom pronouncing the frank word "living." Americans who have stayed in this way for twenty years or more are heard remarking, in solemn tones, "In case I die over here, I am to be taken home to my own country for burial; nothing less could content me." This post-mortem patriotism probably soothes the conscience.

Upon the Saturday already mentioned the Villa Dorio had

but one tenant; for Mrs. Tracy had taken the entire place for a year—the year 1881. She could not occupy it all, even with the assistance of Mrs. North and Dorothy, for there were fifty rooms, besides five kitchens, a chapel, and an orange-house; she had selected, therefore, the range of apartments up-stairs which looked towards the south and west, and the long, frescoed, echoing spaces that remained were left to the ghosts. For there was a ghost, who clanked chains. The spectre of Belmonte, another villa near by, was more interesting; he was a monk in a brown gown, who glided at midnight up the great stairway without a sound, on his way to the tower. The American ladies had chosen for their use the northwestern garden. For the Villa Dorio has more than one garden; and it has also vineyards, olive groves, and the fields of the podere, or farm, in the valley below, with their two fountains, and the little chapel of the Holy Well. The northwestern garden is an enchanting spot. It is not large, and that adds to the charm, for its secluded nearness, so purely personal to the occupier, yet overhangs, or seems to, a full half of Tuscany; from the parapet the vast landscape below rolls towards the sunset as wide and far-stretching as the hidden shelf, one's standing-point, is private and small. When one ceases to look at the view—if one ever does cease —one perceives that the nook has no formal flower-beds; grass, dotted with the pink daisies of Italy, stretches from the house walls to the edge; here and there are rose-bushes, pomegranates, oleanders, and laurel, but all are half wild. The encircling parapet is breast-high; but, by leaning over, one sees that on the outside the ancient stones go plunging down, in course after course, to a second level far below, the parapet being in reality the top of a massive retaining-wall. At the corner where this rampart turns northward is perched a little belvedere, or arbor, with vines clambering over it. It was upon this parapet, with its dizzy outer descent, that the younger visitors were accustomed to perch themselves when they came to Villa Dorio. And Dorothy herself generally led them in the dangerous experiment. But one could never think of Dorothy as falling; her supple figure conveyed the idea that she could fly—almost—so lightly was it poised upon her little feet; in any case, one felt sure that even if she should take the fancy to throw herself off, she would float to the lower slope as lightly as thistle-down. The case was different regarding the Misses Sebright; they, too, were handsome girls, but they would certainly go down like rocks. And as for Rose Hatherbury, attenuated though she was, there would be, one felt certain, no floating; Rose would cut the air like a needle in her swift descent. Rose was thin (her aunts, the Misses Wood, called it slender); she was a tall girl of twenty-five, who ought to have been beautiful, for her features were well cut and her blue eyes lustrous, while her complexion was delicately fair. Yet somehow all this was without charm. People who liked her said that the charm would come. The Misses Wood, however, spent no time in anticipation; to them the charm was already there; they had always believed that their niece was without a fault. These ladies had come to Florence twenty years before from Providence, Rhode Island; and they had remained, as they said, "for art" (they copied as amateurs in the Uffizi Gallery). Of late they had begun to ask themselves whether art would be enough for Rose.

At five o'clock on this April afternoon the three Misses Sebright, Rose, Owen Charrington—a pink-cheeked young Englishman, long and strong—Wadsworth Brunetti, and Dorothy were all perched upon the parapet, while Miss Maria Wood hovered near, pretending to look for daisies, but in reality ready to catch Rose by the ankles in case she should lose her balance. Miss Jane Wood was sitting with Mrs. North in the aguish belvedere. With remarkable unanimity, the group of men near by had declared that, in order to see the view, one must stand.

"Your garden is like an opera-box, Mrs. North," said Stephen Lefevre; "you sit here at your ease, and see the whole play of morning, noon, and night sweeping over Tuscany."

"A view like this is such a humanizer!" remarked Julian Grimston, thoughtfully. "One might indeed call it a hauberk."

To this mysterious comparison Miss Jane Wood responded, cheerfully, "Quite so." She did not ask for explanations (Julian's explanations were serious affairs); she spoke merely on general principles; for the Misses Wood considered Julian "such an earnest creature!" Julian, a wizened little American of uncertain age, was protected by a handsome mother, who possessed a firm eye and a man-like mouth; this lady had almost secured for her son an Italian countess of large circumference and ancient name. Julian so far held back; but he would yet go forward.

"Its most admirable quality, to my mind, is that it's here," Mr. Illingsworth remarked, after Julian's "hauberk." "Generally, when there is a noble view, one has to go noble miles to see it; one has to be out all day, and eat hard-boiled eggs on the grass. You can't think how I loathe hard-boiled eggs! Or else one has to sleep in some impossible place, and be routed out at dawn. *Can* any one admire anything at dawn?"

"There isn't much dawn in this," answered Daniel Ashcraft. "Up to noon the view's all mist, and at noon everything looks too near. It doesn't amount to much before four o'clock, and only shows out all its points as the sun goes down."

"And have you discovered that, Mr. Ashcraft, on your third day in Florence?" demanded Illingsworth, with admiration. "But it's only another instance of the quick intelligence of your wonderful nation. Now I have lived in the town for twenty-five years, and have never noticed that this Carrara view was an afternoon affair. Yet so it is—so it is!"

Daniel Ashcraft surveyed the Englishman for a moment. "Oh yes—our quick intelligence. It makes us feel as though we were being exhibited. Sixpence a head."

More visitors appeared; by half-past five there were forty persons in the garden. Mrs. North received them all very graciously without stirring from her belvedere. Dorothy, however, was everywhere, like a sprite; and wherever Dorothy was Owen Charrington soon appeared. As for Wadsworth Brunetti, his method was more direct—he never left her side.

"They are both her *shadows*," said Beatrice Sebright, in an undertone, to Rose Hatherbury, as they sat perched side by side on the parapet.

"She is welcome to them," answered Rose. "A burly creature like Owen; and that Waddy!"

"Waddy?" repeated Beatrice, inquiringly.

"A simpleton," pronounced Rose, with decision.

Honest Beatrice surveyed her companion with wonder, into which crept something almost like envy; if she, Beatrice, could only think that Owen was burly; and if it were but possible, by trying hard, to regard Wadsworth Brunetti as a simpleton, how much easier life would be! As it was, she was convinced that Owen was not burly at all, but only athletic. And as to Waddy Brunetti, he was simply Raphael's young St. John in the Tribune of the Uffizi—the St. John at twenty-two, and in the attire of to-day. Wadsworth Brunetti's American mother had done her best to make an American of her only child; Waddy could speak the language of New York (when he chose); but in all other respects—his ideas, his manner, his intonations, his hair arranged after the fashion of King Humbert's, his shoes, his collar and gloves—he was as much a Florentine as his father. The Misses Sebright were not mistaken in their estimation of his appearance; he was exceedingly handsome. And the adverb is used advisedly, for his beauty exceeded that degree of good looks which is, on the whole, the best for every-day use; one hardly knew what to do with young Brunetti in any company, for he was always so much handsomer than the other guests, whether women or men.

"Isn't it enough that he allows himself to be called Waddy?" Rose had demanded in the same contemptuous undertone. "Waddy—wadding. What a name!"

"But Madame Brunetti tells us that Wadsworth is one of the very best of American names?" objected Beatrice, timidly, still clinging to her idol.

"She's mad; there are no best American names—unless one cares for those attached to the Declaration of Independence. The thing is, the best American men; and do you call Waddy that?"

Beatrice did. But she dared not confess it.

"Dorothy, I have forgotten my shawl," said Mrs. North, as Dorothy happened to pass the arbor.

"I'll go for it," said Charrington.

"Is it in the drawing-room?" inquired Julian Grimston. "A blue and white, with knotted fringe?"

Dorothy, meanwhile, was crossing the grass towards the house; Lefevre followed her; Waddy accompanied her.

"Nobody can get it but Dorothy—thanks; it is in my own room," said Mrs. North.

Charrington and Julian paused; Lefevre came back. Mrs. North said to Lefevre, "Praise my prudence in sending for a shawl." Then she added, laughing, "You dare not; prudence is so elderly!"

She could afford to make a joke of age; tall, thin, with abundant drab-colored hair and a smooth complexion, she did not look more than thirty-five, though she was in reality ten years older. She was a widow; her husband, Richard North, had been an officer in the American navy, and Dorothy was her step-daughter.

Dorothy and Waddy had gone on, and were now entering the north hall. This vacant stone-floored apartment, as large as a ball-room, with a vaulted ceiling twenty-four feet high, was the home of an energetic echo; spoken words were repeated with unexpected force, in accents musical but mocking. It was one thing for Waddy to murmur, "Give me but a grain of hope, only a grain," in pleading tones, and another to have the murmur come back like an opera chorus. Dorothy paused demurely, as if waiting for the conclusion of the sentence. But her picturesque suitor, still hearing his own roaring "grrrrain," bit his lips and tried to hasten their steps towards the other door.

"Oh, I thought you had something to say!" remarked Dorothy, innocently, when they reached the arcade within. "But you never have, have you."

And with this she crossed the quadrangle to welcome four new guests who were about to ascend the stairway in answer to Giuseppe's "The salon! Signora Tracy!" Waddy went up the stairs also. But he could not hope to follow to the remote region of Mrs. North's chamber, so he accompanied the new guests through the anterooms to the drawing-room at the end of the suite, where Mrs. Tracy, the second hostess, received them all with cordial greetings. Mrs. Tracy's years were fifty. She hoped that she was fine-looking, that epithet being sometimes applied to tall persons who hold up their heads, even if they are stout; even, too, if their noses are not long enough for classical requirements. She certainly held up her head. And she was always very well dressed; so well that it was too well. After saying a few words to Waddy, she passed him on to Miss Philipps, who stood near her. Felicia Philipps despised the beautiful youth. But she was willing to look at him for a few minutes as one looks at—a statue? Oh no, that would never

have been Felicia's word; at wax-works, that was more like it;
Felicia had a sharp tongue. She now chaffed the wax-works
a little, pretending to compliment its voice; for Waddy could
sing.

"As I sing too, Mr. Brunetti, we're companions in soul," she
said. "But, unfortunately, when *I* sing, my soul does not come
to my eyes, as yours does."

"The comfort of Waddy is that you can make mincemeat of
him to his face, when you feel savage, and he never knows it,"
she had once remarked.

There was, however, another side to this: Waddy did not
know, very possibly, but the reason was that he never paid
sufficient heed to Miss Felicia Philipps to comprehend what
she might be saying, good or bad; to his mind, Felicia was
only "that old maid." Mrs. Tracy, for the moment not called
upon to extend her tightly gloved hand to either arriving or
departing guests, expanded her fingers furtively, in order to
rest them, and glanced about her. Her rooms were full; there
was a steady murmur of conversation; the air was filled with
the perfume of flowers and the aroma of tea, and there were
suggestions also of the *petits fours*, the *bouchées aux confitures*,
and the delicate Italian sandwiches which Raffaello was carrying about with the air of an affectionate younger brother.
Waddy, who cherished a vision of Dorothy coming to get a
cup of tea for her mother (Waddy had noticed upon other Sat-
urdays that "my shawl" meant tea), detached himself as soon
as he could from Felicia, and made his way towards the tea-
table in the opposite corner. Here Nora Sebright was standing
behind a resplendent samovar. Mrs. Tracy had purchased this
decorative steam-engine in Russia; but she had not dared to
use it until Nora, seeing it at the villa one day, had offered to
teach her its mysteries. Mrs. Tracy never learned them; but
Nora came up every Saturday, and made the tea in her neat,
exact way. She was number one of the Misses Sebright. Six
sisters followed her. But this need not have meant that Nora
was very mature, because hardly more than a year separated
the majority of the Sebright girls (one could say the majority of them or the minority, there were so many). As it happened, however, Nora was twenty-nine, although Peggy, the

next one, was barely twenty-five; for the six younger sisters
were between that age and sixteen. These younger girls were
tall, blooming, and handsome. Nora was small, insignificant,
and pale; but her eyes were charming, if one took the trouble
to look at them, and there was something pretty in her soft,
dark hair, put back plainly and primly behind her ears, with a
smooth parting in front; one felt sure that she did not arrange
it in that way from a pious contentment with her own appearance, but rather from some shy little ideal of her own, which
she would never tell.

"Do you think they have all had tea?" she was saying anxiously as Waddy came up. She addressed a gentleman by her
side who had evidently been acting as her assistant.

"I think so," he answered, looking about the room with almost as much solicitude as her own.

Her face cleared; she laughed. "It's so kind of you! You have
carried cups all the afternoon."

"I only hope I haven't broken any," responded her companion, still with a trace of responsibility in his tone.

"It is terribly dangerous, with so many people pushing
against one. How you can do it so cleverly, I can't think. But
indeed, Mr. Mackenzie, I do not believe you *could* let anything
drop," Nora went on, paying him her highest compliment.
"This is the fourth Saturday you have given to these teacups; I
am afraid it has been tiresome. Raffaello ought to do it all; but
Italian servants—"

"They are not like yours in England; I can understand that.
But Raffaello, now—Raffaello has seemed to me rather a good
fellow," said Mackenzie.

At this moment Dorothy, carrying a shawl, appeared at the
door; she made her way to the table. "May I have some tea,
Miss Sebright, please, for mamma?"

"I will carry it for you," said Waddy, eagerly.

"Won't you take some tea yourself, Miss Dorothy, before
you go back to the garden?" suggested Mackenzie, in his def-
erential tones.

"I? Do you think I take tea? And how can *you* like it, Mr.
Mackenzie? You're not an Englishman."

Waddy thanked fate that his mother had entered human

existence in New York. Charrington, who was now near the table also, only laughed good-naturedly. On the whole he was of the opinion that Dorothy liked him. Her ideas about tea, or about other English customs, were not important; he could alter them.

"I am afraid I must acknowledge that I do like it," Mackenzie had answered.

"Do you take it in the morning—for breakfast?" inquired Dorothy, with the air of a judge.

Mackenzie confessed that he did.

"Then you are lost. Oh, coffee, lovely coffee of home!" Dorothy went on. "Coffee that fills the house at breakfast-time with its delicious fragrance. Not black, as the Italians make it. Not drowned in boiled milk, as the French drink it. As for the English beverage— But ours, the American—brown, strong, and with real cream! I wish I had a cup of it now—three cups —and six buckwheat cakes with maple syrup!"

The contrast between this evoked repast and the girl herself was so comical that the Americans who heard her broke into a laugh. Dorothy was very slight; there was something ethereal in her appearance, although the color in her cheeks, the brilliancy of her hazel eyes, and the bright hue of her chestnut hair indicated a vivid vitality. As a whole, she was charmingly pretty. The Americans who had laughed were but two—Mackenzie himself and Stephen Lefevre, who had now joined the group. Lefevre wished that his adorable little countrywoman would not say "lovely coffee." But Lefevre was, no doubt, a purist.

Felicia Philipps now came to the table with outstretched hands. "*Poor* Nora, I have only just observed how tired you are! You must have one of your fearful headaches?"

"Oh dear, no," answered Nora, surprised. "I haven't a headache in the least."

"Fancy! But you are overtired without knowing it; you must be, or you would not look so pale. I am sure Mr. Mackenzie sees it. Don't you think, Mr. Mackenzie, that Miss Sebright has been here quite long enough? I'm so anxious to relieve her."

"It's very good of you, I'm sure," replied Mackenzie.

And then Felicia, pulling off her gloves, came round behind the table and took possession of the place with an amiability and a rearrangement of the cups that defied opposition.

"I am afraid this tea will be cold," Waddy meanwhile had suggested to Dorothy.

"Yes, do take it down to mamma, Mr. Brunetti. And take this shawl too, won't you?"

"Aren't you coming?" said Waddy, in a discomfited voice, as, shawl in one hand and teacup in the other, he stood waiting.

"In five minutes; I have taken a fancy for spending just five minutes in that big yellow chair."

"That is wise; I'm very pleased to hear you say it," remarked Nora, who, though dispossessed, still lingered near. "We come up here, stay awhile, and then go away; but you are kept on your feet for three or four hours at a time."

"*You* don't go away, do you, Nora?" said Felicia. "You are so kind. I dare say you have been here since noon?"

"The samovar—" began Nora.

"Dear samovar!" commented Felicia, smiling.

And then Nora, at last understanding the sarcasm of the tone, left the table and crossed the room, her cheeks no longer colorless. Alan Mackenzie, who had heard this little dialogue, thought that the two ladies had been very kind to each other.

Mrs. Tracy, on her way back from the anteroom, whither she had gone to escort Julian Grimston's mother, who was taking leave, now stopped at the tea-table. She drew Felicia aside. "Stay and dine with us, won't you? We are always tired on Saturday evenings, and it will be delightful to hear you sing. The carriage shall take you home."

"You're awfully good," Felicia answered. "But don't trouble to send out the carriage. Ask Mr. Mackenzie too. He will be enchanted to stay, and then we can go down together on foot, and nobody need be bothered."

"You don't mind?"

"At *my* age!" answered Felicia, smiling. Felicia's smile always had a slightly hungry look.

"*We* shouldn't think of it. But then we're Americans," responded Mrs. Tracy. "Over here no woman seems to be safely old."

"Is that why so many of you come over?" demanded Felicia, who at heart detested all American women, especially those who, like the tenants of Villa Dorio, had plenty of money at their disposal. Then curbing her tongue, she added, "What you say is true of wives and widows. But I assure you that old maids are shelved over here as soon and as completely as they are with you in Oregon."

"In Oregon!" repeated Mrs. Tracy. "You English are too extraordinary." And she went away, laughing.

During this conversation Dorothy was leaning back in the gold-colored easy-chair; Charrington and Stephen Lefevre were standing beside her, and presently Julian Grimston joined the group, rubbing his dry little hands together gleefully, and murmuring to himself something that sounded like "Aha! aha!"

"Is it the pure joy of living, Mr. Grimston?" Dorothy inquired. For this was said to have been Julian's answer when an acquaintance, upon passing him in the street one day and overhearing him ahaing, had asked what it meant.

At this moment Waddy came from the anteroom. "And mamma's tea?" Dorothy asked.

"Raffaello was just going down; I gave it to him."

"Oh, thanks. I'm thinking how little mamma will like that." And Dorothy played thoughtfully a soundless tune with her right hand upon the arm of the easy-chair.

Waddy pursed up his lips in an inaudible whistle. Then with swift step he left the room.

Five minutes later he was back again. "It's all right. I caught up with him," he said, briefly.

"Now mark that," began Charrington. "This impostor gave those things to Mrs. North, I'll warrant, with rolling eyes that seemed to say that even to have touched them had been a huge joy." Waddy did not defend himself. "I wouldn't be a cherub, as you are, even if I could," went on Charrington. "You belong to Christmas-cards—your chin on your clasped hands. What is a cherub out of business—a cherub going about clothed, and with an umbrella? It's ghastly."

Mrs. Tracy to Miss Jane Wood: "How do you do, Miss Wood?"

To Miss Maria: "*How* do you do?"

Behind the Misses Wood came Rose Hatherbury and three of the Misses Sebright, who were tired of sitting on the wall. Felicia, very busy, sent tea to them all, Mackenzie carrying the cups. Raffaello presented himself at the table to assist. Felicia did not know much Italian, but she did know her own mind, and she wished for no second assistant; she therefore said to Raffaello, in an undertone, but with decision, "Andate via!" Raffaello, astounded by this unexpected "Clear out!" gazed at her for a moment with wild eyes, and then escaped from the room.

The tea was not good—so the Misses Wood thought as they tried to sip it; Nora Sebright, who was now walking with quick steps through the Via Romana on her way home, would have been distressed to see how bad it was.

"I wonder if there is any one in the garden now?" said Dorothy.

"There are fifty-seven persons," answered Rose, who had seated herself on a sofa near. "I know, because I counted them."

"Then I must go down," said Dorothy, rising.

She nodded to Rose and to the others and left the room, Waddy following as usual. Two minutes later, Charrington, Julian Grimston, and Stephen Lefevre had also disappeared.

Miss Jane Wood (having given up the tea) now began, graciously, "Did you get your ride this morning, Mr. Charrington?"

"Aunt Jane, Mr. Charrington is not here now," said Rose, in her distinct tones.

"Oh," said Miss Jane, bewildered, and fumbling quickly for her eye-glasses, which she had removed when she took her teacup. "He was here a moment ago; I saw him."

"What wonderful elocutionary powers Miss Hatherbury has!" said Felicia, in an aside, to Mackenzie. "I really think she could be heard in the largest hall."

"Upon my word, now that you mention it, I believe she could," answered Mackenzie, admiringly.

Rose divined that she was the subject of Felicia's aside. She said to her aunt, in an interested tone, "How well one sees the Belmonte tower from here!"

Miss Jane came to look, and then (in order that she should see to advantage) her niece pulled the cord and rolled the window-shade up to the top, letting in a broad shaft of sunset light, which fell directly across the tea-table and the persons in attendance there. Rose took this moment to carry her aunt's cup back to the table; and, having put it down, she remained standing by Felicia's side while she began, composedly, a conversation with Alan Mackenzie. Mackenzie responded: his head immediately assumed the little bend which with him signified devoted listening; he stood, meanwhile, exactly where Rose had intended that he should stand—namely, in front of the two ladies, facing them. Felicia, even in her youth, had had no beauty; now all the faults of her sharp features were pitilessly magnified by the same clear light which brought out the fine-grained purity of Rose's complexion and turned her golden hair into glittering glory. Felicia was too intelligent to cherish illusions about her appearance; she quivered under the radiance in which the golden motes danced; she too had color now, but it was an ugly vermilion in spots and streaks. She glanced at Mackenzie; he was listening to Rose; now he was offering one of his civil little questions—those attentive, never-failing small interrogatories for which he was celebrated.

"I should like to strangle him!" thought the older woman, bitterly. "I believe he would keep up those everlasting little questions on his death-bed. In reality, he doesn't care the turn of his finger for that screaming popinjay. Yet he stands there and listens to her, and will do it unflinchingly as long as she talks, if it's all night."

The popinjay at this moment turned, and fired back at Felicia her own gun. "You are tired, Miss Philipps. Doesn't she look tired, Mr. Mackenzie?"

Mackenzie turned obediently; he inspected Felicia's flushed face. "Yes—ah, really, I am afraid you *are* tired," he said, kindly.

Felicia, unable to bear his gaze, seized her gloves and fled.

But the popinjay could not sing, and had no invitation to stay. Alan Mackenzie loved music. As he never spoke of the love, but few persons had discovered it; Felicia was one of the few.

It was nearly eleven o'clock before the song began. They had gone out, after dinner, to the small stone terrace that opened from the drawing-room, in order to look at the valley by the light of the moon. "For we really like our view when we don't have to talk about it," Mrs. Tracy explained. After a while, "Come, Felicia," she said.

Felicia went within and opened the piano; Mrs. Tracy, following, sank into the easiest chair; Mrs. North placed herself in the doorway, with her face towards the moonlight. Dorothy remained outside, using the hammock as a swing, pushing herself to and fro slowly by a touch on the parapet now and then. On the other side of the terrace, in a garden-chair, sat the second guest.

Felicia's voice was a contralto which had not a range of many notes, but each one of the notes was perfect. Her singing was for a room only; it was intimate, personal; perhaps too personal sometimes. The words were, for her, a part of it as much as the melody.

> "Through the long days and years
> What will my loved one be,
> Parted from me,
> Through the long days and years?"

The music upon which these words were borne was indescribably sweet. Dorothy had stopped swinging. But it was the melody that held her vaguely given attention; she paid no heed to the spoken syllables.

> "Never on earth again
> Shall I before her stand,
> Touch lip or hand,
> Never on earth again,"

sang the voice, the strains floating out to the moonlight in a passion of sorrow. Dorothy was now looking at the tower of Belmonte, near by. "I wish our villa had a tower," was the thought in her mind. As her gaze turned, she saw that Mackenzie's eyes were resting upon her, and she smiled back at him, making a mute little gesture of applause.

> "But while my darling lives,
> Peaceful I journey on,
> Not quite alone,
> Not while my darling lives."

And now the music rose to that last courage, that acceptance of grief as the daily portion of one's life, which is the highest pathos. Then there was a silence.

Dorothy made her little motion of applause again, save that this time the applause was audible; the words on her lips, ready to utter, were, "How pretty that is!" Perhaps Mackenzie divined what these words would be, for, with a quick movement, he rose and went to the end of the terrace, where he stood with his back towards her, looking down the valley. But Dorothy had accomplished her duty; she was perfectly willing to be silent; she sank lazily back in the hammock again, and resumed her swinging.

"Mr. Mackenzie, wasn't that exquisite?" said Mrs. Tracy's voice within.

Mackenzie, thus summoned, crossed the terrace and re-entered the drawing-room. Felicia kept her seat at the piano; as Mrs. Tracy was standing behind her, and as Mrs. North's head was turned away, she was freed for the moment from feminine observation, and she therefore gave herself the luxury of letting all the pathos and passion with which she had sung remain unsubdued in her eyes, which met his as he came up.

"Lovely, wasn't it? But so sad," continued Mrs. Tracy.

"Yes," Mackenzie answered; "it *is* rather sad." Then, "What song is it, Miss Philipps?" he inquired. "I do not remember having heard it before."

"'Through the long days,'" answered Felicia, who was now looking at the piano keys.

"Ah! And the composer?"

"Francis Boott."

"Ah! Francis Boott, yes. And the words?" His head had now its attentive little bend.

"They are by John Hay." To herself she added: "You *shall* stop your little questions; you *shall* say something different!" And again she looked up at him, her eyes strangely lustrous.

And then at last he did say, "May I take the music home with me? You shall have it again to-morrow. It is a very beautiful song."

Felicia rolled up the sheet and gave it to him, her hand slightly rigid as she did so from repressed emotion.

At midnight the two guests took leave, Mrs. Tracy accompanying them down to the entrance portal. The irregular open space, or piazza, before the house had a weird appearance; the roadway looked like beaten silver; the short grass had the hue and gleam of new tin; the atmosphere all about was as visibly white as it is visibly black on a dark night.

"It's the moment exactly for our ghost to come out and clank his chains," said the lady of the house. "This intensely white moonlight is positively creepy; it is made for hobgoblins and sheeted spectres; the Belmonte monk must certainly be dancing on the top of his tower."

"Oh no," said Felicia; "it's St. Mark's eve, so we're all under good protection. Hear the nightingales."

She was in high spirits; her words came out between little laughs like giggles. Mrs. Tracy watched the two figures cross the grass and turn down the narrow passage whence the road descends in zigzags to Florence.

"Poor Felicia," she said, when she had returned up the stairs to the drawing-room; "she is talking about St. Mark's eve, in order, I suppose, to bring up the idea of St. Agnes's. It's late, isn't it? They must want to walk!"

"They?" said Mrs. North. "*She.*"

"Well, then, I wish she could," responded Mrs. Tracy. Going to the terrace door, she looked out. "Where is Dorothy?"

"I sent her to bed; she was almost asleep in the hammock. If there is one thing she likes better than another, it is to curl herself up in some impossible place and fall asleep. Would you mind closing the glass doors? The nightingales hoot so."

Mrs. Tracy closed and fastened the terrace entrance for the night.

"What do you mean by saying that you wish she could?" Mrs. North went on. "You wouldn't have Alan Mackenzie marry that plain-looking, ill-tempered old maid, would you?"

"Perhaps she is ill-tempered just because she is an old maid, Laura. And as to looks—if she were happy—"

"Mercy! Are the Mackenzie millions to be devoted to the public charity of making a Felicia Philipps happy?"

"Why, isn't it as good an object as a picture-gallery? Or even an orphan asylum? Felicia would be a great deal happier than all the happiness combined of the whole three hundred orphans out at St. Martin's at a Christmas dinner," suggested Charlotte Tracy, laughing.

"Absurd! Rose Hatherbury is the one—if it's any one in Florence."

"Oh, Rose is too young for him."

"In years, yes. But Rose's heart can be any age she pleases. Alan isn't really old in the least; but he was born middle-aged; he is the essence of middle-age and mediocrity; one always knows beforehand what he will say, for it will simply be, on every occasion, the most polite and the most commonplace thing that could possibly be devised under the circumstances. How came you to ask him to stay to dinner?"

"Felicia made me. Funny, wasn't it, to see Waddy hang on, hoping for an invitation too."

"You might have given him one. It would have entertained Dorothy."

"Well, to tell the truth, Laura, I am a little afraid of Waddy; he *is* so handsome!"

"She doesn't care for him."

"She likes him."

"Yes, as she likes a dozen more. If she has a fancy for one over another, it is, I think, for Owen Charrington," continued the mother. "She would have to live in England. But I dare say his people would take to her; they are very nice, you know—his people."

"How can you talk so! Dorothy is thoroughly American; she would be wretched in England. When she marries—which I hope won't be for five or six years more—she must marry one of our own countrymen, of course. The idea!"

"Very well; I've no objection. But in that case we must take her home again before long," said Laura North, rising. As she spoke she indulged in a stretch, with her long arms extended first horizontally, and then slowly raised until they were perpendicular above her head, the very finger-tips taking part in the satisfactory elongation.

"How I wish *I* could do that!" said Charlotte Tracy, enviously. "But you don't say 'Ye-ough' at the end, as you ought to."

They put out the wax-candles and left the room together, Mrs. Tracy lighting the way with a Tuscan lamp, its long chains dangling. "By this time Felicia, 'delicately treading the clear pellucid air,' is going through the Porta Romana," she suggested.

"Never in the world! She has taken him round by the Viale dei Colli; she won't let him off for two good hours yet," responded Mrs. North.

II

"On Thursday, January 8th, at the English church, Florence, by the Reverend J. Chaloner-Bouverie, Alan Mackenzie, to Dorothy, daughter of the late Captain Richard North, United States Navy."—*Galignani's Messenger* of January 10, 1882.

III

It was St. Mark's eve again, April 24th, and again there were many visitors at Bellosguardo. Upon this occasion they were assembled at Belmonte, the villa with the old battlemented tower, where Mr. and Mrs. Alan Mackenzie were receiving their Florentine friends for the first time since their marriage; they had been travelling in Sicily and southern Italy through the winter months.

"We shall be going home in 1883, I suppose," Mackenzie had said to the ladies of Villa Dorio; "I shall be obliged to go then; or at least it would be better to go. In the meanwhile, as Dorothy appears to be rather fond of Bellosguardo—don't you think so?—I have had the idea of taking Belmonte for a time. That is, if you yourselves intend to continue here?"

"Oh, we shall continue, we shall continue," Mrs. Tracy had answered, laughing. "For detached American ladies, who haven't yet come to calling themselves old—for the cultivated superfluous and the intelligent remainders—there is nothing like Europe!"

The flat highways down in the Arno Valley, west of Bellosguardo, are deep in dust even as early as April; the villages, consisting for the most part of a shallow line of houses on each side of the road, almost join hands, so that it is not the dust alone that afflicts the pedestrian, but children, dogs, the rinds of fruit and vegetables—all the far-reaching untidiness of a Southern race that lives in the street. The black-eyed women sit in chairs at the edge of the dry gutter, plaiting straw; up to middle-age they are all handsome, with thick hair and soft, dark eyes. On this April afternoon they laughed (waiting with Italian politeness until she had passed) as an Englishwoman trudged by them on her way back to Florence. Her plain dress was short, revealing long shoes white with dust; her unbeautiful face was mottled by the heat; she looked tired enough to lie down and die. But to the straw-plaiting matrons she was simply ridiculous, or else mad; for how otherwise should a foreigner be toiling along their plebeian highway on foot, when she could so easily have a carriage? Felicia was finishing her daily walk of miles—a walk without an object save to tire herself. As she passed the olive-crowned heights of Bellosguardo rising on the right, she lifted her eyes.

"He is there, seeing everybody. All the same people who were there a year ago to-day. And what are they thinking— perhaps saying? 'See this dull, middle-aged man, with that flighty little creature for a wife! She cares nothing for him; she turns him round her finger, and always will.' O fool! fool too noble to see or to doubt; simple, generous nature, never asserting itself, always repressed, that _I_ understood, while all these other people, that girl at the head of them, only laughed at it!"

She hastened on, passed through the city gate, and made her way down the dirty, evil-smelling Borgo San Frediano to San Spirito beyond, where, high up in an old palace, she had a small apartment crowded with artistic trumpery. After climbing the long stairs, and letting herself in with a latch-key, she entered her minute drawing-room, and sank into a chair, her feet, in their dusty shoes, like two blocks of wood on the matting before her. And the plates and the plaques and the pots, the bits of silk and tapestry and embroidery, the old sketches and old busts and old shrines that adorned the walls, looked down upon her with their usual heterogeneous glimmer. This time the glimmer seemed personally sarcastic, seemed inhuman.

While she sat there, the people at Belmonte were beginning to take leave. Rose was to remain (with Miss Jane Wood). As Waddy Brunetti was to remain also, the Misses Sebright looked at Rose with envy. Six of the sisters were now united in a single admiration. For Owen Charrington had gone to Australia before Christmas—it was about the time that Dorothy's engagement had been announced—and he had not returned; admiration could not stretch to the antipodes. Waddy, too, had been absent through January, February, and March; but he was now at home again, so there was some use in going once more to teas and receptions.

"How lovely Mrs. Mackenzie is looking!" said Miss Maria Wood on the way down to Florence.

She had accepted a seat in Mrs. Grimston's carriage, and it was that lady who answered her.

"Yes—fairly; it's her youth more than anything else. Strictly speaking, there are but two kinds of beauty—dimpled youth like that, and the noble outline and bearing that come from distinguished birth."

This was a double shot. For Rose certainly had no dimples, and the birth of distinction pointed of course to the widowed countess. But Julian, who sat facing his mother, had no longer any courage to resist; his poor little eyes, like those of a sick monkey, had shed their two slow tears on Christmas eve, when, at last allowed to retreat to his own (cold) room, he had accepted drearily the tidings of Dorothy's engagement, and had given up his struggle against fate.

Mr. Illingsworth walked down the hill with Mrs. Sebright, her girls following at a little distance, two and two. "Don't I miss one of your charming daughters?" he said, gallantly, as, happening to look back at the turn of a zigzag, he caught sight of the procession coming round the higher bend.

"Dear me! I wish he might miss three or four!" thought the mother. But this was nothing worse on her part than a natural desire to translate three or four of them to richer atmospheres —a Yorkshire country-house, for instance, or a good vicarage; even army life in India would do. Meanwhile she was replying, "Yes—Nora; Nora has been at St. Martin's Orphan House, out in the country, since Christmas. She is greatly interested in the work there; so much so that I have consented to let her remain."

Nora's secret only one person had discovered, and this one was the benevolent stranger, Charlotte Tracy, who had happened to see the expression in the girl's eyes for one instant, when the news of Alan Mackenzie's engagement had come upon her suddenly, and taken her (as it took all Florence) by surprise. The American lady, instantly comprehending, had (while her own face showed nothing) screened Nora skilfully from observation for several minutes. And ever since she had kept her knowledge hidden away very closely in a shaded corner of her heart.

"A true Sister of Charity," Mr. Illingsworth had responded to the mother's reply about the orphan house. But as he said this he was thinking, "And if *I* had married, as I came so near doing, I, too, might have had at my heels this moment—great heavens!—just such another red-cheeked, affectionate train!"

That evening the ladies who had dined at Belmonte were taking their coffee in the garden; there was no moon, but the splendid stars gave a light of their own as they spangled the dark-blue sky. From the open door of the boudoir at this end of the house, the light, streaming forth, fell upon Dorothy as she sat talking to Rose. After a while the gentlemen joined the ladies; and then Waddy talked to Rose. But while he talked, his eyes followed the hostess, who was now strolling up and down the honeysuckle path with one of her guests. Some one asked Waddy to sing. Nothing loath, he went within, brought out Dorothy's guitar, and sang one of Tosti's serenades. The song and his voice, a melodious tenor, accorded so perfectly with the old Italian garden that there was much applause. And then Waddy, having moved his chair into the shadow of the trees, sent forth after a while from the darkness, unasked, a second song, and this time the words were English:

> "Through the long days, the long days and the years,
>     What will my loved one be,
>     Parted from me, parted from me,
>   Through the long days and years?"

The lady who had been strolling with Dorothy had stopped to speak to some one, and for the moment the young wife, who had reached the end of the honeysuckle path, was alone. Mackenzie came up quietly and stood beside her as the song went on. When it had ended, she looked up at him.

"Do you like it so much?" she asked, in surprise, as she saw, in the starlight, the expression of his face.

"It's because I have so much more than I ever dreamed of

having, Dorothy," he answered, in a low tone, just touching her hair in the shadow. "A year ago—do you remember? That same song, on the terrace? It expressed what I felt; for then I had no hope. But now—"

Here a voice from the group of ladies said, "Mr. Mackenzie will know; ask him." And Mackenzie, returning to the light, was the attentive host again. Waddy, meanwhile, crossed the grass quickly to the honeysuckle path.

He was the last to take leave; when Mackenzie returned, after escorting Mrs. North and Mrs. Tracy to the Villa Dorio, he was still in the garden with Dorothy.

Fifteen minutes later, through the open windows of Mrs. North's chamber there came the sound of steps.

"Waddy," said Charlotte Tracy, peeping through the closed blinds, and recognizing his figure. "He has outstayed everybody."

"You are no longer afraid of him, I trust?" inquired Mrs. North.

"Certainly not," said the older lady with decision. After a moment she added, "She must always amuse herself, I suppose."

"She has the very best of safeguards."

"Now there you go, with your cold-blooded judgments, Laura! Dorothy has as deep feelings as anybody. I don't know where you get your knowledge of her; you are her step-mother, it is true; but I have been with her as constantly as you have for years."

"Quite so. May I ask how well you knew her father?"

"I don't care!" was Charlotte's reply. She left the room with majesty. The majesty lasted through the hall, and into her own chamber, as she reflected, "*I* have feelings. And Dorothy has feelings. But Laura is a stone!" At this moment she caught a glimpse of herself in the full-length mirror, and majesty collapsed. "Do I look like that? *Do* I? Stout, short-nosed?" And she sank down on a sofa overwhelmed. But presently a laugh broke through her discomfiture. "The very next crumpled little old man I see, I'll be nice to him! I'll ask who is his favorite poet, and I'll get him to quote—yes, even if it's Byron!" Mrs. Tracy's favorite author was Ibsen.

"You will do it if I wish, won't you, Alan?" said Dorothy the next day.

"Why, if you really wish it—if you think it best—" began Mackenzie.

"She doesn't in the least," interposed Mrs. North. "Don't indulge her so; you will spoil her."

Mackenzie's eyes turned towards his wife.

"Don't look at me to see whether mamma is right," said Dorothy, laughing; "invent an opinion of your own about me —do! But let us have something striking; consider me capable of murder, for instance, not of mere commonplace selfishness. Every woman is capable of murder once; I am perfectly sure of it."

"My dear," said Mackenzie, expostulatingly.

"I don't know whether I could quite do it with my own hands," Dorothy went on, stretching out her palms and looking at them. "But Felicia Philipps could; yes, with her long fingers. Brrrr!" And she rushed to her husband and hid her face on his arm.

She had her way, which was not a murder, but a ball. Soon afterwards there was a summer-night party at Belmonte, with music and dancing; the tower and the garden, illuminated, were visible for miles roundabout, like a fairy-land on the dark hill. Then followed excursions, long drives, and, more frequently, long rides; for Dorothy had taken to riding. Mackenzie accompanied the riding-parties cheerfully. But Dorothy was often far in advance with one of the younger cavaliers.

"I believe I should come back from the dead, Alan, to see you pounding along, always at the very end of the procession, with Miss Jane Wood," said the young wife one day. "I know you don't care much about riding. But why do you always escort Miss Jane? She must weigh one hundred and eighty."

"She is a little timid, I think," answered Mackenzie; "at least, I have fancied so. She only goes to see to Miss Hatherbury."

"As you see to me?"

Mackenzie liked long walks.

"But walking is so dull. And the people who take long walks have such an insufferable air of superiority," commented Dorothy. "Not that you have come to that, Alan; with you it's just simple vanity."

And making the motion of turning up trousers at the bottom, she crossed the garden, holding her riding-whip like a cane, with her shoulders put back, her head run out a little, and a long step with a dip in the middle of it—the whole an amusing caricature of her husband's gait when starting on a long excursion. Mackenzie had taught himself that gait; he had even been a little proud of it. But now he joined irrepressibly in his wife's merriment, as she loped down the broad walk, and then came running back to him with her own light swiftness.

Occasionally, however, she went with him for a stroll. One day late in the afternoon they passed Villa Dorio together. The sun, low in the west, was shining on all the square Tuscan towers that dot the hill-tops in every direction. May was now more than half spent, and the air was like that of July in Northern countries. The ladies of Villa Dorio saw them go by; Dorothy's straw hat was hanging by its ribbons from her arm.

"He hates to have her out without her hat," remarked Mrs. Tracy, leaning forward to watch them for a moment.

"Well, in that dress, she doesn't look more than fourteen," answered Mrs. North.

Mr. and Mrs. Mackenzie went on down the hill. When they came to the first zigzag, they left the main road, and, turning, crossed a grassy little piazza; beyond, clinging to the side of the hill, with a cluster of cypresses before it like tall green candles, is the small church of San Vito, commanding a magnificent sweep of the valley below. As they passed, San Vito's chimes rang the Angelus, swinging far out from the open belfry against the sky with all the abandon of Italian bells, which seem forever joyous—almost intoxicated—even for the dead. San Vito's has a path of its own which follows a narrow shelf overhanging the valley; the two pedestrians turned down this path. As the bells ceased, Dorothy began to sing:

"Ring out across the sunset sky, Angelus—"

"Go on; go on," said Mackenzie, delightedly.

"Oh, I can't sing."

"Dear, I think you could; your voice is so sweet. If you would take lessons—"

"Well, by-and-by. We have lots of time for everything, Alan." When they came to the turn where there is a rustic shrine she paused. "I won't go any farther, I think. But don't stop because

I do; you like your walk. Go on, and come back through the olive groves just beyond Belmonte; I will be waiting for you at our wall."

"I don't like to leave you here alone."

"Not under the shrine? What's more, here is the priest."

The priest of San Vito's was coming down the path. He was an old man, with a large, sensible face, and a somewhat portly person dressed in well-brushed black. He aided his steps with a cane. His bearing was serene and dignified. As he passed, Mackenzie saluted him, raising his hat.

"For a Unitarian," said Dorothy, after the worthy man had gone by, "aren't you showing a good deal of courtesy? But you would be courteous to any religion; you would respect the fetich of a South Sea Islander. Do you know, Alan, that you have too many respects? Please go now, so that you can be back the sooner." Mackenzie, who had been leaning against the parapet, turned and began to go down the descent. His wife followed him for a step or two, in order to brush some mortar from his sleeve. "You see it is I that must keep you respectable—in spite of your respects."

How pretty she was! They were alone under the high wall. "My darling," he murmured. And Dorothy, laughing, raised herself on tiptoe to kiss him.

Half an hour later, when he reached the wall near Belmonte, there was no Dorothy. He went within. The signora had gone to Villa Dorio, the servant said. He came out and followed her thither. Yes, Dorothy had been there; but Waddy Brunetti had happened in, and they had strolled down as far as San Vito's.

Mackenzie did not say, "But she has just been to San Vito's." He sat talking with the ladies for twenty minutes or more; then he remarked, offering it as a suggestion for their approval, "I think I will walk on to San Vito's and meet them."

"Yes, do," said Mrs. North. "And make that foolish Dorothy put on her hat."

"It is as warm as midsummer. And the air is perfectly dry, I think; no dew," Mackenzie answered.

"He defends her even when she vexes him," commented Charlotte Tracy, after he had gone.

"He might as well be amiable, seeing that he cannot be interesting," Mrs. North responded.

Dorothy was not at San Vito's. And she had not gone down the zigzags of the carriage-road; he went down to see. He returned to Belmonte. It was now late twilight. But there was still a band of orange light in the west, and, outlined against it, on the top of the tower, were two figures. He recognized them instantly—Dorothy and young Brunetti.

Dorothy waved her hand to him through one of the embrasures. "Send up some one with candles," she called.

"With what?"

"Can-dles; it's too dark now to come down without lights. But don't send immediately; wait fifteen minutes more, so that we can see the moon rise. And, Alan!"

"Yes?"

"Please tell them that Mr. Brunetti will stay and dine with us."

IV

On the 29th of December of this same year, 1882, Reginald Illingsworth was paying a visit to Mrs. Sebright.

"What a career that little girl will have!" he said, with deep gustatory appreciation.

Before this, for half an hour, he had been making remarks of a nature best described by the following examples: "That excellent fellow, Mackenzie! You can't think how I miss him!" "There is something so tragic in such a death—a man who had everything to live for!" "How could they go to Rome! That pernicious Roman fever is the curse of Italy." "Those poor ladies! Directly I heard they had returned to Belmonte, I went up at once to inquire and to leave cards; it is a stricken house!" Having said everything that decorum required, he now finally allowed himself to bring out the thought which was in reality filling his mind: "What a career that little girl will have! Only nineteen, and so very pretty, so charming. He has left her everything without a condition (save in the event—most improbable at her age—of her dying without children, in which case it goes back to his own relatives), and I am told that he had nearly eight millions of dollars; that is, one million six hundred thousand pounds! They are shrewd in their American way—those ladies; Mrs. North is very shrewd. And mark my words, madam, that little girl will make one of the great matches yet; not pinchbeck; something really good!" (His "good" had a deeply solid sound.)

This same afternoon the following words were exchanged in another quarter of Florence:

"Rose, dear," said Miss Jane Wood, "you will go up again to-morrow, won't you, to see poor Dorothy?"

"I have been twice—all that is necessary for appearances, Aunt Jane. Why should I bother Dorothy now?"

"Sympathy—" began Miss Jane.

"Sympathy! She is in a position to extend it to me. I think she is the very luckiest girl I have ever heard of in my life. All another girl can do in the face of such luck as that is to keep away from it, and not think about it—if she can."

Miss Jane Wood: "I am *astonished*!"

Miss Maria: "! ! ! !"

That evening, at Belmonte, Dorothy walked and walked about the drawing-room; now she stopped at a table, took up something and put it down again; now she moved a statuette to another position; now she gazed at the etchings on the wall as though she had never seen them before; now she added pine-cones to the already blazing fire, kneeling on the rug with the hot flame scorching her face; finally she went to the window, and, parting the curtains, stood looking out. It was a dark night without stars; in addition to the freezing temperature, the wind was fierce; it drove furiously against the windows of the villa, it came round the corner of the tower with a shriek like that of a banshee.

"It's dreadfully cold," said the girl at last, as if speaking to herself.

"Surely not here?" replied Mrs. Tracy. Dorothy came wandering back to the fire, and then the aunt drew her down by her side. "Dear child, don't keep thinking of Rome," she whispered. "He is not there; there is nothing there but the lifeless clay." And she kissed her.

"Try not to be so restless, Dorothy," said Mrs. North, from her warm corner. "You have walked about this room all day."

"It's because I'm so tired; I am so tired that I cannot keep still," Dorothy answered.

"I think a change would be a good thing for all of us," Mrs. North went on. "We could go to Cannes for two months; we could be as quiet at Cannes as here."

Dorothy looked at her with vague eyes, as if waiting to hear more.

"It is warmer there. And then there is the sea—to look at, you know," pursued Mrs. North, seeing that she was called upon to exhibit attractions.

"Egypt would be my idea," said Mrs. Tracy. "A dahabeeyah on the Nile, Dorothy. Camels; temples."

Dorothy listened, as if rather struck by this idea also.

"But Egypt would be a fearful trouble, Charlotte," objected Mrs. North. "Who is going to get a good dahabeeyah for us at this time of year?"

"Don't spoil it. I'll get twenty," responded the other lady.

And then there was a silence.

"Well, Dorothy, are you going to leave it to us to decide?"

"Yes, mamma," Dorothy answered. Her eyes had grown dull again; she sat listening to the wind as if she had forgotten what they were talking about.

"It's decided, then. We will go to Cannes," remarked Mrs. North, serenely.

Her Aunt Charlotte's discomfited face drew a sudden laugh from the niece. And this laughter, once begun, did not cease; peal succeeded peal, and Dorothy threw herself back on the cushions of the sofa, overcome with merriment. Mrs. North glanced towards the doors to see if they were well closed. But Charlotte Tracy was so glad to hear the sound again that she did not care about comments from the servants; Dorothy's face, dull and tired, above the dead black of the widow's attire, had been like a nightmare to her.

They went to Cannes. And Mrs. North's suggested "two months" had now lengthened, in her plans, to three. But before two weeks had passed they were again at Belmonte.

"Now that we have made one fiasco, Charlotte, and taken that horrible journey, all tunnels, twice within twenty days, we must not make another; we must decide to remain where we are for the present. If Dorothy grows restless again, be firm. Be firm, as I shall be."

"Surely we ought to be indulgent to her now, Laura?"

"Not too much so. Otherwise we shall be laying up endless bother for ourselves. For we have a year of hourly employment before us, day by day. In the way of seeing to her, I mean."

"She will not make us the least trouble," said Mrs. Tracy, indignantly.

"I am not finding fault with her. But she cannot help her age, can she? She is exceedingly young to be a widow, and she has a large fortune; but for a year, at any rate, if I know myself, gossip shall not touch my daughter."

"A year? I'll guarantee ten," said Mrs. Tracy, still indignant.

"I don't care about ten; three will do. Yes, I see you looking at me with outraged eyes. But there's no need. I liked Alan as much as you did; I appreciated every one of his good points. With all that, you cannot pretend to say that you believe Dorothy really loved him. She was too young to love anybody. The love was on his side, and you were as much surprised as I was when she took a fancy to accept it."

Mrs. Tracy could not deny this. But she belonged to that large class of women who, from benevolent motives, never acknowledge unwelcome facts. "I think you are perfectly horrid!" she said.

Dorothy, back at Belmonte, was troublesome only in the sense of being always in motion. Having exhausted the garden, she began to explore the country. She went to Galileo's tower; to the lonely little church of Santa Margherita; the valley of the Ema knew her slender black figure. Once she crossed the Greve, and, following the old Etruscan road, climbed to the top of the height beyond, where stands the long, blank Shameless Villa outlined against the sky.

"Do you know, I am afraid I am lame," said Mrs. Tracy, the morning after this long tramp to the Shameless.

"Well, why do you go? One of us is enough," answered Mrs. North.

To the walks Dorothy now added lessons in German and Italian. Mrs. North drove down to Florence and engaged Fräulein Bernstein and Mademoiselle Scarletti. Next, Dorothy said that she wished to take lessons in music.

"A good idea. You ought to play much better than you do," said her mother.

"Piano; but singing too, please," Dorothy answered.

Again Mrs. North descended to Florence; Fräulein Lund-borg was engaged for instrumental music, and Madame Fari-nelli for vocal. Dorothy wished to have a lesson each day from each of her teachers. "It's a perfect procession up and down this hill!" thought Mrs. Tracy. There was a piano in the billiard-room, and another in the drawing-room; but now Dorothy wished to have a third piano in her own sitting-room up-stairs.

"But, my dear, what an odd fancy! Are you going to sing there by yourself?" her mother inquired.

"Yes!" said Dorothy.

"Do you think she is well?" asked Mrs. Tracy, confidentially, with some anxiety.

"Perfectly well. It is the repressed life she is leading," Mrs. North answered. "But we must make the best of it. This is as good a place as any for the next three months."

But again this skilful directress was forced to abandon the "good place." Early in March, when the almond-trees were in bloom, Dorothy, coming in from the garden, announced, "I *hate* Belmonte! Let us go away, mamma—anywhere. Let us start to-morrow."

"We took you to Cannes, and you did not wish to stay. We shall be leaving Belmonte in any case in June; that isn't long to wait."

"You like Paris; will you go to Paris?" the girl went on.

"What can you do in Paris more than you do here?"

"I love the streets, they are so bright—so many people. Oh, mamma, if you could only know how dull I am!" And sinking down on the rug, Dorothy laid her face on the sofa-cushion at her mother's side.

Mrs. Tracy coming in and finding her thus, bent and felt her pulse.

"Yes, one hundred and fifty!" said Dorothy, laughing. "Take me to Paris, and to the opera or theatre every night, and it will go down."

"Oh, you don't mean that," said the aunt, assuringly.

"Yes, but I do," Dorothy answered. And then, with her cheek still resting on the cushion, she looked up at her mother. "You will take me, mamma, won't you? If I tell you that I *must*?"

"Yes," replied Mrs. North, coldly.

They went to Paris. And then, for four weeks, almost every night at the back of a box at the opera or at one of the theatres were three ladies in mourning attire, the youngest of the three in widow's weeds. Mrs. Tracy was so perturbed during these weeks that her face was constantly red.

"Why are you so worried?" Mrs. North inquired. "I manage it perfectly; people don't in the least know."

"Do I care for 'people'? It's—it's—" But she would not say "It's Dorothy." "It's ourselves," she finally ended.

"Always sentimental," said Laura.

Midway in the first week of April, Dorothy suddenly changed again. "I can't stay here a moment longer!" she said.

"Perhaps you would like to take a trip round the world?" suggested Mrs. North, with a touch of sarcasm.

"No. I don't know what you will say, mamma, but I should like to go back to Belmonte."

"I have a good deal of patience, my dear, but I must say that you wear it out."

"I know I do; but if you will take me back, I promise to stay there this time as long as you like."

"*I* like—" began Mrs. North; but Dorothy, with a frown, had rushed out of the room.

"What shall we do now?" said the aunt.

"Go back, I suppose; I have always thought Belmonte the best place up to really hot weather. One good thing: if we do go back we can take the opportunity to rid ourselves definitely of both of those villas. My idea is the Black Forest country for August and September. Then we could come here again for a few weeks. For the winter, what do you say to a long cruise towards the South somewhere, in a yacht of our own? We could select the right people to go with us."

They returned to Italy, reaching Bellosguardo again on the 11th of April.

On the 6th of May Charlotte Tracy said, "Laura, to me this is dreadful! Waddy is here morning, noon, and night."

"So many people have left Florence that it hardly matters; nobody knows what is going on up here. He amuses her, and that is something gained."

"I wish he wouldn't be forever singing!" said the aunt, irritably.

"He sings very well. And Dorothy has shown a new interest in singing lately. Don't you remember that she took lessons herself before we went to Paris?"

"You don't mean to intimate that Waddy had anything to do with that?"

"Why not? A girl of that age has all sorts of changing interests and tastes; there will be something new every month or two, probably, for a long time yet."

In June, Mrs. Tracy demanded, "Is Owen Charrington one of your something-news?"

"I dare say he is," Mrs. North answered, smiling.

For Owen Charrington had come back from Australia. He found the zigzags which led to Belmonte very hot and very solitary; there was no Waddy going up or coming down, either on foot or in a carriage, although his ascents and descents had been as regular as those of the postman during the six preceding weeks. Shortly before Charrington's return, Dorothy, entering the boudoir one evening at ten o'clock, said:

"Mamma—Aunt Charlotte—will you tell the servants, please, that whenever Mr. Brunetti calls, after this, they are to say that we are engaged, or not at home? I don't suppose *you* care to see him?"

"What can have happened?" said Mrs. Tracy, when the girl had gone out again without explanation.

"There hasn't been time for much to happen. I have been out there with them all the evening; I only came in for my tea," answered Mrs. North, sipping that beverage.

"Since then he has been singing. At least, I thought I heard his voice—not very loud."

"Perhaps she is tired of his voice—not very loud."

Mrs. Tracy threw a lace scarf over her head and went out to the garden. The long aisles under the trees were flooded with moonlight, the air was perfumed with the fragrance of the many flowers; but there was no Dorothy. She entered the house by another door, and, going softly up the great stairway, turned towards Dorothy's rooms at the south end of the long villa. Here a light was visible, coming under the door of the sitting-room; the aunt did not lift the latch, she stood outside listening. Yes, Dorothy was there, and she was singing to herself in a low tone, playing the accompaniment with the soft pedal down:

> "Through the long days, the long days and the years,
>       What will my loved one be,
>       Parted from me, parted from me,
>   Through the long days and years?"

"She is up there singing; singing all alone," reported the aunt, when she came back to the boudoir down-stairs.

"I suppose you like that better than not alone?" suggested Mrs. North.

Waddy came to Belmonte five times without success. Then he left Florence.

Dorothy did not stroll in the garden with Owen Charrington. If her mother and aunt were outside when he came, she remained with them there; but if they were in the drawing-room or the boudoir, she immediately led her guest within; then she sat looking at him while he talked. Charrington talked well; all he said was amusing. Dorothy listened and laughed. If he paused, she urged him on again. This urgency of hers became so apparent that at last it embarrassed him. To carry it off he attacked her:

"You force me to chatter, Mrs. Mackenzie—to chatter like a parrot!"

"Yes," answered Dorothy, "you must talk; you must talk all the time."

"'All the time'—awfully funny Americanism!"

"And the French 'tout le temps'?"

"Oh, French; I don't know about French."

"Of course you don't. We are willing to be funny with the French. Are you 'very pleased' to be here to-day? Answer."

"Of course I am very pleased."

"And you would say, wouldn't you, 'Directly I returned to Florence, I bought a horse'?"

"But I didn't," said Charrington, laughing; "I only hired one. And that reminds me, Mrs. Mackenzie; you can't think how divine it is now at four o'clock in the morning. Won't you go for a ride at that hour some day soon? Mrs. North and Mrs. Tracy could follow in the carriage" (with a look towards those ladies).

"Ride?" repeated Dorothy. A flush rose in her cheeks. "No," she answered, in an altered voice—"no!"

She said nothing more, and she did not speak again; she sat looking at the floor. Mrs. North filled the pause with her placid sentences. But Dorothy's manner was so changed and constrained that the young Englishman soon went away. The girl had taken something into her head. But it would not last long; nothing ever did last long with Dorothy.

This belief of his was soon jostled by the fact that Dorothy would not see him. Mrs. North covered the refusal as well as she could by saying that her daughter was not well; that she was not seeing any visitors at present. But Florence was empty; there were no visitors to come; it simply meant, therefore, that she was not seeing Owen Charrington. He lingered on through the month, coming every day to Belmonte. Mrs. North received him graciously. But he was obliged to content himself with a close investigation of their plans for the summer. At last, on the 2d of July, unable any longer to endure the burning, glaring Lung' Arno and the furnace-like atmosphere of the Hôtel d'Italie, he took his departure. He went to Baden-Baden, writing home to his family that he should probably spend the summer in the Black Forest country with friends.

The morning after Charrington's departure, illness (real illness this time) seized Dorothy. For a week she remained motionless on a couch, her face white, her eyes closed.

"We must take her to Switzerland; we must go straight up to the snow," said Charlotte Tracy. "When she sees the glacier water she will revive at once. The gray glacier water, you know; one begins to meet it at Chiomonte; it comes rushing over the rocks, gray and cool, with sometimes a little foam; but gray, always gray—a sort of leady gray."

She said gray so many times that Mrs. North cried out at last, "Oh, do call it green!"

Speedy preparations were made for departure; the trunks were packed and sent down to the railway station. Dorothy remained passive, making no objection to their plans, but showing no interest in them. Caroline, her maid, dressed her for the journey. But when the little black bonnet with its long black veil had been put on, and the black gloves, and the young mistress of the house rose to walk to the carriage, after a few steps her figure swayed, and she sank to the floor; she had fainted. She remained unconscious for so long a time that it was evident there could be no travelling that day; they must wait until she was stronger. They waited, therefore, from one day to the next, each morning expecting to start, and each morning postponing departure. The 15th of July found them still at Belmonte. The thick stone walls of the majestic old house kept out the burning sunshine, and Dorothy appeared to like the warm air that came in through the shaded windows; she lay breathing it quietly, with her eyes closed. The American physician of Florence had gone to New York for six months. An English doctor came up daily. But there was nothing to combat. There was no fever, no malady save this sudden physical weakness. Everything possible was done for this, but with small results. At last Dr. Hotham advised them to attempt the journey in any case. A nurse was engaged; Dorothy was to be carried on a couch to the station, where a railway carriage, provided with an invalid's bed, was waiting. But before they had traversed a quarter of the length of the Via dei Serragli, the clatter of the carriage wheels and the other noises of the street threw the girl into a delirium, and they returned hastily to Bellosguardo. The delirium passed away and they made another attempt. This time they were to cross Florence in the middle of the night, and a special train was to take them northward. But the paroxysm came on again, and with greater violence. Before they reached the bottom of the Bellosguardo hill Dorothy threw up her arms like a wild creature; the nurse could scarcely hold her. This time high fever followed; the girl, now in bed, lay with scarlet cheeks and glassy eyes, knowing nobody. Dr. Hotham conquered the fever. Then she was as she had been before, save that the weakness was increased.

With the exception of Dr. Hotham, there was now no one in Florence whom they knew. Nora Sebright remained at St. Martin's Orphan House out in the country; but she knew nothing of events in town. One day Dr. Hotham, having been called to the orphan house to see a child, spoke to Nora of the puzzling illness of Mrs. Mackenzie; he knew that the Sebrights were among the acquaintances of these American ladies. Nora hurried to town, and, although it was evening, drove up to Belmonte without delay. There were now two nurses at the villa. But Nora was the best nurse; and, after seeing Dorothy for a moment, she begged the mother and aunt to allow her to remain and assist.

"You are extremely kind, Miss Sebright. But I do not think you ought to give yourself so much trouble," said Mrs. North. "Dorothy will soon be stronger; the fever, as you see, has entirely disappeared, and in a few days we shall go to Switzerland."

But Nora followed Mrs. Tracy into the next room. "Dear Mrs. Tracy, do let me stay. I am such a good nurse—you can't think. And I am so fond of Dorothy. And I really think she ought to be amused, if possible. Not that I am very amusing; but at least it makes one more."

There was no lamp in this room, but, all the same, Charlotte Tracy seemed to read an expression in the face she could not see. "What has Dr. Hotham said to you?" she asked.

"Indeed, nothing; he never talks. It is only that Dorothy has always been so well; she was well all winter, you know. Even now (for the fever was only the effort of the journey) there seems to be nothing one can take hold of. And so the question came up, as it always does in such a case, could she have anything weighing upon her mind—weighing too much, I mean? But I am sure," continued Nora, her voice calm as usual (but her face, in the darkness, quivering for an instant), "that we need apprehend no danger of that sort; Dorothy's mind is perfectly healthy. And she has been from the very first so brave, you know—so wonderfully brave."

Charlotte Tracy, a prey to conflicting feelings, bent and kissed Nora without a word. Grief for Alan Mackenzie had indeed been more deeply felt at the dreary orphan house down in the dusty valley than in his own home on this beautiful hill. Nora stayed.

August burned itself out. At Belmonte the heavy outer portals were kept closed; within, all the doors stood open in order to create, if possible, a current of air through the darkened rooms. Once in two hours, night and day, Nora came to Dorothy's bedside and offered some delicate nourishment; Dorothy took it unobjectingly. She seldom spoke, but she appeared to like Nora's presence and her gentle ministrations.

Mrs. Tracy had forced herself to speak to Laura about the doctor's question. Some force was necessary, for she was always exasperated by Laura's replies. "I am beginning to be a little frightened about Dorothy, Laura; she doesn't gain. It is no time to mince matters; such things have happened before, and will happen again as long as the world lasts, and it seems that even Dr. Hotham has asked whether there could be anything weighing upon her mind. Now what I want to know is, do you think she is brooding about something?"

"Brooding?"

"Yes. I mean, do you think she is interested in somebody? —Owen Charrington, if I must name him. You used to think that she liked him? And that she cannot bear the separation? Yet thinks it too soon? And that that was the reason she refused to see him again? And now it is weighing upon her?"

"Mercy, what theories! You have always saddled Dorothy with deeper feelings than she has ever possessed. Do leave the poor child alone; don't make her out so unusual and unpleasant; she is like any other girl of nineteen. She is interested in Owen—yes; but not in that exaggerated way; she isn't pining herself ill about him. And let me tell you, too, that if he were to her at this moment all you are imagining him to be, she wouldn't in the least be deterred by considerations of its being 'too soon,' as you call it; she would not even remember that it *was* soon."

Mrs. Tracy's eyes filled.

"Well, what now? Do you wish her to be breaking her heart for Alan? I thought you came in to suggest sending post-haste for Owen Charrington! Do you know really what you want yourself? Dorothy will grow stronger in time. A hot summer in Italy has pulled her down, but with the first cool weather she will revive, and then we can carry out our plans."

Towards the middle of September the rains came, the great heat ended. With the return of the fresh breeze Dorothy left her bed, and lay on the broad divan among its large, cool cushions; she even walked about the room a little, once or twice a day. The first time she walked they saw how thin she was; the black dressing-gown hung about her like a pall.

"Take it off," said Mrs. Tracy, when she had beckoned Caroline into the next room. "Never let her wear it again."

"But I have fear that madame is not enough strong yet to wear a costume," suggested the maid, respectfully.

Mrs. Tracy unlocked a wardrobe and took out a pile of folded draperies. They were white morning dresses, long and loose, covered with beautiful laces and knots of ribbon; they had formed part of Dorothy's trousseau. "Let her wear these," she said, briefly.

Dorothy made no objection to the change. Occasionally she looked at her new attire, and smoothed out the ribbons and lace. Throughout her illness she had scarcely spoken. They had supposed that this silence came from her weakness—the weakness which had made it an effort sometimes for her to lift her hand. But now that she was up again, and walking about the room, the muteness continued. She answered their questions, but it seemed necessary for her to recall her thoughts from some distant place in order to answer. She lived in a reverie, and her eyes had a far-off expression. But these were slight things. When ten days had slowly passed without any relapse, Charlotte Tracy, who had counted the hours, exclaimed, with joy, "Now we can go!" Dr. Hotham was to accompany them as far as Vevey. Nothing was to be said to Dorothy, in order that she should not have even a feather's weight of excitement; but the preparations were swiftly made. On the afternoon before the day appointed for the start, Dorothy suddenly left her easy-chair, crossed the room, opened a door, and looked down a corridor. At the end of the corridor she saw Caroline kneeling before open trunks.

"What are you doing, Caroline? Those are my trunks, aren't they? You may stop; I shall not leave Belmonte."

Nora, who had followed, led her back. "Your mother and aunt are so very anxious to go north, dear," she explained. "Come and lie down; you must not tire yourself before the journey."

But Dorothy resisted. "Please call them, Nora; call them both; I must tell them. I know mamma; she will have me carried. But that is because she does not understand. When I tell her, it will be different. Please call them both."

When they came in—Mrs. Tracy alarmed, Mrs. North smiling

as if prepared to be, outwardly, very indulgent—Dorothy was still standing in the centre of the room, the laces of her white dress fluttering in the soft breeze.

"Mamma," she said, "I must tell you. Aunt Charlotte, you have always been kind to me. I cannot go away; do not ask me."

"Sit down, Dorothy. Nora, make her sit down. You will not be asked to take a step, my daughter; everything is arranged; don't trouble yourself even to think."

"You do not understand, mamma. But I myself have not understood until lately. I cannot leave Belmonte."

"But Dr. Hotham thinks you can," interposed Mrs. Tracy, soothingly; "he knows how much strength you have. We are all going with you, and the journey will be very easy. You used to like Vevey."

"Let me stay here; I wish to stay here."

"But we have never intended to spend our lives at Bellosguardo," answered Mrs. North, drawing her towards the divan and making her sit down.

"Let me stay a little while longer, mamma."

"You mean that you will be willing to go later? But *we* think that now is the time. You have nothing to do save to rest here quietly, and then go to sleep; you will open your eyes in Vevey."

Dorothy, seated, her hands extended on her knees, looked up at her mother. "Mamma, you don't know. There's an ache that will not leave me. I haven't told you about it. But I'm *so* unhappy!"

Mrs. Tracy, hurrying forward, put her arm round the girl protectingly. Mrs. North, her face slightly flushed, whispered to Nora:

"She is wandering. Please go and send some one immediately for the doctor. Write a note for the man to take with him."

In this way she got rid of Nora.

Dorothy, alone with her mother and aunt, went on talking: "I didn't know what it meant myself for ever so long. But now I do, and it's all simple. I shall just stay quietly here. This is the best place. And you mustn't mind, for it makes *me* very happy."

"My darling, have you written? What do you mean?" asked Mrs. Tracy.

"What do I mean?" Dorothy repeated. She smiled; into her white face came a flush of color. "I mean that I shall see him very soon now. It won't be long to wait."

"She has sent for him," thought the aunt. "I was right; it is Owen."

"That is why I wish to stay here," Dorothy went on. "Everything here is associated with Alan; he liked Belmonte so much."

"Alan?" breathed the aunt, amazed, but instantly concealing her amazement. Mrs. North quickly measured some drops from a phial containing a sedative.

Dorothy let her head sink back against the cushions. "In the beginning I didn't in the least know that I was going to feel it so. But that ache came, and it wouldn't stop. I tried all sorts of things—don't you remember? I tried studying. I tried music lessons. He used to urge me to sing. He liked long walks, and I never would go; so then I took long walks. You haven't forgotten them, have you? But the ache went on, and I could not stand it. So I asked you to go to Paris. Paris has always been so funny and amusing. But it wasn't funny any more. When we came back here I thought that perhaps some one coming up every day and staying a long time would make me forget. But having Waddy was worse than being alone, and at last I hated him. Owen Charrington, too! Owen used to make me laugh; I thought he would make me laugh again. But he didn't at all. And when he asked me that last day to ride it was like a knife; for Alan always went with me, and would never say anything to spoil my pleasure. Yet he did not care about it really, though I insisted upon going day after day. That is the way it was about everything. But I'm paying for it now; I miss him so—I miss him so! Alan! Alan!—" And putting her thin hands over her face, Dorothy burst into miserable heart-broken sobs.

Nora came running in; Mrs. North handed her the medicine glass.

"Hysterics," she said. "Give her those drops as soon as you can."

"I look to you, doctor, to get us out of this new difficulty," said this lady the next day to Dr. Hotham. "She has taken this fixed idea that she does not wish to leave Belmonte. But the fixed idea of a girl of nineteen ought not to be a trouble

to you. Can't you suggest something? Has science no resources for such a case?"

Dr. Hotham's resource was to send to Rome for a colleague.
The most distinguished English physician in Italy was called to
Florence, and there was a consultation at Bellosguardo. When
it was over Mrs. North came in to see the great man.

His sentences were agreeable; they were also encouraging.
After a time he spoke of the varying forms of nervous prostration; then he asked whether this very interesting young lady
could have, by any possibility, something weighing upon her
mind?

"No, nothing," replied the mother.

"Ah! In that case time, I trust, is all that is necessary for a
complete recovery."

"My own idea would be to take her north in spite of her
disinclination to go," Mrs. North went on. "A disinclination
ought not to be important. The journey would soon be over.
She could be kept under the influence of sedatives. But Dr.
Hotham will not give his consent."

"I agree with him, madam. Do not force her; the effect upon
the nervous system might be bad. Let her do whatever she fancies. Amuse her. What a pity there is no Corney Grain in Italy!"

"Everything in the way of amusement has been tried. That is
why I wish to take her away."

"Ah! I understood you to say, I think, that there is no hidden
cause, no wish, no mental—ah—err—strain?"

"Nothing of any consequence. She is hysterical sometimes;
but that is owing to her physical weakness," Mrs. North answered. And she said what she believed.

A month later Dorothy, lying on a couch in her room, put
out her hand to Nora. "I must give you some of my money,
Nora, for your poor people—your orphans and the school and
the hospital. I will give it to you to-morrow."

"You can help Nora to distribute it," said Mrs. Tracy.

"Dear Aunt Charlotte, how you hate to hear me speak of
it! But I talk to Nora, you know, just as I please in the night."

"No; talk to me, too. Say whatever you like," answered Mrs.
Tracy, quickly.

"It is so warm this evening that I can have all the windows
open," Dorothy went on. "Take the lamp out, Nora, please,

and let in the moonlight; I like to see it shining across the floor." She lay in silence for some minutes looking at the radiance. They had cut off her hair, thinking that its length and thickness might be taking something from her small store of strength. Her face, with the boyish locks, looked very childlike. "Do you remember that song, Aunt Charlotte, 'Through the long days'? The moonlight makes me think of it. First, Felicia Philipps sang it one moonlight evening over at Villa Dorio. Then, after we were married, some one sang it here in the garden, and Alan said, when it was over— Oh, if I could only tell him once, just once, that I *did* love him! He never believed it—he never knew—"

"Don't cry, dear. *Don't.*"

"No; I don't cry very often now," Dorothy answered, her breast rising in one or two long sobs. "Last spring Waddy dared to sing that song again—Alan's song! I could not see him after that.

"Through the long days, the long days and the years—"

"It will tire you to sing, dear."

"No; I like it." And then, in a faint little thread of a voice, barely audible, but very sweet, she sang, lying there in the moonlight, the beautiful song:

"Through the long days, the long days and the years,
        What will my loved one be,
        Parted from me, parted from me,
    Through the long days and years?

"Never, ah, never on earth again—"

It was her last song. Three days later she died. She passed away so quietly that they did not know it was death; they thought she was asleep.

When at last they learned what it was, Mrs. North, standing beside the couch, white and stern, said, with rigid lips, "The doctors did not tell us."

But the doctors did not know.

# A Transplanted Boy

LORENZO came into the hall, bell in hand.

Putting down his white gloves at the feet of the goddess Flora, he began his promenade: ding-dong past Jupiter and Juno; ding-dong past Mars and Venus, Neptune and Diana, Minerva and Apollo, until the last pedestal on the east was reached; here there was no goddess, only a leaping flame. There was a corresponding tongue of fire on the last pedestal of the west side opposite, and both of these architectural ornaments were made of wood, painted scarlet. On the north side there towered six windows as high as those of a church. These windows faced a flight of stone steps that went down in a dignified sweep, eighteen feet wide, to a landing adorned with a Muse; here, dividing into two wings, the staircase turned to the right and the left in noble curves, and descended to the square hall below. The massive iron-clamped portals of this lower hall were open; they were swung back early in the morning, in order that the horses might pass through on their way to the street; for there were horses in the stables of the court-yard within. They did pass through, making with the carts to which they were harnessed a thundering clatter which would have deafened the inmates of an American dwelling. But the old Pisan palace had been built in another fashion. This lower hall with its heavy pavement and great doors, the gallery above with the rows of life-sized statues, the broad sweep of the stone stairways—all these, a space that could have swallowed many modern houses entire, were but its entrance; and so massive were the floors that no one in the long ranges of rooms above had any intimation of the moment when their hallway was turned into a street. The outer portals remained swung back all day; but the light inner doors were opened and closed on demand by old Bianca, the portress, who lived in a dusky den under the staircase. This evening the sunset was so brilliant that even these inner doors stood open, and Bianca herself had come to the threshold, blinking a little as the radiance fell upon her patient, cloistered face.

She was looking at a boy who was leaning over the parapet

opposite. This boy, with one arm round a small dog whom he had lifted to the top of the wall by his side, was gazing at the tawny water of the Arno as it glided past the house; for the old palace was in the Lung' Arno of Pisa, the sunny street that follows the river like a quay, its water-side lying open to the stream, protected by a low wall. Bianca was evidently thinking of this boy and the summons of the clanging bell above; whether he cared for the bell or not, he seemed to feel at last the power of her mild gaze directed upon his back, for, swinging himself down from the parapet, he crossed the street, and with his dog at his heels, entered the palace. He went up the right-hand stairway, glancing as he passed at the two stone caryatides which upheld the balustrade at the landing; these were girls who had probably been intended for mermaids; but their fish endings were vague compared with the vividly human expression of their anxious young countenances—an anxiety oddly insisted upon by the unknown house-sculptor who had chiselled them according to his fantasy hundreds of years before. Freshly arrived Americans, not yet broken in to the light foreign breakfast, and frozen from January to March, were accustomed to declare that the faces of these caryatides reflected in advance all the miseries of the *pension*, that is, all the hardship of winter life in Italy which assails the surprised and undefended pilgrim from the United States. But the boy who was coming up the stairs, though American, was not freshly arrived; in his mind the caryatides illustrated, more or less, a charming story which his mother had told him—the story of the Little Mermaid; he was fond of their anxious stone cheeks on that account.

The Casa Corti was not an ordinary *pension*. In the first place, it had the distinction of occupying the whole of the Rondinelli palace, with the great shield of the Rondinellis (showing their six heraldic swallows sitting on their tails) over its door; in the second, it had been in the hands of one family for four generations, and was to go down in the same line. The establishment could accommodate seventy persons. Three-fourths of the seventy were always English, drawn hither by the fact that Madame Corti was of English descent. A few Americans were allowed to enter, and an occasional foreigner was received as a favor. In the *pension* phraseology the English were "we," their transatlantic cousins "the Americans," and all the rest "foreigners." As Lorenzo's bell ceased many doors opened, and from the various quarters into which the old Ghibelline residence had for its present purposes been divided—from high rooms overlooking the river and adorned with frescos to low-browed cells in the attic under the eaves; from apartments that looked upon small inner courts like yellow wells, wells that resounded with the jingle of dish-washing from morning till night; from short staircases descending at unexpected points, and from others equally unlooked for which mounted from secret chambers in the half-story (chambers whose exact situation always remained a mystery to the rest of the house)—from all of these, and from two far-off little dwellings perched like tents on the roof, came the guests of the *pension* on their way to the dining-room and dinner. For they were all guests: the word patron or boarder was unknown. In the same way the head of the establishment was not by any means the boarding-house-keeper or the landlady: she was the proprietress. She had inherited her *pension* as other people inherit an estate, and she managed it in much the same autocratic fashion.

When all her guests were seated, this proprietress herself rustled in, a little late. Her attire was elaborate: a velvet gown made with a train, an amber star in the hair, and a chain of large amber beads wound three times round the throat, and falling in a long loop to the belt. She entered with a gliding step, pressing her dimpled hands together as she advanced, and giving a series of little bends from the waist upward, which were intended as general salutation to the company; her smile meanwhile gradually extended itself, until, as her chair was drawn out with a flourish by Lorenzo, it became broad enough to display her teeth as she sank gracefully into her place at the head of her table, and, with a final bow to the right and the left, unfolded her napkin. Her duty as regarded civility being now done, she broke off a morsel of bread, and took a rapid survey of her seventy, with the mixture of sharp personal dislike and the business views which forced her to accept them visible as usual in her eyes behind her smile.

Her seventy appeared, as they always did, eminently respectable. There were three English curates; there were English husbands and wives of the travelling and the invalid varieties; there were four or five blooming English girls with pink cheeks and very straight backs; and there were dozens of English old maids, and of that species of relict that returns naturally to spinsterhood after the funeral, without having acquired, from passing through it, any of the richer tints and more ample outlines that belong to the married state. In addition there were several Americans, and a few "foreigners."

Lorenzo and his assistants were carrying away the soup-plates when two more guests entered late. This was high crime. Madame's eyes, looking smaller than ever, gleamed like two sparks as they passed. For if one were so unfortunate as to be late for dinner at Casa Corti the custom was to make an apologetic little bow to madame as one entered—entered with hasty, repentant step (having passed, outside the door, the whole miscellaneous force of the establishment gathered together with cans of hot water to wash the forks). But these two had made no bow, and madame had known that they would not; so she talked to her right-hand neighbor, Captain Sholto Fraser, R.N., and carefully pretended not to see them. The delinquents were Americans (madame would have said "Of course!"), a pretty little woman who looked much younger than her age (which was thirty-three), and the boy who had adorned the parapet with his sprawling person—a mother and son. They found their empty chairs waiting for them at the far end of the room. The boy's place was at his mother's left hand; on her right she had one of the curates.

"Late again!" began this gentleman. "We shall have to impose a fine upon you, Mrs. Roscoe; we shall indeed." And he made, playfully, a menacing gesture with his large, very well kept hand.

"Ought I to come for the soup?" inquired the lady, surveying the plateful before her with a slight curl of her lip.

"Nay; when it is cold!" remonstrated her neighbor. "Be more reasonable, pray." He regarded her smilingly.

"Oh, reasonable women are horrid!" responded Mrs. Roscoe. "I should never think of coming down until later," she went on, "only Maso—he likes the soup." The boy was eating rapidly. She watched him for a moment. "I don't see how he can!" she added.

"Perhaps Tommaso is hungry," suggested an English lady who sat opposite.

"Maso, please," corrected Mrs. Roscoe; "Tommaso is as ugly as Thomas."

"I dare say he has not nourishment enough," continued the first speaker; "at his age that is so important. Why not order for him an extra chop at luncheon?"

"Thank Mrs. Goldsworthy for her interest in you, Maso," said his mother.

Maso grew red, and hastily crammed so much bread into his mouth that both of his cheeks were widely distended at the same time.

"I have read in the journal, Madame Roscoe, of a gerate fire in your countree—a town entire? I hope you lose not by it?" This inquirer was a grave little woman from Lausanne, the widow of a Swiss pastor.

Mrs. Roscoe gave a shrug. "My interests are not of that kind. Where was the fire, may I ask?"

"But in your countree, Amereekar. Voyons: the citee of Tam-Tampico."

Mrs. Roscoe laughed as she helped herself to fish—a fish tied with yellow ribbons, and carrying a yellow lily in his mouth. "When we were at Mentone an old lady informed me one day of the arrival of some of my 'countrypeople.' 'Now,' she said, 'you will not be the only Americans in the house.' At dinner they appeared. They were Chilians. I said to my friend, 'They are not my countrypeople; they are South Americans.' She answered, severely: 'I suppose you say that because they are Southerners! But now that so many years have passed since that dreadful war of yours was brought to a close, I should think it would be far wiser to drop such animosities.'" No one laughed over this story save an American who was within hearing.

This American, a Vermont man, had arrived at the *pension* several days before, and already he had formed a close and even desperate friendship with Mrs. Roscoe, pursuing her, accompanied by his depressed wife, to her bedroom (she had no sitting-room), where, while trying to find a level place on her slippery yellow sofa, he had delivered himself as follows: "Wife—she kept saying, 'You ought to go abroad; you aren't well, and it 'll do you good; they say it's very sociable over there if you stay at the *pensions*.'" (He gave this word a political pronunciation.)

"All I can say is—if *this* is their *pension*!" And he slapped his thigh with a resounding whack, and laughed sarcastically.

The beef now came round, a long slab of mahogany color, invisibly divided into thin slices, the whole decked with a thick dark sauce which contained currants, citron, and raisins.

"We miss Mr. Willoughby sadly," observed Mrs. Goldsworthy, with a sigh, as she detached a slice. "Only last night he was here."

"I cannot say *I* miss him," remarked Mrs. Roscoe.

"You do not? Pray tell us why?" suggested the curate, eagerly.

"Well, he's so black-letter; so early-English; so 'Merrily sungen the monks of Ely.' In Baedeker, you know."

"He is very deep, if you mean that," said Mrs. Goldsworthy, reprovingly.

"Deep? I should call him wide; he is all over the place. If you speak of a cat, he replies with a cataract; of a plate, with Plato; of the cream, with cremation. I don't see how he manages to live in England at all; there isn't standing-room there for his feet. But perhaps he soars; he is a sort of a Cupid, you know. What will become of him if they make him a bishop? For how can a bishop flirt? The utmost he can do is to say, 'I will see you after service in the vestry.'"

The curate was laughing in gentlemanlike gulps. He was extremely happy. The Rev. Algernon Willoughby, of Ely, had been admired, not to say adored, in that *pension* for seven long weeks.

The dinner went on through its courses, and by degrees the red wine flew from the glasses to the faces. For as wine of the country in abundance, without extra charge, was one of the attractions of Casa Corti, people took rather more of it than they cared for, on the thoroughly human principle of getting something for nothing. At length came a pudding, violently pink in hue, and reposing on a bed of rose-leaves.

"Why, the pudding's redder than we are!" remarked Mrs. Roscoe, with innocent surprise.

Her own cheeks, however, looked very cool in the universal flush; her smooth complexion had no rose tints. This lack of pink was, in truth, one of the faults of a face which had many beauties. She was small and fair; her delicately cut features were

extremely pretty—"pretty enough to be copied as models for
drawing-classes," some one had once said. Her golden hair,
which fell over her forehead in a soft, rippled wave, was drawn
up behind after the latest fashion of Paris; her eyes were blue,
and often they had a merry expression; her little mouth was
almost like that of a child, with its pretty lips and infantile,
pearly teeth. In addition, her figure was slender and graceful;
her hands and feet and ears were noticeably small. To men
Violet Roscoe's attire always appeared simple; the curate, for
instance, if obliged to bear witness, would have said that the
costume of each and every other lady in the room appeared
to him more ornamented than that of his immediate neighbor. A woman, however, could have told this misled male that
the apparently simple dress had cost more, probably, than the
combined attire of all the other ladies, save perhaps the rich
velvet of Madame Corti.

After nuts and figs, and a final draining of glasses, Madame
Corti gave the signal (no one would have dared to leave the
table before that sign), and her seventy rose. Smiling, talking,
and fanning themselves, they passed across the hall to the
salon, where presently tea was served in large gold-banded
coffee-cups, most of which were chipped at the edges. The
ladies took tea, and chatted with each other; they stood by the
piano, and walked up and down, before beginning the regular
occupations of the evening—namely, whist, chess, the reading
of the best authorities on art, or doing something in the way
of embroidery and wool-work, or a complicated construction
with bobbins that looked like a horse-net. There were jokes;
occasionally there was a ripple of mild laughter. Madame Corti,
intrenched behind her own particular table, read the London
*Times* with the aid of a long-handled eye-glass. How she did despise all these old maids, with their silver ornaments, and their
small economies, with their unmounted photographs pinned
on the walls of their bedrooms, and their talk of Benozzo, and
Nicolo the Pisan! She hated the very way they held their teacups after dinner, poised delicately, almost gayly, with the little
finger extended, as if to give an air of festal lightness to the
scene. Promptly at nine o'clock she disappeared; an hour later
her brougham was taking her to an Italian gathering, where
there would also be conversation, but conversation of a very

different nature. Teresa Corti, when she had escaped from her *pension*, was one of the wittiest women in Pisa; her wit was audacious, ample, and thoroughly Italian. There was, indeed, nothing English about her save her knowledge of the language, and the trace of descent from an English great-grandfather in her green eyes and crinkled yellow hair.

Mrs. Roscoe did not remain in the drawing-room five minutes; she never took tea, she did not play whist or chess, and she detested fancy-work. She was followed to the stairway by her curate, who was urging her to remain and play backgammon. "It's not such a bad game; really it's not," he pleaded, in his agreeable voice.

"Nothing is a bad game if one is amused," answered Mrs. Roscoe, severely. She was seldom severe. But this evening she was tired.

"Oh, how early you've come up! I'm awful glad," said Maso, as she entered her bedroom on the third floor. It was a large room, shabbily furnished in yellow, the frescoed walls representing the Bay of Naples. Maso was lying on the rug, with his dog by his side.

"Why are you in the dark?" said his mother. There was a smouldering fire on the hearth; for though the day had been fine (it was the 15th of March), the old palace had a way of developing unexpected shivers in the evening. In spite of these shivers, however, this was the only room where there was a fire. Mrs. Roscoe lighted the lamp and put on the pink shade; then she drew the small Italian sticks together on the hearth, threw on a dozen pine cones, and with the bellows blew the whole into a brilliant blaze. Next she put a key into the Bay of Naples, unlocked a wave, and drew out a small Vienna coffee-pot.

"Are we going to have coffee? Jolly!" said the boy.

His mother made the coffee; then she took from the same concealed cupboard, which had been drilled in the solid stone of the wall, a little glass jug shaped like a lachrymal from the catacombs, which contained cream; sugar in a bowl; cakes, and a box of marrons glacés. Maso gave a Hi! of delight as each dainty appeared, and made his dog sit on his hind legs. "I say, mother, what were they all laughing about at dinner? Something you said?"

"They always laugh; they appear never to have heard a joke

before. That about the bishops, now, that is as old as the hills."
Leaning back in her easy-chair before the fire, with Maso established at her feet, enjoying his cake and coffee, she gave a long
yawn. "Oh, what a stupid life!"

Maso was well accustomed to this exclamation. But when he
had his mother to himself, and when the room was so bright
and so full of fragrant aromas, he saw no reason to echo it.
"Well, *I* think it's just gay!" he answered. "Mr. Tiber, beg!"
Mr. Tiber begged, and received a morsel of cake.

Mrs. Roscoe, after drinking her coffee, had taken up a new
novel. "Perhaps you had better study a little," she suggested.

Maso made a grimace. But as the coffee was gone and the
cakes were eaten, he complied—that is, he complied after he
had made Mr. Tiber go through his tricks. This took time; for
Mr. Tiber, having swallowed a good deal of cake himself, was
lazy. At last, after he had been persuaded to show to the world
the excellent education he had received, his master decided to
go on with his own, and went to get his books, which were
on the shelf at the other end of the long room. It pleased him
to make this little journey on his heels, with his toes sharply
upturned in the air—a feat which required much balancing.

"That is the way you run down the heels of your shoes so,"
his mother remarked, glancing at his contortions.

"It doesn't hurt them much on the *carpet*," replied the boy.

"Mercy! You don't go staggering through the streets in that
way, do you?"

"Only back streets."

He was now returning in the same obstructed manner, carrying his books. He placed them upon the table where the
lamp was standing; then he lifted Mr. Tiber to the top of the
same table and made him lie down; next, seating himself, he
opened a battered school-book, a United States History, and,
after looking at the pictures for a while, he began at last to
repeat two dates to himself in a singsong whisper. Maso was
passing through the period when a boy can be very plain, even
hideous, in appearance, without any perception of the fact in
the minds of his relatives, who see in him the little toddler still,
or else the future man; other persons, however, are apt to see a
creature all hands and feet, with a big uncertain mouth and an
omnipresent awkwardness. Maso, in addition to this, was short

and ill developed, with inexpressive eyes and many large freckles. His features were not well cut; his complexion was pale; his straight hair was of a reddish hue. None of the mother's beauties were repeated in the child. Such as he was, however, she loved him, and he repaid her love by a deep adoration; to him, besides being "mother," she was the most beautiful being in the whole world, and also the cleverest. He was intensely proud of the admiration she excited, and was always on the watch for it; at the table, awkward, constrained, with downcast eyes, he yet saw every glance that was directed towards her, and enjoyed each laugh which her words created. Mrs. Roscoe's purse was a light one; worse than that, an uncertain one; but Maso, personally, had known nothing but indulgence and ease all his life.

While he was vaguely murmuring his dates, and rocking himself backward and forward in time with the murmur, there came a tap at the door. It was Miss Spring. "I have looked in to bid you good-bye," she said, entering. "I am going to Munich to-morrow."

"Isn't that sudden?" said Mrs. Roscoe. "The torn chair is the most comfortable. Have a marron?"

"Thank you; I seldom eat sweets. No, it is not sudden."

"Shall I make you a cup of coffee?"

"Thank you; I don't take coffee."

Mrs. Roscoe pushed a footstool across the rug.

"Thank you; I never need footstools."

"Superior to all the delights of womankind!"

Miss Spring came out of her abstraction and laughed. "Not superior; only bilious and long-legged." Then her face grew grave again. "Do you consider Pisa an attractive place for a permanent residence?" she inquired, fixing her eyes upon her hostess, who, having offered all the hospitable attentions in her power, was now leaning back again, her feet on a hassock.

"Attractive? Heavens! no."

"Yet you stay here? I think I have seen you here, at intervals, for something like seven years?"

"Don't count them; I hate the sound," said Mrs. Roscoe. "My wish is—my hope is—to live in Paris. I get there once in a while, and then I always have to give it up and come away. Italy is cheap, and Pisa is the cheapest place in Italy."

"So that is your reason for remaining," said Miss Spring, reflectively.

"What other reason on earth *could* there be?"

"The equable climate."

"I hate equable climates. No, we're not here for climates. Nor for Benozzo; nor for Nicolo the Pisan, and that everlasting old sarcophagus that they are always talking about; nor for the Leaning Tower, either. I perfectly hate the Leaning Tower!"

Miss Spring now undertook a joke herself. "It is for the moderns, then. You are evidently a Shelley worshipper."

"Do I look like one?" demanded Violet Roscoe, extending her arms a little, with the palms of the hands displayed, as if to call attention to her entire person.

"I cannot say that you do," replied Miss Spring, after surveying her. "I should think New York would please you as a place of residence," she went on, after a moment. "If you do not like Italy, why do you not go home?"

"Why don't you?" retorted Violet, taking a marron and crunching it.

"Well answered. But Newburyport is not to me what I should think New York might be to you; Newburyport has much to learn. However, we all have our reasons, I suppose."

"Mine are not mysterious," said Violet, continuing to crunch. "I have a better time abroad than I do at home; that's all."

Miss Spring gazed at the fire. "I may as well acknowledge that it was those very things that brought me here in the beginning, the things you don't care for; Nicolo and the revival of sculpture; the early masters. But I have not found them satisfying. I have tried to care for that sarcophagus; but the truth is that I remain perfectly cold before it. And the Campo Santo frescos seem to me out of drawing. As to the Shelley memories, do you know what I thought of the other day? Suppose that Shelley and Byron were residing here at this moment—Shelley with that queerness about his first wife hanging over him, and Byron living as we know he lived in the Toscanelli palace—do you think that these ladies in the *pension* who now sketch the Toscanelli and sketch Shelley's windows, who go to Lerici and rave over Casa Magni, who make pilgrimages to the very spot on the beach where Byron and Trelawny built the funeral pyre

—do you think that a single one of them would call, if it were to-day, upon Mary Shelley? Or like to have Shelley and Byron dropping in here for afternoon tea, with the chance of meeting the curates?"

"If they met them, they couldn't out-talk them," answered Violet, laughing. "Curates always want to explain something they said the day before. As to the calling and the tea, what would *you* do?"

"I should be consistent," responded Miss Spring, with dignity. "I should call. And I should be happy to see them here in return."

"Well, you'd be safe," said Violet. "Shelley, Byron, Trelawny, all together, would never dare to flirt with Roberta Spring!" She could say this without malice, for her visitor was undeniably a handsome woman.

Miss Spring, meanwhile, had risen; going to the table, she put on her glasses and bent over Maso's book. "History?"

"Yes, 'm. I haven't got very far yet," Maso answered.

"Reader. Copy-book. Geography. Spelling-book. Arithmetic," said Miss Spring, turning the books over one by one. "The Arithmetic appears to be the cleanest."

"Disuse," said Mrs. Roscoe, from her easy-chair. "As I am Maso's teacher, and as I hate arithmetic, we have never gone very far. I don't know what we shall do when we get to fractions!"

"And what is your dog doing on the table, may I ask?" inquired the visitor, surveying Mr. Tiber coldly.

"Oh, he helps lots. I couldn't study at all without him," explained Maso, with eagerness.

"Indeed?" said Miss Spring, turning the gaze of her glasses from the dog to his master. "How's that?"

Maso was always rather afraid of the tall Roberta; he curled the pages of his History with stubby fingers and made no reply.

"If you won't tell, Maso, I shall," said his mother; "I shall do it to make you ashamed of your baby ways. He divides each lesson, Miss Spring, into four parts, if you please; then, as each part is learned (or supposed to be learned), Mr. Tiber has to sit on his hind legs and wave a paw. Then, when all four parts are done, Mr. Tiber has to lie on the book. Book after book is added to the pile, and finally Mr. Tiber is on top of a monument. But he is so used to it that he does not mind it much. After the last lesson is learned, then Mr. Tiber, as a celebration, has to go through all the tricks. And there are twenty-two."

"Well!" said Miss Spring. She never could comprehend what she called "all this dog business" of the Roscoes. And their dog language (they had one) routed her completely. "Twenty-two!"

"An' *gherry* kinnin, idn't they?" Maso was whispering to his pet.

"Why did you name him Mr. Tiber?" pursued the visitor, in her grave voice.

"We didn't; he was already named," explained Mrs. Roscoe. "We bought him of an old lady in Rome, who had three; she had named them after Italian rivers: Mr. Arno, Mr. Tiber, and Miss Dora Riparia."

"Miss Dora Riparia—well!" said Miss Spring. Then she turned to subjects more within her comprehension. "It is a pity I am going away, Maso, for I could have taught you arithmetic; I like to teach arithmetic."

Maso made no answer save an imbecile grin. His mother gesticulated at him behind Miss Spring's back. Then he muttered, "Thank you, 'm," hoping fervently that the Munich plan was secure.

"I shall get a tutor for Maso before long," remarked Mrs. Roscoe, as Miss Spring came back to the fire. "Later, my idea is to have him go to Oxford."

Miss Spring looked as though she were uttering, mentally, another "well!" The lack of agreement in the various statements of her pretty little countrywoman always puzzled her; she could understand crime better than inconsistency.

"Shall you stay long in Munich?" Violet inquired.

"That depends." Miss Spring had not seated herself. "Would you mind coming to my room for a few minutes?" she added.

"There's no fire; I shall freeze to death!" thought Violet. "If you like," she answered aloud. And together they ascended to the upper story, where, at the top of two unexpected steps, was Miss Spring's door. This door was adorned with a large solidly fastened brass door-plate, bearing, in old-fashioned script, the name "Archibald Starr." No one in the house, not even

Madame Corti herself, had any idea who Archibald Starr had been in the flesh. At present he was nothing but a door-plate. His apartment within had been divided by partitions, so that his sitting-room was now a rain-water tank. Roberta Spring occupied his vestibule. The vestibule was small and bare; in the daytime it was lighted by two little windows, so high in the wall that they were opened and closed by means of long cords. A trunk, locked and strapped, stood in the centre of the floor; an open travelling-bag, placed on a chair, gaped for the toilet articles, which were ranged on the table together, so that nothing should be forgotten at the early morning start —a cheap hairbrush and stout comb, an unadorned wooden box containing hair-pins and a scissors, a particularly hideous travelling pin-cushion. Violet Roscoe gazed at these articles, fascinated by their ugliness; she herself possessed a long row of vials and brushes, boxes and mirrors, of silver, crystal, and ivory, and believed that she could not live without them.

"I thought I would not go into the subject before Maso," began Miss Spring, as she closed her door. "Such explanations sometimes unsettle a boy; his may not be a mind to which inquiry is necessary. My visit to Munich has an object. I am going to study music."

"Music?" repeated Mrs. Roscoe, surprised. "I didn't know you cared for it."

"But it remains to be seen whether I care, doesn't it? One cannot tell until one has tried. This is the case: I am now thirty-seven years of age. I have given a good deal of attention to astronomy and to mathematics; I am an evolutionist, a real-ist, a member of the Society for Psychical Research; Herbert Spencer's works always travel with me. These studies have been extremely interesting. And yet I find that I am not fully sat-isfied, Mrs. Roscoe. And it has been a disappointment. I am determined, therefore, to try some of those intellectual influ-ences which do not appeal solely to reason. They appear to give pleasure to large numbers of mankind, so there must be something in them. What that is I resolved to find out. I be-gan with sculpture. Then painting. But they have given me no pleasure whatever. Music is third on the list. So now I am going to try that."

Mrs. Roscoe gave a spring, and seated herself on the bed with her feet under her, Turkish fashion; the floor was really too cold. "No use trying music unless you like it," she said.

"I have never *dis*liked it. My attitude will be that of an impartial investigator," explained Miss Spring. "I have, of course, no expectation of becoming a performer; but I shall study the theory of harmony, the science of musical composition, its structure—"

"Structure! Stuff! You've got to *feel* it," said Violet.

"Very well. I am perfectly willing to feel; that is, in fact, what I wish—let them *make* me feel. If it is an affair of the emotions, let them rouse *my* emotions," answered Roberta.

"If you would swallow a marron occasionally, and drink a cup of good coffee with cream; if you would have some ivory brushes and crystal scent-bottles, instead of those hideous objects," said Violet, glancing towards the table; "if you would get some pretty dresses once in a while—I think satisfaction would be nearer."

Miss Spring looked up quickly. "You think I have been too ascetic? Is that what you mean?"

"Oh, I never mean anything," answered Violet, hugging herself to keep down a shiver.

"In spite of your disclaimer, I catch your idea," replied her hostess. "But if I should carry it out, Mrs. Roscoe, carry it out to its full extent, it would take me, you know, very far—into complex dissipations."

Her voice took on no animation as she said this; it remained calm, as it always was. She was a tall woman with regular features, a clear white complexion, and striking gray eyes with long dark lashes; her abundant dark hair was drawn straight back from her face, and she carried her head remarkably well. She was what is called "fine-looking," but from head to foot, though probably she did not know it, her appearance was austere.

Violet had given way to irresistible laughter over the "complex dissipations." Miss Spring came out of what appeared to be a mental census of the various debaucheries that would be required, and laughed a little herself. She was not without a sense of humor. "To you it seems funny, no doubt," she said, "for I have never been at all gay. Yet I think I could manage it."

Violet, still laughing, climbed down from the bed; she was too cold to stay longer.

"I knew I should get a new idea out of you, Mrs. Roscoe. I always do," said Roberta, frankly. "And this time it is an important one; it is a side-light which I had not thought of myself at all. I shall go to Munich to-morrow. But I will add this: if music is not a success, perhaps I may some time try your plan."

"Plan? Horrible! I haven't any," said Violet, escaping towards the door.

"It is an unconscious one; it is, possibly, instinctive truth," said Miss Spring, as she shook hands with her departing guest. "And instinctive truth is the most valuable."

Violet ran back to her own warm quarters. "You don't mean to say, Maso, that you've stopped studying already?" she said, as she entered and seated herself before her fire again, with a sigh of content. "Nice lessons you'll have for me to-morrow."

"They're all O. K.," responded the boy. He had his paint-box before him, and was painting the Indians in his History.

"Well, go to bed, then."

"Yes, 'm."

At half-past ten, happening to turn her head while she cut open the pages of her novel, she saw that he was still there. "Maso, do you hear me? Go to bed."

"Yes, 'm." He painted faster, making hideous grimaces with his protruded lips, which unconsciously followed the strokes of his brush up and down. The picture finished at last, he rose. "Mr. Tiber, pim."

Mr. Tiber left the sofa, where he had been sleeping since the termination of the lessons, and hopped to the floor. Here he indulged in a stretch; first, hind legs; then fore legs; then a hunch of his back and a deep yawn. He was a very small black-and-tan terrier, with a pretty little head and face. Maso's voice now gave a second summons from his bedroom, which was next to his mother's, with a door between. "Are you coming, Mr. Tiber? *Very* well!" Mr. Tiber, hearing this, ran as fast as he could scamper into his master's chamber. Here he had his own bed, composed of a flat basket containing what Maso called "a really mattress," and a pillow with a pillow-case, a blanket, and red coverlid, each article bearing an embroidered T in the corner, surmounted by a coronet; for Mr. Tiber was supposed to be a nobleman. The nobleman went to bed, and was tucked in with his head on the pillow. This was Maso's rule; but very soon the head assumed its normal position, curled round on the little black tail.

At eleven, Mrs. Roscoe finished her novel and threw it down. "Women who write don't know much about love-affairs," was her reflection. "And those of us who have love-affairs don't write!" She rose. "Maso, you here still? I thought you went to bed an hour ago!"

"Well, I did begin. I put my shoes outside." He extended his shoeless feet in proof. "Then I just came back for a minute."

His mother looked over his shoulder. "That same old fairy-book! Who would suppose you were twelve years old?"

"Thirteen," said Maso, coloring.

"So you are. But only two weeks ago. Never mind; you'll be a tall man yet—a great big thing striding about, whom I shall not care half so much for as I do for my little boy." She kissed him. "All your father's family are tall, and you look just like them."

Maso nestled closer as she stood beside him. "How did father look? I don't remember him much."

"Much? You don't remember him at all; he died when you were six months old—a little teenty baby."

"I say, mother, how long have we been over here?"

"I came abroad when you were not quite two."

"Aren't we ever going back?"

"If you could once see Coesville!" was Mrs. Roscoe's emphatic reply.

II

"Hist, Maso! Take this in to your lady mother," said Giulio. "I made it myself, so it's good." Giulio, one of the dining-room waiters at Casa Corti, was devoted to the Roscoes. Though he was master of a mysterious French polyglot, he used at present his own tongue, for Maso spoke Italian as readily as he did, and in much the same fashion.

Maso took the cup, and Giulio disappeared. As the boy was carrying the broth carefully towards his mother's door, Madame Corti passed him. She paused.

"Ah, Master Roscoe, I am relieved to learn that your mother is better. Will you tell her, with my compliments, that I advise her to go at once to the Bagni to make her recovery. She ought to go to-morrow. That is the air required for convalescence."

Maso repeated this to his mother. "'That is the air required for convalescence,' she said."

"And 'this is the room required for spring tourists,' she meant. Did she name a day—the angel?"

"Well, she did say to-morrow," Maso admitted.

"Old cat! She is dying to turn me out; she is so dreadfully afraid that the word fever will hurt her house. All the servants are sworn to call it rheumatism."

"See here, mother, Giulio sent you this."

"I don't want any of their messes."

"But he made it himself, so it's good." He knelt down beside her sofa, holding up the cup coaxingly.

"Beef-tea," said Mrs. Roscoe, drawing down her upper lip. But she took a little to please him.

"Just a little more."

She took more.

"A little *teenty* more."

"You scamp! You think it's great fun to give directions, don't you?"

Maso, who had put the emptied cup back on the table, gave a leap of glee because she had taken so much.

"Don't walk on your hands," said his mother, in alarm. "It makes me too nervous."

It was the 12th of April, and she had been ill two weeks. An attack of bronchitis had prostrated her suddenly, and the bronchitis had been followed by an intermittent fever, which left her weak.

"I say, mother, let's go," said Maso. "It's so nice at the Bagni —all trees and everything. Miss Anderson 'll come and pack."

Miss Anderson was one of Dr. Prior's nurses. She had taken charge of Mrs. Roscoe during the worst days of her illness.

"If we do go to the Bagni we cannot stay at the hotel," said Mrs. Roscoe, gloomily. "This year we shall have to find some cheaper place. I have been counting upon money from home that hasn't come."

"But it *will* come," said Maso, with confidence.

"Have you much acquaintance with Reuben John?"

The tone of voice, bitterly sarcastic, in which his mother had from his earliest remembrance pronounced this name, had made the syllables eminently disagreeable to Maso. He had no very clear idea as to the identity of Reuben John, save that he was some sort of a dreadful relative in America.

"Well, the Bagni's nice," he answered, "no matter where we stay. And I know Miss Anderson 'll come and pack."

"You mustn't say a word to her about it. I have got to write a note, as it is, and ask her to wait for her money until winter. Dr. Prior, too."

"Well, they'll do it; they'll do it in a minute, and be glad to," said Maso, still confident.

"I am sure I don't know why," commented his mother, turning her head upon the pillow fretfully.

"Why, mother, they'll do it because it's you. They think everything of you; everybody does," said the boy, adoringly.

Violet Roscoe laughed. It took but little to cheer her. "If you don't brush your hair more carefully they won't think much of *you*," she answered, setting his collar straight.

There was a knock at the door. "Letters," said Maso, returning. He brought her a large envelope, adorned with Italian superlatives of honor and closed with a red seal. "Always so civil," murmured Mrs. Roscoe, examining the decorated address with a pleased smile. Her letters came to a Pisan bank; the bankers re-enclosed them in this elaborate way, and sent them to her by their own gilt-buttoned messenger. There was only one letter to-day. She opened it, read the first page, turned the leaf, and then in her weakness she began to sob. Maso in great distress knelt beside her; he put his arm round her neck, and laid his cheek to hers; he did everything he could think of to comfort her. Mr. Tiber, who had been lying at her feet, walked up her back and gave an affectionate lick to her hair. "Mercy! the dog, too," she said, drying her eyes. "*Of course* it was Reuben John," she explained, shaking up her pillow.

Maso picked up the fallen letter.

"Don't read it; burn it—horrid thing!" his mother commanded.

He obeyed, striking a match and lighting the edge of the page.

"Not only no money, but in its place a long, hateful, busy-bodying sermon," continued Mrs. Roscoe, indignantly.

Maso came back from the hearth, and took up the envelope. "Mrs. Thomas R. Coe," he read aloud. "Is our name really Coe, mother?"

"You know it is perfectly well."

"Everybody says Roscoe."

"*I* didn't get it up; all I did was to call myself Mrs. Ross Coe, which is my name, isn't it? I hate Thomas. Then these English got hold of it and made it Ross-Coe and Roscoe. I grew tired of correcting them long ago."

"Then in America I should be Thom-as Ross Coe—Thom-as R. Coe," pursued the boy, still scanning the envelope, and pronouncing the syllables slowly. He was more familiar with Italian names than with American.

"No such luck. Tommy Coe you'd be now. And as you grew older, Tom Coe—like your father before you."

They went to the Bagni—that is, to the baths of Lucca. The journey, short as it was, tired Mrs. Roscoe greatly. They took up their abode in two small rooms in an Italian house which had an unswept stairway and a constantly open door. These quarters did not depress Violet; she had no strongly marked domestic tastes; she was indifferent as to her lodging, provided her clothes were delicately fresh and pretty. But her inability to go out to dinner took away her courage. She had intended to dine at the hotel where they had stayed in former years; for two or three hours each day she could then be herself. But after one or two attempts she was obliged to give up the plan; she had not the strength to take the daily walk. It ended in food being sent in from a neighboring cook-shop, or *trattoria*, and served upon her bedroom table. Maso, disturbed by her illness, but by nothing else—for they had often followed a nomadic life for a while when funds were low—scoured the town. He bought cakes and fruit to tempt her appetite; he made coffee. He had no conception that these things were not proper food for a convalescent; his mother had always lived upon coffee and sweets.

On the first day of May, when they had been following this course for two weeks, they had a visitor. Dr. Prior, who had been called to the Bagni for a day, came to have a look at his former patient. He stayed fifteen minutes. When he took leave he asked Maso to show him the way to a certain house. This, however, was but a pretext, for when they reached the street he stopped.

"I dare say ye have friends here?"

"Well," answered Maso, "mother generally knows a good many of the people in the hotel when we are staying there. But this year we ain't."

"Hum! And where are your relatives?"

"I don't know as we've got any. Yes, there's one," pursued Maso, remembering Reuben John. "But he's in America."

The Scotch physician, who was by no means an amiable man, was bluntly honest. "How old are you?" he inquired.

"I'm going on fourteen."

"Never should have supposed ye to be more than eleven. As there appears to be no one else, I must speak to you. Your mother must not stay in this house a day longer; she must have a better place—better air and better food."

Maso's heart gave a great throb. "Is she—is she very ill?"

"Not yet. But she is in a bad way; she coughs. She ought to leave Italy for a while; stay out of it for at least four months. If she doesn't care to go far, Aix-les-Bains would do. Speak to her about it. I fancy ye can arrange it—hey? American boys have their own way, I hear." This was meant as a joke; but as the grim face did not smile, the jocular intention failed to make itself apparent. The speaker nodded, and went down the street. The idea that Mrs. Roscoe might not have money enough to indulge herself with a journey to Aix-les-Bains, or to anywhere else, would never have occurred to him. He had seen her in Pisa off and on for years, one of the prettiest women there, and perhaps the most perfectly equipped as regarded what he called "furbelows"; that, with all her costly finery, she chose to stay in a high-up room at Casa Corti instead of having an apartment of her own, with the proper servants, was only another of those American eccentricities to which, after a long professional life in Italy, he was now well accustomed.

Maso went back to his mother's room with his heart in his mouth. When he came in she was asleep; her face looked wan. The boy, cold all over with the new fear, sat down quietly by the window with Mr. Tiber on his lap, and fell into anxious thought. After a while his mother woke. The greasy dinner, packed in greasy tins, came and went. When the room was quiet again he began, tremulously, "How much money have we got, mother?"

"Precious little."

"Mayn't I see how much it is?"

"No; don't bother."

She had eaten nothing.

"Mother, won't you please take that money, even if it's little, and go straight off north somewhere? To Aix-les-Bains."

"What are you talking about? Aix-les-Bains? What do you know of Aix-les-Bains?"

"Well, I've heard about it. Say, mother, do go. And Mr. Tiber and me 'll stay here. We'll have lots of fun," added the boy, bravely.

"Is that all you care about me?" demanded his mother. Then seeing his face change, "Come here, you silly child," she said. She made him sit down on the rug beside her sofa. "We must sink or swim together, Maso (dear me! we're not much in the swim now); we can't go anywhere, either of us; we can only just manage to live as we're living now. And there won't be any more money until November." She stroked his hair caressingly. His new fear made him notice how thin her wrist had grown.

### III

"You will mail these three letters immediately," said Mr. Water-house, in Italian, to the hotel porter.

"Si, signore," answered the man, with the national sunny smile, although Waterhouse's final gratuity had been but a franc.

"Now, Tommaso, I must be off; long drive. Sorry it has happened so. Crazy idea her coming at all, as she has enjoyed bad health for years, poor old thing! She may be dead at this moment, and probably, in fact, she *is* dead; but I shall have to go, all the same, in spite of the great expense; she ought to have thought of that. I have explained everything to your mother in that letter; the money is at her own bank in Pisa, and I have sent her the receipt. You have fifty francs with you?"

"Yes, sir."

"Fifty francs—that is ten dollars. More than enough, much more; be careful of it, Tommaso. You will hear from your mother in two days, or sooner, if she telegraphs; in the meanwhile you will stay quietly where you are."

"Yes, sir."

Mr. Waterhouse shook hands with his pupil, and, stepping into the waiting carriage, was driven away.

Benjamin F. Waterhouse, as he signed himself (of course the full name was Benjamin Franklin), was an American who had lived in Europe for nearly half a century, always expecting to go home "next summer." He was very tall, with a face that resembled a damaged portrait of Emerson, and he had been engaged for many years in writing a great work, a Life of Christopher Columbus, which was to supersede all other Lives. As his purse was a light one, he occasionally took pupils, and it was in this way that he had taken Maso, or, as he called him (giving him all the syllables of the Italian Thomas), Tommaso. Only three weeks, however, of his tutorship had passed when he had received a letter announcing that his sister, his only remaining relative, despairing of his return, was coming abroad to see him, in spite of her age and infirmities; she was the "poor old thing" of her dry brother's description, and the voyage apparently had been too great an exertion, for she was lying dangerously ill at Liverpool, and the physician in attendance had telegraphed to Waterhouse to come immediately.

The history of the tutorship was as follows: Money had come from America, after all. Mrs. Roscoe (as everybody called her) had been trying for some time, so she told Maso, "to circumvent Reuben John," and sell a piece of land which she owned in Indiana. Now, unexpectedly, a purchaser had turned up. While she was relating this it seemed to her that her little boy changed into a young man before her eyes. "You've just got to take that money, mother, and go straight up to Aix-les-Bains," said Maso, planting himself before her. "I sha'n't go a single step; I ain't sick, and you are; it's cheaper for me to stay here. There isn't money enough to take us both, for I want you to stay up there *ever* so long—four whole months."

This was the first of many discussions, or rather of astonished exclamations from the mother, met by a stubborn and at last a silent obstinacy on the part of the boy. For of late he had scarcely slept, he had been so anxious; he had discovered that the people in the house, with the usual Italian dread of a cough, believed that "the beautiful little American," as they called his mother, was doomed. Mother and son had never been separated; the mother shed tears over the idea of a separation now; and then a few more because Maso did not "care." "It doesn't seem to be anything to *you*," she declared, reproachfully.

But Maso, grim-faced and wretched, held firm.

In this dead-lock, Mrs. Roscoe at last had the inspiration of asking Benjamin Waterhouse, who was spending the summer at the Bagni, and whom she knew to be a frugal man, to take charge of Maso during her absence. Maso, who under other circumstances would have fought the idea of a tutor with all his strength, now yielded without a word. And then the mother, unwillingly and in a flood of tears, departed. She went by slow stages to Aix-les-Bains; even her first letter, however, much more the later ones, exhaled from each line her pleasure in the cooler air and in her returning health. She sent to Maso, after a while, a colored photograph of herself, taken on the shore of Lake Bourget, and the picture was to the lonely boy the most precious thing he had ever possessed; for it showed that the alarming languor had gone; she was no longer thin and wan. He carried the photograph with him, and when he was alone he took it out. For he was suffering from the deepest pangs of homesickness. He was homesick for his mother, for his mother's room (the only home he had ever known), with all its attractions and indulgences; he could always play his games there; she was never tired of them nor of the noise and disorder which they might occasion; she was never tired of Mr. Tiber; she was never tired of Indians and war-whoops, nor of tents made of her shawls. She always petted him and made much of him; she was so little serious herself that she had unconsciously kept him childlike; in many things they had been like two children together. In the life they led he had but small opportunity to make friendships with other lads. He had played with the American boys of his age whom he had met here and there, but they were always travellers; they never stayed long. His only comrade had been a lad in Pisa named Luigi. But even Luigi could not play games half as well as his mother could, nor live in the tent half as satisfactorily. He said nothing of his home-sickness to his tutor; Waterhouse thought him a dull, hangdog sort of boy, and also a boy incredibly, monstrously ignorant. "What can that feather-brained little woman have been about not to have sent him to school long ago!" was his thought.

But now Maso was left alone, not only schoolless but tutor-less. When the carriage bearing the biographer of Columbus had disappeared down the road leading to Lucca, the boy went back to the porter, who, wearing his stiff official cap adorned with the name of the hotel, stood airing his corpulent person in the doorway. "Say, Gregorio, I'll take those letters to the post-office if you like; I'm going right by there."

Gregorio liked Maso; all Italian servants liked the boy and his clever dog. In addition, the sunshine was hot, and Gregorio was not fond of pedestrian exercise; so he gave the letters to Maso willingly enough. Maso went briskly to the post-office. Here he put two of the letters into the box, but the third, which bore his mother's address, remained hidden under his jacket. Returning to the hotel, he went up to his room, placed this letter in his trunk, and locked the trunk carefully; then, accompanied by Mr. Tiber, he went off for a walk. The change had been so sudden that he had hardly had time to think; the telegram to Mr. Waterhouse had come only the day before, and until its arrival he had supposed that his life was definitely arranged for several months. Now, suddenly, everything was upheaved. After walking a mile, he sat down in a shady place and took off his hat. His thoughts ran something as follows: "'T any rate, mother sha'n't know; *that's* settled; I ain't going to let her come back here and get sick again; no, sir! She's getting all well up there, and she's *got* to stay four whole months. There's no way she can hear that old Longlegs" (this was his name for the historical Benja-min) "has gone, now that I've hooked his letter. The people she knows here at the Bagni never write; besides, they don't know where she's staying, and I won't let 'em know. If they see me here alone they'll suppose Longlegs has arranged it. I've got to tell lies some; I've got to pretend, when I write to her, that Longlegs has sprained his wrist or his leg or something, and that's why he can't write himself. I've got to be awful careful about what I put in my letters, so that they'll sound all right; but I guess I can do it bully. And I'll spend mighty little (only I'm going to have ices); I'll quit the hotel, and go back to that house where we stayed before the money came. I've got fifty francs—that's lots; when that's gone, I'll go down to Pisa and get some more; they know me at the bank; I've been there with mother; they'll give me some. But I won't take much. Then, as old Longlegs hasn't got to be paid, there'll be stacks left when mother comes back, and she'll be so surprised! That 'll be jolly fun—just elegant fun! Mr. Tiber, pim here."

Mr. Tiber was pursuing investigations by the side of a small watercourse; nothing was visible of him but the tip of a tail.

"*Very* well!"

Mr. Tiber came with a rush. Maso took him up, and confided to him, in the dog language, all his profound plan. Mr. Tiber approved of it highly.

The fifty francs carried the two through a good many days. Mr. Tiber, indeed, knew no change, for he had his coroneted bed, and the same fare was provided for him daily—a small piece of meat, plenty of hot macaroni, followed by a bit of cake and several lumps of sugar. When there were but eight francs left Maso went to Pisa. Mr. Waterhouse, who was very careful about money affairs, had paid all his pupil's bills up to the date of his own departure, and had then sent the remainder of the money which Mrs. Roscoe had left with him for the summer to her bankers at Pisa. Maso, as a precaution, carried with him the unmailed letter which contained the receipt for this sum. But he hoped that he should not be obliged to open the letter; he thought that they would give him a little money without that, as they knew him well. When he reached Pisa he found that the bank had closed its doors. It had failed.

Apparently it was a bad failure. Nobody (he inquired here and there) gave him a hopeful word. At the English bookseller's an assistant whom he knew said: "Even if something is recovered after a while, I am sure that nothing will be paid out for a long time yet. They have always been shaky; in my opinion, they are rascals." The bank, in truth, had never been a solid establishment; during its brief existence its standing

had been dubious. But Violet Roscoe had her own ideas about
banks, and one of the first was that she should be treated "with
civility"; she was immensely indignant if her personality was
not immediately recognized. Generally it was; she was such a
charmingly pretty woman that bankers' clerks all over Europe
remembered that personality without trouble, and handed out
her letters eagerly through the windows of their caged retreats,
stretching their heads through as far as possible to anticipate
her slightest wish. But once, at one of the old banks in Pisa, she
had presented a check on Paris, and had been asked to bring
some one to identify her.

"Such a thing has never happened to me before!" she said,
throwing back her head proudly.

This was true. But, again, it was her appearance, her beauty,
and personal elegance which had helped her; risks had been
assumed now and then simply from these. "She goes it on her
face, doesn't she?" had been the private comment of one clerk
to another in a bank at Rome. Upon this occasion at Pisa Violet had swept out of the place before the older official had time
to find out what the new man was doing at the outer counter.
Soon after this Mrs. Roscoe had selected this smaller establishment as "much nicer." "The office is so handsome, and they
have such nice chairs, and all the illustrated papers. And then
they are polite; they know their business, which is to be civil;
*there* they see what I am!" They did see, indeed.

Maso went back to the Bagni. In the bewilderment of his
thoughts there was but one clear idea: "'T any rate, mother
*sha'n't* know; she's got to stay away four whole months; the
doctor said so."

IV

After a day of thought, Maso decided that he would leave the
Bagni and go down to Pisa, and stay at Casa Corti. Madame
Corti would not be there (she spent her summers at Sorrento),
and officially the *pension* was closed; but Giulio would let him
remain, knowing that his mother would pay for it when she returned; he had even a vision of the very room at the top of the
house where Giulio would probably put him—a brick-floored
cell next to the linen-room, adorned with an ancient shrine, and

pervaded by the odor of freshly ironed towels. It would be no
end of a lark to spend the summer in Pisa. Luigi would be
there; and the puppet-shows. And perhaps Giulio would take
him up on Sundays to the house on the hill-side where his
wife and children lived; he had taken him once, and Maso had
always longed to go again. But when he reached Pisa with his
dog and his trunk he found the Palazzo Rondinelli wearing the
aspect of a deserted fortress; the immense outer doors were
swung to and locked; there was no sign of life anywhere. It
had not been closed for twenty years. It was the unexpected
which had happened. Maso went round to the stone lane behind the palace to see Luigi. It was then that he learned that his
friend had gone to live in Leghorn; he learned, also, that the
Casa Corti servants, having an opportunity to earn full wages
at Abetone for two months, had been permitted by Madame
Corti to accept this rare good-fortune; the house, therefore,
had been closed. Maso, thus adrift, was still confident that the
summer was going to be "huge," a free, banditlike existence,
with many enjoyments; pictures of going swimming, and staying in as long as he liked, were in his mind; also the privilege
of having his hair shaved close to his head, of eating melons
at his pleasure, and of drinking lemonade in oceans from the
gayly adorned, jingling carts. Of course he should have to get
something to do, as his money was almost gone. Still, it would
not take much to support him, and there was going to be an
exciting joy in independence, in living in "bachelor quarters."
He found his bachelor quarters in the Street of the Lily, a narrow passage that went burrowing along between two continuous rows of high old houses. The Lily's pavement was slimy
with immemorial filth, and, in spite of the heat, the damp atmosphere was like that of an ill-kept refrigerator. At the top of
one of the houses he established himself, with Mr. Tiber, in a
bare room which contained not much more than a chair and a
bed. Nevertheless, the first time he came out, locked his door,
and descended the stairs with the key in his pocket he felt like a
man; and he carried himself like one, with a swagger. The room
had one advantage, it contained a trap-door to the roof, and
there was a ladder tied up to the high ceiling, its rope secured
by a padlock; the boy soon contrived means (this must have
been his Yankee blood) to get the ladder down when he chose;

then at night he went up and cooled himself off on the roof, under the stars. There were two broken statues there, for the old house had had its day of grandeur; he made a seat, or rather a bed, at their feet. Mr. Tiber was so unhappy down below that he invented a way to get him up also. He spread his jacket on the floor, made Mr. Tiber lie down upon it, and then, fastening the sleeves together with a cord, he swung the jacket round his neck and ascended with his burden. Mr. Tiber enjoyed the roof very much.

Having established himself, selected his *trattoria*, and imbibed a good deal of lemonade as a beginning, the occupant of the bachelor quarters visited the business streets of Pisa in search of employment. But it was the dullest season in a place always dull, and no one wished for a new boy. At the Anglo-American Agency the clerk, languid from the heat, motioned him away without a word; at the Forwarding and Commission Office no one looked at him or spoke to him; so it was everywhere. His friend, the bookseller's assistant, had gone for the summer to the branch establishment at Como.

Mrs. Roscoe, who detested Pisa, had established no relations there save at the confectioner's, and at the agreeable bank where they saw what she was. But the bank continued closed, and the confectioner objected to boys of thirteen as helpers. In this emergency Maso wrote to Luigi, asking if there was any hope of a place in Leghorn.

"There is sure to be a demand at the large establishments for a talented North American," Luigi had answered, with confidence.

But Maso went up and down the streets of Leghorn in vain; the large establishments demanded nothing.

The boys now came down in their expectations. Upon Maso's second visit to the seaport of Tuscany it was agreed that he should take any employment that was offered; "for of course it is but a temporary thing," said Luigi, grandly. He remembered Maso's mother, and to him Casa Corti, at whose heels, as it were, he had lived, was a highly aristocratic place of abode. Luigi was assistant in a shop where glass-ware was sold; for an hour this morning he was free to accompany his friend in his quest, and together they edged their way along in the narrow line of shade on one side of the hot, white streets. But it made no difference whether Luigi went in first and offered his North American candidate, Maso following a few minutes afterwards, or whether Maso made his demand in person, Luigi entering later, with his best smile, to serve as backer; no one showed any eagerness to secure the services of the small, narrow-chested boy. "Say, Maso, couldn't you *look* a little different?" suggested Luigi, anxiously, as they came out of an office, where, as he was last, he had overheard the epithet "sullen-faced" applied to his American friend.

The two boys spoke Italian; Luigi knew no English.

"Why, I look as I'm made. Everybody looks as they're made, don't they?" said Maso, surprised.

"Ah, but expression is a beautiful thing—a sympathetic countenance," said Luigi, waving his hand. "Now you—you might smile more. Promise me to try a smile at the next place where we go in to ask."

"Like this?" said Maso. And stopping, he slapped his leg violently, and gave a deep, long, sardonic laugh. "I saw a man once who did it like that," he explained.

"Well! If you should go in and ask for a place and do that —well, I don't know *what* they would do to you!" said Luigi, standing still, amazed.

"I didn't want to do it; you made me," answered Maso, nettled.

"I told you to smile with an amiability—a sweetness; I didn't tell you to slap your leg and yell out like that," Luigi remonstrated, taking off his hat and wiping his hot forehead. "Come; here's a window with nice looking-glasses; practise a little, and I'll stand behind and tell you when it's right."

And Maso, standing close to the window, smiled with an amiability—a sweetness. The reflection of his freckled face in the tilted mirror, giving back these grins, was something unearthly. But both of the boys were far too much in earnest to notice that.

"This one will do, I think," said Luigi, doubtfully—"at least, it's the best. I've got to go now, but look in at the shop before you take the train back. Are you hungry? I know a place where things are good and not dear; I'll take you there myself."

This was Luigi's Italian hospitality; he would show Maso his own particular *trattoria*. But Maso was not hungry.

At three o'clock he appeared at Luigi's shop. Luigi was dusting goblets. "Well?" he said, inquiringly.

Maso shook his head.

"Didn't you smile?"

"Yes, I did it as I took off my hat. And every time they seemed so surprised."

"I've a new idea, Maso; behold it: the consul of your country!"

"Is there one in Leghorn?" asked Maso, vaguely.

"Of course there is; I have seen the sign many a time." And Luigi mentioned the street and the number.

The proprietor of the shop, who was packing a case of the slender Epiphany trumpets, now broke one by accident, and immediately scolded Luigi in a loud voice; Maso was obliged to make a hasty departure.

The office of the representative of the United States government was indicated by a painted shield bearing the insignia of the republic, and a brass plate below, with the following notification: "Consolato degli Stati-Uniti d'America." The first word of this inscription rouses sometimes a vague thrill in the minds of homesick Americans in Italy coming to pay a visit to their flag and the eagle. The thrill, however, is immediately followed by a conviction that whatever the syllables may mean (in an unintelligible land), they do not foreshadow, probably, anything so solacing as they appear at first to indicate. Consolato—a consoling-place; if it were indeed that, the bare room would soon be as celebrated as is in Jerusalem the Wailing-place of the Jews. To Maso, however, there was no double meaning. He glanced at the flag; then he went up the stairs and knocked at the door.

As it happened, the consul himself was there alone. Maso, upon entering, took off his hat and tried his smile, then he began: "If you please, I am trying to get a place—something to do. I thought perhaps, sir, that you might—"

He stopped, and in his embarrassment put the toe of his shoe into a hole in the matting, and moved it about industriously.

"Don't spoil my matting," said the consul. "You're a very young boy to be looking for a place."

"I'm going on fourteen."

"And of what nation are you?" demanded the consul, after another survey.

"Why, I'm American," said Maso, surprised.

"I shouldn't have taken you for one. What is your name?"

"Maso—I mean Thom-as Ross Coe," replied the boy, bringing out the syllables with something of an Italian pronunciation.

"Tummarse Errosco? Do you call that an American name?"

"I'll write it," said Maso, blushing. He wrote it in large letters on the edge of a newspaper that was near him.

"Thomas R. Coe," read the consul. "Coe is your name, then?"

"Yes, sir."

"You want something to do, eh? What do you want, and why do you come here for it?"

Maso told his story, or rather a tale which he had prepared on his way to the consulate. It was a confused narrative, because he did not wish to betray anything that could give a clew to his mother's address.

The consul asked questions. "A failure, eh? What failure?"

"It—it wasn't in Leghorn."

"And your mother will be back in September? Where is she at present?"

"She—she is north; she isn't very well, and—" But he could not think of anything that he could safely add, so he stopped.

"We haven't any places for boys. Did you expect me to take you in here?"

"No, sir. I thought perhaps you'd recommend me."

"On general principles, I suppose, as an American, seeing that I don't know anything else about you. And you selected the Fourth as a nice, good, patriotic day for it?"

"The Fourth?"

"I suppose you know what day it is?"

"Yes, sir—Tuesday."

The consul looked at him, and saw that he spoke in good faith. "*You* an American boy? I guess not! You may go." And dipping his pen in the ink, he resumed his writing.

Maso, though disturbed and bewildered, held his ground. He certainly was an American boy. What could the man mean?

The consul, whose name was Maclean, was a lawyer from

Michigan; a short, stout man of sixty, with a yellow skin, bright black eyes, and an old-fashioned black wig with a curled edge all round. "No use waiting, my friend," he said, without looking up; "frauds don't go down here."

"I'm American. True as you live, I am," said Maso, earnestly.

Something in his face made the consul relent a little. "Perhaps you've got some American blood hidden in you somewhere. But it must be pretty well thinned out not to know the Fourth of July! I suppose you've never heard of the Declaration of Independence either?"

A gleam of light now illumined the darkness of Maso's mind. "Oh yes; I know now; in the History." He rallied. "The Indians took a *very* bloody part in it," he added, with confidence.

"Oh, they did, did they? Where were you brought up?"

"In Italy, most; a little in other places. I came abroad before I was two."

"I see—one of the expatriated class," said Maclean, contemptuously. He had a great contempt for Americans who leave their own country and reside abroad. The dialogue ended, after a little more talk, in his saying: "Well, you get me a note from your mother (I suppose you write to her?) telling me something more about you. Then I'll see what I can do." For the boy's story had been a very vague one.

As Maso, heavy-hearted, turned towards the door, Maclean suddenly felt sorry for him. He was such a little fellow, and somehow his back looked so tired. "See here, my son," he said, "here's something for the present. No use telling you to buy fire-crackers with it, for they haven't got 'em here. But you might buy rockets; can't look out of the window summer nights in this place without seeing a lonely rocket shooting up somewhere." He held out two francs.

Maso's face grew scarlet. "I'd rather not, unless I can work for it," he muttered. It was a new feeling to be taken for a beggar.

"You can work enough for that if you want to. There is a printed list on that desk, and a pile of circulars; you can direct them. Show me the first dozen, so that I can see if they'll pass."

Maso sat down at the desk. He put his hat in six different places before he could collect his wits and get to work. When he brought the dozen envelopes for inspection, Maclean said:

"You seem to know Eyetalian well, with all these Eyetalian names. *I* can't make head or tail of 'em. But as to handwriting, it's about the worst I ever saw."

"Yes, I know," said Maso, ashamed. "I've never had regular lessons, 'cepting this summer, when—" He stopped; Mr. Waterhouse's name would be, perhaps, a clew. He finished the circulars; it took an hour and a half.

The consul shook hands with him, the mechanical handshake of the public functionary. "You get me that note, and I'll see."

Maso went back to Pisa. When he arrived at his door in the Street of the Lily, the wife of the cobbler who lived on the ground-floor handed him a letter which the postman had left. The sight of it made the boy's heart light; he forgot his weariness, and, climbing the stairs quickly, he unlocked his door and entered his room, Mr. Tiber barking a joyous welcome. Mr. Tiber had been locked in all day; but he had had a walk in the early morning, and his solitude had been tempered by plenty of food on a plate, a bowl of fresh water, and a rubber ball to play with. Maso sat down, and, with the dog on his knees, tore open his letter. It was directed to him at Pisa, in a rough handwriting, but within there was a second envelope, a letter from his mother, which bore the address of the hotel at the Bagni di Lucca, where she supposed that her son was staying with his tutor. She wrote regularly, and she sent polite messages to Waterhouse, regretting so much that his severe sprain prevented him from writing to her in reply. Maso, in his answers, represented himself as the most hopelessly stupid pupil old Longlegs had ever been cursed with; in the network of deception in which he was now involved he felt this somehow to be a relief. He had once heard an American boy call out to another who was slow in understanding something, "You're an old gumpy;" so he wrote, "Longlegs yells out every day your an old gumpy," which greatly astonished Mrs. Roscoe. The boy exerted every power he had to make his letters appear natural. But the task was so difficult that each missive read a good deal like a ball discharged from a cannon; there was always a singularly abrupt statement regarding the weather, and another about the food at the hotel; then followed two or three sentences about Longlegs; and he was her "affecshionate son Maso. P.S.—Mr. Tiber is very well." He sent these replies to the Bagni; here his friend, the porter, taking off the outer envelope, which was directed to himself, put the letter within with the others to go to the post-office; in this way Maso's epistles bore the postmark "Bagni di Lucca." For these services Maso had given his second-best suit of clothes, with shoes and hat, to the porter's young son, who had aspirations.

The present letter from Mrs. Roscoe was full of joyousness and jokes. But the great news was that she intended to make a tour in Switzerland in August, and as she missed her little boy too much to enjoy it without him, she had written urgently to America about money, and she hoped that before long (she had told them to cable) she could send for him to join her. Maso was wildly happy; to be with his mother again, and yet not to have her return to Italy before the important four months were over, that was perfect; he got up, opened his trunk, and refolded his best jacket and trousers with greater care, even before he finished the letter. For he wore now continuously his third-best suit, as the second-best had been left at the Bagni. At last, when he knew the letter by heart, he washed his face and hands, and, accompanied by Mr. Tiber, tail-wagging and expectant, he went down to get supper at the *trattoria* near by.

The next day he tried Pisa again, searching for employment through street after street. His mother had written that she hoped to send for him early in August. It was now the 5th of July, so that there were only four or five weeks to provide for; and then there would be his fare back to the Bagni. But his second quest was hardly more fortunate than the first. The only person who did not wave a forefinger in perspiring negative even before he had opened his lips was a desiccated youth, who, sitting in his shirt-sleeves, with his feet up and a tumbler beside him, gave something of an American air (although Maso did not know that) to a frescoed apartment in which Singer sewing-machines were offered for sale. This exile told him to add up a column of figures, to show what he could do. But when he saw that the boy was doing his counting with his fingers, he nodded him towards the door. "Better learn to play the flute," he suggested, sarcastically.

Maso was aware that accountants are not in the habit of running a scale with the fingers of their left hand on the edge of

their desks, or of saying aloud, "six and three are nine," "seven
and five are eleven," and "nought's nought." He had caught
these methods from his mother, who always counted in that
way. He clinched his fingers into his palm as he went down
the stairs; he would never count with them again. But no one
asked him to count, or to do anything else. In the afternoon
he sought the poorer streets; here he tried shop after shop.
The atmosphere was like that of a vapor bath; he felt tired and
dull. At last, late in the day, a cheese-seller gave him a hope
of employment at the end of the week. The wages were very
small; still, it was something; and refreshed by the thought, he
went home (as he called it), released Mr. Tiber, and, as the sun
was low, took him off for a walk. By hazard he turned towards
the part of the town which is best known to travellers, that
outlying quarter where the small cathedral, the circular baptistery, and the Leaning Tower keep each other company, folded
in a protecting corner of the crenellated city wall. The Arno
was flowing slowly, as if tired and hot, under its bridges; Pisa
looked deserted; the pavements were scorching under the feet.

As the boy came up the broad paved walk that leads to the
cathedral, he saw two ladies leaving the doorway at the base
of the Leaning Tower; evidently they had been making the
ascent. They went across to the baptistery to see the pulpit of
Nicolo the Pisan. "Now they're going to make the old shed
howl," he said to himself. This was the disrespectful way in
which he thought of the famous echo.

At Pisa the atmosphere clothes the cathedral with a softness which no Northern marbles can ever hope to attain. The
façade, perfect in proportion and beauty, rises with its columns
and galleries from the greensward, facing the sculptured baptistery; on the other side the celebrated and fantastic tower for
the bells stands, like a tree which has been made to slant by the
furious wind, looking across the plain towards the sea.

Maso stretched himself on the grass under the façade of the
cathedral. After a while the ladies came from the baptistery,
and crossed to the Campo Santo. In the relaxation of the dull
season the portal had been left open behind them, and the
boy went over and wandered about within, carrying Mr. Tiber
under his jacket, half concealed, as dogs are not allowed in the
sacred enclosure. He looked at the frescos of Benozzo, at the

"Last Judgment" and the "Triumph of Death." He passed the celebrated sarcophagus without knowing what it was, his attention being more attracted by the modern monuments, the large marble figures, seated and standing, that stared down upon him with their unmoving white eyes. At last he sat down at the base of one of these figures to rest, for the air here was cool compared with the atmosphere outside. The two strangers, in their slow progress, looking at everything, guide-book in hand, had passed him once; now on their second round they stopped near him at the doorway, preparing for departure. "Well, there is nothing more to see in Pisa," said one. "Thank Heaven! Pisa's done. Now we can go on to Lerici."

"We haven't found those plates yet," objected the other.

"What plates?"

"Why, don't you remember? They say there are old majolica plates set in one of the campaniles here—trophies taken from the Moors ages ago. I've stared up at every campanile, and haven't seen a sign. I wonder if that boy would know? What a forlorn-looking creature!"

Maso, in truth, in his third-best suit, and obliged to be economical regarding the bills of the cobbler's wife, who acted as his laundress, did not present an attractive appearance.

The lady, turning towards him, had begun, "Sapete uno posata in campanile—" But resenting her comment, Maso had risen and walked away.

"Evidently he isn't Italian, for he doesn't understand," said the questioner, who was accustomed to declare that it was very easy for her to travel abroad, as she spoke "five languages equally well." "Perhaps he is German—with that light hair." She ran after him. "Tisch," she called, "in thurm. Haben-sie gesehn ein?"

"I speak English," said Maso, stopping.

"You're never English, surely!"

"I'm American."

"American? We are Americans; but I should never have taken *you* for one!" Then she asked her question about the plates. Maso had never heard of them; he told her so, and made his escape, going back to the grass under the façade. "Ugly old things," he thought, "both of them! I just wish they could see *mother*." And forgetting his own mortification, his heart swelled with pride as he recalled her pretty face and pretty step, and the general perfection of her appearance. Only four weeks or so and he should be with her! "Mr. Tiber, pim here. We're going to Switzerland. Do you hear that? I shall take you in a basket and pretend you's lunch. The nobil empress" (this character, in the dog language, was Mrs. Roscoe) "says you mut promit not to bark. But you can bark now. Hi! Mr. Tiber. Hi!"

And Mr. Tiber hied. And then, at the word of command, performed every trick he knew.

V

The cheese-shop was blazing with the light of four flaring gas-burners; the floor had been watered a short time before, and this made the atmosphere reek more strongly than ever with the odors of the smoked fish and sausages, caviare and oil, which, with the cheese, formed the principal part of the merchandise offered for sale. There was no current of air passing through from the open door, for the atmosphere outside was perfectly still. Tranquilly hovering mosquitoes were everywhere, but Maso did not mind these much; he objected more to the large black beetles that came noiselessly out at night; he hated the way they stood on the shelves as if staring at him, motionless save for the waving to and fro of their long antennæ. A boy came in to buy cheese. It was soft cheese; Maso weighed it, and put it upon a grape leaf. "It just gets hotter and hotter!" he remarked, indignantly. The Italian lad did not seem to mind the heat much; he was buttery with perspiration from morning until night, but as he had known no other atmosphere than that of Pisa, he supposed that this was the normal summer condition of the entire world. It was the 27th of August.

On the last day of July, when Maso's every breath was accompanied by an anticipation of Switzerland, there had arrived a long disappointed letter from his mother; the hoped-for money had not come, and would not come: "Reuben John again!" The Swiss trip must be given up, and now the question was, could Mr. Waterhouse keep him awhile longer? "Because if he cannot, I shall return to the Bagni next week." Maso, though choked with the disappointment, composed a letter in which he said that old Longlegs was delighted to keep him, and was sorry he could not write himself, but his arm continued stiff; "probly heel never be able to write agane," he added,

darkly, so as to make an end, once for all, of that complicated
subject. There was no need of her return, not the least; he
and Mr. Tiber were well, "and having loads of fun"; and, besides, there was not a single empty room in the hotel or anywhere else, and would not be until the 6th of September; there
had never been such a crowd at the Bagni before. He read
over what he had written, and perceiving that he had given
an impression of great gayety at the Italian watering-place, he
added, "P.S. peple all cooks turists." (For Mrs. Roscoe was accustomed to declare that she hated these inoffensive travellers.)
Then he signed his name in the usual way: "your affecshionate
son, Maso." He never could help blotting when he wrote his
name—probably because he was trying to write particularly
well. Mrs. Roscoe once said that it was always either blot "so,"
or "Ma" blot; this time it was "Ma" blot.

This letter despatched, the boy's steadiness broke down. He
did not go back to the cheese-seller's shop; he lived upon the
money he had earned, and when that was gone he sold his
clothes, keeping only those he wore and his best suit, with
a change of under-clothing. Next he sold his trunk; then his
school-books, though they brought but a few centimes. The
old fairy-book he kept; he read it during the hot noon-times,
lying on the floor, with Mr. Tiber by his side. The rest of the
day he devoted to those pleasures of which he had dreamed.
He went swimming, and stayed in for hours; and he made Mr.
Tiber swim. He indulged himself as regarded melons; he went
to the puppet-show accompanied by Mr. Tiber; he had had his
hair cut so closely that it was hardly more than yellow down;
and he swaggered about the town in the evening smoking cigarettes. After three weeks of this vagabond existence he went
back to the cheese-seller, offering to work for half-wages. His
idea was to earn money enough for his fare to the Bagni, and
also to pay for the washing of his few clothes, so that he might
be in respectable condition to meet his mother on the 6th of
September; for on the 6th the four months would be up, and
she could safely return. This was his constant thought. Of late
he had spoken of the 6th in his letters, and she had agreed to
it, so there was no doubt of her coming. To-day, August 27th,
he had been at work for a week at the cheese-seller's, and the
beetles were blacker and more crafty than ever.

It was Saturday night, and the shop was kept open late; but at last he was released, and went home. The cobbler's wife handed him his letter, and he stopped to read it by the light of the strongly smelling petroleum lamp. For he had only a short end of a candle up-stairs; and, besides, he could not wait, he was so sure that he should find, within, the magic words, "I shall come by the train that reaches Lucca at—" and then a fixed date and hour written down in actual figures on the page.

The letter announced that his mother had put off her return for three weeks: she was going to Paris. "As you are having such a wonderfully good time at the Bagni this summer, you won't mind this short delay. If by any chance Mr. Waterhouse cannot keep you so long, let him telegraph me. No telegram will mean that he can." She spoke of the things she should bring to him from Paris, and the letter closed with the sentence, "I am so glad I have thought of this delightful idea before settling down again in that deadly Casa Corti for the winter." (But the idea had a human shape. Violet Roscoe's ideas were often personified; they took the form of agreeable men.)

"Evil news? Tell me not so!" said the cobbler's wife, who had noticed the boy's face as he read.

"Pooh! no," answered Maso, stoutly. He put the letter into his pocket and went up to his room. As he unlocked his door, there was not the usual joyful rush of Mr. Tiber against his legs; the silence was undisturbed. He struck a match on the wall and lighted his candle-end. There, in the corner, on his little red coverlid, lay Mr. Tiber asleep. Then, as the candle burned more brightly, it could be seen that it was not sleep. There was food on the tin plate and water in the bowl; he had not needed anything. There was no sign of suffering in the attitude, or on the little black face with its closed eyes (to Maso that face had always been as clearly intelligible as a human countenance); the appearance was as if the dog had sought his own corner and his coverlid, and had laid himself down to die very peacefully without a pain or a struggle.

The candle-end had long burned itself out, and the boy still lay on the floor with his arm round his pet. It seemed to him that his heart would break. "Mr. Tiber, dear little Tiber, my own little doggie—dying here all alone!—kinnin little chellow!" Thus he sobbed and sobbed until he was worn out. Towards dawn came the thought of what must follow. But no; Mr. Tiber should not be taken away and thrown into some horrible place! If he wished to prevent it, however, he must be very quick. He had one of the large colored handkerchiefs which Italians use instead of baskets; as the dawn grew brighter he spread it out, laid his pet carefully in the centre, and knotted the corners together tightly; then, after bathing his face to conceal as much as possible the traces of his tears, he stole down the stairs, and, passing through the town, carrying his burden in the native fashion, he took a road which led towards the hills.

It was a long walk. The little body which had been so light in life weighed now like lead; but it might have been twice as heavy, he would not have been conscious of it. He reached the place at last, the house where Giulio's wife lived, with her five children, near one of the hill-side villages which, as seen from Pisa, shine like white spots on the verdure. Paola came out from her dark dwelling, and listened to his brief explanation with wonder. To take so much trouble for a dog! But she was a mild creature, her ample form cowlike, her eyes cowlike also, and therefore beautiful; she accompanied him, and she kept the curious crowding children in some kind of order while the boy, with her spade, dug a grave in the corner of a field which she pointed out. Maso dug and dug in the heat. He was so afraid of the peasant cupidity that he did not dare to leave the dog wrapped in the cotton handkerchief, lest the poor little tomb should be rifled to obtain it; he gave it, therefore, to one of the children, and, gathering fresh leaves, he made a bed of them at the bottom of the hole; then leaning down, he laid his pet tenderly on the green, and covered him thickly with more foliage, the softest he could find. When the last trace of the little black head had disappeared he took up the spade, and with eyes freshly wet again in spite of his efforts to prevent it, he filled up the grave as quickly as he could, levelling the ground smoothly above it. He had made his excavation very deep, in order that no one should meddle with the place later: it would be too much trouble.

It was now nearly noon. He gave Paola three francs, which was half of all he possessed. Then, with one quick glance towards the corner of the field, he started on his long walk back to Pisa.

VI

"Do you know where you'll end, Roberta? You'll end with us," said Mrs. Harrowby.

"With you?"

"Yes; in the Church. You've tried everything, beginning with geology and ending with music (I can't help laughing at the last; you never had any ear), and you have found no satisfaction. You are the very kind to come to us; they always do."

The speaker, an American who lived in Naples, had entered the Roman Catholic Church ten years before; in Boston she had been a Unitarian. It was the 10th of September, and she was staying for a day in Pisa on her way southward; she had encountered Miss Spring by chance in the piazza of Santa Caterina at sunset, and the two had had a long talk with the familiarity which an acquaintance in childhood carries with it, though years of total separation may have intervened.

"There is one other alternative," answered Miss Spring; "it was suggested by a pretty little woman who used to be here. She advised me to try crystal scent-bottles and dissipation." This being a joke, Miss Spring had intended to smile; but at this instant her attention was attracted by something on the other side of the street, and her face remained serious.

"Crystal scent-bottles? Dissipation? Mercy!" exclaimed Mrs. Harrowby. "What *do* you mean?"

But her companion had gone; she was hurrying across the street. "It isn't possible, Maso, that this is *you*!" She spoke to a ragged, sick-looking boy.

Two hours after her question Maso was in bed in the Palazzo Rondinelli. Madame Corti never came back till October, and the *pension* was not open, but servants were there. The housekeeper went through the form of making protest: "The signora has always such great alarm about fever."

"You will refer Madame Corti to me; I will pay for her alarm," answered Roberta, marching past her to direct the driver of the carriage, who was assisting Maso up the stairs. "It's not infectious fever. Only malarial." Roberta was something of a doctor herself. She superintended in person the opening of a large, cool room on the second floor, the making of the bed, and then the installation of Maso between linen sheets. The servants were all fond of the boy; in addition, Madame Corti was in Sorrento, and Miss Spring's francs were here. Her francs were few, but she spent them for Maso as generously as though they had been many.

The boy, as soon as he was in bed, whispered to Giulio, "Pencil—paper." Then when Miss Spring had left the room, he scrawled on the page, Giulio holding a book under it, "My dog is ded," and signed his name. He told Giulio to give this to her when she came in; then, as he heard her step, he quickly closed his eyes.

Miss Spring read, and understood. "He was afraid I would ask. And he could not speak of it. He remembers, poor little fellow, that I did not care for the dog."

Maso had refused to tell her where his mother was. "She's coming, on the 22d, to the Bagni di Lucca"; this was all he would say. The next morning at daylight she left him with the nurse (for she had sent immediately for Dr. Prior and for one of the best nurses in Pisa), and, driving to the Street of the Lily, she ascended the unclean stairs, with her skirts held high and her glasses on, to the room at the top of the house. Maso had himself gathered his few possessions together after his meeting with her in the piazza of Santa Caterina, but he had not had the strength to carry them down to the lower door. Miss Spring took the two parcels, which were tied up in newspapers, and after looking about to see that there was nothing left, she descended in the same gingerly way, and re-entered the carriage which was waiting at the door, its wheels grazing the opposite house. "Yes, he is ill; malarial fever. But we hope he will recover," she said to the cobbler's wife, who inquired with grief and affection, and a very dirty face.

To find Mrs. Roscoe's address, so that she could telegraph to her, Miss Spring was obliged to look through Maso's parcels. She could not ask his permission, for he recognized no one now; his mind wandered. One of the bundles contained the best suit, still carefully saved for his mother's arrival. The other held his few treasures: his mother's letters, with paper and envelopes for his own replies; the old fairy-book; and Mr. Tiber's blanket, coverlid, and little collar, wrapped in a clean handkerchief. The latest letter gave the Paris address.

*

"My dear little boy! If I could only have known!" moaned Violet Roscoe, sitting on the edge of the bed with her child in her arms. She had just arrived; her gloves were still on. "Oh, Maso, why didn't you tell me?"

Maso's face, gaunt and brown, lay on her shoulder; his eyes were strange, but he knew her. "You mustn't get sick again, mother," he murmured, anxiously, the fixed idea of the summer asserting itself. Then a wider recollection dawned. "Oh, mother," he whispered with his dry lips, "Mr. Tiber's dead. Little Tiber!"

His fever-hot eyes could not shed tears, but his mother cried for him, overwhelmed by the thought of his lonely sorrow. Then she tried to comfort him: "Tiber was an old dog, Maso; he was not young when we bought him, and we have had him many years. Dogs do not live very long, even the oldest; he had to die some time. And he had a very happy little life with you, always; you loved him, and gave him everything, and he loved you. No dog could have had more."

Roberta overheard this attempt; she came to the bedside to add her item also to the consolation. "Perhaps you will see your pet again, Maso. For he had his vital spark as well as we have, though in a less degree. If ours is to reappear in a future existence, I am inclined to think that his will also. Why not?"

Maso did not understand her; his mother's voice alone reached his dulled intelligence. But at least Roberta had done her best.

A month later Mr. Reuben J. Coe, of Coesville, New Hampshire, said to his brother David: "That foolish wife of Tom's is coming home at last. In spite of every effort on my part, she has made ducks and drakes of almost all her money."

"Is that why she is coming back?"

"No; thinks it will be better for the boy. But I'm afraid it's too late for that."

# A Florentine Experiment

ONE afternoon, three years ago, two ladies were talking together on the heights of Fiesole overlooking Florence. They occupied the stone bench which bears the inscription of its donor, an appreciative Englishman, who in a philanthropical spirit has had it placed there for the benefit of the pilgrims from all nations who come to these heights to see the enchanting view. The two ladies were not speaking of the view, however, but of something more personal. It seemed to be interesting.

"He is certainly much in love with you," said one, who was taller and darker than her companion. As she spoke, she gave back a letter which she had been reading.

"Yes, I think he is," said the other, reflectively, replacing it in its envelope.

"I suppose you are so accustomed to it, Beatrice, that it does not make much impression upon you," continued the first speaker, her glance as she spoke resting not upon her companion, but upon the lovely levels beneath, with the violet-hued mountains rising softly up round about them, so softly that one forgot they were mountains until the eye caught the gleam of snow on the summits towards the east. There was a pause after this question, and it lasted so long that the questioner at length removed her eyes from the landscape and turned them upon her friend; to her surprise she saw that the friend was blushing.

"Why, Beatrice!" she exclaimed, "is it possible—"

"No," said Beatrice, "it is not possible. I know that I am blushing; but you must not think too much of that. I am not as strong as I was, and blush at everything; I am taking iron for it. In the present case, it only means that—" She paused.

"That you like him," suggested the other, smiling.

"I like a number of persons," said Mrs. Lovell, tranquilly, gazing in her turn down the broad, slightly winding valley, dotted with its little white villages, and ending in a soft blue haze, through which the tawny Arno, its course marked by a line of tall, slender, lightly foliaged, seemingly branchless trees, like tall rods in leaf, went onward towards the west.

"I know you do," said the first speaker. "And I really wish," she added, with a slight touch of vehemence, "that your time would come—that I should see you at last liking some one person really and deeply and jealously, and to the exclusion of all the rest."

"I don't know why you should wish me unhappiness, Margaret. You have beautiful theories, I know; but in my *experience*" (Mrs. Lovell slightly underlined this word as if in opposition to the "theories" of her friend) "the people who have those deeper sort of feelings you describe are almost always very unhappy."

Margaret turned her head, and looked towards the waving line of the Carrara mountains; in her eyes there was the reflection of a sudden inward pain. But she knew that she could indulge in this momentary expression of feeling; the mountains would not betray her, and the friend by her side did not realize that anything especial could have happened to "Margaret." In excuse for Mrs. Lovell it may be said that so much that was very especial had always happened, and still continued to happen, to her, that she had not much time for the more faintly colored episodes of other people.

Beatrice Lovell was an unusually lovely woman. The adjective is here used to signify that she inspired love. Not by an effort, word, action, or hardly interest of her own; but simply because she was what she was. Her beauty was not what is called striking; it touched the eye gently at first, but always grew. People who liked to analyze said that the secret lay in the fact that she had the sweetness, the tints, the surface texture as it were, and even sometimes the expression, of childhood still; and then, when you came to look deeper, you found underneath all the richer bloom of the woman. Her golden hair, not thick or long, but growing in little soft wavelets upon her small head; her delicate rose-leaf skin, showing the blue veins; her little teeth and the shape of her sweet mouth—all these were like childhood. In addition, she was dimpled and round, with delicately cut features, and long-lashed violet eyes, in whose soft depths lay always an expression of gentle trust. This beautiful creature was robed to-day in widow's mourning-garb made in the severest fashion, without one attempt to decorate or lighten it. But the straight-skirted, untrimmed garments, the little close bonnet, and the heavy veil pinned over it with straight crape-pins, only brought out more vividly the tints of her beauty.

"No," she continued, as her companion did not speak, "I by no means wish for the feelings you invoke for me. I am better off as I am; I keep my self-possession. For instance, I told this Sicily person that it was in very bad taste to speak to me in that way at such a time—so soon after Mr. Lovell's death; and that I was much annoyed by it."

"It has not prevented his writing," said Margaret, coming back slowly from the Carrara mountains, and letting her eyes rest upon the tower of the Palazzo Vecchio below, springing above the city roofs like the stem of a flower.

"They always write, I think," said Mrs. Lovell, simply.

"I know they do—to *you*," said Margaret. She turned as she spoke, and looked at her friend with the same old affection and admiration which she had felt for her from childhood, but now with a sort of speculative curiosity added. How must it feel to live such a life—to be constantly surrounded and accompanied by an atmosphere of devotion and enthralment such as that letter had expressed? Beatrice seemed to divine something of her friend's thought, and answered it after her fashion.

"It is such a comfort to be with you, Margaret," she said, affectionately; "it has always been a comfort, ever since we were children. I can talk freely to you, and as I can talk to no one else. You understand; you do not misunderstand. But all the other women I meet invariably do; or, at least, pretend to enough to excuse their being horribly disagreeable."

Margaret took her hand. They had taken off their gloves, as the afternoon was warm, and they had the heights to themselves; it was early in March, and the crowd of tourists who come in the spring to Italy, and those more loitering travellers who had spent the winter in Naples or Rome, had not yet reached Florence, although it may be said that they were at the door. Mrs. Lovell's hands, now destitute of ornament save the plain band of the wedding-ring, were small, dimpled, very white; her friend Miss Stowe had hands equally small, but darker and more slender.

"You have been happy all your life, have you not, Beatrice?" said Margaret, not questioningly so much as assertively.

"Yes," answered Mrs. Lovell, "I think I have. Of course I was much shocked by Mr. Lovell's death; he was very kind to me."

"Mr. Lovell," as his wife always called him, had died four months previously. He was fifty-six years of age, and Beatrice had been his wife for a little more than a year. He had been very happy with her, and had left her his fortune and his blessing; with these, and his memory, she had come abroad, and had been for six weeks in Sicily, with some elderly friends. She had stopped in Florence to see Miss Stowe, who was spending the winter there with an aunt; but she was not to remain. In her present state of seclusion she was to visit Venice and the Lakes in advance of the season, and spend the summer in "the most quiet village" which could be discovered for her especial benefit on the Brittany coast. The friends had not met for two years, and there had been much to tell—that is, for Beatrice to tell. Her always personal narratives were saved from tediousness, however, because they were not the usual decorated feminine fancies, but plain masculine facts (oh, very plain!); and because, also, the narrator was herself quite without the vanity which might naturally have accompanied them. This last merit seemed to her admirers a very remarkable one; in reality it was only that, having no imagination, she took a simple, practical view of everything, themselves included. This last, however, they never discovered, because her unfailing tact and gentleness lay broadly and softly over all.

"And what shall you do about your Sicily person?" said Margaret, not in the least, however, associating the remark, and knowing also that Beatrice would not associate it, with "Mr. Lovell" and his "memory" (it was quite well understood between them about "Mr. Lovell").

"Of course I shall not answer."

"And if he follows you?"

"He will hardly do that—now. Besides, he is going to America; he sails to-morrow. Our having been together in Sicily was quite by chance, of course; he knows that, and he knows also that I intend to pay, in every way, the strictest respect to Mr. Lovell's memory. That will be fully two years."

"And then?"

"Oh, I never plan. If things do not assert themselves, they are not worth a plan."

"You certainly are the most delightful little piece of common-sense I ever met," said Margaret, laughing, and kissing her. "I wish you would give me a share of it! But come—it is late; we must go."

As they went down the slope together towards the village where their carriage was waiting, they looked not unlike the two seventeen-year-old school-girls of eight years before; Beatrice was smiling, and Margaret's darker face was lighted by the old animation which had always charmed her lovely but unanimated friend. It may here be remarked that the greatest intellectual excitements which Beatrice Lee had known had been when Margaret Stowe had let loose her imagination, and carried her friend up with her, as on strong wings, to those regions of fancy which she never attained alone; Beatrice had enjoyed it, wondered over it, and then had remained passive until the next time.

"Ah well—poor Sicily person!" said Margaret, as they took their places in the carriage. "I know just what you will do with him. You will write down his name in a memorandum-book, so as not to forget it; you will safely burn his poor letter, as you have safely burned so many others; and you will go gently on to Brittany without even taking the ashes!"

"Keep it for me!" said Mrs. Lovell, suddenly, drawing the letter from her pocket and placing it in Margaret's hand. "Yes," she repeated, enjoying her idea and dwelling upon it, delighted to find that she possessed a little fancy of her own, after all, "keep it for me, and read it over once in a while. It is quite well written, and will do you good, because it is not one of your theories, but a fact. There is nothing disloyal in my giving it to you, because I always tell you everything, and this Sicily person has no claim for exemption in that regard. He has gone back to America, and you will not meet him. No—positively, I will not take it. You must keep it for me."

"Very well," said Margaret, amused by this little unexpected flight. "But as I may go back to America also, I want to be quite sure where I stand. Did you happen to mention to this Sicily person my name, or anything about me?"

"No," replied Mrs. Lovell, promptly. "We did not talk on such subjects, you know."

"And he had no idea that you were to stop in Florence?"

"No; he supposed I was to take the steamer at Naples for Marseilles. You need not be so scrupulous; everything is quite safe."

"And when shall I return the epistle?"

"When I ask for it," said Mrs. Lovell, laughing.

The next morning she went northward to Venice.

Two weeks later Miss Stowe formed one of the company at a reception, or, rather, a musical party. She looked quite unlike the "Margaret" of Fiesole as she sat on a small, faded purple satin sofa, listening, rather frowningly, to the rippling movement that follows the march in Beethoven's sonata, opus twenty-six; she had never liked that rippling movement, she did not pretend to like it now. Her frown, however, was slight —merely a little line between her dark eyebrows; it gave her the appearance of attention rather than of disapprobation. The "Margaret" of Fiesole had looked like an animated, almost merry, young girl; the "Miss Stowe" of the reception appeared older than she really was, and her face wore an expression of proud reserve, which, although veiled by all the conventional graciousness required by society, was not on that account any the less apparent. She was richly dressed; but the general effect of her attire was that of simplicity. She fanned herself slowly with a large fan, whose sticks were of carved amber, and the upper part of soft gray ostrich plumes, curled; closed or open, as she used it or as it lay beside her, this fan was an object of beauty. As the music ceased a lady came fluttering across the room, and, with a whispered "Permit me," introduced a gentleman, whose name, in the hum of released conversation, Miss Stowe did not hear.

"He understands *everything* about old pictures, and you *know* how ignorant *I* am!" said this lady, half closing her eyes, and shaking her ringleted head with an air of abnegation. "*I* have but *one* inspiration; there is room in me but for *one*. I

bring him, therefore, to *you*, who have so many! We *all* know
your love for the early masters—may I not say, the *earliest*?"

Madame Ferri was an American who had married a Florentine; she was now a little widow of fifty, with gray ringlets and
emotions regarding music almost too ineffable to be expressed.
I say "almost," because she did, after all, express them, as her
friends knew. She was a useful person in Florence because she
indefatigably knew everybody—the English and Americans as
well as the Florentines; and she spent her time industriously at
work mingling these elements, whether they would or no. No
one thanked her for this especially, or remembered it after it
was done; if republics are ungrateful, even more so is a society
whose component parts are transient, coming and departing
day by day. But Madame Ferri herself appreciated the importance of her social combinations if no one else did; and, like
many another chemist, lived on content in the consciousness
of it.

"I know very little about old pictures," said the stranger,
with a slight smile, finding himself left alone beside Miss Stowe.

"And I—do not like them," she replied.

"If, more than that, you dislike them, we shall have something to talk about. Dislike can generally express itself very
well."

"On the contrary, I think it is one of those feelings we do
not express—but conceal."

"You are thinking of persons, perhaps. I was speaking of
things. Pictures are things."

Miss Stowe felt herself slightly displeased; and the feeling was not lessened when, with a "Will you allow me?" the
stranger took a seat at the end of her sofa, in the space left free
by the gray silken sweep of her dress. There was in reality an
abundance of room for him; other men were seated, and there
was no chair near. Still, the sofa was a small one; the three Italians and two Frenchmen who had succeeded each other in the
honor of standing beside her for eight or ten minutes' conversation had not thought of asking for the place so calmly taken
by this new-comer. She looked at him as he began talking; he
was quite unlike the three Italians and two Frenchmen. He was
not ruddy enough for an Englishman of that complexion; he

had a lethargic manner which was un-American. She decided, however, that he was, like herself, an American; but an American who had lived much abroad.

He was talking easily upon the various unimportant subjects in vogue at a "small party;" she replied in the same strain.

Margaret Stowe was not beautiful; "pretty" was the last word that could have been applied to her. Her features were irregular; she had a well-shaped, well-poised head, and a quantity of dark hair which she wore closely braided in a low knot behind. She was tall, slender, and rather graceful; she had dark eyes. As has been said before, she was not beautiful; but within the past two years she had acquired, her friends thought, an air of what is called distinction. In reality this was but a deep indifference, combined with the wish at the same time to maintain her place unchanged in the society in which she moved. Indifference and good manners taken together, in a tall and graceful person, will generally give that air. Beatrice Lovell had not perceived this change in her friend, but on that day at Fiesole Miss Stowe had been simply the "Margaret" of old.

In accordance with what we have called her good manners, Miss Stowe now gave to the stranger beside her easy replies, several smiles, and a fair amount of intelligent attention. It was all he could have expected; but, being a man of observation, he perceived her indifference lying broadly underneath, like the white sand under a shallow river.

During the same week she met him at a dinner-party, and they had some conversation. Later he was one of the guests at a reception which she attended, and again they talked together awhile. She now mentioned him to her aunt, Miss Harrison, to whom she generally gave, every few days, a brief account of the little events in the circle to which they belonged. She had learned his name by this time; it was Morgan.

"I wonder if he is a grandson of old Adam Morgan," said Miss Harrison, who was genealogical and reminiscent. "If he is, I should like to see him. Has he a Roman nose?"

"I think not," said her niece, smiling.

"Well, describe him, then."

"He is of medium height, neither slender nor stout; he is light, with rather peculiar eyes because they are so blue—a deep, dull blue, like old china; but they are not large, and he does not fully open them. He has a long, light mustache, no beard, and very closely cut hair."

"He must be good-looking."

"No; he is not, especially. He may be anywhere between thirty and forty; his hair in a cross-light shows a slight tinge of gray. He looks fatigued; he looks cynical. I should not be surprised if he were selfish. I do not like him."

"But if he should be the grandson of old Adam, I should have to invite him to dinner," said Miss Harrison, reflectively. "I could not do less, I think."

"I won't poison the soup. But Morgan is a common name, Aunt Ruth; this is the fourth Morgan I have met here this spring. There isn't one chance in a thousand that he belongs to the family you know." She was smiling as she spoke, but did not explain her smile; she was thinking that "Morgan" was also the name signed to that letter locked in her writing-desk —a letter whose expressions she now knew quite well, having obeyed Mrs. Lovell's injunction to "read it over" more than once. They were ardent expressions; it might be said, indeed, that they were very ardent.

But now and then that one chance in a thousand, so often summarily dismissed, asserts its existence and appears upon the scene. It turned out in the present case that the stranger was the grandson of the old Adam Morgan whom Miss Harrison remembered. Miss Stowe, in the meantime, had continued to meet him; but now she was to meet him in a new way—when he would be more upon her hands, as it were; for Miss Harrison invited him to dinner.

Miss Ruth Harrison was an invalid of nearly sixty years of age; she had been for ten years in Europe, but had only had her orphaned niece with her during the past eighteen months. She had a large fortune, and she gave Margaret every luxury; especially she liked to see her richly dressed. But it was quite well understood between them that the bulk of her wealth was to go to another relative in America who bore her family name. It was understood between them, but it was not understood outside. On the contrary, it was generally believed in Florence that Miss Stowe would inherit the whole. It is just possible that this belief may have had a remote influence in shaping the opinion which prevailed there—namely, that this young lady was "handsome" and "gracious," when, in truth, she was neither. But Mr. Morgan, the new-comer, exhibited so far, at least, no disposition to fall in with this fiction. In his estimation Miss Stowe was a conventionally agreeable, inwardly indifferent young lady of twenty-six, who carried herself well, but was too ironical as well as too dark. He came to dinner. And did not change his opinion.

A few days after the dinner Miss Harrison invited her new acquaintance to drive; she was able to go out for an hour or two in the afternoon, and she had a luxurious carriage and fine horses. Miss Stowe did not accompany them; she went off by herself to walk in the Boboli Garden.

Miss Harrison returned in good-humor. "I like him," she announced, as the maid removed her bonnet. "Yes, I think I may hope that the grandson of old Adam is not going to be a disappointment."

"The grandson of Adam—I suppose his name is Adam also —is a fortunate person, Aunt Ruth, to have gained your liking so soon; you do not often take likings to strangers."

"His name is not Adam," pursued Miss Harrison, "and that is a pity; there is character as well as association in Adam. He has a family name—Trafford. His mother was a Miss Trafford, of Virginia, it seems."

Miss Stowe was selecting flowers from a fragrant heap before her to fill the wide-mouthed vases which stood on the floor by her side; but now she stopped. "Trafford Morgan" was the name signed at the end of that letter! It must be he; it was not probable that there were two names of that special combination; it seemed a really remarkable chance. And evidently he had not gone to America, in spite of Mrs. Lovell's belief. She began to smile and almost to laugh, bending her head over a great soft purple heap of Florence lilies in order that her aunt might not observe it. But the large room was dusky, and Miss Harrison near-sighted; she observed nothing. The two ladies occupied an apartment in a house which, if it had not been so new, would have been called a "palace." Although modern, the measurements had been after the old Florentine pattern, and the result was that the occupants moved about in rooms which could have contained entire, each one, a small American house. But they liked the vastness. After a moment Miss Stowe went on arranging her blossoms, but inwardly she was enjoying much entertainment; she was going over in her own mind the expressions of that letter, which now took on quite a new character, coming no longer from some formless stranger, but from a gentleman with whom she had spoken, a person she had met and would meet again. "I never should have dreamed that he was capable of it," she said to herself. "He has seemed indifferent, *blasé*. But it places *me* in a nice position! Especially now that Aunt Ruth has taken a fancy to him. I must write to Beatrice immediately, and ask her to take back the stupid letter." She wrote during the same evening.

The next day she was attacked by a severe illness—severe, although short. No one could tell what was the matter with her; even the physician was at fault. She did not eat or sleep, she seemed hardly to know what they said when they spoke to her. Her aunt was alarmed. But at the end of the week, as suddenly as she had fallen ill, she came back to life again, rose, ordered the maid to braid her hair, and appeared at Miss Harrison's lonely little dinner-table quite herself, save that she was tremulous and pale. But by the next day even these signs were no longer very apparent. It was decided that she had had an attack of "nervous prostration;" "although why in the world you should have been seized by it just now, and here, I am at a loss, Margaret, to imagine," said her aunt.

On the day of her reappearance at the dinner-table there came a letter from Beatrice which bore the postmark of a village on one of the Channel islands. Mrs. Lovell had changed her plans, and gone yachting for a month or two with a party of friends, a yacht probably being considered to possess attributes of seclusion more total than even the most soundless village on the Brittany shore. Of course she had not received Margaret's letter, nor could she receive one—their route being uncertain, but nevertheless to the southward—until her return. Communication between them for the present was therefore at an end.

On the afternoon after Margaret's reappearance Madame Ferri was making a visit of congratulation upon the recovery of "our dear girl." It was a cool day, a heavy rain had fallen, and fresh snow gleamed on the summits of the Apennines; our dear girl, very unresponsive and silent, was dressed in black velvet, whose rich, plain folds brought out her slenderness, and made more apparent than usual the graceful shape of her head and hair. But the unrelieved black made her look extremely pale, and it was her recent illness, probably, which made her look also tired and languid. Madame Ferri, who kept constantly in practice her talent for being charming (she was always spoken of as "charming"), looked at her for a time while conversing; then she rose, took all the crimson roses from a vase, and, going to her, placed one in her hair, meditatively; another in a button-hole of the closely fitting high corsage; and, after a moment's reflection, all the others in a bunch in a velvet loop which was on the side of the skirt not quite half-way down, rapidly denuding herself of pins for the purpose as she proceeded. "There!" she said, stepping back a few paces to survey her handiwork, with her head critically on one side, "*now* you are a picture. Look, dear Miss Harrison, pray look."

Miss Harrison put up her glass and approved. And then, while this climax still lasted, Madame Ferri took her departure; she liked to depart in a climax.

She had hardly gone when another card was brought in: "Mr. Trafford Morgan." He, too, had come to pay his respects to Miss Harrison upon the change for the better in her niece; he had not expected to see the latter person, he had merely heard that there was "an improvement." After he had been there twenty minutes he said to himself that there was, and in more ways than one. She not only looked much better than usual (this may have been owing to the roses), but there was a new gentleness about her; and she listened with a perceptible increase of attention to what he said. Not that he cared much for this; he had not admired Miss Stowe; but any man (this he remarked to himself) likes to be listened to when he is talking better than the contrary; and as the minutes passed he became conscious that Miss Stowe was not only listening, but bestowing upon him also what seemed an almost serious attention. She did not say much—Miss Harrison said more; but she listened to and looked at him. She had not looked at him previously; people can turn their eyes upon one without really looking, and Miss Stowe had excelled in this accomplishment.

During the next week he met her at a dinner-party; she went to these entertainments with a friend of her aunt's, a lady who was delighted to act as chaperon for the heiress. The spring season was now at its height in Florence, and the members of the same circle perforce constantly met each other; on each separate occasion during the two weeks that followed Trafford Morgan was conscious that Miss Stowe was honoring him, although in a studiously guarded and quiet way, with much of a very observant attention. This, in the end, excited in him some curiosity. He had as good an opinion of himself as most men have; but he did not think it probable that the heiress had suddenly fallen in love with him without rhyme or reason, as it were, the "rhyme" being that he was neither an Apollo, an Endymion, nor a military man; the "reason," that he had never in the least attempted to make himself agreeable to her. Of course, if he *had* attempted— But he had not. She was not in need of entertainment; she had enough of that, of all sorts, including apparently the sort given by suitors. She showed no sign of having troublesomely impulsive feelings; on the contrary, she seemed cold. "She is playing some game," he thought; "she has some end in view. But if she wishes to make use of me she must show her hand more. I may assist her, and I may not; but, at any rate, I must understand what it is—I will not be led." He made up his mind that her aim was to excite remark in their circle; there was probably some one in that circle who was to be stimulated by a little wholesome jealousy. It was an ancient and commonplace method, and he had not thought her commonplace. But human nature at heart is but a commonplace affair, after all, and the methods and motives of the world have not altered much, in spite of the gray lapse of ages.

Morgan was an idle man; at present he was remaining in Italy for a purpose, and had nothing to do there. The next time he met Miss Stowe he followed out his theory and took the lead; he began to pay her attention which might, if pursued, have aroused observation. To his surprise she drew back, and so completely that he was left stranded. He tried this three times on three different occasions, and each time met the same rebuff. It became evident, therefore, that Miss Stowe did not wish for the kind of attention which he had supposed was her point; but as, whenever she could do it unobserved, she continued to turn upon him the same quiet scrutiny, he began to ask himself whether she wished for any other. An opportunity occurred which made him think that she did.

It was in the Boboli Garden, where he had gone to walk off a fit of weariness; here he came upon Miss Stowe. There seemed to be no one in the garden save themselves—at least, no one whom they knew; only a few stray tourists wandering about, with Baedeker, Horner, and Hare. The world of fashion was at the Cascine that day, where races were going on. Morgan did not feel like talking; he exchanged the usual phrases with Miss Stowe, and then prepared to pass on. But she said, gently, "Are you going now? If not, why not stroll awhile with me?"

After this, as he mentally observed, of course he was forced to stroll awhile. But, on the whole, he found himself entertained, because his companion gave him an attention which was almost devout. Its seriousness, indeed, compelled him to be serious likewise, and made him feel as though he were in an atmosphere combining the characteristics of a church and a school; he was partly priest, partly pedagogue, and the sensation was amusing. She asked him what he liked best in Florence; and she called it, gravely, "enchanting Florence."

"Giotto and Botticelli," he answered.

"I wish you would be in earnest; I am in earnest."

"With all the earnestness in the world, Miss Stowe, I could only repeat the same reply."

"What is it you find to like in them? Will you tell me?"

"It would take an age—a full half-hour; you would be quite tired out. Women are so much quicker in their mental processes than we are that you would apprehend what I was going to say before I could get it out; you would ascend all the heights, scour all the plains, and arrive at the goal before I came even in sight, where you would sit waiting, patiently or impatiently, as I, slowly and with mortified perception, approached."

"Yes, we are quick; but we are superficial. I wish you would tell me."

He glanced at her; she was looking at him with an expression in her eyes which was extremely earnest. "I cannot deliver a discourse while walking," he said. "I require a seat."

"Let us go to the amphitheatre; I often sit there for a while on the stone benches under the old statues. I like to see them standing around the circle; they are so serenely indifferent to the modern pencil-scrawlings on their robes, so calmly certain that their time will come again."

"What you say is entirely charming. Still, I hardly think I can talk to the statues. I must have something more—more secluded." He was aware that he was verging upon a slight impertinence; but he wished to see whether she would accede —what she would do. He made no effort to find the seclusion of which he spoke; he left that to her.

She hesitated a moment; then, "We might go to a seat there is under a tree at the top of the slope," she said. "It is a pleasant place."

He assented; and they went up the path by the side of the tall, stately hedges, and past the fountain and the great statue of Abbondanza. The stone bench was not one of those sought for; it was not in front, but on the western side. It commanded a view of the city below, with the Duomo and Giotto's lovely bell-tower; of the fruit-trees, all in flower on the outskirts; of the treetops of the Cascine, now like a cloud of golden smoke with their tender brown leaflets, tasselled blossoms, and winged seeds; of the young grain, springing greenly down the valley; and the soft, velvety mountains rising all around. "How beautiful it is!" she said, leaning back, closing her parasol and folding her hands.

"Beautiful—yes; but barren of human interest save to those who are going to sell the fruit, or who depend upon the growth of the grain. The beauty of art is deeper; it is all human."

"I must be quite ignorant about art," she answered, "be-cause it does not impress me in that way; I wish it did. I wish you would instruct me a little, Mr. Morgan."

"Good!" he thought. "What next?" But although he thought, he of course was obliged to talk also, and so he began about the two art masters he had mentioned. He delivered quite an epic upon Giotto's two little frescos in the second cloister of Santa Maria Novella, and he openly preferred the third there—the little Virgin going up the impossible steps— to Titian's splendid picture of the same subject, in Venice. He grew didactic and mystic over the round Botticelli of the Uffizi and the one in the Prometheus room at the Pitti; he invented as he went along, and amused himself not a little with his own unusual flow of language. His companion listened, and now and then asked a question. But her questions were directed more towards what he thought of the pictures (after a while he noticed this), and what impressions they made upon him, than to the pictures themselves or their claims to celebrity. As he went on he made some slight attempts to diverge a little from the subject in hand, and skirt, if ever so slightly, the borders of flirtation; he was curious to see if she would follow him there. But she remained unresponsive; and, while giving no sign of even perceiving his digressions, she brought him back to his art atmosphere, each time he left it, with a question or remark very well adapted for the purpose; so well, indeed, that it could not have been by chance.

She declined his escort homeward, pretexting a visit she wished to pay; but she said, of her own accord, that she would sing for him the next time he came. He knew this was a favor she did not often grant; Madame Ferri had so informed him.

He went, without much delay; and she sang several songs in the dusky corner where her piano stood while he sat near. The light from the wax candles at the other end of the large room, where Miss Harrison was knitting, did not penetrate here; but she said she liked to sing in a semi-darkness, as she had only a twilight voice. It was in truth not at all powerful; but it was sweet and low, and she sang with much expression. Trafford Morgan liked music; it was not necessary to make up a conviction or theory about that; he simply had a natural love for it, and he came more than once to hear Miss Stowe sing.

In the meantime Miss Harrison continued to like "the grandson of old Adam," and again invited him to drive. A month went by, and, by the end of it, he had seen in one way and another a good deal of these two ladies. The "later manner" (as he mentally called it) of Miss Stowe continued; when they were in company, she was as she had been originally, but when they were unobserved, or by themselves, she gave him the peculiar sober attention which he did not quite comprehend. He had several theories about it, and varied between them. He was a man who did not talk of persons, who never told much. If questioned, while answering readily and apparently without reserve, it was noticed afterwards that he had told nothing. He had never spoken of Sicily, for instance, but had talked a good deal of Sweden. This reticence, so exasperating to many women, seemed agreeable to Miss Stowe, who herself did not tell much, or talk of persons—that is, generally. One person she talked about, and with persistence. Morgan was hardly ever with her that she did not, sooner or later, begin to talk to him about himself. Sometimes he was responsive, sometimes not; but responsive or unresponsive, in society or out of it, he had talked, all told, a goodly number of hours with Miss Stowe when May attained its zenith and the season waned.

The tourists had gone to Venice; the red gleam of guide-books along the streets and the conscientiousness of woollen travelling-dresses in the galleries were no longer visible. Miss Stowe now stepped over the boundary-line of her caution a little; many of the people she knew had gone; she went with Trafford to the Academy and the Pitti; she took him into cool, dim churches, and questioned him concerning his creed; she strolled with him through the monastery of San Marco, and asked what his idea was of the next world. She said she liked cloisters; she would like to walk in one for an hour or two every day.

He replied that there were a number of cloisters in Florence; they might visit them in succession and pace around quietly. The effect would be heightened if she would read aloud, as they paced, short sentences from some ancient, stiff-covered little book like *De Contemptu Mundi*.

"Ah," she said, "you are not in earnest. But I am!"

And she seemed to be; he said to himself that he had hardly had a look or word from her which was not only earnest, but almost portentously so. She now began to do whatever he asked her to do, whether it was to sing Italian music or to read Dante's *Vita Nuova*, both of which she had said she did not like. It is probable that he asked her to do a number of things about this time which he did not especially care for, simply to see if she would comply; she always did.

"If she goes on in this sort of way," he thought, "never showing the least opposition, or personal moods different from mine, I really don't know where we shall end!"

But at last she did show both. It was in the evening, and she was at the piano; after one or two ballads he asked her to sing a little English song he had found among her music, not printed, but in manuscript.

"Oh, that is nothing," she said, putting out her hand to take it from him. "I will sing this of Schumann's instead; it is much prettier."

But he maintained his point. "I like this better," he said. "I like the name—of course it is impossible, but it is pleasant—'Semper Fidelis.'"

She took it, looked at it in silence for a moment, and then, without further reply, began to sing. There was nothing remarkable in the words or the music; she did not sing as well as usual, either; she hurried the time.

### "SEMPER FIDELIS

"Dumb and unchanged my thoughts still round thee hover,
        Nor will be moved;
E'en though I strive, my heart remains thy lover,
        Though unbeloved;
    Yet there is sad content in loyalty,
    And, though the silent gift is naught to thee,
        It changes never—
        Faithful forever."

This was the verse; but at the fifth line she faltered, stopped, and then, rising abruptly, left the room.

"Margaret is very uneven at times," said Miss Harrison, apologetically, from her easy-chair.

"All interesting persons are uneven," he replied. He went over and took a seat beside his hostess, remaining half an hour longer; but as he went back to his hotel he said to himself that Miss Stowe had been for many weeks the most even woman he had ever known, showing neither variation nor shadow of turning. She had been as even as a straight line.

On this account her sudden emotion made an impression upon him. The next day he mentioned that he was going to Trieste.

"Not Venice?" said Miss Harrison. "I thought everybody went to Venice."

"Venice," he replied, "is pre-eminently the place where one needs either an actual, tangible companionship of the dearest sort, or a memory like it. I, who have neither, keep well away from Venice!"

"I rather think, Mr. Morgan, that you have had pretty much what you wanted, in Venice or elsewhere," said Miss Harrison, with a dry humor she sometimes showed. Here she was called from the room to see a poor woman whom she befriended; Miss Stowe and Morgan were left alone.

He was looking at her; he was noting what effect, if any, the tidings of his departure (he had named to-morrow) would have upon her. She had not been conventional; would she resort to conventionality now?

Her gaze was bent upon the floor; after a while she looked up. "Where shall you be this summer?" she said, slowly. "Perhaps we shall be there too." Her eyes were fixed upon his face, her tone was hardly above a whisper.

Perhaps it was curiosity that made him do what he did; whether it was or not, mingled with it there was certainly a good deal of audacity. He rose, went to her, and took her hand. "Forgive me," he said; "I am in love with some one else."

It implied much. But had not her manner implied the same, or more?

She rose; they were both standing now.

"What do you mean?" she demanded, a light coming into her eyes—eyes usually abstracted, almost dull.

"Only what I have said."

"Why should you say it to me?"

"I thought you might be—interested."

"You are mistaken. I am not in the least interested. Why should I be?"

"Are you not a little unkind?"

"Not more unkind than you are insolent."

She was very angry. He began to be a little angry himself.

"I ask your pardon with the deepest humility, Miss Stowe. The insolence of which you accuse me was as far as possible from my mind. If I thought you might be somewhat interested in what I have told you, it was because you have honored me with some small share of your attention during the past week or two; probably it has spoiled me."

"I have; and for a month or two, not a week or two. But there was a motive— It was an experiment."

"You have used me for experimental purposes, then?"

"Yes."

"I am immensely grateful to have been considered worthy of a part in an experiment of yours, even although a passive one. May I ask if the experiment is ended?"

"It is."

"Since when? Since I made that confession about some one else?"

Miss Stowe's face was pale, her dark eyes were brilliant. "I knew all the while that you were in love—hopelessly in love—with Mrs. Lovell," she said, with a proud smile. "That was the reason that, for my experiment, I selected *you*."

A flush rose over his face as she spoke. "You thought you would have the greater triumph?" he asked.

"I thought nothing of the kind. I thought that I should be safe, because you would not respond."

"And you did not wish me to respond?"

"I did not."

"Excuse me—we are speaking frankly, are we not?—but do you not contradict yourself somewhat? You say you did not wish me to respond; yet, have you not tried to make me?"

"That was not my object. It was but a necessary accompaniment of the experiment."

"And if I *had* responded?" he said, looking at her.

"I knew you could not. I knew quite well—I mean I could imagine quite well—how much you loved Beatrice. But it has all been a piece of folly upon my part—I see it now." She turned away, and went across to the piano. "I wish you would go now," she said, in a low voice, vaguely turning over the music. "*I* cannot, because my aunt will think it strange to find me gone."

Instead of obeying her, he crossed the room and stood beside her; and then he saw in the twilight that her eyes were full of tears and her lips quivering, in spite of her effort to prevent it.

"Margaret," he said, suddenly, and with a good deal of feeling in his voice, "I am not worth it! Indeed I am not!" And again he touched her hand.

But she drew it from him. "Are you by any chance imagining that my tears are for *you*?" she said, in a low tone, but facing him like a creature at bay. "Have you interpreted me in that way? I have a right to know; speak!"

"I am at a loss to interpret you," he said, after a moment's silence.

"I will tell you the whole, then—I must tell you; your mistake forces it from me." She paused, drew a quick breath, and then went on, rapidly: "I love some one else. I have been very unhappy. Just after you came I received a letter which told me that he was soon to be married; he *is* married now. I had an illness in consequence. You may remember my illness? I made up my mind then that I would root out the feeling if possible, no matter at what cost of pain and effort and long patience. You came in my way. I knew you were deeply attached elsewhere—"

"How did you know it?" he said. He was leaning against the piano watching her; she stood with her hands folded, and pressed so tightly together that he could see the force of the pressure.

"Never mind how; but quite simply and naturally. I said to myself that I would try to become interested in you, even if only to a small degree; I would do everything in my power to forward it. It would be an acquired interest; still, acquired interests can be deep. People can become interested in music, in pictures, in sports, in that way; why not, then, in persons also, since they are more human?"

"That is the very reason—because they are too human," he answered.

But she did not heed. "I have studied you; I have tried to find the good in you; I have tried to believe in you, to idealize you. I have given every thought that I could control to you, and to you alone, for two long months," she said, passionately, unlocking her hands, reddened with their pressure against each other, and turning away.

"It has been a failure?"

"Complete."

"And if you had succeeded?" he asked, folding his arms as he leaned against the piano.

"I should have been glad and happy. I should never have

seen *you* again, of course; but at least the miserable old feeling would have been laid at rest."

"And its place filled by another as miserable!"

"Oh no; it could never have been *that*," she said, with an emphasis of scorn.

"You tried a dangerous remedy, Margaret."

"Not so dangerous as the disease."

"A remedy may be worse than a disease. In spite of your scornful tone, permit me to tell you that if you had succeeded at all, it would have been in the end by loving me as you loved —I mean love—this other man. While I, in the meantime, am in love (as you are kind enough to inform me—hopelessly) with another woman! Is Beatrice a friend of yours?"

"My dearest friend."

"Has it never occurred to you that you were playing towards her rather a traitorous part?"

"Never."

"Supposing, during this experiment of yours, that I had fallen in love with you?"

"It would have been nothing to Beatrice if you had," responded Mrs. Lovell's friend instantly and loyally, although remembering, at the same moment, that Fiesole blush. Then, in a changed voice, and with a proud humility which was touching, she added, "It would have been quite impossible. Beatrice is the loveliest woman in the world; any one who had loved *her* would never think of me."

At this moment Miss Harrison's voice was heard in the hall; she was returning.

"Good-bye," said Morgan. "I shall go to-morrow. You would rather have me go." He took her hand, held it an instant, and then raised it to his lips. "Good-bye," he said, again. "Forgive me, Margaret. And do not entirely—forget me."

When Miss Harrison returned they were looking at the music on the piano. A few moments later he took leave.

"I am sorry he has gone," said Miss Harrison. "What in the world is he going to do at Trieste? Well, so goes life! nothing but partings! One thing is a consolation, however—at least, to me; the grandson of old Adam did not turn out a disappointment, after all."

"I do not think I am a judge," replied Miss Stowe.

*

In June Miss Harrison went northward to Paris, her niece accompanying her. They spent the summer in Switzerland; in the autumn returned to Paris; and in December went southward to Naples and Rome.

Mrs. Lovell had answered Margaret's letter in June. The six weeks of yachting had been charming; the yacht belonged to an English gentleman, who had a country-seat in Devonshire. She herself, by-the-way, might be in Devonshire during the summer; it was so quiet there. Could not Miss Harrison be induced to come to Devonshire? That would be *so* delightful. It had been extremely difficult to wear deep mourning at sea; but of course she had persisted in it. Much of it had been completely ruined; she had been obliged to buy more. Yes—it *was* amusing—her meeting Trafford Morgan. And so unexpected, of course. Did she like him? No, the letter need not be returned. If it troubled her to have it, she might destroy it; perhaps it was as well it should be destroyed. There were some such pleasant qualities in English life; there was not so much opportunity, perhaps, as in America—"That blush meant nothing, then, after all," thought the reader, lifting her eyes from the page, and looking musingly at a picture on the wall. "She said it meant only a lack of iron; and, as Beatrice always tells the truth, she did mean that, probably, and not irony, as I supposed." She sat thinking for a few moments, and then went back to the letter: There was not so much opportunity, perhaps, as in America; but there was more stability, more certainty that things would continue to go on. There were various occurrences which she would like to tell; but she never wrote that sort of thing, as Margaret knew. If she would only come to Devonshire for the summer—and so forth, and so forth.

But Beatrice did sometimes write "that sort of thing," after all. During the next February, in Rome, after a long silence, Margaret received a letter from her which brought the tidings of her engagement. He was an Englishman. He had a country-seat in Devonshire. He owned a yacht. Beatrice seemed very happy. "We shall not be married until next winter," she wrote. "I would not consent, of course, to anything earlier. I have consistently endeavored to do what was right from the beginning, and shall not waver now. But by next January there can be no criticism, and I suppose that will be the time. How I wish you were here to advise me about a hundred things! Besides, I want you to know him; you will be sure to like him. He is" —and so forth, and so forth.

"She is following out her destiny," thought the reader in Rome.

In March Miss Harrison found the Eternal City too warm, and moved northward as far as Florence. Madame Ferri was delighted to see them again; she came five times during the first three days to say so.

"You will find *so* many whom you knew last year here again as well as yourselves," she said, enthusiastically. "We shall have some of our *charming* old reunions. Let me see—I think I can tell you." And she ran over a list of names, among them that of "Mr. Morgan."

"What, not the grandson of Adam?" said Miss Harrison.

"He is not *quite* so old as that, is he?" said Madame Ferri, laughing. "It is the one who dined with you several times last year, I believe—Mr. Trafford Morgan. I shall have great pleasure in telling him this very day that you are here."

"Do you know whether he is to remain long?" said Miss Stowe, who had not before spoken.

"I am sorry to say he is not; Mr. Morgan is always an addition, I think—don't you? But he told me only yesterday that he was going this week to—to Tarascon, I think he said."

"Trieste and Tarascon—he selects the most extraordinary places!" said Miss Harrison. "The next time it will be Tartarus."

Madame Ferri was overcome with mirth. "*Dear* Miss Harrison, you are *too* droll! *Isn't* she, dear Miss Stowe?"

"He probably chooses his names at random," said Miss Stowe, with indifference.

The next day, at the Pitti, she met him. She was alone, and returned his salutation coldly. He was with some ladies who were standing near, looking at the "Madonna of the Chair." He merely asked how Miss Harrison was, and said he should give himself the pleasure of coming to see her very soon; then he bowed and returned to his friends. Not long afterwards she saw them all leave the gallery together.

Half an hour later she was standing in front of one of Titian's portraits, when a voice close beside her said, "Ah! the young man in black. You are not admiring it?"

There had been almost a crowd in the gorgeous rooms that

morning. She had stood elbow to elbow with so many persons that she no longer noticed them; Trafford Morgan had been able, therefore, to approach and stand beside her for several minutes without attracting her recognition. As he spoke she turned, and, in answer to his smile, gave an even slighter bow than before; it was hardly more than a movement of the eyelids. Two English girls, with large hats, sweet, shy eyes, and pink cheeks, who were standing close beside them, turned away towards the left for a minute to look at another picture.

"Do not treat me badly," he said. "I need kindness. I am not very happy."

"I can understand that," she answered. Here the English girls came back again.

"I think you are wrong in admiring it," he said, looking at the portrait; "it is a quite impossible picture. A youth with that small, delicate head and face could never have had those shoulders; they are the shoulders of quite another type of man. This is some boy whom Titian wished to flatter; but he was artist enough to try and hide the flattery by that overcoat. The face has no calm; you would not have admired it in life."

"On the contrary, I should have admired it greatly," replied Miss Stowe. "I should have adored it. I should have adored the eyes."

"Surely there is nothing in them but a sort of pugnacity."

"Whatever it is, it is delightful."

The English girls now turned away towards the right.

"You are quite changed," he said, looking at her.

"Yes, I think I am. I am much more agreeable. Every one will tell you so; even Madame Ferri, who is obliged to reconcile it with my having been always more agreeable than any one in the world, you know. I have become lighter. I am no longer heavy."

"You mean you are no longer serious."

"That is it. I used to be absurdly serious. But it is an age since we last met. You were going to Trieste, were you not? I hope you found it agreeable?"

"It is not an age; it is a year."

"Oh, a great deal can happen in a year," said Miss Stowe, turning away.

She was as richly dressed as ever, and not quite so plainly.

Her hair was arranged in little rippling waves low down upon her forehead, which made her look, if not what might be called more worldly, at least more fashionable, since previously she had worn it arranged with a simplicity which was neither. Owing to this new arrangement of her hair, her eyes looked larger and darker.

He continued to walk beside her for some moments, and then, as she came upon a party of friends, he took leave.

In the evening he called upon Miss Harrison, and remained an hour. Miss Stowe was not at home. The next day he sent to Miss Harrison a beautiful basket of flowers.

"He knows we always keep the rooms full of them," remarked Miss Stowe, rather disdainfully.

"All the same, I like the attention," said Miss Harrison. And she sent him an invitation to dinner. She liked to have one guest.

He came. During the evening he asked Miss Stowe to sing. "I have lost my voice," she answered.

"Yes," said Miss Harrison, "it is really remarkable; Margaret, although she seems so well, has not been able to sing for months—indeed, for a full year. It is quite sad."

"I am not sad about it, Aunt Ruth; I am relieved. I never sang well—I had not voice enough. There was really nothing in it but expression; and that was all pretence."

"You are trying to make us think you very artificial," said Morgan.

"I can make you think what I please, probably. I can follow several lines of conduct, one after the other, and make you believe them all." She spoke lightly; her general tone was much lighter than formerly, as she herself had said.

"Do you ever walk in the Boboli Garden now?" he asked, later.

"Occasionally; but it is a dull place. And I do not walk as much as I did; I drive with my aunt."

"Yes, Margaret has grown indolent," said Miss Harrison; "and it seems to agree with her. She has more color than formerly; she looks well."

"Wonderfully," said Morgan. "But you are thinner than you were," he added, turning towards her.

"And darker!" she answered, laughing. "Mr. Morgan does

not admire arrangements in black and white, Aunt Ruth; do not embarrass him." She wore that evening a white dress, un-relieved by any color.

"I see you are bent upon being unkind," he said. It was sup-posed to be a society remark.

"Not the least in the world," she answered, in the same tone.

He met her several times in company, and had short con-versations with her. Then, one afternoon, he came upon her unexpectedly in the Cascine; she was strolling down the broad path alone.

"So you do walk sometimes, after all," he said.

"Never. I am only strolling. I drove here with Aunt Ruth, but, as she came upon a party of American friends who are going to-morrow, I gave up my place, and they are driving around together for a while, and no doubt settling the entire affairs of Westchester County."

"I am glad she met them; I am glad to find you alone. I have something I wish much to say to you."

"Such a beginning always frightens me. Pray postpone it."

"On the contrary, I shall hasten it. I must make the most of this rare opportunity. Do you remember when you did me the honor, Miss Stowe, to make me the subject of an experiment?"

"You insist upon recalling that piece of folly?" she said, opening her parasol. Her tone was composed and indifferent.

"I recall it because I wish to base something upon it. I wish to ask you—to allow yourself to be passively the subject of an experiment on *my* part, an experiment of the same nature."

She glanced at him; he half smiled. "Did you imagine, then, that mine was in earnest?" she said, with a fine, light scorn, light as air.

"I never imagine anything. Imaginations are useless."

"Not so useless as experiments. Let yours go, and tell me rather what you found to like in—Trieste."

"I suppose you know that I went to England?"

"I know nothing. But yes—I do know that you are going to—Tarascon."

"I shall not go if you will permit what I have asked."

"Isn't it rather suddenly planned?" she said, ironically. "You did not know we were coming."

"Very suddenly. I have thought of it only since yesterday."

They had strolled into a narrow path which led by one of those patches of underwood of which there are several in the Cascine—little bosky places carefully preserved in a tangled wildness which is so pretty and amusing to American eyes, accustomed to the stretch of real forests.

"You don't know how I love these little patches," said Miss Stowe. "There is such a good faith about them; they are charming."

"You were always fond of nature, I remember. I used to tell you that art was better."

"Ah! did you?" she said, her eyes following the flight of a bird.

"You have forgotten very completely in one year."

"Yes, I think I have. I always forget, you know, what it is not agreeable to remember. But I must go back; Aunt Ruth will be waiting." They turned.

"I will speak more plainly," said Morgan. "I went to England during July last—that is, I followed Mrs. Lovell. She was in Devonshire. Quite recently I have learned that she has become engaged in—Devonshire, and is soon to be married there. I am naturally rather down about it. I am seeking some other interest. I should like to try your plan for a while, and build up an interest in—you."

Miss Stowe's lip curled. "The plans are not alike," she said. "Yours is badly contrived. *I* did not tell *you* beforehand what I was endeavoring to do!"

"I am obliged to tell you. You would have discovered it."

"Discovered what a pretence it was? That is true. A woman can act a part better than a man. *You* did not discover! And what am I to do in this little comedy of yours?"

"Nothing. It is, in truth, nothing to you; you have told me that, even when you made a great effort towards that especial object, it was impossible to get up the slightest interest in me. Do not take a violent dislike to me; that is all."

"And if it is already taken?"

"I shall have to conquer that. What I meant was—do not take a fresh one."

"There is nothing like precedent, and therefore I repeat

your question: what if you should succeed—I mean as regards yourself?" she said, looking at him with a satirical expression.

"It is my earnest wish to succeed."

"You do not add, as I did, that in case you do succeed you will of course never see me again, but that at least the miserable old feeling will be at rest?"

"I do not add it."

"And at the conclusion, when it has failed, shall you tell me that the cause of failure was—the inevitable comparisons?"

"Beatrice is extremely lovely," he replied, turning his head and gazing at the Arno, shining through an opening in the hedge. "I do not attempt to pretend, even to myself, that she is not the loveliest woman I ever knew."

"Since you do not pretend it to yourself you will not pretend it to me."

She spoke without interrogation; but he treated the words as a question. "Why should I?" he said. And then he was silent.

"There is Aunt Ruth," said Miss Stowe; "I see the horses. She is probably wondering what has become of me."

"You have not altogether denied me," he said, just before they reached the carriage. "I assure you I will not be in the least importunate. Take a day or two to consider. After all, if there is no one upon whom it can really infringe (of course I know you have admirers; I have even heard their names), why should you not find it even a little amusing?"

Miss Stowe turned towards him, and a peculiar expression came into her eyes as they met his. "I am not sure but that I shall find it so," she answered. And then they joined Miss Harrison.

The day or two had passed. There had been no formal question asked, and no formal reply given; but as Miss Stowe had not absolutely forbidden it, the experiment may be said to have been begun. It was soon reported in Florence that Trafford Morgan was one of the suitors for the hand of the heiress; and, being a candidate, he was of course subjected to the searching light of Public Inquiry. Public Inquiry discovered that he was thirty-eight years of age; that he had but a small income; that he was indolent, indifferent, and cynical. Not being able to find any open vices, Public Inquiry considered that he was too *blasé* to have them; he had probably exhausted them all long before.

All this Madame Ferri repeated to Miss Harrison, not because she was in the least opposed to Mr. Morgan, but simply as part of her general task as gatherer and disseminator.

"Trafford Morgan is not a saint, but he is well enough in his way," replied Miss Harrison. "I am not at all sure that a saint would be agreeable in the family."

Madame Ferri was much amused by this; but she carried away the impression also that Miss Harrison favored the suitor.

In the meantime nothing could be more quiet than the manner of the supposed suitor when he was with Miss Stowe. He now asked questions of her; when they went to the churches, he asked her impressions of the architecture; when they visited the galleries, he asked her opinions of the pictures. He inquired what books she liked, and why she liked them; and sometimes he slowly repeated her replies.

This last habit annoyed her. "I wish you would not do that," she said, with some irritation. "It is like being forced to look at one's self in a mirror."

"I do it to analyze them," he answered. "I am so dense, you know, it takes me a long time to understand. When you say, for instance, that Romola is not a natural character because her love for Tito ceases, I, who think that the unnatural part is that she should ever have loved him, naturally dwell upon the remark."

"She would have continued to love him in life. Beauty is all powerful."

"I did not know that women cared much for it," he answered. Then, after a moment, "Do not be too severe upon me," he added; "I am doing my best."

She made no reply.

"I thought certainly you would have answered, 'By contrast?'" he said, smiling. "But you are not so satirical as you were. I cannot make you angry with me."

"Have you tried?"

"Of course I have tried. It would be a step gained to move you—even in that way."

"I thought your experiment was to be all on one side?" she said. They were sitting in a shady corner of the cloisters of San Marco; she was leaning back in her chair, following with the point of her parasol the lines of the Latin inscription on the slab at her feet over an old monk's last resting-place.

"I am not so consistent as I should be," he answered, rising and sauntering off, with his hands in the pockets of his short morning-coat, to look at St. Peter the Martyr.

At another time they were in the Michael Angelo chapel of San Lorenzo. It was past the hour for closing, but Morgan had bribed the custode to allow them to remain, and the old man had closed the door and gone away, leaving them alone with the wondrous marbles.

"What do they mean?" he said. "Tell me."

"They mean fate, our sad human fate: the beautiful Dawn in all the pain of waking; the stern determination of the Day; the recognition of failure in Evening; and the lassitude of dreary, hopeless sleep in Night. It is one way of looking at life."

"But not your way?"

"Oh, I have no way; I am too limited. But genius takes a broader view, and genius, I suppose, must always be sad. People with that endowment, I have noticed, are almost always very unhappy."

He was sitting beside her, and, as she spoke, he saw a little flush rise in her cheeks; she was remembering when Mrs. Lovell had used the same words, although in another connection.

"We have never spoken directly, or at any length, of Beatrice," she said, suddenly. "I wish you would tell me about her."

"Here?"

"Yes, here and now; Lorenzo shall be your judge."

"I am not afraid of Lorenzo. He is not a god; on the contrary, he has all our deepest humanity on his musing face; it is for this reason that he impresses us so powerfully. As it is the first time you have expressed any wish, Miss Stowe, I suppose I must obey it."

"Will it be difficult?"

"It is always difficult, is it not, for a man to speak of an unhappy love?" he said, leaning his elbow on the back of the seat, and shading his eyes with his hand as he looked at her.

"I will excuse you."

"I have not asked to be excused. I first met Mrs. Lovell in Sicily. I was with her almost constantly during five weeks. She is as lovable as a rose—as a peach—as a child." He paused.

"Your comparisons are rather remarkable," said Miss Stowe, her eyes resting upon the grand massiveness of Day.

"They are truthful. I fell in love with her; and I told her so because there was that fatal thing, an opportunity—that is, a garden-seat, starlight, and the perfume of flowers. Of course these were irresistible."

"Indeed?"

"Do not be contemptuous. It is possible that you may not have been exposed to the force of the combination as yet. She rebuked me with that lovely, gentle softness of hers, and then she went away; the Sicilian days were over. I wrote to her—"

He was sitting in the same position, with his hand shading his eyes, looking at her; as he spoke the last phrase he perceived that she colored, and colored deeply.

"You knew the story generally," he said, dropping his arm and leaning forward. "But it is not possible you saw that letter!"

She rose and walked across, as if to get a nearer view of Day. "I admire it so much!" she said, after a moment. "If it should stretch out that great right arm, it could crush us to atoms." And she turned towards him again.

As she did she saw that he had colored also; a deep, dark flush had risen in his face, and covered even his forehead.

"I am safe—very safe!" he said. "After reading such a letter as that, written to another woman, you are not likely to bestow much regard upon the writer, try as he may!"

Miss Stowe looked at him. "You are overacting," she said, coldly. "It is not in your part to pretend to care so soon. It was to be built up gradually."

"Lorenzo understands me," he said, recovering himself. "Shall I go on?"

"I think I must go now," she answered, declining a seat; "it is late."

"In a moment. Let me finish, now that I have begun. I had thought of returning to America; indeed, Beatrice had advised it; she thought I was becoming expatriated. But I gave it up and remained in Italy because I did not wish to appear too much her slave (women do not like men who obey them too well, you know). After this effort I was consistent enough to follow her to England. I found her in—Devonshire, love-lier than ever; and I was again fascinated; I was even ready to accept beforehand all the rules and embargo of the strictest respect to the memory of Mr. Lovell."

Miss Stowe's eyes were upon Day; but here, involuntarily, she glanced towards her companion. His face remained unchanged.

"I was much in love with her. She allowed me no encouragement. But I did not give up a sort of vague hope I had until this recent change. Then, of course, I knew that it was all over for me."

"I am sorry for you," replied Miss Stowe after a pause, still looking at Day.

"Of course I have counted upon that—upon your sympathy. I knew that you would understand."

"Spare me the quotation, 'A fellow-feeling,' and so forth," she said, moving towards the door. "I am going; I feel as though we had already desecrated too long this sacred place."

"It is no desecration. The highest heights of art, as well as of life, belong to love," he said, as they went out into the cool, low hall, paved with the gravestones of the Medici.

"Don't you always think of them lying down below?" she said. "Giovanni in his armor, and Leonore of Toledo in her golden hair?"

"Since when have you become so historical? They were a wicked race."

"And since when have you become so virtuous?" she answered. "They were at least successful."

Time passed. It has a way of passing rapidly in Florence; although each day is long and slow and full and delightful, a month flies. Again the season was waning. It was now believed that Mr. Morgan had been successful, although nothing definite was known. It was remarked how unusually well Miss Stowe looked: her eyes were so bright and she had so much color that she really looked brilliant. Madame Ferri repeated this to Miss Harrison.

"Margaret was always brilliant," said her aunt.

"Oh, extremely!" said Madame Ferri.

"Only people never found it out," added Miss Harrison.

She herself maintained a calm and uninquiring demeanor. Sometimes she was with her niece and her niece's supposed suitor, and sometimes not. She continued to receive him with the same affability which she had bestowed upon him from the first, and occasionally she invited him to dinner and to drive. She made no comment upon the frequency of his visits, or the length of his conversations upon the little balcony in the evening, where the plash of the fountain came faintly up from below. In truth she had no cause for solicitude; nothing could be more tranquil than the tone of the two talkers. Nothing more was said about Mrs. Lovell; conversation had sunk back into the old impersonal channel.

"You are very even," Morgan said one evening. "You do not seem to have any moods. I noticed it last year."

"One is even," she replied, "when one is—"

"Indifferent," he suggested.

She did not contradict him.

Two things she refused to do: she would not sing, and she would not go to the Boboli Garden.

"As I am especially fond of those tall, ceremonious old hedges and serene statues, you cut me off from a real pleasure," said Morgan.

It was on the evening of the 16th of May; they were sitting by the open window; Miss Harrison was not present.

"You can go there after we have gone," she said, smiling. "We leave to-morrow."

"You leave to-morrow!" he repeated. Then, after an instant, "It is immensely kind to tell me beforehand," he said, ironically. "I should have thought you would have left it until after your departure!"

She made no reply, but fanned herself slowly with the beautiful gray fan.

"I suppose you consider that the month is more than ended, and that you are free?"

"You have had all you asked for, Mr. Morgan."

"And therefore I have now only to thank you for your generosity, and let you go."

"I think so."

"You do not care to know the result of my experiment—whether it has been a failure or a success?" he said. "You told me the result of yours."

"I did not mean to tell you. It was forced from me by your misunderstanding."

"Misunderstandings, because so slight that one cannot attack them, are horrible things. Let there be none between us now."

"There is none."

"I do not know." He leaned back in his chair and looked up at the soft darkness of the Italian night. "I have one more favor to ask," he said, presently. "You have granted me many; grant me this. At what hour do you go to-morrow?"

"In the afternoon."

"Give me a little time with you in the Boboli Garden in the morning."

"You are an accomplished workman, Mr. Morgan; you want to finish with a polish; you do not like to leave rough ends. Be content; I will accept the intention as carried out, and suppose that all the last words have been beautifully and shiningly spoken. That will do quite as well."

"Put any construction upon it you please," he answered. "But consent."

But it was with great difficulty that he obtained that consent.

"There is really nothing you can say that I care to hear," she declared, at last.

"The king is dead! My time is ended, evidently! But, as there *is* something you can say which *I* care to hear, I again urge you to consent."

Miss Stowe rose, and passed through the long window into the lighted empty room, decked as usual with many flowers; here she stood, looking at him, as he entered also.

"I have tried my best to prevent it," she said.

"You have."

"And you still insist?"

"I do."

"Very well; I consent. But you will not forget that I tried," she said. "Good-night."

The next morning at ten, as he entered the old amphitheatre, he saw her; she was sitting on one of the upper stone seats, under a statue of Diana.

"I would rather go to our old place," he said, as he came up; "the seat under the tree, you know."

"I like this better."

"As you prefer, of course. It will be more royal, more in state;

but, to be in accordance with it, you should have been clothed in something majestic, instead of that soft, yielding hue."

"That is hardly necessary," she answered.

"By which you mean, I suppose, that your face is not yielding. And indeed it is not."

She was dressed in cream color from head to foot; she held open, poised on one shoulder, a large, heavily fringed, cream-colored parasol. Above this soft drapery and under this soft shade the darkness of her hair and eyes was doubly apparent.

He took a seat beside her, removed his hat, and let the breeze play over his head and face; it was a warm summer morning, and they were in the shadow.

"I believe I was to tell you the result of my experiment," he said, after a while, breaking the silence which she did not break.

"You wished it; I did not ask it."

If she was cool, he was calm; he was not at all as he had been the night before; then he had seemed hurried and irritated, now he was quiet. "The experiment has succeeded," he said, deliberately. "I find myself often thinking of you; I like to be with you; I feel when with you a sort of satisfied content. What I want to ask is—I may as well say it at once—Will not this do as the basis of a better understanding between us?"

She was gazing at the purple slopes of Monte Morello opposite. "It might," she answered.

He turned; her profile was towards him, he could not see her eyes.

"I shall be quite frank," he continued; "under the circumstances it is my only way. You have loved some one else. I have loved some one else. We have both been unhappy. We should therefore, I think, have a peculiar sympathy for and comprehension of each other. It has seemed to me that these, combined with my real liking for you, might be a sufficient foundation for—let us call it another experiment. I ask you to make this experiment, Margaret; I ask you to marry me. If it fails—if you are not happy—I promise not to hold you in the slightest degree. You shall have your liberty untrammelled, and, at the same time, all shall be arranged so as to escape comment. I will be with you enough to save appearances; that is all. In reality you shall be entirely free. I think you can trust my word."

"I shall have but little from my aunt," was her answer, her eyes still fixed upon the mountain. "I am not her heiress, as you suppose."

"You mean that to be severe; but it falls harmless. It is true that I did suppose you were her heiress; but the fact that you are not makes no difference in my request. We shall not be rich, but we can live; it shall be my pleasure to make you comfortable."

"I do not quite see why you ask this," she said, with the same slow utterance and her eyes turned away. "You do not love me; I am not beautiful; I have no fortune. What, then, do you gain?"

"I gain," he said—"I gain—" Then he paused. "You would not like me to tell you," he added; and his voice was changed.

"I beg you to tell me." Her lips were slightly compressed, a tremor had seized her; she seemed to be exerting all her powers of self-control.

He watched her a moment, and then, leaning towards her while a new and beautiful expression of tenderness stole into his eyes, "I gain, Margaret," he said, "the greatest gift that can be given to a man on this earth, a gift I long for—a wife who really and deeply loves me."

The hot color flooded her face and throat; she rose, turning upon him her blazing eyes. "I was but waiting for this," she said, her words rushing forth, one upon the other, with the unheeding rapidity of passion. "I felt sure that it would come. With the deeply-rooted egotism of a man you believe that I love you; you have believed it from the beginning. It was because I knew this that I allowed this experiment of yours to go on. I resisted the temptation at first, but it was too strong for me; you yourself made it so. It was a chance to make you conscious of your supreme error; a chance to have my revenge. And I yielded. You said, not long ago, that I was even. I answered that one was even when one was— You said 'indifferent,' and I did not contradict you. But the real sentence was that one was even when one was pursuing a purpose. I have pursued a purpose. This was mine: to make you put into words your egregious vanity, to make you stand convicted of your dense and vast mistake. But towards the end a better impulse rose, and the game did not seem worth the candle. I said to myself that I would go away without giving you, after all, the chance to stultify yourself, the chance to exhibit clearly your insufferable and amazing conceit. But you insisted, and the impulse vanished; I allowed you to go on to the end. *I* love you! *You!*"

He had risen also; they stood side by side under the statue of Diana; some people had come into the amphitheatre below. He had turned slightly pale as she uttered these bitter words, but he remained quite silent. He still held his hat in his hand; his eyes were turned away.

"Have you nothing to say?" she asked, after some moments had passed.

"I think there is nothing," he answered, without turning.

Then again there was a silence.

"You probably wish to go," he said, breaking it; "do not let me detain you." And he began to go down the steps, pausing, however, as the descent was somewhat awkward, to give her his hand.

To the little Italian party below, looking at the Egyptian obelisk, he seemed the picture of chivalry, as, with bared head, he assisted her down; and as they passed the obelisk, these children of the country looked upon them as two of the rich Americans, the lady dressed like a picture, the gentleman distinguished, but both without a gesture or an interest, and coldly silent and pale.

He did not accompany her home. "Shall I go with you?" he said, breaking the silence as they reached the exit.

"No, thanks. Please call a carriage."

He signalled to a driver who was near, and assisted her into one of the little rattling Florence phaetons.

"Good-bye," she said, when she was seated.

He lifted his hat. "Lung' Arno Nuovo," he said to the driver.

And the carriage rolled away.

Countries attract us in different ways. We are comfortable in England, musical in Germany, amused in Paris (Paris is a country), and idyllic in Switzerland; but when it comes to the affection, Italy holds the heart—we keep going back to her. Miss Harrison, sitting in her carriage on the heights of Bellosguardo, was thinking this as she gazed down upon Florence and the valley below. It was early in the next autumn—the last of September; and she was alone.

A phaeton passed her and turned down the hill; but she had recognized its occupant as he passed, and called his name—"Mr. Morgan!"

He turned, saw her, bowed, and, after a moment's hesitation, ordered his driver to stop, sprang out, and came back to speak to her.

"How in the world do you happen to be in Florence at this time of year?" she said, cordially, giving him her hand. "There isn't a soul in the place."

"That is the reason I came."

"And the reason we did, too," she said, laughing. "I am delighted to have met you; one soul is very acceptable. You must come and see me immediately. I hope you are going to stay."

"Thanks; you are very kind. But I leave to-morrow morning."

"Then you must come to-night; come to dinner at seven. It is impossible you should have another engagement when there is no one to be engaged to—unless it be the pictures; I believe they do not go away for the summer."

"I really have an engagement, Miss Harrison; you are very kind, but I am forced to decline."

"Dismiss your carriage, then, and drive back with me; I will set you down at your hotel. It will be a visit of some sort."

He obeyed. Miss Harrison's fine horses started, and moved with slow stateliness down the winding road, where the beggars had not yet begun to congregate; it was not "the season" for beggars; they were still at the sea-shore.

Miss Harrison talked on various subjects. They had been in Switzerland, and it had rained continuously; they had seen nothing but fog. They had come over the St. Gothard, and their carriage had broken down. They had been in Venice, and had found malaria there. They had been in Padua, Verona, and Bologna, and all three had become frightfully modern and iconoclastic. Nothing was in the least satisfactory, and Margaret had not been well; she was quite anxious about her.

Mr. Morgan "hoped" that it was nothing serious.

"I don't know whether it is or not," replied Miss Harrison. "Margaret is rather a serious sort of a person, I think."

She looked at him as if for confirmation, but he did not pursue the subject. Instead, he asked after her own health.

"Oh, I am as usual. It is only your real invalids who are always well; they enjoy their poor health, you know. And what have you been doing since I last saw you? I hope nothing out of the way. Let me see—Trieste and Tarascon; you have probably been in—Transylvania?"

"That would be somewhat out of the way, wouldn't it? But I have not been there; I have been in various nearer places, engaged rather systematically in amusing myself."

"Did you succeed? If you did you are a man of genius. One must have a rare genius, I think, to amuse one's self in that way at forty. Of course I mean thirty-five, you know; but forty is a better conversational word—it classifies. And you were amused?"

"Immensely."

"So much so that you have to come to Florence in September to rest after it!"

"Yes."

Miss Harrison talked on. He listened, and made the necessary replies. The carriage entered the city, crossed the Carraja bridge, and turned towards his hotel.

"Can you not come for half an hour this evening, after your engagement is over?" she said. "I shall be all alone, for Margaret cannot be there before midnight; she went into the country this morning with Madame Ferri—some sort of a fête at a villa, a native Florentine affair. You have not asked much about her, I think, considering how constantly you were with her last spring," she added, looking at him calmly.

"I have been remiss; pardon it."

"It is only forgetfulness, of course. That is not a fault nowadays; it is a virtue, and, what is more, highly fashionable. But there is one little piece of news I must tell you about my niece: she is going to be married."

"That is not little; it is great. Please present to her my sincere good wishes and congratulations."

"I am sorry you cannot present them yourself. But at least you can come and see *me* for a little while this evening—say about ten. The grandson of your grandfather should be very

civil to old Ruth Harrison for old times' sake." Here the carriage stopped at his door. "Remember, I shall expect you," she
said, as he took leave.

At about the hour she had named he went to see her; he
found her alone, knitting. It was one of her idiosyncrasies to
knit stockings "for the poor." No doubt there were "poor"
enough to wear them; but as she made a great many, and
as they were always of children's size and black, her friends
sometimes thought, with a kind of amused dismay, of the regiment of little funereal legs running about for which she was
responsible.

He had nothing especial to say; his intention was to remain
the shortest time possible; he could see the hands of the clock,
and he noted their progress every now and then through the
twenty minutes he had set for himself.

Miss Harrison talked on various subjects, but said nothing
more concerning her niece; nor did he, on his side, ask a question. After a while she came to fashions in art. "It is the most
curious thing," she said, "how people obediently follow each
other along a particular road, like a flock of sheep, no matter
what roads, equally good and possibly better, open to the right
and the left. Now there are the wonderfully spirited frescos of
Masaccio at the Carmine, frescos which were studied and copied by Raphael himself and Michael Angelo. Yet that church
has no vogue; it is not fashionable to go there; Ruskin has
not written a maroon-colored pamphlet about it, and Baedeker
gives it but a scant quarter-page, while the other churches have
three and four. Now it seems to me that—"

But what it seemed Morgan never knew, because here she
paused as the door opened. "Ah, there is Margaret, after all,"
she said. "I did not expect her for three hours."

Miss Stowe came across the large room, throwing back her
white shawl and taking off her little plumed hat as she came.
She did not perceive that any one was present save her aunt;
the light was not bright, and the visitor sat in the shadow.

"It was very stupid," she said. "Do not urge me to go again."
And then she saw him.

He rose, and bowed. After an instant's delay she spoke his
name, and put out her hand, which he took as formally as she

gave it. Miss Harrison was voluble. She was "so pleased" that Margaret had returned earlier than was expected; she was "so pleased" that the visitor happened to be still there. She seemed indeed to be pleased with everything, and talked for them both; in truth, save for replies to her questions, they were quite silent. The visitor remained but a short quarter of an hour, and then took leave, saying good-bye at the same time, since he was to go early in the morning.

"To Trent?" said Miss Harrison.

"To Tadmor, I think, this time," he answered, smiling.

The next morning opened with a dull gray rain. Morgan was late in rising, missed his train, and was obliged to wait until the afternoon. About eleven he went out, under an umbrella, and, after a while, tired of the constant signals and clattering followings of the hackmen, who could not comprehend why a rich foreigner should walk, he went into the Duomo. The vast church, never light even on a bright day, was now sombre, almost dark, the few little twinkling tapers, like stars, on an altar at the upper end, only serving to make the darkness more visible. He walked down to the closed western entrance, across whose wall outside rises slowly, day by day, the new façade under its straw-work screen. Here he stood still, looking up the dim expanse, with the dusky shadows, like great winged, formless ghosts, hovering over him.

One of the south doors, the one near the choir, was open, and through it a slender ray of gray daylight came in, and tried to cross the floor. But its courage soon failed in that breadth and gloom, and it died away before it had gone ten feet. A blind beggar sat in a chair at this entrance, his patient face faintly outlined against the ray; there seemed to be no one else in the church save the sacristan, whose form could be dimly seen moving about, renewing the lights burning before the far-off chapels.

The solitary visitor strolled back and forth in the shadow. After a while he noted a figure entering through the ray. It was that of a woman; it had not the outlines of the usual church beggar; it did not stoop or cringe; it was erect and slender, and stepped lightly; it was coming down towards the western end, where he was pacing to and fro. He stopped and stood still, watching it. It continued to approach—and at last brushed against him. Coming in from the daylight, it could see nothing in the heavy shadow.

"Excuse me, Miss Stowe," he said; "I should have spoken. My eyes are accustomed to this light, and I recognized you; but of course you could not see me."

She had started back as she touched him; now she moved away still farther.

"It is grandly solitary here on a rainy day, isn't it?" he continued. "I used often to come here during a storm. It makes one feel as if already disembodied—as if he were a shade, wandering on the gray, unknown outskirts of another world."

She had now recovered herself, and, turning, began to walk back towards the ray at the upper door. He accompanied her. But the Duomo is vast, and cannot be crossed in a minute. He went on talking about the shadows; then stopped.

"I am glad of this opportunity to give you my good wishes, Miss Stowe," he said, as they went onward. "I hope you will be quite happy."

"I hope the same, certainly," she answered. "Yet I fail to see any especially new reason for good wishes from you just at present."

"Ah, you do not know that I know. But Miss Harrison told me yesterday—told me that you were soon to be married. If you have never forgiven me, in the light of your present happiness I think you should do so now."

She had stopped. "My aunt told you?" she said, while he was still speaking. But now, as he paused, she walked on. He could not see her face; although approaching the ray, they were still in the shadow, and her head was turned from him.

"As to forgiveness, it is I who should ask forgiveness from you," she said, after some delay, during which there was no sound but their footsteps on the mosaic pavement.

"Yes, you were very harsh. But I forgave you long ago. I was a dolt, and deserved your sharp words. But I want very much to hear *you* say that you forgive *me*."

"There is nothing to forgive."

"That is gently spoken. It is your marriage present to me, and I feel the better for it."

A minute later they had reached the ray and the door. He

could see her face now. "How ill you look!" he said, involuntarily. "I noticed it last evening. It is not conventional to say so, but it is at least a real regret. He should take better care of you."

The blind beggar, hearing their footsteps, had put out his hand. "Do not go yet," said Morgan, giving him a franc. "See how it is raining outside. Walk with me once around the whole interior for the sake of the pleasant part of our Florentine days —for there *was* a pleasant part; it will be our last walk together."

She assented silently, and they turned into the shadow again.

"I am going to make a confession," he said, as they passed the choir; "it can make no difference now, and I prefer that you should know it. I did not realize it myself at the time, but I see now—that is, I have discovered since yesterday—that I was in love with you, more or less, from the beginning."

She made no answer, and they passed under Michael Angelo's grand, unfinished statue, and came around on the other side.

"Of course I was fascinated with Beatrice; in one way I was her slave. Still, when I said to you, 'Forgive me; I am in love with some one else,' I really think it was more to see what you would say or do than any feeling of loyalty to her."

Again she said nothing. They went down the north aisle.

"I wish you would tell me," he said, leaving the subject of himself and turning to her, "that you are fully and really happy in this marriage of yours. I hope you are, with all my heart; but I should like to hear it from your own lips."

She made a gesture as if of refusal; but he went on. "Of course I know I have no right; I ask it as a favor."

They were now in deep obscurity, almost darkness; but something seemed to tell him that she was suffering.

"You are not going to do that wretched thing—marry without love?" he said, stopping abruptly. "Do not, Margaret, do not! I know you better than you know yourself, and you will not be able to bear it. Some women can; but you could not. You have too deep feelings—too—"

He did not finish the sentence, for she had turned from him suddenly, and was walking across the dusky space in the centre of the great temple whose foundations were so grandly laid six centuries ago.

But he followed her and stopped her, almost by force, taking both her hands in his. "You must not do this," he said; "you must not marry in that way. It is dangerous; it is horrible; for you, it is a crime." Then, as he stood close to her and saw two tears well over and drop from her averted eyes, "Margaret! Margaret!" he said, "rather than that, it would have been better to have married even me."

She drew her hands from his, and covered her face; she was weeping.

"Is it too late?" he whispered. "Is there a possibility— I love you very deeply," he added. And, cold and indifferent as Florence considered him, his voice was broken.

When they came round to the ray again, he gave the blind beggar all the small change he had about him; the old man thought it was a paper golconda.

"You owe me another circuit," he said; "you did not speak through fully half of the last one."

So they went around a second time.

"Tell me when you first began to think about me," he said, as they passed the choir. "Was it when you read that letter?"

"It was an absurd letter."

"On the contrary, it was a very good one, and you know it. You have kept it?"

"No; I burned it long ago."

"Not so very long! However, never fear; I will write you plenty more, and even better ones. I will go away on purpose."

They crossed the east end, under the great dome, and came around on the other side.

"You said some bitter things to me in that old amphitheatre, Margaret; I shall always hate the place. But after all—for a person who was quite indifferent—were you not just a little *too* angry?"

"It is easy to say that now," she answered.

They went down the north aisle.

"Why did you stop and leave the room so abruptly when you were singing that song I asked for—you know, the 'Semper Fidelis'?"

"My voice failed."

"No; it was your courage. You knew then that you were no longer 'fidelis' to that former love of yours, and you were frightened by the discovery."

They reached the dark south end.

"And now, as to that former love," he said, pausing. "I will never ask you again; but here and now, Margaret, tell me what it was."

"It was not 'a fascination'—like yours," she answered.

"Do not be impertinent, especially in a church. Mrs. Lovell was not my only fascination, I beg to assure you; remember, I am thirty-six years old. But now—what was it?"

"A mistake."

"Good; but I want more."

"It was a will-o'-the-wisp that I thought was real."

"Better; but not enough."

"You ask too much, I think."

"I shall always ask it; I am horribly selfish; I warn you beforehand that I expect everything, in the most relentless way."

"Well, then, it was a fancy, Trafford, that I mistook for—" And the Duomo alone knows how the sentence was ended.

As they passed, for the third time, on their way towards the door, the mural tablet to Giotto, Morgan paused. "I have a sort of feeling that I owe it to the old fellow," he said. "I have always been his faithful disciple, and now he has rewarded me with a benediction. On the next high-festival his tablet shall be wreathed with the reddest of roses and a thick bank of heliotrope, as an acknowledgment of my gratitude."

It was; and no one ever knew why. If it had been in "the season," the inquiring tourists would have been rendered distracted by the impossibility of finding out; but to the native Florentines attending mass at the cathedral, to whom the Latin inscription, "I am he through whom the lost Art of Painting was revived," remains a blank, it was only a tribute to some "departed friend."

"And he is as much my friend as though he had not departed something over five centuries ago," said Trafford; "of that I feel convinced."

"I wonder if he knows any better, now, how to paint an angel leaning from the sky," replied Margaret.

\*

"Have you any idea why Miss Harrison invented that enormous fiction about you?" he said, as they drove homeward.

"Not the least. We must ask her."

They found her in her easy-chair, beginning a new stocking. "I thought you were in Tadmor," she said, as Trafford came in.

"I started; but came back to ask a question. Why did you tell me that this young lady was going to be married?"

"Well, isn't she?" said Miss Harrison, laughing. "Sit down, you two, and confess your folly. Margaret has been ill all summer with absolute pining—yes, you have, child, and it is a woman's place to be humble. And you, Trafford, did not look especially jubilant, either, for a man who has been immensely amused during the same space of time. I did what I could for you by inventing a sort of neutral ground upon which you could meet and speak. It is very neutral for the other man, you know, when the girl is going to be married; he can speak to her then as well as not! I was afraid last night that you were not going to take advantage of my invention; but I see that it has succeeded (in some mysterious way out in all this rain) better than I knew. It was, I think," she concluded, as she commenced on a new needle, "a sort of experiment of mine— a Florentine experiment."

Trafford burst into a tremendous laugh, in which, after a moment, Margaret joined.

"I don't know what you two are laughing at," said Miss Harrison, surveying them. "I should think you ought to be more sentimental, you know."

"To confess all the truth, Aunt Ruth," said Trafford, going across and sitting down beside her, "Margaret and I have tried one or two of those experiments already!"

# At the Château of Corinne

O N the shores of Lake Leman there are many villas. For
several centuries the vine-clad banks have been a favorite
resting-place for visitors from many nations. English, French,
Germans, Austrians, Poles, and Russians are found in the circle of strangers whose gardens fringe the lake northward from
Geneva, eastward from Lausanne, and southward from Vevey,
Clarens, and Montreux. Not long ago an American joined this
circle. The American was a lady named Winthrop.

Mrs. Winthrop's villa was not one of the larger residences. It
was an old-fashioned square mansion, half Swiss, half French,
ending in a high-peaked roof, which came slanting sharply
down over several narrowed half-stories, indicated by little
windows like dove-perches—four in the broadest part, two
above, then one winking all alone under the peak. On the left
side a round tower, inappropriate but picturesque, joined itself
to the square outline of the main building; the round tower
had also a peaked roof, which was surmounted by a contorted
ornament of iron somewhat resembling a letter S. Altogether
the villa was the sort of a house which Americans are accustomed to call "quaint." Its name was quaint also—Miolans la
Tour, or, more briefly, Miolans. Cousin Walpole pronounced
this "Miawlins."

Mrs. Winthrop had taken possession of the villa in May, and
it was now late in August; Lake Leman therefore had enjoyed
her society for three long months. Through all this time, in
the old lake's estimation, and notwithstanding the English,
French, Germans, Austrians, Poles, and Russians, many of
them titled, who were also upon its banks, the American lady
remained an interesting presence. And not in the opinion of
the old lake only, but in that also of other observers, less fluid
and impersonal. Mrs. Winthrop was much admired. Miolans
had entertained numerous guests during the summer; to-day,
however, it held only the *bona fide* members of the family—
namely, Mrs. Winthrop, her cousin Sylvia, and Mr. H. Walpole,
Miss Sylvia's cousin. Mr. H. Walpole was always called "Cousin

Walpole" by Sylvia, who took comfort in the name, her own (a grief to her) being neither more nor less than Pitcher. "Sylvia Pitcher" was not impressive, but "H. Walpole" could shine for two. If people supposed that H. stood for Horace, why, that was their own affair.

Mrs. Winthrop, followed by her great white dog, had strolled down towards the lake. After a while she came within sight of the gate; some one was entering. The porter's lodge was unoccupied save by two old busts that looked out from niches above the windows, much surprised that no one knew them. The new-comer surveyed the lodge and the busts; then opened the gate and came in. He was a stranger; a gentleman; an American. These three items Mrs. Winthrop's eyes told her, one by one, as she drew nearer. He now caught sight of her— a lady coming down the water-path, followed by a shaggy dog. He went forward to meet her, raising his hat. "I think this is Mrs. Winthrop. May I introduce myself? I am John Ford."

"Sylvia will be delighted," said Mrs. Winthrop, giving her hand in courteous welcome. "We have been hoping that we should see you, Mr. Ford, before the summer was over."

They stood a few moments, and then went up the plane-tree avenue towards the house. Mrs. Winthrop spoke the usual phrases of the opening of an acquaintance with grace and ease; her companion made the usual replies. He was quite as much at his ease as she was, but he did not especially cultivate grace. Sylvia, enjoying her conversation with Cousin Walpole, sat just within the hall door; she was taken quite by surprise. "Oh, John, how you startled me! I thought you were in Norway. But how very glad I am to see you, my dear, dear boy!" She stood on tiptoe to kiss him, with a moisture in her soft, faded, but still pretty eyes.

Mrs. Winthrop remained outside; there were garden chairs in the small porch, and she seated herself in one of them. She smiled a little when she heard Sylvia greet this mature specimen of manhood as a "dear, dear boy."

Cousin Walpole now came forward. "You are welcome, sir," he said, in his slender little voice. Then bethinking him of his French, he added, with dignity, "Welcome to Miaw-lins —Miaw-lins-lay-Tower."

Ford took a seat in the hall beside his aunt. She talked

volubly: the surprise had excited her. But every now and then she looked at him with a far-off remembrance in her eyes: she was thinking of his mother, her sister, long dead. "How much you look like her!" she said at last. "The same profile—exact. And how beautiful Mary's profile was! Every one admired it."

Ford, who had been gazing at the rug, looked up; he caught Mrs. Winthrop's glance, and the gleam of merriment in it. "Yes, my profile is like my mother's, and therefore good," he answered, gravely. "It is a pity that my full face contradicts it. However, I live in profile as much as possible; I present myself edgewise."

"What *do* you mean, dear?" said Sylvia.

"I am like the new moon," he answered; "I show but a rim. All the rest I keep dark."

Mrs. Winthrop laughed; and again Ford caught her glance. What he had said of himself was true. He had a regular, clearly cut, delicately finished profile, but his full face contradicted it somewhat, showing more strength than beauty. His eyes were gray, without much expression, unless calmness can be called an expression; his hair and beard, both closely cut, were dark brown. As to his height, no one would have called him tall, yet neither would any one have described him as short. And the same phrasing might have been applied to his general appearance: no one would have called him handsome, yet neither would any one have classed him as ordinary. As to what is more important than looks, namely, manner, although his was quiet, and quite without pretension, a close observer could have discovered in it, and without much effort, that the opinions of John Ford (although never obtruded upon others) were in general sufficiently satisfactory to John Ford; and, furthermore, that the opinions of other people, whether accordant or discordant with his own, troubled him little.

After a while all went down to the outlook to see the afterglow on Mont Blanc. Mrs. Winthrop led the way with Cousin Walpole, whose high, bell-crowned straw hat had a dignity which no modern head-covering could hope to rival.

Sylvia followed, with her nephew. "You must come and stay with us, John," she said. "Katharine has so much company that you will find it entertaining, and even at times instructive. I am sure I have found it so; and I am, you know, your senior.

We are alone to-day; but it is for the first time. Generally the house is full."

"But I do not like a full house," said Ford, smiling down upon the upturned face of the little "senior" by his side.

"You will like this one. It is not a commonplace society—by no means commonplace. The hours, too, are easy; breakfast, for instance, from nine to eleven—as you please. As to the quality of the—of the bodily support, it is sufficient to say that Marches is housekeeper. You remember Marches?"

"Perfectly. Her tarts no one could forget."

"Katharine is indebted to me for Marches," continued Sylvia. "I relinquished her to Katharine upon the occasion of her marriage, ten years ago; for she was totally inexperienced, you know—only seventeen."

"Then she is now twenty-seven."

"I should not have mentioned that," said Miss Pitcher, instinctively. "It was an inadvertence. Could you oblige me by forgetting it?"

"With the greatest ease. She is, then, sensitive about her age?"

"Not in the least. Why should she be? Certainly no one would ever dream of calling twenty-seven *old*!" (Miss Pitcher paused with dignity.) "You think her beautiful, of course?" she added.

"She is a fine-looking woman."

"Oh, John, that is what they always say of women who weigh two hundred! And Katharine is very slender."

Ford laughed. "I supposed the fact that Mrs. Winthrop was handsome went without the saying."

"It goes," said Sylvia, impressively, "but not without the saying; I assure you, by no means without the saying. It has been said this summer many times."

"And she does not find it fatiguing?"

The little aunt looked at her nephew. "You do not like her," she said, with a fine air of penetration, touching his coat-sleeve lightly with one finger. "I see that you do not like her."

"My dear aunt! I do not know her in the least."

"Well, how does she impress you, then, *not* knowing her?" said Miss Pitcher, folding her arms under her little pink shawl with an impartial air.

He glanced at the figure in front. "How she impresses me?" he said. "She impresses me as a very attractive, but very complete, woman of the world."

A flood of remonstrance rose to Sylvia's lips; but she was obliged to repress it, because Mrs. Winthrop had paused, and was waiting for them.

"Here is one of our fairest little vistas, Mr. Ford," she said as they came up, showing him an oval opening in the shrubbery, through which a gleam of blue lake, a village on the opposite shore, and the arrowy, snow-clad Silver Needle, rising behind high in the upper blue, were visible, like a picture in a leaf frame. The opening was so narrow that only two persons could look through it. Sylvia and Cousin Walpole walked on.

"But you have seen it all before," said Mrs. Winthrop. "To you it is not something from fairy-land, hardly to be believed, as it is to me. Do you know, sometimes, when waking in the early dawn, before the prosaic little details of the day have risen in my mind, I ask myself, with a sort of doubt in the reality of it all, if this is Katharine Winthrop living on the shores of Lake Leman—herself really, and not her imagination only, her longing dream." It is very well uttered, with a touch of enthusiasm which carried it along, and which was in itself a confidence.

"Yes—ah—quite so. Yet you hardly look like a person who would think that sort of thing under those circumstances," said Ford, watching a bark, with the picturesque lateen-sails of Lake Leman, cross his green-framed picture from east to west.

Mrs. Winthrop let the hand with which she had made her little gesture drop. She stood looking at him. But he did not add anything to his remark, or turn his glance from the lateen-sails.

"What sort of a person, then, do I look like?" she said.

He turned. She was smiling; he smiled also. "I was alluding merely to the time you named. As it happened, my aunt had mentioned to me by chance your breakfast hours."

"That was not all, I think."

"You are very good to be interested."

"I am not good; only curious. Pray tell me."

"I have so little imagination, Mrs. Winthrop, that I cannot invent the proper charming interpretation as I ought. As to bald truth, of course you cannot expect me to present you with that during a first visit of ceremony."

"The first visit will, I hope, be a long one; you must come and stay with us. As to ceremony, if this is your idea of it—"

"—What must I be when unceremonious! I suppose you are thinking," said Ford, laughing. "On the whole, I had better make no attempts. The owl, in his own character, is esteemed an honest bird; but let him not try to be a nightingale."

"Come as owl, nightingale, or what you please, so long as you come. When you do, I shall ask you again what you meant."

"If you are going to hold it over me, perhaps I had better tell you now."

"Much better."

"I only meant, then, that Mrs. Winthrop did not strike me as at all the sort of person who would allow anything prosaic to interfere with her poetical, heartfelt enthusiasms."

She laughed gayly. "You are delightful. You have such a heavy apparatus for fibbing that it becomes fairly stately. You do not believe I have any enthusiasms at all," she added. Her eyes were dark blue, with long lashes; they were very fine eyes.

"I will believe whatever you please," said John Ford.

"Very well. Believe what I tell you."

"You include only what you tell in words?"

"Plainly, you are not troubled by timidity," said the lady, laughing a second time.

"On the contrary, it is excess of timidity. It makes me desperate and crude."

They had walked on, and now came up with the others. "Does he amuse you?" said Sylvia, in a low tone, as Cousin Walpole in his turn walked onward with the new-comer. "I heard you laughing."

"Yes; but he is not at all what you said. He is so shy and ill at ease that it is almost painful."

"Dear me!" said the aunt, with concern. "The best thing, then, will be for him to come and stay with us. You have so much company that it will be good for him; his shyness will wear off."

"I have invited him, but I doubt his coming," said the lady of the manor.

The outlook was a little terrace built out over the water. Mrs. Winthrop seated herself and took off her garden-hat (Mrs.

Winthrop had a very graceful head, and thick, soft, brown hair). "Not so close, Gibbon," she said, as the shaggy dog laid himself down beside her.

"You call your dog Gibbon?" said Ford.

"Yes; he came from Lausanne, where Gibbon lived; and I think he looks just like him. But pray put on your hat, Mr. Ford. A man in the open air, deprived of his hat, is always a wretched object, and always takes cold."

"I may be wretched, but I do not take cold," replied Ford, letting his hat lie.

"John *does* look very strong," said Sylvia, with pride.

"O fortunate youth—if he but knew his good-fortune!" said Cousin Walpole. "From the Latin, sir; I do not quote the original tongue in the presence of ladies, which would seem pedantic. You do look strong indeed, and I congratulate you. I myself have never been an athlete; but I admire, and with impartiality, the muscles of the gladiator."

"Surely, Cousin Walpole, there is nothing in common between John and a gladiator!"

"Your pardon, Cousin Sylvia. I was speaking generally. My conversation, sir," said the bachelor, turning to Ford, "is apt to be general."

"No one likes personalities, I suppose," replied Ford, watching the last hues of the sunset.

"On the contrary, I am devoted to them," said Mrs. Winthrop.

"Oh no, Katharine; you malign yourself," said Sylvia. "You must not believe all she says, John."

"Mr. Ford has just promised to do that very thing," remarked Mrs. Winthrop.

"Dear me!" said Sylvia. Her tone of dismay was so sincere that they all laughed. "You know, dear, you have so much imagination," she said, apologetically, to her cousin.

"Mr. Ford has not," replied the younger lady; "so the exercise will do him no harm."

The sky behind the splendid white mass of Mont Blanc was of a deep warm gold; the line of snowy peaks attending the monarch rose irregularly against this radiance from east to west, framed by the dark nearer masses of the Salève and Voirons. The sun had disappeared, cresting with glory as he sank the soft purple summits of the Jura, and sending up a blaze of color in the narrow valley of the Rhone. Then, as all this waned slowly into grayness, softly, shyly, the lovely after-glow floated up the side of the monarch, tingeing all his fields of pure white ice and snow with rosy light as it moved onward, and resting on the far peak in the sky long after the lake and its shores had faded into night.

"This lake, sir," said Cousin Walpole, "is remarkable for the number of persons distinguished in literature who have at various times resided upon its banks. I may mention, cursorily, Voltaire, Sismondi, Gibbon, Rousseau, Sir Humphry Davy, D'Aubigné, Calvin, Grimm, Benjamin Constant, Schlegel, Châteaubriand, Byron, Shelley, the elder Dumas, and in addition that most eloquent authoress and noble woman Madame de Staël."

"The banks must certainly be acquainted with a large amount of fine language," said Ford.

"And oh, how we have enjoyed Coppet, John! You remember Coppet?" said Miss Pitcher. "We have had, I assure you, days and conversations there which I, for one, can never forget. Do you remember, Katharine, that moment by the fish-pond, when, carried away by the influences of the spot, Mr. Percival exclaimed, and with such deep feeling, '*Etonnante femme!*'"

"Meaning Mrs. Winthrop?" said Ford.

"No, John, no; meaning Madame de Staël," replied the little aunt.

Mr. Ford did not take up his abode at Miolans, in spite of his aunt's wish and Mrs. Winthrop's invitation. He preferred a little inn among the vineyards, half a mile distant. But he came often to the villa, generally rowing himself down the lake in a skiff. The skiff, indeed, spent most of its time moored at the water-steps of Miolans, for its owner accompanied the ladies in various excursions to Vevey, Clarens, Chillon, and southward to Geneva.

"I thought you had so much company," he said one afternoon to Sylvia, when they happened to be alone. "I have been coming and going now for ten days, and have seen no one."

"These ten days were reserved for the Storms," replied Miss Pitcher. "But old Mrs. Storm fell ill at Baden-Baden, and what could they do?"

"Take care of her, I should say."

"Gilbert Storm was poignantly disappointed. He is, I think, on the whole, the best among Katharine's *outside* admirers."

"Then there are inside ones?"

"Several. You know Mr. Winthrop was thirty-five years older than Katharine. It was hardly to be expected, therefore, that she should love him—I mean in the *true* way."

"Whatever she might have done in the false."

"You are too cynical, my dear boy. There was nothing false about it; Katharine was simply a child. He was very fond of her, I assure you. And died most happily."

"For all concerned."

Sylvia shook her head. But Mrs. Winthrop's step was now heard in the hall; she came in with several letters in her hand. "Any news?" said Miss Pitcher.

"No," replied the younger lady. "Nothing ever happens any more."

"As Ronsard sang,

> "'Le temps s'en va, le temps s'en va, ma dame!
>    Las! le temps non; mais nous nous en allons,'"

said Ford, bringing forward her especial chair.

"That is true," she answered, soberly, almost sombrely.

That evening the moonlight on the lake was surpassingly lovely; there was not a ripple to break the sheen of the water, and the clear outline of Mont Blanc rose like silver against the dark black-blue of the sky. They all strolled down to the shore; Mrs. Winthrop went out with Ford in his skiff, "for ten minutes." Sylvia watched the little boat float up and down for twenty; then she returned to the house and read for forty more. When Sylvia was down-stairs she read the third canto of "Childe Harold"; in her own room she kept a private supply of the works of Miss Yonge. At ten Katharine entered. "Has John gone?" said the aunt, putting in her mark and closing the Byronic volume.

"Yes; he came to the door, but would not come in."

"I wish he would come and stay. He might as well; he is here every day."

"That is the very point; he also goes every day," replied Katharine.

She was leaning back in her chair, her eyes fixed upon the

carpet. Sylvia was going to say something more, when suddenly a new idea came to her. It was a stirring idea; she did not often have such inspirations; she remained silent, investigating it. After a while, "When do you expect the Carrols?" she said.

"Not until October."

Miss Pitcher knew this perfectly, but she thought the question might lead to further information. It did. "Miss Jay has written," pursued Mrs. Winthrop, her eyes still fixed absently on the carpet. "But I answered, asking her to wait until October, when the Carrols would be here. It will be much pleasanter for them both."

"She has put them off!" thought the little aunt. "She does not want any one here just at present." And she was so fluttered by the new possibilities rising round her like a cloud that she said good-night, and went up-stairs to think them over; she did not even read Miss Yonge.

The next day Ford did not come to Miolans until just before the dinner hour. Sylvia was disappointed by this tardiness, but cheered when Katharine came in; for Mrs. Winthrop wore one of her most becoming dresses. "She wishes to look her best," thought the aunt. But at this moment, in the twilight, a carriage came rapidly up the driveway and stopped at the door. "Why, it is Mr. Percival!" said Sylvia, catching a glimpse of the occupant.

"Yes; he has come to spend a few days," said Mrs. Winthrop, going into the hall to greet her new guest.

Down fell the aunt's cloud-castle; but at the same moment a more personal feeling took its place in the modest little middle-aged breast; Miss Pitcher deeply admired Mr. Percival.

"You know who it is, of course?" she whispered to her nephew when she had recovered her composure.

"You said Percival, didn't you?"

"Yes; but this is Lorimer Percival—Lorimer Percival, the poet."

Katharine now came back. Sylvia sat waiting, and turning her bracelets round on her wrists. Sylvia's bracelets turned easily; when she took a book from the top shelf of the bookcase they went to her shoulders.

Before long Mr. Percival entered. Dinner was announced. The conversation at the table was animated. From it Ford gathered that the new guest had spent several weeks at Miolans early in the season, and that he had also made since then one or two shorter visits. His manner was that of an intimate friend. The intimate friend talked well. Cousin Walpole's little candle illuminated the outlying corners. Sylvia supplied an atmosphere of general admiration. Mrs. Winthrop supplied one of beauty. She looked remarkably well—brilliant; her guest—the one who was not a poet—noticed this. He had time to notice it, as well as several other things, for he said but little himself; the conversation was led by Mr. Percival.

It was decided that they would all go to Coppet the next day —"dear Coppet," as Sylvia called it. The expedition seemed to be partly sacred and partly sylvan; a pilgrimage-picnic. When Ford took leave, Mrs. Winthrop and Mr. Percival accompanied him as far as the water-steps. As his skiff glided out on the calm lake, he heard the gentleman's voice suggesting that they should stroll up and down awhile in the moonlight, and the lady's answer, "Yes; for ten minutes." He remembered that Mrs. Winthrop's ten minutes was sometimes an hour.

The next day they went to Coppet; Mrs. Winthrop and Mr. Percival in the carriage, Sylvia and Cousin Walpole in the phaeton, and Ford on horseback.

"Oh! isn't this almost *too* delightful!" said Miss Pitcher, when they reached the gates of the old Necker château. Cousin Walpole was engaged in tying his horse, and Mr. Percival had politely stepped forward to assist her from the phaeton. It is but fair, however, to suppose that her exclamation referred as much to the intellectual influences of the home of Madame de Staël as to the attentions of the poet. "I could live here, and I could die here," she continued, with ardor. But as Mr. Percival had now gone back to Mrs. Winthrop, she was obliged to finish her sentence to her nephew, which was not quite the same thing. "Couldn't *you*, John?" she said.

"It would be easy enough to die, I should say," replied Ford, dismounting.

"We must all die," remarked Cousin Walpole from the post where he was at work upon the horse. He tied that peaceful animal in such intricate and unexpected convolutions that it took Mrs. Winthrop's coachman, later, fully twenty minutes to comprehend and unravel them.

The Necker homestead is a plain, old-fashioned château, built round three sides of a square, a court-yard within. From the end of the south side a long, irregular wing of lower out-buildings stretches towards the road, ending in a thickened, huddled knot along its margin, as though the country high-way had refused to allow aristocratic encroachments, and had pushed them all back with determined hands. Across the three high, pale-yellow façades of the main building the faded shutters were tightly closed. There was not a sign of life, save in a little square house at the end of the knot, where, as far as possible from the historic mansion he guarded, lived the old custodian, who strongly resembled the portraits of Benjamin Franklin.

Benjamin Franklin knew Mrs. Winthrop (and Mrs. Winthrop's purse). He hastened through the knot in his shuffling woollen shoes, and unlocked the court-yard entrance.

"We must go all through the dear old house again, for John's sake," said Sylvia.

"Do not sacrifice yourselves; I have seen it," said her nephew.

"But not lately, dear John."

"I am quite willing to serve as a pretext," he answered, leading the way in.

They passed through the dark old hall below, where the white statue of Necker gleams in solitude, and went up the broad stairway, the old custodian preceding them, and throwing open the barred shutters of room after room. The warm sunshine flowed in and streamed across the floors, the dim tapestries, the spindle-legged, gilded furniture, and the Cupid-decked clocks. The old paintings on the walls seemed to waken slowly and survey them as they passed. Lorimer Percival seated himself in a yellow arm-chair, and looked about with the air of a man who was breathing a delicate aroma.

"This is the room where the 'incomparable Juliette' danced her celebrated gavotte," he remarked, "probably to the music of that old harpsichord—or is it a spinet?—in the corner."

"Pray tell us about it," entreated Sylvia, who had seated herself gingerly on the edge of a small ottoman embroidered with pink shepherdesses on a blue meadow, and rose-colored lambs. Mrs. Winthrop meanwhile had appropriated a spindle-legged sofa, and was leaning back against a tapestried Endymion.

Percival smiled, but did not refuse Sylvia's request. He had not the objection which some men have to a monologue. It must be added, however, that for that sort of thing he selected his audience. Upon this occasion the outside element of John Ford, strolling about near the windows, was discordant, but not enough so to affect the admiring appreciation of the little group nearer his chair.

"Madame de Staël," he began, with his eyes on the cornice, "was a woman of many and generous enthusiasms. She had long wished to behold the grace of her lovely friend Madame Récamier, in her celebrated gavotte, well known in the salons of Paris, but as yet unseen by the exile of Coppet. By great good-fortune there happened to be in the village, upon the occasion of a visit from Madame Récamier, a French dancing-master. Madame de Staël sent for him, and the enchanted little man had the signal honor of going through the dance with the beautiful Juliette, in this room, in the presence of all the distinguished society of Coppet: no doubt it was the glory of his life. When the dance was ended, Corinne, carried away by admiration, embraced with transport—"

"The dancing-master?" said Cousin Walpole, much interested.

"No; her *ravissante amie.*"

Cousin Walpole, conscious that he had made a mistake, betook himself to the portrait near by. "Superb woman!" he murmured, contemplating it. "Superb!"

The portrait represented the authoress of *Corinne* standing, her talented head crowned by a majestic aureole of yellow satin turban, whose voluminous folds accounted probably for the scanty amount of material left for the shoulders and arms.

"If I could have had the choice," said Miss Pitcher, pensively gazing at this portrait, "I would rather have been that noble creature than any one else on history's page."

Later they went down to the old garden. It stretched back behind the house for some distance, shut in by a high stone wall. A long, straight alley, shaded by even rows of trees, went down one side like a mathematical line; on the other there was some of the stiff landscape-gardening of the last century. In the open space in the centre was a moss-grown fish-pond, and near the house a dignified little company of clipped trees.

They strolled down the straight walk: this time Ford was with Mrs. Winthrop, while Sylvia, Mr. Percival, and Cousin Walpole were in front.

"I suppose she used to walk here," observed Mrs. Winthrop.

"In her turban," suggested Ford.

"Perhaps she has sat upon that very bench—who knows?—and mused," said Sylvia, imaginatively.

"Aloud, of course," commented her nephew. But these irreverent remarks were in undertone; only Mrs. Winthrop could hear them.

"No doubt they all walked here," observed the poet; "it was one of the customs of the time to take slow exercise daily in one of these dignified alleys. The whole society of Coppet was no doubt often here, Madame de Staël and her various guests, Schlegel, Constant, the Montmorency, Sismondi, Madame Récamier, and many others."

"Would that I too could have been of that company!" said Cousin Walpole, with warmth.

"Which one of the two ladies would you have accompanied down this walk, if choice had been forced upon you?" said Mrs. Winthrop.

"Which one?—Madame de Staël, of course," replied the little bachelor, chivalrously.

"And you, Mr. Percival?"

"With the one who had the intellect," replied the poet.

"We must be even more lacking in beauty than we suppose, Sylvia, since they all chose the plain one," said Katharine, laughing. "But you have not spoken yet, Mr. Ford: what would your choice have been?"

"Between the two, there would hardly have been one."

"Isn't that a little enigmatical?"

"John means that he admires them equally," explained the aunt.

"That is it," said her nephew.

Lunch was spread upon the grass. Mrs. Winthrop's coachman had made an impromptu carpet of carriage rugs and shawls. Percival threw himself down beside the ladies; Cousin Walpole, after trying various attitudes, took the one denominated "cross-legged." Ford surveyed their group for a moment, then went off and came back with a garden bench; upon this he seated himself comfortably, with his back against a tree.

"You are not sufficiently humble, Mr. Ford," said Katharine.

"It is not a question of humility, but of grace. I have not the gifts of Mr. Percival."

Percival said nothing. He was graceful; why disclaim it?

"But you are very strong, John," said Sylvia, with an intention of consolation. "And if not exactly graceful, I am sure you are very well shaped."

Her hearers, including Ford himself, tried not to laugh, but failed. There was a burst of merriment.

"You think John does not need my encouragement?" said the little lady, looking at the laughers. "You think I forget how old he is? It is quite true, no doubt. But I remember him *so* well, you know, in his little white frock, with his dear little dimpled shoulders! He always would have bread and sugar, whether it was good for him or not, and he was so pretty and plump!"

These reminiscences provoked another peal.

"You may laugh," said Miss Pitcher, nodding her head sagely, "but he did eat a great deal of sugar. Nothing else would content him but that bowl on the high shelf."

"Do you still retain the same tastes, Mr. Ford?" said Katharine. "Do you still prefer what is out of reach—*on a high shelf*?"

"When one is grown," said Ford, "there is very little that is absolutely out of reach. It is, generally speaking, a question merely of determination, and—a long arm."

The sun sank; his rays came slanting under their tree, gilding the grass in bars. The conversation had taken a turn towards the society of the eighteenth century. Percival said the most. But a poet may well talk in a memorial garden, hushed and sunny, on a cushioned carpet under the trees, with a long-stemmed wineglass near his hand, and fair ladies listening in rapt attention. Ford, leaning back against his tree, was smoking a cigarette; it is to be supposed that he was listening also.

"Here is something I read the other day, at least as nearly as I can recall it," said the speaker. He was gazing at the tops of the trees on the other side of the pond. He had a habit of fixing his eyes upon something high above his hearers' heads when speaking. Men considered this an impertinence; but women had been known to allude to it as "dreamy."

"'Fair vanished ladies of the past,'" quoted the poet in his delightful voice, "'so charming even in your errors, do you merit the judgment which the more rigid customs of our modern age would pronounce upon you? Was that enthusiasm for virtue and for lofty sentiments with which your delicious old letters and memoirs, written in faded ink and flowing language, with so much wit and so much bad spelling, are adorned—was it all declamation merely, because, weighed in our severer balances, your lives were not always in accordance with it? Are there not other balances? And were you not, even in your errors, seeking at least an ideal that was fair? Striving to replace by a sensibility most devoted and tender a morality which, in the artificial society that surrounded you, had become well-nigh impossible? Let us not forget how many of you, when the dread hour came, faced with unfaltering courage the horrors of the Revolution, sustained by your example the hearts of strong men which had failed them, and atoned on the red guillotine for the errors and follies of your whole generation with your delicate lives.'"

He paused. Then, in a lighter tone, added: "Charming vanished dames, in your powder and brocade, I salute you! I, for one, enroll myself among your faithful and tender admirers."

Mr. Percival remained two weeks at Miolans. He was much with Mrs. Winthrop. They seemed to have subjects of their own for conversation, for on several occasions when Ford came over in the morning they were said to be "in the library," and Miss Pitcher was obliged to confess that she did not feel at liberty to disturb them. She remarked, with a sigh, that it must be "very intellectual," and once she asked her nephew if he had not noticed the poet's "brow."

"Oh yes; he is one of those tall, slim, long-faced, talking fellows whom you women are very apt to admire," said Ford.

Miss Pitcher felt as much wrath as her gentle nature allowed. But again her sentiments were divided, and she sacrificed her personal feelings. That evening she confided to Katharine, under a pledge of deepest secrecy, her belief that "John" was "jealous."

Mrs. Winthrop greeted this confidence with laughter. Not discouraged, the aunt the next day confided to her nephew her conviction that, as regarded the poet, Katharine had not yet "at all made up her mind."

"That is rather cruel to Percival, isn't it?" said Ford.

"Oh, he too has many, many *friends*," said Sylvia, veering again.

"Fortunate fellow!"

At last Percival went. Ford was again the only visitor. And if he did not have long mornings in the library, he had portions not a few of afternoons in the garden. For if he came up the water-steps and found the mistress of the house sitting under the trees, with no other companion than a book, it was but natural that he should join her, and possibly make some effort to rival the printed page.

"You do not like driving?" she said, one day. They were in the parlor, and the carriage was coming round; she had invited him to accompany them, and he had declined.

"Not with a coachman, I confess."

"There is always the phaeton," she said, carelessly.

He glanced at her, but she was examining the border of her lace scarf. "On the whole, I prefer riding," he answered, as though it were a question of general preferences.

"And Katharine rides *so* well!" said Sylvia, looking up from her wax flowers. Sylvia made charming wax flowers, generally water-lilies, because they were "so regular."

"There are no good horses about here," observed Ford. "I have tried them all. I presume at home in America you keep a fine one?"

"Oh, in America! That is too far off. I do not remember what I did in America," answered Mrs. Winthrop.

A day or two later. "You were mistaken about there being no good saddle-horses here," she remarked. "My coachman has found two; they are in the stable now."

"If you are going to be kind enough to offer one of them to me," he said, rather formally, after a moment's silence, "I shall then have the pleasure of some rides with you, after all."

"Yes," answered Mrs. Winthrop. "As you say—after all!" She was smiling. He smiled too, but shook his head. Sylvia did not see this little by-play. Whatever it meant, however, it did not prevent Ford's riding with Mrs. Winthrop several times, her groom following. Miss Pitcher watched these little excursions with much interest.

Meanwhile letters from Lorimer Percival came to Miolans almost daily. "That is the Percival crest," said Sylvia to her nephew, one of these epistles, which had just arrived, being on the hall table, seal upward, as they passed. "*So* appropriate for a poet, I think—a flame."

"Ah! I took it for steam," said Ford.

Now the elder Percival had been a successful builder of locomotives. "John," said Miss Pitcher, solemnly, "do you mean that for derision?"

"Derision, my dear aunt! There is nothing in the world so powerful as steam. If I only had more, I too might be a poet. Or if my father had had more, I too might have enjoyed a fortune."

"Mr. Percival enjoys no fortune," said Sylvia, still solemnly.

"What has he done with it, then? Enjoyed it all out?"

"He tells me that it dissolved, like a mist, in his grasp."

"Yes; they call it by various names," said Ford.

Mrs. Winthrop, dressed in her habit, now came down the stairway; she took the letter and put it in her pocket. That day the groom could not accompany them: the horse he rode was lame. "We are sufficiently brave to do without him for one afternoon, are we not?" said the lady.

"I confess I am timid; but I will do my best," answered Ford, assisting her to mount. Sylvia, standing in the doorway, thought this a most unfortunate reply.

They rode southward. "Shall we stop for a few moments?" said Katharine, as they came towards Coppet.

"Yes; for ten," he answered.

The old custodian let them in, and threw open the windows as before. The visitors went out on the little shelf-like balcony which opened from the drawing-room.

"You notice there is no view, or next to none," said Ford, "although we are on the shore of Lake Leman, and under the shadow of Mont Blanc. They did not care for views in the eighteenth century—that is, views of the earth; they were all for views of the 'soul.' Madame de Staël detested the country;

to the last, Coppet remained to her a dreary exile. She was the woman who frankly said that she would not cross the room to look at the Bay of Naples, but would walk twenty miles to talk with an agreeable man."

"They were as rare then, it seems, as they are now," said Mrs. Winthrop. "But to-day we go more than twenty miles; we go to Europe."

"She did the same—that is, what was the same in her day; she went to Germany. There she found two rather agreeable men —Goethe and Schiller. Having found them, she proceeded to talk to them. They confessed to each other, long afterwards, the deep relief they felt when that gifted woman departed."

"Ah, well, all she wanted, all she was seeking, was sympathy."

"She should have waited until it came to her."

"But if it never came?"

"It would—if she had not been so eager and voracious. The truth is, Corinne was an inordinate egotist. She expected all minds to defer to her superiority, while at the very moment she was engaged in extracting from them any poor little knowl-edge or ideas they might possess which could serve her own purposes. All her books were talked into existence; she talked them before she wrote them. It was her custom, at the dinner-table here at Coppet, to introduce the subject upon which she was engaged, and all her guests were expected, indeed forced, to discuss it with her in all its bearings, to listen to all she herself had to say, and never to depart from the given line by the slightest digression until she gave the signal. The next morning, closeted in her own room, she wrote out the results of all this, and it became a chapter."

"She was a woman of genius, all the same," said Mrs. Win-throp, in a disagreeing tone.

"A woman of genius! And what is the very term but a stigma? No woman is so proclaimed by the great brazen tongue of the Public unless she has thrown away her birthright of womanly seclusion for the miserable mess of pottage called 'fame.'"

"The seclusion of a convent? or a prison?"

"Neither. Of a home."

"You perhaps commend obedience, also?"

"In one way—yes."

"I'm glad to know there are other ways."

"I shall be very obedient to the woman I love in several of those other ways," replied Ford, gathering some of the ripening grapes near the balcony rail.

Mrs. Winthrop went back into the faded drawing-room. "It is a pity there is no portrait here of Madame Récamier," she remarked. "That you might have admired."

"The 'incomparable Juliette' was at least not literary. But in another way she was as much before the public as though she had been what you call a woman of genius. It may be said, indeed, that she had genius—a genius for attracting admiration."

"You are hard to please."

"Not at all; I ask only the simple and retiring womanly graces. But anything retiring was hard to find in the eighteenth century."

"You dislike literary women very much," said Mrs. Winthrop. She had crossed the room to examine an old mirror made of squares of glass, welded together by little leaden frames, which had once been gilded.

"Hardly. I pity them."

"You did not know, then, that I was one?"

He had crossed the room also, and was now standing behind her; as she asked the question she looked at his image in the glass.

"I did not know it," he answered, looking at hers.

"I am, anonymously."

"Better anonymously than avowedly."

"Will you read something I have written?"

"Thanks. I am not in the least a critic."

"I know that; you are too prejudiced, too narrow, to be one. All the same, will you read?"

"If you insist."

"I do insist. What is more, I have it with me. I have had it for several days, waiting for a good opportunity." She drew from her pocket a small flat package, and gave it to him.

"Must it be now?"

"Here and now. Where could we find a more appropriate atmosphere?"

He seated himself and opened the parcel; within was a small square book in flexible covers, in decoration paper and type, a daintily rich little volume.

"Ah! I know this," he said. "I read it when it first came out."

"So much the better. You can give me your opinion without the trouble of reading."

"It received a good deal of praise, I remember," he said, turning over the leaves.

She was silent.

"There was a charming little description somewhere—about going out on the Campagna to gather the wild narcissus," he went on, after a pause.

And then there was another silence.

"But—" said Mrs. Winthrop.

"But, as you kindly suggest, I am no judge of poetry. I can say nothing of value."

"Say it, valuable or not. Do you know, Mr. Ford, that you have scarcely spoken one really truthful word to me since we first met. Yet I feel sure that it does not come natural to you, and that it has cost you some trouble to—to—"

"To decorate, as I have, my plain speech. But if that is true, is it not a compliment?"

"And do I care for your compliments? I have compliments in abundance, and much finer ones than yours. What I want from you is the truth, your real opinion of that little volume in your hand. You are the only man I have met in years who seems to feel no desire to flatter me, to make me think well of myself. I see no reason why I should not think well of myself; but, all the same, I am curious. I can see that you judge me impartially, even severely."

She paused. He did not look up or disclaim; he went on turning the pages of the little volume.

She had not seated herself; she was standing beside a table opposite him. "I can see that you do not in the least like me," she added, in a lower tone.

"My dear lady, you have so many to like you!" said Ford.

And then he did look up; their eyes met.

A flush came to her cheeks. He shut the little book and rose.

"Really, I am too insignificant a victim," he said, bowing as he returned it.

"You mean that I—that I have tried—"

"Oh no; you do it naturally."

For the moment her self-possession had failed her. But now

she had it in hand again. "If I *have* tried, naturally or artificially, I have made a failure—have I not?"

"It must be a novel experience for Mrs. Winthrop."

She turned away and looked at a portrait of Voltaire. After some moments, "Let us come back to the real point between us," she said, as he did not speak—"that is, your opinion of my little book."

"Is that the real point between us?"

"Of course it is. We will walk up and down Corinne's old rooms, and you shall tell me as we walk."

"Why do you force me to say unpleasant things?"

"They are unpleasant, then? I knew it! Unpleasant for me."

"For us both."

"For you, I doubt it. For me, they cannot be more unpleasant than the things you have already said. Yet you see I forgive them."

"Yes; but I have not forgiven you, Mrs. Winthrop."

"For what, pray?"

"For proposing to make me a victim."

"Apparently you had small difficulty in escaping."

"As you say—apparently. But perhaps I conceal my wounds."

"You are trying to turn the subject, so that I will not insist about the little book."

"I wish, indeed, that you would not insist."

"But if I am the sort of woman you have indicated, I should think you would enjoy punishing me a little."

"A little, perhaps. But the punishment would be too severe."

They were walking slowly through the rooms; she turned her head and looked at him. "I have listened to you, Mr. Ford; I have let you say pretty much what you pleased to me, because it was amusing. But you cannot seriously believe that I really care for what you say, severe or otherwise?"

"Only as any right-minded woman must care."

"Say on. Now I insist."

"Good-bye to Miolans, then. You will never admit me within its gates again; that is, unless you have the unusual justice— unusual in a woman—to see that what I say is but the severity of a true friend."

"A friend is not severe."

"Yes, he is; in such a case as this, must be."

"Go on. I will decide afterwards."

They entered the third room. Ford reflected a moment; then began. "The poem, which you now tell me is yours, had, as its distinguishing feature, a certain daring. Regarding its other points: its rhythm was crude and unmelodious; its coloring was exaggerated—reading it, one was cloyed with color; its logic —for there was an attempt at logic—was utterly weak." He paused. Mrs. Winthrop was looking straight before her at the wall across the end of the last room in the vista. Her critic did not lift his eyes, but transferred his gaze from one section of the dark old floor to the next as they walked onward.

"All this, however," he resumed, "could be forgiven. We do not expect great poems from women any more than we expect great pictures; we do not expect strong logic any more than we expect brawny muscle. A woman's poetry is subjective. But what cannot be forgiven—at least in my opinion—is that which I have called the distinguishing feature of the volume, a certain sort of daring. This is its essential, unpardonable sin. Not because it is in itself dangerous; it has not force enough for that; but because it comes, and can be recognized at once as coming, from the lips of a woman. For a woman should not dare in that way. Thinking to soar, she invariably descends. Her mental realm is not the same as that of man; lower, on the same level, or far above, it is at least different. And to see her leave it, and come in all her white purity, which must inevitably be soiled, to the garish arena where men are contending, where the dust is rising, and the air is tainted and heavy—this is indeed a painful sight. Every honest man feels like going to her, poor mistaken sibyl that she is, closing her lips with gentle hand, and leading her away to some far spot among the quiet fields, where she can learn her error, and begin her life anew. To the pity of it is added the certain truth that if the words she sang could be carried out to their logical end, if they were to be clothed in the hard realities of life and set up before her, they would strike first the poor creature who was chanting them, and crush her to the dust. Fortunately there is no danger of this; it is among the impossibilities. And sometimes the poor sibyls learn, and through the teachings of their own hearts, their great mistake." As he ended, for the first time he lifted his eyes from the floor and looked at her.

Katharine Winthrop's face was flushed; the dark color extended over her forehead and dyed even her throat, and there was an expression as though only by a strong effort was a tremor of the lips controlled. This gave to her mouth a fixed look. She was so unlike herself, veiled in that deep, steady, painful blush, that, involuntarily and earnestly, Ford said, "I beg you not to mind it so much."

"I mind only that you should dare to say such things to me," she answered, slowly, as though utterance was an effort.

"Remember that you forced me to speak."

"I did not expect—this."

"How could I know what you expected? But in one way I am glad you made me go on; it is well that you should have for once a man's true opinion."

"All men do not think as you think."

"Yes, they do; the honest ones."

"Mr. Percival does not."

"Oh, Percival! He's effeminate."

"So you judge him," said Mrs. Winthrop, to whose utterance anger had now restored the distinctness.

"We will not quarrel about Lorimer Percival," said Ford; "he is not worth it—at least, he is not worth it to me." Then, as they entered the last room, "Take it as I meant it, Katharine," he said, the tone of his voice changing—"take it as a true woman should. Show me the sweet side of your nature, the gentle, womanly side, and I will then be your suitor indeed, and a far more real and earnest one than though I had become the victim you intended me to be. You may not care for me; you may never care. But only let me see you accept for your own sake what I have said, in the right spirit, and I will at least ask you to care, as humbly and devotedly as man ever asked woman. For when she is her true self she is so far above us that we can only be humble."

The flush still covered her forehead; her eyes looked at him, strangely and darkly blue in all this red.

"Curious, isn't it, how things come about?" she said. "You have made me a declaration, after all."

"A conditional one."

"No, not conditional in reality, although you might have pleased yourself with the fancy. For I need not have been in earnest. I had only to pretend a little, to pretend to be the acquiescent creature you admire, and I could have turned you round my little finger. It is rather a pity I did not do it. It might have been entertaining."

He had watched her as she spoke. "I do not in the least believe you," he said, gravely.

"It is not of much consequence whether you believe me or not. I think, on the whole, however, that I may as well take this occasion to tell you what you seem not to have suspected: I am engaged to Mr. Percival."

"Of course, then, you were angry when I spoke of him as I did. But I beg you will do me the justice to believe that I never for a moment dreamed that he was anything to Mrs. Winthrop."

"Your dreams must be unobservant."

"I knew that he was with you, of course, and that you received his letters—there is one in your pocket now. But it made no impression upon me—that is, as far as you were concerned."

"And why not? Even in the guise of an apology, Mr. Ford, you succeed in insinuating your rudeness. What you have said, when translated, simply means that you never dreamed that Mrs. Winthrop could be interested in Mr. Percival. And why should she not be interested? But the truth is, there is such an infinite space between you that you cannot in the least comprehend him." She turned towards the door which led to the stairway.

"That is very possible," said Ford. "But I have not now the honor to be a rival of Mr. Percival's, even as an unfavored suitor; you did not comply with my condition."

They went down the stairs, past the shining statue of Necker, and out into the sunshine. Benjamin Franklin brought forward the horses, and Ford assisted her to mount. "You prefer that I should not go with you," he said; "but of course I must. We cannot always have things just as we wish them in this vexatious world, you know."

The flush on her face was still deep; but she had recovered herself sufficiently to smile. "We will select subjects that will act as safe conductors down to commonplace," she said. They did. Only at the gate of Miolans was any allusion made to the preceding conversation.

He had said good-bye; the two riding-gloves had formally touched each other. "It may be for a long time," he remarked. "I start towards Italy this evening; I shall go to Chambéry and Turin."

She passed him; her horse turned into the plane-tree avenue. "Do not suppose that I could not have been, that I could not be—if I chose—all you described," she said, looking back.

"I know you could. It was the possibilities in you which attracted me, and made me say what I did."

"*That* for your possibilities!" she answered, making the gesture of throwing something lightly away.

He lifted his hat; she smiled, bowed slightly, and rode onward out of sight. He took his horse to the stables, went down to the water-steps, and unmoored his skiff. The next day Sylvia received a note from him; it contained his good-bye, but he himself was already on the way to Italy.

The following summer found Miss Pitcher again at Miolans. But although her little figure was still seen going down to the outlook at sunset, although she still made wax flowers and read (with a mark) "Childe Harold," it was evident that she was not as she had been. She was languid, mournful, and by August these adjectives were no longer sufficient to describe her condition, for she was now seriously ill. Her nephew, who was spending the summer in Scotland, was notified by a letter from Cousin Walpole. In answer he travelled southward to Lake Leman without an hour's delay; for Sylvia and himself were the only ones of their blood on the old side of the Atlantic, and if the gentle little aunt was to pass from earth in a strange land, he wished to be beside her.

But Sylvia did not pass. Her nephew read her case so skilfully, and with the others tended her so carefully, that in three weeks' time she was lying on a couch by the window, with "Childe Harold" again by her side. But if she was now well enough for a little literature, she was also well enough for a little conversation.

"I suppose you were much surprised, John, to find Katharine still Mrs. Winthrop?"

"No, not much."

"But she told me that she had mentioned to you her engagement."

"Yes, she mentioned it."

"You speak as though she was one of the women who make and break engagements lightly. But she is not, I assure you: far from it."

"She broke this one, it seems."

"One breaking does not make a—breaker," said Sylvia, thinking vaguely of "swallows," and nearly saying "summer." She paused, then shook her head sadly. "I have never understood it," she said, with a deep sigh. "It lasted, I know, until the very end of June. I think I may say, without exaggeration, that I spent the entire month of July, day and night, picturing to myself his sufferings."

"You took more time than he did. He was married before July was ended."

"Simply despair."

"Despair took on a cheerful guise. Some of the rest of us might not object to it in such a shape."

But Miss Pitcher continued her dirge. "So terrible for such a man! A mere child—only seventeen!"

"And he is—"

"Thirty-seven years, eight months, and nine days," answered the lady, in the tone of an obituary. "Twenty years younger than he is! Of course, she cannot in the least appreciate the true depth of his poetry."

"He may not care for that, you know, if she appreciates him," said Ford—Miss Pitcher thought, heartlessly.

During these three weeks of attendance upon his aunt he had, of course, seen Mrs. Winthrop daily. Generally he met her in the sick-room, where she gave to the patient a tender and devoted care. If she was in the drawing-room when he came down, Cousin Walpole was there also; he had not once seen her alone. He was not staying at Miolans, although he spent most of his time there; his abode nominally was a farm-house near by. Sylvia improved daily, and early in September her nephew prepared for departure. He was going to Heidelberg. One beautiful morning he felt in the mood for a long farewell ride. He sent word to Sylvia that he should not be at

Miolans before evening, mounted, and rode off at a brisk pace. He was out all day under the blue sky, and enjoyed it. He had some wonderful new views of Mont Blanc, some exhilarating speed over tempting stretches of road, a lunch at a rustic inn among the vineyards, and the uninterrupted companionship of his own thoughts. Towards five o'clock, on his way home, he came by Coppet. Here the idle ease of the long day was broken by the small accident of his horse losing a shoe. He took him to the little blacksmith's shop in the village; then, while the work was in slow Swiss progress, he strolled back up the ascent towards the old château.

A shaggy white dog came to meet him; it was his friend Gibbon, and a moment later he recognized Mrs. Winthrop's groom, holding his own and his mistress's horse. Mrs. Winthrop was in the garden, so Benjamin Franklin said. He opened the high gate set in the stone wall and went down the long walk.

She was at the far end; her back was towards him, and she did not hear his step; she started when he spoke her name. But she recovered herself immediately, smiled, and began talking with much the same easy, graceful manner she had shown upon his first arrival at Miolans, when they met at the gate the year before. This meant that she had put him back as an acquaintance where he was then.

He did not seem unwilling to go. They strolled onward for ten minutes; then Mrs. Winthrop said that she must start homeward; they turned towards the gate. They had been speaking of Sylvia's illness and recovery. "I often think, when I look at my little aunt," said Ford, "how pretty she must have been in her youth. And, by-the-way, just before leaving Scotland I met a lady who reminded me of her, or rather of my idea of what she must have been. It was Mrs. Lorimer Percival."

"She is charming, I am told," said the lady beside him.

"I don't know about the charming; I dislike the word. But she is very lovely and very lovable."

"Did you see much of her?"

"I saw her several times; but only saw her. We did not speak."

"You judge, then, by appearance merely."

"In this case—yes. Her nature is written on her face."

"All are at liberty to study it, then. Pray describe her."

He was silent. Then, "If I comply," he said, "will you bear in mind that I am quite well aware that that which makes this little lady's happiness is something that Mrs. Winthrop, of her own accord, has cast aside as nothing worth?" As he rounded off this phrase he turned and looked at her.

But she did not meet his eyes. "I will remember," she answered.

He waited. But she said nothing more.

"Mrs. Percival," he resumed, "is a beautiful young girl, with a face like a wild flower in the woods. She has an expression which is to me enchanting—an expression of sweet and simple goodness, and gentle, confiding trust. One is thankful to have even seen such a face."

"You speak warmly. I am afraid you are jealous of poor Mr. Percival."

"He did not strike me as poor. If I was jealous, it was not the first time. He was always fortunate."

"Perhaps there are other wild flowers in the woods; you must search more diligently." She opened the gate, passed through, and signalled to her groom.

"That is what I am trying to do; but I do not succeed. It is terribly lonely work sometimes."

"What a confession of weakness!"

He placed her in the saddle. "It may be. At any rate, it is the truth. But women do not believe in truth for its own sake; it strikes them as crude."

"You mean cruel," said Katharine Winthrop. She rode off, the groom and Gibbon following. He went back to the black-smith's shop. The next day he went to Heidelberg.

But he had not seen the last of Corinne's old château. On the 25th of October he was again riding up the plane-tree ave-nue of Miolans, this time under bare boughs.

"Oh, John! dear John!" said Miss Pitcher, hurrying into the drawing-room when she was told he was there. "How glad I am to see you! But how did you know—I mean, how did you get here at this time of year?"

"By railway and on horseback," he answered. "I like autumn in the country. And I am very glad to see you looking so well, Aunt Sylvia."

But if Sylvia was well in body, she was ill at ease in mind. She began sentences and did not finish them; she often held her little handkerchief to her lips as if repressing herself. Cousin Walpole had gone to Geneva, "on business for Katharine." No, Katharine was not with him; she was out riding somewhere. She was not well, and needed the exercise. Katharine, too, was fond of autumn in the country. But Sylvia found it rainy. After a while Ford took leave, promising to return in the evening. When he reached the country road he paused, looking up and down it for a moment; then he turned his horse southward. It was a dreary day for a ride; a long autumn rain had soaked the ground, clouds covered the sky, and a raw wind was blowing. He rode at a rapid pace, and when he came towards Coppet he again examined the wet track, then turned towards the château. He was not mistaken; Mrs. Winthrop's horse was there. There was no groom this time; the horse was tied in the court-yard. Benjamin Franklin said that the lady was in the garden, and he said it muffled in a worsted cap and a long wadded coat that came to his heels. No doubt he permitted himself some wonder over the lady's taste.

The lady was at the end of the long walk as before. But to-day the long walk was a picture of desolation; all the bright leaves, faded and brown, were lying on the ground in heaps so sodden that the wind could not lift them, strongly as it blew. Across one end of this vista stretched the blank stone wall, its grayness streaked with wet spots; across the other rose the old château among the bare trees, cold, naked, and yellow, seeming to have already begun its long winter shiver. But men do not mind such things as women mind them. A dull sky and stretch of blank stone wall do not seem to them the end of the world—as they seemed at that moment to Katharine Winthrop. This time she heard his step; perhaps he intended that she should hear it. She turned.

Her face was pale; her eyes, with the dark shadows under them, looked larger than usual. She returned his greeting quietly; her trouble, whatever it was, did not apparently connect itself with him.

"You should not be walking here, Mrs. Winthrop," he said as he came up; "it is too wet."

"It is wet; but I am going now. You have been at Miolans?"

"Yes. I saw my aunt. She told me you were out riding some-where. I thought perhaps you might be here."

"Is that all she told you?"

"I think so. No; she did say that you were fond of autumn in the country. So am I. Wouldn't it be wise to stop at the old man's cottage, before remounting, and dry your shoes a little?"

"I never take cold."

"Perhaps we could find a pair in the village that you could wear."

"It is not necessary. I will ride rapidly; the exercise will be the best safeguard."

"Do you know why I have come back?" he said, abandoning the subject of the shoes.

"I do not," answered the lady. She looked very sad and weary.

"I have come back, Katharine, to tell you plainly and humbly that I love you. This time I make no conditions; I have none to make. Do with me as you please; I must bear it. But believe that I love you with all my heart. It has been against my will; I have not been willing to admit it to myself; but of late the certainty has forced itself upon me so overwhelmingly that I had no resource left save to come to you. I am full of faults; but—I love you. I have said many things that displeased you deeply; but—I love you. Do not deliberate. Send me away—if go I must—now. Keep me—if you will keep me—now. You can punish me afterwards."

They had been walking onward, but now he stopped. She stopped also; but she said nothing; her eyes were downcast.

"It is a real love I offer you," he said, in a low tone. Then, as still she did not speak, "I will make you very happy, Katharine," he added.

Her face had remained pale, but at this assertion of his a slight color rose, and a smile showed itself faintly. "You are always so sure!" she murmured. And then she laughed, a little low, sweet, sudden laugh.

"Let him laugh who wins," said Ford, triumphantly. The old streaked stone wall, if dreary, was at least high; no one saw him but one very wet and bedraggled little bird, who was in the tree above. This bird was so much cheered (it must have been that) that he immediately chirruped one note quite briskly, and coming out on a drier twig, began to arrange his soaked feathers.

"Now," said Ford, "we will have those shoes dried, whether you like it or not. No more imprudence allowed. How angry you were when I said we might find a pair in the village that you could wear! Of course I meant children's size." He had drawn her hand through his arm, and was going towards the gate.

But she freed herself and stopped. "It is all a mistake," she said, hurriedly. "It means nothing. I am not myself to-day. Do not think of it."

"Certainly I shall not trouble myself to think of it much when—what is so much better—I have it."

"No; it is nothing. Forget it. I shall not see you again. I am going back to America immediately—next week."

He looked at her as she uttered these short sentences. Then he took her hands in his. "I know about the loss of your fortune, Katharine; you need not tell me. No, Sylvia did not betray you. I heard it quite by chance from another source while I was still in Heidelberg. That is the reason I came."

"The reason you came!" she repeated, moving from him, with the old proud light coming back into her eyes. "You thought I would be overwhelmed—you thought that I would be so broken that I would be glad—you pitied me—you came to help me? And you were *sure*—" She stopped; her voice was shaking.

"Yes, Katharine, I did pity you. Yes, I came to help you if you would let me. But I was not sure. I was sure of nothing but my own obstinate love, which burst out uncontrollably when I thought of you in trouble. I have never thought of you in that way before; you have always had everything. The thought has brought me straight to your side."

But she was not softened. "I withdraw all I have said," she answered. "You have taken advantage."

"As it happens, you have said nothing. As to taking advantage, of course I took advantage: I was glad enough to see your pale face and sad eyes. But that is because you have always carried things with such a high hand. First and last, I have had a great deal of bad treatment."

"That is not true."

"Very well; then it is not. It shall be as you please. Do you want me to go down on my knees to you on this wet gravel?"

But she still turned from him.

"Katharine," he said, in a graver tone, "I am sorry on your account that your fortune is gone, or nearly gone; but on my own, how can I help being glad? It was a barrier between us, which, as I am, and as you are—but principally as you are—would have been, I fear, a hopeless one. I doubt if I should ever have surmounted it. Your loss brings you nearer to me—the woman I deeply love, love in spite of myself. Now if you are my wife—and a tenderly loved wife you will be—you will in a measure be dependent upon your husband, and that is very sweet to a self-willed man like myself. Perhaps in time I can even make it sweet to you."

A red spot burned in each of her cheeks. "It is very hard," she said, almost in a whisper.

"Well, on the whole, life *is* hard," answered John Ford. But the expression in his eyes was more tender than his words. At any rate, it seemed to satisfy her.

"Do you know what I am going to do?" he said, some minutes later. "I am going to make Benjamin Franklin light a fire on one of those old literary hearths at the château. Your shoes shall be dried in the presence of Corinne herself (who must, however, have worn a much larger pair). And while they are drying I will offer a formal apology for any past want of respect, not only to Corinne, but to all the other portraits, especially to that blue-eyed Madame Necker in her very tight white satin gown. We will drink their healths in some of the native wine. If you insist, I will even make an effort to admire the yellow turban."

He carried out his plan. Benjamin Franklin, tempted by the fee offered, and relying no doubt upon the gloomy weather as a barrier against discovery, made a bright fire upon one of the astonished hearths, and brought over a flask of native wine, a little loaf, and some fine grapes. Ford arranged these on a spindle-legged table, and brought forward an old tapestried arm-chair for Katharine. Then while she sat sipping her wine and drying her shoes before the crackling flame, he went gravely round the room, glass in hand, pausing before each portrait to bow ceremoniously and drink to its health and long life—probably in a pictorial sense. When he had finished the circuit, "Here's to you all, charming vanished ladies of the past," he said; "may you each have every honor in the picturesque, powdered, unorthographic age to which you belong, and never by any possibility step over into ours!"

"That last touch has spoiled the whole," said the lady in the tapestried chair.

But Ford declared that an expression in Madame Necker's blue eye approved his words.

He now came back to the hearth. "This will never do," he said. "The shoes are not drying; you must take them off." And with that he knelt down and began to unbutton them. But Katharine, agreeing to obey orders, finished the task herself. The old custodian, who had been standing in the doorway laughing at Ford's portrait pantomime, now saw an opportunity to make himself useful; he came forward, took one of the shoes, put it upon his hand, and, kneeling down, held it close to the flame. The shoes were little boots of dark cloth like the habit, slender, dainty, and made with thin soles; they were for riding, not walking. Ford brought forward a second arm-chair and sat down. "The old room looks really cheerful," he said. "The portraits are beginning to thaw; presently we shall see them smile."

Katharine too was smiling. She was also blushing a little. The blush and slight embarrassment made her look like a school-girl.

"Where shall we go for the winter?" said Ford. "I can give you one more winter over here, and then I must go home and get to work again. And as we have so little foreign time left, I suggest that we lose none of it, and begin our married life at once. Don't be alarmed; he does not understand a word of English. Shall we say, then, next week?"

"No."

"Are you waiting to know me better? Take me, and make me better."

"What are your principal faults—I mean besides those I already know?" she said, shielding her face from the heat of the fire with her riding gauntlets.

"I have very few. I like my own way; but it is always a good way. My opinions are rather decided ones; but would you like an undecided man? I do not enjoy general society, but I am extremely fond of the particular. I think that is all."

"And your obstinacy?"

"Only firmness."

"You are narrow, prejudiced; you do not believe in progress of any kind. You would keep women down with an iron hand."

"A velvet one."

The custodian now took the other shoe.

"He will certainly stretch them with that broad palm of his," said Ford. "But perhaps it is as well; you have a habit of wearing shoes that are too small. What ridiculous little affairs those are! Will twelve pairs a year content you?"

A flush rose in her cheeks; she made no reply.

"It will be very hard for you to give up your independence, your control of things," he said.

But she turned towards him with a very sweet expression in her eyes. "You will do it all for me," she answered.

He rose, walked about the room, coming back to lean over the gilded top of her chair and say, with emphasis, "What in the world does that old wretch mean by staying here so persistently all this time?"

She laughed. Benjamin Franklin, looking up from his task, laughed too—probably on general principles of sociability and appreciation of his fee.

"To go back to your faults," she said; "please come and sit down, and acknowledge them. You have a very jealous nature."

"You are mistaken. However, if you like jealousy, I can easily take it up."

"It will not be necessary. It is already there."

"You are thinking of some particular instance; of whom did you suppose I was jealous?"

But she would not say.

After a while he came back to it. "You thought I was jealous of Lorimer Percival," he said.

The custodian now announced that both shoes were dry; she put them on, buttoning them with an improvised buttonhook made of a hair-pin. The old man stood straightening himself after his bent posture; he still smiled—probably on the same general principles. The afternoon was drawing towards its close; Ford asked him to bring round the horses. He went out; they could hear his slow, careful tread on each of the slippery stairs. Katharine had risen; she went to the mirror to adjust her riding-hat. Ford came up and stood behind her. "Do you remember when I looked at you in the glass, in this same way, a year ago?" he said.

"How you talked to me that day about my poor little book! You made me feel terribly."

"I am sorry. Forgive it."

"But you do not forgive the book?"

"I will forget it, instead. You will write no more."

"Always so sure! However, I will promise, if you acknowledge that you have a jealous disposition."

She spoke gayly. He watched her in the glass a moment, then drew her away. "Whether I have a jealous disposition or not I do not know," he answered. "But I was never jealous of Lorimer Percival; I held him in too light estimation. And I did not believe—no, not at any time—that you loved him; he was not a man whom you would love. Why you allowed yourself to become engaged to him I do not know; but I suspect it was because he flattered what you thought your literary talent. I do not believe you would ever have married him; you would have drawn back at the last moment. To be engaged to him was one thing, to marry him another. You kept your engagement along for months, when there was no reason at all for the delay. If you had married him I should have thought the less of you, but I should not have been jealous." He paused. "I might never have let you know it, Katharine," he went on, "but I prefer that there should be nothing but the truth between us. I know that it was Percival who broke the engagement at the last, and not you. I knew it when I was here in the summer. He himself told me when I met him in Scotland just after his marriage."

She broke from him. "How base are all men!" she said, in a voice unlike her own.

"In him it was simply egotism. He knew that I had known of his engagement to you, and he wished me to appreciate that in order to marry that sweet young girl, who was quite without fortune, he had been obliged to make, and had made, a great sacrifice."

"Great indeed!" she commented, bitterly. "You do well to commend him."

"I do not commend him. I simply say that he was following out his nature. Being a poet, he is what is called sympathetic, you know; and he wanted my appreciation and sympathy— I will not say applause."

She was standing with her back towards him. She now walked towards the door. But her courage failed, she sank into a chair and covered her face with her hands. "It is too much," she said. "You wait until I have lost my fortune and am overwhelmed; you wait until I am rejected, cast aside; and then you come and win from me an avowal of my love, telling me afterwards— *afterwards*"— Her voice broke, she burst into tears.

"Telling you afterwards nothing but that I love you. Telling you afterwards that I have not had one really happy moment since our conversation in this old house a year ago. Telling you afterwards that my life has resolved itself into but one unceasing, tormenting wish—the wish, Katharine, that you would love me, I suppose I ought to say a little, but I mean a great deal. Look at me; is this humble enough for you?"

He drew her hands away; she saw that he was kneeling at her feet; and, not only that, but she saw also something very like a mist in the gray eyes she had always thought too cold.

In the library of Mr. John Ford, near New York, there hangs in the place of honor a water-color sketch of an old yellow château. Beneath it, ranged by themselves, are all the works of that eloquent authoress and noble woman, Madame de Staël.

"You admire her?" said a visitor recently, in some surprise. "To me she always seemed a—a little antique, you know."

"She is antiquity itself! But she once lent me her house, and I am grateful. By-the-way, Katharine, I never told you, although I found it out afterwards: Benjamin Franklin understood English, after all."

UNCOLLECTED STORIES

# Contents

# "Miss Grief"

"A CONCEITED FOOL" is a not uncommon expression. Now, I know that I am not a fool, but I also know that I am conceited. But, candidly, can it be helped if one happens to be young, well and strong, passably good-looking, with some money that one has inherited and more that one has earned—in all, enough to make life comfortable—and if upon this foundation rests also the pleasant superstructure of a literary success? The success is deserved, I think: certainly it was not lightly gained. Yet even with this I fully appreciate its rarity. Thus, I find myself very well entertained in life: I have all I wish in the way of society, and a deep, though of course carefully concealed, satisfaction in my own little fame; which fame I foster by a gentle system of non-interference. I know that I am spoken of as "that quiet young fellow who writes those delightful little studies of society, you know;" and I live up to that definition.

A year ago I was in Rome, and enjoying life particularly. I had a large number of my acquaintances there, both American and English, and no day passed without its invitation. Of course I understood it: it is seldom that you find a literary man who is good-tempered, well-dressed, sufficiently provided with money, and amiably obedient to all the rules and requirements of "society." "When found, make a note of it;" and the note was generally an invitation.

One evening, upon returning to my lodgings, my man Simpson informed me that a person had called in the afternoon, and upon learning that I was absent had left not a card, but her name—"Miss Grief." The title lingered—Miss Grief! "Grief has not so far visited me here," I said to myself, dismissing Simpson and seeking my little balcony for a final smoke, "and she shall not now. I shall take care to be 'not at home' to her if she continues to call." And then I fell to thinking of Isabel Abercrombie, in whose society I had spent that and many evenings: they were golden thoughts.

The next day there was an excursion; it was late when I reached my rooms, and again Simpson informed me that Miss Grief had called.

"Is she coming continuously?" I said, half to myself.

"Yes, sir: she mentioned that she should call again."

"How does she look?"

"Well, sir, a lady, but not so prosperous as she was, I should say," answered Simpson, discreetly.

"Young?"

"No, sir."

"Alone?"

"A maid with her, sir."

But once outside in my little high-up balcony with my cigar, I again forgot Miss Grief and whatever she might represent. Who would not forget in that moonlight, with Isabel Abercrombie's face to remember?

The stranger came a third time, and I was absent; then she let two days pass, and began again. It grew to be a regular dialogue between Simpson and myself when I came in at night: "Grief to-day?"

"Yes, sir."

"What time?"

"Four, sir."

"Happy the man," I thought, "who can keep her confined to a particular hour!"

But I should not have treated my visitor so cavalierly if I had not felt sure that she was eccentric and unconventional —qualities extremely tiresome in a woman no longer young or attractive. If she were not eccentric she would not have persisted in coming to my door day after day in this silent way, without stating her errand, leaving a note, or presenting her credentials in any shape. I made up my mind that she had something to sell—a bit of carving or some intaglio supposed to be antique. It was known that I had a fancy for oddities. I said to myself, "She has read or heard of my 'Old Gold' story, or else 'The Buried God,' and she thinks me an idealizing ignoramus upon whom she can impose. Her sepulchral name is at least not Italian; probably she is a sharp country-woman of mine, turning, by means of the present æsthetic craze, an honest penny when she can."

She had called seven times during a period of two weeks without seeing me, when one day I happened to be at home in the afternoon, owing to a pouring rain and a fit of doubt concerning Miss Abercrombie. For I had constructed a careful theory of that young lady's characteristics in my own mind, and she had lived up to it delightfully until the previous evening, when with one word she had blown it to atoms and taken flight, leaving me standing, as it were, on a desolate shore, with nothing but a handful of mistaken inductions wherewith to console myself. I do not know a more exasperating frame of mind, at least for a constructor of theories. I could not write, and so I took up a French novel (I model myself a little on Balzac). I had been turning over its pages but a few moments when Simpson knocked, and, entering softly, said, with just a shadow of a smile on his well-trained face, "Miss Grief." I briefly consigned Miss Grief to all the Furies, and then, as he still lingered—perhaps not knowing where they resided—I asked where the visitor was.

"Outside, sir—in the hall. I told her I would see if you were at home."

"She must be unpleasantly wet if she had no carriage."

"No carriage, sir: they always come on foot. I think she *is* a little damp, sir."

"Well, let her in; but I don't want the maid. I may as well see her now, I suppose, and end the affair."

"Yes, sir."

I did not put down my book. My visitor should have a hearing, but not much more: she had sacrificed her womanly claims by her persistent attacks upon my door. Presently Simpson ushered her in. "Miss Grief," he said, and then went out, closing the curtain behind him.

A woman—yes, a lady—but shabby, unattractive, and more than middle-aged.

I rose, bowed slightly, and then dropped into my chair again, still keeping the book in my hand. "Miss Grief?" I said interrogatively as I indicated a seat with my eyebrows.

"Not Grief," she answered—"Crief: my name is Crief."

She sat down, and I saw that she held a small flat box.

"Not carving, then," I thought—"probably old lace, something that belonged to Tullia or Lucrezia Borgia." But as she did not speak I found myself obliged to begin: "You have been here, I think, once or twice before?"

"Seven times; this is the eighth."

A silence.

"I am often out; indeed, I may say that I am never in," I remarked carelessly.

"Yes; you have many friends."

"—Who will perhaps buy old lace," I mentally added. But this time I too remained silent; why should I trouble myself to draw her out? She had sought me; let her advance her idea, whatever it was, now that entrance was gained.

But Miss Grief (I preferred to call her so) did not look as though she could advance anything; her black gown, damp with rain, seemed to retreat fearfully to her thin self, while her thin self retreated as far as possible from me, from the chair, from everything. Her eyes were cast down; an old-fashioned lace veil with a heavy border shaded her face. She looked at the floor, and I looked at her.

I grew a little impatient, but I made up my mind that I would continue silent and see how long a time she would consider necessary to give due effect to her little pantomime. Comedy? Or was it tragedy? I suppose full five minutes passed thus in our double silence; and that is a long time when two persons are sitting opposite each other alone in a small still room.

At last my visitor, without raising her eyes, said slowly, "You are very happy, are you not, with youth, health, friends, riches, fame?"

It was a singular beginning. Her voice was clear, low, and very sweet as she thus enumerated my advantages one by one in a list. I was attracted by it, but repelled by her words, which seemed to me flattery both dull and bold.

"Thanks," I said, "for your kindness, but I fear it is undeserved. I seldom discuss myself even when with my friends."

"I am your friend," replied Miss Grief. Then, after a moment, she added slowly, "I have read every word you have written."

I curled the edges of my book indifferently; I am not a fop, I hope, but—others have said the same.

"What is more, I know much of it by heart," continued my visitor. "Wait: I will show you;" and then, without pause, she began to repeat something of mine word for word, just as I had written it. On she went, and I—listened. I intended interrupting her after a moment, but I did not, because she was reciting so well, and also because I felt a desire gaining upon me to see what she would make of a certain conversation which I knew was coming—a conversation between two of my characters which was, to say the least, sphinx-like, and somewhat incandescent as well. What won me a little, too, was the fact that the scene she was reciting (it was hardly more than that, though called a story) was secretly my favorite among all the sketches from my pen which a gracious public has received with favor. I never said so, but it was; and I had always felt a wondering annoyance that the aforesaid public, while kindly praising beyond their worth other attempts of mine, had never noticed the higher purpose of this little shaft, aimed not at the balconies and lighted windows of society, but straight up toward the distant stars. So she went on, and presently reached the conversation: my two people began to talk. She had raised her eyes now, and was looking at me soberly as she gave the words of the woman, quiet, gentle, cold, and the replies of the man, bitter, hot, and scathing. Her very voice changed, and took, though always sweetly, the different tones required, while no point of meaning, however small, no breath of delicate emphasis which I had meant, but which the dull types could not give, escaped an appreciative and full, almost overfull, recognition which startled me. For she had understood me—understood me almost better than I had understood myself. It seemed to me that while I had labored to interpret, partially, a psychological riddle, she, coming after, had comprehended its bearings better than I had, though confining herself strictly to my own words and emphasis. The scene ended (and it ended rather suddenly), she dropped her eyes, and moved her hand nervously to and fro over the box she held; her gloves were old and shabby, her hands small.

I was secretly much surprised by what I had heard, but my ill-humor was deep-seated that day, and I still felt sure, besides, that the box contained something which I was expected to buy.

"You recite remarkably well," I said carelessly, "and I am much flattered also by your appreciation of my attempt. But it is not, I presume, to that alone that I owe the pleasure of this visit?"

"Yes," she answered, still looking down, "it is, for if you had not written that scene I should not have sought you. Your other sketches are interiors—exquisitely painted and delicately finished, but of small scope. *This* is a sketch in a few bold, masterly lines—work of entirely different spirit and purpose."

I was nettled by her insight. "You have bestowed so much of your kind attention upon me that I feel your debtor," I said, conventionally. "It may be that there is something I can do for you—connected, possibly, with that little box?"

It was impertinent, but it was true; for she answered, "Yes."

I smiled, but her eyes were cast down and she did not see the smile.

"What I have to show you is a manuscript," she said after a pause which I did not break; "it is a drama. I thought that perhaps you would read it."

"An authoress! This is worse than old lace," I said to myself in dismay.—Then, aloud, "My opinion would be worth nothing, Miss Crief."

"Not in a business way, I know. But it might be—an assistance personally." Her voice had sunk to a whisper; outside, the rain was pouring steadily down. She was a very depressing object to me as she sat there with her box.

"I hardly think I have the time at present—" I began.

She had raised her eyes and was looking at me; then, when I paused, she rose and came suddenly toward my chair. "Yes, you will read it," she said with her hand on my arm—"you will read it. Look at this room; look at yourself; look at all you have. Then look at me, and have pity."

I had risen, for she held my arm, and her damp skirt was brushing my knees.

Her large dark eyes looked intently into mine as she went on; "I have no shame in asking. Why should I have? It is my last endeavor; but a calm and well-considered one. If you refuse I shall go away, knowing that Fate has willed it so. And I shall be content."

"She is mad," I thought. But she did not look so, and she had spoken quietly, even gently.—"Sit down," I said, moving away from her. I felt as if I had been magnetized; but it was only the nearness of her eyes to mine, and their intensity. I drew forward a chair, but she remained standing.

"I cannot," she said in the same sweet, gentle tone, "unless you promise."

"Very well, I promise; only sit down."

As I took her arm to lead her to the chair I perceived that she was trembling, but her face continued unmoved.

"You do not, of course, wish me to look at your manuscript now?" I said, temporizing; "it would be much better to leave it. Give me your address, and I will return it to you with my written opinion; though, I repeat, the latter will be of no use to you. It is the opinion of an editor or publisher that you want."

"It shall be as you please. And I will go in a moment," said Miss Grief, pressing her palms together, as if trying to control the tremor that had seized her slight frame.

She looked so pallid that I thought of offering her a glass of wine; then I remembered that if I did it might be a bait to bring her there again, and this I was desirous to prevent. She rose while the thought was passing through my mind. Her pasteboard box lay on the chair she had first occupied; she took it, wrote an address on the cover, laid it down, and then, bowing with a little air of formality, drew her black shawl round her shoulders and turned toward the door.

I followed, after touching the bell. "You will hear from me by letter," I said.

Simpson opened the door, and I caught a glimpse of the maid, who was waiting in the anteroom. She was an old woman, shorter than her mistress, equally thin, and dressed like her in rusty black. As the door opened she turned toward it a pair of small, dim blue eyes with a look of furtive suspense. Simpson dropped the curtain, shutting me into the inner room; he had no intention of allowing me to accompany my visitor further. But I had the curiosity to go to a bay-window in an angle from whence I could command the street-door, and presently I saw them issue forth in the rain and walk away side by side, the mistress, being the taller, holding the umbrella: probably there was not much difference in rank between persons so poor and forlorn as these.

It grew dark. I was invited out for the evening, and I knew that if I should go I should meet Miss Abercrombie. I said to myself that I would not go. I got out my paper for writing, I made my preparations for a quiet evening at home with myself; but it was of no use. It all ended slavishly in my going. At the last allowable moment I presented myself, and—as a punishment for my vacillation, I suppose—I never passed a more disagreeable evening. I drove homeward in a murky temper; it was foggy without, and very foggy within. What Isabel really was, now that she had broken through my elaborately-built theories, I was not able to decide. There was, to tell the truth, a certain young Englishman— But that is apart from this story.

I reached home, went up to my rooms, and had a supper. It was to console myself; I am obliged to console myself scientifically once in a while. I was walking up and down afterward, smoking and feeling somewhat better, when my eye fell upon the pasteboard box. I took it up; on the cover was written an address which showed that my visitor must have walked a long distance in order to see me: "A. Crief."—"A Grief," I thought; "and so she is. I positively believe she has brought all this trouble upon me: she has the evil eye." I took out the manuscript and looked at it. It was in the form of a little volume, and clearly written; on the cover was the word "Armor" in German text, and, underneath, a pen-and-ink sketch of a helmet, breastplate, and shield.

"Grief certainly needs armor," I said to myself, sitting down by the table and turning over the pages. "I may as well look over the thing now; I could not be in a worse mood." And then I began to read.

Early the next morning Simpson took a note from me to the given address, returning with the following reply: "No; I prefer to come to you; at four; A. CRIEF." These words, with their three semicolons, were written in pencil upon a piece of coarse printing-paper, but the handwriting was as clear and delicate as that of the manuscript in ink.

"What sort of a place was it, Simpson?"

"Very poor, sir, but I did not go all the way up. The elder person came down, sir, took the note, and requested me to wait where I was."

"You had no chance, then, to make inquiries?" I said, knowing full well that he had emptied the entire neighborhood of any information it might possess concerning these two lodgers.

"Well, sir, you know how these foreigners will talk, whether one wants to hear or not. But it seems that these two persons have been there but a few weeks; they live alone, and are uncommonly silent and reserved. The people round there call them something that signifies 'the Madames American, thin and dumb.'"

At four the "Madames American" arrived; it was raining again, and they came on foot under their old umbrella. The maid waited in the anteroom, and Miss Grief was ushered into my bachelor's parlor. I had thought that I should meet her with great deference; but she looked so forlorn that my deference changed to pity. It was the woman that impressed me then, more than the writer—the fragile, nerveless body more than the inspired mind. For it was inspired: I had sat up half the night over her drama, and had felt thrilled through and through more than once by its earnestness, passion, and power.

No one could have been more surprised than I was to find myself thus enthusiastic. I thought I had outgrown that sort of thing. And one would have supposed, too (I myself should have supposed so the day before), that the faults of the drama, which were many and prominent, would have chilled any liking I might have felt, I being a writer myself, and therefore critical; for writers are as apt to make much of the "how," rather than the "what," as painters, who, it is well known, prefer an exquisitely rendered representation of a commonplace theme to an imperfectly executed picture of even the most striking subject. But in this case, on the contrary, the scattered rays of splendor in Miss Grief's drama had made me forget the dark spots, which were numerous and disfiguring; or, rather, the splendor had made me anxious to have the spots removed. And this also was a philanthropic state very unusual with me. Regarding unsuccessful writers, my motto had been "Væ victis!"

My visitor took a seat and folded her hands; I could see, in spite of her quiet manner, that she was in breathless suspense. It seemed so pitiful that she should be trembling there before me—a woman so much older than I was, a woman who possessed the divine spark of genius, which I was by no means sure (in spite of my success) had been granted to me—that I felt as if I ought to go down on my knees before her, and entreat her to take her proper place of supremacy at once. But there! one does not go down on one's knees, combustively, as it were, before a woman over fifty, plain in feature, thin, dejected, and ill-dressed. I contented myself with taking her hands (in their miserable old gloves) in mine, while I said cordially, "Miss Crief, your drama seems to me full of original power. It has roused my enthusiasm: I sat up half the night reading it."

The hands I held shook, but something (perhaps a shame for having evaded the knees business) made me tighten my hold and bestow upon her also a reassuring smile. She looked at me for a moment, and then, suddenly and noiselessly, tears rose and rolled down her cheeks. I dropped her hands and retreated. I had not thought her tearful: on the contrary, her voice and face had seemed rigidly controlled. But now here she was bending herself over the side of the chair with her head resting on her arms, not sobbing aloud, but her whole frame shaken by the strength of her emotion. I rushed for a glass of wine; I pressed her to take it. I did not quite know what to do, but, putting myself in her place, I decided to praise the drama; and praise it I did. I do not know when I have used so many adjectives. She raised her head and began to wipe her eyes.

"Do take the wine," I said, interrupting myself in my cataract of language.

"I dare not," she answered; then added humbly, "that is, unless you have a biscuit here or a bit of bread."

I found some biscuit; she ate two, and then slowly drank the wine, while I resumed my verbal Niagara. Under its influence —and that of the wine too, perhaps—she began to show new life. It was not that she looked radiant—she could not—but simply that she looked warm. I now perceived what had been the principal discomfort of her appearance heretofore: it was that she had looked all the time as if suffering from cold.

At last I could think of nothing more to say, and stopped. I really admired the drama, but I thought I had exerted myself sufficiently as an anti-hysteric, and that adjectives enough, for the present at least, had been administered. She had put down her empty wine-glass, and was resting her hands on the broad cushioned arms of her chair with, for a thin person, a sort of expanded content.

"You must pardon my tears," she said, smiling; "it was the revulsion of feeling. My life was at a low ebb: if your sentence had been against me it would have been my end."

"Your end?"

"Yes, the end of my life; I should have destroyed myself."

"Then you would have been a weak as well as wicked woman," I said in a tone of disgust. I do hate sensationalism.

"Oh no, you know nothing about it. I should have destroyed only this poor worn tenement of clay. But I can well understand how *you* would look upon it. Regarding the desirableness of life the prince and the beggar may have different opinions.—We will say no more of it, but talk of the drama instead." As she spoke the word "drama" a triumphant brightness came into her eyes.

I took the manuscript from a drawer and sat down beside her. "I suppose you know that there are faults," I said, expecting ready acquiescence.

"I was not aware that there were any," was her gentle reply.

Here was a beginning! After all my interest in her—and, I may say under the circumstances, my kindness—she received me in this way! However, my belief in her genius was too sincere to be altered by her whimsies; so I persevered. "Let us go over it together," I said. "Shall I read it to you, or will you read it to me?"

"I will not read it, but recite it."

"That will never do; you will recite it so well that we shall see only the good points, and what we have to concern ourselves with now is the bad ones."

"I will recite it," she repeated.

"Now, Miss Crief," I said bluntly, "for what purpose did you come to me? Certainly not merely to recite: I am no stage-manager. In plain English, was it not your idea that I might help you in obtaining a publisher?"

"Yes, yes," she answered, looking at me apprehensively, all her old manner returning.

I followed up my advantage, opened the little paper volume and began. I first took the drama line by line, and spoke of the faults of expression and structure; then I turned back and touched upon two or three glaring impossibilities in the plot. "Your absorbed interest in the motive of the whole no doubt made you forget these blemishes," I said apologetically.

But, to my surprise, I found that she did not see the blemishes—that she appreciated nothing I had said, comprehended nothing. Such unaccountable obtuseness puzzled me. I began again, going over the whole with even greater minuteness and care. I worked hard: the perspiration stood in beads upon my forehead as I struggled with her—what shall I call it—obstinacy? But it was not exactly obstinacy. She simply could not see the faults of her own work, any more than a blind man can see the smoke that dims a patch of blue sky. When I had finished my task the second time she still remained as gently impassive as before. I leaned back in my chair exhausted, and looked at her.

Even then she did not seem to comprehend (whether she agreed with it or not) what I must be thinking. "It is such a heaven to me that you like it!" she murmured dreamily, breaking the silence. Then, with more animation, "And *now* you will let me recite it?"

I was too weary to oppose her; she threw aside her shawl and bonnet, and, standing in the centre of the room, began.

And she carried me along with her: all the strong passages were doubly strong when spoken, and the faults, which seemed nothing to her, were made by her earnestness to seem nothing to me, at least for that moment. When it was ended she stood looking at me with a triumphant smile.

"Yes," I said, "I like it, and you see that I do. But I like it because my taste is peculiar. To me originality and force are everything—perhaps because I have them not to any marked degree myself—but the world at large will not overlook as I do your absolutely barbarous shortcomings on account of them. Will you trust me to go over the drama and correct it at my pleasure?" This was a vast deal for me to offer; I was surprised at myself.

"No," she answered softly, still smiling. "There shall not be so much as a comma altered." Then she sat down and fell into a reverie as though she were alone.

"Have you written anything else?" I said after a while, when I had become tired of the silence.

"Yes."

"Can I see it? Or is it *them*?"

"It is *them*. Yes, you can see all."

"I will call upon you for the purpose."

"No, you must not," she said, coming back to the present nervously. "I prefer to come to you."

At this moment Simpson entered to light the room, and

busied himself rather longer than was necessary over the task. When he finally went out I saw that my visitor's manner had sunk into its former depression: the presence of the servant seemed to have chilled her.

"When did you say I might come?" I repeated, ignoring her refusal.

"I did not say it. It would be impossible."

"Well, then, when will you come here?" There was, I fear, a trace of fatigue in my tone.

"At your good pleasure, sir," she answered humbly.

My chivalry was touched by this: after all, she was a woman. "Come to-morrow," I said. "By the way, come and dine with me then; why not?" I was curious to see what she would reply.

"Why not, indeed? Yes, I will come. I am forty-three: I might have been your mother."

This was not quite true, as I am over thirty: but I look young, while she— Well, I had thought her over fifty. "I can hardly call you 'mother,' but we might compromise upon 'aunt,'" I said, laughing. "Aunt what?"

"My name is Aaronna," she gravely answered. "My father was much disappointed that I was not a boy, and gave me as nearly as possible the name he had prepared—Aaron."

"Then come and dine with me to-morrow, and bring with you the other manuscripts, Aaronna," I said, amused at the quaint sound of the name. On the whole, I did not like "aunt."

"I will come," she answered.

It was twilight and still raining, but she refused all offers of escort or carriage, departing with her maid, as she had come, under the brown umbrella. The next day we had the dinner. Simpson was astonished—and more than astonished, grieved —when I told him that he was to dine with the maid; but he could not complain in words, since my own guest, the mistress, was hardly more attractive. When our preparations were complete I could not help laughing: the two prim little tables, one in the parlor and one in the anteroom, and Simpson disapprovingly going back and forth between them, were irresistible.

I greeted my guest hilariously when she arrived, and, fortunately, her manner was not quite so depressed as usual: I could never have accorded myself with a tearful mood. I had thought that perhaps she would make, for the occasion, some change in her attire; I have never known a woman who had not some scrap of finery, however small, in reserve for that unexpected occasion of which she is ever dreaming. But no: Miss Grief wore the same black gown, unadorned and unaltered. I was glad that there was no rain that day, so that the skirt did not at least look so damp and rheumatic.

She ate quietly, almost furtively, yet with a good appetite, and she did not refuse the wine. Then, when the meal was over and Simpson had removed the dishes, I asked for the new manuscripts. She gave me an old green copybook filled with short poems, and a prose sketch by itself; I lit a cigar and sat down at my desk to look them over.

"Perhaps you will try a cigarette?" I suggested, more for amusement than anything else, for there was not a shade of Bohemianism about her; her whole appearance was puritanical.

"I have not yet succeeded in learning to smoke."

"You have tried?" I said, turning round.

"Yes: Serena and I tried, but we did not succeed."

"Serena is your maid?"

"She lives with me."

I was seized with inward laughter, and began hastily to look over her manuscripts with my back toward her, so that she might not see it. A vision had risen before me of those two forlorn women, alone in their room with locked doors, patiently trying to acquire the smoker's art.

But my attention was soon absorbed by the papers before me. Such a fantastic collection of words, lines, and epithets I had never before seen, or even in dreams imagined. In truth, they were like the work of dreams: they were *Kubla Khan*, only more so. Here and there was radiance like the flash of a diamond, but each poem, almost each verse and line, was marred by some fault or lack which seemed wilful perversity, like the work of an evil sprite. It was like a case of jeweller's wares set before you, with each ring unfinished, each bracelet too large or too small for its purpose, each breastpin without its fastening, each necklace purposely broken. I turned the pages, marvelling. When about half an hour had passed, and I was leaning back for a moment to light another cigar, I glanced toward my visitor. She was behind me, in an easy-chair before my small fire, and she was—fast asleep! In the relaxation of her unconsciousness I was struck anew by the poverty her appearance expressed; her feet were visible, and I saw the miserable worn old shoes which hitherto she had kept concealed.

After looking at her for a moment I returned to my task and took up the prose story; in prose she must be more reasonable. She was less fantastic perhaps, but hardly more reasonable. The story was that of a profligate and commonplace man forced by two of his friends, in order not to break the heart of a dying girl who loves him, to live up to a high imaginary ideal of himself which her pure but mistaken mind has formed. He has a handsome face and sweet voice, and repeats what they tell him. Her long, slow decline and happy death, and his own inward ennui and profound weariness of the rôle he has to play, made the vivid points of the story. So far, well enough, but here was the trouble: through the whole narrative moved another character, a physician of tender heart and exquisite mercy, who practised murder as a fine art, and was regarded (by the author) as a second Messiah! This was monstrous. I read it through twice, and threw it down; then, fatigued, I turned round and leaned back, waiting for her to wake. I could see her profile against the dark hue of the easy-chair.

Presently she seemed to feel my gaze, for she stirred, then opened her eyes. "I have been asleep," she said, rising hurriedly.

"No harm in that, Aaronna."

But she was deeply embarrassed and troubled, much more so than the occasion required; so much so, indeed, that I turned the conversation back upon the manuscripts as a diversion. "I cannot stand that doctor of yours," I said, indicating the prose story; "no one would. You must cut him out."

Her self-possession returned as if by magic. "Certainly not," she answered haughtily.

"Oh, if you do not care— I had labored under the impression that you were anxious these things should find a purchaser."

"I am, I am," she said, her manner changing to deep humility with wonderful rapidity. With such alternations of feeling as this sweeping over her like great waves, no wonder she was old before her time.

"Then you must take out that doctor."

"I am willing, but do not know how," she answered, pressing her hands together helplessly. "In my mind he belongs to the story so closely that he cannot be separated from it."

Here Simpson entered, bringing a note for me: it was a line from Mrs. Abercrombie inviting me for that evening—an unexpected gathering, and therefore likely to be all the more agreeable. My heart bounded in spite of me; I forgot Miss Grief and her manuscripts for the moment as completely as though they had never existed. But, bodily, being still in the same room with her, her speech brought me back to the present.

"You have had good news?" she said.

"Oh no, nothing especial—merely an invitation."

"But good news also," she repeated. "And now, as for me, I must go."

Not supposing that she would stay much later in any case, I had that morning ordered a carriage to come for her at about that hour. I told her this. She made no reply beyond putting on her bonnet and shawl.

"You will hear from me soon," I said; "I shall do all I can for you."

She had reached the door, but before opening it she stopped, turned and extended her hand. "You are good," she said: "I give you thanks. Do not think me ungrateful or envious. It is only that you are young, and I am so—so old." Then she opened the door and passed through the anteroom without pause, her maid accompanying her and Simpson with gladness lighting the way. They were gone. I dressed hastily and went out—to continue my studies in psychology.

Time passed; I was busy, amused and perhaps a little excited (sometimes psychology is exciting). But, though much occupied with my own affairs, I did not altogether neglect my self-imposed task regarding Miss Grief. I began by sending her prose story to a friend, the editor of a monthly magazine, with a letter making a strong plea for its admittance. It should have a chance first on its own merits. Then I forwarded the drama to a publisher, also an acquaintance, a man with a taste for phantasms and a soul above mere common popularity, as his own coffers knew to their cost. This done, I waited with conscience clear.

Four weeks passed. During this waiting period I heard

nothing from Miss Grief. At last one morning came a letter from my editor. "The story has force, but I cannot stand that doctor," he wrote. "Let her cut him out, and I might print it." Just what I myself had said. The package lay there on my table, travel-worn and grimed; a returned manuscript is, I think, the most melancholy object on earth. I decided to wait, before writing to Aaronna, until the second letter was received. A week later it came. "Armor" was declined. The publisher had been "impressed" by the power displayed in certain passages, but the "impossibilities of the plot" rendered it "unavailable for publication"—in fact, would "bury it in ridicule" if brought before the public, a public "lamentably" fond of amusement, "seeking it, undaunted, even in the cannon's mouth." I doubt if he knew himself what he meant. But one thing, at any rate, was clear: "Armor" was declined.

Now, I am, as I have remarked before, a little obstinate. I was determined that Miss Grief's work should be received. I would alter and improve it myself, without letting her know: the end justified the means. Surely the sieve of my own good taste, whose mesh had been pronounced so fine and delicate, would serve for two. I began; and utterly failed.

I set to work first upon "Armor." I amended, altered, left out, put in, pieced, condensed, lengthened; I did my best, and all to no avail. I could not succeed in completing anything that satisfied me, or that approached, in truth, Miss Grief's own work just as it stood. I suppose I went over that manuscript twenty times: I covered sheets of paper with my copies. But the obstinate drama refused to be corrected; as it was it must stand or fall.

Wearied and annoyed, I threw it aside and took up the prose story: that would be easier. But, to my surprise, I found that that apparently gentle "doctor" would not out: he was so closely interwoven with every part of the tale that to take him out was like taking out one especial figure in a carpet: that is, impossible, unless you unravel the whole. At last I did unravel the whole, and then the story was no longer good, or Aaronna's: it was weak, and mine. All this took time, for of course I had much to do in connection with my own life and tasks. But, though slowly and at my leisure, I really did try my best as regarded Miss Grief, and without success. I was forced at last to make up my mind that either my own powers were not equal to the task, or else that her perversities were as essential a part of her work as her inspirations, and not to be separated from it. Once during this period I showed two of the short poems to Isabel, withholding of course the writer's name. "They were written by a woman," I explained.

"Her mind must have been disordered, poor thing!" Isabel said in her gentle way when she returned them—"at least, judging by these. They are hopelessly mixed and vague."

Now, they were not vague so much as vast. But I knew that I could not make Isabel comprehend it, and (so complex a creature is man) I do not know that I wanted her to comprehend it. These were the only ones in the whole collection that I would have shown her, and I was rather glad that she did not like even these. Not that poor Aaronna's poems were evil: they were simply unrestrained, large, vast, like the skies or the wind. Isabel was bounded on all sides, like a violet in a garden-bed. And I liked her so.

One afternoon, about the time when I was beginning to see that I could not "improve" Miss Grief, I came upon the maid. I was driving, and she had stopped on the crossing to let the carriage pass. I recognized her at a glance (by her general forlornness), and called to the driver to stop: "How is Miss Grief?" I said. "I have been intending to write to her for some time."

"And your note, when it comes," answered the old woman on the crosswalk fiercely, "she shall not see."

"What?"

"I say she shall not see it. Your patronizing face shows that you have no good news, and you shall not rack and stab her any more on *this* earth, please God, while I have authority."

"Who has racked or stabbed her, Serena?"

"Serena, indeed! Rubbish! I'm no Serena: I'm her aunt. And as to who has racked and stabbed her, I say you, *you*—YOU literary men!" She had put her old head inside my carriage, and flung out these words at me in a shrill, menacing tone. "But she shall die in peace in spite of you," she continued. "Vampires! you take her ideas and fatten on them, and leave her to starve. You know you do—*you* who have had her poor manuscripts these months and months!"

"Is she ill?" I asked in real concern, gathering that much at least from the incoherent tirade.

"She is dying," answered the desolate old creature, her voice softening and her dim eyes filling with tears.

"Oh, I trust not. Perhaps something can be done. Can I help you in any way?"

"In all ways if you would," she said, breaking down and beginning to sob weakly, with her head resting on the sill of the carriage-window. "Oh, what have we not been through together, we two! Piece by piece I have sold all."

I am good-hearted enough, but I do not like to have old women weeping across my carriage-door. I suggested, therefore, that she should come inside and let me take her home. Her shabby old skirt was soon beside me, and, following her directions, the driver turned toward one of the most wretched quarters of the city, the abode of poverty, crowded and unclean. Here, in a large bare chamber up many flights of stairs, I found Miss Grief.

As I entered I was startled: I thought she was dead. There seemed no life present until she opened her eyes, and even then they rested upon us vaguely, as though she did not know who we were. But as I approached a light came into them: she recognized me, and this sudden revivification, this return of the soul to the almost deserted bod, was the most wonderful thing I ever saw. "You have good news of the drama?" she whispered as I bent over her: "tell me. I *know* you have good news."

What was I to answer? Pray, what would you have answered, puritan?

"Yes, I have good news, Aaronna," I said. "The drama will appear." (And who knows? Perhaps it will in some other world.)

She smiled, and her now brilliant eyes did not leave my face.

"He knows I'm your aunt: I told him," said the old woman, coming to the bedside.

"Did you?" whispered Miss Grief, still gazing at me with a smile. "Then please, dear Aunt Martha, give me something to eat."

Aunt Martha hurried across the room, and I followed her. "It's the first time she's asked for food in weeks," she said in a husky tone.

She opened a cupboard-door vaguely, but I could see nothing within. "What have you for her?" I asked with some impatience, though in a low voice.

"Please God, nothing!" answered the poor old woman, hiding her reply and her tears behind the broad cupboard-door. "I was going out to get a little something when I met you."

"Good Heavens! is it money you need? Here, take this and send; or go yourself in the carriage waiting below."

She hurried out breathless, and I went back to the bedside, much disturbed by what I had seen and heard. But Miss Grief's eyes were full of life, and as I sat down beside her she whispered earnestly, "Tell me."

And I did tell her—a romance invented for the occasion. I venture to say that none of my published sketches could compare with it. As for the lie involved, it will stand among my few good deeds, I know, at the judgment-bar.

And she was satisfied. "I have never known what it was," she whispered, "to be fully happy until now." She closed her eyes, and when the lids fell I again thought that she had passed away. But no, there was still pulsation in her small, thin wrist. As she perceived my touch she smiled. "Yes, I am happy," she said again, though without audible sound.

The old aunt returned; food was prepared, and she took some. I myself went out after wine that should be rich and pure. She rallied a little, but I did not leave her: her eyes dwelt upon me and compelled me to stay, or rather my conscience compelled me. It was a damp night, and I had a little fire made. The wine, fruit, flowers, and candles I had ordered made the bare place for the time being bright and fragrant. Aunt Martha dozed in her chair from sheer fatigue—she had watched many nights—but Miss Grief was awake, and I sat beside her.

"I make you my executor," she murmured, "as to the drama. But my other manuscripts place, when I am gone, under my head, and let them be buried with me. They are not many—those you have and these. See!"

I followed her gesture, and saw under her pillows the edges of two more copybooks like the one I had. "Do not look at them—my poor dead children!" she said tenderly. "Let them depart with me—unread, as I have been."

Later she whispered, "Did you wonder why I came to you?

It was the contrast. You were young—strong—rich—praised
—loved—successful: all that I was not. I wanted to look at you
—and imagine how it would feel. You had success—but I had
the greater power. Tell me, did I not have it?"

"Yes, Aaronna."

"It is all in the past now. But I am satisfied."

After another pause she said with a faint smile, "Do you remember when I fell asleep in your parlor? It was the good and
rich food. It was so long since I had had food like that!"

I took her hand and held it, conscience-stricken, but now
she hardly seemed to perceive my touch. "And the smoking?"
she whispered. "Do you remember how you laughed? I saw
it. But I had heard that smoking soothed—that one was no
longer tired and hungry—with a cigar."

In little whispers of this sort, separated by long rests and
pauses, the night passed. Once she asked if her aunt was asleep,
and when I answered in the affirmative she said, "Help her to
return home—to America: the drama will pay for it. I ought
never to have brought her away."

I promised, and she resumed her bright-eyed silence.

I think she did not speak again. Toward morning the change
came, and soon after sunrise, with her old aunt kneeling by her
side, she passed away.

All was arranged as she had wished. Her manuscripts, covered with violets, formed her pillow. No one followed her to
the grave save her aunt and myself; I thought she would prefer
it so. Her name was not "Crief," after all, but "Moncrief;" I
saw it written out by Aunt Martha for the coffin-plate, as follows: "Aaronna Moncrief, aged forty-three years, two months,
and eight days."

I never knew more of her history than is written here. If
there was more that I might have learned, it remained un-
learned, for I did not ask.

And the drama? I keep it here in this locked case. I could
have had it published at my own expense; but I think that now
she knows its faults herself, perhaps, and would not like it.

I keep it; and, once in a while, I read it over—not as a *memento mori* exactly, but rather as a memento of my own good
fortune, for which I should continually give thanks. The want
of one grain made all her work void, and that one grain was

given to me. She, with the greater power, failed—I, with the less, succeeded. But no praise is due to me for that. When I die "Armor" is to be destroyed unread: not even Isabel is to see it. For women will misunderstand each other; and, dear and precious to me as my sweet wife is, I could not bear that she or any one should cast so much as a thought of scorn upon the memory of the writer, upon my poor dead, "unavailable," unaccepted "Miss Grief."

# In Sloane Street

"WELL, I've seen the National Gallery, and *that's* over," said Mrs. Moore, taking off her smart little bonnet and delicately drying with her handkerchief two drops which were visible on its ribbons. "And I think I'm very enterprising. You would never have got *Isabella* to go in such a rain."

"Of course not. Isabella likes to stay at home and read *Memorials of a Quiet Life*; it makes her feel so superior," answered Gertrude Remington.

"Superior?" commented Mrs. Moore, contemptuously. "Mary would not have gone, either."

"No. But Mary—that's another affair. Mary would not touch the *Memorials* with the tip of her finger, and she wouldn't have minded the rain; but she doesn't care for galleries. With her great love for art, she prefers a book, or, rather, certain books, about pictures, to the pictures themselves. For she thinks that painters, as a rule, are stupid—have no ideas; whereas the art critics—that is, the two or three she likes—really know what a picture means."

"Better than the painters themselves?"

"Oh, far!" answered Miss Remington. "Mary thinks that the work of the painters themselves is merely mechanical; it is the art critic—always her two or three—who discovers the soul in their productions."

"The only art critics I know are Mrs. Jameson and Ruskin," remarked Mrs. Moore, in a vague tone, as she drew off her closely fitting jacket by means of a contortion.

"To Mary, those two are Tupper and *Sandford and Merton*," responded Miss Remington. "And I agree with her about Ruskin; all his later books are the weakest twaddle in the world —violent, ignorant, childish."

But Mrs. Moore's interest in the subject was already exhausted. "It's too dreadful that we're forced to be at sea on Christmas day," she said, complainingly. "Philip ought to have done something—arranged it in some other way. At home, already they are busy with the presents and everything. And by the 22d the whole house will be fragrant with the spices and the fruit and the wine for the plum-pudding. If we could only have some oysters, it would not be quite so dreadful. But I have not seen anything I could call an oyster since I came abroad." She sat poised on the edge of the sofa, as though she intended to rise the next moment. Her small boots, splashed with mud, were visible under her skirt.

"The oysters are rather dwarfish," replied Gertrude Remington. "But as England is the home of the plum-pudding, I dare say you can have that, if you like; we could anticipate Christmas by a week or two."

"There's an idea! Do ring." (To the entering servant.) "Oh, Banks, I should like to speak to Mrs. Sharpless for a moment. She is out? Then send up the cook."

"Mrs. Pollikett, mum? Yes, mum," answered Banks, disappearing.

Presently they heard a heavy step coming up the stairs. It stopped outside the door while Mrs. Pollikett regained her breath; then there was a knock.

"Come in," said Mrs. Moore. "Oh, cook, we have taken a fancy to have a plum-pudding, as we shall be at sea on Christmas day! Do you think that you can give us a good one to-morrow night for dinner? Or, if that is not possible, the day after?"

"Hany time, mum; to-day, if you like," responded Mrs. Pollikett, with the suggestion of a courtesy—it was little more than a trembling of the knees for a moment. She wore a print gown, and a cap adorned with cherry ribbons; her weight was eighteen stone, or two hundred and fifty-two pounds.

"To-day? How can you possibly have it to-day? It's afternoon already," said Mrs. Moore, surveying the big woman (as she always did) with fascinated eyes.

"I've one on hand, mum," replied cook, with serene pride. "And an hexcellent one 'tis. 'Twere made a little over a year ago, and the materials being hof the best, 'tis better now than 'tever was; they himprove with keeping, mum. It's large, but what's left you can take with you in a tin box. With care 'twill be as good as hever another year, if you don't require to heat it all now, mum."

Mrs. Moore gave a gasping glance at Miss Remington. Then

she laughed, putting the veil which she held in her hand to her lips, to hide in part her merriment.

"I'll let you know later, cook," she said. "I'll send word by nurse."

And Mrs. Pollikett, unconscious of ridicule, calmly withdrew. Amy Moore put her head down upon the pile of sofa cushions beside her, and ground it into them as if in desperation.

"Plum-pudding a year old, and warranted to keep another year! Hard as a stone, of course, and black as lead. Think of ours at home! Think how light it will be, almost like a *soufflé*! And its delicate color and fragrance!" She took up her jacket, lifted her bonnet, and pinned the little lace veil to it with the long bonnet-pin; then, still laughing, she rose. On her way to the door her eyes caught sight of a figure which was passing the window outside. "There is Philip going out again. How he does slouch!"

"Slouch?" said Miss Remington, inquiringly. She also had seen the figure from her chair by the fire.

"I don't mean slouch exactly; I mean that he is so bent. Curiously enough, it isn't his back either. But up at the top of his shoulders behind, between there and the head, there's a stoop, or rather a lunge forward. But there's no hollow; it's a roll of flesh. The truth is that Philip is growing too stout."

"That bend you speak of is the scholar's stoop," observed Miss Remington.

"I suppose you mean writer's. He could stand when he writes, couldn't he? But probably it's too late now. How do *you* manage to be always so tremendously straight, Gertrude?"

"Don't you know that spinsters—those at least who have conquered the dejection of their lot—are always straight-backed?" said Miss Remington. "Their one little pride is a stiff spine and light step. Because, you know, the step of their married contemporaries is sometimes rather heavy."

"You think you can say that because I happen to weigh only ninety-eight pounds," answered Amy Moore. "But let me tell you one thing—*you* overdo your straightness; your shoulders in those tailor-made dresses you are so fond of look as though they were moulded of iron plate. You'd be a great deal more attractive and comfortable to look at, Gertrude, if you had a few cozy little habits, nice homelike little ways. You never lounge; you never lean back against anything—that is, with any thorough enjoyment. Who ever saw *you* stretched out lazily in a rocking-chair by the fire, with a box of chocolate creams and a novel?"

Miss Remington laughed. "But if I don't care for chocolates?"

"That's just what I am saying; if you cared for them, you'd be much more cozy. A tall thin woman in a tailor-made gown, with her hair dragged tightly back from her face, and all sorts of deep books—why, naturally, all men are afraid of her."

"Are you kind enough to be still thinking of matrimonial hopes for me?" inquired Miss Remington.

"Oh no! For what would become of Philip then?" said Philip's wife. "You are his chief incense-burner; you're awfully valuable to me just for that." She was opening the door as she said this; she went out, closing it after her.

Left alone in the large room, Miss Remington took a newspaper from the table by her side, and vaguely glanced at its page. Her eyes rested by chance upon a series of short lines, each line beginning with a capital letter, like a poem. It was headed "Commercial Matters," and the first four lines were as follows:

"Wool is weaker.
Leather is slow.
Hides are easy.
Rice is low."

Presently the door opened, and Philip Moore entered.

"Oh, you've come back," she said, letting the paper drop to her lap.

"Only went to the corner to put a letter in the box."

"Very wet still, isn't it?"

"Very."

Moore sat down before the fire, extended his legs, and watched the combat between the heat and the dampness of his trousers.

After a while Miss Remington remarked, "We've been to the National Gallery since lunch."

He made no answer.

"We had intended to go to Highgate also," she went on; "but it was too wet for so long a drive."

"To Highgate?"

"Yes. To George Eliot's grave."

Moore's gloom was lightened for the moment by a short laugh.

"You think that's absurd," said his companion.

"Well—yes. Thoughts suitable for the occasion were to have been the attraction, I suppose. But if you can conjure them up in one place, why can't you in another, and save your cab fare? It was your idea, I know—the going to Highgate. Amy is not devoted to such excursions."

"I suppose it was my idea," answered Gertrude. "I thought you liked George Eliot," she went on, after a moment.

"Do you mean her ghost? How can I like a person I have never seen?"

"I mean her books."

"The first two, perhaps," answered Moore, frowning impatiently. "I suppose I may have said so once—ages before the flood, and you never forget anything, you are merciless about that. But women's books—what are they? Women can't write. And they ought not to try."

"What *can* you mean?"

"What I say," answered Philip Moore. "Children's stories—yes; they can write for children, and for young girls, extremely well. And they can write little sketches and episodes if they will confine themselves rigidly to the things they thoroughly know, such as love-stories, and so forth. But the great questions of life, the important matters, they cannot render in the least. How should they? And when in their ignorance they begin, in addition, to preach—good heavens, what a spectacle!" Happening to look up and see the expression of his companion's face, he added, laughing: "*You* need not be troubled, you have never tried. And I'm thankful you haven't. It would be insupportable to me to have any of my personal friends among that band."

"No, I have never tried," Gertrude answered. She hesitated a moment, then added, "My ambition is all for other people."

"You mean my things, of course. I should like you much better if you had never read a word of them," responded

Moore, his impatience returning. "After they're once done I care nothing about them, they are no longer a part of me; they are detached—gone. By the time they're printed—and that is when *you* get hold of them—I'm taken up with something else, and miles away. Yet you always try to drag me back."

Miss Remington bit her lip, a slight flush rose in her cheeks. But it faded as quickly as it had come, and her companion did not see it; he was staring at the fire.

He was a man of forty-five, with heavy features and thick dark hair. His eyes and head were fine. His forehead wore almost habitually a slight frown. He was somewhat under medium height, and his wife's description of his figure and bearing was true enough.

But Gertrude Remington saw him as he once was—the years when he had been full of life and hope and vigor. She also saw another vision of him as he might be now, perhaps, as he would be (so she told herself) under different influences. It was this possible vision which constantly haunted her, troubled her, tossed her about, and beckoned her hither and thither. She was three years younger than Philip, and she had known him from childhood, as her father's house was next to the house of the elder Philip Moore, in the embowered street of the Massachusetts town which was the home of both. When Philip married, he brought his little wife, the golden-haired, blue-eyed Amy, home to this old house, now his own, owing to the death of his father, and the intimacy of the two families had continued. It was almost a matter of course, therefore, that Miss Remington should be one of the party when the Moores came abroad for six months, their second visit to the Old World. Amy was twelve years younger than her husband, and nine years younger than Gertrude Remington.

To Moore's accusation, "You always try to drag me back," Gertrude had replied in a light tone: "That is because one doesn't stop to think. 'Never talk to an author about his books.' I saw that given somewhere as a wise maxim only the other day."

"I saw it too, and in the very review in which you saw it," replied Moore, in a sarcastic tone. "But you have not given the whole quotation; there was more of it. 'Never talk to an author about his books unless you really believe (or can make him feel you believe) that they are the greatest of the great; he will accept *that*!' In your case there is no hypocrisy, I exonerate you on that score; you really do think my things the greatest of the great. And that's the very trouble with you, Gertrude; you have no sense of proportion, no discrimination. If I had believed you, I should have been a fool; I should have been sure that my books were the finest of the century, instead of their being what they are—and I know it, too—half failures, all of them." He got up, went to the window, and looked out. Then he left the room.

Miss Remington lifted the newspaper from her lap, and again perused unconsciously the same column. This time her eyes rested on the second four lines:

> "Beans are steady.
> Sugars are down.
> Truck is in good demand.
> Sweet-potatoes are firm."

This last item brought Florida to her mind, and she thought for a moment of the gray-white soil which produces the sweet-potatoes; of the breezy sweep of the pine-barrens, with their carpet of wild flowers; of the blue Florida sky. Then she put down the sheet (it was an American paper), rose, and going to the window in her turn, looked out. It was the 13th of December. The autumn had been warm, and even now it was not cold, though the air was damp and chilling; fine gray rain had been falling steadily ever since the sluggish daylight—slow and unwilling—had dawned over vast London. The large house was in the London quarter called S.W.; it stood at a corner of Sloane Street, and these American travellers were occupying, temporarily, its ground-floor; it was literally a ground-floor, for there was only one step at the outer door. Miss Remington surveyed Sloane Street. Its smooth wooden pavement was dark and slippery; the houses opposite had a brown-black hue —brown in the centre of each brick and black at its edges; a vine was attached to one of these dwellings, and its leaves, though dripping, had a dried appearance, which told of the long-lasting dusts of the summer. Omnibuses, with their outside seats empty, and their drivers enveloped in oil-skins, constantly succeeded each other; the glass of their windows was obscured by damp, and their sides bore advice (important in the blackest of towns) about soap; each carried on its top something that looked like a broomstick, from which floated mournfully a wet rag. Among the pedestrians, the women all had feet that appeared to be entirely unelastic, like blocks of wood; they came clumping and pounding along, clutching at their skirts behind with one hand, and holding an open umbrella with the other; the clutch was always ineffectual, the skirts were always draggled. These women all wore small black bonnets; and the bonnets attached to the heads of the poorer class had a singularly battered appearance, as though they had been kicked across the floor—or even the street—more than once. Hansom cabs passed and repassed. The horse belonging to those which were empty walked slowly, his head hanging downward; the horse of those that carried a fare moved onward with a gait which had the air of being rapid, because he continually turned his high-held nose to the right or the left, according to the guidance of his driver, making a pretence at the same time of turning his body also; this last, however, he never really did unless compelled, for it would have been one step more. Huge covered carts, black and dripping, devoted (so said the white lettering on their sides) to the moving of furniture, rolled slowly by, taking with cynical despotism all the space they required, like Juggernauts. A red-faced milk-woman appeared, wearing a dirty white apron over her drabbled short skirt, with indescribable boots, and the inevitable small battered black bonnet. The gazer, finding the milk-woman more depressing even than the hansom cab-horses, turned and went to a fourth window, which overlooked the narrow street at the side of the house. Here the battered stone pavement held shallow pools of yellow water in each of its numerous depressions. On the opposite corner a baker's shop displayed in its windows portly loaves, made in the shape of the Queen's crown—loaves of a clay-colored hue, and an appearance which suggested endurance. There were also glass jars containing lady's-fingers of immemorial age, and, above these, a placard announcing "Mineral Waters." Next came a green-grocer's stall, with piles of small, hard, dark green apples. Miss Remington imagined a meal composed of one of the clay-colored loaves, the mineral waters, the lady's-fingers, and the hard apples. A hideous child now appeared, with a white face streaked with dirt, and white eyelashes; it wore a red feather in its torn wet gypsy hat, and it carried a skipping-rope, with which, drearily, it began to skip, after a while, in the rain. A younger child followed, equally hideous and dirty; it was sucking an orange as it trailed after its sister. Neither of the two looked hungry; but, oh! so unhealthy, so depraved. Miss Remington gave it up; she returned to her place by the fire.

Ten minutes later the door opened, and Mrs. Moore came in, freshly dressed. She drew an easy-chair forward and seated herself, putting out two dainty little shoes towards the blaze.

"Those English people upstairs are too ghastly," she announced. "They do nothing but drink tea."

"They have the best of it, then," answered Miss Remington. "For probably they like it, and perhaps it is good. Whereas what we want—the coffee—is atrocious."

"Just wait till I get home," responded Amy, drumming noiselessly on the arm of her chair with her finger-tips, the motion drawing sparkles from her diamond rings. "I have only found one place in Europe where the coffee is as good as ours, and that is Vienna. But as regards tea, they do keep at it, that family upstairs. First, they all drink it for breakfast. Then again with luncheon. Then it goes in a third time at five or six, with piles of bread-and-butter. Then they have it in the evening after dinner. And if they go to the theatre or anything of that sort, they have a cup after they come home. In addition, if any one has a cold, or is tired, or has been out in the rain, there are extra supplies ordered. I should think it would make them nervous enough to fly."

"It doesn't appear to," answered Gertrude. "We look far more nervous than they do. They are remarkably handsome, and pictures of health each one."

"I am sure I don't want to look like them," responded Amy.

Miss Remington made no reply. Amy's firm belief that she had still the beauty of twelve or fifteen years before always rankled a little in the older woman's mind. Amy had been a very pretty girl, the pet of a large family circle, who thought that she had conferred a wonderful favor when she gave her hand to

Philip Moore. Through the years which had passed, they had never concealed this opinion. And sometimes it was apparent also that Amy (in her own mind at least) agreed with them. At present her beauty was gone; in appearance she was insignificant. Her small figure was wasted, her little face was pallid, her blue eyes had lost their bright color, and the golden hair had grown ominously thin.

Presently she began again. "When one is abroad, if it rains, one is ended; one can't get up home occupations in deadly rooms like these; at least I can't. To-night there is *Cavalleria*, but between that and this nothing. Have you any books?"

"I have *Vapour* upstairs. Shall I get it?"

"That analytical thing? I hate analytical novels, and can't imagine why any one writes them. Why don't you talk? You're as dumb as an owl."

"What shall I say?"

"Anything you like. Why people write analytical novels will do as a starter."

Miss Remington, who was embroidering, lifted her eyes. "I suppose you could tell me a great deal about Philip's disposition, couldn't you? All sorts of queer unexpected little ins and outs; oddities; surprises; and trip-you-up-in-the-dark places?"

"I rather think I could," answered Amy, laughing.

"And well as I and all our family believe that we know him, I dare say you could astonish us with details and instances which would show him in lights which we have never suspected?"

"Of course I could."

"Well, if all that you know should be carefully written down, it would be a study of Philip's character which would be very interesting to those who think they know him. My idea is that the persons who write analytical novels, and those also who like to read them, are interested in the study of character generally, as you and I are interested in Philip's in particular."

Amy yawned. "But they put such *little* things in those novels —such trifles!"

"When Philip refused to buy that exquisite little drawing of Du Maurier's that was for sale in Bond Street the other day—refused, though he was longing for it, simply because he had said that he would not buy another article of any kind or description, not even a pin, as long as he was abroad—was it not as vivid an example of his obstinacy (especially as that unexpected check from home had made it perfectly easy for him to indulge his longing) as if he had refused a Senatorship because he had said some time that he would never live in Washington?"

"Oh, I hope he has not said *that*!" answered Mrs. Moore. "Because if he has, he will stick to it, and I shall have endless trouble to persuade him out of it. For there is nothing I should like better than to live in Washington—I've been thinking of it for a long time. He need not have anything to do with the government, you know."

"And when he flung that footstool of yours through the window into the garden last spring, breaking all the glass, wasn't that as much an instance of uncontrollable temper as if he had knocked a man down?"

"The footstool was the embroidered velvet one," answered Amy, "and it was completely spoiled—out all night in the rain. I have to have footstools, because I'm so short; *I* can't stretch my legs all over the room, as you can. I was sitting in the study for an hour or two that day while they were sweeping the drawing-room, and I told Rosa to bring me one; and then when I went out, I forgot it, and there it staid. But it was a very little thing, I am sure, to be so furious about."

"If it had happened only once, yes," answered Gertrude, smiling. "But I seem to have heard before of footstools forgotten in the middle of the floor in the study, and its master coming in after dark in a hurry, and not expecting to find them there."

"Ten times. Ten times at least," responded Amy, gleefully. "It's the funniest thing in the world. There's a perfect fatality about it."

The door opened, and a little boy and girl came in. They were very beautiful children, although slender and rather pale. They went to their mother and kissed her, climbing to her lap and the arm of her chair.

"A story!" demanded the boy. "About the dog who had a house up in a tree."

"No," said the girl. "About Wolla Kersina, the fairy."

"But it isn't story-time," answered Mrs. Moore. "If you have them now, there'll be none when you go to bed."

Fritz and Polly considered this statement thoughtfully; they decided to wait until bedtime.

"Come on, Poll; let's play water-cure," said the boy.

"Well," answered the girl, assentingly. She went to a closet and drew out a box, from which she took forty small china dolls, arrayed in silks and laces. "Here's the passhints," she said, arranging them on the floor.

"I'm the head doctor," said the boy. "Is the passhints ready?" he inquired, in a gruff tone. Kneeling down, he extended his forefinger menacingly towards the first doll. "Good-morning. How are yer? You have a turrible fever, an' you must take twenty baths, and a sitz and a pack, before eating a *mossel.*"

"Fritzy Moore, she'll die with all that," said the girl, indignantly, rescuing the doll. "That's Grace Adelaide, and she's delicate."

Fritz went on to the next one. "Fer you, a shower-bath, and needles, and the deuce, every five minutes."

"I've no appetite, doctor," said Polly, speaking in a very weak voice for a doll whom she drew from the line. "I've been rather anxious because my ten children" (here she hustled forward rapidly ten of the smaller dolls) "have all had typhoid fever most *dangerously* for more than *three* years."

"Vegetubble baths and the *mind*-cure," ordered Fritz.

"I'm going to play I'm a lady who has come with her child to call on a passhint," said the girl. She took a large doll from the closet, drew her own lips tightly together, and, speaking in a melancholy voice, said: "I'm *very* sorry, Maud Violet, that we accepturred Mrs. Razzers's invitation to stay to dinner at this water-cure, for Mrs. Razzers isn't very rich; I don't think she has got more than twenty-five cents; and so we must be very careful. Eat just as little as you *possibly* can, Maud Violet, an' say 'no-thank-yer' to everything, just 'cep' meat and potatoes." Dragging the doll by its hand, she walked with dignified steps towards the side window, where she seated herself on the floor with her back against the wall, the doll by her side. "No-thank-yer," she said, as if speaking to a servant; "no soup. (Maud Violet, say 'no-thank-yer'!)"

Mrs. Moore, meanwhile, had glanced towards the table. "French again? Why are you forever reading French books?"

"Aren't they the cleverest?"

"They have so many s'écriais—he or she s'écriaid—as I always translate that 'shriek,' they go shrieking all down the page," answered Amy. She made a long stretch and took two paper-covered volumes from the table. "Lemaitre? Who is he? Oh, it isn't a novel. And this other one is that Bashkirtseff thing! The most perfectly unnatural book I have ever read."

"I thought it so natural."

"Mercy!"

"I don't mean that it was natural to write it for publication, or even, perhaps, to write it at all; I referred to the ideas, merely. If some invisible power should reproduce with exact truthfulness each one of our secret thoughts, do you think we should come out of it so infinitely better than Marie Bashkirtseff?"

"What extraordinary notions you invent! If I thought that Polly would ever have such ideas as that girl's— But she won't. You spinsters are too queer. You are either so prudish that one can't look at you, or else you're so emancipated that Heaven alone knows what you'll say next! It all comes from your ignorance, I suppose."

"Yes; that answer is always flung at us," responded Gertrude, holding her embroidery at arm's-length for a moment, in order to inspect it critically.

Polly, having overheard her name, had come to her mother's knee. "Want me, mamma?"

"No. Go back to your play."

"We're not playing. Fritzy won't."

"'Cause you're so selfish with your old dolls," said Fritz. "You said they was passhints. Then you came an' yanked 'em all away."

Polly made a face at him. Fritz responded with another, and one of preternatural hideousness, rolling his eyes up to the whites, and stretching out his tongue. This seemed to soothe him, for he demanded, after the effort was over:

"Where's the Noah's ark? You get it, and we'll play crocodile."

"I had happened to read the *Life of Louisa Alcott* just before I began the Bashkirtseff journal," Gertrude went on. "What a contrast! It is true that the Russian girl was but twenty-four when she died, but one feels that she would have been the same at fifty. Miss Alcott worked all her life as hard as she possibly could, turning her hand to anything that offered, no matter what; and her sole motive was to assist her parents and her family, those who were dear to her; of herself she never thought at all. Marie Bashkirtseff's behavior to her mother and aunt showed indifference, and often scorn; her one thought was herself—her own attractions, her own happiness, her own celebrity, and the persons who could perhaps add to the latter two. Her egotism—"

"Children, what *are* you about?" interrupted Mrs. Moore, turning her head; for Fritz and Polly were lying on the floor flat upon their stomachs, and in this position wriggling in zig-zags across the room, with low roars, directing their course towards the animals of Noah's ark, who were drawn up in a line before the sofa.

"We're crocodiles," called Fritz. "We're 'vancing to *scrunch* 'em!"

"Polly, get up instantly; look at your nice white frock! Fritz— Oh, here's Christine at last. Christine, do see to the children," said Mrs. Moore.

The German nurse, who had entered, lifted Polly to her feet and smoothed down her skirts. Fritz sprang up and rushed to the window, for he heard music outside; a street band composed of four men of depressed aspect had begun to play before the house the strains associated with the words:

> "Ever be hap-pee,
>   Wherever thou art,
>   Pride of the pirate's heart—"

"How ridiculous to be tooting away in all this rain!" said Mrs. Moore, irritably.

"It isn't raining now, mamma," called Polly, her nose also as well as Fritz's pressed against the pane.

"As it ees no rain, meeses, I might take de childrens to see dat leedle boy at Norteeng Hill?" suggested the nurse, respectfully.

"Has it really stopped?" answered Mrs. Moore, turning to look. "Well, perhaps it would be better for them to go out. Put on their cork-soled shoes and their water-proofs, and you must be back by five o'clock, or half past—not later."

"I veel at mine vatch look, and take de train shoost in time to be back at half past five," answered Christine, in her earnest, careful fashion. "It ees not much meeneets to Norteeng Hill."

She put the animals back in the ark, and placed it, with the box of dolls, in the closet.

"Take this shilling and give it to that dreadful band. Tell them to go away immediately," said Mrs. Moore.

"Yes, meeses." And taking the children with her, Christine left the room, softly closing the door behind her.

"I do wish Philip *would* go to Washington," said Mrs. Moore, after some minutes of silence.

The band had ceased its wailed good wishes for the pride of the pirate's heart; the room without the chatter of the children seemed suddenly very still; a coal dropping from the grate made a loud sound.

Miss Remington did not answer.

"It's the very place for me," pursued Amy. "There are all sorts of people there—foreigners and Southerners as well as Northerners. Not the seven deadly families, always the same, month after month, that we everlastingly have in New Edinburgh. I love variety and I love gayety, and I especially love dinner parties. I should like to dine out five nights in the week, and have friends to dine with us the other two. I don't see, after all, why we shouldn't go this very winter," she went on, with animation. "I have all these lovely new things from Paris, you know. Think of their being wasted in New Edinburgh!"

"They won't be wasted," said Gertrude. "Everybody will profoundly admire them."

"Profoundly criticise, you mean. Because they are all plain-looking themselves, they think it frivolous to care for looks; and because they are all dull and serious by nature, they think nobody ought to be gay; it's a good strong position, and I dare say they believe it's a moral one! Philip fancies that New Edinburgh is perfect, simply because he has his library there. But books can be moved, can't they? And it is his duty to remember *me* now and then. I suppose he can't appreciate that I have any such needs, because his mother and his five sisters are so different. Dear me! if girls could only know! They never think, when they marry, about the mother and sisters. But no matter what a husband may be as a man out in the world among men, when he thinks of his wife's requirements he seldom gets much beyond what his mother and sisters did and had. Of course Philip's sisters don't long for Washington. Imagine them there! But that's no reason for *me*."

"Philip himself would be a lion in Washington," said Gertrude, her face looking obstinate as she threaded her needle.

"You mean among the literary set? I should not care to have anything to do with *them*, and Philip wouldn't either. I know, because whenever I do succeed in forcing him out, he always likes my kind of people ever so much better. I suppose it wouldn't be hard to get a furnished house as a beginning; one with a good dining-room? But, dear me! what is the use of planning? I might as well be old and stupid and ugly! Philip will stick to New Edinburgh, and stick to New Edinburgh. *You* will like that; you adore the place, with its horrid clubs, and papers read aloud, and poky old whist!"

"I don't think Philip cares for New Edinburgh in itself," answered Miss Remington. "But he has the house, and it is a large place, with all the ground about it. And you know he has spent a great deal in alterations and improvements of many sorts, including all the new furniture."

"And I suppose you charge me with that? But I maintain that I'm not extravagant in the least," said Amy. "I must have things about me dainty and pretty, because I have all those tastes; I was born with them, and they are a part of me; people who haven't them, of course don't understand the necessity. But there's one thing to be said; there is no merit in going without the things one doesn't care for. Philip's sisters are perfectly willing to live forever with nailed-down carpets, hideous green lambrequins and furniture, because they don't know they are hideous. But just attack them on what they *do* care for—their Spanish and German lessons, their contributions to the 'Harvard Annex,' and the medical colleges for women, and there would be an outcry! As to money, Philip could easily make ever so much more a year, if he chose; those syndicate people do nothing but write to him."

"But you would not wish to see him descend to a lower grade of work, would you?" Gertrude's voice was indignant as she said this; but she kept her eyes on her work, and drew her stitches steadily.

"I don't know what you call a lower grade. *I* call it a lower grade to keep us in New Edinburgh, and a higher grade to give us a nice home in Washington—as it's Washington I happen to fancy. Philip *could* make this larger income; even you acknowledge that. Well, then, I say he ought. Other men do—I mean other authors. Look at Gray Tucker!"

"*Philip* to write in the style of Gray Tucker!"

"Now you're furious," said Amy, laughing. "But I'm afraid Philip couldn't do it even if he should try; he hasn't that sort of knack. Of course you are scornful; but, all the same, I can tell you plainly that *I* like Gray Tucker's books ever so much; they're easy to read, and they make one laugh, and I think that's what a novel is for. Everybody reads Gray Tucker's books, and they sell in thousands and thousands."

Miss Remington remained silent for several moments. Then, in a guarded voice, she said, "But if Philip has not that sort of knack, as you call it, surely you would not advise him to tie himself down at so much a year to produce just so many pages?"

"Why not?—if the sum offered is a good one."

"Just so many pages, whether good or bad?"

"They needn't be bad, I suppose. I don't see why he shouldn't keep on writing in the same style as now, but produce more. It simply depends upon his own determination."

"It isn't purely mechanical work, you know," answered Miss Remington.

"Your face is as red!" said Amy, watching her with amused eyes. "There is nothing so funny as to see you get in a rage about Philip. It's a pity he doesn't appreciate it more. Now, Gertrude, listen to me for a moment. I am not in the least frivolous, though you always have a manner that seems to show that you think I am. I have more common-sense than Philip has; I am the practical one, not he. What *is* the use of his persistingly writing books that nobody reads, or, at least, only a very few? To me it seems that a man can have no higher aim than to do splendidly for his own family—for the people that belong to him and depend upon him. I am his wife, am I not? And Fritz and Polly are his children. To give his wife the home she wishes, to educate his children in the very best way, and lay up a good generous sum for them—I confess this seems to me more important than the sort of fame his books may have in the future when we're all dead. For as to fame in the *present* there is no question, that hangs over the volumes that sell; the fame of to-day belongs always to the books that are popular. I know you don't think I'm clever at all; whether I am or not, that's my opinion."

"You're only too clever," said Gertrude, rolling up her work. "If there is any word I loathe, it's that lying term 'popular.'"

"Your eyes are brimming over, you absurd creature!" said Amy, not unkindly. "Yet somehow," she added, as Gertrude rose, "it only makes you look stiffer."

"Oh, do forget my stiffness!" said Miss Remington, angrily. She crossed the room, and began to rearrange the sofa cushions and chairs which the children had pulled about.

The door opened and Philip Moore came in.

"I thought you were writing?" said his wife.

"I can't write on a toilet table or the mantel-piece. Where are the children?"

"They have gone to Notting Hill to see Walter Carberry."

"Did they go by the underground?"

"Yes; Christine, you know, has the whole line at her fingers' ends. She once lived for two years at Hackney."

"Hackney?"

"Well, perhaps it was Putney. Such names! Imagine living at Tooting, or Barking, or Wormwood Scrubs! And then they talk to us about *our* names! But I have something to show them; I saw it in the *Times* yesterday, cut it out, and put it in my purse; here it is. Listen: 'November 28th, at St. Peter's Church, Redmile, Leicestershire, by the Rev. James Terry, rector of *Claxby-cum-Normanby-le-Wold*, Lincolnshire, Algernon Boothby, Esquire, to Editha, daughter of the Rev. J. Trevor Aylmar, rector of *Carlton-Scroop-cum-Normanton-on-Cliffe*, Lincolnshire.' There now! What do you say to that?"

"I don't like their going by the underground," said Moore.

"With Christine they are safe," answered his wife. "Where are our seats to-night?"

"Oh, I forgot to tell you, I've taken a box, after all. I met Huntley and Forrester, and asked them to join us."

"That is just like you, Philip. If I had not happened to ask, you would never have told me at all! Of course for a box I shall dress more," Amy added. "I'll do it for a *box*. And I'd better go and get it done now, by-the-bye, as there is no light upstairs but dull glimmering candles." She rose. "I suppose you are superior to dress, Gertrude?"

"Superior or inferior, whichever you like," answered Miss Remington.

Mrs. Moore went out.

"Do you care about this opera?" inquired Gertrude, returning to the fire.

"Can't say I do," answered Moore. "But they tell me it's pretty, and I thought it might amuse Amy." He had taken an evening paper from his pocket—the *St. James's Gazette*; he began to look over the first page.

Gertrude sat down, took up a book, and opened it. "Amy wishes to live in Washington," she said.

"Yes, I know," replied Moore.

"Perhaps the fancy won't last," his companion went on. She closed the book (it was *Marie Bashkirtseff's Journal*), and with a pencil began to make a row of little rosettes on the yellow cover. "Washington life would not suit you, Philip," she said. "You do not enjoy society; it does not amuse you, but only tires you. That has been proved again and again. And you would not be able to avoid it, either. The circumstances of the case would force you into it. Why isn't New Edinburgh the best place, with your large house, and your library all arranged, and that beautiful garden, and the grove and brook for the children?"

"It's dull for Amy," Moore replied, still reading. "She has been very unselfish about it. I should like to give her a change, if I could. But the first step would have to be to sell the place, and a purchaser for a place of that kind is not easily found."

"You will never get back half that you have spent upon it. New Edinburgh doesn't seem to me so dull," Gertrude continued.

"Amy is so much younger than we are that her ideas are different," answered Moore. He cut open the pages of the *St. James* jaggedly with the back of his hand, turned the leaf, and went on with his reading.

Miss Remington made five more little rosettes in a straight line on the cover. "Why not at least stay until your new book is finished," she said—"the one we all care so much about?" She hurried on, after this suggestion, to another subject. "Washington would only be safe for the children for part of the year. It would be necessary to take them away in April, and they could not return before November. That would be six months of travelling for you every summer—hotels, and all that. You have just said that you could not write on a mantel-piece," she added, forcing a laugh.

"It's very good of you to interest yourself so much in our affairs," said Moore, coldly. "The children would do very well in Washington in the winter; for the summer, I could look up some old farm-house in the mountains not very far away, where they could run wild. That would be even better for them than New Edinburgh. I should like it, too, myself."

"Then you have decided?" said Gertrude, quickly.

"Decided? I don't know whether I have or not," answered Moore.

Banks now appeared with a lamp and a large tea-tray. He placed the tray on a low table which stood in a corner, and drew the table towards Miss Remington; then he set out the cups and saucers in careful symmetry, and after waiting a moment to see if anything more was required, with noiseless step left the room. When the door was closed, Moore turned his head, glancing at the corpulent teapot, the piled sugar-bowl, the large plate covered with slices of bread-and-butter as thin as a knife blade, and arranged with mathematical precision.

"Do any of us ever touch it?" he inquired.

"Never," Gertrude answered. "Yet they send it in every afternoon in exactly the same way. It's a fixed rule, I suppose; like the house-maids always scrubbing the doorsteps on their knees, instead of using a long-handled scrubbing brush; and like the cold toast in the morning."

No more was said. She laid aside her pencil and the book, and took up a newspaper. It proved to be the same one she had had earlier in the day, and mechanically she read another four lines of the commercial poem:

> "Grass seed is middling.
> Pork has movement.
> Lemons have reacted.
> Molasses is strong."

After a while, Amy came in. "When do you intend to dress?" she said to her husband as she sat down by the fire.

"I'm waiting for the children. They ought not to be out after dark."

"It isn't late; they will be here in a few minutes; Christine is like a clock." She lifted her silk skirt and shook it. "It is creased a little, in spite of all the care they took in packing it. But it's a perfectly lovely dress! You need not look up, Gertrude, with that duty expression, as though you were trying to think of something admiring to say; I don't dress for you; or for Philip either, for that matter; he hasn't a particle of taste. I dress for myself—to satisfy my own ideal. And *this* is my ideal of a costume for the opera (that is, if one has a box)—delicate, Parisian, pretty. Philip, do you know what idea came to me upstairs? I want to go home by the White Star Line, instead of the Cunard."

No answer came from behind the *St. James's Gazette*; Moore had found at last a paragraph that interested him.

"Philip. Philip, I say! Why don't you listen?"

"Yes," said Moore.

"You are reading still; you are not listening one bit. Wake up!"

"Well, what is it?"

"I want to go home by the White Star Line instead of the Cunard."

Moore's eyes had glanced at his wife over the top of the newspaper, but there was not full comprehension in his glance.

"When you're absent-minded like that, you look about sixty years old," said Amy. "You've taken to stooping lately, and to scowling. If you add absent-mindedness, too—dear me!"

Moore let his newspaper drop, keeping a corner of it in his left hand, while with his right he rubbed his forehead, as if to rouse himself to quicker modes of thought.

"*Must* I say it again?" inquired Amy, in resigned despair. "You and Gertrude will end by making me lose my voice. No matter what my subject is, yours is always another. I said that I wished to go home by the White Star Line instead of the Cunard."

"But we can't. Our cabins on the *Etruria* have been engaged for weeks," replied her husband.

"They can be changed. At this season there's no crowd."

"But why?"

"I want to see the other line for myself, with my own eyes, so that the next time we cross we can make an intelligent choice."

"The next time? We needn't hurry about that. And it's too late to change now," said Moore, returning to his paper.

"It isn't in the least too late, if you cared to please me. And it's a very little thing, I'm sure. Don't you see that if we are to live in Washington, we must go away early every summer? We ought not to stay there a day after April, on account of the children. So, as I like going abroad better than any of the summer resorts, we shall be over here often. I don't see why we should not cross every year. So far, the three times we have crossed already, you have kept me tied to the Cunards. But I think that's narrow—to know only one line. It's like the New Edinburgh narrowness. They always quote Boston, and go to Boston, as though New York didn't exist. If you see about it immediately —to-morrow morning—I dare say you can arrange it. Promise me you will?"

"No; it's too late; they wouldn't do it. It's unreasonable to ask it."

A flush of anger rose in Amy's thin little face. "I suppose you mean that I'm unreasonable? But if there's anything I'm not, it's that. I always have a motive for everything I do. You have not a single reason for holding to the Cunard, except the trouble it will be to change, while I have an excellent one for wishing to try the White Star. Unreasonable!"

Here there was a knock at the door, and Banks appeared with a scared look in his eyes. "Please, sir, will you step out for a moment?" he murmured, but preserving his correct attitude in spite of his alarm.

Moore threw down his paper, and hurried into the hall, closing the door behind him. Amy, however, had instantly followed him.

A policeman standing at the street door delivered his message: "There is a child injured at the underground station. Don't know how bad it is. The nurse said it lived here at this number."

"Good God!" said Moore. And pushing by the man, he ran down the street towards the station.

Amy, who had overheard where she stood at the end of the

hall, gave a gasp, and leaned for an instant against the wall. Then she too, bareheaded, darted out, and rushed down the lighted street. Miss Remington now appeared at the sitting-room door; seeing the policeman, and catching from Banks the words "child" and "station," she ran back, seized a shawl of her own which was lying on a chair, and then followed the others, Banks accompanying her, but hardly able to keep up with her swiftness.

The Sloane Square Station was near. The stairway leading to the tracks at this station is one of the longest possessed by the underground railway; it does not turn, but goes straight down, down, as if descending to the bowels of the earth. The wicket at the bottom was open, and Gertrude ran through it and out on the lighted platform. There was a group at a distance; something told her that it surrounded the injured child. But before she could reach it, her eyes caught sight of Philip Moore leading, or trying to lead, Amy in the opposite direction, away from this group. Gertrude joined them, speechless.

"It's some other child," said Philip, as she came up. "From our house, apparently. Belongs to that family above us, I suppose. Amy, do come this way; come into the shadow. Think of those poor people who will be here in a moment, and don't let them see you crying."

But Amy seemed incapable of listening. He put his arm round her, and half carried her down the platform towards the deep shadow at the end.

"There is nothing the matter with any of *us*, Amy. Polly and Fritz are safe, and will be here soon. Don't cry so."

But the shock had been too great. Amy could not stop. She clung to her husband in a helpless tremor, sobbing: "Don't leave me, Philip. Stay with me! Stay with me!"

"Leave you?" He kissed her forehead in the darkness. "I'm not dreaming of leaving you. Aren't you more to me than all the world?" He soothed her tenderly, stroking her hair as her head lay on his breast—the thin golden hair, artificially waved to hide its thinness.

Gertrude stood beside them in silence. After a minute she held out the shawl.

"Yes," said Philip, "I am afraid she has already taken cold, with her head bare, she is so delicate." There was deep love in his eyes as he drew the soft folds closely round his little wife, and lifted a corner to cover her bowed head. Then, still keeping his arm about her, he turned her so that she stood with her back toward the distant group, and also toward the stairway by which the other parents must descend.

They came a moment afterwards, poor things! But the noise of an arriving train on the other side covered the sounds that followed—if there were any. Philip, glancing over his shoulder, saw the child borne into one of the waiting-rooms, whose door was immediately shut upon the gazing crowd.

Now came a train on their side—the one from Notting Hill. It stopped, and Christine, composed and cool, emerged, holding Fritz's arm firmly with one hand, and Polly's with the other.

"Don't stop to kiss them now," said Moore; "let us get away from here. Christine, take the children home as fast as possible." He followed the surprised nurse (surprised, but instantly obedient), supporting Amy up the long stairway directly behind Polly's little legs and the knickerbockers of Fritz.

Gertrude ascended behind them. She too was bareheaded; but no one had noticed that. At the door of the station stood Banks. Composedly he presented Philip Moore's hat.

The injured child recovered, though not for many long months. The Moores, however, left the house the next day, for the accident had made the place unpleasant to Amy. They went to the Bristol, Burlington Gardens.

On the passenger lists of the White Star steamer *Teutonic*, January 6, 1892, were the following names: "Philip Moore and wife; two children and nurse. Miss Remington."

Gertrude Remington does not keep a diary. But in a small almanac she jots down occasional brief notes. This is one of them: "New Edinburgh, February 20, 1892. Philip and A. gone to Washington. House here closed."

CHRONOLOGY

NOTE ON THE TEXTS

NOTES

# Chronology

1840–49     Born March 5, 1840, in Claremont, New Hampshire, sixth daughter of Charles and Hannah Cooper Pomeroy Woolson. The only child to receive the middle name "Fenimore," inherited on her mother's side from the Cooper family, which includes James Fenimore Cooper, Hannah's uncle. Two weeks later, scarlet fever epidemic hits the family: Julia, nearly 2, dies March 21; Gertrude, nearly 4, dies March 22; and Ann, 5, dies April 3. Baby Connie and two older sisters (Georgiana, 9, and Emma, 7) survive the epidemic. In the fall, Woolson family visits Cooper relatives in Cooperstown, New York, then moves to Cleveland, Ohio. A sister, Clara, born December 20, 1843. A seventh sister, Alida, born January 8, 1845; after a year of "grief and anguish," dies January 30, 1846. Her only brother, Charles Jarvis, Jr., born September 7, 1846. Attends Miss Fuller's Episcopal school for girls and in the late 1840s, Miss Hayden's coeducational private academy. Around age eight, writes the poem "Symmes' Hole"; it impresses her teacher, who predicts she will one day "excel as a writer."

1850–52     Oldest sister Georgiana marries Samuel Livingston Mather September 24, 1850. Second oldest sister, Emma, marries Rev. Timothy Jarvis Carter May 7, 1851, despite family's concerns about his worsening health. Georgiana gives birth July 13, 1851, to her first child, Samuel Mather, who will become a confidant and financial advisor to his aunt Constance in later years. Timothy Jarvis Carter dies of tuberculosis November 15, 1851. Emma Woolson Carter dies of tuberculosis August 14, 1852; is remembered by her family as having "literally given up her life to love."

1853     Begins a year of coeducational schooling at public Rockwell School. Georgiana gives birth to a second child, Katharine Livingston Mather, September 3. Georgiana dies, probably of tuberculosis, November 2, making Constance, thirteen, the oldest living child, although the sixth born.

1854–57    Attends progressive Cleveland Female Seminary 1854–57,
           taking classes in music, art, and painting, as well as En-
           glish literature, rhetoric, Latin, philosophy, history, chem-
           istry, botany, and trigonometry. In physiology, dissects a
           calf and learns how to assemble a skeleton. Teacher Linda
           Guilford encourages her writing. The Woolsons own a
           cottage on Mackinac Island and spend summers there
           from 1855 to 1857. On Mackinac Island she gets to know
           Zephaniah Swift Spalding, who will become a romantic
           interest and model for many male characters in her later
           fiction. In 1857 goes to Madame Chegaray's French fin-
           ishing school in New York; takes voice lessons, attends
           the opera, and learns French and Italian, among mostly
           southern belles.

1858–60    Graduates from Madame Chegaray's in 1858 with honors
           for her compositions. Family buys her a new set of stylish
           dresses and takes her on a tour of the fashionable East
           Coast resorts, presumably to look for a husband. Accord-
           ing to a family story, she ignores her mother's warning
           not to carry an open inkwell up and down stairs and spills
           ink all over one of her new dresses. Returns to Cleveland
           and begins a period of devotion to her father and mother,
           who suffers from chronic rheumatism. Father takes her on
           long drives in the country, visiting the Zoar community in
           the Tuscarawas Valley. Her hearing begins to deteriorate,
           a condition inherited from her father.

1861–65    During the Civil War, volunteers with the Soldier's Aid
           Society of Northern Ohio, serves as postmistress at a
           Sanitary Fair, sings at fundraising concerts, and greets
           trainloads of wounded soldiers with food and medicines.
           Becomes secretly engaged to Zephaniah Spalding. Reads
           the papers closely, following the great battles and news of
           Zeph's regiment, the Ohio 27th. He leads his regiment to
           victory in the Battle of Corinth in Mississippi and is later
           captured and imprisoned at Cahaba, Alabama, an episode
           that makes its way into her fiction. Many years later she
           will write that "the war was the heart and spirit of my life,
           and everything has seemed tame to me since."

1865–69    After the war's end, Zephaniah Spalding is sent to Hawaii,
           then a sovereign kingdom, as a spy by Secretary of State
           William Seward, a friend of his father's. Within a year he

will become U.S. consul, serving until 1869. Clara Woolson marries George Stone Benedict on January 31, 1867, and gives birth to a daughter, Clare Rathbone Benedict, on December 20, 1868. Woolson's closest friend, Arabella Carter, weds the Rev. Alan Washburn in 1869. Woolson tells her, "The glory of your life has come to you." Begins to call herself a "spinster." Father dies August 6, 1869, of complications of erysipelas and typhoid. Away at Mackinac Island, Woolson feels "eternal regret" at not being at his side.

1870        Decides to begin publishing her writing to support herself and her mother. Travels to New York with brother-in-law George Benedict and meets with magazine editors; *Harper's New Monthly Magazine* wants an exclusive contract with her (she declines). First two signed publications, travel sketches, appear in July 1870: "The Happy Valley" (about Zoar) in *Harper's New Monthly Magazine*, and "The Fairy Island" (about Mackinac Island) in *Putnam's Magazine*. Spends summer in Cooperstown with her mother. First short story, "An October Idyl," appears in *Harper's New Monthly Magazine* in October. Moves to New York with her brother, Charlie, living at 49 West 32nd Street. In December, begins writing "Letters from Gotham" for the *Daily Cleveland Herald*, owned by George Benedict and his father. Publishes six New York letters there through February 1871. Translates George Sand's novel *La Mare au Diable* (1846) but is unable to find a publisher.

1871–72     George Benedict killed in train crash February 6, 1871. Moves back to Cleveland, living with her mother and sister. Zephaniah Swift Spalding weds sugar heiress Wilhelmina H. Makee in Hawaii July 18, 1871. Woolson is devastated but many years later imagines they would both think, "Great heavens—what an escape I had!" Publishes prolifically, including seven short stories, in *Harper's New Monthly Magazine, Appleton's Journal, Lippincott's Magazine, The Galaxy*, and *Harper's Bazar*.

1873        Wins $500 prize from D. Lothrop & Company for her children's novel, *The Old Stone House*, published in their "Sunday school series." *The Old Stone House* appears under the pen name "Anne March," a nod to Louisa May Alcott's *Little Women* (1868). Not happy with the result, gives up trying to write for children and never acknowledges the novel. "Solomon," the first of many stories to be published in the prestigious *Atlantic Monthly*, appears in October, receiving positive notices. Story "St. Clair Flats" published the same month in *Appleton's*. In November, goes to New York with mother, Clara, and her niece, Clare, to see Charlie on his return from Europe. For mother's health they head south, reminders of the recent war at every stop along the way. Spends winter in St. Augustine, Florida, and will winter in Florida until her mother's death in 1879. Continues rapid pace of publication in 1873: six travel narratives, twelve poems, and five short stories.

1874    Meets the critic and poet Edmund Clarence Stedman in St. Augustine in March, forming a lasting friendship. Short story "Peter the Parson" published in *Scribner's Monthly* in September, drawing criticism for its dark ending. In the fall, James R. Osgood approaches her about publishing a collection of her Great Lakes stories. Spends the summer with her mother in Asheville, North Carolina, leaving in November to head back to St. Augustine, stopping at Civil War battlefields along the way. Publishes nine short stories this year, including "The Lady of Little Fishing" (*The Atlantic*, September) and "Jeannette" (*Scribner's Monthly*, December).

1875    Begins to correspond with southern poet Paul Hamilton Hayne after he writes to praise her writing. She and Hannah spend the spring months in Charleston, part of June and July in Cleveland Springs, South Carolina, and July and August in Goshen, Virginia, with trips to Charlottesville, Harpers Ferry, and Gettysburg. Turns down *Harper's New Monthly Magazine* offer to write about her visit to Gettysburg; writes unpublished poem about it instead. Attempts to undertake a novel while in Goshen but suffers from a bout of depression that lasts through the winter. In the fall, in New York, meets Mary Mapes Dodge, Richard and Elizabeth Stoddard, and other writers at the home of Edmund Clarence Stedman and his wife. Writes to him later about how women writers pale in comparison to his unliterary wife, Laura Hyde Woodworth Stedman. Spends November in Charleston then heads to St. Augustine for the winter. Story collection *Castle Nowhere: Lake-Country Sketches* published by James R. Osgood to positive reviews.

1876    Stays in St. Augustine until the weather becomes too warm and spends April and May in Summerville, South Carolina. First Reconstruction story, "Old Gardiston," published in *Harper's New Monthly Magazine* in April. Is warned by one of the Harper brothers, while in St. Augustine, not to write anymore about the postwar South, due to the mounting tensions around the presidential election that year. Spends summer in Cooperstown, New York, visiting her mother's family. Returns to St. Augustine with her mother, Clara, and Clare, for the winter. Feels out of place in the increasingly fashionable resort town, now an outpost of northern high society. Publishes "Felipa" (*Lippincott's Magazine*, June) and five other stories this year.

1877    Publishes the long poem "Two Women. 1862" (*Appletons' Journal*, January and February), drawing mixed reviews; decides to give up ambitions as a poet and focus on fiction. Frightening telegrams from Charlie in Chicago indicate he has broken down mentally and physically, but he returns to Cleveland and seems to be improving by March. In the spring, moves to Yonkers, New York, staying in a house Clara has purchased. *The Atlantic Monthly* publishes "Rodman the Keeper" in March to lead the magazine; it is widely noticed and commended, the Christian Union calling it "one of the few artistically perfect tales that the history of the civil war has inspired." Publishes "Sister St. Luke" in *The Galaxy* in April. Has plans to write a novel, which James R. Osgood expresses interest in. Begins writing for *The Atlantic Monthly*'s "Contributors' Club" in May. In September, Edmund Clarence Stedman visits her and her family in Yonkers. In December, arrives with Hannah at Hibernia, near Green Cove Springs, Florida, a much quieter place to write than St. Augustine.

1878    Publishes "King David" in *Scribner's Monthly* in April. Writes for nine hours a day, completing her first adult novel, *Anne*, in May. Tells Stedman that she is nearly "'finished' too!" Decides to give it to Harper & Brothers, but they will sit on it for two years, deferring her hopes of establishing herself as a novelist. Spends summer with Hannah, Clara, and Clare by the sea in Narragansett Pier, Rhode Island. Works during the day to revise and copy her novel and swims in the afternoon. They all return to Yonkers in the fall, Charlie joining them. Falls very ill in December.

1879        Publishes two reviews of Henry James's *The Europeans* in
            *The Atlantic*'s "Contributors' Club" (January and Feb-
            ruary). In mid-January, barely able to stand, returns to
            Hibernia with her mother, whose own health worsens
            rapidly, a downturn that Woolson will blame on her own
            illness and the care her mother had to give her. Hannah
            Cooper Pomeroy Woolson dies February 13. With sister,
            Woolson brings mother's body north to Cleveland to the
            house of their brother-in-law, Samuel Mather. Spends
            March in Washington, D.C., the summer in Coopers-
            town, and October in Cleveland, consumed with guilt
            over mother's death and burdened with depression. In
            Cleveland, meets the writer John Hay, former secretary to
            Lincoln and friend of Henry James and Edmund Clarence
            Stedman; he will become a good friend. Clara proposes a
            trip to Europe, which she will subsidize. Woolson, Clara,
            and Clare, nearly eleven, sail on the *Gallia*, arriving in
            Liverpool, England, on November 30, amidst the worst
            winter England has seen this century. They spend only
            ten days in London. With a letter of introduction from
            her cousin Henrietta Pell-Clarke, Woolson knocks on the
            door of Henry James's flat, but discovers he is in Paris.
            Her hearing has deteriorated to the extent that others re-
            fer to her as "deaf," although she uses an audiophone (a
            kind of curved fan that directs sounds through the teeth)
            and an ear trumpet. Chased away by the cold weather,
            they travel to southern France and stop in Menton, on
            the Riviera, for the winter. Writes the story "'Miss Grief'"
            sometime that winter (published in *Lippincott's Magazine*
            in May 1880).

1880        In Menton, takes excursions to castles and ruins, but
            complains that the weather is not as warm as Florida's.
            Worries about Charlie, now in California, who has had
            another collapse. Intent on supporting herself in Europe,
            begins to write again, starting the novella "For the Ma-
            jor." Woolson, Clara, and Clare travel to Florence, arriv-
            ing on March 18 at the Casa Molini pension. Writes all
            morning and tours churches in the afternoons with the
            aid of John Ruskin's *Mornings in Florence*. Meets Henry
            James one day at the Casa Molini; for the next three or
            four weeks he guides her around Florence's churches and
            museums in the mornings, taking time away from writing
            his novel *The Portrait of a Lady*. He doesn't know her

work and writes home that she is "old-maidish, deaf & 'intense'; but a good little woman & a perfect lady." She thinks him "a delightful companion." The places they visit together and their differing views on art make their way into her story "A Florentine Experiment" (published in *The Atlantic Monthly* in October). In June, travels with Clara and Clare to Venice, Milan, and Lake Como, and heads to Lucerne, Switzerland, for the hot months, and in the fall to Geneva, where she takes a break from writing and reads the Lake Leman writers, including Madame de Staël. Returns to Florence in December. Second collection of stories, *Rodman the Keeper: Southern Sketches*, is published by D. Appleton and Company to very good reviews, including the one James clips and sends to her from the June issue of the London *Spectator*. In December, her novel *Anne* finally begins its run in *Harper's New Monthly Magazine*, premiering in the first transatlantic edition, published simultaneously in the United States and England. It will appear monthly until May 1882.

1881    After a trip to Siena, arrives in Rome in January with an old friend from St. Augustine. Visits the Vatican, Borghese Gardens, St. Peter's, the Forum, and more. In March, Clara and Clare arrive, and then in April return home to Cleveland. Delighted to be alone in Rome, rents an apartment. Writes for seven hours a day and explores the city, including the Doria Gallery and the Protestant Cemetery, where she visits the graves of Shelley and Keats. James visits her during his two-week visit to Rome. Stays on, despite her family's concerns about Roman fever, until June 4. Then travels to Switzerland, staying until August in Geneva, Engelberg, and Lucerne, writing "At the Château of Corinne," which *Harper's New Monthly Magazine* won't publish while *Anne* is still being serialized. (It won't appear for six years.) In the fall, travels throughout Italy, from Turin to Milan, Padua, Venice, Florence, and Naples, arriving in Sorrento in December.

1882    In Sorrento, writes most of the day in her room overlooking the Bay of Naples. Fan letters about *Anne* arrive daily and, unexpectedly, in February, a letter from Harper & Brothers enclosing a $1,000 check and requesting the right of first refusal on all future works. The Harper brothers will be her exclusive American publisher for the rest of her career. Publishes "The Street of the Hyacinth" in *The Century Magazine* in June. In July, *Anne* is published in book form and goes on to sell 57,000 copies. Reviews compare her to George Eliot and predict an "enduring fame," calling *Anne* "one of the strongest and most perfectly finished American novels ever written." Sees few of the reviews from abroad. *The Atlantic Monthly*'s new editor, Thomas Bailey Aldrich, requests a serial from her, but she declines due to her new contract with the Harpers. Falls ill in the summer and loses sixteen pounds. Returns to Florence and consults a doctor. Joins Clara and Clare, returned from America, in Baden-Baden, Germany, where she works ten- to thirteen-hour days for ten weeks to complete *For the Major*, which will begin serialization in *Harper's New Monthly Magazine* in November. At the end of August, they visit Dresden, then Cologne in September and on to London, from where Clara and Clare sail home. In London, socializes with John and Clara Hay, and with William Dean Howells and his wife, Elinor. In December, follows the Hays to Paris and meets up briefly with James.

1883    Returns to Florence and stays again at the Casa Molini. Becomes part of a social scene that includes Howells and his family, the Hays, old friends from Rome, and a host of British and American writers. Enjoys the respect she receives as a writer in society but laments the time it takes away from her writing. Flees to Venice in April, as do the Howellses, and finds the smaller society there more manageable. Stays at the Palazzo Gritti-Swift; writes in the mornings and spends afternoons in a gondola. *For the Major* continues serialization in *Harper's New Monthly Magazine* through April, followed by the book version in July. Disappointingly, *For the Major* sells only about 5,000 copies. Sampson Low & Company publishes *Anne* and *For the Major* in England. Leaves Venice on July 7 for Engelberg, then travels to Baden-Baden. While in Baden-Baden receives news of her brother, Charlie's, suicide on August 20, plunging her into a deep depression. Arrives in London in October; takes an apartment in Sloane Street and stays for eight months, seeing James often.

1884    In January is feeling more optimistic and starts writing again. By May is working on a new novel, *East Angels*. Moves to Hampstead Heath for the summer; goes to Dover in September, where she meets James; moves to

Salisbury at end of September and spends two blissful months living within the close of the cathedral. James visits September 29 and they go to Stonehenge. Spends winter in Vienna with Clara and Clare.

1885    Stays in Vienna until April. Moves to the Isle of Wight where she falls ill; is unable to write. Retreats to the baths of Leamington with Clara and Clare, who sail home in September. Gradually regains strength and ability to write. Moves back to London for the winter. James introduces her to his sister, Alice James, and her companion, Katharine Loring, and the three become close friends. *East Angels* begins serialization in *Harper's New Monthly Magazine* in January. Asks the Harpers for a larger advance and receives it: $3,500.

1886    Stays in London until spring, finishing book revisions of *East Angels*. Returns to Florence in early April. Learns that manuscript was feared lost on Atlantic voyage and rewrites *East Angels* in fourteen-hour days for two weeks; then learns the manuscript arrived safely after all. Dr. William Wilberforce Baldwin helps soothe the writer's cramp in her arm and back and becomes a close friend. *East Angels* ends serialization in *Harper's New Monthly Magazine* in May, and the book version is released in the U.S. by Harper & Brothers in June, selling about 10,500 copies, and in England by Sampson Low & Company. Critics, including her old friend (and new enemy) Howells, attack the portrayal of the heroine as unrealistic; Woolson defends her portrait in private letters. James facilitates her introduction to his friends the composer Francis Boott, his artist daughter, Lizzie, and her new husband, the artist Frank Duveneck. After summer in Geneva, subleases an apartment in the Bootts' home, the Villa Castellani, on Bellosguardo, a hill overlooking Florence, from September through the end of the year. James comes for a visit December 8, staying for three weeks in the Villa Brichieri, just up the road. Becomes godmother to Lizzie and Frank's baby, named Frank, born December 18.

1887    Moves into the Villa Brichieri after James leaves. Leases it for a year and sets up housekeeping, experiencing settled happiness for the first time since her father died. James's appreciative (although paternalistic) essay "Miss Woolson" appears in *Harper's Weekly* February 12. James falls ill in Venice and Woolson invites him to convalesce in the apartment below hers, with a separate entrance. He stays for six weeks, beginning in April, making daily visits to her upstairs apartment. Woolson falls ill and James helps to care for her. Around this time, they agree to destroy their letters to each other. Only four of hers to him will survive. Poor health prevents her from writing much. Spends the summer in Geneva. Only publication this year is "At the Château of Corrine," in October (*Harper's New Monthly Magazine*).

1888    Renews lease on Villa Brichieri for another year. Begins writing new novel, *Jupiter Lights*, in January. On March 22 Lizzie Duveneck dies of pneumonia in Paris. Helps the grief-stricken father, husband, and son through the summer; they move back to the U.S. in August, leaving Woolson alone and bereft on Bellosguardo. After completing the serial version of her novel, returns to Geneva in October; James stays across the lake and they visit regularly. Publishes "A Pink Villa" in November and "The Front Yard" in December in *Harper's New Monthly Magazine.*

1889    Renews lease on Villa Brichieri for another year. *Jupiter Lights* begins serialization in *Harper's New Monthly Magazine* in January and runs through September. Clara and Clare come and live in the downstairs apartment. The social life they bring with them forces her to stay up at night, writing until dawn, to finish revisions to the book version of *Jupiter Lights.* Starts worrying about money, ability to keep villa; falls into a deep depression; often talks to the departed Lizzie and plays Francis Boott's compositions on the piano, including "Through the Long Days." Visits Venice in June and July. In July, nephew Sam Mather sends her a gift of $15,000, restoring her hope for the future. Visits Richmond, England, in the fall; walks eight miles a day and visits James in London occasionally. Book version of *Jupiter* published in December by Harper & Brothers in U.S. and by Sampson Low & Company in England. Book alternately praised for its power and criticized for its portrayal of domestic violence against women. Sales are modest: 6,000 copies. In December, Woolson breaks up her Villa Brichieri home.

1890    Undertakes journey (begun at end of December 1889) with Clara and Clare to Corfu, Cairo, and Jerusalem.

Returns to Cairo alone, where she enjoys expatriate society and explores Egyptian culture, reporting, "I feel like another person—so broadened in mind by an actual look into the strange life of the East." Sails to England in April and settles in Cheltenham, where she will have few distractions and can write. Receives visits from James, Dr. Baldwin, and Katharine Loring. Grows depressed in the winter. Writes "Dorothy," based on her memories of Bellosguardo (published in *Harper's New Monthly Magazine*, March 1892).

1891     Stays on in Cheltenham. Receives offers from syndicates to write for them and earn more money; she declines and remains loyal to the Harpers. Continues to worry about money as she foresees a time when she will no longer be able to write. In May, Clara and Clare return to Europe and take her on excursions. Moves to Oxford in July, living near Oriel College and then at 15 Beaumont Street. Attends premiere of James's play *The American* on September 26 and meets William James. Tries artificial eardrums to improve her hearing. Two-part essay "Cairo 1890" appears in *Harper's New Monthly Magazine* (October–November).

1892     Falls ill in January, in midst of flu epidemic that closes Oxford University for first time in living memory. Develops splitting headaches, then painful earaches, which she blames on the artificial eardrums, lasting six agonizing weeks. Alice James, on her deathbed in London, sends messages to her, including a final mysterious message probably consigning her brother to her care. The final story Katharine Loring reads to Alice is Woolson's "Dorothy." Alice dies March 6. Henry comes a week later to Oxford and his visits increase through the rest of the year. Publishes "In Sloane Street" in *Harper's Bazar* in June. Earnings dwindle, and Woolson has to draw on her capital, no longer able to live off the small interest her investments earn. Is still unable to start saving for retirement and is already a year late turning in her new novel, *Horace Chase*.

1893     *Horace Chase* begins its serial run in *Harper's New Monthly Magazine* in January. Falls ill again with a bad cold. The labor of writing has left her feeling that the whole right side of her body is "deformed." By March, with two parts of the novel yet to complete, her doctor restricts her activities to writing, eating, and sleeping. Makes plans to leave England's cold winters for Venice. By May, has finally completed *Horace Chase*, which concludes its serial run in August. Visits dentist in London and falls ill with influenza. Severely weakened, leaves for Venice, meeting James in Paris on the way. James plans to visit her in Venice. Lives in Casa Biondetti, writing in the morning and floating out to the lagoons in the afternoons. Socializes with close friends Ariana and Daniel Curtis, Katherine de Kay Bronson, and Lady Layard. Hides her growing depression from them. Works nearly eleven hours a day on book proofs of *Horace Chase*. Friends notice her deteriorating health, and she feels she will not live into old age. Moves into new apartment at Casa Semitecolo on the Grand Canal in September, getting her belongings from Bellosguardo and setting up housekeeping again. James delays his expected visit. The Panic of 1893 spreads across U.S. and Europe, closing banks around Italy. She is terrified of losing her dwindling funds and again draws on her capital, forestalling indefinitely her dream of retiring to Florida. Friends leave Venice for the winter, but she stays, planning to start writing a new novel on January 1.

1894    On New Year's Day, walks through Venice after a snowstorm and writes to her editor, Henry Mills Alden, that she cannot write another novel: "I have given up my broken sword to Fate, the Conqueror." First two weeks of January unusually cold. On the thirteenth, goes for a walk and falls ill. Plans to write her will (which she never does) and requests that her body be brought to the Protestant Cemetery in Rome for burial. After a period of painful vomiting and fever, believed to be influenza but possibly something more serious, seems to be getting better but grows increasingly irritable and dependent on laudanum and morphine. On the night of January 23, doctor refuses to give her a stronger dose. When she wakes up at midnight, either falls or jumps out of third-story window of the Casa Semitecolo, landing on the pavement below. Dies one hour later, in the early morning of January 24. Venetian papers report her death as a suicide and English and American papers pick up the story, pronouncing her eccentric and insane. James plans to come to her funeral from London but is prostrated by grief when he learns her death is considered a suicide. She is taken for burial to the Protestant Cemetery in Rome, where she is laid to rest near the grave of Percy Bysshe Shelley. John and Clara Hay and other friends in Italy attend the funeral on January 31. "A Transplanted Boy" appears in *Harper's New Monthly Magazine* in February. *Horace Chase* is published in February by Harper & Brothers in the U.S. and by Osgood, McIlvaine & Company in England.

1895–96    Harper & Brothers posthumously publishes the story collections *The Front Yard and Other Italian Stories* (September 1895) and *Dorothy and Other Italian Stories* (January 1896), and a volume of travel sketches, *Mentone, Cairo, and Corfu* (January 1896).

# Note on the Texts

This volume contains twenty-three stories by Constance Fenimore Woolson selected from the two short story collections published in the author's lifetime, *Castle Nowhere: Lake-Country Sketches* (1875) and *Rodman the Keeper: Southern Sketches* (1880); her two post-humously published collections, *The Front Yard and Other Italian Stories* (1895) and *Dorothy and Other Italian Stories* (1896); and her uncollected stories.

A popular and critically acclaimed writer in her lifetime who was compared to George Eliot, Woolson published her stories widely in American magazines until 1882, when she entered an exclusive arrangement with the New York firm Harper & Brothers. Thereafter, all her stories, sketches, essays, and books were published by the Harpers. In a letter of 1878 that was printed in *The Ladies Home Journal*, Woolson offered this picture of the busy, unpredictable life of a magazine writer: "When you first begin the magazines pay you about five dollars per page. . . . They pay me now much more, but that is entirely at their option. I get from seventy-five to one hundred dollars for a story; for the pictorial articles more. . . . Messrs. Harper and Appleton pay on acceptance; all others on publication. As they may have to delay publication it follows that authors of accepted manuscripts have sometimes to wait months and months for their pay. One thing is fixed; they won't have the same contributor appear too often; it is against their policy. Supposing you get into 'Harper's,' 'The Galaxy,' 'The Atlantic,' 'Scribner's,' 'Lippincott's,' and 'Appleton's' once each year; you will then have, supposing your article to be of good length four hundred and fifty dollars. . . . But you see there is no certainty about it."

Typically, Woolson revised her magazine stories for book publication; however, she did not make subsequent changes to the stories for later printings in her book collections. *The Front Yard* and *Dorothy* were published by Harper & Brothers not long after the author's death, and it is likely that Woolson prepared the final manuscripts of these Italian stories with book publication in mind. Writing to her nephew Samuel Mather on December 30, 1893, less than a month before her death on January 24, 1894, she refers to a forthcoming "volume of my Italian stories." No manuscripts or typescripts of the posthumously published stories—nor indeed of any others—survive. Furthermore, two of the posthumously published stories were significantly abridged in *Harper's New Monthly Magazine* ("A Transplanted Boy" is discussed below). For all these reasons the texts of the stories presented here are taken from the first edition of the collections in which they appeared, except for the uncollected stories "'Miss Grief'" and "On Sloane Street" (also discussed below). Although Woolson's novels found publishers in London, none of her story collections appeared in British editions.

*Castle Nowhere: Lake-Country Sketches* was published in 1875 by the Boston firm James R. Osgood and Company. Little is known about the composition of these stories, but Woolson drew heavily on youthful memories of the Great Lakes area, rekindled in the years since her father's death by short trips from Cleveland to Detroit and across Lake Huron to Mackinac Island and down the Ohio River. Because Osgood desired at least one unpublished story for the collection, the long title story, "Castle Nowhere," was written for the book and included without prior magazine publication. The other eight stories came out first in magazines, and the six chosen for the present volume appeared as follows: "St. Clair Flats" in *Appletons' Journal*, October 4, 1873; "Solomon" in *The Atlantic Monthly*, October 1873; "Peter the Parson" in *Scribner's Monthly*, September 1874; "The Lady of Little Fishing" in *The Atlantic Monthly*, September 1874; "Jeannette" in *Scribner's Monthly*, December 1874; and "Wilhelmina" in *The Atlantic Monthly*, January 1875. An undated abridged version of *Castle Nowhere* was published as *Solomon & Other "Lake Country" Sketches* by the Canadian publisher J. Neish & Sons. This volume prints the texts of the stories from the 1875 Osgood edition.

Beginning in 1873 Woolson wintered with her mother in Florida (and summered elsewhere on the East Coast), and this change of geography inspired her Southern stories. *Rodman the Keeper: Southern Sketches* was published by D. Appleton and Company to mostly positive reviews in June 1880. Among the favorable notices was one in the London *Spectator* (clipped from the paper by Henry James and mailed to his friend), which praised the collection for its "quite remarkable power." Of the ten stories in the collection eight have been chosen for inclusion; they first appeared in the following magazines: "Miss Elisabetha" in *Appletons' Journal*, March 13, 1875; "Old Gardiston" in *Harper's New Monthly Magazine*, April 1876; "In the Cotton Country" in *Appletons' Journal*, April 29, 1876; "Felipa" in *Lippincott's Magazine*, June 1876; "Rodman the Keeper" in *The Atlantic Monthly*, March 1877; "Sister St. Luke" in *The Galaxy*, April 1877; "King David" in *Scribner's Monthly*, April 1878; and "The South Devil" in *The Atlantic Monthly*, February 1880. In 1886, Harper & Brothers reprinted *Rodman the Keeper*, using Appleton's plates. This volume prints the texts of the stories from the 1880 Appleton edition.

*The Front Yard and Other Italian Stories* was published in September 1895 by Harper & Brothers, the first of two posthumous books that gathered Woolson's Italian stories, all written after her departure from the United States in December 1879 (following her mother's death in February 1879). All six stories in *The Front Yard* appeared in magazines prior to their book publication. The three stories selected for this volume were published in the following magazines: "The Street of the Hyacinth" in *The Century Magazine*, May and June 1882; "A Pink Villa" in *Harper's New Monthly Magazine*, November 1888; and "The Front Yard" in *Harper's New Monthly Magazine*, December 1888. This volume prints the texts of the stories from the 1895 edition of *The Front Yard*.

Harper & Brothers brought out *Dorothy and Other Italian Stories* only four months after *The Front Yard*, in January 1896. The five stories in *Dorothy* appeared in magazines prior to the book's publication. The long story "A Transplanted Boy" (included here) was published soon after the author's death in a significantly shorter version in *Harper's New Monthly Magazine* in February 1894—very likely an abridgment by the magazine's editors. ("A Waitress"—not included here—also appeared in an abridged version in *Harper's New Monthly Magazine* after Woolson's death and prior to its publication in *Dorothy*.) The other three stories selected for this volume were published in the following magazines: "A Florentine Experiment" in *The Atlantic Monthly*, October 1880; "At the Château of Corinne" in *Harper's New Monthly Magazine*, October 1887; and "Dorothy" in *Harper's New Monthly Magazine*, March 1892. This volume prints the texts of the stories from the 1896 Harper & Brothers edition of *Dorothy*.

The first of Woolson's stories to be written in Europe, "'Miss Grief'" was published in *Lippincott's Magazine* in May 1880 and was subsequently anthologized in Scribner's *Stories by American Authors* (1884). Woolson appears to have revised the story for the Scribner's anthology, although the differences between the two texts are primarily minor. An exception concerns the name of the narrator's romantic interest, changed from "Ethelind" in *Lippincott's* to "Isabel" in *Stories by American Authors*, perhaps a nod in the direction of Woolson's friend Henry James and his protagonist Isabel Archer. Woolson did not meet James until spring 1880—that is, after she had written "'Miss Grief'." In a long letter of February 12, 1882, to James, Woolson expressed her admiration for *The Portrait of a Lady*: "I have come slowly to the conclusion that the 'Portrait' is the finest novel you have written. 'Slowly,' because I so much like the others, & hate to desert old friends. I did'nt completely yield until I had read the last two chapters. Then I had to. The scene between Goodwood & Isabel at the end is, in my opinion, by far the strongest scene of the kind you have given to the public." This volume prints the 1884 text of "'Miss Grief'" in Scribner's *Stories by American Authors*.

"In Sloane Street" was published in *Harper's Bazar*, June 11, 1892, and was not reprinted in the nineteenth and twentieth centuries.

This volume presents the texts of the original printings chosen for inclusion here, but it does not attempt to reproduce features of their design and layout. The texts are presented without change, except for the correction of typographical errors. Spelling, punctuation, and capitalization are often expressive features and they are not altered, even when inconsistent or irregular. The following is a list of errors corrected, cited by page and line number: 133.28, "Why,; 137.26, "And; 179.26, organ.; 183.36, "Come, said; 184.24, pace.; 200.5, "Addios,"; 210.30, perhaps.; 215.22, mits; 243.26, he bearish,; 271.15, it's; 314.31, suppose?; 316.38, games."; 322.9, radiance,; 323.7, face,; 333.28, then "cat"; 361.14, I will.; 366.27, Prudence. But; 379.5, 'ain't; 394.37, Vernueil,; 434.7, Sebastian; 493.40, *must?*; 494.1, replies; 518.5, Well!"; 536.15, departure.; 639.34, answewed; 668.10, *Caralleria*; 669.14, to to her; 670.12, 'no-thank-yer"; 677.12, *St. James*.

# Notes

In the notes below, the reference numbers denote page and line of this volume (the line count includes headings). Biblical quotations are keyed to the King James Version. Quotations from Shakespeare are keyed to *The Riverside Shakespeare*, ed. G. Blakemore Evans (Boston: Houghton Mifflin, 1974). For further biographical background than is provided in the Chronology, see Anne Boyd Rioux, *Constance Fenimore Woolson: Portrait of a Lady Novelist* (New York: W. W. Norton, 2016) and *The Complete Letters of Constance Fenimore Woolson*, ed. Sharon L. Dean (Gainesville, Florida: University Press of Florida, 2012).

## CASTLE NOWHERE AND OTHER STORIES

4.14   crash] A coarse weave of absorbent cotton and linen.

4.27   "Santa Margarita"] Saint Margaret of Cortona (1247–1297), patron saint of the orphaned, falsely accused, homeless, mentally ill, midwives, single mothers, and reformed prostitutes.

21.37   gammon] Absurd talk or nonsense.

25.17   Mexico] Here, shorthand for the Mexican-American War, fought from 1846 to 1848.

25.18–19   cloudy heights of Lookout Mountain] In the "battle above the clouds," fought in heavy mist and rain on November 24, 1863, Union troops under Major General Joseph Hooker (1814–1879) drove Confederate forces from much of Lookout Mountain just outside of Chattanooga, Tennessee. Firing between the opposing sides continued into the night, when the Confederates withdrew the rest of their forces.

25.20–21   the great struggle] The American Civil War, fought from 1861 to 1865.

26.8   "O, to escape . . . at rest!"] Cf. Psalm 55:6: "And I said, Oh that I had wings like a dove! for then would I fly away, and be at rest."

27.6   chapters about Balaam and Balak] Numbers 22–24, in which Balak, king of the Moab, asks the Mesopotamian prophet Balaam to curse the Israelites. An angel comes to him and convinces him to bless them instead.

27.7–8   "Let me die . . . be like his."] Numbers 23:10.

29.6   "*une p'tite moue*."] French: a little pout.

702

30.17–18   Macaulay's "Ivry."] Poem by Thomas Babington Macaulay (1800–1859) celebrating Henry IV's Edict of Nantes (1598), which granted religious liberty to the Huguenots, Henry's French Protestant subjects.

31.31–32   Father Piret . . . the Chenaux] Father Andrew D. J. Piret (1802–1875) was a Belgian-born missionary priest stationed at St. Ann's church on Mackinac Island who also ministered to the neighboring Native Americans. Piret built his homestead on the Chenaux Islands.

32.19–20   "*faut que je m' fasse belle.*"] French: I must make myself beautiful.

33.35   *Le Beau Voyager, Les Neiges de la Cloche*] The French song titles translate to "The Handsome Voyager" and "The Snows of La Cloche," the latter a reference to the La Cloche Mountains in Ontario, a southern arm of which extends down to Lake Huron's Georgian Bay.

34.13–35.6   "'Marie, enfin . . . le prisonnier."] An abridged version of "Le Prisonnier de guerre" [The Prisoner of War] by French poet and songwriter Pierre Jean de Béranger (1780–1857). The English translation of 1850 by William Young reads:

> "Marie, 'tis late; put by thy work;
>     The shepherd's star hath risen!"
> "Nay, mother, nay, our village lad
>     Pines in a foreign prison:
> Far off from home on distant sea
> He yielded—but the last was he."
>     "Spin, spin, poor Marie, spin,
>         To send the prisoner aid;
>     Spin, spin poor Marie, spin,
>         For him who's captive made!"
>
> "Well, if thou wilt, the lamp I'll light:
>     But, child, thy tears still flow!"
> "Mother he frets himself to death;
>     The Briton mocks his woe.
> How Adrien loved me, when a boy!
>     With him about our hearth, what joy!"
>     "Spin, spin, poor Marie, spin,
>         To send the prisoner aid;
>     Spin, spin, poor Marie, spin
>         For him who's captive made!"
>
> "Ah, were I not myself too old,
>     I'd spin, child, for his sake."
> "O mother, send to him I love
>     All, all that I can make!
> Rose bids me to her wedding go—
> Hark, there's the fiddler!—no, no, no!"

"Spin, spin, poor Marie, spin
To send the prisoner aid;
Spin, spin, poor Marie, spin
For him who's captive made!"

"Draw near the fire to spin, dear child—
With night it grows more cold."
"Mother, in a floating dungeon groans
Poor Adrien, I've been told:
Stretched are his wasted hands in vain
His scanty ration to obtain."
"Spin, spin, poor Marie, spin
To send the prisoner aid;
Spin, spin, poor Marie, spin
For him who's captive made!"

37.16 'The Harp that once—'] "The Harp that Once through Tara's Halls," an Irish song whose lyrics were written by Thomas Moore (1779–1852) and the piano accompaniment by Sir John Andrew Stevenson (1761–1833).

38.21 "*Moi? C'est aut' chose*,"] French: Me? That's another thing.

38.29 the Prince of the Powers of the Air] The devil; see Ephesians 2:2.

39.3 "*Ce n'est rien*] French: It's nothing.

39.7–8 *Féroce, O féroce . . . c'est joli, ça!*"] French: Ferocious, oh ferocious, like a werewolf! Ah, it's so pretty.

41.39 ordered to Florida] Probably a reference to the Third Seminole War (1858–1868), the last of the wars fought between the U.S. Army and the Seminoles.

42.1 Valley of the Shadow of Death] See Psalm 23:4.

47.25–26 "*Oui, mon cousin . . . fête de Saint André.*"] Jeannette and her cousin, Baptiste, have set their wedding date on the feast of St. Andrew, November 30.

47.33 "*Je vous abhorre; je vous déteste*,"] French: I hate you; I detest you.

47.36 *Allez-vous-en, traître!*"] French: Leave, you traitor!

48.14 *Ah, mon Baptiste, où es-tu?*] French: Oh, my Baptiste, where are you?

48.17 *Je suis femme, moi!*"] French: I am a woman!

50.12–13 glow-worm lamps] Lamps containing adult lightning bugs or their luminescent larvae.

50.32 "Western Reserve."] A tract of land in the northeast corner of Ohio reserved by Connecticut when that state ceded the rest of its western land claims to the United States in 1786. Connecticut transferred jurisdiction over the reserve to the federal government in 1800, and it became part of the newly created Ohio Territory.

50.33–51.2 "Fire Lands," . . . "One-Leg Creek."] Places in northeastern Ohio. Located in the Western Reserve, the "Fire Lands" were given as financial restitution to Connecticut residents whose homes were burned by British troops in the Revolutionary War. The "Donation Grant" refers to land given by Congress to the Ohio Company in 1792. The "Salt Section" of northeastern Ohio is rich in underlying salt rock. Situated along the Scioto River and the city of Columbus, the "Refugee's Tract" was granted by Congress to Canadians who had lost property during the Revolutionary War (as a result of their support of American revolutionaries). The "Moravian Lands" were granted to Moravian missionaries in 1787. "One-Leg Creek" is a tributary of the Tuscarawas River.

52.1 Käse-lab] Or *Käselaib*. German: a wheel of cheese.

52.5 the Community] Zoar, a communal society approximately seventy-five miles south of Cleveland, founded in 1817 by German dissenters from the Lutheran Church. The Zoar commune was dissolved in 1898.

52.32–35 the M.B.'s . . . Mound-Builders] The Mound-Builders of the Great Lakes region, living roughly 2,000 years ago, who built large mounds for burial and ceremonial purposes.

53.12 C——] Cleveland.

54.4–5 list slippers] Slippers made from tightly woven cloth, which would not fray.

55.22 Sandy] Sandusky, Ohio, a town on the shores of Lake Erie, between Cleveland and Toledo.

55.27 Queen of Sheby] In the Bible, the Queen of Sheba came bearing great gifts when she traveled with her retinue to Jerusalem to see King Solomon of Israel. See 1 Kings 10:1–13.

56.7 Judy, Ruth, Esthy] Heroines of the Old Testament. Judith saved her people by seducing and beheading Holofernes. Ruth refused to leave her mother-in-law after her husband's death. And Esther saved the Jews by persuading her husband, the Persian king Xerxes, to reverse his edict to have them all killed.

56.23 chany] China, porcelain dishes.

57.15 "*Où la vanité va-t-elle se nicher?*"] French: Where will vanity settle?

58.5–6 "Ich weisz nicht . . . traurig bin,"] From the German poem "Die Lorelei" (1824) by Henrich Heine: "I don't know what it means / That I am so sad."

58.18–19 "She is quite sure . . . her day."] Cf. Alfred, Lord Tennyson's *Maud* (1855): "Before I am quite sure / That there is no one to love me; / Then let come what may / To a life that has been so sad, / I shall have had my day."

58.22   "A man's a man . . . a woman too,"] Allusion to Robert Burns's popular poem about a poor man's dignity, "A Man's a Man for A' That" (1795), which was also a popular song. Burns makes no reference to women.

62.9   kobold] In German folklore, a spirit that haunts the home and is often invisible but can take the form of an animal.

63.34   rose of Sharon] See Song of Solomon 2:1.

64.18   "Tuscarora] Native American people of the Iroquois League, originally from the Great Lakes region.

65.19   "*Dux nascitur*] Latin: born leader.

70.14–15   the Community of German Separatists] See note 52.5.

70.26   Der Fliegende Holländer] "The Flying Dutchman," a German-language opera of 1843 by Richard Wagner, based on Henrich Heine's retelling of the seventeenth-century maritime legend of the doomed ghost ship. In Wagner's opera, the Dutchman must wander the seas deathlessly until he finds a wife.

71.23–24   "The One Hundred and Seventh Regiment, O. V. I.] The 107th Regiment, Ohio Volunteer Infantry, comprised mostly of German Americans, was organized at Cleveland, Ohio, and mustered out of service at Charleston, South Carolina, on July 10, 1865. The 107th, also known as the 5th German Regiment, participated in numerous battles, including Chancellorsville and Gettysburg.

73.8   the Scriptural phrase . . . milk and honey."] The phrase first appears in Exodus 3:8.

73.10   Wirtshaus] German: tavern.

74.32   Jean Paul . . . the only] Jean Paul, the pen name of Johann Paul Friedrich Richter (1763–1825), German Romantic novelist and humorist, who was called "Jean Paul der Einzige," or "Jean Paul the Only."

75.8   veilchen] German: violet.

75.17   verliebte] German: beloved.

76.18   verlobt] German: engaged.

78.33–35   The statue . . . Pygmalion suffice?] In Greek mythology, Pygmalion fell in love with one of his own sculptures. Taking pity on the sculptor, Aphrodite brought the statue to life.

79.37   *cap-à-pie*] Middle French: head to foot.

80.11–12   "Ruhe ist . . . haben kann,"—] From a hymn ("Ruhe ist das beste Gut") by the German Lutheran theologian and poet Johann Caspar Schade (1666–1698).

84.37   "Das macht nichts,"] German: That doesn't matter.

95.27–28 "In the kingdom . . . Annabel Lee,"] The narrator paraphrases lines from Edgar Allan Poe's "Annabel Lee" (1849).

103.15 crash] See note 4.14.

104.5–17 "The heavens declare . . . Wait—wait."] Adapted from Psalms 19:1, 19:5, 30:5, 65:8, and 102:6–7.

105.18 Napoleon on St. Helena] After the French emperor Napoleon Bonaparte (1769–1821) was defeated at the battle of Waterloo in 1815, he was imprisoned on Saint Helena in the Atlantic Ocean until his death in 1821.

105.31–34 "'The moping bittern . . . the water-lily,'"] Slightly altered lines from the English poet Thomas Hood's "The Haunted House" (1844).

108.29 *Faust*] The opera *Faust* (1859) by French composer Charles Gounod, with libretto by Jules Barbier and Michel Carré, based on the German legend of a scholar who sells his soul to the devil in exchange for knowledge and power.

109.10 *Te Deum*] A Latin Christian hymn of thanks to God.

110.38 "Much learning . . . farmer mad."] Cf. Acts 26:24.

111.22 Prime] William Cowper Prime (1825–1905), American writer known for the book *I Go A-Fishing* (1873).

112.12–15 Bret Harte's "Melons, . . . American youth."] Bret Harte's story "Melons" (1870) features a boy whistling "John Brown's Body," a popular Union song about the abolitionist who tried to spark slave insurrections across the South. Julia Ward Howe wrote "The Battle Hymn of the Republic" (1862) for the same tune.

114.4 delaine] A dress made of high-grade wool from delaine sheep.

116.7–8 "He came flying . . . wind,"] Psalms 18:10.

116.8 Hebrew poet] King David, to whom many of the Psalms are attributed.

117.28–29 "folded their tents . . . stolen away."] See the concluding lines of Henry Wadsworth Longfellow's poem "The Day is Done" (1845).

118.7–9 "close to . . . Bacon got up the phrase] There is no evidence that the philosopher Francis Bacon (1561–1626) coined the phrase "close to the great heart of nature."

120.18 Northwest and Hudson Bay Companies] The North West Company and the Hudson's Bay Company, competing fur-trading companies in British North America forced to merge in 1821 by the British government after a series of skirmishes between the two companies.

121.30 bateaux] Broad flat-bottomed boats, the primary means of transporting men, supplies, and goods in colonial North America and during the fur trade.

124.28   Portage] The mining settlement at Portage Lake, part of the Ke-weenaw Waterway leading to Lake Superior on the Upper Peninsula of Mich-igan. The Portage mine, opened in 1853, was one of many along its shores in the nineteenth century.

124.37   Fort William] Fort erected in 1803 by the North West Company at the mouth of the Kaministiquia River, on the Canadian side of Lake Superior.

125.8–9   Burnt-Wood River] The Bois Brule River, which empties into Lake Superior on the north shore of Wisconsin, about thirty miles east of the town of Superior. The Ojibwa people called the river "Wisakoda," which translates to "burnt woods" or (in French) "bois brûlé."

125.37   'Adeste Fideles.'] The Latin Christmas carol translated into English by Frederick Oakeley in 1841 as "O Come, All Ye Faithful."

128.35   'The minute gun . . . at sea,'] Refrain from the duet "The Minute Gun at Sea" (1814) by English composer M. P. King (1773–1823).

130.29–30   "'Now thank we . . . hands and voices,'] The opening lines to the hymn "Now Thank We All Our God" (1856), translated by Catherine Winkworth (1827–1878) from the German hymn "Nun danket alle Gott" (c. 1636) by Martin Rinkart (1586–1649).

131.15   *voyageurs*] French Canadian boatmen who transported furs, often leg-endary figures in music and folklore.

## RODMAN THE KEEPER AND OTHER STORIES

143.2–21   The long years . . . be alive!] Excerpts of the first and seventh stanzas of American poet Thomas Bailey Aldrich's poem "Spring in New En-gland," first published in *The Atlantic Monthly* in June 1875.

144.19   on that April morning . . . fired on Sumter] April 12, 1861.

156.32–35   "Toujours femme varie . . . plume au vent."] Slightly misquoted or altered from Victor Hugo's drama *Le Roi s'amuse* (1832). Sung by Hu-go's King Francis, the lines translate as "Women are inconstant, / only a fool counts on them; / A woman is often / but a feather in the wind." King Francis I is said to have inscribed the motto "Toute femme varie." above one of the windows at Château Chambord.

160.2   anathema-marantha] Outcast, detested. See I Corinthians 16:22.

162.30–37   "Tell me not . . . the soul!"] First two stanzas of Henry Wads-worth Longfellow's "A Psalm of Life" (1838).

164.9   Southern Memorial Day] Also known as Confederate Memorial Day or Confederate Decoration Day, observed on different dates in several south-ern states since the conclusion of the Civil War.

164.18   "Swing low, sweet chariot,"] African American spiritual, composed by unknown slaves and passed orally throughout the South; first performed onstage by the Fisk Jubilee Singers in the 1870s.

172.2–13 She lived . . . her eyes.] "Sister St. Luke" by John Milton Hay (1838–1905), American poet, former secretary to Lincoln, and friend of Woolson. When Woolson reprinted her story "Sister St. Luke" in *Rodman the Keeper*, Hay wrote the poem for Woolson to use as the epigraph.

172.19 Minorcan] The Minorcans of northeastern Florida trace their lineage to indentured servants brought from Minorca and other Mediterranean islands in 1767 to work on indigo plantations at New Smyrna. The Minorcan colonists revolted and won their freedom in 1777.

173.31 Pelican Island] A made-up name. The island Woolson describes resembles Anastasia Island, off the coast of Florida, just south of St. Augustine.

173.38–39 Fresnel] Lens with concentric rings that reflect light for great distances, invented by Augustin-Jean Fresnel in 1822.

174.17 Queen of the Antilles] Cuba.

174.26 Huguenot] A group of Huguenots, French Protestants fleeing religious persecution, was slaughtered by Catholic Spanish forces near St. Augustine in 1565.

183.9–12 Deep on . . . follow soon—] The first four lines of English poet Alfred Lord Tennyson's "The Eve of St. Agnes" (1837).

185.26–27 Santa Inez . . . Santa Rufina . . . earthen vases.] Santa Inez is the Spanish name of Saint Agnes of Rome, whose name is associated with the Latin *agnus* or "lamb." Agnes is the patron saint of virgins, victims of rape, and gardeners. Rufina and her sister, Justa, are the patron saints of potters. They lived in Seville, Spain, in the third century and were martyred for refusing to sell their pots for pagan rituals.

190.31 primary rocks] A nineteenth-century geologic term for crystalline rocks.

201.2–15 In yonder homestead . . . desolate eyes!] "The Old Mirror" (1877) by American novelist and poet Edgar Fawcett.

201.35 St. Cecilia] The patron saint of musicians.

202.20 sing for me . . . 'The Proud Ladye.'"] Long narrative poem of 1840 by American journalist and poet Spencer Wallace Cone, here adapted for singing.

203.18 *romanza*] A short, lyrical song for voice or instrumental music.

206.9 Minorcan] See note 172.19.

207.16 coquina-walls] Coquina is a limestone made from broken shells, common in Florida and the Caribbean.

208.25 *gondelieds*] A word of Woolson's invention meaning the songs ("Lieder" in German) of the gondoliers.

215.18 Canton crape] A type of soft, wavy, heavy silk.

215.19   Leghorn bonnet] Fine straw hat from Livorno, Italy, called Leghorn in English.

215.21   ruche] Pleated fabric used as decoration.

220.18   *ciel!*] French: heavens!

222.40   Rimmon] Ancient Syrian deity. See 2 Kings 5:18.

223.28   the Paul of this Virginia] A reference to the French novel *Paul et Virginie* (1788) by Jacques-Henri Bernardin de Saint-Pierre, in which the titular characters, brought up as brother and sister, are raised in pastoral innocence on the French outpost of Île de France (now Mauritius) until their sexual feelings for each other are awakened.

224.8   *chaparral*] A thicket of shrubs and small trees. Here, the sandy Florida scrublands.

228.2–17   One by one . . . house go!] The first and eighth stanzas of "Fuit Ilium" (1868) by American poet and critic Edmund Clarence Stedman. The poem addresses the tearing down of New York's historic grand homes to make way for new commercial buildings.

232.20   "Spectator"] *The Spectator*, a weekly London magazine, first published in 1828. On June 19, 1880, *The Spectator* reviewed *Rodman the Keeper* favorably: "These are sketches of life in the Southern States, picturing mostly with a quite remarkable power the condition of things which has resulted from the war. . . . The book will find, we hope, an English publisher."

233.1–4   "Little Cupid . . . a bee,"] Slightly altered lyrics from a popular English song titled "Cupid Wounded," published in *The British Minstrel: A Choice Collection of Modern Songs* (1848).

233.6   Mother Venus's advice] In "Cupid Wounded," Cupid's mother, Venus, tells him to remember "that the rose holds the thorn, and the myrtle, the bee."

240.35   lawns] A lawn is a dress made of fine linen.

250.5   Queen of Sheba] See note 55.27.

252.26–27   No one made courtesies . . . the Lancers.] A lancer is a formal quadrille, or square dance, in which men bow and women curtsy to their partners.

258.2–13   The trees that lean'd . . . black love.] Excerpts from American poet Joaquin Miller's "Isles of the Amazons," published in *Songs of the Sun-Lands* (1873).

261.7   *chaparral*] See note 224.8.

261.27   South Devil] A fictional name, though Woolson's South Devil bears geographic resemblances to Graham's Swamp, south of St. Augustine, Florida.

262.24 Scipio . . . Africanus] Scipio Africanus the Elder (236–183 B.C.E.) was a celebrated Roman general who defeated Hannibal in modern-day Tunisia in 202 B.C.

263.21 San Miguel] Thinly fictionalized St. Augustine, Florida.

264.18 Spanish-bayonets] The Spanish bayonet (*Yucca aloifolia*) is a large yucca plant with sharp spear-like leaves.

269.9 "Gayly the Troubadour touched his Guitar."] Title of a popular ballad by English poet and songwriter Thomas Haynes Bayly (1797–1839).

270.30 *manqué*] French: unsuccessful, failed.

271.10–11 the "Creation,"] *Die Schöpfung* (1798), an oratorio by Joseph Haydn based on Genesis.

274.32–33 Kenton Arctic Expedition—] Woolson's invention, but probably inspired by the lost 1845 Arctic expedition of British explorer Sir John Franklin and by the Second Grinnell Expedition of 1853–1855 to determine the fate of Franklin's crew, led by American physician and explorer Elisha Kent Kane. Kane recounted his party's escape from the ice-bound *Adance* in whaleboats in the best-selling book *Arctic Exploration: The Second Grinnell Expedition in Search of Sir John Franklin* (1856).

283.11–12 San Juan Bautista] Spanish name for Saint John the Baptist.

283.39 fox-and-geese] A board game designed for two players in which the fox tries to capture the geese, while the geese try to hem in the fox. The version played in colonial and nineteenth-century America typically employed thirteen geese.

284.8 "Sweet Afton."] Musical composition of 1837 by American composer Jonathan Spillman, accompanying Robert Burns's poem "Afton Water" (1789), which begins "Flow gently, sweet Afton."

286.13 King's Road] Built by the British Crown along existing Indian trails, the King's Road runs north–south to the west of St. Augustine.

292.2–7 The loveliest land . . . garden spiceries.] Lines excerpted from the long poem "W. Gilmore Simms. A Poem" (1877) by Southern poet Paul Hamilton Hayne (1830–1886), with whom Woolson carried on a long and warm correspondence.

292.9–16 Call on thy children . . . Carolina!] Stanzas from the second and third parts of "Carolina" (1862) by Southern poet Henry Timrod (1829–1867), reprinted in *Poems* (1873), edited by his friend and fellow Southern poet Paul Hamilton Hayne.

293.22–23 "What!" said a country-woman . . . westward, sir?"] See William Wordsworth's poem "Stepping Westward" (1807), which recalls the kind greeting made to Wordsworth and his sister, Dorothy, by one of two passing women, near Loch Ketterine after sunset.

294.36   Giant Despair] In John Bunyan's *Pilgrim's Progress* (1678), Giant Despair captures Christian and Hopeful, halting their progress toward the Celestial City.

297.38–39   "War is cruelty,"] Letter of William Tecumseh Sherman to James M. Calhoun, E. E. Rawson, and S. C. Wells, September 12, 1864: "You cannot qualify war in harsher terms than I will. War is cruelty, and you cannot refine it; and those who brought war into our Country deserve all the curses and maledictions a people can pour out. I know I had no hand in making this war, and I know I will make more sacrifices to-day than any of you to Secure Peace."

298.15   Fredericksburg] The battle of Fredericksburg (December 11–15, 1862), fought in and around Fredericksburg, Virginia, one of the deadliest battles of the Civil War, in which Ambrose Burnside's Army of the Potomac failed to rout entrenched Confederate defenders on the heights behind the city under the command of Robert E. Lee.

298.17   'And pray ye . . . winter'] Matthew 24:20.

299.2–3   'no man knoweth . . . this day.'] Deuteronomy 34:6.

299.12–13   thy tangled Wilderness] The Wilderness, a dense second-growth forest of scrub oak, pine, and underbrush in Spotsylvania County, Virginia, was the scene of two major Civil War battles: the battle of Chancellorsville, May 1–4, 1863, in which Lee succeeded in driving the Union army back across the Rappahannock River, and the battle of the Wilderness, in which Lee attacked the Union army as it moved south through the woods, May 5–6, 1864, but failed to prevent Grant from continuing his southward advance toward Spotsylvania Court House.

299.20–21   'Le roi est mort, vive le roi!'] French: The king is dead, long live the king!

300.31   Appomattox] Outnumbered and surrounded, Lee surrendered the Army of Northern Virginia to Grant at Appomattox Court House, Virginia, on April 9, 1865, effectively bringing the Civil War to an end.

303.17   'Is there any sorrow . . . my sorrow?'] Lamentations 1:12.

303.19–20   the march to the sea?] The scorched-earth campaign of Major General William Tecumseh Sherman (1820–1891), beginning with the departure of Union troops from Atlanta on November 16, 1864, and ending with the occupation of Savannah on December 21, 1864. Sherman's army of 60,000 men marched on a front fifty to sixty miles across, engaging in widespread destruction of both public and private property.

303.21–22   its route . . . flame by night—] Cf. Exodus 13:21.

303.22–23   the march through South Carolina] Sherman left Savannah on February 1, 1865, and began marching into South Carolina, where his army inflicted greater destruction on private homes and property than in Georgia. The Union advance reached Fayetteville, North Carolina, on March 11 and Raleigh on April 13.

307.24–25   a new king . . . not Joseph—] See Exodus 1:8 and Acts 7:18.

308.2–21   Glooms of the live-oaks . . . a shade.] From "The Marshes of Glynn" (1878) by Southern poet Sidney Lanier (1842–1881).

310.24   Minorcans] See note 172.19.

312.38   chaparral] See note 224.8.

315.33   *cui bono?*] Latin: who benefits from it?

320.7–8   cynicism, as Mr. Aldrich says . . . the artilleryman.] Thomas Bailey Aldrich (1836–1907), American writer and editor, in the short story "Marjorie Daw" (1873).

324.39–40   Somebody says somewhere . . . a virtue."] English writer P. G. Patmore (1786–1855), faulting William Hazlitt for his despondency, in *My Friends and Acquaintance: Being Memorials, Mind-Portraits, and Personal Recollections of Deceased Celebrities of the Nineteenth Century* (1845): "Hope is more than a blessing—it is a duty and a virtue."

326.20–25   "Have you felt . . . is she!"] Concluding lines of the fourth part of "A Celebration of Charis in Ten Lyric Pieces" (1640–1641) by Ben Jonson (1572–1637).

329.2–7   I met a traveler . . . an unseen book.] From American poet and journalist Richard Watson Gilder's long poem "The New Day: A Poem in Song and Sonnets" (1876). In later versions of the poem, Gilder substantially altered these lines.

329.17   "the Children of Ham"] In Genesis 9:25, Noah curses his son Ham's children. In the Bible Noah and his family are not characterized in racial terms, but Ham came to be portrayed as black and by the nineteenth century the phrase "Children of Ham" was often used to refer to African Americans, implying that the race was cursed.

329.30–31   mountains of Kong] A mountain range featured on maps of Africa from 1798 until the late 1880s, but which never existed.

330.24   Freedman's Bureau] The Bureau of Refugees, Freedmen, and Abandoned Lands, commonly known as The Freedman's Bureau, established at the close of the Civil War to assist the freed slaves by providing clothing, shelter, and education.

336.13   old Adam] The fallen man, who, like Adam in the Bible, is susceptible to temptation and sin, as opposed to the new Adam, or Christ.

337.23   C.B.] Carpetbagger.

## THE FRONT YARD AND OTHER ITALIAN STORIES

352.16   ring the Angelus] In the Roman Catholic Church, a call to prayer three times a day at 6:00 A.M., 12:00 P.M., and 6:00 P.M., composed of bells ringing three sets of three rings, with a pause between each set.

352.31   Ledham (New Hampshire)] Invented town.

352.35   great triple church of St. Francis] The Basilica of St. Francis in Assisi is composed of two churches and a crypt where St. Francis (1181–1226) was laid to rest. Canonized in 1228 by Pope Gregory IX, St. Francis is the patron saint of Italy.

358.1   Indian pudding] Traditional New England custard made with cornmeal and molasses.

360.27   the Honorable Mrs. Norton] Caroline Norton (1808–1877), an English writer who left her husband, the Honourable George Norton, after which her husband sued Lord Melbourne for seducing her. Caroline Norton's advocacy against the laws that discriminated against married women influenced the passage of the Custody Bill in 1839 and the Marriage and Divorce Act in 1857.

364.16   festa] In Italy, a religious holiday or feast day.

368.30   scaldino] A brazier made of earthenware for holding or burning coal.

377.32   close-reefed] A nautical term: having reduced the area of the sails, particularly in strong winds.

381.23   she read Symonds] John Addington Symonds (1840–1893), English poet and literary critic, wrote on the cultural history of the Italian Renaissance in *Renaissance in Italy* (1875–86), *Sketches and Studies in Italy* (1879), and other works.

381.31   *è troppo grave*,"] Italian: it's too serious.

382.22   Giotto] Giotto di Bondone (1266–1337), Italian artist and architect of the Late Middle Ages, known for his chapel frescoes in Assisi and elsewhere, as well as the bell tower of the Duomo in Florence, considered a masterpiece of fourteenth-century Gothic architecture.

386.6   Queen Margherita] Margherita of Savoy (1851–1926), Queen Consort of Italy, married to King Umberto I.

388.16   Scotch shooting-box] A hunting lodge or, colloquially, a simple, unadorned house.

392.5–6   not afraid of fever] "Fever" here means yellow fever or malaria, widespread in many parts of Italy in the late nineteenth century, both diseases transmitted by mosquito bites.

392.13   Punta Palmas] A Florida town of Woolson's invention.

397.23   Clerkenwell] Area in central London, one of the city's oldest parishes.

398.27 Chevalier Bayard] Pierre Terrail (1473–1524), seigneur de Bayard, a French knight, known as "the knight without fear and beyond reproach."

398.31 "Pioneers! oh, pioneers!"] "Pioneers! O Pioneers!," the refrain in a poem of the same title by Walt Whitman, first published in *Drum-Taps* (1865); the poem celebrates the American frontier spirit.

398.38 prunella shoes] Prunella is a heavy woolen or cotton fabric used for shoe uppers.

401.15 Ehrenbreitsein] A fortress on the Rhine River in Germany, overlooking the town of Koblenz.

403.1–2 "O la douce folie— / Aimable Capri!"] French: "Oh the sweet madness— / Amiable Capri!"

403.25 Trancadillo] A boat song of 1844, also called "O Come, Maidens, Come," with words by American poet Caroline Gilman and music by American composer Francis H. Brown.

404.1 rang the Angelus] See note 352.16.

431.23 *omnium gatherum*] A mock-Latin phrase: a collection of random things or people.

432.30 *res angusta*] *Res angusta domi*, a commonly used phrase meaning poverty, derived from the Latin for "narrowed circumstances at home."

433.7 Doria gallery] The Palazzo Doria in the heart of Rome, home of the Doria-Pamphilj family and site of one of the most renowned art collections in Italy.

433.14 the Borghese] The Villa Borghese, built by Cardinal Scipione Borghese in the seventeenth century as a country home just outside of the walls of Rome. In the nineteenth century, the gardens, home, and extensive art collection were still in private hands, bequeathed to the Italian state in 1903.

433.26 the Caraccis] Agostino Carracci (1557–1602) and his brother Annibale Carracci (1560–1609), artists from Bologna.

434.4–5 the Raphael double portrait?"] *Double Portrait* (c. 1516) by Italian painter Raffaello Sanzio.

434.7–8 the portrait of Andrea Doria, by Sebastiano del Piombo?"] Portrait of Andrea Doria (c. 1526) by Italian artist Sebastiano del Piombo.

434.10 the Velasquez?"] The portrait of Pope Innocent X (c. 1650) by the Spanish painter Diego Velázquez.

434.12 the two large Claude Lorraines?"] French landscape painter Claude Lorrain (1600–1682) spent much of his life working in Italy. Although spelled with an "e" in the nineteenth century, today the artist's name is spelled Claude Lorrain.

434.15 "The Memling?"] German artist Hans Memling's *Lamentation* (1475–80).

440.35 "solferino,"] Purplish red color.

450.12 the Campagna] Pastoral area surrounding Rome, a popular subject for artists and a common site for excursions.

456.35 the Pincio] The terrace in the Borghese Gardens, a popular site for strolling, overlooking Rome.

## DOROTHY AND OTHER ITALIAN STORIES

463.24 Bellosguardo] The hill to the southwest of Florence, where Woolson lived in Villa Castellani in 1886 and Villa Brichieri from 1887 through 1889. In a letter of February 24, 1887, Woolson describes Bellosguardo: "I have taken a villa . . . at Bellosguardo, for a year; perhaps two. Bellosguardo is just outside the Roman Gate of Florence; it is the hill of Galileo; of Hawthorne (where he wrote *The Marble Faun*); of *Aurora Leigh*. Take down that poem, turn to the Seventh Book . . . & you will comprehend the views I have from my windows, & my terrace. It is useless for me to try to describe it after Mrs Browning; but I do believe it is the most beautiful view in the world."

463.31 the Carrara Mountains!] Foothills of the Apuan Alps.

466.16 the Uffizi Gallery] Art museum in Florence, rich in painting and sculpture from the Italian Renaissance.

466.24–25 aguish belvedere] A belvedere is a structure with open sides, usually at rooftop level; the belvedere is "aguish" because it exposes one to the ague, or malaria, a disease transmitted by mosquitos but believed in the nineteenth century to be caused by bad air.

468.3–4 Raphael's young St. John . . . the Uffizi] Raffaello Sanzio's *Young St. John* (1518), known today as *St. John the Baptist in the Desert* and believed to have been executed by his assistants.

468.9 his hair . . . King Humbert's] Umberto I (1844–1900), king of Italy from 1878 to his assassination in 1900, was a tall, striking figure with a large white handlebar moustache and white hair worn in pompadour style.

470.21 *petits fours*, the *bouchées aux confitures*] Tiny cakes and bite-sized pastries with a jam filling.

477.10–13 "Through the long days . . . and years?"] "Through the Long Days" (1878), a song composed by Woolson's friend and Bellosguardo neighbor Francis Boott (1813–1904), with lyrics by another friend, John Hay (1838–1905). In a letter of February 23, 1887, to John Hay, Woolson wrote of the piece: "Words & music are both supremely beautiful. I sing the song (under my breath), & play it, every morning of my life."

481.1–2   Viale dei Colli] A scenic route in Florence, extending from the Porta Romana on the south side of the Arno River to the Niccolò Bridge west of the city. It is made up of three roads: Viale Michelangelo, Viale Galileo, and Viale Machiavelli.

481.8   *Galignani's Messenger*] An English-language daily newspaper published in Paris from 1814 to 1904.

482.24–25   Borgo San Frediano to San Spirito] Borgo San Frediano is the name of a street running parallel to the south side of the Arno, which was the meat district of Florence. On its western end it turns into the Via San Spirito, named for the Basilica di San Spirito.

484.21   Tosti's serenades] Neapolitan singer and composer Francesco Paolo Tosti (1846–1916) wrote immensely popular sentimental love songs and ballads.

487.31   "Ring out . . . Angelus—"] Cf. "The Angelus" (1883), with words by Frances L. Mace and music by Woolson's friend Francis Boott: "Ring soft across the dying day, Angelus! / Across the amber-tinted bay, / The meadow flushed with sunset ray,— / Ring out, and float, and melt away, Angelus." See also note 352.16.

488.28   San Vito's] Here, not the church but Via di San Vito, an east–west street on Bellosguardo.

489.26   Roman fever] See note 392.5–6.

490.2   pinchbeck] An alloy of zinc and copper used in the eighteenth and nineteenth centuries to simulate gold.

491.9   dahabeeyah] A large, shallow-bottomed passenger boat, the primary means of transportation on the Nile in the Victorian era.

492.25   Galileo's tower] From 1617 to 1631, Italian scientist Galileo Galilei lived in the Villa dell'Ombrellino on Bellosguardo, where he made many astronomical observations from his tower.

497.22   Lung' Arno] Road next to the Arno River in Florence, on which many fashionable hotels were situated.

498.23   Via dei Serragli] Road that runs from the west side of Bellosguardo to Florence.

501.23   Vevey] A Swiss town on Lake Geneva that was a popular resort for British and American tourists.

504.22   Corney Grain] The stage name of Richard Corney Grain (1844–1895), a popular British actor and entertainer.

511.11   black-letter] Old-fashioned. Black letter is heavy Gothic type predominant in printing from the thirteenth to fifteenth centuries.

511.11–12 'Merrily sungen the monks of Ely.'] Old English song that dates to at least 1300, author unknown.

511.12 In Baedeker, you know."] Meaning conventional. The German publisher Baedeker began to issue its popular guidebooks in English in 1861.

512.34–35 Benozzo, and Nicolo the Pisan!] Benozzo Gozzoli (c. 1421–1497), a Florentine Renaissance painter; Nicola Pisano, a classical Italian sculptor (c. 1220–c. 1284), sometimes called the father of modern sculpture.

513.34–35 shaped like a lachrymal . . . catacombs] Lachrymatories, or tear-vessels, found in large numbers in Roman catacombs, had long necks and small bulb-like bodies. Despite their name, they held unguents.

513.36 marrons glacés] Candied chestnuts.

516.7 old sarcophagus . . . talking about] The elaborately carved Phaedra sarcophagus, or stone coffin, from the second or third century C.E. in the Camposanto, or Monumental Cemetery, in Pisa.

516.31–32 Campo Santo frescoes] Frescoes dating to the fourteenth to seventeenth centuries, some of them by Benozzo Gozzoli, in the Monumental Cemetery in Pisa.

516.34–517.2 Shelley and Byron . . . Mary Shelley?] Percy Bysshe Shelley's first wife, Harriet, drowned herself two years after Shelley had abandoned her for Mary Wollstonecraft Shelley. Shelley and Mary Wollstonecraft Shelley lived at the Palazzi di Chiesa on the Lungarno Galileo Galilei from 1821 until his death in 1822; Lord Byron lived across the Arno River, in the Palazzo Toscanelli. After Shelley drowned in a storm off the coast of Lerici, near Pisa, his friends Lord Byron and Edward Trelawny burned his body on the beach.

519.29 Society for Psychical Research] Founded in England in 1882, a society dedicated to the scientific study of paranormal, supernatural, or psychic phenomena, such as mind-reading, premonitions, and spectral visitations.

519.29–30 Herbert Spencer's works] The English philosopher and sociologist Herbert Spencer (1820–1903) made a significant contribution to the acceptance of the theory of evolution through his application of Darwinian ideas to social transformation.

523.3 the Bagni] The Bagni di Lucca, a spa town approximately twenty-five miles north of Pisa.

526.22 Aix-les-Bains] Spa town in the French Alps.

526.32 "furbelows"] Trimmings, flounces, or decorations.

529.23 Lake Bourget] Lake on which Aix-les-Baines sits.

542.15–16 majolica plates] Majolica is decorated and glazed Italian Renaissance pottery.

542.16 campaniles] Bell towers in Italy, often freestanding.

542.23–24 "Sapete . . . campanile—"] Mangled Italian: Do you know a cutlery in the bell tower?

542.30–31 "Tisch . . . gesehn ein?"] Mangled German: Have you seen a table in the tower?

544.9 peple all cooks turists] Thomas Cook & Son of London published Cook's Tourist's Handbook, a series of popular English guidebooks aimed at middle-class travelers. The company also organized tours.

550.3 Fiesole] The hills of Fiesole, including the town of the same name, three miles northeast of Florence, a popular nineteenth-century tourist site.

551.15 Carrara mountains] See note 463.31.

552.15 the Palazzo Vecchio] Florence's Town Hall, dating from 1299, with its tall bell tower rising far above the city.

553.16 the Lakes] Northern Italian lakes, chiefly Lake Como, Lake Garda, and Lake Maggiore.

559.13 the Boboli Garden] The Medici family's extensive, lavish gardens and sculpture collection, behind the Pitti Palace in Florence.

562.11–12 an Apollo, an Endymion] Apollo, the Greek and Roman god of the sun, associated with intellectual light, music, and poetry; Endymion, in Greek mythology, a youth of great beauty, visited every night by the moon goddess Selene.

563.7 Baedeker, Horner, and Hare.] Shorthand reference to popular guidebooks. Baedeker, see note 511.12; Horner, *Walks in Florence* (1873) by Susan and Joanna Horner; Hare, *Cities of Central and Northern Italy* (1876) by Augustus Hare.

563.8 Cascine] Extensive public park on the north bank of the Arno River in Florence.

563.21 Giotto and Botticelli] Giotto, see note 382.22; Botticelli, Sandro Botticelli (1445–1510), one of the most famous painters of the Italian Renaissance, although his reputation was only beginning to grow in the nineteenth century.

564.14–15 the great statue of Abbondanza] In Florence's Boboli Gardens. See also note 559.13.

564.17 the Duomo] Florence's cathedral, its famed dome designed by Filippo Brunelleschi (1377–1446).

564.34–35 Giotto's two little frescoes . . . Santa Maria Novella] In *Mornings in Florence* (1875–1877), John Ruskin describes "two small frescoes" in Santa Maria Novella's second cloister (the Cloister of the Dead), which he attributes to Giotto, "that on the left, the Meeting of Joachim and Anna at the Golden Gate; and that on the right, the Birth of the Virgin."

564.36–37   the little Virgin . . . in Venice] *The Presentation of the Virgin at the Temple* in the Tornabuoni Chapel at Santa Maria Novella is now attributed to Domenico Ghirlandaio (1449–1494). The version by Titian, or Tiziano Vecelli (1488–1576), is in Venice's Gallerie dell'Accademia.

564.38   round Botticelli of the Uffizi] Either *Madonna of the Magnificat* (1481) or *Madonna of the Pomegranate* (1487), both round paintings by Botticelli in the Uffizi.

564.39   one in the Prometheus room at the Pitti] Most likely Botticelli's *Madonna and Child with Young St. John* (c. 1495). Florence's Palazzo Pitti, the chief residence of the Medici family from the mid-sixteenth to mid-eighteenth centuries, contains several museums.

566.15   the Academy] The Academy, the Galleria dell'Accademia in Florence, the home of Michelangelo's *David* (1501–1504).

566.17   the monastery of San Marco] The former monastery in Florence in which visitors can glimpse the renowned frescoes of early Renaissance painter Fra Angelico (1395–1455).

566.25   *De Contemptu Mundi*] Latin for "On Contempt of the World," the title of various works, including a fifth-century epistle by St. Eucherius, a twelfth-century book by Innocent III, and a sixteenth-century three-thousand-line poem by Bernard of Cluny. All three critique the vanity of the material world.

567.13–21   "SEMPER FIDELIS . . . faithful forever."] The poem is Woolson's.

573.33   "Madonna of the Chair."] Painting by Raphael with the Italian title *Madonna della Siggiola* (1513–1514). Henry James extolled its beauty in his "Florentine Notes," published in *Transatlantic Sketches* (1875) and reprinted in *Italian Hours* (1909).

573.38–40   one of Titian's portraits . . . young man in black.] Titian's *Ritratto Virile* or *Portrait of a Young Englishman* (1540–1545), also praised by James in "Florentine Notes."

579.21–23   Romola . . . the remark."] George Eliot's novel *Romola* (1863), set in Renaissance Florence, portrays the union of the scholarly Romola and the charming but unfaithful schemer Tito.

580.3   St. Peter the Martyr] Most likely Fra Angelico's *The Triptych of St. Peter the Martyr* (1429) at San Marco. See note 566.17.

580.4–13   Michel Angelo chapel of San Lorenzo . . . sleep in Night.] After completing his design and architectural work on the Medici Chapels of Florence's Basilica of San Lorenzo in 1524, Michelangelo turned to the sculptures and the sarcophagi, among them the allegorical figures Dawn and Dusk for the tomb of Lorenzo, Duke of Urbino and Day and Night for the tomb of Giuliano, Duke of Nemours.

582.12 "Spare me . . . 'A fellow-feeling,'] English playwright David Garrick's *Prologue on Quitting the State* (1776) contains the often-reprinted line "A fellow-feeling makes one wondrous kind."

582.19–20 "Giovanni . . . golden hair?"] The warrior Ludovico di Giovanni de' Medici, also called Giovanni dalle Bande Nere (1498–1526), was buried in his armor. Leonore of Toledo, or Eleanor de' Medici (1522–1562), the wife of Cosimo I, Grand Duke of Tuscany, had brown hair, but portraits show it pulled back and covered with a gold mesh snood.

587.32 "Lung' Arno Nuovo,"] The extension, or new part of the Lung' Arno, today called Lungarno Amerigo Vespucci.

587.38 Bellosguardo] See note 463.24.

590.22–23 frescos of Masaccio at the Carmine] The Brancacci Chapel frescoes in the Church of Santa Maria del Carmine by early Renaissance Florentine painter Masaccio, born Tommaso di Ser Giovanni di Simone (1401–1428).

590.25–26 Ruskin . . . pamphlet] Allusion to English art critic John Ruskin's *Mornings in Florence* (1875–1877), published in pocket-sized pamphlets with maroon covers, considered the definitive guide to Florence's art and architecture for English-speaking travelers.

591.9–10 "To Trent . . . Tadmor,"] Trent could be the northern Italian city Trento or the village Trent in southern England. Tadmor is the Arabic name for Palmyra, in modern-day Syria.

594.15 golconda] A source of great wealth or advantage, derived from the diamond-rich Golconda mine in India.

597.2 Lake Leman] The French name for Lake Geneva, along the border of Switzerland and France.

598.4 If people supposed . . . Horace] An allusion to English writer and art historian Horace Walpole (1717–1797), known for his multivolume *Letters*, published in the nineteenth century, and his Gothic novel *The Castle of Otranto* (1764).

601.10 Silver Needle] Probably the mountain known today as Silberhorn, which has an arrow-like peak. References in nineteenth-century texts indicate a mountain near the Jungfrau in the Alps bore this name.

603.5 Gibbon lived] Edward Gibbon (1737–1794), English historian, writer, and politician, author of *The History of the Decline and Fall of the Roman Empire* (1776–1788).

603.39–40 Salève and Voirons.] Mountains in France to the south and east of Geneva, respectively.

604.1 the Jura] Swiss mountain range northeast of Geneva.

604.18–25 Coppet . . . meaning Madame de Staël,"] Coppet is a Swiss town north of Geneva on Lake Geneva where French-Swiss writer Madame de Staël (1766–1817) had a family home, the Château de Coppet, to which she fled after being exiled by Napoleon; the Château de Coppet became a meeting place for displaced writers and thinkers. "Etonnante femme" is French for "astonishing woman."

605.18–19    "'Le temps . . . nous en allons,'"] From "Sonnet à Marie" by French poet Pierre de Ronsard (1524–1585), also a popular song. The lines mean "Time goes on, time goes on, my lady! / Alas! time does not, but we pass away."

605.30    "Childe Harold"] *Childe Harold's Pilgrimage* (1812), a long narrative poem by Lord Byron.

605.31    Miss Yonge] Popular English novelist Charlotte Yonge (1823–1901), best known for *The Heir of Redclyffe* (1852).

607.21–22    the phaeton] Small open carriage with large wheels.

608.1    The Necker homestead] The family home of Madame de Staël, whose maiden name was Necker. See note 604.18–25.

608.33–34    the 'incomparable Juliette' . . . gavotte,"] Parisian salon hostess and famous beauty Juliette Récamier (1777–1849), born Jeanne Françoise Adélaïde Benard, known for excelling at the gavotte, a French dance.

609.10–11    Madame Récamier] See note 608.33–34.

609.12    the exile of Coppet] Madame de Staël. See note 604.18–25.

609.19    Corinne] Titular heroine of Madame de Staël's novel *Corinne, ou L'Italie* (1807), possessed of poetic genius and often likened to the author. Though Corinne achieves public recognition, she dies of a broken heart when spurned by her lover for a conventional woman.

609.23    *ravissante amie*] French: ravishing friend.

610.15    the Montmorency] French statesman Mathieu de Montmorency, duc de Montmorency-Laval (1767–1826), a lover of de Staël.

615.34–35    thrown away her birthright . . . mess of pottage] Cf. Genesis 25:29–34.

617.8    Campagna] See note 450.12.

629.28    Madame Necker] Madame de Staël's mother, Suzanne Curchod (1737–1794), herself a noted writer and salon hostess.

## UNCOLLECTED STORIES

637.23    "When found, make a note of it."] From Charles Dickens's *Dombey and Son* (1848).

639.10    Balzac] Honoré de Balzac (1799–1850), French novelist and one of the originators of literary realism. *La Comédie humaine* (*The Human Comedy*), a lifework of interlinked novels and stories, is often seen as offering a comprehensive portrait of French society.

639.37   Tullia or Lucrezia Borgia.] Two infamous women of Italian history often portrayed as dangerously seductive. Tullia D'Aragona (1510–1556) was a highly esteemed Renaissance poet and philosopher as well as a great beauty and courtesan. Lucrezia Borgia (1480–1519) was the daughter of Pope Alexander VI and member of the ruthless Borgia family of Rome, around whom salacious rumors of incest and murder swirled.

645.28   "Væ victis!"] Latin: Woe to the vanquished!

650.29   like the works of dreams  . . .  *Kubla Kahn*] Samuel Taylor Coleridge claimed his famous poem "Kubla Kahn: or, A Vision in a Dream: A Fragment" (1816) came to him in its entirety in a dream but was interrupted in its composition by a visitor from Porlock.

657.37–38   *memento mori*] Latin: reminder of mortality.

659.7–8   *Memorials of a Quiet Life*] English writer Augustus J. C. Hare's two-volume life story of his adopted mother (published in 1872 and 1876), who, he says in the introductory note, would be surprised to learn that "anything she could do or say would have an interest beyond the loving circle in which she lived."

659.24   Mrs. Jameson and Ruskin] Anna Brownell Jameson (1794–1860), Anglo-Irish art historian and author of the influential *Sacred and Legendary Art* (1848); John Ruskin (1819–1900), the most prominent art authority of the nineteenth century and author of the multivolume *Modern Painters* (1843–1860).

659.28–29   Tupper and *Sandford and Merton*] References to Martin Farquhar Tupper's collection of moralizing maxims *Proverbial Philosophy* (1838) and the popular children's book *The History of Sandford and Merton* (1783–1789) by Thomas Day.

664.34–35   'Never talk to an author about his books.'] The maxim is Woolson's own invention.

665.29   Sloane Street] A fashionable shopping and residential street in the Belgravia district of London. Woolson lived there in 1884.

668.10   *Cavalleria*] The opera *Cavalleria Rusticana* (1890) by Pietro Mascagni, which had its British premiere in London on October 19, 1891.

668.12   *Vapour*] Woolson's invented title for a vacuous novel.

668.37   Du Maurier's] French-born British writer George du Maurier (1834–1896) was known for his popular novels, such as *Trilby* (1895), as well as his illustrations for *Punch*, *Harper's*, and other magazines.

670.3   water-cure] A prevalent treatment in the nineteenth century for various ailments, in the form of showers, sitz-baths, enemas, douches, or simply the drinking of mineral water.

670.23   "Vegetubble baths and the *mind*-cure,"] Vegetable baths were infused with herbs, seaweed, or leaf extracts. The mind cure was a popular belief in the power of positive thinking to heal the body.

671.4    Lemaitre?] French literary and drama critic Jules Lemaître (1853–1919).

671.5–6   that Bashkirtseff thing!] *The Journal of Marie Bashkirtseff* by Russian-French artist Marie Bashkirtseff (1858–1884), published posthumously to great acclaim and criticism for its frank portrayal of the author's extraordinary ambitions to become a famous artist. An English translation by Mathilde Blind appeared in 1890.

671.35–672.3   *Life of Louisa Alcott* . . . thought at all.] *Louisa May Alcott: Her Life, Letters, and Journals*, edited by Ednah Cheney, was published in the United States and England in 1889. In a tribute to Alcott years earlier, Woolson published her children's novel, *The Old Stone House* (1873), under the pseudonym Anne March.

672.24–26   "Ever be hap-pee . . . pirate's heart—"] From "The Pirate's Chorus" of Irish composer Michael W. Balfe's opera *The Enchantress* (1845).

674.30   lambrequins] Pieces of cloth draped over mantels or atop doors or windows.

674.32–33   'Harvard Annex,'] The Society for the Collegiate Instruction for Women, popularly known as the Harvard Annex, led by Elizabeth Cary Agassiz and founded in 1879. Forerunner of Radcliffe College, established in 1894.

675.6    Gray Tucker] A made-up name.

677.12   *St. James's Gazette*] A London evening paper published from 1880 to 1905, known for its conservative politics and highbrow literary content.

# THE LIBRARY OF AMERICA SERIES

Library of America fosters appreciation of America's literary heritage by publishing, and keeping permanently in print, authoritative editions of America's best and most significant writing. An independent nonprofit organization, it was founded in 1979 with seed funding from the National Endowment for the Humanities and the Ford Foundation.